PENGUIN BOOKS

HELEN OF TROY

Margaret George, a tenth-generation American, is the author of the bestselling *Mary, Called Magdalene*; *The Autobiography of Henry VIII*; *Mary Queen of Scotland and the Isles*; and *The Memoirs of Cleopatra*. When not continuing research for her novels in places such as Egypt, Israel, Rome, and England, she lives with her husband in Madison, Wisconsin.

To request Penguin Readers Guides by mail (while supplies last), please call (800) 778-6425 or e-mail reading@us.penguingroup.com. To access Penguin Readers Guides online, visit our Web site at www.penguin.com.

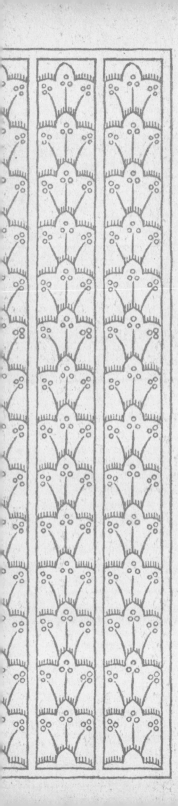

HELEN of TROY

MARGARET GEORGE

PENGUIN BOOKS

PENGUIN BOOKS

Published by the Penguin Group

Penguin Group (USA) Inc., 375 Hudson Street, New York, New York 10014, U.S.A.
Penguin Group (Canada), 90 Eglinton Avenue East, Suite 700, Toronto,
Ontario, Canada M4P 2Y3 (a division of Pearson Penguin Canada Inc.)
Penguin Books Ltd, 80 Strand, London WC2R 0RL, England
Penguin Ireland, 25 St Stephen's Green, Dublin 2, Ireland (a division of Penguin Books Ltd)
Penguin Group (Australia), 250 Camberwell Road, Camberwell,
Victoria 3124, Australia (a division of Pearson Australia Group Pty Ltd)
Penguin Books India Pvt Ltd, 11 Community Centre,
Panchsheel Park, New Delhi – 110 017, India
Penguin Group (NZ), 67 Apollo Drive, Rosedale, North Shore 0745,
Auckland, New Zealand (a division of Pearson New Zealand Ltd)
Penguin Books (South Africa) (Pty) Ltd, 24 Sturdee Avenue,
Rosebank, Johannesburg 2196, South Africa

Penguin Books Ltd, Registered Offices:
80 Strand, London WC2R 0RL, England

First published in the United States of America by Viking Penguin,
a member of Penguin Group (USA) Inc. 2006
Published in Penguin Books 2007

1   3   5   7   9   10   8   6   4   2

Copyright © Margaret George, 2006
All rights reserved

Map by Jeffrey L. Ward

ISBN 0-670-03778-8 (hc.)
ISBN 978-0-14-303899-3 (pbk.)
CIP data available

Printed in the United States of America
Set in Adobe Garamond
Designed by Francesca Belanger

To my daughter,
Alison Rachel,
dear friend and companion

And to her grandmother, my mother,
Margaret Dean,
a last great Southern belle

Acknowledgments

My thanks to:

My thoughtful Greek friends—Artemios and Evie Kandarakis and Xenia Vletsa—who helped me at their country's archaeological sites, and in many other ways; Katie Broberg Foehl and Nikos and March Schweitzer, enthusiastic Graecophiles who were comrades in my quest; Brian and Mary Holmes, who helped me shape the story; and Jane and Bob Feibel, at home in the ancient world.

Birgitta Van der Veer and the curators of Istanbul Archaeological Museums, for arranging personal access to the Troy collection; Dr. Dan Gibson of WPI, for clarifying the chemistry of Tyrian purple dye production from *Murex* snails; Eric Shanower, who generously shared information; Beena Kamlani, gifted editor and friend of Homer's; Professor Stephen G. Miller, University of California, Berkeley, for reviving and organizing the Ancient Nemean Games and letting me participate; Professors Barry B. Powell and William Aylward at the University of Wisconsin, who were always willing to share their expertise, and whose classics department symposium "The Trojan War: The Sources Behind the Scenes" taught me many things.

. . . Troy, with walls still far from old
Had been destroyed, that noble, royal town
And many a man full worthy of renown
Had lost his life—that no man can gainsay—
And all for Helen, the wife of Menelay,

When a thing's done, it may then be no other.

John Lydgate, *Troy Book,* circa 1412–1420

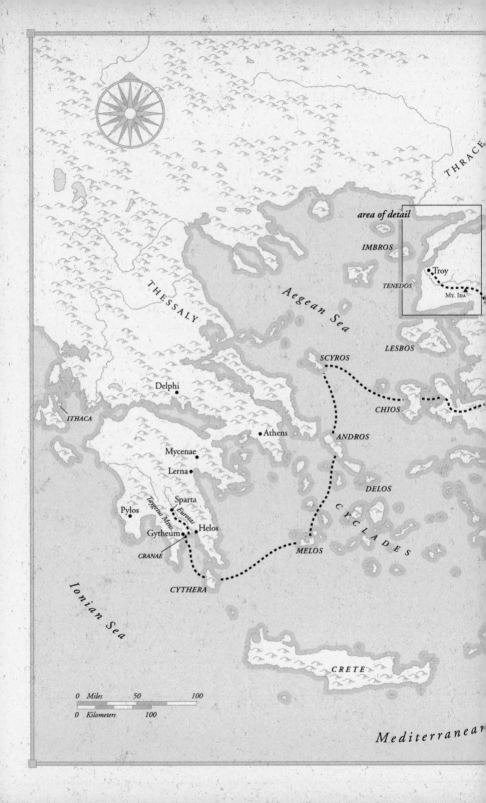

THRACE

area of detail

IMBROS

Troy

TENEDOS

Mt. Ida

LESBOS

THESSALY

Aegean Sea

SCYROS

Delphi

CHIOS

ITHACA

Athens

ANDROS

Mycenae

Lerna

DELOS

Taÿgetus Mnts.

Sparta

Eurotas

Pylos

CYCLADES

Gytheum

Helos

CRANAE

MELOS

CYTHERA

Ionian Sea

CRETE

0   Miles   50   100

0   Kilometers   100

Mediterranean

The World of the Trojan War

Black Sea

PAPHLAGONIANS

AMAZONS

YSIANS

PHRYGIANS

MAEONIANS

CARIANS

LYCIANS

IMBROS

Hellespont

Simois

Troy

TENEDOS

Scamander

MT. IDA

Thebe

CYPRUS

Sea

- - - Helen and Paris's journey
from Sparta to Troy

© 2006 Jeffrey L. Ward

❧ PROLOGUE ❧

I flew back to Troy. No, it was more like floating, for it was a steady flight, no dipping or soaring. I had no wings, although my arms were extended, but they served to steer me, not propel me. I could feel the wind sliding between my fingers. I was lost in the wonder of being able to go to Troy, and so effortlessly.

I could see the brilliant singing blue of the sea, passing over its sparkles and its white-foamed waves, over the islands that reared themselves like barren backs of beasts, shorn of their fur. They were brown, and their bones showed in the hills that were their spines.

Where were the ones Paris and I had visited on our way to Troy, our stepping-stones? From so high above it was impossible to tell.

A gull swooped near me, the wind from his flapping wings disturbing my flight. For an instant I felt myself falling, then I righted myself and floated serenely on. My gown ruffled out, wafting like smoke around me.

Far below I could see ships. Whither were they bound? Whom did they carry? Impossible to know, or, really, to care. This was how the gods viewed us—as trifling amusements. Now I understood. At long last, I understood.

The shore of Troy came up—so soon! I had only one concern, one burning drive: to behold Troy again. To enter its gates, to walk its streets, to touch the buildings, yes, even the buildings I had never cared for. Now they were all precious. I righted myself and set myself down gently just outside the south gate, the grandest one. When I had beheld it on my first entrance to Troy, its top seemed to reach the sky, but now that I had seen it from above, I knew it stopped far short of the clouds.

Oddly, when my feet touched down upon the soil, they raised no dust. But I was dazed with the heady joy of knowing I was back at Troy. I could hear the birds in the meadow around me, could smell the drowsy scent of fields at noonday. To my right I saw herds of dun-colored horses grazing, the famous horses of the Trojan plain. All was peaceful and ordered. In the distance I could see a small stone farmhouse, with a tiled roof, in a grove of trees. I wanted to go there, knock on its door. But it was far away, and I turned back to Troy.

Troy! The magic of Troy rose before my eyes, dancing against the blue of the sky. Its towers were the highest possible for man to build, its walls the strongest and the most beautiful, and inside it . . . ah, inside it lay all the glories of the world! Troy shimmered like a mirage, hovered teasingly, whispered its secrets, lured me toward it.

I walked toward the gate. To my surprise, it was open. The thick, bronze-sheathed doors were gaping wide, and beyond them the path up to the citadel lay broad and beckoning. I passed through the usually guarded gate and did not ask myself why there were no guards, no soldiers. Once inside, I found it was quiet—no sound of groaning wagons, no laughter, no voices at all.

I kept walking up toward the citadel, that cluster of palaces and temples crowning the top of Troy. I could see its glimmer in the distance, its white stone beckoning like a goddess.

It was utterly deserted, and now I began to listen for the echoes in the empty houses as I passed. Where had the people gone?

I was seeking the citadel, where all my people would be. Priam and Hecuba would be in their palace, Hector and Andromache in theirs, the many sons and daughters of Priam and Hecuba in their own quarters behind the royal palace—fifty sons and twelve daughters, each with his or her own home. And between the temple of Athena and the palace of Hector would be mine and Paris's, standing high and proud.

It was there. It was perfect, as perfect as Paris and I had first imagined it, long before a single stone had been laid. When we had lain together on our fragrant bed and amused ourselves imagining our perfect palace. Here it was.

As it never was. The stones had not been exactly like this, no, we could not get the red ones from Phrygia and had had to substitute darker ones from Lesbos. Yet here were the red ones, mortared and in place. For an instant I was puzzled by this, and stood staring at it. *No, it was not like this, except in our minds,* I murmured, as if the stones would shimmer and rearrange themselves at my words. Yet they stubbornly remained as they were.

I shrugged. No matter. I entered the palace and made my way across the wide megaron and then up the stairs into the most private of our quarters, the rooms where Paris and I withdrew when the business of the day at last closed and we could be alone.

My footfalls echoed. Why was it so empty? It was as if a spell had seized it. Nothing stirred, no voice made itself heard.

I stood at the threshold of the chamber. Paris must be in there. He was waiting for me. He had returned from the fields, from exercising the wilder horses as he loved to do, and would now be taking a cup of wine and rubbing a bruise or two from today's work. He would look up and say, *Helen, the white horse I told you about* . . .

Resolutely I pushed the doors open. The chamber was dreadfully quiet. It also looked dark.

I walked in, the whispering of my gown around my feet the loudest noise. "Paris?" I said—the first word I had spoken.

In stories, people are turned to stone. But here they had vanished. I turned and turned, seeking someone in the rooms, but there was nothing. The shell of Troy remained, her palaces and walls and streets, but she had been stripped of what truly made her great—her people.

And Paris . . . where are you, Paris? If you are not here, in our home, where are you?

I saw sunlight and was thankful that someone had thrown the shutters open. Now Troy could begin to live again; now sunshine would flood her. The streets would fill with people again and spring back into life. It was not gone, merely sleeping. Now it could awaken.

"My lady, it is time." Someone was touching my shoulder. "You have slept overlong."

Still I clung to Troy, standing in the bedroom of my palace. Paris would be there now. Surely so! He would come!

"I know it is difficult, but you must rouse yourself." It was the voice of the lady of the chamber. "Menelaus can be interred but once. And today is that day. My condolences, my lady. Be strong."

Menelaus! I opened my eyes and gazed about me wildly. This room—it was not my room in Troy. O the gods! I was in Sparta, and Menelaus was dead.

My Spartan husband Menelaus was dead. Trojan Paris was not there. He had not been there for thirty-odd years. Troy was gone. I could not even call it a smoking ruin, for its smoke had long disappeared into the sky. Troy was so dead even its ashes had been scattered.

It had all been a dream, my visit to Troy. Even what had remained in the kindly dream—the walls, the towers, the streets, and the buildings—was gone. There was nothing left. I wept.

A gentle hand on my shoulder. "I know you sorrow for him," she said. "But still, you must—"

I swung my feet over the side of the bed. "I know. I must attend the funeral. Nay, more than that, I must preside over it." I stood up, slightly dizzy. "I know my duty."

"My lady, I did not mean—"

"Of course not. Please select my garments." There, that would get rid of her.

I pressed my fingers to my temples. Menelaus dead. Yes. That was as it was. His confession to me, his plea—it was all one. I forgave him. It was so long ago. And Paris: *People yet unborn will make songs of us,* I had told him. What a young fool I had been. He had vanished. He was nowhere in my dream—and I knew it, now, for a dream. Paris and I were no more.

No matter. The dream had shown me the way. I would return to Troy after the funeral, after things were set right in Sparta. I must see it again, empty and ruined though it might be. It was where I had lived, most fully lived, where Helen truly took form as Helen, became Helen of Troy.

In life I had soared, if only for a brief time: in that the dream spoke true. Once there was a Helen and she had lived most fully in Troy. Make of that what you will. In my time I called forth hatred, war, and death. I was said to be the woman with a wreath of bronze swords framing her face rather than flowers.

Yet that was never my doing, never my intention. I lay that guilt at the feet of the men who pursued me.

I speak of Helen as if you knew. But who is Helen?

Listen, and I shall tell you. Hold your breath, and you will hear her speak.

PART I

Sparta

❖ I ❖

Helen. Before I could speak, I heard my name and learned that I was Helen. My mother whispered it, but not sweetly; she whispered it as if it were an ugly secret. Sometimes she hissed it, close to my ear, and I could feel her hot breath tickling my skin. She never murmured it, and she never shouted it. Murmuring was for endearments, and shouting was for warning others. She did not want to call attention to me that way.

She had another pet name for me, Cygnet, and when she used it, she smiled, as if it pleased her. It was private, our little secret, for she never used it in front of anyone else.

Just as the mists that cling to hills gradually thin and disappear, and the solid form of the rocks and forests appear, just so a life takes form out of early memories, which burn away later. Out of the swirl of jumbled memories and feelings of my childhood, I remember being at a palace where my mother's family lived, and where she had grown up. My grandmother and grandfather were still alive, but when I try to recall their faces, I cannot. We had all gone there—fled there—because of trouble with my father's throne in Sparta. He had been driven from it, and now was a king in exile, living with his wife's family.

I know now that this was in Aetolia, although of course then I knew nothing of locations, places, names. I only knew that our palace in Sparta, high on its hill, was more open to the sun and the wind than this one, which was dark and boxlike. I did not like being there and wished I could return to my old room. I asked my mother when that might be, when we could go back home.

"Home?" she said. "This is home!"

I did not understand, and shook my head.

"This was my home, where I grew up. Sparta was never my home."

"But it is mine," I said. I tried not to cry at the thought I might never be able to return there. I thought I had stopped the tears at the corners of my eyes, but my trembling lip gave me away.

"Don't cry, you baby!" she said, gripping my arm. "Princesses do not cry, not even before their mothers!" I hated the way her face looked as she bent down and put it up to mine. It was long and narrow and when she frowned it seemed to grow even longer, stretching out to look like an animal's with a muzzle. "We will soon know how long we will be here, and where we are to go. Delphi will tell us. The oracle will reveal it."

We were jouncing in a cart across land that was wild and forested. It did not look like the land around Sparta, cupped in its gentle green valley. Here rough hills, covered with scrub and scrawny trees, made our journey difficult. As we approached the mountain where the sacred site of Delphi hid itself, we had to abandon the carts and trudge along a rutted path that clung to the ascent. On each side of us, tall thin trees with trunks like needles sought the sky but gave no shade, and we had to skirt around boulders and clamber over obstacles.

"It makes the arrival all the more special," said one of my brothers, Castor. He was some five years older than I, dark-haired like Mother, but of a friendly and light disposition. He was my best friend among my siblings, cheerful and heartening, amusing yet always thoughtful and watchful of me, the youngest. "If it were easy to find, it would not be the prize it is."

"Prize?" Coming up beside us, puffing and thumping, was Castor's twin, Polydeuces. He was as fair as Castor was dark, but he lived in the shadows of caution and doubt, belying his looks. "I see no prize, just a dry and dusty ascent up Mount Parnassus. And for what? For a seer to tell us what to do? You know if Mother does not like what she hears, she will just ignore it. So why bother to come, when she could just stay in her chambers, call a seer, and have a divining rite there?"

"It is Father who must know," said Castor. "He will give weight to what the oracle says, even if Mother does not. It is his throne, after all, that is in question."

"It is his brother who has driven him from it. Now, dear brother, let us clasp hands and vow to avoid such strife."

"We can rule together. I see nothing to prevent it." Castor laughed.

"If Father does not regain his throne, we will hardly be likely to follow him," said Polydeuces.

"Well, then, we'll make our way boxing and wrestling, win all the prizes, have lots of cattle and women—"

"You'll always make your way, I am sure." Suddenly the eldest was beside us, our sister Clytemnestra. "That is a great gift." She turned to me. "Are you tired?"

I was, but would not admit it. "No, not at all!" I walked faster to prove it.

At sundown we reached Delphi at last. We had climbed and climbed, until we finally passed a spring, where others—who seemed to have come from nowhere—were refreshing themselves, splashing water on their faces and filling their waterskins. The spring emptied into a pool, a pool shaded by overhanging trees, with dappled sun playing on its surface. It was very calm there, very restful, and I dipped my hands into the surprisingly cold water, letting it restore me.

It was too late to go to the oracle, and so we spent the night in the field that lay just below the sacred buildings. Many others were there as well, sleeping in the clear open air. The stars above us were bright and cold. I looked at them and promised myself to ask my brothers to tell me the stories about them. But this night we were so tired we all fell asleep instantly.

The sun hit my eyes and woke me up very early. It did not have to peek over a mountain, as in Sparta, but flooded the sky with light the instant it rose. All around me others were stirring, folding their blankets, stretching, eager to seek the secrets of Delphi.

Father was not himself. I could tell by the way he greeted the other pilgrims around us. He spoke to them but did not seem to hear their answers. And his response was vague, beside the point.

"We must hurry, so we are first at the oracle." He looked around at all the others, taking their measure. "Their concerns are everyday ones, not the very future of a throne." He pushed us to be on our way.

The oracle. The future. Omens. Prophecies. Until then, I was free. I was a child of no importance—or so I believed. After this, they ruled my life, the soothsayers, the fixed limits of the gods, the parameters that defined me.

Father was hurrying toward the oracle, leaning forward against the wind in his haste to get there first, when suddenly a shriek rang out from a rock on the path. Perched on it was a crone, a woman who, in her dark robes and hood, looked more like a vulture or a raven than a person.

"You! You!" she—I swear it—cawed.

Father stopped. All of us stopped. He went over to her, stood on tiptoe to hear her as she leaned over on her rock and spoke to him. He scowled, then shook his head. He was arguing with her! I saw him gesturing. Then he came over to me and dragged me over to her.

I did not want to go. Why was he forcing me? I twisted and tried to get away.

"Child, child!" she cried in her ugly, high voice. Father lifted me, squirming and trying to escape, and held me fast. He thrust me up to her. She leaned forward and grabbed my head, and her voice changed. She began uttering strange, unearthly cries. Her hands felt like talons, gripping me so tightly I feared my head might burst open.

"Bring her up in Sparta, then!" Her voice was now a sound like the water in the pool we passed at the entrance to Delphi, distant and dim. "But she will be the ruin of Asia, the ruin of Europe, and because of her a great war will be fought, and many Greeks will die!"

"Let me go, let me go!" I cried. But Father held me fast, and the woman breathed in and out harshly, a horrible sound, half gasping and half roaring. Mother stood there, too, rooted and unmoving. My parents' helplessness frightened me most of all. It was as though she had by some power paralyzed them.

"Troy," she muttered. "Troy . . ."

Then suddenly the spell was broken. She stopped her labored breathing and released my head. My scalp tingled and I fell back into Father's arms.

We continued the march up the path to the oracle, the famous one who sat in a secret place and breathed in fumes—or conversed with the god Apollo—and Father sought her out. But what she said I do not know. I was still shaking after the assault of the woman.

"The Sibyl," corrected Clytemnestra. "She is the Herophile Sybil and she wanders about giving prophecies. She is more ancient than the oracle, more important." Clytemnestra knew such things. She was six years older than I and made it her business to know such things. "What she says always comes true. Whereas what the oracle says—well, there are tricks to it. It does not always happen as people think."

"Why did she grab Helen?" Polydeuces demanded.

Clytemnestra looked at him. "You know why," she said.

"*I* don't!" I said. "Please, please, tell me!"

"It is not for me to tell you," she said. "Ask Mother!" At that, she gave a wild laugh almost as frightening as the Sibyl's.

We hurried—or so it seemed—back to the palace of my grandparents. Mother and Father secluded themselves, conferring with the old king and queen, and I was left to wander about my barren chambers. Oh, I did not like them, and my scalp still hurt from the grip of the Sibyl. I touched it gingerly and felt the ridges of scabs there.

Great war . . . many Greeks will die . . . Troy . . . I did not know what it meant, but I knew it alarmed Mother and Father—and even Clytemnestra, who was usually fearless, the first to drive a chariot with unruly horses, the first to break a rule.

I picked up a mirror and tried to see the injury on my head. I turned the mirror this way and that, but the injury was too far back for me to see. Then Clytemnestra snatched the mirror from my hands.

"No!" she cried. There was real alarm in her voice.

"Can you see the top of my head?" I said. "I cannot. That is all I want to do."

She parted my hair. "There are grooves there, but nothing deep." She kept the mirror firmly clenched in her hand.

❖ II ❖

Thus it was that I learned I was forbidden to use a mirror. It was such a simple thing—a polished bronze surface that reflected back a poor image in any case. I had seen little when I held the mirror up to my head. The face I saw, fleetingly, was not the face I had imagined.

Can we envision our own face? I think not. I think we imagine ourselves invisible, with no face at all, able to blend perfectly with everything around us.

Mother looked at herself in a mirror often enough. It seemed that every time I came into her room she was peering into it, raising her eyebrows, turning her head to see a different side of her cheek, or licking her lips. Sometimes what she did brought a smile to her face, but more often it brought a frown, and a sigh. She always put the mirror down when she saw me, even going so far once as to sit on it so I could not take it up.

Was my mother pretty? Attractive? Alluring? Fair? Lovely? Beautiful? We have so many words to describe the exact degree in which a person pleases our senses. Yes, I would say she was all of these things. She had, as I have said, a long thin face, which made her unusual; in our family, the faces were round or oval. Her nose was a perfect thin blade that set off her wide-set, slanted eyes—that was what you noticed when you looked at her: those large slanted eyes, which never met yours directly, and dominated her face. The most arresting quality about her was her vivid coloring. She had very white skin, very dark hair, and cheeks that always seemed flushed and glowing. She had a long thin neck, too, very elegant. I would have thought she would be proud of that, but once when someone said she had a swan's neck she ordered her out of the room.

Her name was Leda, a lovely name, I thought. It meant "lady" and she was always dainty and graceful, so in choosing that name for her my grandparents had given her something to grow into.

My own name, Helen, was less certain. I asked Mother one day—when I had again come upon her peering in the mirror, and she hastily put it away—why I was named that, and what it meant.

"I know that Clytemnestra means 'praiseworthy wooing,' and since she is your firstborn, I thought that meant that Father's wooing had won you."

She threw back her head and gave a low, amused laugh. "Your father's wooing was such as he is, political." Seeing the puzzlement on my face, she said, "I mean by that he was in exile—again!—and took refuge with my mother and father. And they had a marriageable daughter, and he was eager to be married, so eager that he promised great gifts to them if they would surrender me, and so they did."

"But what did you think of him, when you first saw him?"

She shrugged. "That he was not displeasing, and I could abide him."

"Is that all a woman can look for?" I asked, very hesitant, and also a little shocked.

"Yes." She looked hard at me. "Although in your case I think we can ask for more than that. Drive a harder bargain. Now, as to the others' names: Castor means 'beaver,' and indeed he has grown up to be very industrious, and

Polydeuces means 'much sweet wine.' Your brother could use more wine, if it would serve to lighten his spirits."

"But my name! My name!" Children are most interested in themselves. I was impatient to hear my story, the special story of myself from before I could remember, a mystery to which only Mother and Father held the key.

"Helen." She took a great deep breath. "It was hard to choose your name. It had to be . . . it had to reflect . . ." She nervously began to twirl a lock of her hair, a habit she reverted to in times of uncertainty or agitation; I knew it well. "It means many things. 'Moon,' because you seemed touched by the goddess; 'torch,' because you brought light."

"I was a baby. How could I have brought light?"

"Your hair was bright and shone like the sun," she said.

"Moon—sun—I cannot be both!" Why was this so confusing?

"Well, you are," she said. "Their light is different, but it is possible to be both. To have attributes of both."

"But you also call me Cygnet. What does that mean?" I might as well have it all, have all my names explained.

"Cygnet means 'little swan'—a tiny one, just out of the egg."

"But why did I remind you of that? You don't even like swans!" One day we had been walking near the lake at my grandparents' and a flock of swans had made their way toward us. My mother had turned her back on them and hurried away, and Father had yelled and thrown stones at them. His face had turned red and he had yelled, "Get away, you filthy monsters!"

"Oh, I used to like them well enough," she said. "They were my favorite birds when I was a little girl and living here with my own parents. I would go out to the lakeshore and feed them. I loved to watch them float on the water, with their lovely curved necks and their white feathers."

"But why did you change your mind about them?"

"I learned more about them when I was grown up. My wonder at them fled." Suddenly she bent down and took my face in her long thin hands— long and thin like her face. "Do not look too closely at something, do not come too near, or you might lose the wonder. That is what separates children from adults." She stroked my cheek. "Believe in everything now. Later you cannot." She gave one of her dazzling smiles. "Once I loved them, and I still love the swan in you."

"Then I shall go and see the swans every day," I said stoutly. "While I can still like them, before I find out . . . whatever it was that changed your mind."

"Hurry, then. We will be leaving here soon. Your father has his throne back, and we return to Sparta. The swans come there only rarely. They do not live there, do not touch down often."

Oh, it was good to be back! Back in our lovely sprawling palace, high on its hill above the valley of the Eurotas River, looking down over the city of Sparta on the plain. I had missed it so. I loved my chamber, with its paintings of birds and flowers on the white walls, and the old pear tree just outside my window. And all my toys were still safe in the chest, just where I had left them when we fled so quickly.

Of course, no one would take toys, but Father was most concerned to check his storerooms and see what had been plundered while his brother had usurped his throne and lived in his palace. Father had emptied the treasure room himself and hidden its goods, buried them in the foothills of the surrounding mountains.

"But you cannot guard against everything!" he said. "And I consider every tile that is damaged an outrage, every cloak that was taken a violation! *He* lived here, he dared to invade my palace!" Again he was getting red-faced, and Mother tried to calm him.

"Tyndareus, these are little things. The only important thing is your throne. It is here. You have reclaimed it."

"My brother—the swine—!"

"Your brother is dead," said Mother flatly.

"I hate him anyway!"

Overhearing these things, I wondered how a brother could come to wrong another brother so that he would feel that way. But oh! I had yet to learn of the vile things one family member could do to another. I did not understand, because I loved my brothers and sister and they loved me, and I could not see how it could be otherwise.

My life there was full of sun and wind and laughter. I had the run of the palace, I could have anything I wished. I sang and played and learned my lessons from the amiable old tutor they brought for me. I lacked nothing, desired nothing that was not to hand. I look back on that time as my most innocent, my happiest—if happiness consists of no desires at all, no concerns, a dreamless floating.

But, as will happen, I looked up one day, when my eyes and heart were older, able to discern, and saw the high wall surrounding our palace, blocking me from anything beyond it. I began to ask to be taken outside, to see what lay in the meadows and the mountains and the city. I was met with a stern refusal.

"You must stay here, within the walls of the palace grounds," Father said in a voice that discouraged argument.

Of course, children always ask why, but he would not tell me. "It must be as I have said," was all he would utter.

I asked my brothers, but they demurred, which was most unlike them. Castor, who was usually adventurous, said that I must respect Father's wishes, and Polydeuces hinted darkly that he had his reasons.

I hated being the youngest! The others could come and go as they pleased, but Helen must say inside, a prisoner! Would I never be delivered, never be freed?

I made up my mind to demand that I be allowed outside. I should be taught to hunt; I should be able to go out in the mountains with a bow, it was embarrassing that I was seven years old and still had never even held one! I marched toward Father's quarters, shoving aside the guards on either side of the megaron. I felt odd, pushing them like that, as I was only a third their size, but I was a princess, and they had to obey me.

Today the megaron—the great chamber with its open fireplace and its polished pillars, where important guests were welcomed—was dark and empty. The private chambers of the king, separate from those of the queen, which were upstairs and near the megaron, lay on one side of the palace, across from the children's quarters. More guards appeared when I approached the inner chambers, and I shoved them aside as well.

I heard Father's voice. He was there! Now was the time to speak to him! I would tell him of my longing to go outside the palace grounds. But then I heard my name. I stopped and listened.

"Helen," he said. "Can we do it?"

Do what? I felt my heart stop, then start racing.

"It will mean you have to admit to it." Mother's voice. "Are you able to do that? For she is worth much more if—"

"I know, I know!" Father barked. "I realize that." Now I could hear the pain in his voice. "But can we—can you—prove it absolutely? They will want proof—"

"Look at her!" Mother's voice was triumphant.

"But there is nothing definite, I mean, beauty, yes, but you, my sweet, you are also beautiful—"

I heard her make a noise of dismissal. "The hair," she said. "The color of the hair."

What of it? I did not understand.

"There must be more," said Father. "Have you nothing else?"

The silence told me the answer was no.

"How could you have been such a fool?" he cried. "You could have asked for *something*."

"If you had ever had such an experience, you would know how stupid you sound!"

"Oh, so I am stupid!"

And then it ran along the same old channel as their usual arguments, and I knew there was nothing more to be learned. I stepped brightly into the room and made my request to leave the palace, see what lay beyond it. They both frowned and denied me. Father said it was because I was too young, Mother because I had everything I needed here.

I grew older. I was eight, then nine. I stayed behind the walls, but I made a habit of dragging a log over to one stretch of them and, standing on it, spying out the valley lying at the foot of the palace mountain.

At length I won a small victory: persuading Mother and Father to let my brothers take me hunting. They allowed me to go into the private royal hunting grounds in the Taygetus Mountains behind us, where no outsiders could trespass.

"We will start you off with hares," said Castor. "They cannot turn on you, but they move fast and are a challenge to hit with a bow and arrow."

The forest glades and mountain glens became my world. I cared less about hunting than chasing the game. I loved running through the woods. I was fleet of foot, so much so that my brothers called me Atalanta, after the woman whom no one could outrun. In the legend many suitors raced against her, but she defeated them all; only a trick of Aphrodite allowed a man to finish ahead of her.

"That Aphrodite," Castor had said, when he teased me about my swiftness. "She will make sure you trip."

"But, my dear sister, perhaps a suitors' race would not be a bad idea,"

Polydeuces said. "You are sure to win the first few rounds, and that will delay the inevitable."

I sighed, leaning back against an oak tree, letting its bark press into my skin. Father had begun talking about Clytemnestra's marriage; he said it was soon time she be wed. All the eligible young men of our surrounding area, and even as far away as Crete or Rhodes, might compete for her. For with the hand of Clytemnestra came a crown: her husband would be king of Sparta after Father—unless he was a king in his own right, and then he would take Clytemnestra away to his realm.

"In olden times, did not the losers have to die?" I asked.

"Those are the legends," said Polydeuces. "In truth, I think men are much more cautious."

"Then if I made it a condition for my contest . . . it would discourage men?" I said, meaning it as jest, but suddenly the Sibyl's words *many Greeks will die* came into my mind. "No, I don't mean it," I quickly said.

As I gained skill, my brothers let me range on my own; they did not shadow me everywhere. Often when I was pursuing game I let it go, and stopped to linger in the green glades of the foothills of the lofty Taygetus Mountains. There were misty glens with carpets of moss where the sun was reduced to pale shafts seeking the ground. I loved to stay here, where it felt so private that even the sun could not penetrate.

Then I would forget the arguments I heard more and more when I came unexpectedly upon the king and queen, their sharp voices as they sparred with each other. In the forest, animals did not jeer, nor did the trees make me feel uneasy. You knew which animals were dangerous and likely to attack you. In the forest there were no secret enemies.

❖ III ❖

Nine winters had passed since I was born, and now I was almost as tall as my mother. Lately she had insisted we stand back to back whenever I was summoned to her chamber, so she could see how I had grown. She called for a stick to be laid across the tops of our heads, and would ask her attendant,

"I am still taller, am I not?" and the attendant would dutifully nod. I wondered what would happen on the day the stick would tilt and I would be taller. I wished that day would never come, for I knew it would displease her, only I did not know why.

When she called me into her chamber, often it was on the pretext of asking me what my tutor was teaching me. If I told her we were learning the family of the gods, she would ask questions. At first they were easy: Name the Olympian gods, she would say. Only the twelve who live on Mount Olympus, none of the others. And I would recite them. But later she put much harder questions to me. One day she asked me to name all of Zeus's offspring.

"Do you mean the immortal ones, or all of them?"

She gave a strange smile. "Begin with the immortals."

I named them—Athena and Persephone, Apollo and Artemis, Ares and Hermes. I added that Hera was his sister, and that Aphrodite was not the child of Zeus but of his grandfather Uranus.

"Aphrodite was not born, strictly speaking," said Mother with a dry little laugh. "But Zeus has made sure that Mount Olympus teems with his children. Since he will never die or step down from his throne, he need not worry who will succeed him. They can bicker and brawl to their hearts' content, it makes no difference. None of them will die, none will have to go into exile." She paused, settling herself down on a bench, extending her long legs beneath their thin linen gown. I could see them through the fabric, the flesh turning the white linen pinkish.

She saw me looking and smoothed the linen over her thighs. "The best, from Egypt," she said. "I would have preferred blue, but we are last to receive anything here. It comes first to Mycenae, after it has gone through Troy and Crete and the gods know where else first."

She was about to begin her lament on Sparta's isolation. "Still, it is very lovely," I assured her.

"Now for the mortal children!" she suddenly said. "Name them!"

"The ones Zeus had by earthly women? Oh, Mother, how could I ever count them all?" I laughed. The tutor had told me the most important ones, such as Perseus and Minos, and, of course, Heracles, but some were unknown.

"Someone *did* count them all; Zeus has singled out one hundred and fifteen mortal women to give his . . . his attention to."

"And of course they all had children," I said. The gods could never take up with anyone, god or mortal, and not leave proof.

"Yes, always," she said.

"But it is so—so—peculiar that the women can't look at the god, at least not in his divine form. Now, when he is disguised as a bull, or a shower of gold—."

"He does that for their protection! You know what happened to that foolish Semele, who wished to gaze on his divinity."

Yes, no less a woman than the mother of Dionysus had seen Zeus in his godhood and had instantly been turned to cinders. "It was very sad," I agreed. She seemed agitated, as if it were very important what the tutor had taught me. I sought to soothe her. "So it seems that curiosity can be dangerous," I said.

She took a deep breath. "Just so. Now, what of the other ones, besides Heracles and Dionysus?"

I tried to remember. "They are the most famous because they became gods themselves, which is very unusual. The rest of them just die in the regular way. There's Perseus, he lived near here, at Argos, and then there's Niobe, Zeus's first mortal woman, and her son Argus, and oh, Mother, there are so many of them! Zeus was everywhere, it seems, and—no, I cannot name them all." It was hopeless. Even the tutor most likely could not. "Alcmene, the mother of Heracles, was the last," I said. "Zeus comes no more amongst us." For that I was thankful—no more additions to memorize.

Now she burst out into that laugh I hated. "Is that what he's told you?"

"Yes, it is." I backed up a step or two. She was frightening when she gave that laugh. "He said that Zeus—that that time had ended."

"Not entirely," she said. She opened her mouth as if to speak more, but gave a great sigh of resignation. "Now it has. Now it has. But not with Heracles. There are younger children of Zeus. Now, did your tutor point out any odd thing about the offspring of Zeus?"

I could not imagine what she meant. "No," I finally said. "Of course, they are all lovely, and tall, and strong, and have—what is the saying, 'more than mortal beauty'?—but aside from that, I do not know. They are all very different."

"They are all men!" she cried, leaping up from the couch so quickly my eyes could barely follow her. "Men! All men!"

"Perhaps he has daughters, but does not recognize them," I said. "Perhaps he feels it is not fitting to sire daughters, and so he will not claim them." It seemed as if Zeus might believe that.

"Nonsense!" She was trembling. "He has daughters, divine ones on

Mount Olympus, and he is proud of them. Perhaps mortal women did not give him any daughters worthy of him. If they did, you can be sure he would be proud of them. If he knows of them. If he knows of them!"

"I thought he knew everything."

Now came that dreadful laugh again. "Oh, Hera fools him all the time! No, it is entirely possible he has overlooked his mortal daughter, if she has been hidden away, in a place where no one comes, no one sees her."

Suddenly I had this dreadful feeling, as her words rang in my ears. *Hidden away, in a place where no one comes, no one sees her.* They had kept me hidden away, and few visitors came to Sparta, and there was so much whispering about me between Mother and Father . . . and there were the forbidden mirrors. And Mother so fierce about Zeus, so adamant about him. But no, that was a foolish fancy. All children like to think they are special, or even unique.

I suddenly remembered something. Perhaps it was what she had been hinting at. "I am descended from Zeus!" I cried. "Yes, he told me that Zeus and a nymph of the mountain, Taygete, had a child, Lacedaemon, and that child is Father's ancestor." I expected her to reward me, to clap and say, *Yes! Yes!*

She shook her head. "That was a very long time ago, and I see nothing godlike in your father. The blood has run very thin, if indeed it ever stretched back to Mount Olympus."

She was trembling. I touched her shoulder, wishing I could embrace her, but knowing she would push me away. "Well, it is of no matter," I said. "I cannot see how it would affect us in any way." What happened long ago, in a story, was of no moment.

She looked very hard at me. "It is time we go to the Mysteries," she said. "The goddesses Demeter and Persephone are bound to our family. You are old enough. We will all go to the shrine on the mountain, and there you will learn of your guardian goddess. And she can reveal much, if she so chooses."

It was decided that we would go at the time of the celebration of the Greater Mysteries, in the autumn. I could begin my initiation now so that when I arrived at the sanctuary I could experience the secret rites in their fullest measure. Only those who had trained and been accepted by the goddesses could look upon their secret nature.

An older woman who had served my mother since childhood instructed me in private. We are forbidden ever to reveal what we learned, but I can tell of the things everyone knows. Mother's friend Agave began by taking me on a walk through the newly planted fields, while telling the story in a singsong voice. I was forced to wear a veil to hide my face lest any of the field-workers see me. It made the clear day seem overcast. Tramping beside us were two guards, armed with stout swords. They, too, were initiates.

Though my sight was dimmed, I could still hear, and the birds and cries of human voices told me it was that exultant time of year when the earth rejoices as it warms again. I could smell the musty odor of just-turned earth, and hear the snorting and deep rumbles of oxen pulling the plow. Behind the curved plow came the farmer scattering the seeds, dropping them into the furrow, and behind him, a boy with a mattock to cover them over again. Cawing and wheeling around his head, the crows were looking for a meal. Even the low rasp of their cries sounded happy to me. The boy yelled and beat them off with his hat, laughing all the while.

"The earth rejoices, and why?" Agave suddenly stopped, so abruptly that I ran into her. She turned around and peered at me, but she could not see me through the veil.

"Because Persephone has returned from the underworld," I dutifully recited. Everyone knew that; you did not have to be an initiate.

"And?"

"And now her grieving mother, Demeter, who withered all the blooming and growing things, will bring them back to life again. And that is why we have the planting, and the flowering of the fruit trees."

She nodded. "Good. Yes. And might we see and hear Demeter? Walking here amongst us?"

I was puzzled. "I am not sure. If we did, I think she would be in disguise. She disguised herself when she went searching for Persephone, did she not?"

"Yes." Agave took my hand and we began walking again, skirting between two fields—one of barley, one of wheat. Now the rows were just little green hairs, looking very fragile. "While the daughter is with her, the mother will be gracious to us all," she said. "But when she leaves again, then it is we who are punished. The vines shrivel and the cold kills the flowers, and we call it winter."

"And we hate it!" muttered one of the guards. "Blue toes, stiff fingers, still we're expected to fight as if it's summer. The fields get to rest, the bears to sleep, but a Spartan soldier must carry on."

Agave laughed. "No wars are fought in winter, so you cannot whine about that."

"Kings must be guarded in winter. Princesses, too." He winked at me. "Yes, and where were Persephone's guards that day that Hades got her? If Demeter had been a good mother, she wouldn't have left her unprotected like that."

"Don't demean her or she'll strike these fields, and you, my friend, won't be eating," said Agave.

"No danger of anyone making off with Helen here. The king keeps a guard on her at all times, even though she's locked up in the palace grounds. What's he so worried about, I ask?"

"It is best you *don't* ask," said Agave. Her voice changed. "Demeter may be in these very fields, so watch your words," she told us all. Then to me she said, "But the correct answer to my question is just that. We might see her here. But you will surely see her at the Greater Mysteries. That I promise you."

I felt a shiver of excitement just thinking of that. But it was Persephone I most wanted to see. She was young, like me.

Persephone chose the time of year when the days and nights were equal to come and go, from a special cave at a place called Eleusis. But that was far from Sparta, close to Athens, over the mountains from us. Since no one in our families came from there, I wondered why the goddess and her mother had chosen us to protect.

Mother told me that because Demeter was the goddess of crops and plenty, it was natural that she would favor Sparta, as our valley was so rich and fertile. We lay protected on both sides by high mountains, and through our flat green valley ran the Eurotas River, broad and swift, watering our crops. Fields of grain, trees heavy with their burden of apples, pomegranates, olives, and figs, vines twining themselves around oak trees and hung with grapes, all would please Demeter, proclaim her power in our lives.

"You saw how barren it was in Aetolia," she said. "Or perhaps you don't remember, you were so young. But there's no place as lush as Sparta and our valley, no, not for all the airs of Argos or Tiryns or Mycenae. Even Pylos cannot match us." The unmistakable lilt of pride filled her voice. "For this Demeter loves us."

"Or are we this way because Demeter loves us?" I asked. "Which came first?"

She frowned. "Really, Helen, you are most argumentative and contrary."

"I didn't mean it that way."

"You often sound it nonetheless. I don't know the answer to why the Eurotas Valley is rich, or which came first, and I don't think it matters. What matters is that Demeter is our goddess. She has blessed this land we rule over, and she thereby blesses us."

"But what if we didn't have the land? Would she still bless us?" After all, if I married and left Sparta, I would no longer be in that fertile land. Would Demeter then dismiss me?

She bent her head and closed her eyes. Was she angry? Had I offended her? She was breathing heavily, almost as if she had fallen asleep. But when she spoke, her voice was quiet and hesitant. "You have spoken true," she said. "Often kings are driven from their thrones, lose their kingdoms. Your father has almost lost his, twice. Kings have drowned themselves in the Eurotas. In Mycenae, the family has a curse on it because of the fighting between the brothers for that throne. Dreadful things were done . . ." She gave a shudder. "Perhaps then the gods abandon us," she said. "They do not like to involve themselves in our troubles."

We had been sitting in the bright courtyard of the palace, caressed by the sunny day. In summer, the open area was a rustle of leaves from the ornamental trees scattered throughout, and birds, expecting food, hopped from branch to branch. They were so tame they would swoop down and strut at our feet, darting toward our toes to grab a crumb or two. Then they would chirp, jump back, and fly swiftly away, over the palace roof and far away. When she saw them flying, Mother would laugh, a thrilling low laugh, and I could look at her and see that she was beautiful. Her dark eyes would follow the flight of the birds and I could trace them by looking at her.

"Come with me, Helen," she suddenly said. "I wish to show you something." She stood up and held out her slender hand, weighted with rings. When she squeezed my hand, the rings bit down and hurt. Obediently I followed her, back into her quarters.

Now that I was growing older, I was aware that her rooms were furnished more richly than the rest of the palace. Usually there were few stools and the tables were plain three-legged things, their tops bare. But in Mother's rooms there were chairs with arms, couches to lie upon in daytime, spread with soft coverlets, tables with ivory inlays, carved ornamental boxes and alabaster bowls on them. Sheer curtains shielded the room against the stabbing sunlight of noon, softening it while rippling with the breeze. Being so high meant we always caught the best breezes, and Mother's rooms were a cool dim haven.

On one of the tables flush against a wall she kept her favorite precious items: I always saw several cups and round boxes of purest gold, and her ivory-handled mirror lay face down. Several long bronze pins, their ends tipped with crystal, were arranged side by side between them. I had a desire to grab the mirror and look long and hard at my face.

She saw my eyes go in that direction and she shook her head. "I know what you are thinking," she said. "You long to see for yourself what is the object of curiosity for so many. Well, on the day you are betrothed, and we know you are safe, then you may look. Until then . . . I have something for you." She opened an oblong box and drew out a shimmering piece of what looked like a cloud. But it was attached to a circlet of gold. She waved it to and fro, so that the cloth danced and the sunlight played through it. Little rainbows chased across it, disappearing in a wink. She settled it on my head, pressing the circlet down. "It is time you had a proper veil," she said, as the fuzziness blurred my vision.

I yanked it off. "I won't wear it! There's no need, here in the palace, everyone knows me, I can't bear it!" I squeezed the material in my hands, trying to ruin it. But no matter how hard I crumpled it, it refused to wrinkle. Such was the hateful fineness of the cloth.

"How dare you?" she said, wrestling it from me. "This cost a fortune. I had it woven specially, and the gold circlet could have made a fine cup!"

"I won't do it anymore, I won't hide behind a veil. There must be something wrong with me. You pretend I'm beautiful, but I must be a monster, to be hidden from sight. *That's* why you won't let me look in the mirror. Well, now I will!" Before she could stop me, I leapt across the room and seized the mirror. I rushed between the columns and beyond the curtains and for an instant, before she clutched my arm, I saw my face in the brightly polished surface of the bronze, saw it in the sunlight. Or rather, saw part of it—the eyes, which were fringed with thick black lashes, and the mouth and cheeks. In that fleeting instant I saw my flushed face, the bright green-brown of my eyes. That was all, for the mirror was wrenched from my hand, and my mother stood before me. I expected her to strike me or shake me, but she did not. For an instant it crossed my mind that she was afraid of me, rather than what I later learned—she was afraid of damaging me if she did that, and she took good care of her possessions. "You are not a monster," she said, "although sometimes you behave as one!" Then she laughed, and all at once the ugly moment had passed. "Then you need not wear it here, but you must promise me you will never leave the palace grounds, not without a guard or your instructor, and in that case, you will cover yourself. Oh, Helen . . . there are many people who wish us all harm, who would kidnap a princess easily enough. We do not want that, do we?"

I shook my head. But I knew it was more than that. There seemed to be more worry that I would be kidnapped than that any of her other children would.

❖ IV ❖

The days grew long, twilights lingered, and the hot blast of summer poured down on us. I could almost feel Helios in his chariot directly overhead, the heat radiating out from his pathway, drying up the earth beneath him. Under his hand the leaves, dulled with dust, hung limply from their branches, and we in the palace fanned ourselves to create our own breezes. In the stillness of noon even the white butterflies hid themselves, and it seemed that nothing stirred.

All the while I was learning the rites and secrets of the mysteries of Demeter, and it took all summer. There were so many of them—there was the story of her wandering in search of her daughter, who was snatched away by Hades as she gathered the spring flowers, which must be reenacted. The priestesses even knew which flower she had been gathering—a rare yellow narcissus. Her mother, in seeking her, had briefly dwelt with mortals and assumed the guise of an old woman caring for a baby prince. Did she wish to take him for her own son? She tried to make him immortal by passing him through a flame, but his mother discovered it and brought a hysterical end to the attempt.

"She did not understand that this would kill him, rather than make him immortal," old Agave said.

These gods seemed to have little regard for us, I thought, and little understanding for how fragile we are. Truly they were frightening. I was thankful that Demeter was our patron, but I hoped she would not ask anything of us. It might be something deadly.

I learned to mix and partake of the special drink that was used in the rites, a barley gruel flavored with mint that Demeter drank on her sorrowful journey. We also had a sacred basket, the *cista mystica,* that contained ritual objects. We were given long torches that were to be carried in procession to the site, and used in a sacred dance to imitate Demeter searching in the dark for her lost daughter. I was to practice walking with it, holding it high, and then learn to dance with it in only one hand.

But there was one final thing, perhaps the most important thing. Without it I could not proceed to the initiation. "You must be of an unblemished moral character," said Agave solemnly. "Your hands must be absolutely clean and your heart immaculately pure."

I trembled before this order, imagining myself to be smudged and spotted by all my childish shortcomings. I know now that the only thing that bars an initiate is being a murderer, but I suppose it is good for children to start out vigilant against all failings. Even being a murderer does not keep you from the Mysteries forever, for if you atone and are purified, you may approach them once again.

If being a murderer kept one permanently from the rites, then Father could hardly be going, and he was enthusiastically readying himself for them. I had learned, by listening and asking questions, that Father had stopped at little—I started to say *nothing* but that would be untrue—to regain his throne and to keep it. With enemies such as he had, he needed to be as hard as they. And the land was filled with warriors, with murderers and rivals and bad people. I smile as I say "bad people" because it became a joke with my brothers. "There are bad people there," they would say, when speaking of just about anywhere I mentioned. Crete. Egypt. Athens. Thessaly. Thrace. Syria. Cyprus.

"Do you mean everyone in Egypt? Everyone in Thrace?" I would say. "Surely not!"

"Oh, that's what Polydeuces always says," Castor would say, laughing. "But I—I would only say that there are a great number of bad people about, mixed in with the good ones. We trade with all those peoples, and without them our palace would be bare indeed. Bare, anyway, of all the luxuries Mother likes."

"So be on guard, little sister, for all those baaaaaad people!" Polydeuces' deep voice rumbled. Then he laughed. "Many foreigners pour in for the Mysteries, although they tend to favor Eleusis. But it is strictly required that they speak Greek, so that eliminates the uncivilized, if not the truly bad."

The days began to shorten. At first barely noticeable, only in that we could see the stars a little sooner. Then the morning light began slanting differently into my chamber, and the winds that blew into the palace shifted. They whispered through the west side, bringing cool nights for sleeping. Now, at last, it was time to go to the shrine of the Mysteries and meet our goddesses.

We would set out at dawn, and rose even before that to partake, in silence, of the new harvest grains, and to taste the new wines. Then we attired ourselves in the gold and green tunics and mantles we wore in their honor—the color of growing things—and took up our torches. A cart, groaning with our offerings from the fields and trees, was ready to trundle away with us. By the time the sun broke over the horizon we were already in the gentle hills leading up to the shrine.

I wore the hated veil as I had promised, intoning the hymns to the goddesses I had been taught. We were not supposed to talk, but I could hear Mother and Father speaking in low voices to one another. Clytemnestra walked behind them, her head meekly downcast, but she was most likely straining to overhear them. The air was fresh and filled with the scent of reaped fields. I suddenly felt overcome with the beauty and fullness of autumn.

As we made our way, the paths grew steeper, and soon the cart could not climb with us. Servants took the offerings off and bore them on slings, the fat jars of grain and the baskets of fruit swaying. The sacred basket with the ritual objects was borne separately on its own platform. As we ascended, streams of other people joined us, coming from the huts and houses in the foothills. Mother turned to make sure I was wearing my veil.

All were equal in the rites, so the people could jostle and jockey for a place near us, freely walking as our companions. Our guards—who were also initiates—kept them from crowding right up against us, and my brothers, although their lips were forming the words of the hymns, were looking around sharply to protect us. No weapons would be allowed into the sacred precinct, but for now they could have their swords at the ready.

The path began to rise sharply, growing narrow at the same time. It squeezed us pilgrims into a narrow file, and suddenly made a sharp turn around a grim gray boulder that blocked our way. I felt a shudder ripple down my body before I knew why, and then I saw it all again in my mind: the rock with the Sibyl on it, shrieking her dreadful prophecy. There was something on this boulder now, too, and I flinched, bracing myself for whatever lurked there.

Huddled around the rock, rag-clad people jeered and reviled us. "Tyndareus! Haven't seen you at the market! Why not? You are always trying to sell your daughters, aren't you?" yelled one.

"Only the cygnet!" cried another.

How dare they call my secret name? How did they know it?

"Look to your wife! Look to your wife!" they chorused. "Blow the feathers from her thighs!"

"What next?" Now they attacked Mother. "A bull, like the queen of Crete? Try a porcupine!"

One perched on the rock and flapped his arms, his mantle flying out. "Fly away! Fly away! The great bird has flown!"

Father and Mother kept their heads down, which was very unlike them, and made no retort.

Clytemnestra passed by them with only insults to her stockiness and big hands, and then it was my turn. They started moaning and trilling, and one tried to grab off my veil, cooing, "Does she have a beak? Does she have a beak?"

Now that someone wanted to take it, I fought to keep the veil. I clutched at the gold circlet and held it on my head, grimacing.

"She's a fighter!" cried one. "Her face must need protecting."

"Where's the eggshell? How big was it?"

There was more, but I do not remember it. I hurried past them as fast as I could go without running, for I did not want to show fear, but I was trembling. As we emerged on the other side, and the taunts were directed at those behind us, I rushed to Mother.

"It is over," she said. "We could not tell you, for it is part of the initiation to pass through a wall of insults. But you did well." There was pride in her voice.

"Why is it necessary?" It seemed cruel and pointless to me.

"To make us all equal," said Father. "Kings and queens must bear the insults along with everyone else, and no matter what they say we cannot ever punish them for it. That is the rule." He laughed as if it were no matter, but I knew he would brood over it.

"It teaches us humility," said Mother. "All people need to know the worst that is said of them, the more so if surrounded by flatterers."

We were stopped, waiting for Polydeuces and Castor to emerge from their drubbing.

"They say we learn lessons from it," said Father, his mouth working in that odd way it did when he was thinking. "I have just learned one: what we must call Helen from now on. We will put it about that she is the most beautiful woman in the world. Yes. That is what we shall claim for her. She must keep wearing the veil, it will increase curiosity and drive her bride-price up."

"I am far way from being married . . ." Oh, I hoped so! I was only ten years old, too soon to speak of it. "The veil . . ."

"What people cannot readily see, they imagine. They long for. They become consumed with. And things longed for are very dear, and people will pay highly for them. If there were rainbows every morning, they would be ignored. If we have a rainbow here, in you, then let us proclaim it but allow few to see it."

Mother narrowed her eyes. "The most beautiful woman in the world. Do we dare? Dare claim that?"

Just then my brothers came galloping up, laughing and reeling. "They know too much!" Castor said. "They seem to know all about us!"

"They know what will hurt us," I said. "I am not sure what else they know. It is simple to know what will wound a person."

Clytemnestra looked approvingly at me. "Helen is right. To insult someone is an easy task. To rise above the insult, not so easy. We remember it far longer than we remember praise. That is just the way we are made."

"Then it must be the way the gods are made as well, for they seem to take our praise and costly sacrifices for granted, but hold grudges for omissions and slights forever," Father said with a grunt. He looked up at the trail. "Come, we lose time."

Peaceful now that we were past the raucous taunting, we let the sharp air of the mountain cool our flushed cheeks. I puzzled over the angry words, the strange references. Beaks? Eggshells?

We were still climbing. The Taygetus Mountains were so high that the snow lingered on their jagged tops long past the time when the blossoms of the apple and quinces in the valley had blown away, and it came early, before the crops were gathered in. There was not one mountain but many, making a great wall down the middle of our country. On one side of them lay the fearful Stymphalos Lake, where Heracles had killed the evil birds; on another lay Nemea, where he had slain the lion with the impenetrable hide. A fierce longing to see these things seized me.

You have indeed left the palace, I told myself. Is that not a beginning? The dismal lake of Stymphalos, the other places where Heracles performed his labors, must wait. But you will see them, yes, someday you will see them.

Daylight was waning by the time we approached the sacred site, as it was meant to be. A grove of black poplars came into view, rearing above the other trees, swaying in the evening breeze, whispering their mysteries. We walked between the narrow aisle they created and then at once emerged onto flat ground where hundreds of torches flared.

"The goddesses greet you." By my side a robed priestess held out a long slender vessel and bade me drink. I tilted it up to my lips and recognized the mint-flavored potion made of white barley harvested from Demeter's sacred field. She gestured me toward a man standing with flaming torch, from which I must light mine. I obeyed.

My torch aflame, I was directed to join the swirling lights in the field before me, which transformed the grounds into a sky full of stars. Hundreds of devotees were dancing, turning, and weaving intricate patterns and chains of movement in the gathering dark, holding their torches.

"We dance for the goddesses," a priestess whispered in my ear. "Do not be afraid, do not hold back. Offer them yourself."

Surrounded by the worshippers, I found myself borne away, whether I would or no. The dark ground was uneven and it was hard to keep from stumbling, but the dancers seemed to float over the ground, and in joining them, so did I. I lost my parents, lost my brothers and sister; I left the Helen that had to wear a veil, and keep hidden, and obey, and soared free. I felt Persephone take my hand. I heard her murmur, "When they take you away, it is not captivity but freedom." I could sense the brush of her sweet soft hand, smell the richness of her hair. Although I could not see it, somehow I knew it was red-gold.

At once everything grew still. The dancing ceased, and the priestess held up her hands. I could barely see her in the dim light.

"You have drunk the sacred beverage," she said. "You have taken the goddess into yourselves. Now you must recite your secret promise."

The rumble of hundreds of voices mixed, impossible to decipher. But the pledge was thus: *I have fasted. I have reached into the sacred basket and, having worked therein, left a residue in the ritual basket. Then, withdrawing from the ritual basket, I have returned to the sacred one.* I can recite it here, knowing that it is incomprehensible to those outside the mysteries. I betray nothing.

Satisfied, she motioned for us to make a huge spiral on the sacred dance ground. Its tip would go first into the initiation hall, and the rest would uncoil behind it. As we entered, we were to douse our torches in a large stone trough just outside the building. Each torch plunged into the water made a last, singeing protest.

Inside, it was utterly dark. A deep and dreadful dark, like the dark of the tomb, like the dark when you awaken and know not if you still live. Only the press of the other bodies around me reassured me I had not died, was not lost.

"Happy is he among men upon earth who have seen these Mysteries; but he who is uninitiated and who has no part in them, never has a good portion once he is dead, down in the darkness and gloom," a faraway, echoing voice cried.

"Bow before the goddesses," we were directed. I felt, rather than saw, a movement in one direction, and I followed. Ahead of me I heard sighs and moans, and as I approached I could barely make out the dim shapes of statues of Demeter and Persephone. The mother, dressed in radiant color, was in front, and behind her, shadowy in black, was the daughter. We passed before them quickly, not allowed to linger, as we were herded into another, smaller hall.

An overpowering scent of flowers filled the air. I was not sure which ones, it seemed that there were several blended together. Were there irises, hyacinths, narcissus, piercing sweet and crushed? But it was not the season for those flowers, so how could the images of the goddesses have come by them?

"These were the last flowers I gathered before I was taken," a ghostly voice spoke, floating in the heavy perfumed air. "You can feel what I felt, smell what I smelled . . ." The voice trailed away sadly.

We were plunged into even deeper darkness, as if we had descended with her into the chasm. I felt myself falling.

At the bottom, where I landed after a long glide, I was alone. I pulled myself to my feet, and fought to know where I was. All around me was black, dark, smothering night.

"This is what all those above must face." A soft voice whispered against my cheek. "But for you—you need never come to this place of darkness. That is the fate of mortals."

"I am mortal." I was finally able to frame the words.

"Yes, somewhat." Now a gentle sigh, almost a laugh. "It is up to you how mortal you are."

The voice . . . the presence . . . I had come for the Mysteries, and they promised that the divine epiphany would manifest itself. It had happened, then. "I do not know what you mean," I said.

"Your mother has done you a great disservice, then," she—I knew it was a she—said. "She should tell you the truth of your engendering."

"If you know, I beg you, tell me," I cried. I seemed to be alone with her, having a private audience. There was no one around us. Had I fallen into a secret pit?

"You and I are sisters," she said. "That is all I may say."

If only I knew who she was, then I would know what to ask. "Who are you?" I murmured.

"Whose shrine is this?" She sounded displeased.

Oh, let her not be displeased! "Demeter and Persephone's."

"Just so. And who am I?"

It must be the daughter! "Persephone?"

Now I felt a warmth spreading out, engulfing me. "You speak true." A great pause. "But my mother is worthy of praise as well," she said. "And you would be wise to heed that. Even though a daughter is grown it does not mean that the mother stops requiring homage."

At that time I did not know what she meant. Later I was to know all too well.

She stepped down, approached me. I could feel her near me. "Sister," she murmured. "You may trust me. I will always be with you. Beware any other goddess."

How could she think of any other goddess, or imagine I might? Her radiance, a radiance that penetrated the darkness and shone in my mind, overwhelmed me. "Yes," I mumbled.

"And now I await others," she said.

Of course: the goddess is always ready to attend to the next, whereas we mortals look back, at what just passed, at what we have just seen. In that, I was entirely a mortal. My eyes were blinded with the radiant vision of her, although I had never truly beheld her face. That was as she intended.

In the great hall we huddled, waiting. It was far into the night, though we had no way of knowing exactly how far it had crept. Time had flown like a raven on black wings. Everything had dropped away, and I stood stripped of all I knew, all I was, all I had felt. I was naked before the godhood, awaiting their revelation.

A light blazed; the answer came in the final ritual enacted for us. I saw the miracle, the deep kernel of the secret. From that moment on, death held no fear for me. I knew it for what it was. I could transcend it.

V

For a time what I had seen in the inner chamber consumed me, and I basked in the splendor of that vision long after I returned home. I contented myself with my lessons, I practiced the lyre—which I was now old enough to learn—and I was proud when I outgrew the little bow of elmwood that Castor had fashioned for me and was able to draw a larger one, as well as hunt larger game. No more hares; now I could take aim at wild goats.

The autumn faded in a blaze of glory, ebbing away, its bronze turning brown, its fruits picked, its fields fallow and sleeping. We huddled indoors, rubbing our stiff hands before the hearth fire in the great chamber, enduring the dull songs and poems of the bards who visited us. Not all singers are gifted, and those that were not seemed especially drawn to Father's palace.

I thought the experience at the shrine would last longer, stilling my desire to see more, but by spring I was chafing at my imprisonment more than ever. Escaping for a little while had only made it worse. No matter that our palace was open to the breezes that blew across it, caressing it like the strings of a lyre. But the green valley and its little city below murmured beguilingly to me, as the forbidden always will.

Clytemnestra came upon me as I was standing on tiptoe, peering over the wall on a rock, and she grabbed my shins and shook me. I almost fell off.

"Stop craning your neck, you'll stretch it out." She laughed and held out her arms and I jumped into them. She was so strong she did not even sway as my weight hit her.

"Take me there!" I suddenly said. "Please, please!"

She looked around to see if anyone was listening. But we were quite alone. "Now?"

"Yes, now!" I said. "No one is paying any attention, we can be back before they miss us. Oh, please, please, you can go whenever you like, but I am kept tied up here like a slave. No, not even a slave, slaves aren't bound."

I could see her thinking. Clytemnestra always liked a dare.

"Unless you're afraid?" I said, knowing she would have to prove she was not.

She scoffed. "Me?" She took a deep breath. "All right, let's hurry!"

Looking around nervously, we slipped out the postern gate and hurried down the slope of the hill. The shade from the hill's olive and cypress trees gave way to bright sunshine once we were out from under them, making the green of the meadows dazzling.

"It's prettier than jewels!" I said. I ran into the open meadow, feeling the cool grass against my legs, surprised by the flowers hidden in the grasses— little purple ones, lacy white ones, clusters of pink blooms.

"Helen!" Clytemnestra's usual commanding voice held a note of worry. "Helen!"

My head was barely taller than the stalks of grass and weeds, and I waved my arms at her. "I'm here."

"Come out now, before I lose you," she said. "The grass here is too high."

We stayed on the path that led to the river, making our way down to the banks. Here, once again, we had shade—under the tamarisks and willows that grew near water, their freshly budding branches throwing shadows on banks and stream. The muddy water swirled past, turning and flipping up little flecks of white.

"The water nymph is waving," said Clytemnestra. She seemed to remember something that made her smile.

"Which one lives here?" I wondered.

"I don't know her name," Clytemnestra said. But somehow I knew she did. She just did not want to say it. Perhaps it was sacred.

I came close by the edge of the water, to a place where the rushes grew. "I would like to see her." I had to speak loudly for my voice to carry over the murmur of the water in the rushes. I stuck one toe in, and found it chilly. The snows on the Taygetus Mountains were still melting.

Clytemnestra came and stood beside me. Our reflections were rippling in the water beneath us. I bent over to see mine better, but Clytemnestra pulled me back.

"Don't," she said.

I felt I must see what I looked like. I found a surprising strength to push against Clytemnestra, who was so much larger than I. Her grip loosened for an instant, and in that instant I lunged forward and saw a face staring wide-eyed back at me, as startled as I was in beholding it.

I looked nothing like I had imagined, although I already knew—from my furtive look in Mother's mirror—that my eyes were green-brown and had thick dark lashes, and that my lips were full and curved. Now I could see it all, see my face as those around me saw it.

I leaned farther over, until I almost touched the water, and then my nose did touch it, and the image broke into ripples and shards, dancing away. I held my breath and waited for it to become still, so that once again I could gaze on my image and see what others had been seeing and had been denied me, could study it and memorize it. It dictated my life, it kept me a prisoner, so should I not know what it was?

"No." Clytemnestra pulled my arm back. "Stop, or you'll end up like Narcissus." She took a deep breath. "The man who fell so in love with his own reflection in the water that Apollo turned him into a flower. Is that what you want?" She kept her voice light, but she could not hide the fear from me. What was she afraid of?

"No," I said, obediently stepping back, for she had succeeded in frightening me. "I would not want to be rooted in any one place, even a place as lovely as this riverbank."

But once we were back on the sunny path leading to the city, my apprehension faded away. I had seen nothing, after all, but a reflection, and no face had any power in and of itself, at least no human face.

The path meandered, sometimes ranging far out into the meadow on its way to the city, sometimes turning back to hug the riverbank again. By now the sun was high enough even in this early spring to make the shade welcome whenever we walked under trees again by the water. At one point the river widened, making a dark pool. Swimming serenely on its surface were three large swans, circling one another in stately majesty, their curving necks held high, their gleaming white feathers looking impossibly pure against the murk of the water.

I stopped, holding my breath. Behind me Clytemnestra came to a halt.

"They are so beautiful," I whispered, as if they did not truly exist and the smallest sound could make them disappear.

I had never seen swans this close before, but I was held motionless by their imperious, conquering grace. I stared and stared; they glided past as if they were spirits, never acknowledging any other creature on the river.

One of them then turned his head, swiveling it around smoothly and fixing his surprisingly small eyes on me before he swam in our direction. He was making for a grassy spot on the bank, an inviting one with irises and violets making spangles on the green.

He seemed to have a purpose, seemed deliberately to be coming toward us. Honored and excited, I stepped back one little step and grasped Clytemnestra's hand. The swan, the largest of the three, I now saw, was not stayed by the little, distracting motion I had made.

His eyes held mine with a dark stare.

We had dogs at the palace, hunting dogs, and my father and brothers had told me, "An animal will always look away when you stare at him; he will drop his eyes first. That is because man is master over the animals. Unless, of course, he isn't an animal at all, but a god disguised . . ."

Gods were fond of disguising themselves as animals, at least they were in olden times, when the stories we love so much were born, but this swan was of my own time. And he was bold.

He was almost up to us; he was making for the bank where we stood. His face was turned toward us; and above his black and orange beak his eyes were closeset and unfathomable.

"No!" Clytemnestra cried, and rushed forward, waving a stick. "Not again! Don't come here again, you raping, cruel creature!"

The swan halted, then swam furiously toward us, raising his wings and clambering up on the mud, emitting a harsh sound.

He was huge. With his wings spread, he dwarfed Clytemnestra, who backed up and found a stone to throw at him. It hit his beak, turning his head.

Any other creature would have fled, but the swan attacked. Hissing, he flew toward Clytemnestra and, ramming his neck back and forth, pecked at her in a series of jabs and bites. She fell face downward in the mud and threw up her hands to protect her head. The swan trapped her and started pecking at the back of her neck and her arms, all the while making the most horrible rasping hiss, like steam escaping from a boiling pot. The other two swans continued their serene circling in the water.

I rushed forward and flung myself on the swan's back. What else could I do to save Clytemnestra? I clawed at his feathers. They were thick and shiny and smooth, and I felt the power underneath, and the muscles. This was no pillow or cloud, but strength and glory and pitilessness under the misleading beauty of the white feathers and the grace of form.

"Leave her! Leave her!" I cried, and then I grasped the swan's neck—a swaying tube that felt like a striking snake.

As if my hands had no strength, he turned that neck beneath them and looked directly at me. His little black eyes seemed to expand until they filled all my vision, holding me in their power.

"Stop it," I whispered, my lips almost touching the hard beak.

The beak opened and grasped my cheek. There were little ridges inside it, tiny points, and I could feel them pinching my flesh. He held the skin gently, swaying his head a bit, as if he were caressing—or kissing. Then he let go and pulled back to look at me again. He ruffled his feathers, making them rise up and unseat me, so that I slid off. He stood for a moment, regarding me. Then he arched his neck once more and patted my hair with his head. He then turned and reentered the water, floating serenely away to join his companions.

Clytemnestra sat up, gasping and puffing. Her arms were covered in mud, and her face was smeared with river ooze.

"I curse you!" she cried after the swan.

"No!" I grabbed her arm. "It is dangerous. Do not—he may take revenge!" This was no ordinary swan.

Then she uttered mysterious words. "What else can he do?" she asked bitterly. "The deed is done." She stood up and called out over the water, "I curse you! I curse you!"

The swans had glided away into the darkness of the shaded water.

The rest of the walk toward the city we made in silence, shaken from what had happened on the riverbank. For a moment I thought of returning to the palace, but once we were back it would be difficult for me to get out again—I would be guarded more closely than ever.

Tight-lipped, Clytemnestra trudged on, holding my hand. Her cheek was dirty where it had rubbed on the riverbank. On the back of her cloak I could see the muddy imprints of the webbed feet of the aggressive swan.

I tugged at her hand. "Please, can we slow down a bit? And could you smile? I think you will frighten the people in the city."

She shook her head and a little smile crept up the corners of her mouth. I could always make her smile when others could not. Then she laughed, a bit shrilly. "You are right," she said. "We can only laugh about it. Together. No one else would believe us." She went down on one knee and looked directly into my eyes. "You must not tell anyone."

"But why? It was so—" The words died on my lips as I saw her expression. "No, I won't," I said.

"Good. No one must know. It must be our secret."

The city came upon us in a bend of the path, which had widened out and become big enough to permit carts to lumber along it. One moment we were on what looked like a country path, surrounded by meadows, grazing cattle, and gardens, and then we were passing into the city of Sparta.

It was not a very big city, I know that now, but then it seemed huge—so many buildings, so close together, and so many people. We passed through the gates—small in comparison with those I later saw in Troy—and into the streets.

Suddenly there were people everywhere, moving like an enormous bee-hive. They were rushing in all directions, as if they had all been summoned to a vital job at the same instant. I expected to hear buzzing, but the sounds were much louder than that—yelling and creaking and the crack of whips.

A few laden donkeys were plodding along the street, bumping against the sides of houses, lumbering under wineskins or pottery jars, but mostly there were people, people carrying baskets of grain and bolts of cloth.

"We'll go to the market—you'd like that, wouldn't you, Helen?" Clytemnestra asked. She stood closer to me and took me partly under her arm, as if to shield me, hide my naked face.

Nodding, I tried to wiggle free so I could see better. But her arm held me firmly as she steered me down the street.

We reached the marketplace, an area where several streets came together to make an open space. I could see rows of people sitting on the ground on mats, with their baskets of dried figs or mint leaves and their pots of honey and other foods.

There was something gleaming in one deep basket, and I bent over to peer into the dark depths of it. Far down I could see some kind of trinket that caught the sunlight, and I put in my hand and drew one out.

It was a bracelet of twisted wire, cleverly made so that part of the wire was flattened and would flash in the light.

The seller was quick to take my hand and slide another bracelet over it, but Clytemnestra was even quicker to push it off, along with the first one. She jerked my hand back.

"No, you mustn't," she whispered. "Come." She tried to turn me around, but it was too late. The woman's eyes had left my arm, an arm like any other prospective customer's, and gone to my face to cajole me into buying. But instead of the usual banter and urging, she let loose with a shriek. Her eyes, until then seeing nothing but a possible sale, widened in disbelief.

"It's her! It's her!" she cried. She jumped up and grabbed my arms, pulling me toward her, knocking over the basket of bracelets and spilling their glitter all around.

Clytemnestra, muttering, pulled me back, and they began tugging at me as if I were a sack of grain.

"Help me! Help me!" the merchant called to her fellows. "Hold her! It's *Helen!*"

They rose up as one and rushed over to us. Clytemnestra was stronger than the bracelet-woman and had wrenched me away from her grasp, hiding me in the folds of her cloak, but we were completely surrounded. Only armed bodyguards could have held them back.

Clytemnestra held me fiercely to her side, so tightly that I could see nothing, but I could feel the trembling of her body. "Stand back!" she ordered, her voice gruff. "Stand back, or you will answer to the king for this! Let us depart in peace."

"Let us see her face!" a voice from the crowd demanded. "Let us see her face, and then you may depart!"

"No," Clytemnestra said. "It is not your right to look upon the princess."

"We see your face," another, deeper voice said, "and you are also our princess. I say, let us see Helen! Unless she is a monster, has the beak of a swan, the beak of her father—"

"Her father and mine are the same—your king, Tyndareus. Let such slander stop," Clytemnestra said, her voice ringing.

"Then show us!" a man's voice demanded. "Why has she been hidden away all these years up in the palace, never showing herself to us as you have been shown, as Castor and Polydeuces have been shown, openly, coming to the city, playing in the open fields, unless it's true—she's the daughter of Zeus, who came to the queen as a swan, and was hatched from an egg—"

"An egg of hyacinthine blue," another voice cried. "I've seen the eggshell—preserved—"

"What nonsense!" Clytemnestra bellowed. "You've been too long at the shrine of Hyacinthus nearby, he's put these fantasies in your heads—"

"No, the egg is real, its shell really was blue—"

"Someone saw the swan and the queen down by the riverbank. And the swan sometimes still comes back, as if he's lovesick. He's bigger than the others—stronger—whiter—"

"Let us pass!" Clytemnestra commanded. "Or I'll curse you!"

A moment of quiet followed as they considered her words. I still could not see anything, enveloped as I was in the folds of her cloak.

A voice broke the silence. "She's a monster! That's why you hide her!"

"A monster! A monster like the Gorgon. A hideous apparition!"

"Let us go!" Clytemnestra repeated. "Or perhaps . . . if she is a monster, I will let you see her, and that will be the curse. Remember the power of the Gorgon to turn onlookers to stone."

A quiet murmur followed the threat. I should have felt safer, but Clytemnestra's hint, even if was clever, hurt me. She was willing to paint me a monster, dreadful to look upon, and leave the people of Sparta believing that, rather than give in to them.

I twisted out from under Clytemnestra's grip and flung off my cowl, baring my head before the crowd.

The crowd was a large one—a circle of people several rows deep. I had never seen so many faces.

"I am Helen!" I cried. "Look your fill!" I held my head high and braced myself.

There was silence. Utter, deep silence. The faces turned toward me, like moonflowers following the moon as she makes her nightly journey across the sky. The expressions drained away, replaced by a calm as serene as if they were under that moonlight.

Finally someone murmured, "It *is* true. Only the daughter of Zeus could have such a face."

"So terrible . . . it blinds . . ." they murmured. But what they were truly seeing in my face was also the power that would set in motion so much strife and destruction.

We turned, leaving them standing there, truly like stones, as a Gorgon would have turned them, and made our way through the streets, stunned as if under a spell.

But it was I who was stumbling and under a spell. Zeus. They had called me the daughter of Zeus, said he had mated with Mother as a swan. The swan that attacked us—was he—could he be—my *father*?

The sunshine was still as bright, but all I could see was the white of the swan and his pitiless eyes, and the stares of the townspeople as they gaped at me and were paralyzed by looking at me. So that was what the veil was for, that was why I was guarded, and that was why Mother had hurried from the swans at the lake near my grandparents', and that was why Father had thrown stones at them and called them filthy monsters. And that was why she called me Cygnet, little swan . . . Everything around me swirled, and I fell to the ground.

VI

I knew nothing, until I awoke in Clytemnestra's arms as she labored up the hill. She was gasping and panting as she clutched me against her; I was astonished by her strength and agility as she clambered over the rough path, climbing uphill all the while.

"I—I—" I wanted her to stop, I wanted to ask her about all of it while we were still alone. No one was near; we must have left the pursuing villagers behind.

"Don't talk!" she said. The words were stern, but her voice was trembling.

"But I have to! You have to tell me, everyone knows things about me but me, even the Spartans knew things—"

She stopped and let me down. "It was foolish of Mother and Father not to tell you. They made us all promise not to tell you. As if you would not know someday. All of it—the veil, the mirrors, the imprisonment! How stupid of them!"

The gates of the palace loomed ahead; they were closed as always, but Clytemnestra cried, "Open! Open in the name of mercy!" and the doors swung wide. Just inside, she dropped me down and turned around to aid the guards in pushing the doors shut and bolting them. No one seemed to be behind us, but we could not be sure.

We thought we were safe, and Clytemnestra was just whispering to me to go directly back to my chamber before we could be caught, when suddenly Father strode from beneath the portico. He looked around, frowning, and saw us just as the gates groaned shut. In an instant he was beside us, jerking Clytemnestra's arm.

"You'll be punished for this!" he said. "Severely punished. You have disobeyed my orders. You"—he stuck his face up into Clytemnestra's, and in that instant it struck me how alike they were—"are old enough to know better, and so you shall suffer the worst punishment. You"—he swung around at me—"could have been injured. You risked yourself, and put us in danger."

"The only thing in danger is your bargaining rights with Helen, had she been physically damaged in some way," snarled Clytemnestra.

Father drew back his hand and struck her across the cheek, but she did not budge, only narrowed her eyes. "To your quarters, to await my punishment!" he ordered her.

Surprisingly, she obeyed, leaving me with Father. He kept staring at me and I realized that Clytemnestra had spoken the truth: he was inspecting his wares for damage. Satisfied there was none, he relaxed and released me. "You also, to your quarters." He put his hand firmly on my back to steer me.

Just then Mother emerged from her chambers and saw us. We stood and waited for her as she rushed toward us, her gown fluttering. Her face was a mask of worry. She grabbed my shoulders and began sobbing.

"Control yourself, Leda, she is safe," Father said abruptly.

"Oh, where did you go, and what did you do?" she asked.

I must be properly contrite. "Oh, Mother, I am sorry. It was not Clytemnestra's fault. The wrong was mine. I persuaded her to take me from the palace, I wanted to see Sparta. We went into the town, and some people saw me and got excited . . ." Mother was breathing heavily but kept silent, so I continued. "And on the way I played in the fields, and by the riverbanks . . ." I shouldn't say it, I had promised Clytemnestra I would keep the secret, but suddenly I knew this was the only way to force Mother to betray her own, much greater secret. "A huge swan was there, and he chased Clytemnestra and attacked her, and I beat him off, and then he looked at me, and he—he *kissed* me." I glanced at her innocently. "He seemed to be fond of me, for some reason. Mother, it was as if he recognized me!"

She gave a little choking cry. "Oh, how could you . . . how could he?"

"It was as if he wanted to tell me something."

She drew herself up, as if she were issuing a command to her body. "Tomorrow morning, Helen, come to my chamber. After you have fulfilled your punishment."

Clytemnestra was taken to the whipping place, where youths were initiated into manhood and punished with rods. I was sent to my room and given nothing to eat, and made to sleep on the stone floor rather than my bed. I also had to sleep in the dark. The oil lamps were taken away. I spent a cold and frightening night, and I kept seeing the swan and his black eyes, and the eyes of the townspeople when they converged on me. I was frightened not by what had already happened, but in dread of what I would hear tomorrow from

Mother. For I would not leave her chamber ignorant of my true self. I was determined now to know the truth.

The sun was barely up when I wrapped myself in a wool mantle and sought my mother's chambers. Her quarters were not far from the huge throne hall with its open hearth, situated so the queen could discreetly retire when a formal evening went on too long, which happened all too often.

She was just arising, and a servant was draping a soft cloak the color of old ashes around her shoulders as I came into her room. I could see that her rising was only for show. She, also, had not slept.

The new-risen sun was spilling its early light between the pillars of her room, reaching across the floor like thin arms.

"My dear child," she said. "Here, eat something with me." She indicated a tray holding a honeycomb and some bread. But she did not eat, and neither did I.

"Helen, I am sick with worry about you," she said. "You knew you were not to leave the palace grounds. Certainly your sister knew that. She has become unmanageable, and it is time we find a husband to govern her. But something dreadful could have happened—something dreadful almost *did* happen." She gave a little shudder.

No more evasions. The truth must be stabbed, dragged out into the open. "But Mother, what truly could have happened? Those people are your subjects, and they would not have harmed their princess. Perhaps if I were to see them more often—"

"No!" She clapped her hands together to silence me. "No."

"It is that prophecy," I said. I knew that somehow the Sibyl was part of the reason I was kept locked up. That and the swan. Begin with the Sibyl. "Long ago . . . when we went to Delphi . . . there was that witch, that prophetess, I don't know really what she was, but she made a prediction about me . . . something about being the ruin of Asia, the ruin of Europe, the death of Greeks. Are you trying to prevent it by holding me prisoner?"

I expected her to deny it, but she nodded. "Yes. We hoped to trick the fates."

In my lessons I had heard the legends: how Perseus's grandfather had known his daughter's son would kill him so he sent them away, to no avail—the son killed him anyway; how Oedipus had been told he would kill his father and marry his mother, so he had taken himself off to Thebes, and on the way had killed his father unknowingly and as a reward was given his mother to wife, again unknowingly. It was futile to try to avoid what was foreordained.

I remembered Father's words: *To know is to arm. An enemy seen a far way off cannot surprise. An enemy seen from a distance can be outwitted and avoided.*

So far no enemy had come. But the Sibyl had not said when the trouble would come. Nor from what direction. Nor in what form. Despite Father's brave words, it is hard to arm against something that you cannot recognize. Oedipus learned that.

"Mother, you know it is impossible to avert what has been foreordained."

"But we must try." She turned from me to the table where she kept her jars of unguents and scented oils and poured a little oil into one of her palms. She held it out to me, and when I nodded she took one finger and spread the fresh oil on my cheeks.

"Such lovely skin," she said. "My little Cygnet."

I grabbed her wrists. "Mother! It is time you tell me of what seems to be common knowledge. Cygnet. Little swan. Am I a little swan, Mother? Do not seek to divert me with talk about my gracefulness, my white linen tunics, and so on, as Father has. What is the truth of it? What is the truth of what everyone in Sparta speaks of—that you and the swan—but it was not a swan, it was—it was—" I could not say it, it sounded too presumptuous. "I saw the swan, and his feathers were shining white, a white that dazzled, like the clouds before the sun bursts through them, and they hurt my eyes."

Mother stood for an instant, unmoving. She bowed her head and I knew she was taking counsel of herself, weighing how much truth it was wise to speak. I could see the top of her head with its shining dark hair—so unlike mine—but could not see her face, could not see the struggle taking place within her. Finally she raised her head and I knew she had won her battle. She would tell me the truth.

"Come," she said, drawing me over beside her on her couch. She clasped me tightly to her, so I could feel her body next to mine. I waited. "Dear child," she said, "there is no way to say it but this: When your father was away, the father of all the gods, the ruler of Olympus, came to me. He chose me, I know not why. And yes, he came as a mortal creature, a swan. To look upon him in his glory means death for a mortal, and he did not wish me to die. He departed at sunrise—just at this time, so there is no morning that comes that I do not bid him farewell again, feel his leaving. And yes, our child was born, and it was you."

Suspicions, fears, dreams—those are not the same as hearing it for a fact. I felt dizzy, and leaned against her.

"You are his only daughter," she said. "Oh, he has many sons, but you are his only mortal daughter, by a mortal woman. He will protect you, regardless of what the Sibyl said. That is why we sought to thwart her, for Zeus is more powerful than a mere Sibyl."

"But . . . Father . . ."

"He knows. But he pretends he does not. Perhaps it is better that way. One must give men their pride. He calls you 'the most beautiful woman in the world' but does not dare to admit how that can be. Of course the daughter of Zeus will be of immortal beauty, while she lives." Her voice grew sad. "But the children of gods and mortals are always mortal," she said. "That is inevitable. You will die as I will die. But while you live, we seek to protect you."

I bowed my head in acquiescence. Now all was revealed; now I understood.

She took a strand of my hair and held it next to hers. "Mine is of the earth, yours is of the heavens. See how it shines, full of gold!"

"Mother, did he leave you nothing?" I knew, from the stories, that the gods were hard, lusting after mortals but discarding them afterward. But sometimes they left them a token.

"Only what I took," she said. She rose and walked dreamily toward a wall niche, taking down a carved ivory box with a domed lid. She plucked off the lid and thrust the box toward me. Inside were four long gleaming swan feathers, so pure they glimmered and gave off a light of their own, an entirely unnatural light.

Feathers. When she might have asked for the world.

❦ VII ❦

True to their word, Mother and Father immediately sent out the announcement that their elder daughter, the most illustrious princess Clytemnestra, was of an age to be married. Her advantages were stressed: an impeccable pedigree—she was descended from the earliest rulers of Sparta, and with her hand might even come the inheritance of that throne—and she was of good childbearing stock, pleasing to look upon, and healthy. Nothing, of course, was hinted of her obstinate and rebellious nature, nor of her indifference to women's tasks, nor of her physical strength, comparable to a man's. Father said that he hoped a high bidder would come along, and wanted to open the contest to foreigners as well as Greeks.

"I'm willing to consider an Egyptian, or a Syrian," he said.

"Egypt would be wasted on Clytemnestra," said Mother, smoothing her hair with long nervous fingers. "The linen so sheer it floats, the enameled bracelets, the perfumes—one might as well offer them to a wolf."

"It is true, your daughter is unlike you. I know it's you who covets such things, and would begrudge them to Clytemnestra." He chuckled, as if he enjoyed knowing her envy. "But, my dearest, we must think only of what the match might bring to Sparta, not of the luxuries you are missing."

"A foreigner, no matter how rich, would be a failure. Others would look down upon us."

I had tiptoed into their room and now I barely dared to breathe, lest they hear me.

"Let them look. Down, up, or sideways, as long as we have a connection to a rich port over there."

"I've never heard of a foreigner come courting here, nor of such a marriage taking place," Mother said. "And Sparta has no port, so how could a connection with a foreign one help us? The trade would all go to Mycenae, where it goes already."

"Troy," Father suddenly said. "That's much closer, and Egypt trades through *it*, so we needn't bother with an Egyptian. Besides, Trojans are richer than Egyptians."

"Better-looking, too," said Mother. Now it was Father's turn to be needled. "They say they are so striking, even the gods can't keep their hands off them. Zeus took up with Ganymede, and Aphrodite herself could not contain her passion for that shepherd, what was his name? Why, once when you were away, one came on a diplomatic mission. I entertained him alone, of course." She smiled. "It was not a difficult task."

I could almost feel the swan feathers stirring in the little box, mocking Father.

"All right, no foreigners," Father finally said. "There should be enough of our own kind to choose from."

I was about to make my presence known when suddenly Mother said, "I think it is time. Time for Helen to be seen. Then the word will spread, and when she is old enough to wed, bidding will be at a frenzied peak."

"Yes! And we can let it be known that she's the most beautiful woman in the world!" Father sounded jubilant, trumpeting his favorite phrase.

Mother frowned. "But wait . . . might that not detract from Clytemnestra's chances? Perhaps the suitors will decide to wait for Helen."

"Ummm . . . yes, that could be a problem," Father admitted. "But it seems a shame to keep her hidden when all these people gather. When would we have such an opportunity again?"

"There are advantages either way," said Mother. "Let us think about it, do nothing hasty."

In the glorious summer, when the sun was at his height, the suitors came for Clytemnestra. One by one they climbed the steep hill to the palace, bearing their hopes and their gifts. One by one they were received by the king and queen, and settled in their quarters.

The rules in the competition for the hand of the king's daughter had been observed since the days of long ago, and they were rigid. Father must feed and house the suitors until one was chosen; it was permissible for a suitor to send a representative rather than come in person, if he lived far away or was too powerful to appear as a supplicant; there might be some sort of contest, like a footrace or an archery match, although the results were no longer binding.

As I watched the parade of hopefuls arrive, I wondered where all these men would stay. Beds were laid out under the wooden porticoes, where they could sleep still partially protected but in the open air. Mother had gotten hold of every spare woven blanket and sheep's fleece to serve as bedding, and the goatherds brought in their kids and ewes and began the slaughtering to feed the crowd. Endless jars of grain and oil were produced and the great amphoras of wine were opened for drinking and libations. It was as important for Father's wealth and hospitality to appear limitless as it was for the suitors to pose as guardians of the door of promise.

Some twelve came—an impressive number. Among them were the prince of Tiryns, two sons of Nestor of Pylos, a warrior from Thebes, a cousin of the royal house of Theseus of Athens, and a young king of tiny Nemea. The rest sent emissaries—these came from Rhodes, Crete, Salamis, and faraway Thessaly. And then, on the last day, the brothers Atreus—Agamemnon and Menelaus of Mycenae—climbed the hill and stood before the palace gates.

Mother turned visibly pale, and her hand fluttered up to her white neck. "No . . ." she breathed, so low that only I, standing close by her side, could hear.

Father's face betrayed nothing. He welcomed them as he had welcomed the others, with a set greeting: *Noble guest, come into my home.*

I knew about the curse on their house. Everyone did. In a land where we children grew up on tales of ghastly murders and betrayals, the story of the sons of Pelops still stood out, a story that had not ended yet and was therefore even more frightening.

Briefly, then: The king Pelops had two sons, Atreus and Thyestes. In struggling for supremacy, Atreus killed the three sons of Thyestes, and cooked them into a stew, which he then served to his brother. In horror, Thyestes cursed Atreus and all his descendants. Atreus had two sons, Agamemnon and Menelaus.

There was much more to the story, adulteries and more murders, unnatural liaisons, treachery, and lies. But now the embodiment of the curse, Agamemnon, had come to seek Clytemnestra's hand.

Agamemnon was a dark-haired, stocky man with a heavy beard and thick lips. His eyes were oddly large and his nose fleshy; his neck was short and so his head seemed to spring directly from his shoulders. If he needed to look to the side, he almost had to turn his entire body around. I saw how muscled his arms were, hanging down by his side, and suddenly a picture of him strangling someone flashed through my mind. That he could do it barehanded, I had no doubt.

A servant behind him was carrying a long thin gold-inlaid box, holding it out like a precious sacrifice.

"Is that the scepter?" Father asked.

"Indeed, yes. Did you think I would come without it?" Agamemnon's voice was as heavy and dolorous as the rest of him.

Father then turned to greet the other man, Agamemnon's younger brother. "Menelaus, noble guest, come into my home."

"I thank you, great king."

Menelaus. My first glimpse of him. Like his brother, he was wide-shouldered and heavy with muscles. But his hair was a lighter, reddish gold, thick and wavy like a lion's mane, and his mouth turned up in a smile rather than down in a frown. It was hard to believe that he, too, carried a dark curse, for there was nothing in his person to suggest it.

"I come, dear King Tyndareus, to bolster my brother's courage in seeking for the princess's hand." This voice was plainspoken, but not rough. It was very deep, making him seem larger than he was, but it was a reassuring deepness.

"I do not understand," said Father. "You do not come as a suitor yourself?"

"There has been too much rivalry between brothers in our house," he said. "Has it not caused enough sorrow? No, it is enough that I may personally encourage my brother's suit." He bowed his head in an oddly formal manner, and at that moment he saw me. Like all the others, he stared. Everyone who had stepped into the palace, who had passed the royal family and me, had likewise been rooted for a moment. Some stammered. Others swallowed.

He smiled a little, said nothing, and followed his servant.

Thank you for saying nothing! I thought. Thank you, thank you! I was instantly grateful.

For I had been granted my wish: to stand before people without any barrier, without a veil. It had been unpleasant. After the first two men had acted as if they had seen an apparition, I became embarrassed and then frightened and then angry. I was more trapped without a veil than I had been behind one. Yet had I not requested this very thing?

The men drew lots for the order of the day of their appearance. No one wanted to be first; somewhere near the end was most advantageous. Had this been a performance with no prize in sight, then to appear toward the end would have been bad, because by then the audience would be restless and inattentive. But in this case, the man who went first might find himself forgotten by Clytemnestra by the time she had to choose.

Euchir, the young king of Nemea, had the misfortune to be first. He bore himself well. He spoke of Nemea in its valley, saying it lay far enough from Sparta that Clytemnestra could feel she truly had a new home, but close enough that she would never be severed from her family. He promised a crown that was uncompromised by other claimants or prophecies. (Clever point! The brothers Atreus must have hated that.) Then, charmingly, he ordered his trunk opened, and displayed part of the impenetrable hide of the lion of Nemea that Heracles had slain—the city's pride.

I could tell from Clytemnestra's face that she was not impressed. He was a sapling to her, too slight and too green for consideration. She confirmed my thoughts by declining to ask him anything, and he had to take himself and his lion skin away.

At the feast afterward, the bard plucked his lyre and sang of the deeds of Euchir's ancestors. His voice was increasingly lost in the rising noise of the hall as more wine made men speak loudly. He glared at them; this bard was not blind as many were.

After a great long while it was over, and we could go to bed.

And on and on it went for days. After the first few, they all began to blend together. Perhaps they seemed indistinguishable to me because Clytemnestra showed no interest in any of them.

The two sons of Nestor of Pylos were as long-winded as their father, she said.

The prince of Tiryns was as heavy and gray as his city's fortifications.

The warrior from Thebes would be awkward in a palace. He probably sleeps under his shield, she quipped.

As the numbers still to present their suits dwindled, I wondered what would happen if the last spoke his piece and she was still unmoved. Must we hold this contest year after year, hoping someone new would appear?

Agamemnon was the next-to-last to present his suit. He strode out into the center of the hall and took his stand, planting his legs like posts. His head lifted, he looked once around at all the faces, then fixed his attention on Father.

"I, Agamemnon, son of Atreus, do here present myself as husband for your daughter. If chosen, I shall make her my queen, the queen of Mycenae. She shall be honored and obeyed throughout all Argos, and I shall strive to assure that she shall never have an unfulfilled wish, if it lies within my power."

"And what do you bring to show us?" Clytemnestra spoke.

There was a deep silence. This was the first time she had asked anything of a suitor.

Agamemnon grinned. I thought it made his face sinister, as the heavy black beard parted, revealing his gash of a mouth. "Princess, I will show it betimes." He left his place and fetched the long inlaid box from its resting place beside a pillar. Placing it carefully in the center of the megaron, near the hearth, he opened it with great ceremony. Then he reached in and took out the scepter, holding it aloft, turning so everyone could see.

"Behold the work of the god Hephaestus!" he cried.

It looked like any other scepter to me—the length of a man's arm, about the same thickness, too. That it was of bronze made it unusual.

"Tell me, King, the story of this scepter." Clytemnestra was leaning forward.

"I am honored to do so," he said. His voice resounded like thunder that is too close. "Hephaestus fashioned this in his heavenly forge for Zeus. Zeus presented it to Pelops, who then gave it to Atreus. From Atreus, Thyestes took it, and then it came to me as its rightful wielder."

"Shall I wield it, too?" Clytemnestra was almost standing now in her excitement, and her voice also sounded loud as thunder.

Agamemnon looked startled, but quickly recovered. His eyes finally joined his mouth in smiling. "I shall have to ask Zeus's permission," he said. "After all, it is Zeus's, and so far it has only passed through the hands of men."

"Do not ask Zeus," Clytemnestra said. "He is prejudiced because of his dealings with Hera, and will always deny the wife. I ask *you*."

For just an instant he hesitated. Then he gestured to her. "Come here and take it yourself."

I saw Father go stiff. This was against all protocol, and he moved to disqualify Agamemnon. But as he rose, Clytemnestra stepped from her place and went over to Agamemnon. Briefly they looked into each other's eyes, testing for mastery. Neither looked away, and, still keeping her eyes on Agamemnon, Clytemnestra grasped the shaft of the scepter, closing her fingers around it.

"It seems you have decided the matter," Agamemnon said. "Now I need not ask of heaven."

The feast and gathering following this could not but be affected by the couple's extraordinary actions. People were so stunned that they could not help talking about it, even if they were reduced to whispering amid the pleasantries.

"A woman has touched the god-hewn scepter."

"Does she mean to wrest it from Agamemnon?"

"If the gods permit such a thing, does that mean that they would allow a woman to rule alone?"

I overheard all these questions nestled between comments on the roasted kid, the quality of the firewood, and the near-full moon.

I stayed close to my family, especially wanting to know what Mother thought. But, queen that she was, she betrayed nothing, nor would she speak her true thoughts where there was the slightest chance that anyone might overhear.

Father was more transparent, and I could tell by his glowering that he was highly displeased. Castor treated it as an amusement—"Clytemnestra looked regal with the scepter"—whereas Polydeuces found it offensive—"To spar in public like two boxers demeans them both." I myself did not care for Agamemnon, but I had to admit that he brought out Clytemnestra's fire and that perhaps they were well suited.

I left Castor and stood for a moment at the edge of the hall, where the covered porch gave way to the open courtyard and, beyond that, the moonlit grounds. Looking up, I saw that the moon had only one more night before it was full. It shone brightly, casting sharp shadows from the edge of the roof and the tall poplars swaying in the wind, the same wind that ruffled the shoulders of my gown.

Someone came and stood beside me, disturbing my solitude. I thought that if I ignored him he would turn away. Instead he spoke.

"I fear my brother's behavior has displeased you." It was Menelaus.

"No," I said, feeling bound to answer. "Not displeased, but surprised. Yet it seemed to appeal to my sister, and after all she is the one whose favor must be won."

"It was bold of him."

"A gamble that may pay off."

"Does boldness appeal to both sisters?"

I could look at the moonlit grounds no longer, keeping my profile to him. "I do not care for boldness for its own sake," I finally said, turning to him.

"Nor do I," he said. "I am not sure I am capable of it myself. I am quite different from Agamemnon."

"As I am from Clytemnestra," I said. "Brothers and sisters are never mere copies of one another."

Outside in the night I heard the call of a nightingale. The warm winds of spring stirred it, the same warm winds that were stirring the hems of our garments.

"No," he said. "And sometimes there's more in common between unrelated strangers. Clytemnestra and Agamemnon are both dark-haired, and we are both light."

I laughed. "Yes, that is one thing." His hair was a redder gold than mine, but they were similar. And we had both chosen to stand apart from the crowd at the feast, to look out into the night: another similarity.

A long silence now descended. Although I had wished him not to speak, now that he was beside me and had ceased doing so, it felt awkward. Why did he not reply? The nightingale called again, sounding very close.

He seemed content just to lean on the little balustrade and keep looking out onto the moonlit courtyard. The edge of it cut into his muscled forearms, but he did not move them. His hands were finely made, perfect and strong. They hung loosely, relaxed. I thought of Father's, nervous and veined like a monkey's, and always plucking at something. Father's were also festooned with rings. I saw that Menelaus only wore one, so that his hands looked naked for a man of standing.

"What are you thinking?" he finally said.

I was startled at his directness. "I was wondering about your ring," I admitted. "That you wear only one."

He laughed and held up his hand. "I need my hands to be free, not weighed down, even with gold."

"What is on it, then? What does it show?" I could see it was incised with figures.

He pulled it off and gave it to me. In the deep hollows of the oval I could barely make out two dogs flanking a curved object. Their heads arched toward the edges of the oval, making a graceful half circle. As I turned the ring to catch the carvings in the dull light, I realized how thick it was and how much gold it held. The House of Atreus was rich; in that Clytemnestra had made a good match. *Zeus gave power to the House of Aeacus, wisdom to the House of Amythaon, but wealth to the House of Atreus*: I had heard that saying from Father's lips.

"My two hunting dogs," he said. "When we were fleeing from Mycenae, they faithfully accompanied us. They are gone now, but I keep them with me this way."

"You are loyal to them as they were loyal to you."

He smiled as he drew the ring back on. "Yes. I shall never forget."

And we cannot forget, either: the reason you were driven away, the dreadful curse of your house, I thought. At the same time, he must have been remembering the unspeakable thing hanging over our house, my mother's deed. We were both defined by our family histories, yet must not speak openly of them. I laughed, a quiet, sad laugh.

"This amuses you?" he said. "Loyalty?"

"No. What amuses me is the weight we both carry, and must not speak of. Yet you seem to carry it lightly enough."

"I try to make it look that way." He gave a smile, and won my admiration.

"Oh, so here you are!" A loud drunken voice cut through our privacy. "Little brother!" Agamemnon swaggered up, rubbing his belly in satisfaction, and reeled, sagging, against Menelaus. "Hiding? You should be celebrating with me. I've found the wife I need!"

Menelaus pushed him away, and Agamemnon swayed back and forth on buckling knees, eyeing me. "Ehhh . . ." he murmured. "Is she really the most beautiful—"

"Silence!" ordered Menelaus. "Drink more and cease your stupid babbling."

Thus the hated phrase was stopped halfway through. I signaled my thanks to Menelaus, then slid away from the distasteful brother hanging on his shoulder, the man soon to be my own brother-in-law.

❖ VIII ❖

I was awake before dawn, watching the moon set behind the trees on our hilltop. The breeze was still stirring, stealing into the room between the columns. There was a faint stale scent of the megaron fire, burned out now.

Being up so early, I was able to assist Clytemnestra in her dressing. Only one more day for her to dress formally; only one more day to attire herself in what must appear to be the fourteenth different costume. In truth, she combined her gowns and mantles and brooches in changing ways to make it appear that she had many.

"Bring me the bright scarlet!" she ordered her servant as I stepped in. She was magisterial that morning, her color vivid. There was something different about her.

The servant returned, bearing a bolt of cloth so red it would make a poppy look pale. Clytemnestra smiled and picked it up. "Yes!" she said.

"It is the color of blood," I said. Are you sure you wish to . . . to look like a warrior?"

"A warrior-man needs a warrior-woman," she said, holding the cloth under her face.

"So your mind is still settled on Agamemnon?"

"Yes. I shall wed him. I shall go to Mycenae." With no hesitation she stripped off her sleeping gown and stood naked for a moment before sliding the red wool over her body. She had an unusually strong body, broad-shouldered but not like a man's. Her face was likewise strong of feature, but not masculine in the least. It was her spirit that was so bold.

"I shall miss you," I said, my voice low. I was just realizing how much. From my earliest memories she had been there, protecting me, teasing me, playing with me. Now her chambers would be empty.

"But we knew this must happen," she said. She was so straightforward. Her thinking was thus: I am a woman. I must wed. When I wed, I may leave Sparta. What is the surprise in that, in the what-must-be?

Her acceptance of it—of leaving me—hurt. "But Agamemnon!" I said. "What about the—the—"

"The curse?" She was pinning the shoulders of her gown. She did not reply until she had gotten them just right. Then she turned and looked searchingly at me. "I cannot explain it, not even to myself. But the curse is part of the reason I want him."

I was horrified. "Why do you wish to bring self-destruction upon your head?"

"Because I believe I can thwart it—even overcome it," she said, lifting her chin. "It has issued a challenge. I will take up that challenge."

"But to bring *our* house into this circle of destruction! Oh, please do not!"

"Are you forgetting we also have our bad prophecies? Aphrodite has vowed to Father that his daughters will be married several times and leave our husbands—did he ever tell you that? If you intend to be faithful to your husband, then you also will be trying to challenge a prophecy, to overcome it."

I wanted to say, *Please don't leave our house! Don't leave me behind. And don't marry Agamemnon. I don't like him!* But I would never voice those words. When a daughter left home to wed, there was always an empty place in the family.

"One more to get through," she said, laughing. "And then I can have the man I want."

The pitiful last contender, an envoy from a Cretan suitor, had little to offer and no one was paying much attention to him, so when his brief speech was over, he slunk away. He knew—as did everyone else—that the choice had already been made.

At the closing gathering, Father presented all the suitors with guest-gifts of bronze cauldrons and thanked them. Then he announced that his daughter Clytemnestra would wed Agamemnon of Mycenae.

Hearing the actual words *wed Agamemnon of Mycenae* was so dreadful and final, I flinched.

They were married two months later. Clytemnestra rode with great gladness in the marriage chariot that took her to Mycenae, determined to best the prophecy that had been laid out for her.

It felt lonely without Clytemnestra, and at first we kept looking for her to return for visits, as some daughters did. But she stayed mostly at Mycenae, and the journey was just long enough to give one pause in making an impromptu visit. My brothers helped fill the gap, and Father seemed content with the match he had made. He also was pleased that his "most beautiful woman in the world" ploy seemed to have taken root in the popular imagination. The rejected suitors spread it everywhere, so that it became a fervid belief in the minds of the Greeks: Helen, princess of Sparta, is the most beautiful woman in the world. This meant that from the moment Clytemnestra was betrothed, they began to ask him when I would be ready to wed. I was only eleven then, but Father put them off, not to keep me at home and preserve the last of my childhood, but to drive the price up and attract more suitors.

Mother was kinder and genuinely wanted to keep me with her a while longer. As we expected, I had finally grown taller than she. And one day she pronounced that I had eclipsed her in beauty, and she was content with that.

Looking into my face, she said, "A mother always imagines it will hurt, when she must surrender her throne to her daughter, and so she fights it. But when the time comes, it feels natural." She smoothed my hair.

"You have lost no throne that I can see," I reassured her.

"The throne of youth, my dear, and all the loveliness that attends it." She tilted her head a little. "It may not happen to you at all. Your aging may be . . . different."

Four years later, when I reached fifteen, Father decided that my own turn had come to follow in the ritual of the suitors and the choosing. But before that could take place, I wished to be allowed to follow an ancient custom, still occasionally observed in my day, of a race for unmarried girls. It was reputed to go back to the bride of Pelops—the grandfather of Agamemnon. She had raced before her wedding day with fifteen maidens in honor of Hera, the patron of marriage. Afterward the girls dedicated a garment to a statue of the goddess.

I begged him to let me enact this last rite of the girlhood and the freedom I was leaving behind. "For you know I am a fast runner," I said.

"Yes, but—"

Mother broke in. "Let her run. Let her have this day." She looked at me knowingly. "I never had that opportunity." She took my face in her hands. "Dear child, you shall run free down by the banks of the Eurotas." She smiled a private smile. "As is fitting."

Because that is where I was conceived? I thought. The swan feathers were still in her box; I had recently looked. They had lost none of their blazing whiteness.

"First you must weave a garment for the goddess," Father said.

That was a joy for me. I had become a good weaver, and even learned to put patterns into the cloth. For the goddess I would create a pattern showing her favored bird, the peacock. It would be challenging, but yes, I could do it. With pure white wool, then green dyed from nettle and moss, then a border of blue.

It was early spring, to my mind the most beautiful time of year. Tiny leaves created green auras around the tree branches when the sun shone through. A thousand minute flowers—white, gold, purple—were winking in the meadow. Once again I stood by the banks of the Eurotas.

Beside me were fifteen other girls, all selected by their villages or their families as fleet of foot. Some were younger than I, I could tell by looking. Others were older. The day that I ran the race I was fifteen.

I had reached my full growth. I was taller than some, but not all. We were each to wear a short tunic that reached only to our knees, and which bared our right shoulder. We were barefoot.

The sun was slanting through the willows lining the riverbank when we lined up for the race. Our heads bowed, we asked the blessings of Hera and dedicated our strengths to her.

"You will race along the riverbank until you reach the boulder in the field of barley. Then turn left and run along the footpath beside the field. When you come to the end of it, turn left yet again, until you come to the two shields that will be set up as gateposts, with a thread stretched across them. The first one to break that thread is the winner," a young priestess of Hera announced.

We each put our left foot forward, ready to dash. I felt my knees tremble. But not for fear of losing; it was for eagerness of running. At last I could run as fast and as hard as I wished with no hindrance.

"Fly!" the race-master cried.

I flung myself forward; my right leg acted as a bowstring; the trembling muscles leapt and I sprang out.

How can I describe the lightness and freedom of running free? I felt immensely strong, filled with power, and there was no barrier to it. Whatever was there, I would leap over it. I had that strength.

The river fled past; I was vaguely aware of the shaded waters flowing on my left, but I ran on. I saw only those girls on either side of me.

We reached the stone in the barley field and rounded it. Two others were still level with me. Panting, I rounded the stone and aimed at the straight path ahead. It was mine.

There was more speed in me, and my legs moved faster as I commanded them to.

Atalanta. She is Atalanta. My brothers had called me that all my life, when they watched me run. Atalanta: the swiftest woman who had ever raced.

But no one threw a golden apple in my path to distract me as Atalanta was distracted. The muddy course, and the race itself, were mine to claim. I told my chest to take in air, to breathe; I pumped my arms; above all, I called up all the strength I might have hidden in corners of myself.

One yet ahead of me. She was short and strong, her powerful legs shooting her along the path, showing muscles in the thighs bared by the short tunic. She was the one. She was the one who thought to win.

Hera, help me! I cried.

But no surge of strength came into my limbs. We reached the end of the barley field. The other girl and I swung left again; we were so close in the turn that I could see the sweat on her shoulders.

She bolted ahead, and for an agonizing few minutes she left me behind on the path. Ahead I saw the shields marking the finish.

Now, I told myself. Give it all your strength. Give it even the strength that you do not have.

I saw her back; I commanded myself to catch up to it. I told my arms to pump harder.

Was the gap closing? I ran as hard as I could. I no longer told my body to do anything; I *was* my body.

Closer . . . closer. Her back was getting larger. Larger.

I came abreast. I looked over at her. Sheer surprise was written on her face.

I pulled ahead of her, broke the slender thread. Collapsed on the ground. For I had run better and faster than I was able. Something all athletes understand. You have done as well as you are capable, I exulted to myself. Nay, even better. Better than your best, who can explain it?

My maidenhood was over. It ceased with the victory in that race. It was my sacrifice to Hera—my swiftness, my strength. My wind-fed freedom to race.

❖ IX ❖

They were coming, approaching from all sides. Mother laughingly said that the hills were dark with them, like an army of locusts. She said it with a shudder, but a touch of pride as well.

"Truly I have never witnessed a greater number of suitors for any woman's hand," she assured me. She was pleased. I, on the contrary, wished that there had been far fewer of them.

Since Clytemnestra's wooing, Father had decided that this time each suitor must present a token that spoke for his person, and display his prowess in some manner, be it by sword, spear, race, gold, crown, or promise of deeds to come.

"He will address us here, in the megaron," Father said, pointing to the freshly painted chamber, its thick pillars shining and its hearth scrubbed. "Then you, Helen, may question him further, as much as you like."

"You are becoming lax in your age," said Mother. "Letting Helen speak as much as she likes!" But she said it with approval. It was only fair that I be allowed to question the man freely to satisfy myself rather than defer to Father or my brothers.

"Now, as to the men who woo by proxy—they must be able to answer as their master would. We must assume the master has confidence in the friend's words. Perhaps the friend can even speak better than his master, and that's why he was chosen."

"May I ask him that?" I asked.

"Certainly, but be prepared for him to lie. After all, his task is to win you, perhaps by making his master seem more attractive than he really is."

"I think I shall not choose anyone unless I see him with my own eyes," I decided. "So the men who are sending proxies are wasting their efforts."

Father laughed. "But not before they have presented their gifts!"

Now was the time to say it, the thing I had decided. "I refuse to choose anyone who utters the phrase 'the most beautiful woman in the world,'" I said. "He would be doing it only to please you, and in any case, it isn't true, which also makes him a liar."

Father looked alarmed, but then said, "You may make that a condition in your own mind, certainly, but we will not announce it."

Even now, to recall the suitors is to make me smile. All told, there were some forty of them. And what an assortment of men! They ranged in age from six(!) to sixty. The extremes of age were provided by two who came not to woo but to accompany ones who did: old Nestor, king of Pylos, at least sixty, came with his son Antilochus, and Patroclus brought the boy in whose household he lived, six-year-old Achilles.

There was a huge hulk of a man, Ajax of Salamis. There was a courtly man from Crete, Idomeneus, who, even though a king, came in his black-sailed ship to woo in person. There was a barrel-chested red-haired man, Odysseus from Ithaca. Men of every size and shape and character had assembled under our roof. Since each contestant would have a whole day to himself, that promised forty days of Father's hospitality.

"We'd better pick a rich one," Father muttered the first afternoon when he lifted the curtain to look out and see how many were gathered in the megaron. "To repay my expenses!"

Now we must emerge and take our places on the thrones to one side of the room. My hair was covered under a veil, and my shoulders were hidden as well, but still I braced myself for the predictable staring and silence when I appeared.

Dear Persephone, I prayed, oh, cannot one of them *laugh*? I swear, I would fall in love with him on the instant.

"Greetings," Father said, taking his time in looking around the room.

The suitors lined every wall. Some were in shadow and I could not see their faces clearly, but there was a great variation in height. The man I later knew as Ajax stood a head taller than everyone else, and Odysseus almost a head shorter. There was an enormous man shaped like an olive-oil jar, who turned out to be Elephenor from Euboea. I had my first glimpse of Patroclus, a handsome young man, with the glowering boy pressed to his side. At the time all I thought was, what is that surly child doing here?

"You do us honor to come seeking the hand of my daughter Helen," Father said. "Now let us pour libations before beginning the contest." He gestured to a servant, who gave him a rhyton of unmixed wine. He solemnly poured it out in the special floor trough near the throne and asked the gods to look with favor on us.

"Who will be first?" he said. This time he made them choose their own order.

All of them stood there dumbly. Some of them were still staring at me.

"Come, come, you warriors, why be bashful?" Father said. "The first to speak is the first to be finished, to enjoy himself the rest of the time."

Elephenor, the rotund man from Euboea, stepped forward timidly. "Very well, great king." He bowed and looked moonstruck at me, like the people in Sparta all those years ago. "But I am no warrior." He shrugged. "I can only say that, if Helen were to choose me, she would have the most ordinary of lives, where each day passes in peace."

But I already had that, and longed to escape it. The rest of his suit went almost unheard, as the life he offered did not tempt me, and he was not rich enough to interest Father.

By the time his presentation was over, the smell of roasting ox wafted in, telling us it was time to go outside and partake of the feast. We approached the grounds, where many spits were turning, sending clouds of smoke heavenward. Every night Father would have to provide such fare.

"Helen!" Suddenly I was embraced in a tight hug. When I turned, I saw it was Clytemnestra. "We've come! Menelaus is a suitor!" Her voice was low and thrilling. "Not in person, of course. Agamemnon will represent him." Behind her stood her lord, grown heavier and more florid in the four years since they had wed.

"Greetings, great king," I said dutifully. I had seen as little of my brother-in-law as possible whenever Clytemnestra and I had visited. Mycenae was a gloomy place, a gray palace of heavy stone set in the wrinkle between two steep hillsides in Argos. Outside of providing an excursion—one of the few times I journeyed from Sparta, and even then in a closed cart so that no one could see me—it did not lure me. I much preferred it when Clytemnestra visited me, bringing her fair-haired little daughter, Iphigenia.

I had also seen little of Menelaus, who never seemed to be at Mycenae when I was, but Clytemnestra had always spoken glowingly of him. In a subtle way, she had been his champion all along.

"Why does he not come himself?" I was remembering our little talk in the moonlight long ago as I asked.

"Some border problems with Sikyon," said Agamemnon. "He rode out with some warriors—we cannot know how long it will take." His voice, never pleasant, was unnaturally loud. He always called to mind a snorting bull.

"No, he's just bashful," whispered Clytemnestra. "He does not like competitions. He does not fare well in them."

"I'll speak for him," boomed Agamemnon. Several heads turned at the sound.

"Welcome!" Father extended his arms in greeting. "Welcome to my favorite son-in-law."

"Your only one." Agamemnon liked stating the obvious. "But not for long."

People were swirling around us in the great open courtyard, some faces seen easily in the yellow torchlight, others in shadow. There were so few women; a handful of contenders had brought sisters or cousins, but the men had mostly come alone. I noted that many of the warriors had brought their gear; presumably they planned to use it in their trials.

"Hail, great king of Sparta!" The red-haired, thick-chested man appeared next to Father and held out a cup in salutation. "And most gracious queen," he added, bowing to Mother.

"Hail, Odysseus of Ithaca," said Father. "What surprise do you have hidden under your helmet for us? What display do you have in mind?" He held out his own cup, which was promptly refilled by a slave.

"Why, none, Your Highness," said Odysseus. "I know I cannot compete with these wealthy men who have come from all over Greece and across the Aegean Sea. Ithaca is a poor island, rocky and barren. No, I can offer nothing."

"Oh, come, now," said Father. "You did not come all this way from your island off the western coast to offer nothing."

He grinned. "Only advice, sir, only advice. And it is to benefit you in making your choice."

Father groaned. "Advice I have aplenty. Pray spare me advice, if you wish to remain my friend."

"My advice will enable you to keep the men gathered here your friends. Without it, there will be enmity."

Father looked up sharply. "What do you mean?" he asked.

"I mean that the losers may not accept your choice. They may turn these weapons from tools of friendly competition to instruments of deadly intent."

Mother gave a little intake of breath and brought her hand up to her throat. But she kept her eyes from widening or blinking.

I knew we—Father, Mother, and I—were hearing again the shrill voice of the Herophile Sibyl crying, *Because of her a great war will be fought, and many Greeks will die!* But Odysseus had not heard those words; he could not know.

"And what is your proposal?" Father asked, looking keenly at Odysseus.

"Ah! Before I reveal it, I must ask your promise for something in exchange."

Father grunted. "I knew it. You do in fact want something."

"I do. But not the hand of Helen. I am not worthy"—he looked at me and smiled—"but perhaps I could join your family in another manner."

"Oh, speak up! Spit it out, whatever it is you want!" I could tell Father was troubled by the ugly prospect Odysseus had raised about the disquiet; it was filling his mind.

"I would like you to speak on my behalf to your niece Penelope," he said. "It is she I long to wed."

Father looked relieved. "Is that all?"

"To me it is everything."

"Very well. I shall do my utmost for your suit. And may the gods do the rest! Now your part of the bargain!"

"It is simple. This is the way to avert any trouble. You will announce that all the suitors must swear an oath to uphold Helen's choice of husband, to be content with it. If anyone should seek to disrupt the marriage or dispute it, then all the others will make war on *him*."

"But why would they agree to that?"

"Because, men being men, each will imagine himself the winner, and enjoying the benefits of this oath."

"You said 'Helen's choice,'" I said softly.

"That is right, little beauty," said Odysseus. "It must be your choice. That way no one can hold it against your father."

"But that's unheard of!" said Mother.

"I am sure she will listen to the wise advice of her parents," said Odysseus, all but winking. "But in the end"—he turned to me—"it is you who must speak the words. The words that say, 'I choose you to be my husband.'"

I felt a strange excitement at the prospect of it.

Odysseus slipped between two large men and disappeared.

A tall, wrinkled man, his head bobbing, was weaving his way toward us, turning adeptly to slide between people. He never stopped talking to a man trailing alongside him.

"Ah, to behold you again is worth the journey from Pylos," the wrinkled man said, throwing his hands up in exultation. "Ah, and along the way, there were repairs on the road, we had to take a detour. Although it was not as rough as the time in that battle with the Epeans when my chariot wheel came off—do you remember?—no, you were too young, you were not there. Well, it seems—"

"Greetings, King Nestor," said Father, when Nestor had paused to gulp in a breath. "We welcome you. But we thought you had a wife already!"

One who, preferably, was deaf, I thought.

"Oh, I do, I do! It is my son who seeks a wife. Antilochus here!" He clapped the young man on the back, and his son winced in response.

Antilochus was of medium height, with one of those faces that are inherently pleasing—whether by expression or the contours of the nose, cheeks, and eyes, it is hard to say. It was a face I felt I could trust.

"And what do you plan as your part of the competition?" asked Father abruptly. He was still distracted by what Odysseus had said about the strife.

"What, and ruin his surprise?" Nestor shook his finger at Father. "Really, Tyndareus, I'm surprised at you! You know better!"

"You're not *my* father, Nestor. Pray don't scold me!" said Father.

"I will either demonstrate my swift running or drive my chariot," said Antilochus. "But I will not say which yet."

"Oh, he's the swiftest—wins races all the time . . ."

Father moved away, leaving Nestor talking. I could barely keep myself from laughing out loud.

The night air was cool and soothing, and overhead the stars were coming out, looking like specks of silver dust. Some of them were blotted out by the clouds of smoke rising from the fires for roasting the meats. The breeze stirred; soon I would need a light cloak.

"I've never lost a race; no, nor a wrestling match, either . . ."

"What? You haven't been to the oracle at Dodona? Pity! Where do you go, then?"

"I've found a shrine that doesn't require any blood sacrifices; the goddess accepts grains and milk instead. Saves me a fortune! Do you want the location?"

How amusing it was to stand absolutely still and listen to these snatches of conversation, the revealing little snippets of people's concerns.

"When's it to be ready? By Hermes, I'm about to faint!" The jug-shaped Elephenor came by, rubbing his stomach. He let out a rumbling hunger-burp that he did not trouble to hide. He sidled up to one of the fires and eyed a platter of meat that the servants had begun carving from the roast and snatched a piece dripping with fat. He tore it with his hands and then dropped pieces of it down his gullet.

"No!" Suddenly at his side was a boy who barely came up to his waist. "Stop it! That's rude!"

Elephenor lowered his head and peered over his waist to see who was speaking. "What?" he muttered, his words choked by the meat in his mouth.

"I said it's rude, to help yourself like that! Are you a thief? You act like one!" The boy was glaring at him.

"Who speaks to Elephenor of Euboea thus?" Elephenor swallowed his food quickly.

"Achilles of Phthia," the boy said.

"Who in Hades is Achilles of—Phthia?" He made *phthia* sound like a loud spit.

"Son of Peleus and the goddess Thetis!"

"He needs a lashing, whoever he is." Elephenor turned away, wiping his greasy hand surreptitiously on his garment.

"I saw that!" the boy yelled.

Elephenor whirled around, like a big melon, and bent down. "Enough from you!" he said. "If you don't shut up, I'll lash you myself. Where's your mother?"

"I told you, she's a goddess, and—"

"Hush, Achilles!" A tall youth appeared. "Leave this man alone." He turned to Elephenor. "Excuse him, please."

"No, I won't. He's a loudmouthed brat." Elephenor drew himself up. The grease stains were smeared darkly on the side of his tunic.

"*He's* a loutish thief!" Achilles cried. "I hope you don't think the princess would ever hold *your* greasy hand!"

"Enough," said the boy's companion. He had a calming effect on him.

"All right, Patroclus." I was surprised to hear the boy give in so easily. Suddenly he saw me. "It's Helen!" he cried, pointing at me.

"Oh. Yes." Patroclus nodded to me. "Princess, I fear to speak to you privately ahead of my time. I would not be presumptuous."

I liked him. "It would seem pretentious not to. Or—what the word you are so fond of, Achilles?—rude to pretend we don't see each other. Besides"—I felt emboldened by Odysseus's plan that I should make my own choice—"I am free to speak to anyone, at any time everyone is gathered here."

"I must be one of the youngest of the suitors," said Patroclus. "I would not wish to be seen as speaking out of turn."

"Well, how old are you?" Now that he had mentioned it, I had to ask.

"Fourteen," he admitted.

He looked older than that. I said so.

"No wonder!" said Achilles. "He killed a playmate when he was even younger, and his father brought him to live with me and my father, and made him my squire. So he's been treated like a man for years!"

"It was an accident," said Patroclus softly. "I didn't mean to harm him."

"But blood once spilled must be avenged," I said. "I am glad you found safety." I knew all about the blood feuds, the relatives that had to even out a death, even an accidental one. Only fleeing to another land, and seeking purification from a god, would avert more killing. Hoping to lighten the mood, I said, "You are not the youngest, then. I've been told there is a genuine suitor here who is ten." Somehow I suspected that around Achilles, the mood was never light.

"You would have to put him in a storeroom and let him mature, then," said Patroclus. "Like wine."

We laughed, and the evening seemed gentler.

X

Libations poured, places taken, faces fresh from rest, and Father standing beside his throne in the megaron, forty men waiting to hear what he would say.

"One of our guests spoke yesterday—the noble Elephenor." He nodded toward the man, who was now wearing a clean robe. "Many more will speak in the days to come. But before any other man takes his place before us, I must announce that I have decided to add another condition to the contest."

Now an uneasy silence fell over the group, so lighthearted an instant before. I watched Father, thinking how sure he always seemed, wondering what it would feel like to be so certain of all my actions. He did not seem to mind changing the rules after the contest was under way.

"There are some forty of you; thirty-nine will be disappointed. Disappointed men sometimes do not accept results they dislike. With such strong and trained warriors, this might lead to ugly strife. I want everyone here to return to his home as able-bodied as when he left it."

In the pause that followed, some men began muttering, but as Father started speaking again, a hush fell over the crowd. "Therefore," he continued, "I want it to be clear who has chosen: Not me. It will be Helen herself. And surely you can accept the choice of the woman you claim to love."

Everyone stared at him. This was unheard of. Was he a coward, afraid to make a choice and stand by it? Hiding behind his daughter?

"This is Helen's wish." Father looked at me. "Helen?" He motioned to me.

I stood. "I will choose my husband." I spoke slowly. "As I must pay the price for a wrong choice, I will be doubly thoughtful, doubly careful to safeguard my own happiness."

Father looked satisfied. I sat back down, gripping the arms of the throne, my hands cold.

"But I demand something further," Father said. "All of you must pledge to respect Helen's choice, and should anyone—*anyone,* no matter who he be—dispute it or attempt to disrupt it, all of you must defend the chosen man, with arms, if necessary."

"What?" cried Ajax of Salamis, a gigantic slab of a man. "You insult us!"

Instead of arguing, Father just cocked his head. "Perhaps, although that is not my intention. I have my own prophecies to consider, none that you need know, but this will assure peace. Believe me, it is for your own good, whether you know it or not."

Ajax grunted.

"You must go and take the oath now," said Father, "before we proceed any further. Any man who does not wish to follow me to the solemn site may withdraw his suit."

The whole company followed Father out of the megaron and from there out of the palace. Three priests led a horse to be sacrificed. He was a sturdy little horse from Thessaly, but now his strength and his blood would be poured out in order to bind these men and to prevent a war—the dreadful war that only Father knew about.

Some hold that fates are fixed, and that even Zeus cannot alter them, while others feel that they are more fluid than that, and ever-changing. But when a gruesome fate awaits us, it is in our nature to try to change it, or, at least, not to walk willingly toward it.

It was a long distance from Sparta; I had not expected to walk so far. We went in silent procession down the long hill, past the city. A crowd came out to watch us pass. It seemed unseasonably chilly, and I shivered inside my light wool gown. I walked between Father and Mother, with Castor and Polydeuces behind us. Clytemnestra and Agamemnon were just behind them.

Father looked grim as he trudged along, and Mother no less so. It was clear that with each step they took, they felt as if they were challenging the oracle, trespassing the will of the gods. Yet they had to do it.

A shady clearing against the side of a rocky hill with a thin cold waterfall on one side: just the sort of place a tree or water nymph would call home. Dark cypresses ringed the edge of the glen; the ground was spongy with moss. Silently, as if in a ceremony for one of the Mysteries, the men made a circle around the clearing. Father took the reins of the horse and led him into the center. With a trembling exhalation of breath, the horse shivered and his hide twitched, little ripples passing across it.

"Proceed." Father nodded to the priests. They stepped forward with bronze swords and knives. One twisted the horse's halter, forcing his head back to better expose the throat, while the second stroked his withers and murmured calming words. Then the third moved swiftly, taking one long sword and slicing the horse's neck open in one motion. The horse reared but could make no sound; he fell to his knees and his head pitched forward, hitting the ground with a crack. Spouts of blood erupted from the neck, so much that the head disappeared beneath its red torrent. A cloud of steam surrounded the flood as its warmth met the cold air, and a horrid thick metallic smell filled the air.

A pool of blood surrounded the horse; he lay sprawled as if on a red sail. When several moments had passed without the horse moving, Father nodded again to the priests. They walked across the circle of blood and began dismembering the horse, using short knives to sever limbs and joints and lay open the insides. The only sound in the clearing was that of their hacking and sawing, of sinews snapping and joints ripping, of soft tissues gurgling as they spilled their contents.

Methodically, the priests arranged the pieces in a circle, then withdrew, their legs bloody up to their knees, their cloaks soaked with gore.

Father raised his arms. "Take your places," he commanded the men. "There are enough pieces for all of you. You must each stand on one of the pieces and make your solemn vow."

Even though many were warriors, the men looked uneasy at this ghoulish request. Glancing at one another and then back at Father, slowly they came forward and put at least one foot on part of the bloody carcass.

"I do swear before this company and all the gods on high Olympus that I will defend Helen of Sparta and her chosen lord against anyone who seeks to wrong them," they intoned together in their deep voices.

"Thus shall it be," said Father. He turned to the priests. "Bury the horse," he said. "Raise a mound to it, so that it remains a memorial to this day and this oath." Then, with a smile, he said, "Come now, let us return to the palace." The smile was almost the worst thing of all, as if he had played god and succeeded in altering our fate.

XI

A fresh day, cleanly created for us by the gods, the remains of the horse moldering under a heap of earth.

We gathered again for the contest to continue in our tidy and warm megaron. It was the turn of Ajax of Salamis to speak.

Agamemnon was sitting with the men, but Clytemnestra was beside me and Mother on Father's right hand.

"He probably cannot even speak," Clytemnestra whispered into my ear. "There is something so . . . bestial about him."

I agreed. He was a huge man; most men would not even reach his shoulders. His outsized head with its oddly small features did resemble the head of a bull. Under his thick unruly hair there might be tiny horns. I shivered and thought of the Minotaur, that ghastly offspring of a woman and a bull.

Ajax took his place; in adjusting his cloak he managed to sweep it into three men's faces. They fell back, pushing others behind them.

"My pardon!" Ajax made a stiff bow, his body like a creaky hinged door. "Great king, queen, princess . . ." He went on and made his formal declaration. He was Ajax, son of Telamon, king of Salamis. "I am very strong!" he said, stating the obvious. "And why am I so strong? Because of Heracles! Yes, Heracles visited my father once, and spread out his famous lion skin and stood on it and decreed to my father that his newborn son should be as strong as the skin!" Ajax looked around proudly. "Yes, in Nemea they still have a patch of the skin, but I was formed by its strength!" He nodded, pleased with himself. "And I have a special shield. It's called . . . the Shield of Ajax." I could not help myself; a small laugh escaped from my lips.

He looked puzzled at the amusement. "But, Princess, that *is* what it is called. It's made of seven layers of bull hide, and—here, let me show you!" With surprising nimbleness, he darted off to get his shield.

Now everyone openly laughed. But they hushed when Ajax returned, hoisting his gigantic shield over his shoulder. He planted it in front of him, where it stood like a tower. "Tychios, the best worker in hides, made this from the skins of seven bulls. And over it, there is a layer of bronze. Nothing can penetrate this!" He thumped it up and down on the floor.

"Why would a woman care about his bull-hide shield?" Clytemnestra said with a giggle. "Truly, do men ever understand what appeals to a woman?"

"Thank you, Ajax," said Father, shouting over the banging of the shield. "Now, what do you bring as your prize for Helen? Unless it is to be the shield?"

"I— Great deeds! I offer great deeds! My prowess in cattle-rustling. Cattle equal wealth. I can deliver many heads of cattle, all stolen from the people of Troezen, and Epidaurus, and from Megara and Corinth and Euboea."

At that Elephenor cried, "You offer to plunder my lands! How dare you!" and rushed over to Ajax, who brushed him off like a bothersome insect. The rotund man, seemingly so difficult to budge, went flying.

"Ajax . . ." Father chose his words carefully. "It is not appropriate to offer stolen goods as a bride-price."

Ajax looked confounded. Behind him Elephenor was getting to his feet, ready to assault again. "But prizes won in battle are the most precious of all!"

"Salamis is not at war with Euboea, nor Corinth, nor Epidaurus," said Father. "Have we not just taken a vow to avoid strife and war?"

I rose and looked at Ajax. I gave him what I hoped was a compensating smile. "I wish no violence ever to be laid at my feet," I said.

"Oh!" Ajax's face grew almost as dark as his beard. "Well, then, if you spurn the great Ajax . . ." He swirled around and dragged his shield after him, then pushed his way through the crowd and stalked out.

"You're well rid of him," said Mother. "Imagine the tempers he could get into. Imagine being on the receiving end of them."

That was not something I cared to imagine. I was content to let the bull-man retreat and leave Sparta.

The third day of the contest: the suitor was Teucer, the half-brother of Ajax, also the son of Telamon, but evidently born after the telling visit of Heracles. He was of average size and strength; no lion-skin promises had been made on his behalf. I liked him better for it.

I studied him carefully. His looks were pleasing, and he was of a goodly age—perhaps some five or six years older than I, making him twenty or so. There was gold in his hair, and his eyes were green-flecked.

"Oh, those Trojans!" Clytemnestra purred. "No one can compare to them in looks."

"He isn't a Trojan," I whispered back.

"He's half Trojan," she replied. "And if this is what one looks like when he is only half Trojan, I'd like to see a full-blooded one!" She sounded hungry.

"Who is his mother, then? He shares a father with Ajax." I should have studied all this, but there were so many suitors, and all their lineages were so complicated.

"Hesione," she said. "The sister of Priam, the king of Troy. She was kidnapped by Heracles and taken off to Salamis and given to Telamon. A long time ago."

"Has she been kept a prisoner all this time?"

Clytemnestra shrugged. "I don't know. Perhaps she grew to like Salamis and didn't want to return. Perhaps she is fond of Telamon." She rolled her eyes.

As it turned out, Teucer's skill was archery, and his demonstration was most impressive.

The fourth day. Already this was becoming wearisome. Had it not been for Clytemnestra's presence at my side and her evaluations and comments about each man, it would have been unendurable. This fourth day, Idomeneus, king of Crete, took his place facing Father and us.

He was a bit older than the others had been; from the story of his life on the island kingdom and the battles he had fought, I assumed he was in his early thirties—at least twice my own age. After declaring his lineage—as a grandson of the mighty Minos—and recounting his wealth and the title as queen that he could offer me, he was confronted by Father's asking, "Most kings do not come in person; they send an envoy to represent them. This is all the more true when the distance is great, and Crete is four days' sail from Gytheum, our nearest harbor. Yet you have come all this way."

Idomeneus just smiled, not defensive at all. "I do not trust to rumors or to other men's eyes. I wished to come in person to see for myself this Helen of Sparta, who is reputed to be the most beautiful woman in the world."

I stood up, trembling. "Sir! That is not true!"

"That I wished to see you in person, that is true."

"I am not the most beautiful woman in the world! You must stop this!" I looked around, pleading with all of them in the room.

Idomeneus looked saddened. "Princess, you *are*." He said it as if he were pronouncing an incurable illness.

And by this time it felt like one. Silently I sank back down in my seat.

"What do you bring to offer Helen as your wife?" Father asked.

"I bring her the title of queen of Crete. I lay Crete at her feet, Crete to share with me, a goodly kingdom that is rich in pastures, in olives and vines and sheep, surrounded by the deepest seas, protected by our ships. "We are a proud people, Princess," he said to me. "Come and live amongst us."

"And what is your skill?" Father went directly to the point.

"Words, mighty king. I tell epic tales, fit them to verse. My lyre is best played by a more talented bard, but I taught him the words." He indicated a young man who until then had remained quietly in the shadows of a column, clutching his tortoiseshell lyre.

The bard took his place beside Idomeneus, and although it was full daylight and no wine had been drunk, the beauty of the poem and the music moved us first to silence and then to tears. He sang of the love of Adriadne for Theseus, and the bravery of that hero.

But I could not choose him. Had I not promised myself that anyone who spoke the "most beautiful woman in the world" words would be disqualified? And, appealing as he was, he lived far away and the thought of being separated from the rest of my family by a wide stretch of ocean frightened me.

The moon, a crescent to begin with, grew full and waned and became a crescent again, and yet the contest dragged on. By that time we were so weary of speeches, of roasted ox, of wine, of lyres and archery and chariots and footraces, we vowed never to indulge in them again once this was over.

Agamemnon, who had gone home to Mycenae after the first few days, returned to be the final contestant, speaking for his brother.

Stocky, thick legs spread wide in challenging stance, he stood beside the megaron hearth, his manner impatient.

"My brother Menelaus has trusted me to speak for him. A humble man cannot sing his own praises, even when they are deserved. And my brother is a humble man." He made it sound like a fault. Or perhaps he just meant that his brother's humility was now inconvenient for him, Agamemnon. "But of all men, he has least reason to be! His lineage is of the noble House of Atreus!"

There. He had flung out his greatest liability as if it were his greatest asset. The House of Atreus—its founder Tantalus, and his son and grandson Pelops and Thyestes.

"Yes, we carry a great burden, but so does Atlas! Atlas bears the world on his shoulders, but we bear the burden of the curse of a brother to a brother: that of Thyestes to Atreus. So be it. He cursed all of Atreus' sons, forever and in all generations. But no mortal has the power to do that, only the gods. And Menelaus and I are living proof of that. We hold no enmity for one another—quite the contrary. We are close as brothers can be, and would go to one another's defense on the instant. I am pledged to protect him, and he, me. The curse is dead!"

I saw Father tighten his lips and frown. Beside me Clytemnestra was silent. Did she believe this?

Agamemnon looked around, gauging the expressions in the room. But the faces were guarded. "Princess, at your feet he will lay the precious stores of oil and grain and robes and gold that fill the vaults of Mycenae, as well as twenty black-hulled ships and the spoils of the islands we raided. Besides that, there are all the cattle of the Plataean region."

He was promising more wealth on his brother's behalf than he himself held.

"And as a final bride-price, he dedicates the entire city of Asine, lately captured from the Tiryans."

Now the room stirred, and I saw anger flush across the broad face of Menestheus, until then the suitor with the greatest pledge. He was from Athens and immensely wealthy; he had pledged ships and palaces and gems, but nothing like this. He was outbid.

"Had my brother a kingdom, Princess, he would pledge it all to you." Agamemnon's dark eyes bored into mine until I almost felt pain at the back of them. "I myself hold the kingdom of Argos and Mycenae, but on his behalf I pledge it all, all except the title itself." He paused. "He offers you all he has."

"And much he does not," muttered Clytemnestra.

"With his body he will defend you, with all his treasure he will endow you, with this necklace he will wed you." Agamemnon then drew out a thick chain of gold, its heavy links clanking as he held it up, its bright unmistakable luster proclaiming that its gold was pure. True gold is a piercing, almost garish yellow. He turned, holding out the necklace, so that everyone in the room could see it. Then he stopped, facing Father and me.

"This is most generous," was all Father allowed himself to say.

Fortunately, I was not required to speak.

"Now for your feat . . . ?" Father pressed.

"It is not my feat, but Menelaus's. Here it is: If you choose him, Princess, he will present himself here and undertake any task you set him. He will complete it, though it take all the rest of his life."

"But it is a requirement that he perform it now!" Father rose. "All the others have."

"What the others have done is perform a limited exhibition. What my brother proposes could require a lifetime—or, at the least, a warfaring season."

"You are asking for one man to compete on a promise, while the others performed for our eyes. There is no competition that cannot be won in the imagination, and a promised feat is always perfect." Father's fists were clenching. He was ready to disqualify Agamemnon.

I rose. "Father is right. A promise is not a deed. Therefore let him prove himself. Let him—"

"Princess, the condition was that you have chosen him first." To my shock, Agamemnon interrupted me.

"As I am the prize, I set the conditions," I snapped back. "If he is really so eager for me as you claim, then he will comply. Let him race from Mycenae to Lerna, where Heracles slew the Hydra, without stopping. It is a full day's walk, but he must not walk, he must run. Bring me word how he does. Mind you, if he stops and rests, or slows to walk, he has lost."

Agamemnon's face flushed dark. I could see his mouth working, fighting not to spit out words of fury. "Very well," he finally said in a low, cold voice.

Around the room spirits now lightened. I had set, they believed, an impossible task for Menelaus. How could an ordinary man run so far without stopping?

But I had not specified how fast he must run, and I had already known that Menelaus was a strong runner. He did not remember, but Agamemnon himself had told me at Mycenae while bragging about his own hunting prowess. He had complained that Menelaus seemed more content to chase the quarry than to slay it, and that he was capable of staying on his feet and running all day.

So I aided Menelaus in his suit. Some might even say I fixed the contest, but that is not true, for he had given me leave to choose whatever feat I wished. Did I want him to win? Even today I cannot answer that.

"You have prolonged the contest," grumbled Father. "Who knows how long this will take now? Menelaus may be far away, and— What came over you?"

"I could see that you were ready to dismiss the suit."

"You were right. It was absurd. Does Agamemnon think just because he's king of Mycenae he doesn't have to follow the rules?"

"Clearly that is the case. But we should not punish Menelaus on his behalf."

"Menelaus is a fool if he chose Agamemnon to speak for him, and that alone should disqualify him!" Father barked. "It was most revealing of his character, his judgment—or lack of it!"

"But Father—"

"He is right, dear." Mother was standing beside us. "For the most serious decision in his life, he chooses his hotheaded, arrogant brother to speak for him? A poor choice. A very poor choice. What does it say about Menelaus?"

Now I felt compelled to defend him, to defend my soft-spoken companion in the moonlight. "Who else could he have chosen? Would it not have seemed most peculiar had he bypassed his brother the king and chosen someone else?"

"Why didn't he come himself? Anything would have been better than Agamemnon, I don't care how stumblingly he speaks."

"He doesn't speak stumblingly!" I said.

"Why, child, are you defending him?" Mother pressed.

"I'm not!" I cried. "I don't even know him!"

"I'll tell you why he didn't come," said Clytemnestra, pushing herself between us. "He was afraid. He was afraid he would fail, and then he could not live with himself. He could not trust his words, his feelings were so strong."

We all stared at her. She went on.

"He wants you more than anything in the world," she told me. "Menelaus does not want things, not like Agamemnon, who is greedy for everything he sees. Menelaus is content. But since he saw you, all those years ago, he finally found something he wanted. He was too afraid that he would lose it for himself."

"So he would allow another to lose it for him?" I was incredulous.

"He thought Agamemnon, not caring so desperately, would actually speak better." Clytemnestra paused. "I know this. I heard them talking. I have kept silent until now, so you could make up your own mind. But now, apparently, you have."

"No, I haven't! Let me see first how he runs!"

❖ XII ❖

Deep night. Alone, lying silently on my bed, my chamber attendants—more like companions than slaves, in truth—stolen away to pallets of their own, I allow myself to relive the extraordinary closing day of the contest.

It has not been as I imagined. I had longed for the end of it all, for the ceremonies and the presentations to cease. I was weary of judging men, of noting every nuance in their words, and more than that, of what lay beneath their words. Clytemnestra's constant jokes and cynicism had worn thin, and I could feel the mounting strain on Father and Mother. For me there was the fear of making a wrong choice, for I wasn't simply choosing a man, I was also choosing a way of life.

Father was right to question me about what I had demanded of Menelaus, but I had no good answer. I was curious about Menelaus. His absent presence lit my imagination and created a man I was hungry to know.

The night is chill, as nights in spring are. Yet I am so restless I keep throwing off the light wool covers and shivering in the darkness. Through my mind troop the suitors, in a ghostly file, looking at me accusingly.

Choose me . . . look with favor upon me . . . I can give you . . . I am the best . . . I risk all . . .

If I choose one, will they truly all go away? So they had vowed, bloodying themselves with the slain horse to do so.

I do not want to marry a king. I do not want to go away to some foreign city or realm. If I marry someone less than a king, he can stay here with me in Sparta. I will not have to leave all that I know, family and home. As if by magic, the kings vanish from the ghostly line.

I do not want to marry someone much older than I, or much younger. Someone older would treat me like a daughter, being either strict or stupidly fawning. Someone younger would defer too much to me, and would know less than I. Out fly Idomeneus, Menestheus, Patroclus, and the ten-year-old from Corinth.

I do not want to marry anyone whose face—or the rest of him, for that matter—does not please me. Instantly the fat man from Euboea careens away, followed by a number of others whose looks displease me for one reason or another. Among them is Odysseus, although I know he is not a true suitor in any case. There is something in his eyes that makes me uncomfortable; I do not trust him. Although he affects a careless, amiable manner, I can see the calculating opportunist in him. Penelope was welcome to him.

I open my eyes and lean against the frame of the window, gazing once more out into the night.

There are still too many left, too many still to choose from. I cannot do it, and there are only a few days left until the contest must end. Oh, help me!

To whom have I cried?

"Oh, my dear goddesses, please look down and help me choose." I search the heavens as if I believe I will see them. All I see are the scattered stars wheeling around me.

"Hera, sweet goddess of marriage, guide me! You who hold marriage most dear, be merciful to me. Beautiful Persephone, who left maidenhood with such a struggle, help me in mine. To go from maid to wife is no light matter, and you were torn. Take my hand and guide me."

My senses strain, but I feel nothing in the black expanse.

For long moments I stand shivering in the dark, waiting to feel their presence. The perfume from the fruit trees comes to me on puffs of wind, like the goddesses' breath.

I turn and seek my bed, believing all is well. But I had forgotten to include Aphrodite, I had slighted the greatest goddess of men and women and their love. As my father had once neglected her, thereby incurring her wrath, so did I.

"He is on his way!" Clytemnestra grasped my forearm in a painful pinch. "He didn't stop at Lerna! He's still running, coming directly here!"

"All that distance?" It seemed cruel, and I would never have set that task for him.

"He is determined to meet your test and to go beyond it," she said. She released my arm. "I didn't know he had it in him."

We were surrounded by people; the suitors were still on hand to await the judging, but boredom had sowed its seeds and everyone was eager for distraction. Menelaus and his race were providing it. Now ears strained to overhear us. I had been told that the men had taken bets as to whom I would choose, and therefore anything they might overhear could help their odds.

"Come." I motioned to Clytemnestra and we retreated into the guarded inner courtyard of the palace. Seated on a low bench, we spoke in whispers.

"What do you mean?" I asked her.

"I just meant that Menelaus has seldom shown much passion about anything. So this is a surprise."

I could not imagine that it was for love of me, as he really did not know me. We'd had only those moments in the night long ago. "So you think he covets the throne he will get from Father?"

She tilted her head and considered this. "Perhaps. To live in Agamemnon's shadow might have been difficult all these years, although he never showed it. He is a hard man to know."

"Perhaps he only wants to brag about winning me."

"My dear, they all do."

"So he is a lackluster fellow, one who shows no passion?" I pressed her.

"Usually. Of course, Agamemnon has enough passion for both of them, and too much passion is as bad as too little." She glanced around and lowered her voice even more. "But he does not even have a mistress. He never avails himself of any of the captured slave women, never requests any as his lot when spoils are divided."

I was apprehensive. "Could it be . . . does he prefer men?"

"No. No men, either."

"Has he taken a vow to Artemis? But grown men do not—"

"What are you two whispering about? You look like conspirators!" Castor bounded out of the palace toward us.

"We are," I said. "We are forced to be."

"Well, have you made your decision?" he asked, grinning. He crossed his arms and waited. "I won't tell, I promise." He made a silly sign of a solemn vow.

"Who would you choose?" I asked him. I did value his opinion, and up until now both my brothers had kept remarkably quiet about the contest.

"It would depend on what sort of life I wanted," he said. "A quiet one—a warfaring one—a wealthy one—I'm not you, little sister."

"I haven't chosen yet," I admitted. "I have eliminated some impossible ones, but there are still far too many left."

"Dear, you should be flattered. No one in living memory, or even in legend, come to think of it, has been sought by so many."

"No, I'm only confused," I said. "I don't really want to be married at all, but I know I must."

"Don't go away!" said Clytemnestra suddenly. "Don't leave us!" She shook her head. "I've tried to say nothing, but just now, the thought of your going so far away was painful. I was lucky, Mycenae isn't very far, and we've not been separated, but—oh, I don't think I could bear it!"

Her outburst shocked me. Even Father and Mother had not said as much, seemingly resigned to losing me. I was deeply touched.

"Dear sister," I said, embracing her. Castor came and put his arms around us both. I looked at them, flooded with emotion. "It would be impossible for me ever to love anyone as much as I love you, my family."

Even as I said the words, I could hear Aphrodite, the one I had scorned, laughing at me—her laughter cruel and mocking.

"They've sighted him." Mother came into my chamber before the dawn. I opened my eyes in the semidarkness to see her bending over me. She touched me lightly.

"So soon?" I murmured, pushing up on one elbow. I wanted to delay the inevitable; my future was beginning to claim me already.

"Child, little Cygnet," she whispered, sitting down beside me on the bed. She drew me up and held me close to her.

"Oh, will no one rescue me?" I cried. Oh, I did not wish to be married! I did not want to go with a man. But at the same time, I wanted to be free to see the world without a veil, to be released from this cage where I was being held. Only marriage could open this trap, lift the bars, and let me out. Yet, in truth, I would choose neither a cage nor a man, but run away from both.

"That is what the suitors wish to do," Mother said. Her face betrayed her sorrow. She wished to be rescued, too, from this onrush of time that, in taking away her youngest, made her old. A woman whose daughters have married is no longer a woman to catch Zeus's fancy. That, too, would end for Mother, even the daydream of it. The feathers would turn yellow—if not yet, then soon.

"But they will change everything!" I cried.

"Only one of them will, child. The rest will go home and change some other woman's life." She brushed her tears away and smiled. "Thus has it been always."

"I'll stay close to you!" I promised. "I won't go away!"

She smoothed my hair. "You must not choose a man for that reason. You must choose the one who appeals the most to you, not just one who will consent to live here in Sparta."

"We must be up to receive Menelaus," I said, rising.

The goddesses would, must, guide me. I had to believe that.

Mother looked knowingly at me. "Wear your most flattering gown, Cygnet. But I have a feeling you would have without my telling you."

I selected a gown and robe of the sheerest wool, a blush of dawn-pink. I had been told since childhood that it was my most flattering color. It wrapped around me like a mist. I put on gold and amethyst earrings and a heavy gold bracelet. No necklace; that would spoil the effect.

When I left the chamber and walked out onto the raised porch, my gown and robe swirled around my ankles like mist and made me feel like part of the dawn.

"He's reached the outskirts of Sparta," said Polydeuces, returning from the palace gates. "He will be here before the messenger can come and go again. Shall we throw open the gates and welcome him?" The rising sun struck his golden hair, and for a fleeting moment I thought how handsome my brother was.

"Yes!" said Father, coming up behind us. "That young man deserves our salute." He clapped his hands and motioned for servants to open the bolted gates that stood, poised, overlooking the steep road up from the river. "He's put me to shame. I don't remember what I did for your mother, but it wasn't running for days and nights."

It was not what you did in the beginning, I thought, but what you did later—overlooking the whispers about Zeus.

Castor joined us, then Mother. Clytemnestra, always a late sleeper, was unlikely to be up before the sun.

We stood at the gates, looking down the slope. Far below we could see the misty green of willows overhanging the riverbank. The meadow path was lined with curious people; I could see them milling down below, perhaps not even knowing why they were there. Then the sound of cheers and clapping, and a figure was moving, slowly, along the path, lifting his legs painfully, his arms swinging.

"He isn't very fast, is he?" asked Polydeuces. "He wouldn't win any crowns from *our* contests."

Always so critical, my golden brother. "We have no races that go on for days," I said. "I doubt that anyone else—even you—could run continually so long."

He shrugged.

"We'll know his tale when he arrives," I said. And, as a runner, I was eager to hear it. I wanted to know what it was like to run over rough ground, boulders and hills and soggy meadows, and not stop. It was a different sort of running, not about speed but endurance.

"I can beat him!" Beside me that strange child, Achilles, had suddenly appeared. He dashed out through the palace gates and bolted down the hill. I saw him meet up with Menelaus at the bottom of the hill. The dark boy turned on his heel and began to race Menelaus up the slope. He had all the speed of someone who had rested all night and only had a short distance to go. Pumping his arms, he passed Menelaus, throwing gravel up in his wake.

Legs flying, Achilles flung himself back through the gates, panting, then turned triumphantly, hands on hips. "I'm faster!" he crowed.

Father paid him little mind, merely nodding and ushering him aside. Achilles started jumping up and down to attract attention. But all eyes were on the laboring Menelaus, doggedly climbing the hill. He was barely running at all, and seemed so weary, his feet barely left the ground.

From the corner of my eye I saw Patroclus come out and make a fuss over Achilles, doubtless praising him. In any case he calmed down; Patroclus knew what to say to the excitable boy.

Closer now: Menelaus was just coming up over the last crest before the palace gates. For a moment he disappeared from view, then suddenly his reddish hair appeared, catching the sunlight, making an aureole. He gasped and stumbled toward his goal, his legs still lifted, still running, his chest heaving. He burst through the gates, then spun and almost lost his feet. Great tearing sobs of gasps came from his mouth. He staggered and would have fallen, but Castor grabbed him and held him up. His eyes rolled upward and he was about to faint. Without thinking, I rushed over to him and helped Castor to hold him up. He was limp and so covered with sweat he was slippery like a new-caught fish.

Just before he fainted, he looked directly at me and murmured something I could not make out.

Now the contest was over. Now I must make my choice, with no delay—if Father hoped to have any resources left from his extensive hospitality for all the suitors. I would not be so thoughtless a daughter as to drag this out one day longer.

But yet again I had the dreadful, throat-closing feeling of being hurried along, forced to walk a path I was not ready for. I discarded my dawn robes and had myself prepared for the evening ceremonies. My women removed the airy gown of day and brought out the robes of night—blue and dark as the sky just before full night comes.

"My lady, you are lovely," one said.

"My hair ornaments," I said.

"Yes, my lady." She brought out the twisted wires of silver, with their tiny ornaments, and patiently fastened them into my hair, which I let fall free over my shoulders and my back. "The silver shows well," she said. "Gold gets lost in your hair, since the colors are so similar." She unstoppered a bottle of narcissus flower oil and rubbed a bit across the bend of my elbows and along the sides of my neck. "I don't want it to stain the necklace," she said. "Which one shall you wear tonight?"

Silver and deep blue—what would go with those colors? "Perhaps the clear one, the crystal?" Let everything be icy and clear tonight. If only my thoughts could be as well!

After I was bedecked, I dismissed both attendants. I stood for a few moments alone in my chamber. I still did not know what I would do, who I would choose. But I *would* make a choice. I must end this uncertainty, for myself and everyone else. I took several deep breaths and then walked slowly out the door, entering the private courtyard that the inner rooms gave out onto. I looked up at the sky, feathered now by the fresh tree leaves.

I searched for the constellation of the lion, my dear constellation that told the tale of Heracles at Nemea that I loved so, as if somehow the answer hid itself in the bright twinkling of the stars, as if I could decipher something there.

Oh, what must I do? I had to choose. Over and over I begged Hera and Persephone for their guidance. But nothing came. Then a dull resignation mixed with determination, like that of a soldier facing a stronger enemy, stole over me. Very well. I must choose. I *would* choose. I would shut my eyes and whomever I saw first in my mind, that was the one.

I heard a crunching of gravel in the courtyard, and the image of Menelaus running up the hill filled my vision. Some person, all unaware, walking nearby, had thereby decided the matter. Yes. It would be Menelaus. It was meant to be Menelaus. Now my reasons tumbled over one another like unruly children. Had I not been granted that special private meeting with him long ago? Obviously the gods had arranged it. Had I not felt something for him even then? And now had he not proved himself superior in the task I had set before him? And was our hair color not similar? Even that now seemed imbued with secret meaning.

Menelaus. I felt relief. I even felt warmth and contentment. I took a deep breath and turned to carry out my duty.

The megaron was barely large enough to hold everyone, and they all were jammed in. A small fire was lit against the chill of the night, but the heat of the crowd made it unnecessary. As I walked in, everyone looked at me and a hush settled over the company. Father held out his hand and drew me over to him beside the throne.

Everyone had eaten earlier, devouring oxen and sheep and downing seas of wine, and they looked quite content. They now stared back with dull eyes, the eyes of men satiated. Good. They would accept my decision placidly.

Father stood and made the customary libation—poured out to honor Zeus, the liquid made a harsh sound against the dust as it struck.

"My daughter, it is you who must make the choice," said Father. "Have you reached a decision?"

"I have," I said. The unknown walker had made it for me, conjuring the image of Menelaus in my mind. I moved forward, ready to speak to the company.

"Then, my dear?" Father stood and put his arm around me.

I looked out at all the men. The upturned faces stared back at me. Patroclus. Idomeneus. Ajax. Teucer. Antilochus. Agamemnon and Menelaus, so many, many more who I have not described here.

This was the moment. Whatever I said, whatever steps I took, would bind me forever. Father placed a wild olive wreath in my hands.

"Crown him," he said.

Only at that moment did I realize that he had not asked me my choice; he did not know, either; he trusted me to select the man who would succeed him on the throne. "Thank you," I said.

I walked toward the group. I felt the hem of the robe stirring around my feet, felt the faint pulses of heat coming from the fire, but I walked on, like someone in a dream.

"You are my husband," I said to Menelaus, placing the wreath on his head. I did not dare to look at his face. I did not need to see him now. Having made my decision, I did not want any last-minute feelings to intervene.

"Princess!" He knelt, and his lovely head bent forward, almost losing the wreath.

I drew him up. "Rise," I said. "Stand here beside me." He did so, and still I did not dare to look at him.

"My daughter has spoken," said Father. "Let us all rejoice!"

A resounding cheer tore through the megaron—relief, release. It was over.

Menelaus squeezed my hand, turned to me.

"Princess, I am not worthy," he said. Still I feared to look at him. I could not gaze on his face. He noticed.

"Princess," he said, "it is not my face you should be afraid to look upon. I am just an ordinary man. If I can gaze at your face, which takes more courage, then you should have no fear of looking at mine."

Before we could speak further, Father came over and embraced Menelaus. "Son!" he said.

Castor and Polydeuces also made their way over. If they resented losing the throne to Menelaus, they did not show it. Had both Clytemnestra and I left Sparta to marry, they would have inherited Father's title.

"Welcome, new brother," said Castor.

Polydeuces clapped him on the back. "We'll race sometime, you and I," he promised. "But you've won the race that counts."

Mother took both his hands, and Clytemnestra embraced me. "Now we will be double sisters," she whispered. "Oh, I'm so happy."

"When will it be?" asked Agamemnon. "You can take a newlywed journey to Mycenae and stay with us—in privacy, of course."

"Soon," I said. "As soon as all arrangements can be made. And there will be few of them, as all the family is already here."

Suddenly I felt ready to embrace my future, and rushed to meet it.

❖ XIII ❖

The gods themselves chose the day—the warm height of spring, when the countryside was erupting with life. We would pledge ourselves in the private forest stretching behind the palace. Father and Mother had wanted it in the little enclosed courtyard, but as I had gazed on that every day of my life, I wanted another place for this sacred moment.

For this day I would wear my finest golden robes, and the evening before, I fasted and dedicated myself to the marriage. I did everything—O you gods, I did!—to ensure that this marriage would be blessed.

The grove was hushed; the sweet murmur of wind in the uppermost branches of the trees was soothing. Mother and Father escorted me into the clearing. My face was veiled with the sheerest linen, as I was guided toward the place where the rite would be held. I felt as though I were walking in a dream, for it could not possibly be true, what I was doing. But when they lifted the veil, there was Menelaus beside me. He smiled hesitantly, his face pale.

A priestess of Persephone, to whom our family was loyal, would conduct the ritual. She was young and her mossy green gown seemed the same shade as the ground beneath her feet. She looked first at my face, then Menelaus's.

"Menelaus, son of Atreus, you stand here in sight of all the gods of Olympus to pledge yourself," she said. "You seek to take Helen of Sparta to wife."

"Yes," said Menelaus.

"You do this knowing all the decrees of the gods through their prophecies—upon your house, and upon the house of Tyndareus?"

No, he didn't know the prophecy of the Sibyl, how could he?

"Yes," said Menelaus. "We are right with the gods."

She held out a garland of flowers and bade him bind our wrists together. "As these flowers of the field are twined together, so must your houses be."

She nodded to one of her acolytes and a gold pitcher was brought and placed in her hands. "The sacred waters of the Kastalian Spring at Delphi," she said. "Bow your heads." She poured some over us. "May this impart wisdom." She unwound a bright red thread from around her waist and told us to touch it. "Whosoever touches this has touched the belt of faithfulness and will remain true." She motioned to another acolyte and she circled around us, carrying a bowl of smoking incense. "Let the prayers ascend."

We stood in silence. I had not so far been asked to say a word.

"Close your eyes and circle one another," she ordered us. Slowly we shuffled past one another. "Forever after, you will be within one circle, one house."

Still no words, no promises, were asked of me.

"She is yours," said the seer abruptly. "Take her hand."

Menelaus reached out and grasped my wrist, in the ceremonial gesture indicating someone taking a wife. It harked back to the days when a man abducted a woman for marriage; now, of course, it was symbolic.

But Menelaus had another, private gesture. He motioned to his servant, who brought forward a carved wooden box. Opening it, Menelaus drew out the big gold-linked necklace that Agamemnon had flourished. Reverently, he lifted it up and put it over my head. It sank down around my neck, so heavy it felt like a yoke. Its lower links fell below my breasts, tangled in my hair—the great weight of marriage, and of what I had entered into, tugged earthward.

The gleam of the gold and its thickness dazzled the onlookers. I might say it blinded them—all they could see was the yellow and the glitter.

Back in the palace, the marriage feast began. The entire central portion of the palace, with the megaron giving out onto the private enclosure, had been transformed. Cut branches of flowering myrtle and roses twined around the columns, clouds of sweet incense rode the wind, and great stacks of braided flower garlands awaited the guests. Everyone must feast, everyone must rejoice before setting out for home, back to their gray-walled fortresses and sea-dashed houses.

Now I must walk with Menelaus, not Father. Forever after, it must be Menelaus, and not Father. Hesitantly I held out my hand and he took it. He must have felt the cold in it.

Pulling gently, he drew me to him. He pressed me against his cloak, whispered, "I cannot believe that you are mine, that we will see each other every morning as long as we live."

Nor could I. "We must think only of tonight, and of tomorrow, the first morning to come," I said. It was all I could manage. And I did not know what to think of them. I was not prepared, I could not imagine how to live through them.

"Now, my brother!" Castor interrupted us, but it was not unwelcome. Menelaus turned to him. We still belonged to others, at least for now.

I embraced my mother. Was she trembling, or was that my fancy?

"Dear child," she said. "I am happy for you, and happy for me, that I shall not lose you."

"You will always have me near," I said. And that was a comfort.

Father came to us. "It is done," he said briskly. "And well done." He gestured around to the company. "They will go home content. And I will be content that they have gone home!"

The sweet sound of flutes rose through the human voices.

"This is your wedding day," said Mother.

I felt tears starting behind my eyes.

"So look about you, see everything, remember it, hold it close to your heart."

What did I see? A great company of men, the disappointed suitors. There they were, the lives I might have had, had I gone with those men. There were many cakes—poppy, linseed, sesame, honey, sweet oil—laid out on the tables. There were piles of the sweetest dried figs—as it was not the season for fresh—and dates from Egypt and barley bread and honey from a mountain near Athens. There were slices of roast meat of all varieties—ox, kid, sheep, heifer—still steaming on their platters, just sliced from the turning spits. There were huge amphoras of the best wine, some from as far away as Mount Ismarus in Thrace, and so many lined up that our stores seemed inexhaustible, trumpeting our generosity.

But all of it faded—the music, the talk, the food, the wine—as I was terrified by the realization: *I am married.* I, Helen, was a married woman.

What does it mean to be married?

We went away. We went away in a chariot just at twilight, making for Mycenae. Menelaus took the reins and I stood beside him, and the horses made for his home. We rattled down the hill—on the gentler side, the path that horses and chariots could descend. The guests ran out after us, pelting us with quince apples, with myrtle leaves, and then, in a shower from heaven, thousands of braided violets. They landed in the chariot, they struck our feet, and we crushed them underfoot, releasing their delicate slight scent.

Menelaus's quarters in the gray citadel of Mycenae: a great winding labyrinth of stone passages and little rooms, each with its own hearth. The attendants

welcomed us gladly, and lit the fire in the chamber that had been laid, awaiting Menelaus's return.

We were alone. Just he and I, standing in this chilly stone chamber, watching, awkwardly, the fire lapping against the wood. We were as stiff as the wood,
as unmoving as the stone around us.

Menelaus finally spoke. "Helen . . ."

I turned to him. "Yes. I am here."

Silently, he enfolded me in his arms. He was much taller than I, and
when he enveloped me, I was pressed against his chest and all the rest of the
world was black.

"I cannot believe my fortune, that you chose me . . ."

I turned my face up to his. I had never kissed anyone before and did not
know what to expect, what to do, but it felt natural.

We kissed. He embraced me, pulled me tight against him. It was so odd to
be touched this way, to have someone be so familiar with my person. Now this
stranger was putting his mouth on mine. It frightened me and I felt trapped.

Now his hands were clasping the sides of my face, pulling me up toward
him, as if I were not close enough. His fingers got caught in my hair, pulling
it, and it hurt. But I dared not cry out, say anything. Somehow I sensed that
if I did so, this first time, I would insult him.

"Helen . . . Helen . . ." he was murmuring, and his breath was coming
faster.

I felt nothing. Nothing but my heart pounding in panic. *Stop!* I wanted to
say, but I knew it was hopeless, and at the same time I felt foolish. What had
I truly expected, when I asked what it meant to be married?

"Helen . . ." He stumbled toward the wide flat sleeping place that sat in
one corner of the room, spread with fur pelts and fair linens.

I followed him; I let him take my wrist (again, the old symbolic gesture).
I was short of breath. I did not know what to do, only that there was one
dread test left to me, this test that must be passed in private.

Softly, he led me to the flat linen-spread surface, and knelt on it, drawing
me after him. My hands felt icy. I breathed slowly.

Do not think about it, I told myself. I folded myself by his side.

"Helen . . ."

He reached out to pull away my gown. I stiffened and wanted to stop
him, but I commanded myself, Do not interfere. He has the right to touch
you, to take off your garments.

Do not think about it.

The fire was flickering, making snapping noises. Menelaus seemed glad to notice it, to comment on it. Then he turned back to me.

"My dearest," he whispered. His hands stroked my shoulders. I shuddered at the touch, but willed myself to stay still. "My dearest . . ." His words were lost against my throat.

He drew the last of the clothing separating us aside. I felt chilled, embarrassed, vulnerable. Let this be over!

He was holding me, he was . . .

Oh, I cannot relate it. It was painful, and invading, and then it was over. So quickly.

"Helen . . ." His head rested against my shoulder. "Helen . . ." With a great sigh, his voice trailed off. He slept.

In the teasing light of the fire, when he was absolutely still, I moved and drew up the soft woolen covers. It grew cold in the chamber. I slid as far away as I could, pulling the covers after me.

❖ XIV ❖

The day stole into the chamber cold and gray. The glorious sunshine of the day before had fled, and I felt the encroaching, encircling grasp of the stone walls like the heavy weight of Menelaus's arm flung across my shoulders.

He slept, his light-lashed eyes closed. In the dim light I could study him, watch his face—the first time I was able to do so.

He was my friend, my ally. I had sensed that from the moment I met him; and if one must marry, then let it be to a friend. That I had felt uneasy at the final surrender that was part of marriage should not undermine the rightness of my choice.

He breathed in, out, sleeping carelessly. He had done so much to win me; now he rested.

Like Heracles after his labors, I thought, and giggled. A man must rest.

But the labors of last night . . . why had I found them so off-putting? I was supposed to swoon at the ministrations of Aphrodite, but they had left me unmoved.

Aphrodite. I solemnly invoked her in my mind, not daring to murmur the words aloud. If by any human failure or weakness I did not call out to you at the time I desired guidance in choosing my husband, please forgive me. Your greatness may have blinded me, so I looked past the most obvious goddess of all. I, Helen, beg you to come to me now.

For a life without passion will be too long, even if it is short.

Menelaus stirred and looked at me. He moved his arm—its dead weight lightened as it came to life again. Then he reached out both arms and enfolded me.

"Dear Helen," he murmured. "Now it begins. Our life together."

I laid my head on his shoulder, smooth with its relaxed muscles. "Yes. May the gods grant us a blessed one."

All would be right. It would have to be. I had chosen, and there was no going back.

Clytemnestra and Agamemnon arrived the next day, although before that we had ventured out into the palace and played a bit with their daughter, pretty Iphigenia, sturdily walking, and babbling away with words that were enchanting, even when they were incorrect.

"Well, well!" Agamemnon chuckled, as he did everything, loudly. He had an ugly gleam in his eyes that he tried to mask, but it was unmistakable. He kept looking at me, looking at Menelaus, narrowing his eyes. I knew he had spent last night with us in the chamber, in his mind at least—the chamber that he had promised us was ours in privacy.

Menelaus tried to keep his face expressionless—out of respect for me, I suppose. But what would he say when he and his brother were alone, as would happen sooner or later? Clytemnestra, too, was eager to speak to me in confidence. I dreaded it; I wished they would go away. I did not care to speak of it; I felt it would be a dreadful betrayal of Menelaus. Or was it a betrayal of myself?

"And after you drove away in the chariot, and everyone's hands were stained from the flowers and fruit they had tossed after you, we went back into the palace and . . ." It had been quiet after we left, with the strange hush that descends after great bustle.

"And now," said Clytemnestra, holding her arms wide, "you have all the years of your lives to be together!"

"I wonder how long that will be?" asked Menelaus.

"Do you mean, how long will you live?" Agamemnon demanded.

"Yes, I suppose that's what I mean. People in our families do not live a long time."

"How morbid! Why would you speculate about that today, of all days, Menelaus?"

"I was just . . . wondering how many years of happiness I'd be granted."

"How old is the oldest person you have known—or known about?" I asked Menelaus, trying to steer the subject onto more cheerful ground.

Agamemnon answered. "I suppose Nestor, and he isn't all that old. There was a man in Argos who claimed to be eighty—a wizened little cricket of a human who lived in a tiny house. I saw him once, with Father. But of course no one could prove how old he really was."

"Do you think anyone could ever live to be a hundred?"

"No," said Menelaus. "That would be impossible." He smiled and took my hands. "But fifty years of happiness will equal a hundred dull years."

We stayed in Mycenae for ten days, and Menelaus showed me all his haunts and the secrets of the landscape. The citadel itself was built halfway up a hill between two mountains, and from its ramparts you could see the sea—something we never could do in Sparta. The first time I saw it, a flat shining expanse, I cried out in excitement. I had never seen the sea.

"My love, how can that be?" he asked.

"I was kept locked up," I said. "It was . . . it was for my own protection."

"Now I will protect you," he said. "And if you wish to see the sea, you may look your fill."

"Can we go closer? Even sail on it?"

"Let us go closer first," he said. "Sailing can come later."

There were caves in the high hills where he and Agamemnon had played as boys, and where he still knew hidden entrances, overgrown with vines. I liked imagining him as a boy, wondered what he had looked like then.

He showed me the great storeroom of the citadel where the treasures of his house were kept—huge stores of olive oil, of finely woven cloth, of gold and silver, and of bronze tripods and armor. The armor had been captured from various foes in raids and battles, most forgotten now, remembered only for the spoils they had yielded. They gleamed on in the dark of the storeroom while their owners had long ceased to gleam.

"Take what you like!" he said, gesturing around the room. But I had no desire for any of it. When I did not reply, he opened a cypresswood box and took out a gold goblet.

"My wedding gift," he said, presenting it to me.

It was as large as a bucket, and very heavy. "This is not for mortals," I said. "Unless it be Ajax of Salamis." My arm ached with holding it. It had a pattern of little circles stamped all over its body and its handles were pleasingly curved. I handed it back to Menelaus.

"I said it is yours." He pushed it back at me.

"You have already given me wedding gifts," I said. "Truly, I am content."

"I want you to have something from my father's house," he said. "Atreus won this in battle, and he always prized it. My mother kept it by her place at feasts, and now you must, too."

The gold was warming under my hands, and I saw I must not refuse. But still I was loath to take it.

Menelaus took a strand of my hair and wound it around the cup. "The same color," he said. I could see the pride and possessiveness in him as he entwined his cup with my hair. "Oh, Helen!" he said. "You never saw the sea, you could not look upon it. Now I will take you there. You can have your fill of it now." He leaned forward and kissed me.

Our last night in Mycenae: cold, as I suspected all nights were there, even in high summer. We ate together at a long wooden table, and I dutifully kept the large goblet by my place, although I never could have drained it. Menelaus kept refilling it, as if to secure it to me. Afterward we lay back on pillows in the megaron and enjoyed the warmth of the fire and the sweet music of the bard, who sang of battles and brave deeds of men who lived before our times.

"Always before our times," said Menelaus. "The age of heroes is over, now that Heracles is dead."

"How do you know?" said Agamemnon. He never missed an opportunity to question or contradict. "Did the heroes themselves know they were living in the age of heroes? Did it have a big sign saying, 'All ye underneath, know that you live in the age of heroes'?"

"Agamemnon, you sound so stupid sometimes!" Only Clytemnestra would dare say that to him, although I had thought it. She laughed.

"It's not a stupid question! I think heroes make their own age," he said.

"And only later, someone calls it the age of heroes." He looked around, his eyes again seeking mine. I wished he would stop it. I dropped mine. "It is not over yet. Not if we decide it goes on."

"You need to fight mighty foes," said Clytemnestra, "and I don't see any about. Heracles killed them all off." She leaned forward and tickled his ear. "No, my lion, you will have to content yourself with cattle raids and minor skirmishes. That is the problem with times of peace. But who would wish otherwise?"

Agamemnon grunted and brushed her hand away as if it were an annoying fly. But Clytemnestra, feeling playful, kept on.

"Cheer up, my love," she said. "Perhaps a dragon will come along and menace a city. Or another sphinx."

"Stop it," Agamemnon warned her. "I won't be teased."

His raised voice caused the bard to stop singing, tuck his lyre under his arm, and steal away.

Back in our cold chamber, we would huddle under the wolfskin covers that overlay the wool blankets. Menelaus would encircle me with his strong arms and begin to murmur endearments, moving against me ever more insistently. I had not overcome my revulsion for the sexual act and continued to fight the impulse to push him away, to put both my palms on his wide chest and shove.

In the past ten days, something alarming had become clear: I hated to be touched. I had never realized that before, as anyone touching me had done so only in a passing manner. Even my mother, when she embraced me, did not linger, nor did she invade my person. My attendants, when I bathed, averted their eyes and used sponges to apply the perfumed oil and the olive oil to rub on my back afterward. My brothers draped their arms carelessly over my shoulders, but only lightly, and only for a moment.

This was different. And my aversion to it was growing; I was not becoming accustomed to it. I dared not show it and found for the first time in my life how difficult it was to pretend—something I had never had to do. I knew without anyone telling me that I must, at all costs, keep it from Menelaus. But how could I, forever? For a little while, yes, but . . .

Where was Aphrodite? Why did she spurn my abject apology? Without her I would never cross to that other land, that fabled place where women not only welcomed such behavior but sought it out and . . . sometimes . . . instigated it themselves. Every morning I begged her to come to me in the evening; every night it was clear she had turned deaf ears to my plea. As Menelaus moved closer to me, his breath warm against my ear, I was as cold inside as the waters of the Styx.

In the sunlight it seemed of much less import, of course. The next morning, as we jounced in our chariot toward Sparta, it was easy to forget the secrets of the dark. I looked at Menelaus's strong forearms as he stretched them out to hold the reins; now—perverse goddess!—I found them appealing, now that they were not reaching for me.

"Our new quarters will be waiting," he said, flicking the reins. "What shall we find, do you think?"

While we were away, Father and Mother were readying our apartments, the place where I would live as a married woman. My old chambers, the chambers of girlhood, would be left behind—until I had a child of my own to fill them.

"They are on the east side of the palace," I said. They had stood empty for many years; I had heard stories about a great-aunt who had lived in them with a pet monkey and poisonous plants. The monkey had eaten some of the leaves and died—but she, with her knowledge of herbs, had given him an antidote and he had recovered. Or so the tale went. We children were forbidden to explore the rooms.

"Morning sun," he said. "Good to wake up to." He laughed and flicked the reins again, and the horses leapt forward, making the chariot lurch; the woven leather-strap floor bounced. I clutched his arm to keep my balance, and he looked fondly at me.

We were keeping to the green lowlands of the river watering the valley of Mycenae, leading to the coast. We passed through Argos and by Tiryns with its high walls. We would keep the sea on our left for a good long time before turning inland toward Sparta. I could hear the roar of the waves against the shore and smell the salt air; two small boats were bobbing farther out. I had a great wish to set sail and feel the water all around me.

"You have sailed, have you not?" I asked Menelaus.

"Oh, yes. To Rhodes—Troy—Crete. My grandfather is in Crete, and we used to visit him often."

"Someday I wish to meet him," I said. But what I really wished was to see Crete. I would have gone to meet him there even if his grandfather had been a parrot.

We jounced along in silence. Then I said, "And you've been to Troy? Is it as splendid as everyone says? Is it true that jewels encrust the walls of the palace?"

"Nothing like that," he said, amused. "The walls look like any other walls, except for the paintings on them. The colors are very bright, brighter than ours. Perhaps that started the rumor about jewels."

I wanted to ask him about the handsome men there but thought it would sound peculiar. "Do the people there look like everyone else?" I finally asked.

He laughed. "Yes—how else should they look? Hair made of leaves or five ears?" The chariot lurched as we swerved to avoid a rock. "They seem well fed and strong," he said. "They have that look—that look of a people who are proud, though. A people who know they command not only themselves but also the land around them. Even the king, old Priam, is an impressive figure, almost unnaturally strapping and youthful. He has fifty sons! I suppose making them keeps him young."

"Are they all by the queen?" Surely not! Unless she had had a series of twins.

"No, but ten of them are." He laughed. "Come to think of it, the queen is surprisingly sturdy to have survived all those births. Perhaps there *is* something about Troy . . ."

Eventually we left the coast road and turned east, climbing into the hills. The horses strained and the chariot creaked; the wheels ground into the gravel and the hard-packed earth. Occasionally we rumbled over little bridges built of boulders—rough but better than becoming stuck in a streambed.

Even in late spring, the peaks of the mountains were snow-covered and blue; Sparta lay nestled between two big ranges, the Parnon and the Taygetus. I had not realized how green and fertile my land was until I saw the drier and rougher places en route; truly Lacedaemon, the region where Sparta lay, was a blessed place.

"Your new home," I said to Menelaus. "Is it not a fair exchange for Mycenae?"

"Even were it not as magnificent as it is, it is better to be first in a small place than second in a large one." Behind his light words lurked the years of being shaded by Agamemnon's bulk and the prospect of remaining there forever. I had freed Menelaus, even as he had freed me—freed me to remove my face veil and move about in the world. Now—why, now I could even go into Sparta myself, walk the streets!

"My dearest," I said, standing on tiptoe to kiss his cheek. At that moment, I felt overcome with warm love for him.

As we passed through the palace gates, everyone was out to welcome us—the runners had seen us approaching as we rolled alongside the riverbank.

Father, Mother, Castor, Polydeuces, my dear old attendants, even the palace dogs, cried out in greeting. We were swept out of the chariot and into embracing arms. Home. We were home, a home that would now be different.

"Helen, you left us a maiden and now you return a married woman. It is only right that we present you with the tokens and emblems of your new station." Father spoke the words that began the traditional ceremony in which a Spartan woman is recognized as an adult about to enter her own household.

We were standing at the threshold of the apartments Menelaus and I would share.

As my father called them out, my mother presented me with the items befitting my station one by one. First, the cloth that would replace my maidenly robes: an intricately woven fabric with glittering silver-blue threads worked into it. Next, a large silver brooch to fasten the two edges of cloth at my shoulder. And finally, the earrings.

Mother handed me a cedarwood box that held two huge circular gold earrings with open weaving and little spikes decorating the rims. They were so heavy they could not be worn through the earlobes but must be suspended by wires behind the ears: symbol of my womanhood.

"I thank you," I said, lifting them from the box and cradling them in my palms.

Father took them and fastened them properly on my ears, pushing back my hair to do so.

"Wife," said Father, "last of all, present our daughter with the signs of her womanly toil."

Mother brought forward a little silver basket on wheels to hold yarn ready for weaving. Inside it were four balls of the finest wool yarn in natural white, dark brown, and two dyed colors: delicate pink and lightest blue. There was another basket of unworked wool, needing to be spun.

"Spinning and weaving belong to the realm of women's secrets," said

Father. "It is proper that your married life begin by invoking the three Fates; Clotho, the spinning fate; Lachesis, who assigns to you your fate; and Atropos, who represents what you cannot avoid. The three goddesses who control the span of a mortal life, from birth to death."

I took the baskets and clasped them to me.

"And now," said Father, "all rites being done properly as should be, pass into your new quarters and take possession of them."

I took Menelaus's hand and we stepped over the threshold into what would be our new home.

Inside, the sheer linen serving to shade the windows blurred the light and gave everything a blue tint, like earliest dawn. Swimming in the haze, we could make out the tall chairs, stools, and three-legged tables scattered about the painted floor.

"Look!" I cried, pointing down. "Patterns! We've never had them before." They must have been painted while we were away. They made the room seem very rich. And now my eyes saw the paintings on the wall—water lilies, reeds, and birds. "Oh, how lovely." I would never grow weary of looking at them.

I saw that the high-seated chairs were inlaid with spirals in blue-enameled ivory; their footstools had a matching pattern.

In the adjoining room Menelaus's bedstead was heaped with the lightest fleeces over a fine linen sheet. A brazier filled with cedar and sandalwood made sweet warmth.

Menelaus held out his arms and I went into them. He clasped me tightly to him, so tightly that I could feel the warmth of his chest through his tunic and mantle. He bent his head down toward me. He was turning toward the fair-spread bed.

Now! Surely now I would feel my heart leap, at least feel a spreading warmth that would make me desire him.

But instead I heard noises coming from just outside the windows, reminding me that others were nearby. The moment's possibility was gone. I slid away from his grasp and pretended to go on examining the new chamber. I did not dare look at his face; I could not bear to see the anger or the disappointment there. I thought I heard faraway laughter: Aphrodite's?

Only one last custom to be enacted before my new life would truly begin. Down by the Eurotas, Father and Mother transformed the broad meadow into a field of celebration and welcomed all of Sparta, so that Menelaus could encounter the people he would come to rule someday.

The open fires in the field were crackling; above them oxen were turning, roasting. Anyone who thrust a cup out would have it filled with Father's finest wine. Townspeople thronged the meadow, the artisans to spread out their pots and jewelry, the weapons-forgers their knives and swords. Housewives offered their barley-meal cakes and fig paste; would-be bards plucked their lyres and sang. I saw shepherds, swineherds, and goatherds milling about. Far on one side of the field athletic contests were in progress—boxing, wrestling, and running. Anyone from Sparta or the surrounding area could compete. I was thinking nostalgically of my last race as a maiden. Today only boys and men were on the field. Beside them horse breeders offered their animals, hoping for a sale. Ours was not the area for the finest horses, but one took what was available.

Menelaus and I wandered in and out of the crowd. I felt the eyes upon me, but with his arm around my shoulder I knew freedom for the first time. I need hide no longer. I grasped his hand and squeezed it. He could never understand how grateful I was.

"Fortunes! Fortunes!" We passed an elderly woman who plucked at our clothes with her clawlike hands. "Fortunes! Fortunes!" she rasped.

"Let go! Can't you see—" Menelaus began. Then he realized she was blind, her eyes sealed like an old leather purse. He recoiled.

"Potions!" a woman beside her said. This one could see, all too well: her sharp black eyes looked like a bird of prey's. "Pay her no mind. Whatever the fortune, a potion can undo it!" She thrust a vial into my hand.

"Don't. It's poison," said another voice, calmly. "You'd need an antidote before you walked fifty steps." The speaker was a man. "Halia, really, are you still trying to peddle that deadly potion? And to our future queen? What's wrong? Don't you like her?"

The woman drew herself up. "It was for the *use* of the queen," she said. "You did not give me a chance to explain further."

"So the queen can poison her enemies? Why don't you give a demonstration of its powers? Otherwise we might think you are passing off plain old sheep's fat."

Menelaus was staring at the man who had appeared so suddenly, wearing a dusty red cloak.

The potions-seller shrugged. Without any hesitation, she grabbed her companion's dog, which had been dozing beside them on the ground, and smeared its muzzle with the cloudy paste. The dog growled and licked its lips.

The enigmatic man raised one eyebrow and looked down at it. "These things can take a while," he said. There was a restrained humor, or judgment, hanging on his words. In some way he was baiting the woman; or perhaps he was teasing, or perhaps he did not care in the least. His tone of voice could be interpreted any of those ways.

The dog lurched up, unsteady on its feet. It made aimless little circles before sinking down again and starting to whine and tremble.

"Better have the antidote nearby," the man said.

The dog's owner began shaking it, crying out.

The potions-seller was calmly rummaging through a basket, finally producing a little bottle of liquid. "Ummm . . . here it is." She pried the dog's salivating mouth open a crack and poured the liquid into it.

"Very impressive, Halia," said the man. "I see you know your plants. What was that . . . nerion?"

She glared at him. "I'll not tell you all I know."

"And what did you use to reverse it? Juice of the belladonna?"

"I said, I'll not tell you!"

Menelaus and I began backing away, and the woman protested. "After all that, you won't buy?"

The mysterious man had disappeared. Menelaus and I looked at each other.

"Did we really see him?" I asked.

"One can't be sure," said Menelaus. "Somehow he was more disturbing than the poisons. I can explain poisons, but he seemed to have an extraordinary knowledge of such things."

"We don't know that, not really," I said. "All we know *he* knew was the woman's name and how two poisons worked."

"I had the feeling he knew much more."

"Aha! Here you are, hiding yourselves in this humble section!" a commanding voice boomed out behind us. We whirled around to find ourselves face to face with Odysseus. He was grinning—his marriage to Penelope had been approved and the wedding day set. He had what he wanted. "You're in disreputable company." He indicated the fortune-teller and the potions-seller.

"Did you see that man who was with us a moment ago?" asked Menelaus.

"No, why?" Odysseus was hitching up one shoulder of his tunic and adjusting his hat. "Was he a pickpocket?"

"I don't think so," I said.

"Then what's the concern?" He laughed. "So. You look content." Now he reached up to put his arm around Menelaus's shoulders. "I must congratulate myself on supporting your suit. Have you had any rumbles of discontent from any of the leftover suitors? The vow we took in that bloody field should put a stop to any mischief."

"When is the wedding?" asked Menelaus. "I heard about the footrace. Of course you won."

"Of course. I made sure of that." He winked. "Suddenly I outstripped all Penelope's suitors. We will wed before the moon is full again. Then I return to Ithaca, with my bride. Her father, of course, is not eager to let her go. But I don't wish to linger here. I want my island again. I like its rocks and loneliness."

Two men passed us, both preposterously handsome, one older and the second in that first flush of maturity when a boy is just turning into a man. The man was golden-haired and the boy very dark, with thick eyebrows. They were not villagers but soldiers, I could tell by the way they walked.

"Well, well," said Odysseus. "Where might they be from? Mount Olympus, perhaps?"

Returning to Father's side, I saw that newcomers had joined him. A company of soldiers surrounded him, decked out in linen breastplates and carrying short swords. A swaggering fellow with a shiny face and gloating expression had his ear.

"Whoever they are, we'll smash them," he was saying. His fellow soldiers nodded, murmuring.

What was he talking about? Who needed smashing? We were at peace.

"Your place will be ready by tomorrow," Father said.

"You Spartans are too trusting," the blustering soldier said. "It's high time you had some protection. Why, it's said you don't even have spies."

"If a king is just and his soldiers strong, it doesn't matter what evil the enemy is planning," Father said. "Therefore we don't need spies. Whatever they are planning will come to nothing."

There was a short low laugh behind me. I turned to see who it was but saw only more of the soldiers. Then, out of the corner of my eye, I caught a glimpse of a dusty red cloak. That man again! Why was he here?

I grabbed Menelaus's arm. "Get hold of him!" I whispered. "The man—he's a—he must be . . . a spy. For whom?"

Menelaus turned and looked, but the man seemed to have disappeared once again.

"Now, Lynceus, will you as general be content to share the barracks with your men?" Father was asking the bombastic man.

Lynceus nodded condescendingly.

"If you value your throne, Tyndareus, I would keep him in full view in the palace, not out of sight in a private barracks," came a quiet voice from the throng around Father.

"Who's speaking?" Father craned his neck.

The man in the red cloak stepped forward. "I seek only to offer some commonsense advice," he said. "Something I am sure you would have seen for yourself before long." *But by then it might have been too late,* his tone hinted.

"I said, who's speaking?" Father insisted.

"I am Gelanor of Gytheum."

"A seaman? A harbormaster?" Gytheum was the nearest seaport to Sparta, although to reach it by nightfall you would have to set out shortly after dawn.

"Neither of those, although my father goes to sea."

"Why haven't you followed him?"

"More interesting things happen on land."

"Name one!" the truculent general bellowed at him.

"Man," said Gelanor. "Man happens on land, and he is infinitely more interesting than fish."

"You haven't answered me," Father said. "What is your livelihood? You don't have the look of a soldier."

"Nor a swineherd," whispered Menelaus, and we both stifled laughs. The man did not stink, after all.

"I make things . . ."

"What things?" demanded Father.

"I make things happen."

"What sort of an answer is that? Are you a magician?"

Gelanor laughed. "No. All I meant is that if someone wants something, I can help him bring it about. Only"—he held up his hands—"by my wit and experience. I have no magic arts. Nor do I traffic with the gods. I have found, august king, that the mind is the only magic art one needs."

Father shrugged. "Here's another mad fellow." He waved him away. Then the general whispered in his ear, and he turned back to Gelanor. "Perhaps I can use you . . ."

We wandered away from the soldiers with their unappetizing leader.

"What is all this about?" I asked Menelaus. "Why has Father taken up with these men?"

"Their leader is a man looking for a war," said Menelaus. "Perhaps it is useful to have such a person about."

We politely refused the slave weaving about the crowd refilling cups. The sticky-sweet wine was overpowering and needed watering down.

"But there is no war," I said. "So what shall Father do with him?"

"Perhaps feel safer," Menelaus said. "That fellow does not look as if much would get past him."

"Which fellow? Gelanor or Lynceus?" The general or the man in the red cloak?

"Both of them. Gelanor's mind is sharper and Lynceus's arm is stronger—an interesting contest, if ever it came to that."

"But as long as they both serve Father, they will work together." I meant it as a statement, but it was more of a question. Menelaus did not answer it.

We were approaching the tent where the bards were performing; the sweet sounds of the lyre strings carried through the air.

Sparta was known for its music-making and its poets, and I was eager to hear them. This was all part of my new freedom. I was eager to taste it all, to gorge on every new dish.

"Don't listen to him." A dark little man standing near the tent entrance made a disparaging gesture. "He loses all the contests."

His music sounded well enough to me.

"And I suppose you win them?" asked Menelaus.

"Indeed," he said with a shrug, as if to say, *Winning against such people is hardly a victory.*

"Let us judge this man for ourselves," I said, edging toward the entrance.

The bard inside was just finishing up; he was singing of the mighty deeds of Heracles, especially his victory over the Nemean lion.

". . . the claws! Oh, so sharp that they alone could cut the hide! Oh, the strength of Heracles, beyond the ken of mortal man! Oh, Heracles!"

"I think the fellow outside was right," whispered Menelaus, echoing my own thoughts.

Soon he was ushered off, and the stranger we met outside took his place. He looked at us as if to say, *Now it will be worth your while.*

"I shall sing of something that has happened in our time," he said, bowing, taking his lyre in hand.

"Heracles was but a little while ago!" someone objected.

"True, but this is nearer." He plucked at his mantle where the brooch was pinned, adjusting it like an athlete preparing for a contest.

"I, Oeonus of Therapne, will sing of the marriage feast of King Peleus of Phthia and the sea goddess Thetis."

"That may not be wise," someone muttered from the back. The voice was low, but the man heard it.

"Bards must sing of what is true, and that is not always wise." He took up his lyre and began. He did have a pleasing voice and his skill on the instrument was impressive—it seemed to be part of his own speech. He lost himself in the words and it seemed as if he were feeling them from within himself. Then the silvery notes died away.

The listeners roared their approval of his song.

As he made his way out, we stopped him. "You were right," I said. "About both yourself and the other singer."

Just beyond the tent a man was holding forth to a crowd of interested onlookers. He held up a wooden box with a handle on it.

"It works! It works!" he proclaimed. "No more mice!"

"A house snake is better," someone said.

"Oh, it's true." His face broke into a smile. "Nothing beats a snake for ridding you of mice. But can you keep a snake? He's here one day, vanished the next. When you most need him, he's slithered away." He patted his box. "Now, this is always waiting. You bait it like this"—he lifted the door and put a morsel on it—"and the trap works like this." He touched it with a twig and the door slammed shut. "Take two!" He held another aloft.

But no one bought his wares, and the man trudged to another group.

"Tell me, friend, have you been at this long?" Menelaus asked, falling in beside him.

"Only a year or so," he said. "Before that, I was—I had a most unpleasant job."

"Can you tell me what that was?"

"I was the one who took the babies to the Taygetus Mountains."

The Spartan babies deemed not worthy to live—whether because of weakness or disease or merely a bad prophecy—the ones who were put out to die of exposure on the slopes of the mountains. No wonder he had changed to making mouse-catchers.

"Did you ever . . . try to save them?" I asked.

"Twice or thrice," he said. "If the baby was doomed only because of a prophecy, and if there were shepherds or hunters about who could take it home and care for it. But that happened seldom."

"What about those stories of bears and wolves suckling the babies?" I asked. Everyone had heard them.

He shook his head. "A she-wolf would eat them. A she-bear would probably kill them with a swat. That's all they are—stories."

"Who does that duty now?"

"I don't know," he said. "Someone. They always find someone."

Shuddering, we turned aside. We did not have far to seek for another pull at our attention as we reached the edge of the athletic field.

A panting group of young men had just crossed the finish line of a race and now they reeled on the grass, tumbling and gasping. The sun hit their glistening bodies, the sweat marking out every muscle, shining it like buffed stone. Against the green of the new grass, their youth seemed eternal, fixed, guaranteed forever.

Mocking that was an older man leaning on a staff nearby, watching them. He was massaging his knee, then swinging it to and fro to loosen the stiff joint.

"Oh," he muttered. "Oh, that hurts!" He smacked the knee. "Damn ointment-sellers, charlatans!" He bent over and sniffed the knee. "It stinks, but it doesn't work!" He picked up a little clay pot at his feet and thrust it at us. "Take a whiff!" he commanded.

Menelaus sniffed at it and winced. "Friend, you are right. What a stench! Reeks like rotten goat guts."

"It probably is," the man grumbled. "They sold it as ground pearls and oil of narcissus, and so it smelled the first day, but now . . ." With a hiss, the man threw it over his shoulder. It flew far, surprisingly far.

He glanced back at the young athletes. "As they are now, so once was I," he said knowingly. "Don't believe me? My javelin arm is still strong, and once I could have raced any one of these lads into the ground. Twenty years ago, back when Agamemnon was first born." He paused, thought a moment. "Well, more like thirty years ago," he admitted.

"That is better," said Menelaus. "For my brother Agamemnon is nearer thirty than twenty. Even I am nearer thirty than twenty."

"Menelaus! Forgive me, I should have recognized you." The man bowed from the waist.

"Tell me, friend," said Menelaus, "you say you were a famous athlete thirty years ago. Where did you run? Against whom?"

"I ran for Sparta in many races, as far away as Argos and Nauplia," he said. "I even beat Callippus of Athens in the double *stadia* twice. My fans carried me through the city on their shoulders." His voice first swelled with pride and then grew soft at the cherished memory of a vanished time and a vanished strength. "I boxed, too," he said. "Won a few bouts. Paid for it, too." He indicated his scarred ears, peeking out from under his graying hair. "I was a better runner," he admitted.

"Tell us your name," I said.

"Eudelus," he said.

"Eudelus, Sparta should be proud of its son," Menelaus said.

"It was—once," he said. He looked over at the athletes on the field, up on their feet now, drinking refreshing water and carrying the winner about on their shoulders. A crown of meadow flowers hung askew on his head.

"Save that crown," he said. "My lad, save that crown."

We mingled with the crowds and as darkness fell, the crowds began to thin, leaving a smaller group to gather around the fires and eat more, then linger to hear the bards, who never seemed to tire. But the artisans, the mouse-catcher-sellers, the fortune-tellers, and the athletes disappeared, and just as the moon rose, the royal party returned to the palace, the new contingent of soldiers accompanying us. The walk back up the hill was a pleasant one in the early evening, lit by torches and caressed by the wind whispering as it passed over us.

Father and Mother paused before we went our ways to our separate quarters.

"Behold your kingdom!" Father said. "Today you took stock of it and it took stock of you. Did you like what you saw?"

"Indeed," said Menelaus. But his response sounded oddly distant.

"I liked being *able* to see it, at long last," I said.

"Little Cygnet, now you may glide on the waters all you like," said Mother.

Back in our chambers, lamps had already been lit, and sweet-scented herbs had been crushed in a dish to make the air fragrant. I was happy and excited; surely now that excitement would carry me through, lift me aloft on a tide of desire, as the athlete had been carried on the shoulders of his fellows. The events of the day would propel me into Menelaus's arms and straight into the sun of his desire. My coldness would melt in that sun.

But it did not happen; the moon, that cold goddess, looked down on our silver bed through the window and her chill air banished love.

❖ XVI ❖

And now my life was beginning—or was it over? I had so longed to be free, and that happy day down by the Eurotas I thought that time had come, but Menelaus, in opening the door to one cage, had merely ushered me into another. I could not help but think of the mouse-catcher and his traps. Menelaus, who had appeared at first so strong and uncomplicated, now seemed taciturn and mysterious to me, keeping his thoughts locked up inside himself. He spoke, but he did not speak of anything vital; he was pleasant, but in a remote way. I had thought he would be my friend; instead I had a protective and stolid companion. A friend can be a companion, but a companion is not necessarily a friend, as I was discovering.

Artemis, the cold virgin goddess who guides the moon, had looked down upon us in our chamber after that lovely day in the meadows and must have taken pity on us. She somehow must have persuaded the gracious Demeter, who presides over fertility and loves the house of Tyndareus, to grant us her blessings in spite of the absence of Aphrodite in our bed. She was able to do so because passion is not needed for fecundity, nor does fertility invoke desire—although the two usually keep company.

Three months after the marriage, I was with child.

No one thought I was too young. I would be sixteen when the baby was born, as Mother had been when she bore Clytemnestra, nearly as old as Clytemnestra was when she bore Iphigenia. Even I did not think I was too young. It seemed entirely natural to me that I could suddenly become a mother. It did not require wisdom, it only required love and strength. Or so I—and everyone else—believed.

Now the door of my cage slammed shut in earnest. Menelaus treated me as a fragile bird whose nest could blow away in a day's breeze. He forbade me to wander the slopes of the Taygetus Mountains alone, warned me not to run fast, and as for playing and wrestling with Castor and Polydeuces, who still involved me when their wine was not watered enough, he was adamant that that must cease immediately. I was to be protected and quiet. Those were his orders. Only the smile and gentle tone in his voice when he spoke of it betrayed how pleased he was.

Mother was fluttering and flustered, as if the idea of a new grandchild were both thrilling and unsettling. It meant she was older; it also meant that her lineage would go on. At times she was solemn, warning me about all the dangers of birth and infancy. At others she was giggly and giddy. "Zeus," she burst out one day, "is to become a grandfather!" She clapped her hands to her mouth and laughed. I did, too.

"Mother . . ." I chose my words carefully. "I know I am mortal. And so must my child be. But do you think . . . do you believe . . . that Zeus might bestow a special blessing? The truth is, I know nothing of how the gods treat their grandchildren."

"I fear they lose interest in them," she said sadly. "Just as they do with mortals they have . . . been temporarily taken with. But the glory of the gods remains in the lineage. That, little Cygnet, cannot be taken away. It is ours forever. Our reward, if you will, for risking ourselves." Then, briskly, "Let us think about names . . . and you need a midwife, the finest that Sparta can offer . . . they know many things, things I do not. There's a woman—she has magic hands, she's never lost a child, nor a mother . . . I'll send for her."

Nor a mother. Stark words, a stark reminder that I was not like a tree, a peaceful tree that never yet died of bringing forth a pear or an apple.

"Call me Piele, 'plump,'" the bulb-nosed woman pronounced. "Everyone else does." She put her hands on her hips and inspected me. "I saw you once already,'" she said as a disclaimer. "I watched that maidens' race. So don't think to blind me with your beauty. I'm not concerned with your face, but with your inner organs. And I'll warrant they are the same as anyone else's. In any case, we can't see them." She paused to take a breath. "The question is: are they working properly? That's all we need be concerned with. Lie down here on this bench and let me inspect!"

Dutifully I stretched myself out and let her knead with her fingers and put her ear against my belly. Her hands were gentle, even if her manner was not.

"All seems to be in order," she said, grunting as she lurched back up to her feet. "You say you expect the babe in the depths of winter?"

"No, more toward the end of it."

"Good. I could not struggle up the hill were it covered in ice." She sighed and settled herself down on the bench next to me. "Now, my child, you must be sure to eat only the foods that ensure water, not the ones that are fiery and might incite early labor. That means no leeks, no vinegar. Sorry, it means a very dull plate." She shrugged. "But what you want is a dull labor. A very dull labor. Well." She stood up. "Send for me whenever you have any questions." Leaning near my face, she whispered as if it were a secret, "Most people know nothing about birth or babies. Do not listen to their foolishness! Always ask me!"

Piele was a godsend, and patience itself when it came to answering my many questions about childbirth. But on the most important question of all—why my silhouette had not changed—she could only answer, "It varies, my dear, it varies."

But I wondered if it was the goddess part of me that was keeping me slender for so long. And I wondered, too, if it was possible for a woman with any goddess in her to die in childbirth. Did it protect against that? And I could not ask her that, as she would have no experience with it.

Menelaus acted more like an old woman than my mother did, fussing and fidgeting and warning me against dangers. He draped his arm protectively about me whenever we were together. Once he even tried to make me wear the dreadful heavy gold marriage chain as if for protection, but I made him leave it in its box. I could not bear its weight.

Next he began to collect arms and armor for what he assumed would be a son. "He'll be a warrior," he said, holding up a newly worked bronze shield and sword, presenting them proudly.

I ran my hands over the finely inlaid surface of the sword hilt—depicting warriors chasing a lion, in gold and silver. It gleamed in the early morning light. All swords gleam beautifully when you first see them, before they are used for their deadly business.

"And what shall we name . . . him?" I asked.

"I have the name already!" he said proudly. "Nicostratus! It means 'victorious army.'"

"I know what it means," I said. "But must he bear the weight of such a name?"

Menelaus looked downcast. "I can think of no higher honor."

"What if it is a daughter?"

He shrugged. "Then she should be named after something pretty—a flower, a nymph."

"I was thinking of Hermione."

"'Pillar-queen'? Why?" He laughed.

"Because I want her to be strong. The sort of woman others look to for support. A great ruler."

"Who says she would rule at all? No woman rules alone." He seemed petulant as he packed the sword and shield away.

Menelaus withdrew after that, and seldom called for me to join him in his bedchamber. He said it was out of care for the child, that he wanted me to be alone so it would not be harmed, but I wondered what he was doing when he was by himself all those nights. He seemed morose; at times I would find him wandering in the halls of the palace, looking pensive. He always gave a wistful smile as he brushed by me.

After a time I grew more awkward and bulky and felt more and more constrained, but my puzzlement about Menelaus grew as well. He was not happy, so it seemed, but I did not know why. He had wanted to marry me, had performed that spectacular feat to win me, and now was about to have an heir. He would inherit the throne of Sparta. Yet he walked in gloom. It could not be the lack of passion in our marriage, surely. A man would not notice its lack as much as a woman.

No, I concluded. It had to be something else.

Perhaps he had found life with us the same as life with Agamemnon, always following behind. Father was king here, and what was Menelaus to do? Had he no purpose other than to order new armor and wait for Father to die? That would break a proud man like Menelaus, faster since he was also a kind man and would never consider speeding along his inheritance.

But if I spoke to Father, asked him if he might be willing to share the throne, even as a formality . . . perhaps he might consider it. And that could go a long way toward freeing Menelaus from the grip of his dolor.

I sought him out one afternoon as he was just dismissing foreign merchants from Gytheum. Leaving the palace, they chattered and clutched the gifts Father had presented to them as they descended the hill, their bright robes making them easy to see even from a distance.

"Syrians," Father said. "They are always so loud—both their voices and their garments. No wonder they wanted to make arrangements to procure some of the purple dye from our shores. But I am not sure I wish to deal with them. I can get a higher price from the Egyptians."

"Oh, Father, always looking for the highest price!" He would never change; one thing I admired about Menelaus was that he seemed unconcerned with such things.

He smiled and held out his hands to welcome me. "Would you prefer that I look for the lowest one?" He laughed. "That is no way for a king to think."

"It's being a king that I have come to talk to you about," I said. He had made it easy for me.

"How so? You can never be one, dear, so you needn't concern yourself with the duties of kingship." He drew himself up. "And I myself am healthy, so you have no worries there." He did look strong and vital, younger than his years.

"I am grateful to see that with my own eyes. No, Father, it's Menelaus I wish to discuss. He's young and healthy, too, and yet is forced to be idle. It is eating at his spirits, I fear."

Father gave a snort. "He needs a war! What else is a young man to occupy himself with? A warrior needs a war. This peace is what's distressing him. That's only natural."

"Peace is a blessing."

"To women and farmers, but not to men," said Father. "Men need action. Without it they wither away. Now, me, I've had my wars and my fights, and now can rest content in the megaron and listen to bards. But Menelaus—find him a war."

"I can't create a war."

"I'll listen and see if I hear of any battles nearby he can indulge himself in. All the Greeks do is fight—there's sure to be one going on this very moment."

"Let him share some of the duties of being a king with you," I said. "That would be better than a war."

"I am not sure a man is fit to be king if he hasn't fought in a war."

"Menelaus has fought, in battles around Mycenae," I reminded him. "Oh, could you not make him a co-ruler?"

He looked at me gravely. "You must truly care for this man," he said.

"He is my husband," I said. "I want to help him."

"I will consider it, but I make no promises," he said. "And I warn you, the consideration may require a very long time."

My slenderness was gradually replaced by fullness, but it was a rounded and graceful fullness. As the year revolved, as each crop and beast followed its appointed time—the ewes dropped their kids, the olive trees bore their fruit—I felt cupped in the hand of our Demeter, watched over by that benevolent goddess of the crops. When she began to grieve because her daughter had departed from the warm earth, I prepared myself for her absence. But by that time I had learned what I needed from the midwife, had gathered all the things necessary for the care of the baby, and surrounded myself with all the people who loved me. *I* need not fear the goddess's abandonment.

The darkest time of the year came and went. The sun began to rise farther east and set farther west, and climb a bit higher in the sky, although it was still cold and damp. I knew my time was nearly here, and I had readied myself as much as I could for something I only knew would be nothing like what I expected—an impossible thing to prepare for.

The old midwife was right: it was unmistakable.

I had been at my loom, weaving what I thought was a complicated pattern (that was before I saw what they did at Troy), when I felt a slight twinge. Still I kept on weaving, kept bending down and feeding the shuttle and telling myself, No, not yet. This might be only a flutter or a false start.

But the twinges persisted and grew stronger. Excited, I put down the shuttle and sought out Mother.

"Oh, Cygnet!" she cried. "Come quickly into the birth room. I'll send for the midwife!"

She led me into the room, kept deliberately bare and unfurnished. There was nothing in there but a hard wooden bench, blankets, and some jugs and buckets. I clutched at her hand and climbed up onto the bench. Looking about me, all I saw was bare whitewashed walls.

"There is no purpose in having beautiful wall paintings," she said. "They will give you no pleasure and afterward whenever you looked upon them you would shudder."

The waves of pain came crowding in on one another, coming now so fast they overpowered me, and soon I was gasping.

I looked up and saw Piele's face. "Get hold of yourself!" she barked. "You cannot fall behind now. It will be a long time until you can rest again!"

"How long?" I cried.

"A long time!" she said. "A great long time!"

It seemed an eternity, but those who were there said it was only one night and part of a morning. I saw it grow dark—lamps and torches had been lit, so it was hard to tell—and I thought I saw it grow light, but I was seeing little by then. There was a window in the room and I believe it changed color, but I cannot remember. What I do remember is the acute pain and how I cried out, "Father! Can you not spare me this?" and when the pain continued unabated, I knew that my mortal side was by far the stronger one within me. A goddess would not feel the agony I did.

At last, after a great crest and surge of pain, it abruptly stopped.

"It's here!" the midwife cried. "It's here!" Dimly I heard something—a scurrying, a murmuring. But no cry. Then it came. A loud wail.

"Helen has a daughter!" Piele cried, holding up a loud red bundle.

A daughter. "Hermione!" I whispered. My pillar-queen.

Piele placed her in my arms and I looked at her little wrinkled face. Just at that moment she opened her mouth and showed her tiny pink tongue. Her cries grew louder.

"Dear one," I said. I welcomed her with all my heart, and felt at that instant nothing would ever sunder us. We were one.

Later that morning, after we had been moved out of the stark birth room and to our regular quarters, Menelaus hurried in to see us. He held out his arms, and smothered us in them.

"Here is Hermione," I said, pulling away the encircling cover from her face.

He gazed at her face in rapture. Finally he spoke. "She takes after her mother," he said slowly, his voice a mere whisper.

"Almost as beautiful as Helen was when first I beheld her," said Mother. "Almost."

Later Mother sat by my side and handed me a hard little object of brown clay. I held it up and saw that it was a doll, with red paint outlining its head and eyes and the pattern of its dress. From the bottom of the clay skirt, sturdy legs, which were secured with a peg, dangled.

"It was yours, Cygnet," she said. "Now it can be Hermione's."

The sun shone on our shoulders as we stood in a small circle around a fresh-dug hole in the earth. There were two priestesses of Demeter, one holding Hermione, and the rest of us spread out on either side. Beside the prepared hole a little plane tree was waiting to be planted, its leaves already drooping a bit.

Father stepped forward. "We have a new member of our family, the first of the new generation to be born here in the royal palace of Sparta. In her honor, we will plant a tree, which will grow along with her. When she is small, she can play at its base. When she is older, she can measure herself against it. When she is a grown woman, she will see it attain its growth as well. She can sit in its shade and enjoy its gifts. And when she is old, she can be comforted that the tree is still in its vigor and youth."

He took a spadeful of earth and threw it, ceremoniously, into the hole. Then one priestess came over and poured a libation. Mother leaned over and buried something in the earth. Castor and Polydeuces did likewise. What had they bequeathed to the tree? Menelaus laid a dagger in the hole, saying that the man who wished to claim his daughter would have to recover it. Last of all, I stepped to the rim of the hole and scattered flower petals. Little Hermione just looked on solemnly.

The gardeners set to work, moving the little tree and setting it aright, then mounding the earth around it. They emptied great jugs of water around its roots, pronouncing it to be thirsty. "But it should thrive!" they predicted.

Father then took his place before the tree. "Now that Helen and Menelaus have brought forth a child," he said, "I see the line will continue. And being a bit weary of my duties, I wish to appoint Menelaus to take the helm as king of Sparta, by marriage to Helen, queen of Sparta by rights of descent."

Father! I had not wished him to abdicate, only share some of his duties with Menelaus. I was shocked.

"I do not wish to grow old on the throne and dodder," Father said, before anyone could object. "The throne's scepter belongs in a young man's grasp. It is he who can most savor it and guard it. No, I am not old . . . but how will I know when I am? They say—the wisest men say—that in old age you feel no different than when you were young. So what—or who—will tell me when it is time to step down? No one. Now I feel in my heart it is time, and I will obey myself. Better that than to bow reluctantly before another's decision."

I looked over at Menelaus. He was as stunned as I was; nay, much more so.

"Your Majesty—" he began.

"I have spoken," said Father. "And the king's dictate is binding." His eyes caught mine and he gave an almost imperceptible nod.

The ceremony continued, but I heard little of its conclusion. I was light-headed from the force with which the heavy mantle of responsibility had been dropped on me as well as Menelaus.

"Menelaus," I said quietly when we were alone. "Father's generosity has left me dazed. You are ready to be king, but I am not prepared to be queen."

"You will be a magnificent queen," he said. "I must strive to be worthy to stand by your side."

"Stop such talk," I said. "You will be a king worthy of Sparta." He would be fair and generous; he did not have any of Agamemnon's ferocious self-absorption and ambition. His thoughts would always be of what was good for Sparta.

"So we go forth to claim our scepters?" My voice was shaky.

"We do what we are called to do," he replied, as he put his arm around me. He had not recovered from the surprise; it was too early yet to tell if he was pleased.

The scepters were ones that had been fashioned in the palace workshop—a shaft of ash with each end sheathed in finely worked gold. The conferment ceremony was equally simple. Father and Mother, each clutching the scepters, gave them to us with only a few words. Father acknowledged that Menelaus was his chosen successor and that all men must obey him. Mother handed me her scepter and said, "I have longed to give you this since the day you were born. I knew it was your fingers that should grasp it. And now the gods have answered my request, and it is yours." She thrust it out to me, and I took its slender shaft in my hand.

"Rule well and wisely," said Father.

The witnesses—my brothers, the commander of Father's palace guard, the treasurer of the kingdom, the head scribe, the priestesses of Demeter—all nodded to indicate their acceptance. Then I saw a face among them that puzzled me. It was Gelanor of Gytheum—the spymaster Father had recruited at the great festival of the kingdom when first I married. The man who knew about poisons. How had he attained such a high position that he was present at this solemn ceremony?

I had the feeling that he knew exactly what I was thinking. Especially when he shrugged. I found myself staring at him, longing to ask him what he was doing here.

But when I looked for him after the ceremony, he had vanished, as mysteriously as he had appeared.

❖ XVII ❖

I had arisen that morning as a princess and I retired to my bed as a queen. I prayed that I would be able to carry out the duties faithfully. Immediately my life now demanded daily audiences in the megaron, and my attendants were increased so that I had six of them—three young and three older.

I had a wet nurse for Hermione, but still I nursed her as long as I was able. Holding her close was something I was loath to relinquish, even after it was clear I was not providing enough nourishment and she would not grow properly. I consulted with Piele about my nursing and she responded by bringing more of the cheese she had recommended in my pregnancy.

"For cheese is but curdled milk, my lady," she said. "So to bring forth more milk, cheese is the best way. You *could* drink flagons of goat milk, but I know you do not care for it." I did as she urged.

Menelaus found me cutting up a platter of the cheese, putting it on slices of cucumbers. He teased me about it, saying that I would turn into a great wheel of cheese.

"But it is for Hermione!" I said.

"Helen," he said, "why don't you just give her over to the wet nurse?" He took one of the slices of cucumber with the cheese atop it. He tasted it and then shook his head.

Was he happier now? Certainly he was busier, and had less time to brood. But he had no more time for me, and sometimes we seemed as formal with one another as we were with the foreign envoys that we received in the megaron. He did not come often to my chamber and when he invited me to his, our coupling was tepid and forgettable: pleasant enough, like that light wine from Rhodes, but like that wine, it did not make you lose your head. You could memorize a list afterward or drive a chariot without swerving.

I stopped petitioning Aphrodite and ceased thinking about it. It was not to be part of my life. Well, I could exist without it. No one ever died for lack of Aphrodite, but many had died from the surfeit of foolishness she invoked. I should be thankful I was spared that.

I did not feel well. I had not felt well for some time, but it had happened gradually . . . a headache, a lassitude, a weakening of the limbs, a loss of appetite. Then my hair began to fall out, and when my chamber-woman combed it she held big chunks of it in her hand.

"Often women lose hair after childbirth," she said, seeking to reassure me.

I knew that. But it was now six months later, and the hair loss was increasing. And then there were the other symptoms.

I looked long and hard into my polished bronze mirror. My face looked strained, and I thought I saw blotches, but the mirror did not offer a good reflection. Polished bronze is not even as good as water in giving you back your face.

I peered into water basins, but the light was too bad—for always my head was blocking it—to show me a true portrait of myself.

But day by day it was growing more difficult for me to do the things I must do. I did not sleep well, and all day I had the sensation of dragging myself from one thing to another.

I first spoke to Menelaus about it, but all he could say was, "Consult a physician." I did, and he suggested I spend the night in a temple of Asclepius. But the nearest temple was several days' journey away at Epidaurus.

One day, after drooping my way through my public duties and then seeking a seat in the shaded portico, a man came over to me.

I had not spoken directly to him since the festival. I shaded my eyes and looked up at him. "Gelanor of Gytheum, is it not?" I said.

"The same, Your Highness," he said, bowing slightly. Then he looked straight at me with those eyes that missed nothing. "You are not well?" he asked.

"Just tired," I said.

"Are you sure?" Again his eyes held mine. And there was no deference in them, no groveling. "I fear you may have been feeling this way for some time."

"How do you know that?"

"I have been present at many ceremonies."

"Yes, and how has that happened? When Father first met you and indicated an interest in you—"

"What you mean is, 'How did a humble man from Gytheum rise so quickly'—don't you?"

"Well—yes." I was a bit taken aback by his bluntness.

"I had skills the king needed, and valued," he said. "The former king, that is. The new king has yet to discover my . . . talents. And so I may be departing for Gytheum before long." He paused. "But I am concerned about your health."

"Oh, you needn't be—" I began, turning my head in what I hoped was a lighthearted gesture. A clump of hair fell out.

Palace protocol demanded that it be ignored. Gelanor bent down and picked it up. "This is alarming," he said.

"It is?" My voice rose. Everyone else had sought to soothe me about it.

"Yes. This sort of hair loss usually means . . . poison."

"Oh, yes, that's right, I remember, you are the expert in poison!" I attempted to laugh.

"Fortunately, yes," he said. "There is nothing mysterious about poison. It is quite obvious when it is employed."

"If you have eyes to see," I said.

He gave what I was later to know as his characteristic sad smile. "It should not take trained eyes to spot this," he said. "Now tell me your other symptoms."

I had recounted them to the court physician, only to be told to go to a temple. But Gelanor listened attentively. He wrote nothing down, but I knew it was all being entered into the records of his mind.

There was only one thing left for him to ask: When had it begun?

It was hard to tell, since I had been weakened by childbirth and the recovery took some time, thus disguising the true onset of the illness.

"Hmmm . . . yes, very clever. Disguise it, mix it in with a normal recovery." He sat back and frowned. "Who has been closest to you during this time?"

There was Mother, of course. And the three new attendants. And the midwife, who had taken such good care of me. I could not think any one of them would wish to harm me. No, that could not be. It was impossible . . .

"Do not think of the personality of the suspects, but only of their possible motive and their access to you," Gelanor said.

"Must you call them 'the suspects'?" I asked.

"That is the first step in seeing them as they are. Forget their names, forget their kind words, and transform them in your mind to 'the suspects.'"

"That is horrible!" How could I do that?

"That will uncover the truth. What is horrible is not labeling someone 'the suspect' but what they, under the guise of trust, are seeking to do to you." He leaned over and whispered, "They are not interested in whether your hair falls out or not. That is just a side effect of the poison. They mean much greater harm than that. And look to your daughter." He stood up abruptly. "I will examine some things in your chamber, with your permission. And also, with your cooperation, I will test the foods brought to you. Please, without attracting attention, save samples for me. And watch. Remember there may be more than one—several may be working together. Make sure no one suspects that *you* suspect."

So I surreptitiously and cleverly—so I thought—secreted bits of whatever I ate and turned them over to Gelanor, sometimes meeting him at the palace portico, other times leaving them wrapped and hidden beneath a certain rock in the garden. I looked carefully at all those who served me, and I could not begin to discern who was the culprit.

My three young attendants: Nomia, who was the daughter of the chief of Agamemnon's guard; Cissia, the daughter of one of Mother's lifelong maidservants; Anippe, about my age, whom I had known from my cradle. It was possible the latter two might have had some grudge against me, but I could not fathom what it might be. As for the first, she surely would not jeopardize her father's position—Agamemnon was not noted for his mercy.

The older ones: Philyra, wife of Father's head archer; Dirce, a priestess of Demeter, who maintained the goddess's shrine in the palace woods; and Eurybia, wife of the leading citizen of the town of Sparta below us. Why would any of these women wish to harm me?

There were the palace cooks—one must not overlook them. And there were other ways to be poisoned besides food. There could be tainted ointment, lethal smoke from fires or incense, poisoned wine or water. My clothes could have been imbued with some sort of poison. There was, after all, the shirt of Nessus that had killed Heracles.

A thousand things to think of. A thousand things to prevent!

Gelanor laughed. But "those are only means of last resort," he admitted.

Well, that was a relief. Because once I started trying to analyze every single thing I came in contact with, the task loomed as Olympian.

"You want to know why," he said. Yes, I had, but I had not asked that. "The reason is simple. These other methods dilute the poison. Think about it. Poison wafting about in smoke—ineffective. You would have to be enveloped in it for hours at a time. What happens when incense fills the room overmuch? We flap cloths and force it out. And putting drops of poison in bathwater—not enough. You would have to bathe for hours in pure poison. As for the clothes—unless you have poison from the Hydra, as Nessus did in his blood, it is a very ineffectual way of trying to kill someone. Someday evil people will perfect poison so that only a tiny drop is needed to kill," he said. "But that time is a long way in coming."

"What about poisonous snakes?" I asked.

"Yes, the snake has perfected that. But I know of no one who has been able to tame snakes and teach them to kill. And I know of no one who has been able to milk a snake to extract the poison. If he could"—Gelanor's face lit up—"then all he would have to do is smear a drop or two on a cut of the victim. Did you know that you could drink a cup of snake poison and walk away as sound as ever?"

"How can that be?" I asked.

"Swallowing it does not harm you," he said. "Only if it gets into a wound. So the snake creates its own wound to make sure. Therefore I think we can discount these other poisons, although anything is possible. But food and drink are the most likely. Continue to watch them."

Once I began to suspect people, everyone began to seem dangerous. There was the man who brought jugs of heated water to fill the bathtub—was it ordinary water? There was the man who perfumed the oil that went into the tub, which floated in shiny, sinister, drops upon the water. The scent—of lilies—had always pleased me. Now it seemed a death odor. Perhaps Gelanor was right in saying that poisoning by bathing was not likely—but was it impossible?

Or perhaps it was on the wooden combs my attendants used to comb through my hair? And lately—they had pricked me several times when fastening my bronze shoulder brooch.

Dressing, I slid my feet into my goatskin sandals and noticed how slick the leather was—could it be polished with some poisonous substance? I stared at it, trying to see any suspicious powder.

As for the food, I could no longer eat any of it, and I asked Menelaus himself to fetch me water from the spring so that I would have my own supply. Menelaus was the only person I could be sure of. At the same time, I had to pretend that I was eating and drinking as usual, which entailed so much deception I did not know how long I could go on with it. Spitting out the wine when no one was looking, moving food around on the plate to make it look as if I had eaten, were not easy to do convincingly.

"Menelaus, I am ready to do as your physician so wisely suggested some time ago. I must go to Asclepius!" I had to get out of the palace.

"Yes, my dear, I can see that you have not improved. And . . . these demands of yours, about the water . . . ?" He looked so eager that for an instant I thought, Is it you? And then realized that he was hoping this all meant I was with child again.

"I must go so that what we hope . . . can happen," I assured him.

"Will you take Nomia and Eurybia?"

"No!" I must get away from them. From everyone here. "It is—I have been told I must go alone."

"By whom?"

"By Apollo," I lied. Menelaus would not argue with a god, as he would with Gelanor. Apollo, as everyone knew, could cause sudden illness with his arrows. Perhaps he was in back of this—or so Menelaus might think.

"I will take a bodyguard of soldiers," I said. "I shall be safe enough." I regretted that I could not confide in Menelaus. Once I had thought I could, that he would be my true friend as well as my husband, but he had turned out to be only my husband, and I did not now want to invite him to raise a premature alarm.

Gelanor would stay behind, observing. I had left him enough samples of food and drink and ointment to keep him busy. He had also fabricated an arrow-testing experiment for Menelaus's archers that would provide an excuse for him to be on the palace grounds at odd hours.

As I made ready to go out to the waiting chariot, he grasped my forearm. "Be careful. Keep your senses about you, even as you sleep, if possible." His usual smile had faded, revealing the worry in his eyes.

"I shall," I assured him.

Now, after a long dusty journey, I stood in the dimly lit stone hall where the altar to Asclepius stood. Before it were offerings left by supplicants seeking help from this god of healing. The sacred serpents, companions to Asclepius, coiled around its base. Tame, fed by the priests, they only betrayed their life by an occasional movement.

I was almost too weak to stand erect; I could feel my knees trembling, and when I held up my hands, my arms ached. But I raised them higher and spoke directly to Asclepius, that man whose gift not only of healing but even of bringing back the dead had angered Zeus and Hades, as he was intruding on their domains. So Zeus struck him down with a thunderbolt and here he lay, in Epidaurus. Even his bones had power, however, and he continued to heal from the grave.

"Restore me," I whispered. "Reveal to me what I must know to recover." I bent down and added my offerings to the others heaped about.

One of the priests came over to me, moving as silently as one of the sacred snakes.

"Helen? Helen of Sparta?" he whispered. He had recognized me. Even in my present ravaged state, I could not pass as just another supplicant.

I nodded in assent. "I have come to seek a cure," I said.

"The other patients will retire to sleep outside," the priest said. "But you should remain here, near the god's altar. Wait, and he will come to you."

The floor was hard stone, but I felt safety and peace here at the foot of the altar.

The dim light gradually faded completely and the great stone chamber grew dark as a moonless sky; small votive lamps here and there provided only twinkles of light, like stars.

Creeping as close to the altar as possible, I stretched out on my thick traveling cloak and lay still. The soft pulsing of the little lamps seemed to keep time with my own heartbeats, and I fell asleep.

I felt a cold current. It was coming in two streams, twining themselves around me. I swam up through layers of sleep and fought to open my eyes, but they were being held shut. There was something cool and scaly over them.

Then I felt it move, sliding forward. I felt my ears being touched, being tickled by something flicking against them. I dared not move. Was all this part of a dream?

A hard rounded object was burrowing against the opening of my right ear, while the other ear was being—caressed, soothed, licked. Cautiously I moved my right arm up behind my back where something heavy was lying on it, and felt the rounded body of a snake.

The sacred snakes! The sacred snakes had come to me and were curling about my head . . . licking my ears with their tiny darting tongues.

This must be a message, must be symbolic. I was honored that they would come to me. Asclepius had answered my plea, but how? I could not understand the snakes, if they were trying to tell me something.

They coiled around me a long time, and only slithered away when the hint of footsteps vibrated across the floor. Dawn must be coming; the priests must be making ready to come inside.

Raising my head up slowly, I watched the serpents retreating back to the unhewn stone altar, their pale backs glistening in the faint light from the few oil lamps that had not burned out. I lay there with racing heart, unsure of what exactly had happened.

When the unmistakable sounds of morning flooded into the shrine, I knew I would have to rise. I folded my cloak and stood up. There were two priests already at the altar. They were setting out dishes of milk for the snakes.

I went over to them. I wanted to tell them what had happened, so perhaps they could explain it. At the same time, I did not want to betray the secret meeting between the snakes and me—if it *was* a secret. Perhaps it wasn't. I did not know. I did not want to make a mistake.

"They came to you," the first priest said.

How did he know?

"It was revealed to me. I know them, and they know me. Daughter, do you know what it means?"

"No," I admitted.

"With the permission of Asclepius, they have transmitted three gifts to you." He paused. "Now you must discover what they are."

XVIII

All the way back to Sparta, in the bumping and jouncing chariot, I felt light-headed. I kept clutching my head, as if I could rattle it and have answers come tumbling out like dice. What gifts had the serpents bequeathed to me? How would I recognize them? In what form would they manifest themselves?

As I held my hands over my temples, I felt the sparseness of my once-abundant hair. The gifts of the serpents were not to be spurned, but the reason I had come to Asclepius, my weakness, was more pressing. I had received no knowledge about it, but in spite of my dizziness, I did feel somewhat better. The trembling in my arms and legs was due to excitement, not weakness. It was not such an effort to stand erect.

The countryside passed before me, but I barely saw it—I, who had so longed to see beyond my circumscribed world of Sparta. Now I was so shaken and preoccupied, I was unable to feast my eyes upon it and was only dimly aware of the rocky hills, the high-tinkling bells of the sheep, the sweet sound of the rushing streams. From the heights I spied the sparkling sea, which I could never see from Sparta, but it meant little to me now.

Instead, I was consumed to know what Gelanor had discovered in my absence. What a relief it would be if he had pinpointed the source of the poison and discovered the culprit. If only it were so!

We arrived back in Sparta late on the third day of traveling. Menelaus, Mother, Father, all rushed to greet me and all but drag me from the chariot.

"You look better," Mother pronounced. "Your color has returned."

"Yes!" Father concurred.

Menelaus encircled me with his arm and, murmuring endearments, steered me toward our apartments.

Suddenly there was a shout from the chariot. The grooms, taking the reins of the horses and removing the mantles and floor covering, let out a yelp.

"Serpent! Serpent!"

Pushing Menelaus aside, I rushed back to the chariot. There, coiled in one of the mantles, was a small pale snake—a baby. It reared its head, looked at me, and flicked its tongue.

"This must be one from the sacred precinct," I said. "Somehow it entered our chariot when we left it standing beside the building at night, and hid itself there." It was as if we had been given our own sacred snake. "It belongs near our family altar," I said. "I will assume its care."

I followed Menelaus back to his chamber, but quickly asked if Hermione was well. He assured me that she was.

"And you, sweetheart, you *do* look better," he said. "The roses are back in your cheeks."

I went into the nursery and picked up Hermione; she slept so soundly that the movement did not awaken her. Yes, they were right. She seemed healthy and her color was good.

"Oh, thank all the gods!" I said.

"Apollo has spared her," said Menelaus solemnly.

Not Apollo, I wanted to say. My enemy, whoever he or she is.

It was not until the next day that I had an opportunity to speak to Gelanor in private. I had spent the time resting in my chamber, the curtains drawn to keep the glaring light of noon out. I let the food the attendants brought sit; eventually the flies found it and that was my excuse for not eating it.

He came into the darkened chamber and took a seat on the little bench by the shaded window.

"You look better," he said, echoing the others.

"I feel stronger," I said.

Instead of ascribing my cure to Asclepius as all the others had done, he said, "That means you have not been exposed to the means of the poison for at least six days." He shook his head. "I am sorry to report that I have been unable to discover the source of the poison. I tested all the foods you gave me, all the ointments, and the obliging animals I gave them to are as frisky as ever. I wiped the shoes and took the flowers from the vases and inspected the incense burners. I even tested the fleeces on the bed and the bedding and your robes. Nothing. Nothing at all."

"The combs? Did you test them?"

"Yes, I did."

"The points of my brooches?"

"Nothing."

"But it is somewhere! We know that. And once I was away from it—wherever it might be concealed—I began to recover."

"I am at my wits' end," he admitted. "I cannot think of anything I have not inspected or tested."

My attendants were especially high-spirited as they dressed me on my second morning back.

"While you were away I thought of this fillet for your hair," Cissia said. "It will grace your forehead and lift your hair." She slipped the cold metal around my head and it felt like a band of death. But nothing stung.

"Thank you," I said.

"And these new robes," Anippe said. "This dye is such a pale pink, like the inside of a seashell, and you always favored that color." The robe was fastened around me and I felt nothing.

"Your bracelet," said Eurybia, waving my favorite bright gold snake bracelet. She twined it around my upper arm. I thought of the other snakes, the real ones, and their twining.

"Thank you," I said. I had always been fond of that bracelet; now I knew why, now I knew my affinity for the creatures, and they for me.

The next day I did not feel so well, and the day after that I had slipped back even further. I prayed to Asclepius to renew his cure, asking him to extend his power beyond his burial place at Epidaurus, and I made sure the snake was well looked after at our family altar. But it was all to no avail—day by day I felt the weakness creeping up upon me, leaching me.

I forced myself to dress every day and go out, if only to anger my enemy. Every day that he or she saw me walking about the palace grounds (oh! what willpower it took to do that, and do it without shaking) would arouse anger, and possibly carelessness and desperation. Then the poisoner might become bolder, and easier to detect. If only I might survive the boldness!

Gelanor visited me at the time of twilight, when I was lying listlessly on my couch. I could barely hold up my head. In fact, I could not, and rested it on the pillow.

"Forgive me for my rudeness in not sitting up," I said. Even my voice sounded shadowy to me. I tried to raise my arm in greeting and found it difficult. Tremblingly, I peeled the arm bracelet off, as if that would lighten my arm enough to make a difference. I laid it on a tray, where it rocked back and forth, the gold glinting, the carved scales of the snake catching the shadows and the light. They were very realistic. I marveled at it.

Gelanor was tense and looked worried. "I cannot seem to find the means to stop this," he said.

In the dark hours of the night I was terrified, but now I wished to at least appear brave. "It may be beyond our ability to find," I said.

He looked around the room. "What can it be? It must be something you come in contact with. It should be obvious—something that rubs up against you. But I have tested the bedding and the clothes—" His eyes suddenly came to rest on the snake bracelet. "Did you take this with you to Epidaurus?" he asked.

"No. I did not want to wear jewelry before the god, and it is foolish to travel with anything valuable."

"Hmm." He picked it up and held it this way and that, letting it catch the light. "How many days were you free from wearing it?"

"At least seven."

He rose suddenly. "I am taking it. That will assure you don't wear it to-morrow. If anyone asks, tell them you must have lost it. Then look to see who searches for it the hardest."

He hurried from the chamber clutching the bracelet.

The sun stole into my chamber. I watched as the light threw long fingers across the floor and gradually made the curtains glow with power.

But I had no power. I was as drained as an empty wine flagon and my arms hung limply over the side of the bed. My eyes could still discern the lovely light patterns and my mind could think upon them, but my body was all but useless.

Who would want to do this to me? For I did not believe it was a god. It was another person.

It must be someone who was envious of me. I was a queen, I was—rumored to be—daughter of Zeus. And the eyes of others who beheld me re-flected their belief that my beauty was unnatural and disturbing. I was imprisoned by my own good fortune, my unasked-for gifts, and made a target for others' discontent.

But this was all their fancy. Had anyone lost anything because of me? Anyone who was near to me? I could not think of anyone.

And the things they could easily see did not reveal the lacks in my life as Menelaus's wife.

* * *

My attendants, chattering and happy, trooped in to dress me. Philyra swirled the gowns around in the air. Dirce made a show of selecting the proper sandals. And Nomia looked through the jewelry box.

"These earrings, I think, the ones with amethyst," she said. She held them up, dangling them.

"And your favorite, the gold snake," said Eurybia. She poked around searching for it. Finally she looked up. "It does not seem to be here. Did you lay it down somewhere?"

"I don't remember," I said casually, noticing her concern.

I watched as she began methodically searching the box, and then the surfaces in the chamber.

"Oh, it does not matter, Eurybia," I said.

"I am only looking hard because I know how fond you are of it," she assured me.

"Oh, you needn't trouble yourself," I said.

That afternoon, on my slow but determined walk, I chanced upon a campfire where shepherds were roasting meat. I asked them for some—for I knew they could not be involved—and had the first meal free of worry I had had in a great long time. The burned lamb was the most delicious meat I had ever tasted. It was free of evil.

When I awoke the next morning, my arms were not so limp and I felt a bit stronger. During the day I made a point of seeking out the shepherds again, and eating as much as I could, so that I could decline the offerings at our palace meal.

Again, the next morning, I was stronger. Some fallen hair still covered the pillow, but my arms and legs were no longer tremulous.

I went to my loom. I had become quite a good weaver, creating new patterns to tell stories. A repeating abstract pattern could be lovely, but how much better to illustrate a tale. I was depicting one of the labors of Heracles—the one in which he confronted the Hydra of Lerna, the many-headed monster with one immortal head. The twisting necks gave a pleasing symmetry, enabling me to make a better picture than using another popular motif, the octopus. The octopus had only eight arms, whereas the Hydra had a hundred heads. Weavers shied away from the Hydra because she was evil, but as an artistic pattern, she was superb.

Suddenly Gelanor was beside me.

"I have it," he said.

His words were a shock. Without knowing it, I had given up hope of discovering the source of my ill health.

He waved the snake bracelet. "This is it." He said.

I took it from him. "Careful," he said. He raised one eyebrow as I took it gingerly. "But first—are you feeling stronger? And how often did you wear the bracelet?"

"I—most days, I think. It was one of my favorite pieces of jewelry."

"As I thought. Very well. Look at its underside." He took it back and spread the spirals apart. "This should be smooth. It is not. Look at these grooves." He stayed my hand. "Do not touch it. Look here. See the scratches and uneven surfaces within it? Someone has made those hollows to put poison in, knowing it will be in contact with your skin for at least all the daylight hours. I found a waxen substance in them and tested it. It was filled with poison. Your skin was drinking it in."

"No!" I said, taking the bracelet back. "No!"

He thought I was lamenting over the evil use of the beautiful bracelet. "We can make you another one," he said.

"It is not that," I said. "It is—this means it is someone close to me."

"Yes," he said. "It is."

We like to imagine that only those who do not know us would wish us ill. To think that those we walk among, eat with, laugh with, hate us and plan to harm us, is soul-chilling. An enemy disguised as a friend is the deadliest of all.

Menelaus visited me, eager to show me the specially weighted arrows that Gelanor had designed for him.

"That man," he said, shaking his head. "His mind is always searching, ferreting. I am thankful he is working for me rather than my enemies."

"Which enemies?" I asked, I hoped offhandedly.

"It's just a figure of speech," he said, rising and stretching. "But they say there is no one whose death is not a relief to *someone*."

A chill passed through me.

"So in that way, we all have enemies." He looked about for Leucus, his body-servant. "Where is that lad?"

Lying in bed the next morning, I watched, with slitted eyes, my own attendants gather in the chamber. There came Nomia, slender and tall, invariably—sometimes, I had to admit, gratingly—cheerful. Her father was the opposite: one of Agamemnon's most glowering soldier-guards. Perhaps she had determined to be pleasant after a childhood darkened by her father's pique.

Next were Cissia and Anippe, both of whom I had known since childhood. I had always found Cissia's sensible placidity soothing, the sort of antidote I longed for after my upsets and excitements. I relied on her more than I liked to admit, if only for a foil to myself. And Anippe had shared my love of dolls and clothes.

Could any of these three hate me? Or could they be acting under the orders of others?

Who would be relieved at my death?

They were moving about the chamber, opening the curtains and filling pitchers of water. Their sweet voices murmured to each other.

No, it could not be either of them!

Next came Philyra, the wife of Father's chief archer, to whom at this very moment Gelanor's arrows were being presented. She, like me, had fair hair, and we had often laughed about the subtle difference in color. She had flattered me by proclaiming mine to be pure gold, whereas hers tended more toward the red-gold of sunset. "I think the sunset is more precious," I had said. And I had truly thought her hair to be the lovelier.

The priestess of Demeter, wise and proper Dirce, strode in. Dirce's presence always overpowered anyone else in the room, and today was no different.

I watched the moving shadows in my room. It seemed that I could see more than I normally could; my vision was taking in more than it ever had before.

I could not see anything in these five women that would cause alarm.

Last to arrive was Eurybia, because she had to come all the way up the hill from the village. She was a heavy woman, muscular, with a head of hair that must have weighed so much she needed her neck to be as thick as it was to carry it.

She bent over me, detecting that I was awake.

"Dear Helen," she said, "are you feeling better today? Oh, please tell me you are!"

I raised up on my elbows. "Yes, Eurybia," I said. "I believe so. I hope so."

She smiled. And as I saw that smile, I saw something more. I cannot describe exactly what it was, but there was something else.

I swung my legs out of bed, and she offered her hand. I took it and stood up. The chamber swam, but I commanded my legs to stay straight.

My attendants all swarmed around me, and helped support me. They brought out my clothes and offered me many selections, omitting the ones that would wrinkle badly when I—sooner or later—had to lie down. They offered trays of jewelry—large chunky necklaces of agate and rock crystals, anklets of fine gold. Tactfully they did not bring out the tray of gold hair ornaments, which would get crushed when I lay upon a pillow.

"Your bracelets," said Anippe, holding up a tray of them.

They all looked too heavy. I waved them away.

"We still have not found that snake bracelet, have we?" asked Eurybia. "It is light to wear and does not . . ." What she meant was, I could lie down while wearing it, if need be.

"No, we have not," I said. "Perhaps it was stolen." I looked around at each of them, one at a time.

When I got to Eurybia, I knew. It was something—something I could see beyond just what my eyes were receiving. I heard her words, but now it was as if I had a secret translation of them, and of their true meaning.

"But we must find it!" she said.

"Why?" I said. "There are many other pieces to choose from."

"Yes, of course." She quickly looked away.

Now. Now was the time to do it, now, in front of the others. I would never have been so bold before, but that was changed, too.

"Eurybia, why are you trying to kill me?" My voice was so unnaturally calm it did not even sound like mine. "I know it is you."

That was the gift of the serpents, I suddenly knew—I could discern character in times of danger, almost as if I were a god. That was what they had given me.

My sudden attack caught her off balance. "I—I—"

"It is you!" I pointed at her.

The others just stared.

"Why have you done this?" I confronted her, calling on all my power to appear strong and not shake.

I expected her to deny it, to say that it was my illness that was causing me to speak so.

Instead she drew herself up and put down the jewelry tray with great dignity.

"So. I am doomed. I will die anyway for threatening the safety of the queen. Very well. Let me tell you, you blind, stupid girl. Yes, girl. For you are only a girl, yet you have had the entire world handed to you! And why has all this come about? Simply because of your face. I wanted to see you up close, to see what it was that entitled you to all this adulation. What I see does not impress me. So I decided to remove it."

I fought for words. "Is that all?"

"No! You weren't content with all the worshipping of your looks, but you were greedy and had to take things from other people. You didn't need to win that race! You had everything else. Why did you take it from my daughter?"

She was the mother of the girl I had beaten in the maidens' race!

"*She* would never have become queen. She never would have had forty suitors, coming with big bags of gold. She's as mortal as they come. But her speed—she would have always been able to cherish the memory of winning that race. You robbed her of it!"

"I didn't rob her," I said. "I won it. I was a faster runner."

"Yes, because you cheated."

"Cheated?"

"You were Zeus's daughter. Of course you had extra speed."

"No, I didn't. The child of a god—even if that is true—is mortal. Didn't you know that?"

"They are fleeter, they are more lovely—they aren't like the rest of us."

"Can't you understand?" I pleaded with her. "Imagine all that anyone ever talked about was your face. Would you not want to be recognized for something else? I knew I was a fleet runner, and I needed to run. If your daughter had been faster, she would have surpassed me."

"No!" she said. "You cheated."

"What kind of poison did you put into the snake bracelet?" I asked her.

The others in the chamber had been shocked into silence.

"I won't tell you," she said. "It has long served my family. And just because you, with your special powers, have found me out—"

But it was Gelanor, with his human powers, who had found her out. I was immensely glad, like Menelaus, that he was not working for our enemies.

I called the guards. "Take her away," I said. "Take her away."

Father, and Menelaus, would want her executed. I did not. All I wanted was some assurance that she—or an accomplice—would never have access to me again.

Now it became clear to me—finally, and what sweet knowledge this was—what the serpents had blessed me with: prescience, which is its own kind of wisdom.

❖ XIX ❖

Clytemnestra had come for one of her ever more frequent visits, and we were sitting together under Hermione's tree. Or perhaps "under" is a bit exaggerated; in the five years since it had been planted, it had grown higher than my head, but its lower branches were still too close to the ground for us to sit directly under. We were stretched out on the sweet meadow grass beside it, having our favorite picnic fare, watching our girls play on the hill below us, running and throwing a ball. Iphigenia was eight and my Hermione was five.

"Ah, she's a runner like you," said Clytemnestra. "Look how she's catching up to Iphigenia." Both girls were running as fast as they could, tearing through the grass. I shivered, remembering my poisoner.

"My racing days are, I fear, over," I said. It was indeed a pity that women's contests ended with marriage.

Clytemnestra seemed restless to me, and she declined the rest of the wine. That was how I knew. "Why, you are pregnant!"

She nodded. "Yes. Agamemnon is pleased, of course, for he hopes for a son, a son he wants to name Orestes . . . 'the mountaineer.' Zeus only knows why he would choose that name. He does not come from the mountains."

"Perhaps he believes that the name will somehow bring about the event. That Orestes will scale high mountains."

She laughed. "He just wants a warrior son. I think . . . he is eager for a war. He is bored, I can tell. Overseeing a peaceful kingdom does not satisfy him."

The one thing most rulers prayed for was peace, I thought, deeply grateful that in the five years that Menelaus had been king of Sparta, things had been quiet.

"Of course, he does not endure deprivation patiently," she said, almost under her breath.

I knew what she meant, and that familiar flash of jealousy tore through me. She meant that she and Agamemnon, in the bedchamber . . . But I would not think of it.

Over the years I had tried to disguise my cold bed from Clytemnestra, believing it to be a form of disloyalty to Menelaus to reveal it. What passed—or did not pass—between us in the dark was private. But it grew harder and harder to pretend, especially when I should have been knowledgeable about things I knew not of. I was surprisingly good at pretense, but I hated it.

"Yes!" I attempted a knowing smirk.

"I am afraid that he will satisfy himself with one of the slaves around the palace," she murmured.

"If so, he will forget her the moment you come to him again." Oh, let us leave this subject, before—

"You have never had this worry about Menelaus?" Her eyes searched mine.

"I—I—" I could feel blood rushing to my cheeks.

She laughed. "Oh, forgive me! I forgot how modest you are. You should be beyond this . . . this reticence." She paused. "After all, you're twenty-one and have been married for six of those years. What else can we married women speak of?"

Oh, anything else! I thought. Please, anything else! "Well, there are our children . . . I see that Iphigenia is a gentle girl, but the poetry she composes to accompany her lyre is worthy of . . . well, Apollo must inspire it!"

She nodded. "Yes, she is a poet. I treasure that; it is rare. Truly, as you said, a gift from Apollo."

Just then the two girls came running up, breathless, and threw themselves on the blanket.

"She always wins the race!" said Iphigenia, pointing at Hermione.

"Just like her mother," said Clytemnestra. "But come, you can do things she cannot. Like compose for the lyre."

Iphigenia smiled and brushed a strand of hair from her sweaty forehead. She was a pretty girl, with the dark curly hair of her father and the clear skin of her mother. "Yes, I like that best."

Hermione rolled over, holding her skinned knees. She spent most of her time outdoors, and would not go near a lyre. Her uncles, my brothers, delighted in teaching her to ride and shoot. My little doll, given to her by Mother, lay neglected.

Menelaus doted on her, but of course he was assuming she would eventually have a brother. "Oh, my dearest one," I said, leaning forward and running my hand through her curls. Her hair was bright gold, like mine, and we sometimes played at mixing strands and trying to separate them based on color. We couldn't, of course, but it made us feel close to see that our hair was identical.

I looked over at Clytemnestra and felt something . . . something dark and oppressive. It was that unasked-for gift from the serpents, illuminating, hinting at things in people's hearts. I could see something around them, could hear echoes from deep inside them. Now I saw it with Clytemnestra.

I had seen too many things I wished I had not, in the years since the snakes had licked my ears; I had been given insight into private matters that should have been barred from me.

And the priest had said there might be three gifts. Thus far only this one had manifested itself. But perhaps, I consoled myself, there would be no others.

"Clytemnestra, dear sister"—I almost held my breath in saying it—"is anything amiss?"

"Why, no," she said. "Why do you ask?"

So it was not yet, not yet. And pray Zeus, it might never be. But the color that surrounded her was dark and murky. A chill of fear passed over me, like a wind blowing over a field.

Dead winter. Nothing could move on the waters—ships were lying ashore, their hulls filled with rocks to keep them stable on the pelted seashore, and only the most brave—or foolhardy—would risk actually voyaging on the high seas. Between cities the roads were ice-bound and slippery, and few would venture out. Menelaus and I were among those few. Agamemnon had summoned us to Mycenae—for what we knew not. The message was vague.

The ground between Sparta and Mycenae lay bleak and the forests were leafless. Hermione tugged at my cloak. "I'm cold," she said. I could feel her shivering next to me. I peeled off the fleece that rested on my shoulders and fastened its thickness around hers.

"There, now," I assured her. "If this can keep a ram warm in the field, it can help you."

She smiled back at me. Eight years old now, and still our only, treasured child.

"What does Uncle Agamemnon want?" she said.

"We don't know," I answered. "Perhaps he has a surprise."

"I don't want a surprise from Uncle Agamemnon," she said. "He is scary. But I like seeing Iphigenia and Elektra."

In spite of Agamemnon's hopes, the baby had been a girl. They named her Elektra, meaning "amber," because her eyes were a lovely golden brown. Iphigenia was eleven now, but unlike other girls her age, she seemed content to play with her younger cousin. I wondered when Agamemnon would insist on arranging a marriage for her—and to whom.

Ahead of us, golden in the fading winter sun, I could see the carved stone lions guarding the gateway of Mycenae, rearing over the entrance. I always felt a mixture of awe at their splendor, and dread at what awaited me once I was past them. Mycenae was not a pleasant place to visit, in spite of its grand vistas across the mountains and out to the sea. The palace squeezed me, squeezed me between heavy walls built of enormous boulders and guarded ramparts, and the air was always heavy and damp.

Once past the lions, we made our way up the steep path that led to the main part of the palace, perched on the highest part of the hill.

A flock of retainers surrounded us as we climbed. Someone had run ahead to alert Agamemnon, and now he stood at the top of the pathway, the sun behind him, a great looming figure.

"Welcome! Welcome!" he cried. He swung into view, no longer obliterating the sun. It made him smaller. He stepped forward to embrace Menelaus. "Dear brother!" he cried, clapping his back.

"Brother!" Menelaus echoed back.

Together they mounted the great staircase that led up to the palace courtyard.

We were seated in the megaron in the heart of the palace. A wide hearth held a lively fire, with heaps of pungent cedarwood upon it, and the smoke—not all of it escaped through the round roof-hole—perfumed the air in the hall and softened the faces of the people gathered there.

Agamemnon still had not revealed why he had summoned us, but from the rank of the guests—all kings or chieftains of nearby cities—I knew it was political. He seemed distracted, nervous, in spite of his attempts to be jovial. The serpent-vision I had been granted enabled me almost to overhear his own thoughts. They were angry and confused. Yet he smiled and smiled.

He made sure we all had gold cups to drink from—each of them shallow, decorated with circles and swirls, and smooth and glorious yellow, a bright, happy yellow, as only gold can be. Since there were over thirty of us in the megaron, this advertised his wealth, as he thought, discreetly.

His guests were Palamedes of Nauplia, Diomedes of Argos, Poliporthis of Tiryns, and Thersites of Corinth, as well as a number of others I did not recognize, as they had never visited us in Sparta. Agamemnon strode amongst them bluffly, slapping their shoulders, throwing his head back and roaring like one of his lions at the gateway.

Menelaus stood about, looking lost. He did not relish such gatherings, being a quiet and private person. I kept myself by his side. Taking his hand, I intertwined my fingers in his. I felt a wearisome need to protect him.

There were few other women present; women were not usually admitted to such gatherings. Clytemnestra and I were the exception: Clytemnestra as the host of Mycenae, and I because Menelaus would not be parted from me, and I was sister to Clytemnestra.

"Ah, my friends!" Agamemnon bellowed. "Welcome, welcome! I am touched that you would come all the way here in the dangerous travel time of winter." He looked about. "Drink, eat! I slew a late-season boar and it has hung and cured to perfection, so I share it with you!"

More boasting about himself, I thought.

"It is roasting even now!" He stood, swaying slightly in his thick boots, his fur-clad shoulders making him look like a formidable bear.

Clytemnestra came over to us, trailing her long robes. "That man has no sense of time," she muttered. "It will be hours before it is ready. I told him to start it earlier—"

I leaned over and kissed her cheek. "No matter, dear sister. We are happy just to see you. We did not come for the boar. Indeed, we are not sure why we have come—aside from an opportunity for Hermione to see her cousins again. Perhaps that is the most important, and lasting, thing that will come of this."

She rolled her eyes. "Agamemnon wants to assess the support he can count on."

"For what?" Menelaus asked. "Everything is quiet. We are at peace."

"Agamemnon does not like peace," she said.

"But surely he does not mean to provoke war? And with whom?" Menelaus was upset by the sudden news.

"He has entangled himself with the cause of Hesione," she said. "Which is foolish," she hastened to add. "Although the Trojan king claims otherwise,

Hesione seems perfectly content to live in Salamis with Telamon. It has been almost forty years since she was taken from Troy."

"Troy," muttered Menelaus. "A place better left alone. All that happened in another generation, and although some may call me coward for it, I say the happenings of the day should be confined to that day and time, and not spill out and contaminate another."

Clytemnestra raised her eyebrows. "How radical!" she said. "But sensible," she allowed.

Agamemnon walked up and down the megaron, his rough features illuminated by torches stuck in wall sockets. In some lights he was handsome; in others he looked like a satyr. Perhaps it was the beard and the deep-set eyes.

"The boar is coming, I say, it is coming!" he said, holding up his arms. "But friends, while we wait, I must exhort you to think upon the wrongs done to us by the insults of the Trojans. That aged princess of theirs, Hesione, sister to their king Priam, was awarded to Telamon of Salamis years ago. But they never cease agitating for her return! They even threaten to send out a party to rescue her. They say she was taken against her will, by Heracles. I say, nonsense! She shows no desire to return to Troy."

The loud voice of Thersites broke through the crowd. "Has anyone asked her?"

"I assume her husband Telamon has! Or her son, the matchless archer Teucer!" Agamemnon yelled. He threw back a cup of wine.

"Could she speak freely before them?" Thersites persisted.

"Surely after forty years—" Menelaus began.

"Women cannot always say what they wish." To my surprise, the voice was mine. I had not meant to speak out. But it was true.

"What do you mean?" My brother-in-law rounded on me. All eyes were fastened on me.

"I mean that a married woman, who has regard for her family, for her husband and child, cannot always frame the true feelings in her heart in words—for they may be contradictory." I took a breath. "The love for one family does not smother the love for the first one." I had been fortunate—I had both my first family and my chosen, second one about me. But that did not always happen.

"She has forgotten Troy!" Agamemnon pronounced. "She has proved it by her actions."

"Conflicted loyalties can cause great pain—and lead to silence," I said. I saw his brows contract. I did not relish his attention, but how could I remain quiet? His misconceptions might lead to bloodshed, for clearly he had convened these warriors in hopes of rousing and using them.

"If the Trojans persist in making these accusations, we'll answer them with warships and with bronze!" he cried. He looked around to see who would echo his cry. There were a few halfhearted cheers.

"Troy is arrogant," said Thersites. "It lurks beside the Hellespont and hinders our trade farther in, all the way to the Black Sea. I'd be just as happy if it vanished."

"It isn't about to vanish," said Agamemnon. "It will persist, as a spear in our sides, until we *make* it vanish."

"Troy has many allies surrounding it," said Diomedes. "They would come to its aid."

"Stop!" said Menelaus. "You talk as if a war is a given. There is no reason, no purpose, for a war with Troy. It is cheaper, to be frank, to pay whatever bribes and tolls they require than to muster an army. This is the way of trade—barter, taxes. They were given their position near the Hellespont by the gods, just as we were given ours on the Aegean. We must respect that."

There was a low groan in the room, although Menelaus spoke intelligently. Intelligent objections were not what they wanted—not in the flickering torchlight and the half shadows and half-truths floating about in the wintry chamber.

"So you just want to sit in your great hall in Sparta, warming yourself by the fire, and die with no glorious deeds to be recited when the funeral pyre is lit?" Diomedes asked.

I felt Menelaus stiffen beside me. He had to answer. "I believe . . . I believe . . ."—he searched for words—"that whether there are glorious deeds to be sung at a man's funeral depends upon what tasks the gods set before him to test his character. We accept the cup the gods give us. We must. Peace is also a gift."

"Bah!" cried Diomedes. "I can fill this cup with whatever potion I desire!" He lifted his golden cup high.

"But the cup itself was given you by another." Again, it was my voice speaking. I could not bear his cockiness. "Perhaps you are not as free as you would wish."

He glared at me, and then at Menelaus, as if to say, *Curb your wife!*

"Leave quivering old Priam alone," a voice sounded from the back of the hall. Perhaps the mood was turning; perhaps Menelaus's sensible advice was seeping into men's minds.

"Priam! He's an old fool. A decadent potentate from the east. He has fifty or so sons—all lodging in his palace at Troy," Agamemnon said.

"Is that a reason to attack him?" asked Menelaus. "Let him have his fifty sons!"

He hid it well, but I heard the pain in his voice. Fifty sons—oh, let me have one. Only one! All men wanted sons. Menelaus ached for one.

"It's not seemly," muttered Agamemnon, also sonless.

"I heard he just added another," Palamedes said. "A grown one."

"Oh, one of those slave offsprings?" Poliporthis laughed. "A king's halls are full of them."

"This one is different," Palamedes persisted. "This one, a legitimate son, was cast away because of a bad omen, and has returned to claim his inheritance. And he cuts a pretty figure, they say, with prowess in contests of all sorts, as well as a stunning face. They call him Paris, 'pack,' because he was tucked into a pack when he was being taken out to the mountain as a newborn to die."

"Oh, how affecting!" Thersites bowed, sneering. "What a lovely story!"

"So old Priam sits happy on the lookout of windy Troy, knowing he is safe!" Agamemnon all but spat. "What matter whether he have forty-nine sons or fifty, whether one is pretty or not?"

"What matter to *you*, Agamemnon?" a strong voice spoke out. "You speak non—you speak without thinking."

No one told Agamemnon he spoke nonsense—no one except Clytemnestra. And then not in public. Agamemnon glared, searching the room for the man who had spoken. "It matters to me because Priam is the brother of Hesione. It is he who keeps reminding the world that she was taken from Troy—by Greeks. He hates us!" Agamemnon lowered his chin, as he always did when he was crossed, looking like a truculent bull.

"That's your imagination," said Menelaus. "I have heard he is an even-tempered and sensible man, not given to hatred."

"Well, if he's sensible, then he should fear us!" Agamemnon motioned and two men emerged from the shadows—an older one with a shiny face and a gloating expression, and a younger one with much hair and dark slashes for eyebrows. I had seen them before—where?

The older one was carrying an armful of protective clothing and armor, and the younger one bristled with weapons—spears, swords, arrows, and shields. Perched on his head was an impressive helmet made up of rows of boars' tusks.

"Lynceus, show them what you've brought!"

Obligingly, the man spread out his linen breastplate, his bronze greaves and helmet, and one huge winding spiral of metal to cover a fighter from shoulder to thigh. It would also require superhuman strength to move and fight in it.

"This outfits the warrior," he said proudly.

"I have a storeroom full of these," said Agamemnon. "I am prepared for any challenge."

"It seems you may issue the challenge yourself," said Diomedes. "Once you have such weapons, do they not raise their own cry to be used?"

"Better that than to be needed and be lacking," said Agamemnon. "Now, Cercyon, show the rest of it."

The young man quickly obeyed, kneeling down and displaying the weaponry at his feet. "Ah, but the best course is to have such superior weapons that the enemy never has a chance to strike."

He motioned to a group of swords and daggers at his feet. "Long swords are too awkward. A shorter sword is better. Stronger. It won't suddenly crack and leave you unprotected. And it's meant for thrust-and-cut rather than just the old-fashioned puncturing. Of course, a dagger is the best for close fighting." He brandished one, relishing its heft. "But the disadvantage is that you must *be* close." He laughed.

"The ideal would be a weapon that could kill from afar. In fact, if you look at swords, you can see that each improvement is an attempt to kill at a greater and greater distance from the body of the attacker." Suddenly Gelanor was standing beside the young man. "What you want is a long sword that also slashes. *That* would be a warrior's dream."

Why was he here? Had Agamemnon taken him from Menelaus's service?

The thought of his no longer being in Sparta was intolerable. We would demand his return. How had Agamemnon recruited him?

"Your boar-tusk helmet." Gelanor pointed at it. "Very pretty. But we have better things now."

Cercyon looked crushed. He pulled it off and squeezed it.

"You need something more rigid to protect your head better," said Gelanor.

He stood over the display of arrows and their bows. "Arrows need to fly farther," he said.

"Arrows are a coward's way of fighting!" said Diomedes of Argos.

"Oh? How bullheaded! No, my friends, arrows are but the next step in the long and unfinished story of war weapons. They allow you to kill from far afield. If you do not perfect them, someone else will."

"What is the farthest an arrow can shoot and kill?" someone asked.

"With these bows and arrows, seventy paces. But with mine, you can hit a target three hundred paces away."

"Impossible." Agamemnon stood beside him. "I have great faith in Gelanor, but this is impossible."

"The problem lies in your bows," said Gelanor. "The arrow can go only as far as the tension in the bowstring. If you could stretch the string farther back, to your ear, or even farther, your arrows will astound you."

"We don't have such bows, nor bowstrings," said Lynceus.

"Not yet. Let us build them. It can be done. And fairly easily, I think."

"So you don't actually have these bows?"

"No, but I am confident they can be made. Using hair with the sinews, to increase the spring—"

"Bah!" Lynceus grabbed the bow that Cercyon had put on the floor. "This is good enough for me!"

But Cercyon tellingly pulled Gelanor aside to question him.

"I'll embrace any method that kills more Trojans!" said Agamemnon. "Just show me how to get them!"

After the men stopped swarming around the weapons, they were removed and a bard was summoned into the hall. I was able to go to Gelanor's side and whisper, "Have you deserted us?"

He looked at me, his peculiar half-smile in his eyes, not his mouth. "Never, my lady. I stand always ready to deflect your enemies."

Because no enemies had reared their heads since the poison episode, I had seen little of him. "You must not stay in Mycenae," I suddenly said. "I order you to return to Sparta with us."

Now his mouth smiled. "I obey." He laughed. "Agamemnon's pay is bad. And he clearly does not mean to pursue any of my ideas. They will cost too much, and the man is stingy."

* * *

The bard stood in the hall, waiting for the company to grow quiet. He clutched his lyre and shut his eyes. Outside, the wind was gathering itself and I could hear it tearing around the corners of the building. Someone threw more wood on the fire, but all the same the cold was creeping in, stealing between the stones.

"Sing of the voyage of the Argonauts," someone said. "Jason and the Golden Fleece."

"We're heard that a hundred times," said Cercyon. "No, do Heracles and the Hydra!"

A groan rippled around the room. "No! Boring!"

"Do Perseus! He founded Mycenae, so they say."

"Perseus and the Medusa!"

"No!" Agamemnon shouted. "Sing of Priam and his quest for his sister Hesione."

The bard looked sadly at him. "I know not such a song, sir."

"Then compose it! Do you not have the Muse at your call?"

The bard looked uncomfortable. "Sir, it is a story without an ending. Such is not suitable for an epic song."

"Then let us write it, by all the gods!" cried Agamemnon. "Then you can sing it well enough!"

The fire was dying down, and no one threw more wood onto it. Outside, the wind was ferocious, and guests were eager to get to their beds, to pull a warm fleece over themselves, wrap their arms around their shoulders, and hope for sleep.

Menelaus and I were assigned to the best of the guest chambers, the ones we had occupied on our wedding visit. When we stepped out of the megaron, we were slapped by a wind so strong and cold it felt like a garment of ice, with a hint of sleet. We shivered and huddled together as we made our way across the passage leading to our chamber.

To be here again, after all that had passed in the intervening years . . . But in truth, I cared not; I was so sleepy I could barely see anything.

Menelaus was groaning, as always, to indicate how tired he was. He took off his fur, removing it from his shoulders, but they seemed no less burdened.

He stooped. I had never noticed it before, but he was bent over—unlike that eager young warrior Cercyon, who had stood as straight as a quivering new sword. Menelaus was older, of course, although no war had sapped him—only time.

His stooping was dear to me. His weakness drew me. I stood beside him, compassion for him brought on not from his strength but from his human burdens.

Dear Menelaus. I *did* care for him.

We embraced; we lay down together. I felt him near me, my dear friend, my lord. But what followed was the same as always. Aphrodite had failed me again; she had withheld her gifts. There remained the gifts of love, respect, devotion, that the other gods had showered upon us. Lying in Menelaus's strong arms, I thought wistfully that I must content myself with them. I was fortunate to have been granted even these. And had not Menelaus been my ally since the beginning? That was our start, and that would be our finish.

❖ XX ❖

Seeing Sparta come into view, spread out along the banks of the Eurotas, my spirits rose as they always did. My city was fair, open, set in its groves of trees—it was everything the cold, guarded Mycenae was not. Both palaces were set high, but ours was a golden beacon over the plain.

Hermione was happy to be back home, where she could roam in the open corridors. All that was missing for her were cousins for playmates; there were the children of the attendants and slaves about, of course, but no one of her own blood. She confided in me that this time Cousin Iphigenia did not seem so interested in playing, that she had accumulated a collection of ivory combs and bronze mirrors and perfumed oil, and spent much time in arranging them.

"Well, she is near the age when she might have to marry," I said. "I suppose she is only making ready for it, in her own mind."

"And Elektra is too little, she's a pest, and no fun. She's just annoying; all she does is ask questions."

I laughed. "That is what being three means," I said. "So did you."

She shook her head furiously, making all her curls dance. "No, no, I didn't!"

"There's no shame in it," I assured her. "Better to ask too many questions than too few."

Questions . . . I had so many myself. Why did Agamemnon want war so badly? Was he bored, and this was what bored men did? Was he jealous of Priam, with all his sons? Did I want Menelaus to go to war? Would my life be more interesting, or less, if he were gone?

Winter clung with bony, gripping hands to the land, squeezing it pale and lifeless. As we shivered in our mantles and kept the braziers lit indoors, I had the irreverent thought that Demeter did not need to go to such extremes lamenting the loss of Persephone. As soon as I thought it, I hastily begged apology; not knowing the pain of the loss of a daughter, I did not want to provoke the goddess into allowing me to find out.

Gelanor asked leave to return to Gytheum, saying that with little to do here in Sparta he should use the time to gather up the purple-bearing shellfish along that seashore so that when the traders came calling in the spring his family would have a ready supply of them to sell. He said harvesting them was not so difficult in foul weather, if you could be sure of a warm fire afterward.

"Even the Phoenicians do not sail in this weather," he said. "But they'll be the first ones out as soon as the storms break."

I did not want him to go; I always found him so amusing to talk to. The women in the palace talked only of weaving, marriages, deaths, and children; the men only of hunting, trade, and war. Somehow, although Gelanor would speak of these things, it was as if he were standing on a high rock and describing them from above, rather than being part of them, or having any concern for the outcome. Suddenly I had an idea—something that would cure the boredom of both of us. "Take me with you!" I said.

He just looked at me quizzically. "So you can scamper on the rocks and gather the shellfish?"

"No, so that I may see Gytheum. And the sea. I've never stood on the shore, nor heard a wave."

"You are queen of the dry land," he said. "And so you shall remain, until Menelaus takes you out on the sea. Isn't his grandfather from Crete? Why don't you go there with him?"

"His grandfather is ailing, and Menelaus"—Menelaus himself did not like the sea, I realized, and avoided sailing anywhere if possible—"goes there as seldom as possible."

While we were talking, a gust of wind blew my head covering off. Gelanor laughed. "I'll take you to Gytheum when the worst of these winds are gone.

Now you would only be drenched in sea spray and chilled to death, and Menelaus would execute me for robbing the fair Helen of her health." He squinted out at the horizon, pretending he could see the sea. "Poseidon loves this time of year, when he can rage and stir up mountains of water and waves, but prudent people keep far away from him."

"Then why are you going?"

"I never said I was prudent, and anyway, enforced idleness has a way of destroying prudence."

Menelaus was amenable to my going; he trusted Gelanor. I would say he trusted him like a brother, but I had the feeling that he did not trust Agamemnon, not completely. His only condition was that I wait to accompany him until the worst of the winter storms were past, and that I not take Hermione with us, and keep two bodyguards nearby.

In truth, Menelaus seemed amenable to most things these days; he had a calm air about him. Perhaps at last he was finding that being king satisfied his talents. "Bring me one or two of the shellfish when you return," he said. "I understand that they themselves have no color at all, but only release that purple fluid when they are crushed."

"I will," I promised, my blood singing at the thought of walking beside the sounding sea, at last.

There is a time of year when winter and spring lock themselves in a wrestling match and take turns throwing one another: first one is down, then the other. One day is cold, the next warm. The cautious leaves stay furled; the more reckless open themselves to the sun. At such a time Gelanor and I set out to Gytheum, a very long day's walk, the bodyguards trailing behind. But I welcomed it, and wore sturdy shoes and a warm cloak. I knew enough to take a face veil. I was used to people staring, but Gelanor was not and it would be a nuisance as we tried to cover the ground as swiftly as possible. I wanted to pass with no hindrance.

"Well, you are quite a sight," said Gelanor as I joined him just before the palace gates.

"What do you mean?" I looked down at my feet and my cloak.

"I have only seen you bedecked as a queen," he said. "Never as a wayfarer." He smiled. "Come!"

He must have had doubts about my ability to keep up, because by the time we had passed the site of Artemis Orthia—that dark and mysterious place where boys had to undergo secret physical trials—he stopped, pulling out a skin filled with water. "My, my," he said. "You certainly can move. I am a bit out of breath."

"I once was a runner," I said. But that seemed long ago.

"Ahh," said Gelanor. "I am thankful, then, we are not competing." He passed the water to me.

On down the dirt path to Gytheum. At first we kept to the valley of the Eurotas; the river, swollen by melting snow and spring rains, sought the sea as we did. Along the way were villages, small farms. The fields, sown in late winter, showed barley and emmer, already knee-high. No one paid any attention to us, which delighted me. I said as much to Gelanor.

"Tell me," he said. "I have never wanted to ask you, as I did not want to be intrusive. But—what is it like to be stared at, no matter what you do?"

"Horrible!" I said. "Dreadful past description!"

"But what of the opposite, the person who wants to be noticed and is always invisible?" he asked.

"How can I know of this? How could I compare them?"

"It is my opinion that these invisible people cause all the trouble in the world. They want to be looked at, and do anything to command attention. They kill, they make false accusations, they brag and lay claim to deeds they have not achieved."

"That is a harsh judgment," I said. "Sometimes a very visible person wants even more. He or she is greedy." I thought of Agamemnon, clearly chafing at his quiet life in Mycenae, though he was its king. "And many simple people are happy with their lives."

Gelanor grunted. "Still, show me a man who feels overlooked . . ."

By late afternoon we faced a very high ridge of hills, rearing up like a fence. The sun, hanging over them, made them look formidable. "Just over this, Gytheum and the sea await," Gelanor said. "And we don't have to climb them. There's a pass."

We trudged over the pass and there, spread out glittering before us, was the sea. It was enormous, spreading out wider and longer than any land. The horizon twinkled far away. It was truly a kingdom: the kingdom of Poseidon.

Just before sunset, we reached the rocks, where the surf was dashing, despite the clear day. "At dawn tomorrow we'll be back here," he said. "That's the best time for gathering."

I inhaled the odd smell of the sea, a strangely metallic odor, from the seaweed and moss on slippery rocks.

We spent the night at the home of Gelanor's family. They tried not to stare at me; Gelanor tried not to boast in any way that he served me. They were open and simple people. I could sense that Gelanor was nothing like them, and that was why he no longer lived there.

Cold, dark, wet. Gelanor had insisted that we come down to the shore at this hour, before dawn broke. He was ready to wade out into the water to gather the shellfish while I waited on the shore and watched.

"You said you wanted to do this." He wagged his finger.

"How long will you be gone?" I asked.

"Oh, I don't know," he said, shrugging. "Until I can no longer find any purple-bearing shellfish."

I was to mind the sack where he would store the captured shellfish. I tried to guard it carefully, but after some time, when he had vanished behind a set of rocks, I moved it to where it would be safe and he could find it, and clambered off the slippery rock and made for the shore. I could not sit there any longer, staring out at the horizon, though the sunrise had been glorious. I was shivering and soaked by the sea spray.

I decided to walk along the shore, picking my way carefully between the rocks, hoping that the movement would warm me. I ordered the guards to stay with Gelanor. I shook my legs and tried to walk briskly. There was not another human being to be seen anywhere; it was still too early for fishermen to be out. I watched as the waves broke amongst the rocks and then reached along the beach like searching fingers tipped with foam, frothy and white.

I could see a small island offshore not far away. It was covered with trees, trees that bent with the wind; the island seemed to call out to me.

I walked and walked; the sun came up, hitting my back and warming me at last. Then I saw something ahead on my left, a cave or opening where a cliff appeared on one side of the shoreline. I made my way toward it, I know not why. As I approached it I felt a warm wind coming from inside.

Impossible, I told myself. Caves are colder than the outside air. But I sought it out, stumbling into the dim recess of its mouth. It was warm as summer in there.

The warmth grew. A soft wind caressed me. It smelled of roses. Roses like wild ones I had come across in the fields and meadows—the ones with a hundred petals, the ones that bloomed where they would and perfumed the air, but resisted gardens, refused to grow there.

Roses did not grow in caves! They sought sun, they needed sun!

My heart was hammering. I could hardly breathe. I clasped my throat. The air around me was permeated in roses, was pure roses. I fell to my knees immediately. I knew this was from the gods.

I bowed my head and shut my eyes—less out of reverence than fear. What was I going to see? I could not bear it.

"My child," a voice whispered. "Listen to me. I have called you. It has been a long wait. Your father disdained me, neglecting my offerings. And you yourself, on the eve of your wedding, forgot me. How could you? As far as marriage goes, I am the goddess without whom you cannot thrive. Hera? Oh, forget her! She knows nothing of what binds a man and a woman. Why, she cannot even satisfy Zeus! She has begged to borrow my belt, which bestows desire."

"Aphrodite?" I whispered.

"Yes, my child," she said. "You are my very likeness. I have tried to forget you, because of your and your father's insults to me, but I cannot. It is not often that a mortal woman is nearly my equal, but you are. So we are kin, and I have come to acknowledge that at last." She paused. "Come inside. Come inside the cave."

I had never liked caves and grottoes; they frightened me. But I obeyed and stepped past the rocks guarding the true opening of the cave. Instead of darkness, it was suffused in a glowing light, and the air grew even warmer. A burst of color erupted on either side—banks and banks of roses, all in full bloom, reds as deep as wounds, pinks as delicate as the lining of shells, as exuberant as the swirl of clouds at sunset, crimsons the match of any field poppy. Petals fell as I watched, in a gentle shower. The floor of the cave was carpeted with them, carpeted so deeply that their cool smoothness caressed my ankles and I waded in them.

"Show yourself to me," I murmured. I needed to see her, to see this goddess.

"That is dangerous," she said. "To see a god or goddess face to face can kill a mortal."

"Is it always so?" I so longed to behold her.

"One never knows," her soft voice said. "Sometimes it is safe. But for you, dear Helen—is it worth risking death? Zeus, your father, would be angry at me if I caused it. You are his only daughter by a mortal woman. He dotes on you. I dare not incur his wrath. Yes, even we goddesses dread it! So, my child, you must take me on faith. But someday, perhaps, you shall gaze safely upon me."

What did she mean? That I would become a goddess, go to Mount Olympus?

"Do not assume that, for few go to Mount Olympus."

Her reading of my mind was swifter and more thorough than that ability which the sacred serpents had bestowed upon me, but it was the same gift, in kind.

"Pass before me," I begged her. "Let the roses stir."

She laughed, a laugh that was rich beyond honey and deeper than desire. Or rather, it was all desire in a single sound. The roses trembled and moved, and their petals fell. "There," she sighed.

"Why . . . have you summoned me here?" I asked her, after I had inhaled the wondrous fragrance.

"My child, you summoned me."

"No—how—"

"You have long sought me, wished for me. My lack in your life—deliberate, I now confess—has been a torment to you."

"No, not a torment . . ." I had, after all, learned how to live without it, something I had never tasted. Can one truly miss what one has never known?

I heard her low, thrilling, intimate laugh.

"Oh, do not be ashamed. Many people have sought me, many have cursed me—when I ignored them. But you! Oh, I think you should not dismiss gifts you know not of. Those who dwell in a cave—I surmise that you do not care for them—might belittle sunlight, but they have no experience of it. So I need show you what you lack in your life. You lack me, and it is a grievous lack."

"Then give me your gift. Touch me with it. Open my eyes." I hoped that sounded humble enough; and as I thought that, I smothered it. She could hear thoughts.

"Gladly. With all my heart."

"What must I do?" I beseeched her.

"Stand very still, close your eyes. Reach out and touch roses on either side. When you return to the seashore, wade out into the water and wait for a foam-laden wave. Let it wash over you, drench you. Then you will be suffused with me."

I extended my arms and grasped clusters of rose petals, crushing them. An explosion of scent flooded the air.

"Close your eyes," Aphrodite said. "You need your other senses now."

As soon as I closed my eyes, I felt the warmth of the air, inhaled the intense rose smell, heard the whisper of her voice more clearly.

"I touch you," she breathed by my side. "I give you my vision. Zeus is your father, but I am your sister. And I will never depart from you. I shall be at your side all your days."

Did I feel anything? A glow, a warmth? No. I only heard her sweet whisper.

"Open your eyes."

I opened them and the roses were brighter than before; they pulsated with a richness I had never imagined. I looked up at the ceiling of the cave; its dark and shadowy recesses seemed rich and mysterious and full of infinite promise, not dank and cold.

"You now see things through the veil of Aphrodite," she said. "It is a different vision."

I sensed that I was being dismissed, that the goddess was through with me.

"Oh, no," she assured me. "You are my chosen, my daughter as well as my sister. Why . . . I have never had a daughter. About time, I would say. Did you know, gods and goddesses usually give birth to males? So you are alone in being a female among us."

"But I am not a goddess!"

"But nearly so," she sighed. "And many will treat you as such. You have certain privileges reserved for us."

"What are those?"

"Oh, when others would be killed or traded—" She stopped and laughed. That disarming laugh! "But I forget—you mortals like surprises. That is why the oracles speak in riddles. To tell you too much is to spoil the suspense." She paused. "I would not rob you of it."

And then, suddenly, she was gone. The cave was dark and dripping. No roses. No warm air.

Why do the gods depart so abruptly? To tease us, to punish us, to laugh at us? I was forced to stumble out, feeling my way. I wanted to grab her shoulders, shake her, say, *How dare you treat me this way?* But there was no recourse.

The gods were as they were; we mortals were as we were. Sometimes we could speak and understand one another; usually not.

Time had not existed, had not passed, in the cave, but when I emerged it was midday. The sun was high in the sky, turning the ocean into a mirror. I returned to the spot I had left. I could see the collecting sack was still safe; I was thankful for that.

Gelanor was standing near it, hands on hips, looking everywhere for me. I waved at him, although, truthfully, I did not wish to speak to him or anyone else. I wanted to sink down alone on the sand and think of what had happened to me.

"Helen! Helen!" Gelanor was waving his arms, signaling to me.

I walked toward him, feeling the soft give of the sand beneath my feet, smelling more acutely than ever before the sand—sea—salt.

"Where have you been?" he demanded.

"It was cold and so I left the sack—in a safe place—and walked to warm myself."

"I told you it would be cold!" he scolded.

Oh, what matter? I wanted to tell him. All those things of ordinary life have passed away.

I came abreast of him. "What have you gathered?" I knew it was a question I should ask.

"I got many." He patted the bulging sack. Then he wheeled on me. "What's wrong with you?"

I stared at him. "Nothing. Nothing."

"You act like a sleepwalker."

The sun striking the rocks was glorious. They seemed more than rocks, they seemed some special offering of the gods. Why had I not seen it before?

"Nothing," I repeated. "Nothing."

"I don't believe you." He grasped my arm. "You are ill."

Just then a huge wave surged offshore—rearing itself up, it crested and raced toward us. I tore away from him, ran down into the tide, stood braced and waiting for the wave to wash over me, arms upraised, as Aphrodite had commanded me.

"No!" Gelanor cried, running after me.

But he was too late. The huge wave engulfed me, swallowed me up in a great green swallow. I gave myself to it, and it was warm, as warm as the breath of someone's mouth against my neck, as warm as water that sat out in high summer in a clay jar in sunlight. And half of it was foam, light frothy foam, foam that enveloped me, bathed me. The wave receded and I stood coated with foam, white as a spirit.

"You are mad," said Gelanor, encircling my shoulders with his strong arms. "This water is lethally cold . . ." He stuck his hand in it. "It's dangerous."

Couldn't he feel its warmth? Or was it warm only for me?

He insisted on enveloping me in a blanket and hurrying me up above the water line. "Whatever has come over you?" he asked, shaking his head, dabbing the foam off me.

I said nothing. The foam had anointed me. I was now Aphrodite's. But it was our secret, our private pledge.

Far off on the horizon, the outlines of an island showed itself. I realized I must think of something to say to Gelanor, something innocent. "What island is that?" I asked.

"Cythera," he said shortly. "It is two days' sail from here with a fair wind."

"It beckons me."

"It is where Aphrodite was born, where she was washed ashore on a seashell, emerging from the foam. Better to have your sights on nearby Cranae." He pointed to the island just offshore that had intrigued me. "It is far easier to attain."

❧ XXI ❧

The way back seemed short; perhaps I also had fresh strength in my legs. Gelanor had put the shellfish into a stone tank near the shore filled with seawater for his parents to sell to the Phoenicians when they arrived. He had gathered heaps of them; they almost filled the tank.

"Better than farming," he said. "The dye itself will fetch ten to twenty times its weight in gold."

I had selected two fat ones to show to Menelaus, and we were carrying them carefully in a sealed jar of water.

Now I eagerly looked at the landscape as we walked through it, the guards trudging a respectful distance behind. We were climbing the hills that screened

Gytheum; when we passed beyond it, the sea would vanish from sight. Oaks and yews clung to the slopes, stubbornly pointing skyward. I heard the goat bells of herds that grazed on the hills; I saw their keepers sleeping under the trees, dozing in the shade.

"Let us stop," I asked Gelanor. I had an overwhelming urge to sit down on this hill near the goatherds; why, I did not know.

He looked at me quizzically. "We have barely started," he said. "Tired already?"

"No, not tired."

"What, then?"

"I wish to linger a few moments," I said, and sat down. I leaned against the trunk of an old myrtle—sacred to Aphrodite—and closed my eyes. The high tinkling sound of the goatherds' bells played like lyres in the air. A pungent, sweet smell of wild thyme rode the breeze.

Suddenly time and place vanished, as it had in the cave. I kept my eyes shut—had not Aphrodite told me they interfere with the other senses?—and stilled the racing of my heart. I let my mind drift free; I smelled the scents around me, heard the sounds, felt the hard, pebbly ground under my feet. I saw another mountain, a higher one, with green meadows and wildflowers and butterflies playing in and out; I heard the splashing of a stream, falling down into a pool; I felt the shady coolness. Somehow, too, I smelled cattle, their hot, thick scent, and heard them low—so different from the bleats of sheep and goats. And then I saw—somewhere in my head, in this waking dream—a herdsman sleeping, dreaming, his head pillowed with green grass and meadow flowers. He had a smile on his face. And I could see inside his dream, and that there were goddesses parading before him, three of them.

In the man's dream, he rose and conferred with Aphrodite. I could not hear what passed between them, but there was smiling and agreement. Then the goddesses all vanished and the man awoke, rolling over and sitting up. He clasped his knees with his hands and sighed.

"We must get up," Gelanor said. "We have a long day's walk."

Yes. We must go. I stood, the images still swirling in my mind. These goddesses—that herdsman—the steep mountainside with its cascading streams—what had they to do with me? As we descended from the hills—not really mountains—the fields and forests around us were very different.

It was past sunset when we reached Sparta. The last trudge up the hill to the palace seemed very long, coming at the end of the journey. As we passed through the gates, I saw Agamemnon's horses and chariot in the outer courtyard, and smelled roasting ox. We had visitors, official ones.

Exhaustion gripped me. My feet were dusty and aching from the journey; all I wished was to send for a quiet supper in my quarters and retire. I turned to Gelanor. "Oh, no," I said.

He shook his head. "My lady, this is where being an ordinary man is more desirable than being queen. For I may rest and you may not."

"It is not fair!" I said.

He laughed, and leaned over to kiss my cheek. "Courage!" he said, saluting me.

Should I go to my chambers and wait to be summoned? Or should I go directly to the megaron and have it over with? I decided it was best to go to the gathering. Once I reached my chambers it would be hard to leave.

I walked through the open porch and the portico of the vestibule and entered the great megaron. To my relief, there were not many people there.

Menelaus hurried up. "Dear wife, we have had some tragic news."

Agamemnon followed him. "Our grandfather Catreus on Crete has died. We must go and make obsequies for him." He held up his hands to check condolences. "It was not unexpected. And he has lived a long time, longer than our father." He drew in a heavy breath. "But we must delay for nine days."

"Why is that?" I did not understand.

"At the very same time that I received the news of Grandfather, these . . . visitors . . . appeared. We have two conflicting protocols. One is that a family funeral must be attended; the other that a foreign guest or envoy must be entertained for nine days."

Menelaus nodded. "So I will hold them here, feast them, and so on. Agamemnon will return to Mycenae and ready the ships for our journey to Crete."

Crete! "May I accompany you?" I asked. I had so longed to see Crete.

"No," said Menelaus. "You are not of his direct blood. Besides, I must leave you here in charge of Sparta while I am gone."

"But Father or Mother—"

"No. You stay here." Did he say this to satisfy Agamemnon?

"Who are these envoys?" I was not to go to Crete. Would I ever see anything? Even the journey to nearby Gytheum had required special permission.

"They are from Troy! Troy!" muttered Agamemnon. "One is Priam's son, the other his cousin. Paris and Aeneas."

"Troy?" I found it hard to believe.

"Indeed. They came on an embassy about their aunt Hesione. Priam sent them. I see he fears war!" Agamemnon chuckled.

"Or perhaps he thinks it would be foolish, and hopes to lay all this strife to rest," said Menelaus.

Such a possibility did not please Agamemnon, yearning for war, even one based on an old woman content with her lot. "Bah!" He laughed and turned a smiling face to me. "Come. Come and meet them."

Menelaus held out his hand and I took it. Together we entered the hall.

He had not asked me about the shellfish; I hoped Gelanor could keep them alive until morning.

The two visitors were standing by the open hearth in the middle of the megaron. They turned, almost in unison, as we approached. One wore a deer-skin and the other a purple-dyed mantle held over the shoulder with a brooch.

They were both handsome—one was dark-haired, with almost perfect features. (No wonder; later I was to learn he was Aphrodite's own son.) But it was the other one, the light-haired one, broad-shouldered and tall, that I stared at.

It was the herdsman in my dream. And he was staring hard at me.

"Paris," he said, inclining his head.

"Aeneas," said the dark one.

They were like gods. They were gods. That was what they said of the Trojans—that they were so beautiful even the gods themselves carried them off. *Trojans are most like to gods of all mortal men in beauty and stature,* Aphrodite whispered to me, as she brushed by me in the evening like a moth, delicate and white.

I struggled for speech. Then I berated myself. This was absurd.

"Helen," I said.

"The immortal Helen," Paris said. His face seemed lit with a glow of gold.

"No, not immortal," I said. "I shall perish as everyone else."

"Never."

All this passed in an instant, but our words did not matter. We kept looking at one another. For the first few minutes I wanted to tell him my dream of him on the mountain, ask him what it meant. But even that passed away, as a great stillness fell upon me and I was content just to look at him.

"We are come in the name of peace," he said. "We are distressed that Priam's inquiries about his sister have been so rudely rebuffed."

Even his voice resonated, lovely as the pipes of Pan in glens. "But she is content where she is," I said.

"Helen is not to speak of political matters." Agamemnon's harsh voice cut across the night. "My brother and I are the ones empowered to negotiate, not his wife!" Obedient, subservient laughter rose from around the room.

"I am a woman," I persisted. "And I think I can speak of what women feel."

"Her feelings are immaterial!" bellowed Agamemnon.

Paris and Aeneas kept silent; I thought the more highly of them. But I could not keep my eyes from Paris. For the first time perhaps in my entire life, I felt desire course through me. I wanted to possess him, devour him, take him away in a chain and have him always at my command. At the same time I wanted to give him anything he desired; anything. And I wanted to be with him every instant. And so far we had not spoken a single private word.

Oh, Aphrodite! I cried in my thoughts. You are indeed the most powerful goddess, you have subjugated my sense and my thoughts and reason.

Yet I did not wish to be freed. I felt more alive than ever before, even as I was an abject prisoner.

I walked, as lightly as a nymph, back to my chamber. Had I felt weary? No longer. Now I felt as fleet as I had the day I raced beside the banks of the Eurotas, but I wanted to run toward Paris, not away from a starting line.

Dreamily I let the attendants remove my clothes, attire me for sleep. I raised my arms, reaching for the ceiling; I felt them untying my hair, letting it fall down my back. Light robes swirled as they dropped them over my head down to my ankles.

"Dear Queen," one said, gesturing toward the bed, bowing. Then, impulsively, she reached for an alabaster vial of rose oil, unstoppered it, and stroked some of the oil across my throat. "Until the true roses bloom," she said.

Oh, but they had. They had! I took her hand and squeezed it. "Thank you," I said.

I lay down, pulling the linen over me, aching to be alone, to think. I shut my eyes, and went back to the cave and the roses and the foam and the anointing. And then, the dream and the herdsman in it. The herdsman who was here. But he was no herdsman, he was a prince of Troy. None of it made sense. My head spun.

Paris. His name was Paris. Had I not heard earlier . . . somewhere . . . of him? Paris. Yes . . . that child who had been exposed, set out to die, and who had later returned to his father, Priam.

But why would they want to leave him to die? He had no blemishes, he was not impaired. Why would a mother and father expose such a son? Sometimes a daughter might be exposed, her only fault being that she was a daughter. But a royal son . . . Of course, Priam had so many, he need not miss one. Had not an omen been mentioned?

To think that Paris might not have lived. I could not bear even to contemplate it, to think it was only chance that he lived, and breathed, and was here in Sparta.

Paris. Why was I drawn to him and not to Aeneas, who was also handsome? I could not say; only that the sight of Paris had . . . inflamed me, that was the only word for it.

A loud noise made me open my eyes; a thump as something was thrown down; Menelaus was tossing his mantle with its heavy brooch onto a chest. So he had come to me tonight. The attendants had left a lamp burning, and in the dim light I saw him standing, stretching, his skimpy tunic leaving his broad, muscular shoulders to gleam faintly. I saw them move as he lowered his arms.

Had Aphrodite touched me in regard to him? At last, could I see him with eyes of desire? That would be far better than anything else, far, far better. Give me that Aphrodite vision, bathe my vision of my husband in it! Let me be one of those fortunate wives! Let the net of desire fall over my faithful husband, Menelaus!

He came closer. I closed my eyes. When I opened them, how would I see him?

"You have had a long journey," he said, sitting on the edge of the bed; it gave under his weight. "I hope you have enjoyed it?" His voice was warm and soft.

"Indeed, I have. And we brought you"—I opened my eyes—"a sample of the shellfish, as you requested."

"Thank you." His voice was gentle. He reached over to touch my cheek.

I recoiled. It was all I could do not to shudder.

The net did not fall over him. It was exclusive to Paris.

"Oh!" I cried, close to a sob. I did not want this to be the answer, Aphrodite's cruel answer. I turned away.

* * *

We lay side by side, quietly, as we did so many nights. I drifted away into dreams—but slight, fractured things—and kept emerging out into consciousness, like the moon sliding out between clouds. At length I felt so wide awake that I stole from the bed and put on my mantle.

I did not know where to go, what to do. I could not stay in this chamber for fear of making noise and waking Menelaus. The rest of the palace slept in darkness; the guards kept watch outside, but everything else was quiet.

My fingers trembling, I pulled open the door and slipped out. Immediately I felt calmer. I merely needed to be alone, truly alone, for a time. I needed to think, not to have to speak to anyone. Gelanor was very dear, but he examined everything and asked questions. Menelaus—no, I could never tell Menelaus.

Perhaps I should go to the shrine of—no, it was the gods who had caused this. But . . . the household altar, the shrine where the sacred snake lived, the snake I had brought back from Asclepius's temple . . . yes, that might be what I sought. There was no particular god there, just the spirits of our house and dynasty.

I walked out across the portico; the rising moon made long shadows of the pillars. I walked through them, a forest of shadow-trees with bright clearings.

The small, circular marble room nearby, with its altar in the center, glowed with reflected moonlight. Two votive lamps flickered on the floor. I sank down on a bench along the wall and clasped my hands in my lap.

Yesterday's honey cake offering for the snake lay to one side of a lamp. I had been diligent in taking care of him, as I had promised. He had grown a great deal in the eight winters since he had come here. And he was fond of me; at least, I liked to think so. It is hard to know what a serpent thinks. But he always glided out to see me. Where was he tonight? Perhaps he slept, as all the world did.

This was the first private breath I had taken since the cave had beckoned me. I wanted to transcend myself, the palace, Menelaus, even Aphrodite herself. You, my pet snake, you are the only one I want to touch and speak to, I thought. And as if in response to a command, he glided out from behind the altar.

I got up and came over to him, being careful to move smoothly, with no jerky movements—snakes do not like them. I bent down and stroked his slick head.

"My friend," I whispered, "I rejoice to see you."

He raised his head up and flicked his tongue.

"You protect our household."

No answer from him; but he did move over toward me and approach my feet.

"Oh, I cannot even tell you what has happened," I murmured to him, "but I know you guard our household and you will warn us if there is any danger."

He reared himself up and, surprisingly, coiled around my ankle. Then he tightened his grip.

"Dear friend, can you not speak more clearly?" Was he trying to warn me? I reached down and tried to uncoil him, but he clenched even more tightly. It became painful. "I cannot translate what you are saying," I told him. "But you must release my foot. You are causing me distress." I tried again to uncoil him. His strength was surprising. I could not unwind him without injuring him.

A soft voice came from the shadows. "He is trying to tell you something."

No. Even here, even here I could not be alone. I whirled around.

"Who is there?" I demanded. The snake still clung to my ankle.

There was no answer. Only the shuffling of footsteps. Then, out into the dim, white-tinged light, stepped Paris.

"Oh!" My hands flew to my mouth.

He came closer. I could not breathe. "Oh," I repeated mindlessly.

"Shall I help you with the snake?" He knelt down and touched it, gently, but the snake had already loosened himself and was moving away. Paris leaned forward and kissed my ankle, at the place where the snake had been entwined. His lips were warm and set me to boil. I snatched my foot away.

"He—he is gone," I said. It was all I could say.

Slowly Paris straightened himself and stood to his full height, a goodly height. He looked down at me.

"I came here because I could not sleep," he said. Ordinary words.

"Nor could I." More ordinary words.

We could not sleep. We could not sleep for thinking of one another, but who could say it?

"Yes," I finally managed. "Yes."

"Helen—" He paused and took a very deep breath, a breath meant to stop the next words. But it was an inadequate dam; the words spilled over it. "You are all they say you are. Oh, you know that all too well! How many fool-ish fumbling mouths have spat it out? Yes, your beauty is . . . godesslike. But it is not your beauty that draws me, it is something else, something I cannot even frame in words." He looked up at the dark ceiling and laughed. "You see how it robs me of speech, how it cannot be expressed? But not being able to express it makes it no less real. I feel you, Helen, in my deepest part, and yet I have no words to describe it."

"I saw you in a waking dream," I told him. "I saw you on a mountain, in a meadow, with goddesses."

"Oh, that was a foolish dream," he said quickly. "But if it made you think of me, then I must be grateful for it."

"I am married."

"I know that."

"And a mother."

"I know that. That is what makes it so unthinkable."

"The gods delight to sport with us."

"Yes."

He was standing there, all desire gathered into one being. I reached out, embraced him. He was no dream; he did not vanish. He clasped me to him, and he was so real his arms around me hurt in their strength. I kissed him. His lips unlocked a rush of desire in me, the first I had ever felt.

I had longed for this, hungered for it, imagined it, but never tasted it. Now it exploded with all the gush of sweet fruit fresh from the tree, of honey new-smoked from the hive, too rich for use.

"Helen," he murmured.

A moment longer and I would have lain down beside the marble altar and taken him to me. But no, it was all too soon, and I tore myself out of his arms.

"Paris," I said. "I do not know—I cannot—"

"Do you love me?" he asked. Only four words. Four simple words. He stood there in all his beauty and asked them. They were, after all, all that mattered.

"Yes." I choked. "But—" I turned and ran away.

How could I love a man I did not know?

But I did know him. I had known him since the beginning of the world, from its very formation. Or so it felt. I knew him better than I knew Menelaus, better than I knew Clytemnestra, better, in the deepest sense, than even I knew myself.

Yet I did not know him, truly, at all! Only through Aphrodite did I know him. And what sort of knowing—true or false—was that?

What are they really here for?" I asked Menelaus sleepily as I opened my eyes and saw him fastening his cloak. My head ached; I felt as if I had been struck on the back of my neck. I could not believe that what I remembered about the night had really happened. Surely it was a dream. I reached down and touched my ankle, and it was a bit sore from my encounter with the snake. But even if I had gone to the shrine, perhaps I had been walking in my sleep. Now Menelaus would turn to me and say, *What is who here for? I don't know what you mean,* and I would sigh in relief.

"King Priam sent them," he said. "That's what they claim. Word of Agamemnon's mutterings have reached Troy, evidently. So they came on Priam's behalf to request that Hesione be returned to her native home, or at least that they be allowed to speak to her."

I sat up. So it was true. Trojans were here. "And were they?"

Menelaus snorted. "No, of course not. Agamemnon could not allow that. Hesione would say she was content, then Priam would have to stop lamenting about it, and Agamemnon would have nothing to complain against Priam about." He sighed. "The young men, to their credit, do not seem exactly on fire to free Hesione. I suspect they came to humor the king, and to see Greece. Young men like to roam."

I stood up and clapped my hands for my attendant to come. "I am sorry about your grandfather," I said.

"Yes," he said. "As soon as this entertaining is over, I go to Crete. Protocol . . ." He shook his head. "Of course, guests are sacred, and obligations must be honored."

Yes. Even when someone was dying, or had died. We all knew the story about how King Admetus entertained Heracles in the palace even though the queen was dying, because hospitality demanded it. Heracles only found out there was anything amiss when he heard the slaves wailing.

"Yes," I said. "Such is custom."

Nine days for Paris to be our guest. Nine days . . . I was afraid to come out of my chambers and see him again. I was equally afraid not to see him again.

* * *

So that Agamemnon could be quickly on his way, it was decided to hold the traditional ceremonial feast for the guests that night. So—any dream I had of hiding in my quarters was gone. I gave orders that the food be prepared, and the cooks worked from noon on with no rest. I set the servants to work decorating with budding branches of wild pear and almond trees, and ordered the most skilled players of the lyre from the town to present themselves at twilight. I sent word to Mother, Father, and my brothers, as well as Hermione, that they were to be present. It no longer felt strange to summon my mother and father; I had walked in the sandals of a queen, worn the gold diadem long enough, that I truly presided over the palace. I made sure I issued all these commands from my own chambers; I did not want to venture out into the rest of the palace yet, lest I encounter Paris.

The hour of twilight, the time of the blue light and what some called "first dark" had come. The sun was gone, and in his wake the bright star of Aphrodite gleamed on the horizon, white and full. A light wind, warm and soft, sprang up from the south.

I needed to dress, and I allowed my maids to choose something for me; I scarcely knew what it was. Truly it did not matter; I wished to be invisible, and had I a robe that made that possible, that was what I would have chosen. As it was, I had to endure the weaving of gold ornaments into my locks, the fastening of the gold diadem with its sun-spiral patterns across my brow, and the murmurs of appreciation for it all.

"You are so oddly quiet tonight, my lady," said one of my attendants. "I believe we could put a sow's bladder on your head and you would not object."

Her chatter set me on edge. "Oh, do be silent," I told her. I saw her give the other attendant a look, a raised eyebrow.

Full dark had come, and torches were blazing in the hall. I heard the musicians playing, saw the light spilling out across the vestibule entrance. I took a deep breath and stepped forward. I had barely walked three paces before I could feel my head throbbing behind the diadem.

Inside, I saw Mother holding Hermione's hand, pointing out the strangers.

"Dear daughter," said Mother, turning to me. "I think this is a good way to teach Hermione about courtly feasts. After all, she is nine, and her lifetime will include many of them." Mother and I had long since stopped alluding to the possibility of Hermione having a brother or sister.

"Mother!" Hermione bowed to me. "You look—you look like a queen!" My daughter usually only saw me in my everyday attire, as we played together in the palace or took walks.

"She *is* a queen," said Mother proudly.

"As are you," I reminded her. I bent down and smiled at Hermione. "As you someday will be, Princess. It is not so difficult. Why, it only means wearing special clothes occasionally. For the rest of it, a queen's life should be like any other's, only it should be able to bear being watched more closely."

"Why is that?" Hermione asked. She knitted her brows.

"Because many people watch a queen and, sad to say, they look for faults in her."

"They'll find none in you!" she said stoutly.

I could not help but smile at her wholehearted loyalty. O, let me be worthy of it! "Oh, as you grow older you'll see faults aplenty," I assured her.

"These men," said Mother. "I like them not." She was frowning in the direction of the crackling hearth fire of cedar and sandalwood that perfumed the air. "I fear they are here to spy upon us, that Priam has sent them to find our weaknesses. I think he means to attack us."

"Over his elderly sister?" Her suspicion surprised me.

"We all know that is just an excuse," she said. She drew closer to me and I could smell the faint scent of lily, her favorite oil. "Troy finds us tempting to invade, and Agamemnon has already decided in his heart to attack Troy. Oh, I am filled with fear!" Her soft voice trembled. "I smell a war not far away."

I remembered the weapons and war talk not long hence at Mycenae. "I pray you are wrong," was all I said, while my heart felt a chill.

"Come, I want to see them!" Hermione was tugging at my hand.

Menelaus turned as we approached, his face filling with pleasure. He opened his arms to welcome us. Just beyond his embrace I could see Paris, standing stiffly. I could only see part of his face, but from that glimpse, I felt the hot and cold run through me. *It was still here. It had not vanished with the night. It was no dream.*

"Our honored guests," Menelaus said, stepping back slightly and turning me toward them. "Paris, son of King Priam of Troy, and Aeneas, prince of Dardania and son of—"

"Oh, please no," said Aeneas quickly. He was actually blushing.

"—Anchises," finished Menelaus. He turned to me. "Helen, I was speaking to them of my own voyage to Troy." He squeezed me closer to him. "Yes, in my youth. I am familiar with it. Tell me." Oh, he was straining so hard to be bright and cheerful. "The citadel on the crest of the city, the shrine to Athena—I remember it so well—is it the same?"

It was Aeneas, not Paris, who spoke. "Oh, yes. The shrine with its sacred image of Athena, the one we call the Pallas Athena, remains as it was first built. We honor it with festivals and sacrifices."

"And are the heights still so windy?" He laughed. "Of course they would still be, if my memory serves. Winds do not change. Once I set down a leather pouch—heavily laden, I can tell you—on a bench near the oak growing on the northwestern edge of the summit. I thought ridding myself of the weight would help me to keep my footing. As I watched, the wind moved the pouch to the edge and finally toppled it over. It hit the ground with a thud."

Paris laughed. "It has been that way since I have been there."

That voice. That inimitable voice! I heard it again and my heart sang.

"He hasn't been there long enough to know about the winds." An ugly voice intruded itself. Agamemnon was speaking. "Have you?"

If he expected Paris to shrink before this slap, he thought wrong. Paris just smiled and laughed, as light as a butterfly. "No, I haven't." He turned to the rest of us, confiding, "All my life I've been a prince, but I've only known it a short time."

"And why is that?" Agamemnon persisted.

"My fortune reversed itself overnight," Paris said. "But let us wait until everyone can hear. It is a tale that wears out in much retelling."

Agamemnon grunted. He flourished a gold cup filled with wine. "I trust everyone has wine?" he asked pointedly. Our guests' hands were empty.

Menelaus went into a flurry of apologies. I cringed to see him doing so.

"There is wine aplenty if the guests will just avail themselves of it." I was glaring at Agamemnon as I spoke.

"I sense that the guest gifts must be presented or we shall never proceed to the feast itself." Paris gestured to one of his Trojan retainers. "I cannot accept another moment of hospitality at the hand of the great king and queen of Sparta without offering my profound respect."

Two men struggled into the hall balancing a tall bronze tripod, exquisitely fashioned. Its three feet had eagle claws grasping globes, and from them rose braided legs to hold a wide bowl for offerings.

"No fire has ever touched it," said Paris. "It has waited for you."

Menelaus stepped forward and stroked one of its legs. I looked upward at the subtly convex bowl crowning it. It was truly a work of art.

"Magnificent," said Menelaus.

"I am pleased that it has found favor in the eyes of the king."

"The artisans of Troy are cunning." The heavy voice of Agamemnon—as heavy as the weariness at day's end, of a tedious cousin, of an overstuffed bag.

"We pride ourselves on our skill," said Paris. "But it is all at your service."

This effusion was revolting. Yet it was customary. Now Menelaus must present him with our gift—something smaller that he could carry away easily.

I give you Helen, my wife. Here, take her. You will find her of finest workmanship. I trust she will please you. Menelaus takes me by the wrist and leads me to Paris.

I saw it all in my mind, in a perfect picture. Oh, if only it could have been so simple, so easily accomplished. For it came to that in the end.

Two of our slaves rolled in a large bronze cauldron. Paris and Aeneas affected surprise and pleasure.

"This, too, has never seen the touch of fire," said Menelaus. It was all part of the ritual of gift exchange. A never-used vessel was of the highest value. No one ever used the vessels hereafter, either. They stored them as proof of how they were esteemed by others. The most precious materials and skill were thus lavished on things never to be desecrated by actual use.

Then lesser gifts followed. Swords, bowls, goblets.

"And strongest of all, stronger than bronze," said Menelaus, "is the sacred bond between host and guest, *xenia*. Zeus himself sets the rules for it, the rules of trust and honor."

Paris and Aeneas bowed their heads.

"Now let us go in to feast," said Menelaus, raising his arm in signal.

One end of the megaron had been laid out with a long table where we were to seat ourselves and eat. Ordinarily we ate at many small tables, even with a large company, but Father seemed keen on being able to hear all the conversations and miss nothing.

The long table—a huge board propped on trestles—seated the Trojans, the present royal family, and the former royal family. My brothers joined us, belatedly seating themselves, murmuring apologies. I was seated between

Paris and Menelaus. I dared not ask that Paris be moved, but I longed to. The nearer he was, the more difficult it was for me.

"My sons," said Father. "Castor and Polydeuces."

"The famous wrestler and boxer," said Paris. "It is a privilege to meet you."

"Paris is a boxer," said Aeneas, from the other end of the table.

"No—" Paris shook his head.

"Oh, but he is. Or rather, he claimed his inheritance through boxing."

"Really? Tell me!" Polydeuces, the boxer, said.

Paris rose and looked around at the company. His knuckles rested on the table and I felt the table move. "I promised you, King Agamemnon, to tell you of my late coming to my father's household. This is part of the story. But I fear our dinner will be greatly delayed if I tell it all."

"It will only increase our appetite," said Father. "Whereas if we wait until our bellies are full, we may be dull of hearing. Pray, tell it."

Paris must have smiled; I could not see his face, but I could hear it in his voice. "Very well. I shall try to make it short, unlike bards, who string out a story for days." He took a breath. "I was raised as a herdsman on the slopes of Mount Ida," he said.

"The mountain near Troy where Zeus was raised," intoned Hermione, who had spent much time learning all these things. "It has many goodly springs and flowers."

"Indeed, Princess," said Paris. "That is why I was happy there. I tended cattle and—"

"He routed a band of cattle thieves when he was little more than a boy," said Aeneas. He nodded toward us. "He is too modest, he will never tell it all."

Paris shook his finger at Aeneas. "Quiet, or we shall never get through the story. I discovered that I had a way with bulls. I could control them, and soon I was sought after for local bull-judging contests. I had a reputation for fairness, that's why. And then one of my prize bulls was taken from me to be sacrificed at Troy in a tribute. I lost my temper—I loved that bull, I had raised it from a calf! Why did the selfish king of Troy demand him? I decided to follow after, to compete in the tribute games, and win the bull back." He bent over—he was still standing, although the rest of us were seated—and took a long drink of wine. Looking up, I saw his throat moving. I quickly looked away.

"My father tried to stop me. I did not know why. He warned me against going to Troy; he told me to forget the bull. 'The king's whims are law, my son,' he had said. But nothing more.

"I brushed this aside, and set out for Troy. Out on the plain before the city gates a contest field was laid out. I had never seen such an elaborate thing—all my races had been barefoot through mountain meadows, but these were formal, along a track. Still, I was so angry about the bull, I entered them. And I won. Anger gave my feet wings. And then there was the final contest, boxing. I had never boxed before, but, as I said, anger pushed me forward. I won that as well. But I do not know if I could ever repeat it. I do not understand how I accomplished it. I had no training, no method."

"He accomplished it through courage rather than skill," said Aeneas. "That was the fair judgment. But it qualified him as the champion of the tribute games. And he was ready to ask for the bull as a prize when suddenly the sons of Priam turned on him and tried to kill him, they were so angry at being defeated by a herdsman, a rustic from the mountains. Only when his father—who had followed Paris there—begged them to stop because he was their *brother* was all revealed." He took a breath. "I mean, that he was not truly his father but had merely raised him. Paris was the son of King Priam. So, after it was proved, Priam said, 'Better Troy should fall than that my wonderful son should be lost again.' And thus the household of Priam gained a son."

"As if he did not have sons enough," said Agamemnon.

If he heard it, Paris took no notice. "Aeneas, dear cousin, I see you will not allow me to recite my own story. So be it." He took another drink of wine. "I might have taken longer and detained these good hosts even longer from their food. This we must not have!" He sat down and set his goblet on the table.

"Why had your father King Priam cast you aside? Why were you lost in the first place?" Of course it was Agamemnon who asked that, the indelicate, unspeakable question.

The servers were bringing in platters of food—boiled goat and mutton, roasted wild boar—and we had to suspend our talking as our plates were filled.

"Because there was—"

A second set of servers appeared, bearing herb-flavored sausage, and then pots of honey smoked from the hives, and bowls of wild figs and pears, and finally containers of goat cheese and nuts.

People began to talk to their companions, talk of pleasant, inconsequential things. But Agamemnon's voice cut through the murmurs. "Tell us, good prince. Tell us why your father cast you out of the palace," he persisted.

"Mmmm . . ." Paris was chewing the meat.

"Oh, young man, seek not to evade the question!" Agamemnon tried to sound jolly.

Paris took his time finishing the mouthful of meat and at length said, "If you are determined to have it, here it is, though I fear it may sound the wrong note in this happy company. There was an omen about my birth, an omen that said I would be the destruction of Troy. So they sought to prevent that." I could hear the tiny tremor in his voice. Curses to Agamemnon for forcing him to say this—this which must cause him distress!

"So that is what Priam meant when he said, 'Better Troy should fall than that my wonderful son should be lost again,'" said Father. "I see." He wiped his mouth. "Well, that's a brave father!"

"Now, wouldn't you do the same for us?" teased Castor, leaning toward Father.

Father laughed. "I don't know. Perhaps I'd be better off if I'd sent you off to the Taygetus mountains, like other parents do bad children."

"Well, you would have had to send both of us," said Polydeuces. "We do not tolerate being separated."

"It doesn't happen very often," said Agamemnon. "Royal families hardly ever expose infants nowadays. Only the most dreadful situation would require it." He took a long, slow drink from his cup, then set it down slowly, precisely. Then he gave Paris a riveting look, settling back in his chair.

Mother, beside him, looked at both the guests and asked brightly, "And are you married?" But I knew the question was not innocent and was meant for Paris, not Aeneas.

"Yes, madam, I am," said Aeneas. His dark hair shone like a raven's wing as he dipped his head politely, catching glints of the torchlight. "I have the privilege to be married to Creusa, the daughter of King Priam."

Mother raised her eyebrows. "My, my. The son-in-law of the king himself! But isn't—wasn't—there a prophecy about your descendants ruling Troy, and so—"

"Enough, enough prophecies!" Paris waved his arm in dismissal. "They take away our appetites, our appetites for this fine food, and make us rude guests."

So far I had not really looked at him; because he was so close beside me, I could not see him unless I turned my head completely around. I started to do so and caught Mother staring at me.

"And are you married, Paris?" she persisted.

"No, I am not," he said. "But I pray daily to Aphrodite, that she will send me a wife of her choosing."

Castor burst out in a laugh that made him spray wine out of his mouth all over the table. He smeared it around, attempting to clean it up. "Oh, oh, my boy, you have quite a sense of humor."

"He's so used to saying it, I think he's come to believe it," said Aeneas. "He just keeps repeating it whenever his family urges him to marry."

"He isn't old enough," said Menelaus. I realized those were the first words he had spoken during the meal. "He is intelligent enough to know that."

"How old *are* you, Paris?" Mother asked, with that artificial brightness. Why had she taken a dislike to him?

"Sixteen," he said.

Sixteen! Nine years younger than I!

"A mere lad," said Agamemnon. "But then, that's what cowherds usually are—lads."

"He isn't a cowherd!" I said.

"Oh, but I *was* a cowherd, and a very good one, too," said Paris quickly. "Those were dreamy days, there in the mountains—the cedars with their blue and purple shadows, the south wind in the trees, the waterfalls and meadows of flowers—yes, memories I cherish, those days with my cattle."

"Is that Zeus mountain very high?" asked Hermione.

"Yes, very high indeed, and big, wide, with lots of little mountains around it. Mind you, it's not as high as Mount Olympus, which no man can climb, but it's high enough to get foggy and cold and let you lose your way."

Just then there was a flourish and a special course was announced. One of the slaves, a pretty girl, gestured toward a cauldron being wheeled in and said, "The famous black broth of Sparta!" A slave behind her set out bowls for each of us.

The black broth of Sparta: supposedly it could be stomached only by true Spartans.

I had grown up drinking it, and did not find it distasteful, although even I preferred clear almond broth. The blackness of the broth came from swine's blood; its pungent taste from the vinegar and salt mixed with it. The slave ladled some into my bowl and sprinkled it with goat cheese. The characteristic odor of the soup, reminiscent of standing downwind from a fresh sacrifice, wafted up from the bowls.

When Paris and Aeneas were served, all eyes fastened on them. They both smiled, but after the first sip Aeneas looked to be in pain. He held the liquid in his mouth and had to command his throat to open and accept it. Then it was Paris's turn. He turned the bowl up to his mouth and I could hear him gulping it down. Then I saw the empty bowl set back on the table. He had swallowed it all in only one gulp.

"Ah," he said. "Justly famous."

I knew he must have swallowed it so swiftly to avoid savoring and actually tasting it.

Mother motioned to the server. "More for Prince Paris," she said, and his bowl was refilled.

"Your kindness is striking," said Paris. He picked up the bowl and held it in his fingers. "And what of the others?" he asked. No one else had a second helping. But it would not have mattered; we were inured to it.

"I'll have some," said Agamemnon, holding out his bowl.

There was no help for it, and Paris drank his down. I could sense his throat trying to close, but he mastered it.

"Bravo! Bravo!" said Castor. "And he didn't even grimace."

"I suppose you must be used to rough fare, having grown up in that cowherd's hut," said Mother. "This is probably dainty to you."

"No, madam," said Paris. "Hardly dainty, but distinctive. And in the hut of my foster father we ate well enough, simple food, but simple is best—closest to that which the gods give us."

"So you are most at home in huts?" Mother could not have sounded more puzzled and disapproving.

"I can be at home anywhere," said Paris. "Even in a foreign place like Sparta. Fortunate, isn't it? The world is my home."

"Yes, that is fortunate," said Menelaus. "That means you can never be an exile."

A noise near the hearth behind us caught our attention. I turned, just as Menelaus said, "Here are the dancers! Let us leave this table."

Ten lithe boys, wearing only short tunics, stood in line, holding balls in each hand. Their leader bowed to us and explained their dance; they came from Crete. At the mention of Crete, Menelaus sighed. Soon he would be sailing there.

At a hand clap, the dancers began to weave and move swiftly in a pattern that seemed very intricate to me, coming together in a circle, then falling back, then exchanging places in an elaborate design. Just when it seemed most confusing and complicated, they began tossing balls to one another, catching them as they moved, so the dance was a swirl of movement and color. Their skill at throwing and catching while moving was breathtaking.

We stood around them in our own circle, and I was on the side opposite from Paris. I could only glimpse him through the movement; in the dull light he was almost hidden.

The dancers pranced out of the hall and the singers filed in, clutching their lyres. Bowing, they looked around and addressed us all, saying the usual things about not being worthy, and so on. Menelaus waved his arm impatiently for them to get on with it. This was the part of a ceremonial feast where everyone was ready to depart but custom demanded extensive entertainment, and the higher-ranking the guests, the more extensive.

The singers stood straight as the columns in the hall, holding their lyres out and closing their eyes. One by one they sang, sweet songs of dawn and dusk and the beauty of the stars. Paris had crept closer to me; now only Hermione was between us. I saw her pull on Paris's hand and point to a lyre.

"That's made of a tortoiseshell!" she murmured.

"Yes, indeed," said Paris brightly.

"That's wrong!" said Hermione, her voice too loud. "They shouldn't kill them for that!"

Paris bent down and made a "quiet" signal to her, but she went on. "I have them for pets. People shouldn't kill them for their shells!"

"Not even for sweet music?" said Paris.

"Not even!"

Paris now knelt on one knee. "And where do you keep these pets?" he asked. "Will you show them to me?"

"They're in a secret place," said Hermione.

"But will you show me? I am a special visitor."

"Yes . . . they're only secret from the singers, because I don't want any of them to steal my pets!"

"Tomorrow, then? Do you promise?"

"Yes," she said, bowing her head and feeling very important. "But you must meet me here, at midday, and I'll take you."

"May I come, too?" I asked her. I did not know about these secret tortoises.

"No," she said. "You're friends with the singers, you might tell them."

"I'm not friends with them. I've never met them before."

"Oh, let her come," said Paris. "I promise she will not tell anyone about them."

"How do you know that?" said Hermione. "You aren't her!"

Yes, I am, his mouth soundlessly said.

"All right," said Hermione. "If you really want her to . . ."

The singers were finishing up, at long last, and we could end the evening. The foreign guests each had to make a little speech, and so did Father and Menelaus and I. I merely said, politely, I was thankful that the gods had sent them to us.

❊ XXIII ❊

The next morning I watched Menelaus standing listlessly while his attendant helped him dress, bringing out several tunics and mantles before he selected one. He set others aside to take with him to Crete.

"Do you not wish to go to Crete because you dislike traveling by water, or because the death of your grandfather saddens you?" I asked.

"Both," he said.

"Then you can be happy that he reached the end of his life quietly," I said. "You know that common wisdom—until the last day of life, we can count no man fortunate."

"Yes, I know. Fortunes reverse themselves overnight. Thus we are always in a race to the grave, to get there unscathed."

From outside, the spring noises of birdsong and playing children intruded into the chamber. "Oh, let us not be so gloomy. Life is more than that. They also say that our best revenge against death is to live each day and extract its joys to the full."

"Like stepping on a grape?" Menelaus laughed. "My dear wife, when did you become such a philosopher?"

Since Paris came. I seek to explain it all to myself, to set it in ways I can grasp . . . I smiled back at him and shrugged.

Menelaus would be busy that day, preparing for his journey. His usual attendants came in, as well as women. One of them—that pretty girl I had noticed presenting the black broth—brought in a small locking box that she claimed was waterproof.

"For the voyage," she said, smiling.

I was wondering why a kitchen slave was now bringing personal items, when I received a message from Mother, requesting that I come to her chambers.

I found her at her loom, surrounded by skeins of dyed wool. She had several wheeled baskets arrayed around her, each holding different colors; I saw light blue, pale pink, bright red, yellow, and a startling deep purple, made from the type of shellfish Gelanor had collected. I thought of the live ones we had brought back to Menelaus; by the time he had seen them, they had died. I bent down and picked up one of the balls of yarn, this one a green as dark as cypress.

"What story are you telling?" I asked her.

"The unfinished story of our house," she said. Her face, fuller with the years, was not soft today. Its lines and planes seemed etched.

"Where have you got to?" I moved beside her, trying to see the pattern.

"As far as I dare," she said. She looked around to be sure we were alone. "And you have gone as far as you dare, if you do not wish to destroy the tapestry of our family!"

My first thought was, She knows! My second was, But there is nothing to know, it is all in my mind and heart. No one can see into that. My third was, How can I answer this? I gave the predictable, giveaway reply: "I don't know what you are talking about."

She got off her stool beside the loom. "Oh, please, Helen. You are talking to me. Leda. Leda. I say Leda, not Mother. You understand."

Yes, I understood. Leda, the name forever linked to the Swan. I nodded. I was exposed. At least it was by my mother, by someone who had faced something similar, and before any damage had been done. Nothing had been done! I assured myself.

"Zeus is different," she said. "A husband will tolerate Zeus. It cannot be helped. But . . . ." she blushed. "Oh, to think I must discuss such things with my daughter!"

"Mother . . ."

"Even with Zeus, it was not easy," she said. "Things were never the same again with your fa—with Tyndareus. They try to forget, they try to overlook it, but how can they? Could you overlook such an . . . excursion . . . by them?"

"I don't know," I admitted. Women were expected to, I knew that.

"But this Paris! A child, and the child of foreigners, possible enemies. Oh, I can see how he might dazzle one's eyes—but Helen! Think!"

I cannot think, thanks to Aphrodite, I thought. I can only feel. I smiled feebly at her.

"I know things have not been . . . passionate with Menelaus. In the past Aphrodite was angered at Tyndareus; perhaps she is taking revenge on him through you. Such is the behavior of the gods. But I beg you, sacrifice to her, seek her favor. She will listen to your request."

No, the cruel goddess only listens to her own desires, I thought. For some unknown reason she has come down to me and enveloped me. She fulfills her secret reason, I suffer. Such sweet suffering! I sighed, and Mother looked sharply at me.

"Oh, Helen!" she said. "Do not cast yourself away on this . . . boy!"

I was tempted to say, *At least he's human, and not a swan!* But I held my tongue. Instead I embraced her, clasping her close to me. "Mother," I whispered, "it is both a pity and a joy that we are so much alike."

"Helen, no . . ." she murmured against my neck.

"Would you take it back?" I asked her. "That is the only real question."

"Yes! Yes, I would! It changed too many things."

"Then you would make me not to be." I was stunned. If that would truly be Mother's choice, then I had been cast away, too, like Paris.

Thus Paris had already caused me to sever a deep link to my family, in my own mind. So far it had not happened outside that realm of the mind, my sad farewell to my mother. Outwardly everything was preserved like figs floating in honey; inwardly the substance was altered, translated into something utterly different.

I waited in the shadows of the colonnade around the forecourt. The shadows were short: it was noon. I nervously fingered my bracelets, distressed about what Mother had said.

Hermione came strolling up, hand in hand with her favorite attendant, Nysa. As always, the sight of her buoyed my spirits. Her long hair spilling out of the little fillet she always wore, her ready smile, touched me. Daughter of my heart. Can any daughter truly know what she means to her mother?

Perhaps I had been hasty about Mother; perhaps she would not really have forgone the encounter and erased me. But why had she said it? If it was to quash my feelings for Paris—

"Paris!" Hermione squealed, much more delighted than she had been at seeing me.

But he was closer to her own age . . . a boy! Mother called him a boy!

"Hello, little friend!" Paris was kneeling in front of Hermione, his golden head bent. "I am eager to see these creatures that you hold so dear," he said.

"Hello, Paris," I said. Without standing, he raised his head and looked at me. Our eyes locked together. His were a deep amber, the color of a certain kind of brown honey that glows if held up to the sun.

"We are to go on an adventure together," he said, rising to his feet.

"Yes." I took a deep breath. "Hermione will lead us."

Hermione must be with us. If we fled—why was I thinking of this?—she must come with us.

Flee. Leave Sparta and flee? But I was the queen. The queen did not flee. Why was I even thinking of this? He had not asked me to flee.

But what else can happen? I thought. He cannot stay on here as a guest.

No, no, it is impossible! I shook my head.

"Mother, you look possessed!" Hermione giggled. "You are shaking and jumping when there is no reason."

Possessed. Yes, I was possessed.

Paris laughed, a golden laugh. "Come, I am eager to see your pets." He steered her away, so that she was looking down the path, before he turned back to look at me.

The way through the palace woods quickly seemed as secret as the hidden pen itself. Tall trees closed overhead, their tops whispering. Early spring flowers poked up through the forest floor, white against the shade, where they would bloom and fade unseen. I let Paris and Hermione go far ahead of me; I wanted them to get to know one another. I prayed that she liked him.

But why? Helen, why? It can have no purpose. Yet the fearsome roar of Aphrodite in my soul was as loud as . . . as loud as a waterfall I heard off to one side of the path.

I slowed my steps and turned to see where it might be. The sweet sound of flowing water always drew me. There seemed to be a grotto of some sort in the dim light ahead. Strange I had never discovered it in all my wanderings.

A breeze was murmuring with cool breath from that direction as I approached. I saw a gushing spring tumbling over rocks to empty into a deep oval pool, where its ripples spread out to stony edges. All was green, black, and white—green plants, black pool, white spray. And then, movement: the flash of human flesh.

Lovers were hidden here! I almost laughed at my own shock. Was I still so innocent? If I moved, they would surely see me and freeze. Feeling benevolent, I did not wish to disturb them. I was content to wait to make my escape. I sat down and held my breath. My only concern was that the path to Hermione's pets might branch off and I would not know which to choose. Oh, let these lovers be quick about it! I thought, then chastised myself for being so uncharitable. Their voices drifted over to me, amplified by the pool.

"I feared you would be cross," the woman was saying. There followed a silence.

Then, "No, I am happy. Happy beyond my telling. The gods smile on me at last, if they grant me a son." That voice—it was that of Menelaus!

"Or perhaps two. I think there may be two in my womb." I did not know this voice—or did I?

"That is too much to hope for! I am content with one." Oh, it *was* Menelaus! No mistake.

I saw a stirring across the pool; bushes moved and I glimpsed an arm, a back. I could not think. I backed away, hoping they would not see me. But the bushes had closed over them again.

I stumbled back onto the path, running now to catch up. Menelaus. Menelaus and some woman. Who? It must be a palace servant, a slave girl. That girl who lingered at the feast, who brought Menelaus the locking box for his sea-journey.

Instead of horror, or betrayal, or lamenting, *How could he? Why?*, my first feeling was a rush of relief. I was free. Menelaus and his slave girl had set me free. Had Aphrodite arranged that as well? How well the goddess knows everything about us!

I ran and ran and eventually caught up with Paris and Hermione. I stopped and caught my breath.

"How you run!" said Paris, looking at me. "Your tunic flying out behind you, white against the deep shade of the forest—you could be a wood nymph."

"Mother was a runner," said Hermione. "When she was *young,*" she added.

"And how long ago was that?" asked Paris, winking. "A long time?"

"Before my wedding, when I was fifteen, I raced—and won. But once I married . . ." I shrugged.

"You could still beat them all," said Paris.

"I will never know," I said. We continued on the path. Menelaus! I could not cast the image from my mind. Everything I knew, everything I assumed about him, had been turned into disarray.

Then, suddenly, I was angry with him. Why must he add this complication? Then, just as suddenly, I started to laugh, and Paris and Hermione turned around. I had been overtaken with wild love, longing, desire for a foreign prince, and I blamed Menelaus for making things difficult?

Had any other queens fallen into a mad passion for a stranger? I could not think of any; but then, I was not thinking well. Phaedra's passion for her stepson Hippolytus—also brought about by cruel Aphrodite—was within her own family. I could think of no other examples of what might befall us. Poor Phaedra killed herself, and Hippolytus was killed by Poseidon. But I would not kill myself, nor would Paris commit suicide. Why should we?

"Hurry up!" Hermione was gesturing. "And stop that silly laughing, Mother! If you don't stop, I won't let you see them!"

"Yes, my dear." I joined them on the path. "My daughter, you have ventured far from the palace."

"I wanted a secret place," she said. "And my uncles hunt throughout the forest, so I had to find a place where they would not come. A place where no game could be. It's a stony place, a place only tortoises would like."

"Yes, they do like stony places," said Paris. "There are many of them around Troy."

"Near the sacred mountain of Parnassus there are many large ones, and they are all sacred to Pan," said Hermione solemnly. She seemed so wise and old. Oh, my child . . . but are you old and wise enough to survive what must come? I was thankful she was as clever and mature as she was, beyond her years. But even so . . .

"We must make an excursion there someday," said Paris. "I myself am longing to see this famous Parnassus." He added softly, "There are so many things I wish to see. I think I could live forever and not be content, as there would still be things unseen before me."

"Here we are," cried Hermione. We rounded a bend in the path and came to an improvised pen made of branches and logs. She leaned over the edge and her voice rose in happy excitement. "Oh, oh! You have been naughty!" She climbed over the fence and disappeared from our sight. But Paris and I sought each other, drinking in one another's image. His face filled my eyes, my soul, my mind. I could not take my eyes from him. He was looking back at me, silent. Already we did not need words.

Hermione's head popped up. "Here he is, my prize one!" She was clutching a large tortoise with a scarred shell. "His name is Warrior!"

I looked at the creature. When faced head-on he looked disgruntled. His beady black eyes, set far apart, stared straight ahead with Olympian disdain. *It is all the same to me, what you do,* his expression implied. I wondered fleetingly whether a god inhabited him. The gods are all like that, I thought. They look at us, but they are never moved.

"And why do you call him Warrior?" asked Paris. He seemed genuinely, infectiously, interested.

"He battles the others," said Hermione. "They hit each other like rams, and try to turn each other over. He just keeps on and on; he hammers away and always wins."

"Perhaps you should have named him Agamemnon, after your uncle," I said.

"Or Achilles," said Paris. "That youngster—oh, he cannot be any older than I—who has already got such a reputation for fighting."

"How have you ever heard of Achilles?" Could he mean that aggressive child who had come with Patroclus and the other suitors?

"Oh, in Troy they are much preoccupied with noble deeds at arms," he said. "It is a passion in Troy. And this Achilles has made a name for himself, even reaching across the sea."

"For what, I cannot imagine," I said. "He was a horrid child."

"Horrid children make the best warriors," he said. "That is why I shall never make a great one. I was not horrid enough." He laughed, and all the joy of a summer noontide was in it. Was I in love with him, or with his glad grace, his bask in the sunlit side of life? There are such people, rare people who promise to open the portals of secret joy to us.

"Here are more," she said. "Come and look!" We leaned over the side of the pen and saw a carpet of moving creatures. They were all different sizes—some as small as an oil lamp, others large as a discus. They all wore a pattern of yellow and black, but no two bore the same markings.

"Why do you like them so?" asked Paris. "I must confess, I never thought about them one way or another." He climbed over the fence easily and bent down to stroke the head of a venerable-looking one.

"I don't know," Hermione said. "I found one in the garden and he was so . . . I don't know, calming. I could sit and look at him for a long time. He seemed so . . . wise. Like nothing could ever bother him or upset him. I want to be like that!"

I longed to ask, *What upsets you or bothers you?* But Paris said, "We all wish to be like that." Perhaps we must not examine too closely, look too hard, at another. Even at our own child.

"Even grown-ups?" asked Hermione.

"Yes. Especially grown-ups," Paris assured her.

Hermione gathered leaves and flowers for the tortoises, putting them in a big heap. The creatures moved slowly over to them and began eating, their leathery jaws clamping down on the greenery. It was very hard not to laugh. Finally I said, "I am sorry, my dear, but I do find these animals amusing."

Hermione stroked one's back. "I'll never let them use you for a lyre!" she promised it.

The way back was lazy; we strolled along. I kept thinking of Menelaus and the slave girl, wondering how long this had gone on. My anger and amusement had drained away, and only curiosity remained. Aphrodite must have led him into it, as she had me. Perhaps it was her delayed punishment of Father for her grudge against him. We would never know; we could only accept. We had no power to do otherwise.

As Hermione walked along, head held high, I said, "Good, Hermione, that is the way queens walk. Isn't it, Paris?"

He cocked his head. "My mother doesn't have so much spring in her step," he said. "Of course, she's older. *Much* older. She's had nineteen children, sixteen who live."

Just the thought of it was head-spinning. "Nineteen!" How did Paris feel about his mother and father, truly, knowing they had put him out to die? How could he overlook that, forgive it, forget it? I never could have. I had been hurt by Mother even hinting at renouncing her encounter with Zeus, which she may not even have meant.

"Of course, whether Hermione is a queen or not depends on whether she marries a king," said Paris. "If she marries a . . . a tortoise-keeper . . ."—Hermione giggled at this—"then she'll only be Queen of the Pen."

"Oh, she'll be queen," I said. "In Sparta it is the woman who holds the title. Her husband becomes king through her." As I made Menelaus king. Well, my slave girl, you need not think that your child will ever follow Menelaus onto the throne, as he has no power to pass it on, I thought.

"Interesting," said Paris. "Unusual."

On our way back into the palace, we passed the Hermione plane tree. It had grown tall enough to give good shade now; its leaves were just opening, and it would spread out in the summer sun. But would I be there to sit in that shade?

The palace looked the same, but suddenly I was a visitor, joining Paris, seeing all through his eyes. This colonnade . . . these stout gates . . . the way the shadows of the pillars stretched out across the courtyard . . . all known to me since my earliest days, now newly foreign.

Preparations for Menelaus's journey to Crete were complete. Tonight marked the end of the ninth day since Paris's and Aeneas's arrival, and now no custom need hold Menelaus here.

Menelaus. The slave girl. I could not get the image of them from my mind, but it was an image bereft of any pain. Menelaus was not the faithful spouse I had supposed. Perhaps he, too, was tired of waiting for Aphrodite to anoint our union. I could not blame him.

The curtain was pushed aside and Menelaus stepped in. He was dirty and sweat-stained, and he quickly peeled off his tunic and kicked off his sandals, heading for the bathhouse.

I did not wish to talk to him, lest I betray what I knew, what I had seen. I merely nodded as he hurried through. As soon as he was gone, I summoned my own attendants and had myself dressed for the supper that I knew would be the last. Even so, I was surprisingly careless of my attire. Anything would do. The only thing I paid attention to was my jewelry. It seemed oddly important that I wear my favorites—my chunk-amber necklace, my gold cuff bracelets with the hunting scenes, my hanging drop earrings, delicately fashioned of gold filigree.

The sun vanished and deep blue twilight stole into all the chambers like a fog, until the yellow of oil lamps banished it. We gathered around a smaller table on one side of the megaron; the dark rest of the hall gaped like a cave around us. No singers this time, no dancers. Just the few of us—Father, Mother, my brothers, Menelaus, Paris, and Aeneas.

"What message will you take back to Troy?" Menelaus asked Paris.

Paris shrugged. "I received different ones from you and your brother," he said. "But neither of you seem inclined to let us speak to Hesione, and my father will be unhappy about that." He raised his heavy gold cup and studied it as if its decorations held something of great import.

"Is that truly why you came?" asked Menelaus.

"Why else should we have come?" Paris sounded surprised.

"My brother was of the opinion that you were spies," Menelaus said.

Paris and Aeneas both laughed. "As if we would come in person for that!" they said, almost in unison. "As you must know, there are plenty of spies about, experienced ones, and we need not be so obvious."

"Ah! But no spy would have an invitation to our private table here," said Menelaus.

I wished he would hush. He sounded so heavy-handed, so obvious. For the first time I saw the familial resemblance between him and Agamemnon.

"There may be less revealing talk here than at a mess hall or a ship," said Aeneas. "Royal tables are not known for divulging information."

"I have admitted you to my palace," Menelaus said. "I have let you see what no other spy would see."

Oh, let him stop!

"You have dined with my wife, an honor sought by many," he continued. "You have looked upon her famous face."

"You make me sound like a prize sow," I said. I was angry at him, angry at his clumsy threats and brags—and now he was dragging me into it. "Here!" I leaned over the table, looking directly into the face of Aeneas. I could not do so to Paris, as he was seated right beside me. "Look your fill!"

Aeneas coughed and drew back, embarrassed, as any polite person would.

"Helen!" said Mother.

I sat back down and glared at her.

Menelaus cleared his throat and raised his goblet. "I merely meant that I have taken you into the bosom of my family," he said.

"Yes," said Paris. He had spilled a bit of his wine on the table and was drawing patterns with it, like a child. "Yes." Then I looked down at what he had done: written *Paris loves Helen* in the wine, bright against the table.

My heart stopped. What if someone saw? I moved my left hand up and smeared it, but I saw Mother looking. At the same time I was overwhelmed by his daring.

Then out of the corner of my eye I saw my wine cup—the special one, the one Menelaus had given me as a wedding gift—move as Paris slid it over to himself and took a slow sip, placing his lips exactly where mine had been. I was shocked into frozen stillness, holding myself rigid, searching the faces and eyes of the others for a response.

"We shall be returning to Troy forthwith," said Aeneas quickly. He had seen. "Our ship is waiting at Gytheum."

"Not near Mycenae?" asked Menelaus. "I thought you landed there."

"We did," said Paris. "But our men have brought the ship around the Peloponnese so it is close and we do not have to track back to Mycenae."

"I leave from Gytheum myself," said Menelaus. "In fact—it is time. Forgive me, but I must take my leave shortly."

He had waited the exact nine days, and not an hour longer. I suddenly hated his preciseness.

He drank his last wine, spoke some farewell words, then indicated that we must all leave the table along with him.

I turned to speak a formal parting to Paris and saw his lips forming the silent words, *The sacred snake.* I closed my eyes to show I had received the message: I must meet him at the altar of the sacred household snake.

In the meantime I must tread stately steps and follow Menelaus to his chamber to wish him farewell. He strode off quickly, leaving me behind.

I followed, slowly. It was quiet now, so quiet, in the palace.

I entered his chambers, which were strangely darkened, although one or two lamps burned in the far corner. But I heard a low murmur of voices coming from the connecting chamber. I stole over to the door and listened. I dared not look in and betray my presence. I knew well enough what it was. Perhaps I merely wanted to confirm what I had seen earlier in the day, vindicate my own decision.

For a moment the voices stopped and that meant the people were kissing and caressing. No ordinary conversation stops in midsentence—only the murmurs of lovers.

Then they resumed. *Oh, I hate to let you go . . . Take care upon the high seas, have you sacrificed to Poseidon? . . . No, it is you who must take care, you carry my son . . .*

I peeked around the doorframe and saw them—Menelaus and that woman, that slave woman who had brought him the decorated locking box. And hers was the same voice I had heard near the waterfall.

I stepped into the room. I said nothing, but I let the curtain fall behind me, and its sound made them jump. Two startled faces turned toward me. Menelaus pushed the woman—did she have a name?—away.

"Helen!" he gasped. He looked horrified; she looked annoyed. "It is not what it seems," he blurted out.

Still I said nothing.

"I swear, she means nothing to me—"

Poor, foolish Menelaus. What a cruel, stupid thing to say in front of her. For a moment I sided with her. But in truth, I still felt nothing.

The woman shrank back, whispering, "How could you?" and stole away, sobbing, running for the door at the far end of the chamber. Menelaus did not follow, or pay any attention.

Instead, he turned directly to me, holding out his arms. "Oh, my dearest Helen, please, please—this means nothing—I beg you, forgive me—oh, please . . ."

I stood there like one of the pillars in the courtyard. How could I go to his arms when I myself had transgressed already in a much greater way? I loved Paris, was mad for him, although we had barely touched. Menelaus had lain down with this woman, but his loyalty was uncompromised. Who was the greater adulterer? And if I embraced Menelaus and "forgave" him, what would he think later of my hypocrisy?

"Oh, Helen, please—oh, do not fix that stony look upon me—I will make it all up—I will sell her, send her away—I care not, nothing matters but you . . ."

Still I could not speak, but out of honesty, not calculation. It only served to spur him on to higher emotion.

"I esteem you above all things. Nothing—not even the gods, may they forgive me—means more to me. I will give you my life . . ." He continued holding out his arms.

I should have gone into them. But I could not, and call myself honest. And above all, I had to be honest to myself. "Menelaus, you must depart. The ships await. You must go." I turned away. I could do nothing else.

"Let the ships wait!" he cried. "My grandfather is dead already." Now his obedience to rituals vanished.

"Your brother Agamemnon is sailing with you. You cannot disrupt ceremony and protocol for a . . . personal matter. Go with the blessings of the gods. And mine." I smiled wanly at him, then turned away.

Oh, let him not follow me! Let him depart! I fled beyond our chambers and back out into the courtyard to elude him. But there were no footsteps behind me.

He, too, was relieved to defer all this.

Neither of us realized it would be deferred for nigh on twenty years, and that we would meet again only at Troy, with the fires of destruction blazing around us.

✦ XXIV ✦

I waited a long time in the courtyard, standing beside a flowering tree. I heard the retainers come for Menelaus, heard him depart. I thought I heard him hesitate, looking for me. But then he was gone, and the sounds faded away as the men marched out of the gates.

The sanctuary of the sacred snake . . . I was free to go there now. No one could question my movements or behavior. I passed through the courtyard, and into the farther reaches of the palace until I came to the little shrine. It was empty.

I was relieved. I so badly needed to sit and think. And if I were to leave, I needed to tell the household guardian snake why, and why he could not come with me.

How could I leave all this? It was part of me, my own self. I sank down on the stone bench and waited. A flickering votive light illuminated the altar. The honey cake and the saucer of milk were there, but there was no sign of the snake.

I felt a great calmness stealing over me. It was done—whatever happened, it was done. How odd, to say that something that had not yet come about was done. Yet I felt that truth deep inside me. Perhaps it had already been done before I was born.

A small movement, a twitch. The snake was coming. He glided out from behind the altar and raised his head, looking about him.

I was overcome with a love for him. He had pledged himself to me, and my family, leaving his life at Epidaurus behind. As I must leave this life behind. The snake would understand. I bent down and told him about it. He looked at me and flicked his tongue out. He had given me his blessing.

"How can I ever say what I love best about you?" Paris was standing at the far corner of the little chamber. "Perhaps it is that you treat all creatures about you as worthy."

I stood up, flew into his arms. For a moment there was nothing but frantic embracing and kissing. I reveled in the feel of his arms, in his shoulders, his flesh.

At length he pulled away, held me at arm's length to keep me from burrowing in his arms. "Helen," he said. "What shall we do?" He paused. "It is all up to you. I will take you with me to Troy, but it is you who will leave all this behind. For you it is loss, for me everything is gain. Therefore I cannot make the decision."

Odd how, although we had never spoken directly of it, we both knew this was the only choice. Stay and part, or flee and be together.

"I cannot let you go!" I cried, clinging to him. No, let the whole earth perish, let the palace of Sparta crumble to dust, but do not let Paris live his life out of my sight.

"But what of Hermione?" he asked. "You are a mother. You are another man's wife, yet I have managed to set that aside in my mind. Wives can be replaced; mothers cannot. Believe me, I know."

"We'll take Hermione with us!" I said. Yes, let that be the answer!

"But you said that she is to be the next queen of Sparta," said Paris. He was more levelheaded—or feeling more guilty—than I. "How can you deprive Sparta of that?"

"We'll ask her!" I said. "Let her decide."

"Helen," he said slowly, turning me around and looking at me. Those eyes—those golden eyes, honey-deep even in the lamplight. "She is nine years old. Can you force her to make such a decision? Any child of that age will decide to go with her mother. It does not mean that is what she would choose later."

"But—"

"You cannot lay such a burden on her shoulders, a burden she will question for the rest of her life."

"So we should just steal away? Leave her with no farewell?"

"A farewell, yes. But do not ask her to make a decision. She will hate you for it later."

"How can I leave my child?" I cried.

"Because you love her, and would not expose her to danger," said Paris. "And you love Sparta, and will not leave it bereft of a queen."

"But she will not know that! She will not understand."

"In time, she will." He clasped me to him. "In time, she will. Just as I did about the actions of my mother and father."

But had he truly? They had left him out to die!

"Helen," he said. "If we are to leave, we must do it now. When Menelaus discovers it, there will be . . . turmoil. We should leave as quickly as possible after him, to get the greatest head start. Everything is at the ready. It must be tonight."

"No! Not tonight! Not on the heels of Menelaus!"

"Yes, on his heels . . . but we will sail in a different direction."

O all the gods! Tonight, while Mother and Father slept, and my brothers, and Hermione—!

"Whatever it is, it is always too soon," said Paris. "We are never ready."

I looked at him in wonder. "You are only sixteen. How can you know that?"

"My sixteen years have been filled with unexpected turns and reversals," he said. "I have been jolted out of one comfortable life already," he said. "It was painful. But that gives me more experience in this than you."

"You left a family but not a kingdom," I said. "Nor did you leave a wife."

"I left a way of life, a belief that I was one man when in fact I was another," he said. "And true, I did not leave a wife, but a companion of the mountains, a woman who loved me. But she did not belong in the palace. Helen, sometimes there are hard choices to be made. I know many people try to keep both ways, but sometimes you cannot. Is it me, or Menelaus? It is that simple. I cannot claim your loyalty. That belongs to him. I can only appeal to whatever brought us together. Aphrodite and her magic—or her poison."

The snake was gliding out across the floor, and he reached our ankles. He twined himself about them, binding them together. I felt his cool smoothness linking us.

"The sacred snake has spoken," I said. "He indicates that ours is the true union."

"I knew that," said Paris. "I only wanted you to realize it as well."

* * *

We parted; he to rouse Aeneas for our escape, me to say my private farewells. If this were an orderly departure, we would have been taken by chariot down to Gytheum with a royal escort in broad daylight, after a ceremonial leave-taking. As it was, we would have to steal the chariots in the dead of night; we would have to use the speed of the chariots to arrive in Gytheum by dawn and sail away. No leisurely walking this time; we could not afford that.

How could they get the chariots and the horses without alerting the guards? I shuddered. I must leave that to them. If they were caught . . . of course it would be they accused of theft and dishonesty, they who must bear the punishment.

"Don't fail!" I whispered to Paris, gripping his arm. "We cannot afford to fail. We have only this one chance."

"It will be difficult," he said. "Aeneas and I do not even know the layout of the royal stables and chariot house. And we cannot make any noise."

"Do not think of the difficulties," I said. "Do not, for an instant, think of them, or you will be undone. Now go, my love. Think only of its being done, and what lies before us." I turned away, but not before I pointed in the direction he must go. I watched him steal away, a shadow in the moonlight.

The moonlight. Was that a help or a hindrance? It meant we would not stumble about and did not need to light torches. It also meant that our movements would be visible as we descended the hill and onto the roadway beside the river. It meant that any Spartan who was sleepless and watching out his window would be able to tell the searchers what direction we had traveled.

The moon, round and dazzling, hung in the middle of the sky like a white torch. Shadows were short; everything was bathed in an eerie cold light, making things that were soft and rounded by sunlight sharp and hard. It was impossible, of course, but things actually seemed clearer than in daylight.

The palace . . . every flagstone, every carving on the doors, every jutting corner of the roof was burned into my consciousness. Now I paced it, looking my last at it. I wanted to touch each post, each doorknob, and bid farewell.

All was hushed. All was holding its breath. I looked at the entrance of the great building.

You will return. And in moonlight.

Where had those words come from, whispering in my mind? The snakes of Asclepius . . . was that another of their gifts? Could I discern the broad outlines of the future? Oh, let it not be so. It would be a curse rather than a gift.

And yet the overwhelming feeling remained. I would return here, walk these paths again. Beyond that, nothing. No knowledge.

Never mind! I told myself. Those are phantoms, spirits of the future. To-night there is work to do, action to take.

I glided—as silently as one of the snakes—into the rooms of my mother and father. They slept soundly. The guards outside slept as well, and I did not wake them. The reflected moonlight showed them well enough, breathing evenly and lying calmly upon their beds, the thick fleeces spread over them for the still-cold night.

I bent over them. I looked at them, then shut my eyes to call up their images, then looked again to fix them in my mind.

I longed to lean over and kiss them, but I feared to wake them. My heart ached. "Farewell, Mother and Father," I bade them silently. "Do not condemn me, do not hate me."

I turned away; I could bear to stay no longer. I made my way into the chamber of Hermione. I meant to say my silent goodbye, but when I saw her, I knew I could not leave her.

I leaned over her, looking at her sleeping peacefully, a slight smile on her lips. She was so lovely; she was so much a part of me, and my days with her were not finished.

I touched her shoulder. "Hermione," I whispered.

Slowly she opened her eyes and looked at me. "Oh . . . Mother," she murmured.

"Hermione," I said, speaking in as quiet a voice as I could, "would you like to go on an adventure?"

She sighed and wiggled around in the bed. "I don't know . . . what?" She was still half asleep.

"Paris and I are going to visit his home. It's far away, across the seas, in a place called Troy."

She struggled to sit up, but failed. She was still drowsy. "How long will you be gone?"

"I—we don't know," I said. "That's the thing about adventures—when you go, you do not know how long it will take. Usually it takes longer than you expect."

"Oh," she said. "No, I don't think I want to go."

No! She couldn't say that. "But Hermione, I want you with me."

She shook her head stubbornly. "No, no. I don't want to leave. I have my friends and my tortoises that I have to take care of and I don't really want to see Troy. I don't care about Troy." She smiled and stretched her arms over her head.

"But Hermione—I will miss you so much. I need you to come with me."

"But what of Father?" she asked. "Is he coming, too?"

"No," I said.

"Oh, well, then. You'll be back before long." She giggled.

No, I wanted to say. *No, I won't.* But I could not. "Oh, Hermione. Please come."

"Oh, let me think about it. Why are you waking me up to ask me?"

"Because I must leave now."

"In the dark?"

"Yes. It has to do with the ship . . ."

She flung her arms around me. "I can't go now, not in the middle of the night. It's dark. I don't want to."

"But there's a full moon. We can see very well."

"Mother, I don't want to go on your adventure," she said. "Full moon or no." Her voice was firm.

"Hold me, then," I said, trying to keep my voice steady and the tears contained within my eyes. I could not tell her anything further. I could not explain. I could only say goodbye, and clasp her to me one last time. Yet surely it was not the last time.

No. You will gaze on her again, hold her to you. But she will be a grown woman, older than you are now.

The vision of the future, the mystery I had been granted. A blessing, then, a blessing. I would hold her again! That was all I needed, all I asked to know.

"Goodbye, my love," I whispered, pressing my cheek up against hers.

"Oh, Mother . . . don't be so serious . . ." She lay back down and was instantly asleep.

Sobbing, I left the chamber. I leaned against one of the moonlit columns until the scene before me stopped swimming in my tears and my vision cleared.

Aphrodite must have stolen down between the columns, because I could hear her gentle urges and whispers.

What else do you need to know? Your daughter will be waiting . . . you will not lose her . . . now you may seek your destiny with Paris . . .

Cruel goddess! I shot back at her. To you and the undying gods, time is nothing. But to us, us mortals, it is everything. Twenty years is a long time to us, ten, all those years that mean nothing to you. We change; Hermione long hence will not be the little girl snuggling, drowsy and warm, in her bed, flinging her arms around me, talking of tortoises. But all that is of no matter to you!

No, it isn't, she admitted; I could almost see her shrug. *And you are giving it too much importance yourself. Do you wish to grasp at all that life can allow for you mortals, or do you wish to hang back, say "I cannot, alas, I am not strong enough"?*

Strength has nothing to do with this, I argued. It has to do with decency, and honor, and all those things you seem not to comprehend.

Then I abandon you, she said. *Goodbye, Helen.*

I could feel, for an instant, her leaving. I could feel her draining away, leaving me dull and colorless, as my life had been before the roses. No! I cried. No, don't leave me!

Very well, then. Do as I say. Let us have no more of this nonsense, these second thoughts. Go to the stables! Paris is waiting. Obey me! Or . . .

With a wrench I tore myself away and ran toward the stables. The palace was behind me. I passed the plane tree, with its reaching branches and its thickening trunk. Tree of my marriage, new-planted when I was a bride and new mother. I shielded my eyes from it and ran on.

Aeneas and Paris had harnessed horses to two chariots. They were busy loading their goods onto them when they looked up and saw me.

I had never felt more unearthly or detached from my surroundings. I was leaving. I needed to take some of my possessions. I could not take Hermione, I could not take my sacred snake. Perhaps I was possessed with a sort of madness, a feeling that I must take something, something beyond my person and the clothes I was wearing. "I will take my jewels," I said. "They are mine. And some of the palace gold. I am queen; they are mine by right. We may . . . we may need them!" I bolted back into my quarters, scooping up boxes of jewels, even the hideous heavy gold marriage necklace, although if I had been thinking clearly, I would have shunned it as an evil omen. Then I went into the palace treasury and took gold goblets and platters, stuffing them into baskets. I dragged them back into the stables.

"Helen!" cried Paris. "This is madness! They will slow the chariots!"

"I must take something!" I shrieked, until Paris put his hand over my mouth to silence me. Peeling it off, I said, "I must have something, I must take something. You forbade me my daughter!"

Paris shook his head. "I told you all the reasons why she should not come. I did not forbid you, I have not that power."

No, it was not Paris who had denied me. It was Hermione herself. "We need these things!" I said.

Paris tried to take them off the chariots. "They will call me a thief, and I am no such thing. Or rather . . . I steal only the queen. Nothing else. We have gold aplenty in Troy."

Aeneas stayed his arm. "She needs to take them," he said. "She is, after all, the queen. These things are hers by right. And she wishes not to be a supplicant or a beggar but to have means of her own. She does not wish to cast herself as a refugee upon the shores of Troy."

Paris shook his head. "It will slow us down."

"If it soothes her and quiets her spirits, let it be."

I watched as Paris deferred to his older cousin—an unusual thing in youth. Yet Paris was wise in unexpected ways. "Very well," he said, and shoved the baskets back onto the chariot. "Now come!" He leapt into the chariot and motioned for me to join him. Aeneas took the second one, and we urged the horses forward, out of the stable and away from the gate.

"We cannot go through the main gate," I said. "The guards will stop us and question us. I can command them to open the gates, but why let them know what we are about? There is another, little-used back way. Here." I pointed toward it.

Thanks be for the bright moon! We could find the rutted pathway that led around the palace; it waited to join the main road until it reached the banks of the Eurotas. The way was steep, but we were able to traverse it. The rich goods, stuffed into the baskets, jounced and pinned our feet to the floor of the chariot. The hill rushed past us; it was going too fast, too fast, and I could barely glimpse the dark trees around us, let alone grieve over the leave-taking.

Flat ground: we were on the meadows that bordered the river, running the chariots through the wild fields, searching for the road. We jumped and flew over dirt clods and gulleys; with each jounce we wanted to cry out, in fear and exuberance for this mad venture, but we had to remain silent. The city lay just ahead and we must get past it. The walls were high and in the searching moonlight I could see the shadows between the giant boulders forming them, deep and secret. I murmured something about their strength to Paris.

"Wait until you see the walls of Troy!" he said. "They are smooth and three times as high as this—this childish defense here!" He waved dismissively at the rounded stones. "No handhold or toehold on the walls of Troy!"

Now we had found the road and were rushing alongside the Eurotas, which was also rushing, swollen from the melting snow in the mountains. I could see white foam upon its surface.

How different this was from my leisurely walk with Gelanor. Then we had trudged along the path, stopping to eat and drink and rest whenever we wished.

Gelanor! What would he think when this news reached him? was my horrified thought. Then the next quickly followed: It is Gelanor they will send to track us down. And he will find us. But will he find us in time?

"Hurry!" I urged Paris.

On the flat ground, we made the horses gallop. The chariots flew behind them, sometimes leaving the ground. Overhead the moon swam in and out of clouds. When it emerged, the landscape lay clear before us like a finely carved scene. When it disappeared, our surroundings became a dream—indistinct, fading, changing.

With the horses, we reached the sea well before dawn. Had we been on foot, we would still have been a long way off. The sea, the rocks—the cave of Aphrodite, where all this had started. Was it even still there? Had it existed at all? I craned my neck to try to see it, but it was lost in the shadows amongst the rocks upon the shore. And perhaps I should never gaze upon it again. The first time it was magic; any other time it might be just another cave, empty and dank.

"The ship awaits." Aeneas pointed to a large vessel anchored nearby.

A small boat came to transport us to the larger one. My foot left the sands of my homeland as I stepped into it, dripping water. I watched the trailing drops, falling with finality.

I boarded the Trojan ship. My first ship, the first time I had ever left land. I had nothing to compare it to, but it seemed a fair one. All the men lined up on deck to salute Paris and Aeneas, and the captain bowed. "My princes, only tell me where to steer us, and there we shall go."

"Cast off from here," said Paris. "We must leave these shores as quickly as possible."

"It is dangerous to sail before we have full light," said the captain.

"But we must get away!" said Paris.

"There is a small island a piece out," said the captain. "It is called Cranae. We could anchor there, out of sight, and set sail in daylight for farther ports."

"Then do so!" said Paris. "Do so!"

We negotiated the heaving seas around the island of Cranae; even I, as un-knowledgeable as I was about the sea, saw that a small island near the shallows of shore had more turbulent waters around it than farther out in the sea. It took great skill for the captain to bring the ship in on the far side of the is-land, on a shore not visible from land.

"They cannot glimpse us here," he said. "Any search party will think we have sailed far away."

I looked at the eastern sky, still dark. "We will rest here ashore," I said. Indeed, I was exhausted. We had not slept at all.

In the dim light the island was sheltering and hushed. It was covered in tall trees, trees that swayed in the stiff breeze. Here and there were clearings, for fishermen must come here sometimes, but no one lived here.

"Build a shelter," I said to Paris.

"We have tents on board," he said.

"Have one sent," I said.

I stood, waiting, while it was brought from the ship. Paris insisted on dis-missing the men and setting it up himself. "I know well enough how to do this," he said. "I've built many a shelter in my day."

"More than your princely brothers at Troy, I'll wager," I said. I thought of pampered royal sons, unable to loft themselves from a couch.

He gave me a quizzical look, but continued setting up a makeshift tent. Eventually he stood before it and ushered me inside.

"My queen, your quarters are ready," he said.

I crawled in through the tiny opening. Inside, it was dark, even though the skies outside had started to lighten. He had unrolled blankets and even made pillows for us out of linen bags stuffed with clothes.

"Is this what you use at Troy?" I asked.

He laughed. "No. You must have heard that Troy is known for its luxu-ries. No, this is the proper fitting for a vagabond, a pirate." He patted the blanket. "Are you not tired of being a queen? Sample what it is to be a runaway, having to live in the fields."

I sank down on the blanket. I was so tired, this rough blanket on hard ground was as welcome as swans' down. I was so exhausted I could not think, could not turn over in my mind the momentousness of what I had just done.

I rolled over on my back. Paris was looking at me, propped up on one arm. Outside, I heard the crashing roar of the waves against the nearby rocks.

"On a small island the noise of the waves is ever-constant," said Paris. "Wherever we go, we may not escape it."

"They provide a welcome chorus," I said. And indeed they did. The resounding repetition of wave crashes was like a drumbeat, a drumbeat that drowned out all thought. The loud waves, the hissing, long withdrawals, pounded in my head. I looked at Paris, but even his face wavered before me.

I am here, I thought. Here with Paris. We have left Sparta behind. Everything is gone—everything but us. I reached out and encircled his neck with my arm, drew his face down to mine.

Paris. I kissed his lips, those lips I had watched forming words as he teased Hermione, parried insults from Mother. I had seen them lingeringly caress the rim of my wine goblet. I had watched them as they moved, wanting to feel them against mine, having only tasted them that once, briefly. They were everything I had desired, drawing me further into his world, himself. I pressed him to me. I felt his strong young body against mine and I laughed aloud.

"What?" he asked.

My head fell back against the blanket. "Oh, I cannot decide what I wish to do with you," I said, stroking his cheek. "I want to touch you, I want to revere you, I do not know what I wish!"

"Do not revere me," he said, his breath close to me. "It is too distant. It is what I should be doing to you, but I wish instead to touch you." He lay down beside me and encircled me with his arms.

At that, all thought of revering and worshiping went out of my head. The touch of flesh on flesh set all else in motion. I shivered with the actual touch of him. In the wonder of it, I did not even stop to marvel at it, at this thing I had never felt before, had prayed for, had begged for, had longed for. It was here, here, and so resounding that it overwhelmed me. I laughed again.

"What is it? Why are you laughing?" Paris murmured. He was afraid I was laughing at him.

"Only at the joy of the gods," I said. "Only at the joy of the gods. They bless me at last!"

Laughter-loving Aphrodite . . . yes, they called her that. She smiled on lovers, but she also knew, in her wisdom, they must laugh.

"Make me your wife," I said, pulling him toward me. Oh, let him! Let me be a wife at last!

Around us the waves grew louder, making it difficult to talk. I had to put my mouth directly up against his ear for him to hear my words. We were in our own citadel, our own fortified city, encircled by waves and rocks and the cries of water dashing against them.

All that had been denied was now, suddenly, granted me: Aphrodite was a generous goddess. I ached, I throbbed, I pulsed with desire for Paris. The slightest hesitation, the slightest barrier between us was insufferable, I must tear it away. I must have him, I must have him in the extreme, nothing else mattered. And the glory of it was worth the loss of a kingdom, the loss of all.

Afterward we clung together, bound in whatever awaited us. What was done could not be undone. But who could think of undoing that magnificence?

I lay looking at the tent ceiling in the darkness. This is what people speak of. Oh, my deepest thanks, Aphrodite, for granting it to me. I know now that to die without tasting this is truly not to have lived. In this, and this only, have we lived: to feel all, to dare all, to try all.

❖ XXV ❖

All the remaining night the stars wheeled around us as we drowsed and woke and embraced over and over again, until there was no telling the waking from the sleeping or our rest from our lovemaking. I could glimpse the sky through the openings in the rude tent Paris had set up for us, the draped cloaks sagging and revealing the heavens. Enveloping my ears was the constant sound of the sea. All my senses had been touched by newness: my eyes with the unknown vista of Cranae and of Paris, unclothed; my nostrils with the scent of the special wildflowers of this island, and the smell of Paris's skin with my face pressed against him; my hands, the touch of his body, so slender and warm, so different from Menelaus's; my tongue, the taste of his neck when I kissed it; my ears, the murmur of Paris's voice, slow and sleepy, barely discernible above the noise of the waves.

The night lasted seemingly forever, much longer than an ordinary night. I knew that the gods could make days or nights longer if they chose, and perhaps that was Aphrodite's wedding gift to us.

Gradually the stars faded and the sky turned gray. In the growing light I could see my dearest one sleeping, could study his every feature. I thanked Aphrodite for giving me this opportunity, for I had never had the chance to truly look at him, or rather, to look my fill. Our time together in Sparta had been passed in the company of others, others to whom I could never betray myself, so I never let my eyes linger on him.

I felt no shame, no remorse, nothing but a wild excitement and happiness; a happiness beyond happiness, a fine ecstasy. I was free. I had seized the gift dangled before me, I had passed the test of courage, the test of whether I truly wanted this prize. Now my life would begin.

I forced myself to stand up and, throwing on a cloak, I left the tent, left the warmth and protection of it. Outside, the wind was ripping through the pines and blowing dust along the path. Dark clouds scudded across the sky. I stood on tiptoe and looked out to sea. On the other side of the island I could have seen Gytheum, but already I did not want to see it. I did not want to look for the movement of men on the shore, searching for me. I wanted to look out across the open water, to the horizon as far as I could see.

But when the sun rose, emerging from the waters and turning them into a glittering golden pathway, shapes swam out of the mists. And far away on the horizon I could see an island floating. That must be Cythera. Gelanor had told me about it when I had sighted it from Gytheum. Suddenly I wanted very badly to get there, as he had told me I could not. I wanted to do all the things that I had been told I could not.

"Would you leave me so soon?" Paris was standing behind me, and he clasped me to him from the back. I felt his strong arms encircle me. For a moment, as I watched them twining, I thought of the sacred snake. I bent my head over and kissed his forearms.

"Never," I said. "I will never leave you."

"Nor I, you," he said. "Nor I, you."

"Awake, I see!" Aeneas's voice interrupted us. "That's good, we need to get under way." He walked up to us. I could see him searching our faces, intensely curious as to how our hours had gone: those hours which would cost everyone so dear. Out of habit I banished the expression from my face so it could not be read. "We need to be far away before the hue and cry is raised. They are probably just now waking up and missing us."

I pictured Mother opening her eyes, yawning, and turning over; Father swinging himself out of bed; Hermione still dreaming. Hermione. I would not think of her now!

As we boarded the ship, I caught sight of the figurehead and laughed: it was Eros. "How came that to be carved?" I asked.

Aeneas glanced at it. "Paris commissioned it," he said.

We cast off. The men raised the square sail and we ran before the southwest wind, blowing us toward Cythera. To speed us along, the rowers fell to as well. We were heading for the open sea.

"We'll have to spend the night on the high seas," said the captain. "We have no choice; there is no anchorage between here and Cythera. Pray to Poseidon that we don't reach the tricky currents while we are still in the dark."

"What do you mean?" asked Paris.

"Cythera is a dangerous passage," he said. "Lots of shifting currents and hidden rocks. Those are the natural perils. Then there are pirates, but they tend to stick closer to shore. There's a saying: round Malea and forget your home. We must pass to the west of the Malea promontory to reach Cythera."

Paris hugged me. "My dearest, you wanted adventure," he said. "And we shall have it." He steered me toward the railing. "If only we could make love on the high seas. Now, that would be a challenge, with all the bucking and rolling. Like making love on horseback, I should imagine."

"What? Have you?"

He laughed. "No, but it would be a very Trojan thing to do."

"Why?"

Now he turned and looked carefully into my face. "You really don't know, do you? Did they not let you learn anything? What about that palace wizard, that man who knew so many things? Didn't he teach you things?"

His accusation, true as it was, hurt: hurt *because* it was true. "Gelanor taught me many things, but only the things that I had occasion to ask him. He was not my tutor."

"I'm sorry. I did not mean to accuse or belittle. It's just that—well, Troy is famous for its horses. My brother Hector is known as 'Breaker of Horses.' So of course, in Troy, there are many feats of horsemanship. Probably somewhere there is someone renowned for his ability to make love on a galloping horse."

I laughed. "Then I suppose the ship will be good practice for us. We can dazzle everyone with our prowess when we reach Troy." Aphrodite had made me ready to hide away with Paris again, and it had only been a short while since we had held one another. The goddess made me like a devouring fire. I was concerned that we have privacy on the ship; I whispered my request to Paris.

For an instant he looked embarrassed, as his eyes swept around the ship with its large crew. It was a man's domain, a place where there would be little privacy and no niceties. "I was only joking about the practice for the horses. I—I think we must wait until we reach shore. There is no way that we can have more than a small place to rest, and no possibility of shielding ourselves from all these eyes." He gestured toward the rowers at their oars. He pinched my shoulder. "Helen," he murmured, "you will just have to control yourself. We must wait."

"Wait. All I have done, all my whole life, is wait," I said.

He laughed, to show he was teasing. "Let us hope this passage will be quick, then. Waiting is a most exquisite form of torture."

The waters grew rougher as we left Cranae behind; the island, with its clumps of trees, grew fainter in our wake. The winds began to buffet us and the rowers had to strain as the ship listed. As we made our way out into the open water, all the land seemed equidistant, faint images on the horizon to the left, right, and ahead of us. Gulls followed us, wheeling and diving, crying loudly, their calls snatched away by the winds.

"Lower the sail," the captain ordered at sunset. "We need to slow ourselves in darkness, and besides that, we do not want to pass anywhere near Malea at night. We must be fully alert and able to see when we make that run."

Shivering, I sank down in a protected place near the rear of the ship. Paris brought me food; the ship was well provisioned, as such provisions go, but they were cold and meant to be eaten as quickly and unceremoniously as possible, washed down with wine. I took a long drink, laid my head back against the side of the ship, and started laughing. To think I had imagined this voyage as a place of private indulgence. How naïve I was! How sheltered I had been—not even to know what a voyage would be like. How much I had to learn!

Paris brought a blanket for me to wrap myself in and use as a pillow. He was treating me as I treated Hermione. But here he was the elder; he was right, in some ways he had lived longer than I, if experience constituted longevity.

"Close your eyes," he said, kissing my eyelids. "I will keep watch. Of course, I don't think there will be any pirates, not in the dark, but I won't sleep." Poor Paris—his voice betrayed how tired he was. Neither of us had had true sleep that night on Cranae.

I squeezed his hand and tried to relax on the swaying, rolling ship. I felt as though I were suspended in a hammock, being rocked by a giant hand. I tried not to think of the depths of cold water under me. It did not help that the captain had said, "Only three fingers' width of wood separates us from the sea."

Sheer exhaustion forced me into a kind of sleep, as though my head were being pushed down into the realms of dreams. I cannot recall any of them, and for that I am thankful. Had there been omens, I could not have borne it. I did not want any omens. I was mortally tired of them. They had ruled me from my birth—nay, before it. Now I left the omens behind, as I had left Sparta.

Let me live each day as just a day, I thought. Let me see neither more nor less than just what is contained in that day.

Paris still held my hand. This was sufficient for me, all I would need.

Dawn rose. I was stiff and cold; my hands felt numb. Lying beside me and under the blanket was Paris.

"I thought you were going to stay awake all night," I whispered, touching his ear with my lips.

"I did," he said. "I only lay down when it began to get light. The seas were clear." He sat up, shaking his head. "Only one more day to go."

Until we arrived at Cythera. And then . . . but now I was not to think in those terms. I was to think only of the day's voyage to Cythera. And once on Cythera, to think only of that day there, and then . . .

"Here comes the dangerous part," said the captain, striding toward us. "We're in the worst part of the currents, the ones that sweep through the channel, and we're approaching Malea. Look there. You can see Cape Malea away on our left, and Cythera straight ahead."

I stood up, my legs quivering. The wind smacked me in the face, stinging cold. I could see the headland of Malea, and dead ahead the mountain of Cythera. It had resolved itself out of the mists of a dream.

"At last! At last I shall set foot on it!" I said.

"Not so hasty, lady," said the captain. "There's them to get by first."

"What?" Paris asked.

"Them." The captain pointed to a small ship, barely visible, near Malea.

Paris laughed. "That little thing? It will never catch us, and even if it did, what matter?"

The captain shook his head. "Did you not know, Prince, that pirate ships are small and light? They have to be, for speed and hiding. And this has all the look of a pirate ship to me. I don't think it's an innocent fishing boat, although it may be disguised as one." He turned to the rowers. "Faster! As fast as you are able!" He motioned to the crew. "Sail up! Sail up! Let's harness this wind!"

The men rushed to unfurl the sail and hoist it high, and it jerked as it filled with the impatient wind. The ship flew over the waves. The suspicious boat was left far behind.

The captain seemed to relax a bit, but he kept squinting astern, keeping the boat in his sights. He motioned to the men manning the steering oars to turn right, and they did. Then, a few moments later, he ordered them to turn left, quickly, and they obeyed. A dark look spread across his face.

"What is it?" I asked.

"It's pirates, all right. They are altering their course whenever we do."

"Mightn't it just be a smaller boat using us as a safe means of charting a course?" asked one of the younger men.

"Possibly," the captain admitted. "And now that we have the wind, and a larger sail than they do, we are outdistancing them. If we are fortunate, then we will reach Cythera far ahead of them."

"But we'll have to camp far inland," said the man. "Pirates raid coasts and carry people off!"

"Then we'll have to go up the mountain and live there for a while," said Paris, his lips close to my ear. He made it sound like a paradise there, a retreat where we could linger for a very long time.

"The pirates like to swoop down on festivals where women and unarmed men are celebrating," the young man wailed. "My aunt was carried off that way; we never saw her again."

Pirate raids furnished most of the slaves sold for household work; in peacetime, without any war captives, pirates supplied that need. I shuddered.

"Courage, lad," said the captain, not unkindly. "It's harder to take a whole ship of men. There's only one woman aboard, and she'll fetch such a ransom that she will be safe." He winked at me. "Faster!" he ordered the rowers.

But Cythera was farther away than it seemed, or perhaps we had been carried away to one side by the current. As the sun neared the horizon, Cythera was still a distance away. And then the wind, abruptly, stopped, as if it were descending beneath the ocean with the sun. The sail fell slack, hanging limply, uselessly. Our speed dwindled, and we moved now only by the power of the rowers.

And the mysterious following ship now grew larger behind us. When the wind was blowing, our bigger sail had carried us over the water faster; but without the wind, their rowers could propel their lighter boat faster. They were catching up, and no matter how hard our rowers strained, the gap between us was closing. I clutched the railing of the ship. Was my freedom to end after only a day? Were one night and one day with Paris all I was to be granted? Was I to be captured, trussed up, and sent back to Sparta like a penned animal?

"No!" I cried. "No, no!"

They were close enough now that we could see how many were aboard—some thirty or so, all grim-faced. There did not seem to be a captain; it was all rowers. Perhaps all pirates were equal, or all could take turns in being the captain. I supposed it was necessary, since so many must get killed on raids.

"Arm yourselves!" Paris and Aeneas ordered their men. The Trojan soldiers fastened their corselets and breastplates and put on their helmets. Now, surely, at the sight of armored men, the pirates would turn away. But no, they kept coming, coming even faster, as if they were gleeful that a true fight was in the offing.

As the waters grew shallower near Cythera, the pirates came alongside us. Now, instead of slowly patrolling the waters looking for an opening through the rocks to beach the ship on shore, the captain had to order the rowers to continue pulling their oars to keep us away from jagged rocks while we took a stand against the pirates. They would, of course, try to force us onto the rocks. Our situation was a pirate's dream.

Paris pulled me into the middle of the ship, between the two banks of oarsmen, and surrounded us with soldiers. "You must be in the middle of the middle, protected on all sides!" he said. I could hear a scrabbling sort of sound—the pirates were scaling the sides of the ship, climbing over. Then piercing yells—from the pirates, meant to terrorize us. Then the ship began rocking madly as the men fought, battling on every little scrap of space. Large as it was, I feared the ship would tip on its side into the sea, take on water, and sink. At one point I was thrown to my knees as it listed suddenly to the left, when the fighters piled up there. I clutched at the boards beneath my fingers and clung to Paris's leg, and all the while I could see nothing, protected by the wall of men guarding me.

The noise rose—screams of pain now mingled with the war cries, metal hit metal, wooden oars were smashed, and someone brought the sail down, so it enveloped us all, making the men fight as if in a net. I lost my grip on Paris's leg and then I lost Paris. He was gone, and the solid circle of soldiers around me broke up, and as I rose I saw the melee on the ship, the men caught in the sail, the others fighting desperately, the dead bodies lying where they fell, some draped across the oars. I saw Paris and Aeneas slashing at pirates together, saw Paris spit one with his dagger—Paris looked as surprised as the pirate at his success. The man sagged and grabbed at his belly with fluttering hands, and I saw then that he was no man but a boy. He died with surprise still on his face. Had this been his only foray into the world of plundering? Was this his first day as a pirate?

Paris saw me nearby and yelled, "Get away! Get away!"

But where could I go? The entire ship was a battle scene, from the figurehead to the stern, with the rowers trying gamely to keep rowing as soldiers fought all around them. Some had abandoned their posts to join the fight, others were disabled by the fallen sail. Somewhere in the midst of this was the chest with the Spartan treasures in it; I had not thought of it until this late. Had anyone gone near it? But no, it was safe under the sail. I looked around wildly to see where I might escape the fray, but all I could do was dodge and slither around the grappling men.

Again the ship listed, so sharply water sloshed onto the deck; several men were washed off and now the armored soldiers fared the worse, as the weight of their corselets dragged them down. Some hit the rocks with a dull metal clang; the pirates who hit sent up a spray of red. The sucking of the waves around the rocks mingled with the groans of the dying men to make a long mournful moan. On board the din of fighting rose to the pitch of a screaming wind.

Slowly the greater numbers of soldiers and their better arms began to best the invaders. More and more of our men crawled out from under the sail to join their brothers in the fight, and finally the last two pirates were cornered up near the bow of the ship. Aeneas and another soldier were pinning them down on the railing, and a crush of other men piled up behind, so much that the pirates were more likely to be suffocated than to be killed by the daggers of Aeneas and his companion.

Aeneas barked orders that the others were to back away; catching his breath, he demanded, "Who are you? Where is your hideout?" he asked one of the pirates.

The pirate shook his head and refused to answer.

"Talk or you'll die," said Aeneas.

"I'll die, talk or not," he said. With a stunning display of cunning and skill, taking advantage of the tiny space between himself and his captor, he suddenly twisted himself free and leapt onto the Eros figurehead. There he crouched like a cat.

"Trojans, I see," he cried, mockingly, sweeping off his hat. "And what brings you so far from home? Pretty armor you have, and pretty soldiers, too. And a pretty treasure to go with the pretty woman, I'll warrant."

Aeneas lunged forward, almost flying through the air, and grabbed the pirate's leg. But the man kicked free and retreated farther out on the figure-head, while Aeneas lay sprawled just out of reach.

"Farewell," said the pirate. "I throw myself on the mercy of Poseidon." With that, he flung himself off into the water. Muttering, Aeneas peered over the side and shook his head.

"Disappeared," he said.

In the confusion with that pirate, attention turned from his companion, still pinned against the railing. With a cry, Paris suddenly ran forward and stabbed him. This time neither victim nor killer looked surprised. The pirate grunted and slumped forward, and Paris pulled out his dagger and wiped it on his tunic, his face grim.

"Oh," I cried, rushing over and embracing him. He clasped me to him with trembling hands.

Death lay all around us, bodies like fallen flowers on the blood-soaked deck.

We waded ashore, leaving the men to clean up the ship and dispose of the dead. But walking through the churning waters, we had to pass between floating bodies bobbing on the surface, and once I stepped on one that had already sunk to the bottom. It was still warm, and when my foot touched it I cried out. Paris grabbed my arm and steered me past it.

The waters grew shallower around my legs; now I would not step on anything hidden. Suddenly Paris let go of my arm and leapt ahead of me, jumping over the waves and rushing to the shore. "Now!" he cried, holding his arms wide. "Stop. Stand there."

I could not imagine what he was doing, but I halted and looked at him.

"There. Don't move. Don't ever move."

Was he mad? I could not stand there forever. I took another step.

"Now I have seen her," he said.

"Who?"

"Aphrodite coming forth from the foam, the foam where she was born," he said, holding out his hand to draw me onto the beach. "This is where she came ashore, you know." He flung his arms around me. "And in you I have seen her." He started kissing my neck. "But you are more lovely yet."

"Do not provoke her," I whispered. But I knew that she had already heard. And behind us I could feel the gazes of the men boring into us. While they threw dead bodies overboard and scrubbed the deck free of blood, these young fools were embracing. That was what they saw. At least they could not blame me for the pirate attack itself.

So I had reached Cythera, where I had set my sights. But how different the arrival than what I would have wished.

We camped deep inside the island, leaving only a few men to guard the ship. They broke up the pirate boat and sank it, after stripping it of anything useful—ropes, baskets, oars, and the few remaining weapons. Quickly they made basic shelters and gathered wood to set a fire; they built a big one, placing some of the wood from the pirate boat close by to dry out. The sun had set on us during the fight, and now the light was fading quickly. In a few minutes the stars would be out.

They passed around wineskins and we all drank from them. Usually—I assumed—there would have been tired, lazy talk, reliving the day's journey, planning the next. Now they all sat dully staring at the fire, saying nothing. The silence, except for the snapping of wood in the fire, was not unwelcome. I feared what they would say if they could truly speak their minds.

What they were thinking was, *Helen brings death.* I had not been gone from my home more than a day and already we were surrounded by dead bodies. Was it my fault? No, how could it have been? But fault and cause are not the same thing. If honey attracts flies, the honey is the cause of the swarm. But it is not the fault of the honey, it is merely its nature to attract flies.

Was it my nature to attract death? The Sibyl and what she had said . . . *many Greeks will die.*

Were the pirates Greeks? I quibbled to myself. Perhaps they weren't. But the one who had spoken to Aeneas—he sounded Greek enough.

"Glum, glum, my fellows." It was Aeneas who spoke, as if he had overheard me thinking about him. "Cheer up. They say a journey that starts badly ends fairly. And it did not end as badly for us as for the pirates." He laughed; a forced laugh at first that grew genuine as some of the men joined in.

"Here, here," one of them said, squirting wine into his mouth, then passing the wineskin to the man beside him.

"Now!" One of the others grabbed a piece of wood from the pirate boat and heaved it onto the fire. It sizzled and spat from the water still within it. "Burn. Burn so we have something useful from you." He spun around and said, "Isn't it unusual, instead of taking something, the pirates have left us something?"

"No loot, though," another man said. "Apparently we were the first victims to be attacked. It would have been better if we were the last—then we'd have inherited their booty."

The first. He was probably right, then: that boy was probably on his first foray. Death was always ugly, but ugliest in the young. I shuddered.

"You dispatched a couple," said Aeneas, pointing to Paris. "Your first, I assume? Not much killing before you came to Troy, I'll warrant."

But much killing afterward. Who whispered that in my mind?

"Yes. It was . . . easy." Paris looked down, embarrassed. "It isn't supposed to be."

"Who said that?" one of the men said. "It's a lie that it's not easy. It's one of the easiest things in the world. That's why there's so much of it."

The captain joined in. "It's especially easy when you know he's about to kill *you*." He roared with laughter. "But you made such a mess of my ship!" Another gust of laughter. "Can't you men kill more cleanly?"

"Let us hope that the clean-scrubbed decks will see nothing else the rest of the journey," said Aeneas. "Let us pass to Troy as quickly as possible."

"We will have to pick our way in and out of islands almost all the way to Troy," said the captain. We'll be able to anchor and put ashore, but we won't be safe until we reach the bay by Troy."

I wondered how long it would take to reach Troy. Strange, I had not asked before, and now I realized even under the best of conditions it would take many days. Was someone following us? How long would it be until Menelaus found out and came in pursuit? He was still on Crete; he would remain there for the funeral games. Someone might sail to Crete to tell him, but by the time they reached him he would be almost ready to return. Suddenly I laughed. Why, he had not even arrived at Crete yet! We had left at the same time, and Crete was much farther than Cythera. I felt safe. We would be safe in Troy before he could rally any followers.

"What's so amusing?" Paris leaned over.

I could not tell him I was laughing in relief that my husband was not a threat. "Nothing . . . I was just laughing out of weariness."

"Yes, let us go to our tent." He did not need much encouragement, nor did I. I did not want to remain at the fire much longer.

This time our tent was more substantial, with wooden supports from the planks of the pirate boat and drapings of goat-hair cloth. Paris still left an opening in the center so we could breathe the fresh night air. He had spread the ground with heavy wool blankets and set our cloaks atop them. The treasure trunk was resting within our sights.

"Not that I don't trust the men, but . . ." He smiled. "What do you think of our palace?" He gestured proudly.

I leaned back against him. "I think you have learned a great deal about setting up tents in just a day. By the time we reach Troy, you will be the best tentmaster in the Aegean." And it was true—he was clever and obviously resourceful. He will learn, I whispered to myself, and everything he learns will make him more and more outstanding among men, until there is no touching him. I excited myself just thinking of it—of the young man beside me and the man he would grow into.

Even though the tent was chilly, we would kindle heat from naked bodies that would not shiver from cold but from desire. Again that wild desire swept over me that made me want to disappear into him, and at the same time to caress every piece of him, to worship his body.

Paris sank down on his knees and pulled me with him. Delicately he unpinned the shoulders of my gown and the fine wool fell off, light as a baby's breath. Then his own breath replaced it, warm and caressing, on my shoulder. Oh, it was sweet as the murmuring wind that passes over flowery meadows.

I tilted my head back, and my hair fell all the way to the makeshift pallet, like a column. He plunged his hands into it, tangling his fingers in it, squeezing it.

"Your hair . . . your glory . . ." he was saying faintly. His voice sounded far away and was hard to hear. His hands in my hair pulled me backward. He toppled with me and playfully took handfuls of my hair and covered my face with them. "Now you cannot see," he said.

It was so dark in the tent—and we could have no lighting because of fire danger—that I could not see in any case, but the hair was a strange mask: warm from his hands, thick and heavy with a scent that only now I realized was my own. He parted it and kissed my lips. My hair fell away on both sides.

I loved the shape and feel of his lips—they were curved like a hunter's bow, and smooth as only a young man's could be. Menelaus's were harder and unyielding, and in those fleeting moments I wondered if Paris's would become inflexible in time, but now they were soft and spoke only of pleasure. I could—I would—never tire of kissing them.

He slipped his arms under my shoulders and I ran my hands across his back, delighting in the feel of each muscle and sinew.

"Cattle herding must be arduous." I heard my own voice giving form to my thoughts. It was true: he had grown a warrior's body from everyday tasks. The things that normal men do in a day's job may be harder than a prince's training. "It is good you did not become a prince until you had first been a man."

From somewhere I heard a drowsy laugh. "I was always a prince. I did not know it."

I pulled him closer. "Your cattle knew it," I said. "Animals know."

"You are very silly sometimes," he murmured. Then all banter ceased, as our bodies silenced us.

"Paris," I said, "Paris, I and all my fortunes are yours."

I gave myself to him with all my being, and took him with all of mine. I could not hold him close enough. We rolled over together on the mantles, cold from the air around us, and tumbled over and over until we rested on the bare ground. "Now," I whispered. "I can wait no longer." And it was so—my body was on fire, and I must have him.

"Nor I," he murmured.

There was no one time, no one coming together. Even in the darkness, the tent seemed to glow with red and yellow and the colors of desire and the sun. When at last we fell back onto the blankets and pulled the mantles over us, it was only because we were perfectly and utterly fulfilled.

Yet sleep was beyond me. I gazed outward through the opening in the tent and saw the diminished moon only now high enough in the sky to shine through to us. A bright shaft of light fell onto Paris, illuminating his sleeping face.

His face was so perfect it would arouse the envy of the gods. I raised myself on my elbow and looked upon it. His eyelids were closed and he slept deeply. Beauty. What an exacting master or mistress it is over us. What I hated others doing to me, I was doing to Paris.

I tore myself away, rose to my feet. I pushed aside the tent flaps and went outside, wincing at the first brightness of the moonlight. It threw shadows from the moving branches on all sides of the tent. I stood on tiptoe and drew in my breath—the air was cold and pine-scented, bracing. I could hear the sea, but it was far away. This was a much bigger island than Cranae, with forests and animals.

The moon overhead was eaten away on one side. Just so much had it lost since the night Paris and I had run away. It was a relentless mistress of time, measuring our life together.

❖ XXVII ❖

The dawn came up around me, stealing across the sky, draining the moon of its light, turning it into a milky ghost fleeing toward the west. The sea seemed white as well, stretching away on all sides. Somewhere, out of sight, lay Troy.

I had no picture in my mind of Troy. I had words: Rich. Strong-walled.

Broad-streeted. Windy. But still that did not tell me what it would look like. Nor how it would feel to be there. Nor what I would find amongst the people there.

The tent flap moved; Paris stepped out, rubbing his eyes. The rising sun struck his face, making him wince, turning his skin to gold. He shook his head and looked about him. Seeing me, he came over and embraced me.

"Are you not cold?" He took his mantle and placed it around my shoulders. Not until then had I realized I was chilled.

"Thank you," I said, leaning back against him. The chill fled.

Together we wandered over the island, exploring it. It was large, so much so that when we were walking through its woods or climbing its hills it was easy to forget that we were on an island. It was richly forested and filled with running brooks, and the birdsong made it seem magical.

"It is a fitting place for the birthplace of Aphrodite," I said, as we passed the white ribbon of a tumbling waterfall making for a green pool far below. It seemed the most delightful garden of pleasurable things I had ever seen.

We found a grove of myrtles, huddled like a family of women: there was the old matriarch, standing tall and wide above her daughters and granddaughters, who were more slender and were still flowering. The scent was so rich I could almost touch it.

"Here. Here it is," said Paris. "The place where we must build her shrine."

We began to search for stones to fashion an altar for her, to honor her. We found them in plenty lying in the streambed and scattered about the myrtle grove. Heaving them up was another matter, and it took all our strength and maneuvering ability.

"Perhaps we should call some of the men," I said. "They could do this easily and quickly."

"No," said Paris. "It must be built by our hands alone." And so we struggled all afternoon, moving and arranging the stones. But by sunset we had a lovely altar underneath the overhanging branches of the old myrtle. They encircled it protectively.

Paris's hands were torn and raw from the rough stones. I took one and kissed it. These hands had killed men during the pirate raid, but their wounds came from attempting to honor Aphrodite. Aphrodite was more demanding than Ares, then.

"Now we must consecrate the sacred grove," he said.

I looked at our half-empty wineskins. We had drunk a great deal to quench our thirst while we labored for the goddess. "Will she be satisfied with our leavings for her libations?" I wondered.

"We shall not be giving her only these libations, but the one she most prizes." Paris took the wineskin and solemnly emptied it out on the ground, invoking her presence. Then he turned to me.

"You know the rite the goddess treasures," he said, putting his hands on my shoulders. "We must do it in her sight and before her sacred altar."

I started to demur, but then the goddess herself overpowered me again, coming to us in the rustling of the myrtle branches. I could hear her laughter just beneath the murmur of the leaves. I could almost see her, half hidden in the shadows.

Consecrate my grove, my child, she whispered. *Make it holy by what you do here.* She pushed me toward Paris and I fell into his arms.

At once it was as if the hard ground were replaced by the softest grasses of a meadow, and as we sank down into it, crushing it beneath us, the scent of a thousand tiny flowers filled the air. In bruising them we rubbed their perfume upon us. We were the two most blessed people on earth, or so it seemed under the spell of the goddess. Each gesture was filled with infinite grace, each word was music, our coming together a dance of beauty, as we joined ourselves together as man and woman. In our earthly tent the night before we had stoked a fire of happy, unthinking animals; now, in the soft filtered daylight of the sacred grove, we were creatures of the air and heavens.

Later I lay back, looking up at the blue sky. I turned my head, reached over, and stroked Paris's cheek. He sighed with delight.

I could still see the goddess, a dim image hovering just at the corner of my sight. And behind her, another form: a darker one, one that crowded close to her and vied for her attention, draping his arm over her shoulder. I saw the shield. It was Ares, her lover. Then he stepped forward and took his place beside her, boldly. She tried to push him back, but he would not retreat. She smiled at me as if to say, *I tried to banish him, but he insists on being here.*

The god of war, hand in hand with Aphrodite. She had called me, and then he had followed. We each had our lovers. What had I expected? If I had mine, hers would invite himself along as well.

Suddenly the grove was no longer a place where I cared to linger. *He* was here, that ugly god, ruining the beauty around us. I sat up and began to seek my discarded gown. Paris withdrew his hand.

"What is it?" he asked, puzzled.

Could he not see the hateful war god? "Aphrodite has brought another," I said. "I do not wish him to gaze upon us."

"What—who—?" Paris scrambled to collect his clothes.

He did not know. He could not see. Fortunate Paris.

"Come," I said. "We have honored the goddess. Now we should go before darkness falls."

"No, let us stay here all night and celebrate her rites!" Paris eagerly embraced me.

"No," I said. We must leave this place. I stood up and reached for my mantle.

There was a movement in the bushes behind us. Had Aphrodite and Ares taken human form? Oh, we must prepare ourselves! I clenched my fists and tried to still my racing heart. We would not, must not retreat. Gods hate a coward.

The sound in the bushes grew louder. Something was thrashing about, breaking the branches, muttering. Then, out into the clearing, Gelanor appeared.

Had Aphrodite stepped out, I was prepared. Even had Ares accompanied her, I would have stood my ground. But now I staggered back, shocked.

"No!" I shrieked. This had to be an apparition.

Another person emerged from the bushes, brushing herself off—an old woman, with a face like a winter's apple.

"No!" I cried again, grabbing Paris and pulling him away.

"What a disappointing welcome," the Gelanor-apparition said.

"Go away!" I cried. "You cannot be real!" Yet a few moments ago I had welcomed the phantom image of Aphrodite.

"You know better than that," he said, walking toward me. "Living people remain in their flesh. Only dreams and gods are smoke and visions. Perhaps you have seen too many visions of late?"

I covered my eyes with my hands. When I raised them again, he would be gone.

But when I peered out between my fingers, he was still there, and only an arm's length away.

"Helen, this is very foolish of you." He took my arm, and his hand was all too real, and it pinched my wrist. "You must return to Sparta with me, before Menelaus knows any of this. It is not too late."

"No!" I pulled my arm away. "Never!" Then, staring at him, I blurted out, "How did you come here? How did you find me?" Yet had I not known from the beginning that it would be Gelanor they would send after me?

"She did," he said, indicating his companion. "She knew you had gone—she saw you visit the household shrine and then she heard the noises in the stable. She saw the two chariots tearing out down the hill."

I stared at the old woman.

"She has poor eyesight, but she has the other sight." He shrugged. "It is a talent I lack—you know I rely only on my own reasoning—but you are right, my reasoning could never have led me here. Except . . . you were so curious about Cythera. So perhaps we each were led here by different means."

"So you were not . . . sent?"

He frowned. "No. I did not go near the royal quarters—I had no reason to. Doubtless your mother and father and daughter have discovered your absence, but if you return now you and I can concoct a reasonable explanation. Or it need not even be reasonable. People believe what they wish to believe, what soothes them. They do not question, especially when the answers to the questions might be painful."

So. I could undo it all. I could have had my adventure with Paris, could have proved my daring to myself, and be none the worse. I had not thought to repair the damage so easily. A transgression with no price.

I looked over at Paris, at his face. His mouth framed a smile. "Go if you must," he said. "I shall treasure what I was given."

I went to his side. "No. I shall not go."

"Helen, please!" Gelanor shook his head. "Think. Only think."

"I have thought, and thought, and thought. All those years at Sparta, I thought."

"You will not return?" He sounded forlorn.

"I cannot. To return is to choose death." But why had Ares appeared in my new life? He had never been there before. And he trailed death. But must I leave all my old life behind? Perhaps I need not. "Gelanor—come with us. Come with us to Troy!"

"What?" His face registered—what? Surprise? Disgust? Horror?

"Yes. Come with us to Troy. Oh, please do!" Suddenly I wanted him above all from Sparta to accompany us. I had missed him more than I knew. "Oh, Gelanor, I need you with me! You can do much good in Troy, you can be . . ." I knew not what, but I knew I needed him.

"I have no wish to go to Troy," he said. "Neither should you go. It is a dreadful mistake, it is wrong!"

"I am going, wrong or not!" I said. "That said, come with me!"

"Go with her." The old woman suddenly spoke. Her voice was like an echo down a well.

"Who is she?" I rounded on Gelanor.

"Why, she is the old wool-carder from the palace," he said.

I barely remembered her. Perhaps that was because I did not venture into those quarters often.

"Oh, my lady, I remember you well." She answered my thoughts, not my words. "I have seen you grow up."

I tried not to dislike her, though she had laid bare my secret escape. Had it not been for her, perhaps Gelanor might never have found me.

"I brought you something you should not have departed without," she said, holding out a rough hemp sack.

"What is this?" I said.

"Open it," she ordered, walking toward me with extended arms. There was movement inside the sack.

I did not wish to obey, but I did, curious. I opened the mouth of the sack and saw inside the household snake. "Oh!" I cried.

"You will need him in your new life," she said. "He will advise you, protect you."

But . . . I had trusted the snake to guard Hermione, to keep her safe in my absence. And now he could not! A dreadful fear for her, and her future, swept over me.

I reached in and stroked the snake's head with trembling fingers. "Do not forget my daughter," I begged him. To her, I said, "Tell Gelanor again, he must come with us."

She shook her head. "I have told him once. He has good ears. He has heard."

"Two on a foolish quest do not halve the foolishness," said Gelanor. "No, I cannot come. Come back with me."

"Just as you cannot come with me, I cannot come with you. But you have not told me how you found me."

"Yes, I have. Evadne knew where you would be. She was granted an image of the island in her mind. We knew you would be going by sea, for Paris had a ship. She described the island, and I knew it for Cythera. We set out at once."

"I see."

We stood, stubbornly staring at one another. "Join us at least for the night, before you return to Sparta."

"I suppose we cannot leave until morning, anyway. It was dangerous enough in full light." He sounded angry that he had to stay even another moment, and he turned his head away as if he disliked looking at me. We took a few steps before he said, "Perhaps you and your paramour ought to finish dressing yourselves before you set out."

Only then did I look down at my breasts, partially uncovered. I had not finished pinning my up gown when these intruders had arrived. "You came upon us without our knowledge and interrupted—"

"Not *that*, at least!" Paris laughed merrily.

"No. Aphrodite spared us that sight." Perhaps Paris, not knowing him well, did not hear the sarcasm in Gelanor's voice, but for me it was insulting. I was shaken and angry that he had found me so quickly; at the same time, his having come this far, I might as well have him with me at Troy. And the fact that he did not wish to come angered me further.

Using makeshift torches in the growing twilight, we found our way back down the hillside to the camp. Little was said as we walked; we were focusing all our attention on our footing as we descended. I took the arm of the old woman to help steady her; it felt as fragile as a brittle, dry stick. Paris held the sack with the snake, cradling it in his arms. He had a fondness for the snake, I knew, because it had favored us—something no one else was likely to do. Gelanor's stern arrival drove home to me the consequences of my flight; Gelanor was right in that if I returned now, much trouble could be averted. And what awaited us at Troy? Were the Trojans likely to welcome me? They might see me as fair exchange for Hesione, but did anyone in Troy really miss Hesione but her brother?

The men jumped up as we approached. "What's this?" they cried. Three rushed over to Gelanor and surrounded him with swords. "A surviving pirate?"

Gelanor laughed. "Nothing so wild and scary," he said. "I am just a craftsman from the court of Sparta. You flatter me, taking me for a pirate."

They circled him, their blades out. He did seem flattered, as men of the mind always are when they are taken for dangerous men of the sword. "It is true," he said. He looked toward me to tell them.

"Yes," I said. "He is from Sparta. He and this woman have chased us here out of loyalty to Menelaus."

"For a craftsman, you must be an expert sailor," said the captain, coming over to him, ordering his men to lower their weapons. "This is no easy passage."

"I grew up in Gytheum," said Gelanor. "My father is a fisherman."

"Ahh," said the captain. "I see."

"Odd how certain skills one thinks forgotten can return in crucial moments," said Gelanor. "We beached on the other side of the island; the current took us there."

"Returning will be a different matter," said the captain. The currents are against you, as are the winds. Unless you have a huge sail and many rowers . . ."

For the first time since I had known him, I saw something take Gelanor by surprise—unpleasant surprise. Had he not considered the return passage? Or had he assumed he could persuade the captain to turn his large ship and take us all back to the mainland? Perhaps he been so bent on his goal he did not think of anything beyond that. What had driven him to pursue us so furiously?

"I will manage," he said stiffly.

The captain motioned for us all to gather around the fire, which was already blazing. "You are welcome here," he told Gelanor and Evadne. The wineskin was making its rounds, and someone handed it to Gelanor. He took a deep swallow and passed it on.

Aeneas came over to us. "Who did you find?"

"He found us," Paris said. "Someone from Helen's court, coming to take her back. But he wasn't sent, he just came on his own."

Aeneas glanced down at him. "Brave man," he said. "So the alarm hasn't been raised yet for our flight?"

"Gelanor and this woman left by daybreak, only a few hours after we did. Of course, by now we have been missed—all of us," I said.

"Who is this man?" asked Aeneas.

A meddler, I thought. My dear friend, too. "He serves as an adviser to Menelaus on many things," I said. "He is very clever."

"Well, what sort of things?"

"Oh . . . weaponry, supplies."

"He's a military man?"

"No, not a soldier."

"I don't understand," said Aeneas. "If he isn't a soldier, how would he be expert in soldiering? Why would his advice be valuable?"

"He just knows many things," I said. "I told you he was clever. I cannot explain it any further than that."

"We could use such a man in Troy."

"Exactly what I told him. But he refuses to go. He just wants to return to Sparta."

"You are a stubborn man, Gelanor," said Paris, raising his cup to salute him. "But as one myself, I must honor that." He took a long swallow of wine.

"Is your loyalty to Menelaus so absolute, then?" asked Aeneas.

"My loyalty is to Helen," he said. "The court at Sparta without her has no hold on me. So I shall search elsewhere for a place to employ my talents."

"Come to Troy, then!" said Aeneas.

"I said my loyalty was to Helen," said Gelanor. "I did not say I was owned by Helen, going wherever her fancy took her."

Suddenly I knew how to reach him. "Gelanor," I said, "the best service you could do for both Menelaus and me would be to accompany us to Troy and then return to Sparta to report that we have arrived safely. That way you would have seen me to the end of my journey and also stayed loyal to Menelaus, able to set his mind at ease. He will know then exactly what has happened and not be at the mercy of rumor and guessing, and can act accordingly."

Act accordingly. What might he be moved to do? No matter. The walls of Troy were high and strong. And we would be safe inside them by then.

I took a deep breath and looked into his eyes, innocently, I hoped. "Is this not the most reasonable course of action, the one that will satisfy everyone's honor?" Reason never failed with him; let it prevail now!

Instead of answering me, he shook his head and made a sound of annoyance, sitting down on the sand and joining the men around the fire. He had not said no. He was delaying his answer. Once he gave his word, I had never heard him change it. "What food are you offering a hungry man?" he asked.

Soon everyone was eating and talking. The men had explored the island during the day, and the captain and some of the soldiers had repaired the damage to the ship from the pirate attack, and hasty landing, making ready to set sail.

"It's ready, men," said the captain. "Now the true voyage can begin!"

"The dangerous part, you mean," said Paris.

"What, weren't the pirates and the bad current dangerous enough for you?" asked Aeneas.

"It's all dangerous," the captain admitted. "But if we are in favor with the gods, we should arrive safely enough in Troy."

"What route will we take?" Aeneas asked.

"We'll go from here to the island of Melos—from there to Andros. And from there, Scyros, and then to Chios—"

"Chios?" Gelanor asked.

"Yes, Chios. And then we are right upon Troy. Each jump will involve night sailing again. It's risky, but there is no other choice. The distance between these islands is too great. And I am thankful for the islands, because without them we would face too long a stretch over open water between here and Troy." He took a deep draught of wine and wiped his mouth. "So drink up tonight, get your fill of lying on the earth."

Soon all had drifted away to their sleeping places. Overhead the sky was clear and the stars friendly and white. But out on the open sea, with only blackness under us, how much comfort would we find in them?

❖ XXVIII ❖

The winds were brisk when we arose and went down to the beach in the early dawn. "A good sign," said the captain. "Let us be on our way!" The men were loading the wineskins and sacks of grain on board.

I looked around for Gelanor. But he was not there. I was disappointed but not surprised. More than anything, I was sad I would never see him again. And I worried about his safety in sailing back to Sparta alone. Would he not even speak with me before we parted?

A rustling by my side surprised me, and I turned and saw Evadne, her face almost invisible in the folds of her hood. "The snake and I are coming," she said. "He would have it no other way." She patted the bag affectionately. "This morning we were able to catch some mice for him, and that will satisfy him until we reach his new home."

I was touched that this woman, whom I had barely known all my years in Sparta, was willing to make this journey with me. So she and the snake would be all of my old life that would travel with me. That and the gold and jewels. But the woman and the snake were more precious. "Thank you for coming," I said.

"Everyone aboard," ordered the captain, and we filed down to the side of the ship and one by one climbed over the sides and took our places. Just as the last of the soldiers were mounting the ship, someone banged on the side.

"Let me speak to the captain!" Gelanor demanded. I peered out and saw him standing there, cloaked, looking impatient.

"Yes, what is it?" the captain sounded equally impatient. "We must sail straightaway."

"You said you were going to Chios," he said.

"Yes, that's what I said," he snapped.

"Can you promise that?"

The captain laughed, but it was not a happy laugh. "Ask Poseidon. Only he can promise that."

"Is it your solemn *intention* to go to Chios, and put in there?"

"Yes, how many times do you need to hear it?"

"All right, then. I shall come." He jumped up on the boulder the soldiers were using to climb in and joined us. He did not look at me or Paris, but took a seat a distance from us.

What was so special about Chios? I asked myself. Whatever it was, apparently it meant more to him than all my pleas that he come with us. It meant more to him than *me*. I glared at his back. Well, then, let him have Chios and whatever was on it!

The sky lightened and turned a clear ringing blue. We sped across the waves toward Troy.

Oh, that journey, that journey. In it I was suspended between my worlds, outside any world at all, for life on a speeding ship has no bearing on a life elsewhere. Each day held its own wonders, each night its own dangers, and so there was never a moment of feeling less than vibrantly alive. Each day seemed five years' worth of newness, yet it passed in a flash like a dream.

Our first stint, to Melos, was a very long one, and the wind failed us halfway there. The rowers had to put their strength to the oars and keep rowing at night. As it came into sight at last, the captain warned us that Melos was also a haunt of pirates, who hid in the sea caves at the base of the towering cliffs. But we passed unhindered into the curved, protected bay and beached at last in a fine harbor. Eagerly we climbed out of the confines of the ship and frolicked on land, stretching our limbs and waving our arms and whooping with joy. Paris and I danced a little dance on the sands. Evadne took the snake out of his bag and draped him around her neck and sang. Aeneas challenged Paris to a race along the seashore. Gelanor walked off by himself to inspect the seashells along the tide line.

We stayed there for several days, replenishing our water and exploring the island. I had never seen anything like it—the strange rock formations, and black stone from old volcanoes. Gelanor seemed especially interested in that—he collected shiny sharp pieces of it, saying this was obsidian and it made good knives. "Good when there's no bronze to be had." It was almost the only thing he had said to me since we had left Cythera. I made a polite, cool response, and moved away. I was still stinging about his strange turn-around in voyaging with us, and his silence about it.

In contrast to Gelanor, Evadne was very talkative, although she tended to mutter and mumble the way old women often do. I could not tell how old she really was—she seemed Sibyl-like to me and I wondered, truly, how long she had been at Sparta. Could she have been there all the way back to the reign of Oebalus or even Cynortas? She kept her eyes shaded with an overhanging flap of her head covering, saying that the bright light bothered her.

On the third day we were suddenly confronted with a crowd of islanders. The news of our arrival had spread and they came to see us. I was not fast enough in covering my face and so it caused the usual gasps and gapes. We must go before it got worse. So we left the island, thankful that we had filled up the water skins first.

"Always a problem when you travel with Helen," Gelanor told the captain. "Next time you can expect it."

Did he mean to be funny? I did not find it amusing. But Paris laughed. "A problem every other man in the world would love to have!" he said, embracing me possessively.

On we sailed to Andros, another long journey. On the way we saw other islands where we could have put in, but the captain warned us that would slow our journey a great deal. "I know we are all eager to reach Troy," he said.

The night sailing was difficult—it was impossible to sleep, and so when we reached Andros at twilight the second day I was thankful we would be spared another night at sea. Night was falling rapidly, but in the failing light I could see how majestic the island was, how high the mountains.

So it proved in the daylight—magnificent slopes, covered in green forest, with waterfalls tumbling down the gorges. "There's even a river or two here," said the captain, "good water for us. It's unusual for an island to have rivers."

We rested there for several days, rejoicing in the simple pleasures of being able to walk freely, something I had never appreciated before this voyage.

On to Scyros. When we reached it we would be at the halfway point of our journey. It was a small island, with two mountains rising up like breasts on either side of a flat area. We had not even brought our ship up to shore when soldiers appeared on the shore to question us.

"This is the island of King Lycomedes," their commander called. "Who are you? In whose name do you come?"

Paris started to answer, but Aeneas hushed him. "I am Aeneas, prince of Dardania," he said. "I am returning to my home from an embassy to Salamis."

"You are welcome, Prince, you and your men," the commander said. "We shall escort you to the palace."

Oh, no! Now we would be discovered, and our route known. Or—worst of all!—we would be captured and detained. Paris could lie about his identity, but when they saw me . . .

I went to Aeneas and spoke into his ear. "Beg for a bit of time. Say we must attend to something or other on the ship."

"Good men, let us recover a bit. It has been a tiring journey," Aeneas called.

"You can refresh yourselves at the palace. There are hot baths there, dainty food." They planted themselves stubbornly beside the boat.

"Here." I felt a tug at my cloak. Evadne was beside me. "Smear your cheeks with this." She slipped a little clay jar into my hand. "It will age you."

"Forever?" That seemed a drastic remedy.

"Until you wash it off," she said. "I call it my Hecate-cream. It is a gift from the old goddess herself."

I think you are that old goddess, I thought suddenly. How did I even know this woman was a human and not a goddess? I could not be sure she had ever even been in Sparta. And for her to appear so oddly, along with Gelanor, and carrying the sacred snake . . . I was cold with apprehension.

"A wool-carder learns much about skin and how to treat it," she explained, as if to soothe my fears. "There is a substance in wool that preserves youth. Look at my hands." She held them out, and indeed they were smooth, the hands of a girl—in contrast to her wrinkly face. "There are other substances that mimic age." She pressed the jar into my palm. "Hurry, my dear." The soldiers were peering into the ship. I bent down and smeared my face with the thick gray clay. It spread surprisingly easily, and I could barely feel it on my skin. "Pull your hair back," she said, taking it roughly in her hands and twisting it up in a knot. Then she took a coarse wool scarf and wound it about my head to hide my hair completely. "Remember to bend as you walk. Forget your usual walk. Now your hips ache and your feet are swollen."

I was barely finished with this transformation before we were being herded off the ship and marched on a path up the mountain, to the palace perched at its summit. I tried to remember to hunch over and walk painfully. I even requested a stick to lean on. Paris kept abreast with Aeneas and I hobbled along with Evadne.

Suddenly we were on a smooth plateau and the palace appeared before us—polished pillars and a shaded porch fronting a wide two-story building. Courtiers scurried out and ushered us in, under the shaded gallery and into the smaller courtyard. The climb had been a steep one and it was not difficult for me to remember to pant and keep bent.

Soon the king appeared, hobbling out. He was as old as I was pretending to be. "Welcome, strangers. You will dine with us and spend the night," he said.

Now there must be a long ceremonial dinner, presentation of gifts. I was thankful that protocol forbade his asking us our names or our business until after the dinner—that would give us longer to rehearse our stories to ourselves.

He led us into the great hall, and suddenly we were surrounded by a host of young girls, like a flock of butterflies. "My daughters," he said. "I have more daughters than any other king, I'll warrant."

"No sons?" asked Aeneas.

"The gods did not send me that blessing," he said. But he held out his arms to embrace several of his daughters, laughing. "What the palace lacks in warriors, it makes up for in beauty."

The banquet was as all banquets—ordered, predictable, mildly pleasant. Has anything of importance ever happened at a banquet? I was seated with the women and girls, since I was supposed to be a member of Aeneas's entourage of no special rank. The king's eldest daughter was on one side—her name was Deïdameia and I guessed her to be fifteen or sixteen. Her gown was a light creamy green. Again I thought of a butterfly. Beside her was a girl who looked older and bigger, but I had been told specifically that Deïdameia was the eldest. This girl said little and kept her eyes down. The arm that emerged from her tunic when she cut her meat seemed oddly muscular.

"Pyrrha, can you not speak to our guests?" Deïdameia coaxed.

Pyrrha lifted her eyes and for a moment they looked familiar to me. Then she blinked and seemed to struggle for words. "Have you had adventures along the way?" she asked in a low voice.

"Once we ran into pirates," I said.

"Oh, where?"

I started to tell the truth but then realized I must not indicate we had been anywhere in the vicinity of Cythera—too close to Sparta. Instead I said, "Near Melos."

"What happened?"

"There was a fierce fight, but our men beat them."

"By Hermes, I'd like to have been there!" she said fiercely.

"Oh, Pyrrha!" Deïdameia gave a tinkling laugh.

Pyrrha wanted to know all about the weapons the pirates had used, and what type of boat they had used to overtake us. But she was interrupted in her string of questions by the launching of the ceremonial part of the dinner. Gifts were presented from Lycomedes to Aeneas, and Aeneas proffered some bronze from the ship. Then, and only then, did Lycomedes ask, "And who are you, friend?"

"I am Aeneas, prince of Dardania."

"Welcome, Prince Aeneas!" Lycomedes said in a quavering voice. "And who have you with you?"

Paris stepped forward, "His cousin, good king. His cousin Alexandros."

The king nodded. "And these others—your guards and attendants, yes?"

"Yes," he said. He did not introduce Evadne, Gelanor, or me, except to say, "These are trusted servers of my counsel and chamber."

"You are all most welcome," the king repeated.

Afterward there were hours to fill, and the king arranged an exhibition of dancing acrobatics for us, with boys and girls leaping over ropes and flipping themselves across the backs of carved wooden bulls, using the horns to vault themselves over.

"In Crete, they say, they leap over the horns of real bulls," said Paris.

"Too dangerous," said the king. "I prefer that all my acrobats return home without blood."

One of the dancers slipped under a rope when he missed his beat to jump it, and pretended nothing was amiss.

"I saw that!" Pyrrha's rough voice rang out.

The words were spit out just as ones I had heard once before. *I saw that.* Three simple words, but spoken with singularly distinctive disdain and venom. *I saw that.*

"Saw what?" the king asked, but his tone said, *That's enough, Pyrrha.*

"I— Oh, never mind!" She hunched her shoulders and turned away, going to lean against a pillar.

How tall she was. Taller even than the king. Had his queen been exceptionally tall? I went over to her.

"Go away," she muttered.

I was shocked at this rudeness. One never ordered a guest to go away, especially one older than oneself. Before I could utter a word, she turned and glared at me. And I recognized the eyes of Achilles, that angry child I had last seen ten years ago mingling with the suitors in Sparta.

A boy! A boy disguised as a girl, here on the island of Scyros. Why? No wonder he was angry, having to pretend to be a girl.

As he looked at me, I saw that he also recognized me. *Helen*—his mouth silently formed the word. *Helen!*

"Shh," I said. "Say nothing."

Then we both began to laugh, trying to stifle ourselves. Achilles disguised as a girl looked out at Helen disguised as an old woman servant. And neither of us could ask why.

Just then the courtyard was filled with clattering, and we turned to see the king's youngest daughters trotting in on tiny horses, clutching their manes. We both looked to the courtyard. Even standing on tiptoe, I had trouble seeing over all the heads crowding around, but Achilles would be able to see easily.

"These miniature horses—where did they come from?" I asked him. But there was no answer. I turned to see that he had gone, slipped silently away from the column.

I pretended to watch and applaud the riders, but all I could think of was,

Achilles is here, in hiding! Did the king know? Did Deïdameia? Did anyone besides me?

Now I remembered Paris telling me that Achilles was already spoken of in Troy. But in what way? He could not be older than sixteen. That would make him the same age as Paris. How could he have made a name for himself as a warrior, with no wars to fight? There were always local skirmishes and disputes, but a great soldier does not arise from such.

And a great soldier is not of a character to hide among women!

The little horses were trotting in circles around the courtyard to loud applause. To me they looked as horses shrunken down to fit the children, a magical sight.

"These horses come from wild herds farther down the mountain," said Deïdameia. "No one knows why they live only on this island. Even if they are descended from some that were brought here and escaped, where were they brought from? No other place has such tiny ones."

"Perhaps the brisk sea air or special plants here stunted their growth." Gelanor was standing beside us, staring intently at the horses. This was just the sort of puzzle he liked.

I longed to whisper the secret about Achilles into his ear; my confusion about it overpowered my lingering pique at his earlier behavior. But I could not. Somehow I knew that this knowledge was a secret I must keep to myself until we had left Scyros. Achilles trusted me with it, as I trusted him with mine.

We could not linger on Scyros, unless we fancied day after day of the king's hospitality. By dawn we were descending the hill, accompanied by servants bearing supplies for us, and by midmorning we had set sail for Chios. When we were safely away, and the wind billowed the sail, I flung off my head covering and splashed seawater on my face to wash off the Hecate-cream. I was tired of being old. How wonderful to be able to wash it away!

"Thank you," I told Evadne. "Your quick thinking and your help saved me. Saved me from . . . being Helen."

The island was receding behind us. When it is out of sight, I thought, I will tell Paris and Gelanor about Achilles. But even when Scyros dwindled and disappeared on the horizon, I could not. And I hoped that, far behind me, Achilles likewise respected my own secret.

* * *

Chios meant more night sailing, and through rough seas almost due east. We clung hard to the stays and handholds to keep from being thrown out, but even so we were drenched as the waves broke over the sides of the ship. Shivering and miserable, we stared at the horizon, hoping to see Chios. But all we saw was the rising sun, shining out over the heaving waves.

I began to feel seasick, an illness that I had been spared up until now. "Look out at the horizon, my lady," Evadne told me. "Lift your eyes away from the waves. And here, suck on this." She handed me a salted piece of pork. "Salt helps."

The bitter taste of the meat seemed to promise more stomach-churning, but she was right; somehow it countered the seasickness. I kept my eyes fastened straight ahead, over the waves, and was one of the first to see Chios when it emerged from the mists of twilight.

Like the others, it had mountains; unlike the others, it was very large, a massive piece of land lying just off the coast—the coast where Troy itself lay. This would be the end of the floating, free run that I had had—like the race I had run before my marriage. In one I had flown over the grass, in this I had flown over the sea. Now all that must end.

Grateful to be ashore, everyone disembarked. There were people here on this island; it was known for its fine wine. I knew I would have to disguise myself again, but surely that could wait. Surely no one would find us before morning.

A camp was set up, and speedily: this being our sixth stop, we had become expert in what to do. Soon we were sitting around the fire, waiting for our food to be done, drinking our wine—which was turning sour now.

"Perhaps we can refill our skins here at Chios," said the captain. "That would improve matters!"

"What do we have to exchange?"

"A lot of leftover bronze," said Paris. "We came well equipped with gifts."

"A cauldron for an amphora. Sounds like a fair trade."

The wine, on top of the residual seasickness, made me light-headed. The stars overhead seem to turn slowly as I watched. My head fell back on Paris's shoulder. I remember nothing more about that evening.

I was one of the first to awaken and leave the tent shelter. I walked down to the sea and let the steady rhythm of the waves help clear the fog of sleep from my mind.

"You won't see Troy from this side of the island."

I turned to find Gelanor standing beside me. The noise of the sea had drowned out his footfalls.

"I am not sure I wish to see Troy," I replied.

"A little late to think of that."

"You've turned into a scold. As soon as we reach Troy, you can turn around and go back. That is what you want. So you must be pleased that we are within a short journey of your escape." Let him go. Let him leave. His presence had been oppressive on this voyage.

"I haven't yet had what I want from this journey."

"What is that?"

"I am about to grasp it today. I will head south and find it."

"Find what?"

"A certain kind of shrub that produces a sweet sticky gum. It grows elsewhere, but only here does its sap harden naturally if the stem is bled."

I was disgusted. So that was what made him change his mind and come on board. *That* was what Chios offered him—a tree sap.

"Come and see," he said. "It will be fascinating to find. I think there could be many uses for such a substance. It could serve as incense in place of expensive myrrh, or as an ointment, or as syrup, or—oh, when I smell and taste it, I'll know."

"I have no interest in it," I said.

"Oh, Helen, once you would have. Do not change, do not take on the lightness of . . . those you associate with."

"He is not light!"

"So shall we wait and include him?" Gelanor looked up at the sun. "However, it might be a long wait. He does not emerge from his tent until midmorning sometimes."

"No. It would be too late to start then."

"I thought you were not coming." He laughed. "Oh, do. It would be a good stretch of your legs. They must be cramped from sitting so long on the ship. I know mine are."

So it was decided. I was going with him. It had been a long time since we had walked side by side—since the fateful trip to Gytheum.

Chios was a lovely island, but less green than Andros. Fewer tall trees meant that the wind whipped across it faster. I fancied that the wind came from Troy—brisk and energetic. The hillsides were covered in scrub and bushes.

"How will you ever know the bush you seek?" I asked him.

"I've seen its dried leaves," he said. "I will recognize them. And we may see cuts on the trunks where people bleed them for the sap."

As we walked along, I saw bright yellow and pink orchids in the limestone crags. "I've never seen so many," I said, bending down to pick one. I tucked it behind my ear.

"Nor I," admitted Gelanor. "This island must favor them." Suddenly he stopped and grabbed my arm. "There!" He pointed to a nondescript bush. Then he hurried over to it and knelt down, inspecting the leaves. Taking out a small piece of the sharp obsidian from Melos, he made a neat cut across the stem. Immediately a clear sap oozed out.

"Now we wait." He sat down beside it. "For how long, I don't know." He pointed out across the sea. "But look, while we wait—your new home."

I shaded my eyes. The water was bright and the sun was reflecting off it, making a glare of everything around it. But beyond it—yes, there was land.

"The land of Troy," Gelanor said. "Fabled Troy."

I could tell nothing about it, save that it had hills and was somewhat green.

Beside me, he laughed. "What did you expect? Walls of gold?"

"There has to be a city before there can be walls, of gold or stone. I see no city."

"That's farther away. This is merely the region surrounding Troy, its neighbors. The Carians, the Lycians, the Mysians. People just like anyone else. Disappointed?"

"That—or relieved." In truth I did not know.

"Oh, come, now—you did not turn your world inside out to find yourself back among ordinary people."

He did not understand. He had never been touched by Aphrodite. He could not see that it was Paris—Paris, not Troy or the Trojans or walled cities—that called to me, held me fast in a net. To those whom the goddess had never visited, all this was incomprehensible. So I merely smiled and said nothing.

"Look!" He was turning around and scrambling over to the bush. The sap had turned amber-colored and formed little beads. Gelanor broke one off and rolled it between his fingers. It was springy, and when he squeezed it, it plumped back into its original shape. He sniffed it, then handed it to me.

I played with it and tried crushing it. When I mashed it, a delightful scent filled the air, much like smoky incense. But when it resumed its shape, the odor vanished. I nibbled on it and found the taste to be stinging, much like pine sap.

"What wondrous things people could do with this!" he said. "If we find the collectors of the sap, we'll ask them what they use it for here on Chios. I know it is traded abroad, but only for mending things or making them watertight."

I hoped we did not see anyone. It was so tiresome, being Helen. It was likewise tiresome pretending not to be Helen.

"So now you've seen it," I said. "What you endured the long sea voyage for." I could not keep the bitterness from seeping into my voice.

"Oh, Helen, you know better than that."

"Or perhaps you just could not face the dangers of sailing back through the Cythera channel by yourself. The captain painted a black picture of it. So you hid your fear with this excuse of wanting to come to Chios. Now you can safely return over land. A long way, but doubtless you will find many rocks and trees and poisons along the journey to entertain you and make it worthwhile."

"Helen." He was looking hard at me. "You know better than that," he repeated.

"No. No, I don't."

"Must you force me to say it? I had changed my mind, and yes, you are right, I needed some coloration for it. I could not let myself be seen as an indecisive, silly boy. But the reason I had changed my mind was that I needed to see you safe to Troy."

I laughed. "Did you not trust the captain, and Aeneas and Paris and all those soldiers? Are you better protection than they?"

"Perhaps not, but I had a bond of honor with myself. I said there on the beach of Cythera that my loyalty was to you, not Sparta. Leaving you there would not be an act of loyalty. Quite the opposite. So I have come all this way, and I will stay until you are ushered inside the walls of Troy." He took the ball of resin back from me. "So you see, you have been angry with me all these days for no good reason."

I shook my head as if it were of no matter. But I felt secure again. My friend was back. Indeed, he had never gone away, except in my own mind. Keeping him in Troy . . . that would be another matter. Another challenge.

* * *

We waited and collected a small bag full of the mysterious sap, then walked back to the ship. As we passed a wooded site in the hills, I was suddenly over-come with a feeling for the significance of this place, that it would be of im-mense importance to me, to Paris, to all of us. I stopped and stared at it. There was nothing there. No hut, no herds, no garden, no people. Yet some-day there would be.

"What is it?" asked Gelanor. "You are staring at nothing, at the empty air."

"No, not empty." It was thick with something.

"Is it evil?"

"No. It is—it is glorious. Something wonderful will come from here."

PART II

TROY

❖ XXIX ❖

The crossing to the mainland where Troy lay was not exciting. It should have been, but it was not. I should have felt the brushing of Aphrodite's wings against my cheeks, should have beheld omens or heard faraway music, but everything was ordinary.

The soil where I stepped was ordinary: plain dirt with a few straggling blades of grass. A distinctly ordinary breeze was blowing, and it brought no unusual perfumes or scents. I sighed, oddly disappointed.

"What is it, my love?" asked Paris, who heard my slightest breath. "We are almost home!"

Your home, I thought. Your home. "I am nervous," I admitted.

He looked surprised. "Helen is nervous? Why, the world always bows before you."

That was about to end, I thought. And had I not longed for it to end? Had I not complained endlessly about it to myself?

"A new world for you to conquer!" he said.

"You are more certain of that than I."

We were walking slowly toward a clump of—ordinary—trees, where we would ready ourselves for the last stage of the journey. Behind us Aeneas was shouting orders at the men, and the captain was barking about how to secure the ship.

"Come!" Paris took my hand and ran with me to a knoll, where he pointed north. The endless, featureless landscape fell away before his finger. "If you could fly directly, like an eagle, there lies Troy." He turned my shoulders and held me to him. "But you would not be an eagle; no, you would be one of those bright-colored birds that live somewhere far to the south. I've never seen one, but I've seen the feathers—yellow and red and brilliant green."

If I were a bird . . . but my feet were standing on rocky soil, and it was my feet that must carry me to Troy. I said as much.

"We could have horses," he said. "You are now in the land of horses. I told you Troy was famous for them. We can get chariots and wagons—"

"No! I do not want them to know we are coming. Horses and chariots will announce us."

He looked puzzled. "Why should they not know we are coming?"

"I want—I want it to be unexpected," I said. Somehow I thought that would be safer. But safer in what way? Would it postpone the disfavor and dismay I now dreaded?

"But they will want to welcome us properly."

"Before we arrive, you must tutor me all about the Trojans. All your family, and the court. I need to know what they look like, what their strengths and weaknesses are, and how you feel about them. I want to be able to recognize them the first time I see them." Somehow I felt that would give me protection. And I wanted very much to know those whom Paris held dear—and the others whom he did not.

We traveled very slowly through the landscape. We had landed on a long narrow cape that jutted far out into the sea, as if it were reaching rocky fingers toward Chios. For a bit we could see the sea on both sides, but soon we were enveloped by the gentle hills and plains.

The roads—such as they were—were rough and narrow, and we passed no cities. Few people came out to see us, and those who did were farmers and herdsmen.

"Where are the allies of Troy you told me about?" I asked Paris as we walked along.

"A bit farther inland," he said. "We have the Lycians and the Maeonians. You'll see them soon enough." He laughed. "Perhaps even the Amazons will come to court to greet you."

"Amazons. Are there really such things?" I had learned that Paris liked to tease. Sometimes I wondered if he was ever truly serious.

"Oh, yes. Beyond the Black Sea."

"Have you ever actually seen an Amazon?"

"No . . . but my brother Hector has. Remember, I myself have not been long in Troy. Hector said that the one who came to court was as tall as he was, and had great muscular arms—she was quite frightening!"

{ 234 }

"Tonight—you must tell me all about Hector and the rest. You promised!" In only a few days we would arrive in Troy and I must know.

"Ah, yes!" He cupped his hands and called to Aeneas. "Dear cousin, tonight you and I must put on a show!"

The fire burning brightly, we sat on woven mats and lay back, wine cups in hand. "No more delays," I told Paris. "Let me learn so I can recognize them and greet them by name." I called Gelanor and Evadne over to join us.

"Very well." Paris motioned to Aeneas, who stood up and turned his back on us. In a moment he turned around and stood facing us, a scowl on his face, thumping a large staff, which I assumed was to mimic a spear. "Who is it?"

"That must be Hector." He was the oldest son, the finest warrior there that I had heard of. But was he also fierce and unpleasant?

Paris laughed. "Fooled you! We wouldn't start with the most obvious. You will learn better if they're all mixed up. This is Deiphobus, a bit older than I. He wants to be Hector, but isn't. Pity." He waved to Aeneas. "Next."

Aeneas returned partially stooped, wearing a woman's headdress. Earrings made of string hung from his ears and he seemed to have a wig on, but one suspiciously strawlike.

An older woman . . . but he couldn't mean Queen Hecuba, could he? Shuffling along like that, bent over? "An old priestess?" I ventured.

"No, no! There *is* a high-ranking priestess of Athena, named Theano. But she's younger. This is my mother, Queen Hecuba."

"So old?" I asked.

"Well—we exaggerated," Paris admitted. "After all, my brother Troilus is younger than I am, and there's a daughter and son younger yet. So she is not so far away from childbearing."

"Tell me about Troilus," I said.

"He's very handsome, and he loves horses. He's a great tamer of them, a great charioteer. But although he's good-looking, he seems unaware of it and he's very friendly and loving."

Aeneas came back in, still wearing the wig, but now with a mantle draped backward over him to suggest a gown. He whirled around, pointing and mouthing silent cries.

"Oh, she'll never get this one," said Paris. "That isn't fair. She doesn't even know about her."

"Doom! Doom!" rasped Aeneas.

"Cassandra," said Evadne in a low voice.

Paris started. "How can you know that?"

"The less I see with my eyes, the more I hear from far away. Other minds tell me things, even in Sparta. This is your sister Cassandra, the one who prophesies doom to Troy."

Aeneas stopped acting. "It seems that you may be a prophetess as well."

"No," said Evadne. "I merely use what is brought to my senses. But this Cassandra—has she not been your enemy, Paris?"

Paris gripped my hand so hard it tingled. "I have no enemies."

"But when you returned, did not this sister try to have you cast out again?" Evadne persisted.

"No!" said Aeneas quickly. "No, nothing like that. And no one listens to Cassandra. She is mad."

"Not mad," said Evadne. "You know that. Just cursed by Apollo, because she spurned him. So the great god of prophecy revenged himself on her by making it so that she had the gift of prophecy but no one would believe her. What crueler punishment for a seer?"

"It wasn't Apollo who made her a seer," said Paris. "She and her twin brother Helenus had their ears licked by serpents when they were infants, and that gave them the gift of prophecy."

Serpents. The call to prophecy. We were siblings in that gift. Would we recognize one another?

"But it was Apollo who twisted the gift into a curse for her," said Aeneas.

Would Aphrodite have twisted mine into some sort of curse if I had rejected her? I shuddered. Obey them, resist them—either way the gods inflict misery on us.

Paris heaved himself up from the mat. "My turn," he said. Aeneas took his place, watching.

Paris strutted his way across our vision, his head held high, grasping a stave.

"A councilor of some kind," I said. But was he a good councilor or a bad one?

Paris preened a bit, inspecting his sleeves.

"Even I cannot know who you mean," said Aeneas. "We have many pompous councilors."

"Pandarus," said Paris. "I admit, there are many Pandarus-like fellows about."

"Pandarus is an irksome fool," said Aeneas.

"You can take his place!" said Paris, pointing at Gelanor. "We need some new blood in the council chambers."

Gelanor laughed. "A Spartan serving as a Trojan councilor? I think not."

I noticed that he did not add, *and besides, I am not remaining at Troy.*

"But the queen of Sparta will now serve as . . . princess of Troy. People can change countries. Yes, and she will be honored beyond anything you can imagine!"

"I shall watch the ceremonies, then, as a guest," said Gelanor. "Before returning home." I was disappointed to hear those words.

Paris kept his staff but dropped the flourishes. Instead, he struck a monumental pose.

"Still a councilor . . . or perhaps a seer," said Aeneas. "But a respectable one. Oh!" He smacked his cheeks. "Of course! His brother Calchas!"

"Excellent. Excellent." Paris bowed. "Yes. Helen, Calchas is one of our most trusted seers and councilors. He is embarrassed by Pandarus, but we cannot choose our relatives."

"Exactly what your brothers may say about you when they see what you have brought back to Troy," said Aeneas quietly. "Paris, have you thought how you will present Helen?"

"As my wife," he said. His face was open and brave.

"But she is not your wife," said Aeneas. "She is someone else's wife."

"No! She has renounced him. Let us marry now, this moment, so I can look the king, my father, in the eye and tell him honestly that Helen is my wife."

"But . . . we have no power to perform that rite!" Alarm rose in Aeneas's voice.

"Power? There is no special power needed. The gods will hear us! All we need is to clasp our hands and vow ourselves before witnesses. There are three witnesses here. That is sufficient."

So: here, on this plain ground somewhere on the way to Troy, sometime in the evening, but at no hallowed time—neither at sunset nor midnight nor sunrise—wearing only traveling clothes, with no bridal dowry or gift, I would wed Paris.

"Yes," I said. "Let us do this." I turned to the others. "I ask you, bring what you find to help celebrate this. Let us make it our own, using only what is at hand."

My mantle was dull brown, stained with sea spray and dirt. My gown was rumpled and its hem smeared with mud. My hair was bound up in a coil, my feet dusty from the path.

Bridal attire was supposed to have prophetic powers. What did this mean—that Paris and I would be dusty wayfarers? That we would be reduced to poverty? I could not see how this would be, but I no longer scoffed at the idea that the unimaginable could come about.

Gelanor brought his bag of dried mastic resin from Chios; Aeneas a skin of wine and clay cups; Evadne the sack with the snake. Paris took a torch and went out into the fields searching for night-blooming flowers, but it was too early in the season for them.

Aeneas planted two torches before the entrance of our tent and then beckoned us over to the fire. "Now say what you must," he said.

Paris took my hand and led me to the warmth of the fire. A light, chilly wind had arisen, and was blowing across the fields and out to sea. My hands were cold as he took them, covering my fingers with his. How many times had we held hands? Yet this felt different, heavy with intent.

If I just slid my fingers away, pulled back . . . then all could be undone. If I did not, now, then I was bound forever. The grip of his hands on mine felt imprisoning, like clamps. I could not move my fingers.

"Speak," said Aeneas. "It is only you who must speak now. No priest, no priestess, no mother, no father. As it is when all those things fall away and you are alone."

Paris shut his eyes and bowed his head, thinking. He had never looked more boyish, more disarming. His light hair fell forward in glorious waves. The firelight turned his perfect skin to gold. In this light, even his garments were turned to gold. Had Midas touched him, turning him from a living being into a statue of metal?

"I am Paris, son of King Priam and Queen Hecuba of Troy," he said, lifting his head. "I was born to them the night my mother had a dream that she gave birth to a flaming brand. One of my brothers proclaimed that it meant I would bring fire and destruction to Troy. So my mother and father cast me out, left me to the will of the gods. But their will was that I should live, and they gave me a glorious childhood in the glens and meadows of Mount Ida, the mountain where Zeus himself resides." He stopped and took a deep breath. "Then, when I was ready, the gods brought me back to my true home and family."

The fire crackled and leapt up at that moment, and Paris laughed. "I thought nothing was lacking in my happiness then. I knew my mother, my father, my family—cousins like Aeneas. I belonged to their world. But that happiness was as pale as dying smoke compared to the fire that consumed me when I first beheld you, Helen." He took my face and turned it full to his. "Since then it has been as if the sun has never set, there is no night. And so before you here, I pledge myself to Helen for the rest of my life. I shall care for nothing but her, look at nothing but her, think of nothing but her, as long as I shall live. I offer myself to you utterly, Helen. Please take me."

His eyes pled with me, as if this were the first time we had ever spoken. As if it was all only starting now.

"I take you, Paris," I answered, my voice low. I had trouble speaking, I was so affected by the solemnity of this moment. "I am yours forever." I could not speak of how much and what this meant. Surely those four words said everything.

"We stand as witnesses to these promises," said Aeneas. "And now we will drink a cup of wine together." He measured out the portions and handed the cups around. Before we drank, he poured a libation on the ground and invoked Hera as goddess of marriage. "Bind them, O goddess," he beseeched her, "in the sacred union of marriage."

We all raised our cups and sipped the sweet wine in silence.

Gelanor took a handful of the resin beads and cast them into the fire. The smoky fragrance of the renowned mastic rose, dense and compelling.

Evadne stepped forward and held out the snake in both her arms. "Take him," she said. "Let him bind you." She placed him around our necks, where he curled, seeking our warmth.

He had bound us once before, in Sparta. Now he sealed our union, tying the past, the present, and the future together in his graceful coils.

Aeneas motioned us to the tent. "Now take yourselves to your new home. Here, we will accompany you the short distance with torch and song, as if this were a regular marriage procession."

Our short and subdued little parade walked over to the tent, and then we left them and went inside.

Even the familiar tent now seemed different. The quick improvised vows felt more genuine than the lengthy ceremony I had undergone with Menelaus, with its heavy gold necklace, traditional promises, priestesses, and sacrifice, all a blur now. But I would never forget the look in Paris's eyes as he made those sweeping, wild promises to me.

"Your gift," he said, kneeling and handing me a jar.

I opened its covering and peered in. A light flutter showed itself against the clay.

"A big white moth," he said. "I caught it when I was looking for moon-flowers. I think the moth was looking, too."

"Oh, it is lovely," I said. The white wings were pulsing gently at the bottom of the jar. "But we must let it go. Tonight, all creatures must be as free as we are. Come." Together we stood at the entrance of the tent and shook the jar, setting the moth free. It floated away, seeking the fields.

"We are that moth," I said. "Now we are free in the fields, the fields that belong to neither kingdom, not to Troy or Sparta or Argos or Mysia." I threw my arms around him, all hesitations flown away with the moth.

❖ XXX ❖

Troy. It shone before us, floating up over the featureless plain like a vast and impregnable ship on a swelling sea. Behind us lay Mount Ida; we had skirted its pine-covered flanks and now nothing stood between us and Troy.

As we came closer and it loomed larger, it seemed less and less real. Its walls were of gleaming, fitted masonry. Massive towers, square and lowering, guarded the circuit of the walls, and spread out like a flung mantle beneath those walls were countless houses. It was as grand as Mycenae and Sparta and Pylos and Tiryns all put together—more delicately wrought and yet more formidable.

I walked, keeping it ever before my eyes, seeing it grow to fill more and more of my vision. Beside me, Evadne kept her face toward it, but her expression did not change.

"You cannot see it," I said. "But if you could—you would know it is something you have never beheld in Greece."

She turned her head rapidly and said, "Oh, yes! I know! It gleams!"

"How did you know that?"

"I saw it."

"But you cannot see . . . you told us so."

"My lady, it is very odd. I cannot see straight on, but sometimes, if I move my head quickly, I can glimpse something just out to the side. But if I then turn to face it and look, it disappears. It is so maddening. It means I can only see the shadows and hints of things, and never look directly at them. But I saw Troy, for that tiny instant. And it shines like a crystal."

"So you have a bit of sight. Perhaps that is why your eyes do not look like a blind person's; they appear as clear and bright as anyone's."

"So I have been told. I fear I must have angered some god and this is how I am being punished, but I cannot for my very life know what I have done."

"Not everything that happens is from the hands of the gods." Gelanor came up beside us.

"Do not let them hear you say that!" Evadne laughed. "They might strike me again to make their point. Look, what do you see when you see Troy?"

"Power and beauty," he said.

"Wealth?" I added.

"Wealth and power are the same thing. And together they underpin beauty. The world of nature can give us beauty cheaply, but the world of man requires wealth to make beauty."

"Here it lies, Helen!" Paris came running, light of foot, and took my hand. "Troy. My home. Now yours as well."

Troy will never be home to me, I thought fleetingly. "Will I . . . will I be able to speak easily to the people?"

"Of course, to the people at court. We speak much as you do—a few odd words here and there may be different. But, after all, we are related, we Trojans and Greeks. We share common ancestors—Atlas and Pleione, at least the old tales tell us so. The workers and people in the big city below the walls, they are a bit hard to understand, unless you have grown up with common people as I have. But I'll translate for you—just as I do for Hector and the rest of my family." He hugged me close to him. "Helen, I'm so proud—to show Troy to you—and you to Troy."

Troy did not seem curious to see me. I should have been thankful for that—had I not wished to cease being an object of curiosity? But now it hinted at something amiss. The high towers, standing like sentinels, must have guards inside, guards whose duty was only to spy out anyone approaching the city. The parapets encircling them looked like jagged teeth, and the height would make anyone inside dizzy.

. . . *And burnt the topless towers of Ilium.* The words twined themselves around my mind. *Topless towers of Ilium* . . . someone else framed those words, and whispered them to me then, someone who lived so long afterward

that he saw Troy only in his dreams, but he saw it clearer than anyone standing beside me that day I first approached it, he told of Troy when men had
forgotten her, and now she lives . . . or perhaps Troy was always only a dream.

"How long since we sailed away?" Paris asked Aeneas. "Time has ceased to
pass for me. But for Troy . . . how long might they have been expecting us?"

"Some two full moons since we left," said Aeneas. "But since the duration
of our mission could not be predicted, nor could the winds promise a certain
return, we may take them by surprise."

We reached the outskirts of the city, protected by a stout wooden palisade
fence; its sharpened tips turned the top into a row of spears. Now, in the
peace of noonday, the outer gate was wide open, and people were streaming
in and out, chattering and carrying baskets and bundles. They smiled and
greeted us, calling out playfully to Paris, but other than that paid us little
mind. However, like the ripples of a wave, word of our arrival raced ahead of
us as we walked through the streets.

"These streets seem like any other streets," I told Paris.

"Of course," he said. "Did I not assure you that Troy would not seem foreign to you?"

"I meant, they are not very wide. Whenever Troy is spoken of, people say,
'broad-streeted Troy.' But it is not so."

He laughed. "Wait until you get inside the walls, into the *real* Troy—or
rather, the famous Troy. The one that all men speak of. When they say Troy,
they do not mean *this*." He flung out his arm to encompass the small houses
and shops all around us.

Behind us our guardian soldiers trooped, stopping to swig new wine they
bartered for their smiles and promises. All the time we were walking uphill toward the high walls, which seemed to elongate and reach for the sky even as
we approached. The houses fell away and left a broad swath before the glistening, slanted masonry. A square guard tower jutted out almost to the nearest house; before it were stone pillars holding statues.

"The gods who protect Troy," Paris said. "Apollo, Aphrodite, Ares, and
Artemis."

Glancing at them, I thought how unlike the glorious gods these stone
representations were. Plain, squat, broad-featured: surely the gods would renounce these likenesses. But no one knew how to make better ones. We fashioned the gods in their splendor only in our minds.

"This is the south gate," Paris said. "Some people say it is the grandest, but they are all grand."

I looked overhead at the large beckoning entrance and I could not see how it could be grander.

"Inside, inside, my love—my wife. See my city!"

We passed through a dark tunnellike entrance through the walls, some fifteen paces wide—oh, such wide walls above us!—and then out into the sunlight and a wide paved courtyard.

"Oh, are we already at the palace?" I asked.

Paris laughed. "No, no. This roadway circles the walls. It makes a broad street for us to parade upon, walk upon, merely to look upon. We do not permit houses next to the walls."

I had never beheld such a thing. A street only to give space. The sunlight seemed to fill every aspect.

"The palace, the temple of Athena, the living quarters of the king's children—they are all farther up, at the summit. All Father's sons and daughters live in apartments surrounding the palace, but now I'm going to build my own. We need not be like all the others!"

"Perhaps we should not insist—" We were asking so much already.

"Nonsense!"

A young man flew toward us, almost tripping over his sandaled feet as he rushed down the sloping street.

"Troilus!" Paris's voice was warm with affection. This, then, must be his favorite younger brother.

"Is it really you, Paris?" Troilus stopped, panting, clutching Paris's mantle. He was light-haired and freckled, with an open, sunburnt gladness about him.

"Your eyes see true," Paris said.

Troilus turned them toward me. "What—who—?"

"I have brought home a wife!" proclaimed Paris.

"But how—?"

"I will explain all to our father, and thereby tell it once—although I would gladly tell it a thousand times, for I love the telling of it."

"Aeneas?" cried Troilus. "I see you have brought my brother safely home, as you promised."

"I have brought him home," said Aeneas. "Safely is another matter."

Again poor Troilus looked perplexed. "He looks well enough."

"Aye, there's the pity. Had he looked less well, then . . ." He shrugged. "All will become clear in time."

We resumed walking, Troilus falling in beside us. Then a woman came flying down the street, arms outstretched. She rushed to embrace Aeneas.

"My wife, Creusa," he finally mumbled, when he could get his breath.

She was small, fair, and fine-featured. Her eyes missed nothing. Now they looked me over. There was none of the usual squinting or pandering. "Who is with Paris?" she asked.

"He calls her wife," said Aeneas.

"But where—"

"I shall explain all once I see the king and queen, my father and mother," Paris said again.

"Oh." Creusa turned back to him, losing interest in me.

What a novel experience! Did it sting? Or was it a relief? A bit of both.

As we walked toward the top of the city, more and more people came out of their houses, drawn by the large company of soldiers tramping behind us. They were well dressed and only then did I notice how handsome the men were. Just so: the godlike Trojan men, renowned everywhere. So it was true.

Opening up before us was a wide pavement—a level courtyard. We must have reached the top at last. It had been a long walk, much farther than walking from the palace in Sparta down to the banks of the river and to the city. Troy was, then, truly immense.

The view was dazzling. A tree-dotted plain spread out before us on three sides, and on the fourth the sea shone a hard reflective blue. The buildings crowning the courtyard were of two stories, surrounded by brightly painted pillars, and boasting wide welcoming porches with overhanging roofs. One of them was fronted with stately columns; this looked to be the temple.

Just then there was a stirring in the portico of the largest building, and an elderly man stepped out, shading his eyes. I knew immediately it was Priam. He was tall and commanding even in his advanced years; his tunic did not hang limply around the frame of a shrunken man, but rippled as from the shoulders of a warrior.

"Father!" Paris held out his arms and walked swiftly toward him.

"Oh, my dear son!" Priam came forward and embraced him. "Welcome home!"

Aeneas inclined his head with respect. "You bade me bring him home safely," he said. "That I have done."

"You shall tell me all!" said Priam. "Tonight. We'll have such a feast—" He suddenly looked around. "No Hesione? What did she say?"

"We did not see her, but from all accounts she does not care to leave Salamis," said Paris. "She is old, she is content . . ." He shrugged. "What would be the point in abducting her? Would your joy in beholding her offset her sorrow in leaving her home?"

"This was her home!" Priam thundered, and I thought of Zeus.

"Homes change," said Paris. "Mine did, from the slopes of Mount Ida and a herdsman's hut, to Troy." He took my hand and drew me to his side. "And hers has changed as well. From Sparta to Troy."

"What do you mean?" His voice was sharp. "Who is this, Paris?"

"Do you not recognize her?"

"I have never seen her before in my life."

"But nonetheless you should recognize her. Just look upon her face."

He narrowed his eyes and looked at me. Then he shook his head. No one had ever done that before.

"Oh, Father, come now. There is only one person in the world who could look like that, and you know who it is."

"Yes," said Priam. "And that face has told me I am a liar, something I have never been. Never!"

"What do you mean?" Paris dropped my hand.

"They have already come looking for her, threatening me if I did not return her—the queen of Sparta, Helen! I told those envoys from Menelaus in the sternest terms that I knew nothing of this, that Helen was not here, nor had you abducted her. I sent them away with warnings. Now I see . . . you have made a liar of me!"

"But Father, how could you have known? You spoke the truth as you thought."

"I should have known the character of my son! That should have stood surety for your actions. But no—I see I do not know you at all. They warned me, they said you had not been brought up as a prince, that you did not have a noble mind—but I sent those naysayers packing. To my sorrow!"

All the while I was standing there while they argued over me. I felt I must say something.

"Priam, great king." I stepped forward. But I knew to come no closer, nor to make any gesture of either supplication or familiarity. "It is true, I am Helen of Sparta, former wife to Menelaus. I came with Paris on my own accord.

It was no one's doing but my own. I do not wish to cause unhappiness to any-one in Troy—bitter enough that I must cause it in Sparta. Often the happi-ness of one person must cause the unhappiness of another. But I have found happiness, the first true happiness I have ever known, with your son Paris, and I rejoice in it. I only regret any sorrow it may cost anyone else."

His eyes grew so large the whites showed all around the irises, as if he would burst from within like an overripe fruit. "How dare you blather such nonsense, when you have put us all in danger? And how dare you compromise the honor of Troy in such a fashion?"

"Father!" said Paris. "She is my wife!"

"What do you mean?" Priam shouted.

"We have pledged ourselves, and before witnesses. The gods brought us together, they guided us, and now they must protect us."

"Bah!" yelled Priam.

"Great king," I said. "Please have mercy."

"Oh, I'll have mercy." He whirled around and pointed to the guards on each side of the palace, to the people gathering in curiosity in the courtyard. "But the rest—the council of elders, the Trojan people, our allies, and the far-away Spartans—will they?"

"We must hope—" I began.

"Oh, if it were just me," he said, "I would welcome her." He put his leathery, lined face very close—too close—to mine. "I would kiss her hand in welcome"—he did so, elaborately—"and praise my newfound son for finding such a bride. Who could not? To have such a one about the palace would be like harnessing the sun, so it would always be bright. But alas, she comes trail-ing sorrows and dangers."

He was still looking at me, and I felt him soften. People always did if they looked long enough. I had despised this gift; now I poured out silent thanks for it.

"Hesione did not wish to come, and I did. One princess for another," I said.

"Do not speak to me of my sister!" he barked, and I realized I had over-stepped the delicate bounds.

"You were willing to risk war and sorrow for her," said Paris, "when she did not even wish to come!"

"That was a matter of blood," said Priam.

"What is happening?" a high voice sounded from the porch. "Priam?"

A small woman, wearing the finest light wool gown, had appeared. Her voice showed her to be an older woman. This, then, must be Hecuba. Head held high, she descended the steps and came over to us, dripping dignity.

As soon as her eyes fastened on mine, I knew she was the hard one, not Priam. She would never melt, she was an eternal snow capping the highest mountain. Like the snow, her complexion was very pale, and when she was younger, it must have been exquisite.

"Paris? You have returned, then." She held out her hand for him to take.

"Yes, Mother." He bent over the hand, then took it in both of his and squeezed it.

"And he's brought us a pretty prize—oh, our son has been a-plundering!"

"Gold? Slaves? Cattle?"

"Nothing so useful," said Priam. "He's stolen the wife of Menelaus. The queen of Sparta." He gestured toward me.

"Helen!" Her voice was a hiss, a soft slither of sound. "So it is all true, then."

I longed to know what was true, what she meant, but I knew to keep silent and look respectful before this formidable little woman. I bent my head.

"Are you a statue, girl? Can't you speak?" she said.

Oh, I can speak, I thought, but if I speak my mind I might anger you. "I would not presume," I murmured, in what I thought was a conciliatory manner.

"A mealymouth, then!" Hecuba said. "You've gone to all the trouble to kidnap a timid little milksop. Her face will soon seem as wheylike as her manner!"

"She's my wife!" Paris said loudly. "I command you to stop insulting her!"

Everyone in the square overheard him, and pressed forward eagerly to hear more.

"Command, do you?" she said. "Will you flick me with a whip like you did your cattle when you herded them?"

"Cease!" Priam ordered them. "Come inside, out of this public place."

"Do you invite me to enter your palace, then?" I said, without moving one step. I knew that to be invited inside the palace meant that they accepted me—or the marriage, that is.

Hecuba raised an eyebrow. "She can speak!" She puckered her mouth. "At least there's that. Yes, of course, get yourselves inside!" She made fluttering movements with her hands.

We stepped over the marble threshold, and in so doing, I thereby became a Trojan.

Inside, it was cool and dark, and for a moment I felt I was back in the cave with Aphrodite, a sensation made stronger by a faint scent of roses. But in a moment I saw smoke rising from an incense burner and knew this was the source of the perfume. I was not in a magic cave but standing in the palace of the richest city in the world, facing all-too-human critics.

"Now, my child," said Priam, "we may speak freely."

"Yes." Hecuba took her place by his side. She barely came up to his shoulders. Her voice did not invite speaking, free or not.

Paris gestured toward the pillows heaped around the walls. "Can you not invite us to sit?"

"In good time," said Hecuba briskly. She continued standing.

Must it be I who spoke first? I looked about, hoping someone would spare me that obligation. But all faces, and mouths, were closed. I drew up my courage and prayed to Aphrodite to guide my words.

"Blood is a sacred thing," I began tentatively. I did not know how sacred the Trojans held it. "We share our blood. Closely, through my father Tyndareus, we are cousins. Atlas had two daughters and they are the ancestors of Lacedaemon and Dardanus, our forefathers."

"Not so close," said Priam. "And no blood at all, if it is true that your father is not Tyndareus after all." As my eyes grew accustomed to the dim light, I could see him more clearly. His face showed no emotion, no recognition. Yet he was appraising me. I knew that look well enough.

"Great king, I cannot speak for that." I bowed my head—submissively, I hoped.

"I can," said Hecuba crisply. "There is no Tyndareus there. Look at the light that shines around her. The very chamber has brightened." She sounded vexed.

"But you and I, most exalted queen, share blood that cannot be denied." I turned to her. "On my mother's side, we claim Phoenix as our common ancestor."

She grunted. "And how is that?"

I was ready. I had teased it out of Paris and Aeneas in preparation. "Agenor is the ancestor of Phoenix. Do you truly want me to relate all the threads in between, leading to my mother Leda and you?" I could do it, but so tedious!

"No," she replied. "I know it as well as you."

Silence for a moment. The smoke poured from the incense burner in clouds.

"It seems that Paris has chosen his wife," Priam finally said. "We had urged him to marry. He has done so. They have lived together publicly as man and wife, taken vows. It is not to be undone. Helen is, distantly, of our blood. We must—" He shook his head. "We must welcome her as a daughter."

I bowed my head.

"But a daughter who weakens us," said Hecuba. "I thought marriage alliances were to strengthen dynasties, not threaten them." She turned a hard face toward me. "The envoys from your husband, lady, were insistent that you be returned. In all truth we replied that we knew nothing of this matter. But this is no longer the case. When you fail to return, what will their response be?"

"Nothing!" cried Paris. "Nothing has ever come of such a thing. In all respect, Father, nothing has come of Hesione being in Salamis, nor of Medea being stolen from Colchis by Jason. Nor the abduction of Adriadne by the Athenians. The Greeks will fulminate, curse, send envoys. In the end they will sit down content before their fires and make sad ballads about Helen, the lost queen."

" 'People yet unborn will make songs of us,' " I said.

"What?" demanded Hecuba. "Is that all this means to you? Songs?"

"I—I—" In truth I knew not where those words had come from. They came from somewhere outside me. "I did not mean it to sound light," I said.

"What else could it be?" she snapped.

"Helen knows of things we do not," said Paris.

"What can you possibly mean?" asked Hecuba.

"I mean, because of gifts bestowed upon her in a temple, she can see things we cannot. Her attendant has brought the sacred serpent from her household altar. Let us find a suitable home for him here."

"Troy is filled with seers!" said Priam. "Too many of them. Helen, you are welcome here as the wife of Paris, but as a seer—no!"

Now he had come around, as I knew he would. "I will keep my serpent, then, only as my special companion, a treasured thing I have brought from Sparta."

He smiled. Men were so easily won.

"I suppose you will retire to your old apartments?" Hecuba asked. Women not so easily won.

"Only for now," said Paris. "I will build splendid new ones for Helen and me."

"What, desert all your brothers and sisters who lodge in the royal apartments? Are you to be set apart, then?"

"Dear Mother," Paris said, stepping forward and taking her face between his hands, "I am already set apart, because fair Helen is my wife." He held out his hand to me. "Come, my wife. If my mother and father do not invite us to sit, I do." He gestured toward the brightly colored pillows. We sank to the floor—a floor covered with woven tapestries, but ones unlike any I had ever seen before.

"Here in Troy do you put your fine weavings upon the floor?" I asked. I ran my hands over one, marveling at the design.

"Oh, these come from the East someplace," said Paris. "We get them from the passing caravans before they proceed any farther. It is one of the privileges of living in Troy—to intercept trade." He laughed.

"Since you have already done so, I invite you to sit," said Hecuba. "Would you care for refreshments?" Now she extended all the trappings of hospitality, in a measured way.

"Yes," said Paris. "Yes, we would."

Priam nodded to a waiting slave. "Bring him what he desires."

"It seems the gods have already done that," said Hecuba tartly. She took her seat nearby. "So you like our floor coverings? They come from farther east. We call them carpets. Novel idea, to cover the floors. But warm. It gets very cold here in winter." She smiled at me, a distant smile. "You will see."

❖ XXXI ❖

Aeneas, who had been sitting quietly all the while, stood and made to leave.

"Say nothing to Creusa!" Hecuba ordered him. "Swear it, before you leave this room."

Aeneas frowned. "But she has already seen us. She met us on our way through the city, and I am eager to be with her again."

"Be with her all you like," said Hecuba. "But say nothing. You men excel at that—being with a woman and saying nothing of import."

"She has seen me as well." I felt I had to speak. "She knows I am here, and who I am."

"Let that be all she knows!" Hecuba glared. "You should never have allowed your face to be seen in the streets of Troy. Henceforth, you must wear a veil."

"No, I will not." I kept my voice low, but I was trembling. I could not go back to that, I could not bear it. "I am not an animal to be trussed up. Covering my face is like being bound. Let people see it, and do as they will. I saw that no woman in Troy wears the veil."

"You are not a Trojan." Priam finally spoke. "Do not invoke the customs of Troy for yourself."

"She is a Trojan now!" Paris leapt to his feet. "Henceforth she will be known as Helen of Troy, not Helen of Sparta. Let her therefore be treated as a Trojan."

"I fear that cannot be," said Priam. "One is as one is born. Just as Hesione was, and always will be, Trojan, not Greek."

Aeneas shook his head. "Great king, I think she is Trojan no longer, and we must turn our eyes from that idea."

Priam grunted.

"Go to Paris's quarters," Hecuba ordered us. "Stay there until I summon you. This must be dealt with swiftly. I must think of what to do. In the meantime, stay out of sight."

"Like a thief or a murderer?" Paris cried.

"You *are* a thief!" said Hecuba. "What else can we call a wife-stealer?"

"He did not steal me," I said. "I came of my own accord."

"That is not what the Greeks will say," said Priam. "It would insult their honor; to keep their honor they must maintain that you were stolen."

"Raped, even!" Hecuba snorted. "I can hear it already."

That would compromise my own honor. Let it not be said!

"No," I protested. "It is not so."

"Can you prove that to your kinsmen, far away? No, they will cling to that belief." She stood up, straight as a shaft of light. "Go now. Go to your quarters."

I had not been ordered about like this since I was a child. I would have answered back, but Paris, reading my mind, took my hand.

"Let me show you where I lived before setting sail for Greece," he said.

We left the small chamber and wandered out beneath the brightly painted inner portico whose zigzag reds, yellows, and blues made me blink. We passed through a small passageway and then out into an immense oblong courtyard with shady porches protecting each doorway.

"Here is where all the sons and daughters of Priam live," said Paris, sweeping his hand over the vista.

It was as big as a city. I said so.

"Indeed," he admitted. "And we have all the trappings of a city—a ruler, power struggles, scandals, and bribes."

"And who is the ruler of this city, if it be not Priam?"

"Hector, of course," Paris said. "The most illustrious of the princes. It does not hurt that he is also the eldest. That eliminates quarrels about rank and worthiness. It is always convenient when those qualities keep company."

I thought of Agamemnon and his rank and worthiness. I hoped that Hector was more likable.

"My quarters are halfway down the portico."

Rather than beneath the dim covered portico, we walked in the open courtyard, where potted plants made the semblance of a sacred grove. Their leaves rustled in the stiff breeze, making a dry sound.

"Troy trades with many lands," said Paris. "These plants were all bartered for other goods. Some of them are valuable, like these myrrh bushes. Others have flowers with unusual colors. Hector's wife, Andromache, wanted a garden with flowers of every color. She has come close. Her collection is here." He led me over to a dense grouping of pots. "She said she now has all the colors except black, and flowers do not come in black. But there is a legend that a black flower blooms on the banks of the River Styx. Is it true? Have you ever been to the Styx?"

"No," I said. There were so many places I had never been, even ones near my old home. "But I know that Persephone's sacred groves have black poplars. I think she would claim a black flower as her own." I looked over the flowers, seeing violet, red, pink, yellow, white, waving bravely in the wind. Happy colors. "Andromache would not want black," I said. Just then a gust of wind blew dust in my face. How could it be so windy in this enclosed space? "Where does this wind come from?" I sputtered.

Paris laughed. "Windy Troy. Have you not heard of our famous wind?"

"Yes, but this seems a magical wind, to leap over a thick barrier like the apartments." I clutched at my cloak.

"It blows steadily from the north most of the year," said Paris. "It makes a native Trojan easy to identify. He is the one who walks with a slant at all times. I must confess, I have not got used to it yet, so I still walk straight."

Attacked by the wind again, we ran for the portico, laughing as our clothes billowed out around us.

Each doorway was painted a vibrant red and had fastenings of bronze, ceremonial bolts that artists had adorned with depictions of stags, boars, and lions.

"Here are Hector's former apartments, before he built his own palace," said Paris, flicking his hand. Its glossy red door reflected my face; its gleaming bronze mirrored our movements. We passed it and then Paris said, "And here is the house of Helenus," he said. "My brother the augur, the twin of Cassandra who also prophesies, but more understandably."

"Is he the one who interpreted the dream of Hecuba?" The dream that made her cast Paris away!

"No. That was Aesacus. I could not endure being polite to Helenus had it been he. As it is, I do not have to see Aesacus very often." He stopped in front of a door that looked identical to all the other doors.

"Here!" He lifted the bronze bolt and opened the shining door. I stepped in, acutely aware of entering Paris's home. I lifted my feet and crossed the threshold entirely of my own volition. There was no abduction, no rape, no force.

The room seemed enormous—larger than Father's throne room. Was everything in Troy, then, bigger and more spectacular than anyplace else on earth? The small apartments grander than a king's megaron? "Oh!" I said, surveying it.

The shaded windows at either end admitted dim filtered sunlight, robbed of its intensity. Stretching down the length of the chamber was another of those weavings, laid on the floor to be trampled on, or stepped upon, carelessly. Such was the wealth of Troy. What others hoarded and treasured was here trod underfoot.

Paris raced through this large room and beckoned me on to the smaller ones. "This is where I truly live," he said. He flung open a door; a chamber with high windows near the ceiling revealed itself to me.

So this was where Paris felt most at home. The walls were washed with an earth color, and the floor was smooth stone, stained a deep red. Around the walls were stools with leather seats, and bows and arrows were strewn about the low shelf running along one wall. Off in an alcove was a bed, spread with a red and yellow weaving.

Oh, this was a happy place. I felt it instantly. "Paris—we need not leave these rooms. We can make our home here."

He caught me up in his arms. "Never. For the fairest woman in the world, she needs the fairest quarters in the world."

"These rooms where you live are fair enough for me." I meant it. They had his spirit, which drew me.

"No, no," he murmured. "I must build you something worthy of you. I cannot bring you here to live in my bachelor apartments."

"Why not?" I asked. "Are you not trying to please me? Should I not be allowed to select the place where I shall live?"

"No." He smoothed the wind-mussed hair from my forehead. "No, for you have not seen the new rooms yet and cannot compare."

"Nor have you," I said.

"Ah, but I see them in my mind," he said, "which you cannot do."

"Paris, you want to make me happy," I said. "But I am happy just having found you."

"We are happy with one another just so," he said. "But the others, they do not share our joy. And so we need a citadel, a fortress where we can barricade ourselves against their hostility. I am afraid, my love, that that is why we must have new apartments. To protect our love."

He spoke true. We were alone against the world, and its constant buffetings would wear us away, and these flimsy apartments, for all their glorious decorations, would not shield us. They were too near others.

"Very well," I said.

"But in the meantime . . ." He led me to the tapestry-covered bed and drew me onto it. "It has been a long time since we held one another," he said. "And we must not forget what that feels like."

Ah, Paris. To be loved by Paris was . . . to be loved for myself. If the gods could love, they would love you only for what you are. But the gods do not love. And so we seek for that one person who can love us as we all long to be loved.

An announcement from Hecuba: we were to wait in the privacy of the family courtyard after sundown, and meet with all the family at once. In the meantime we were not to go out, and the passageway into the courtyard was to be shut tight. This was not the joyful homecoming Paris had hoped for.

The summit of Troy was the last place where the sun lingered, but soon enough the rays ebbed, and the ruddy afterglow faded from our window. When the first of the stars became visible, I knew we must leave the apartment and go out into the courtyard, obeying Hecuba. I shivered, and not from the night air, although I did cloak myself against it.

They were all already there: a vast throng of them. It was like the time the suitors had all descended on Father, except that these people had not come to seek my hand, but to inspect Paris's folly. I braced myself for their hostility.

"Paris!" A friendly tone. The braziers illuminated the face of Troilus. He gripped Paris's arm. "You said you would tell us everything. Is that why Mother has summoned us?"

"One reason," said Paris. "One never knows with Mother."

"Well, well." A man with a handsome face and a sour expression came up behind Troilus. "So our wayward brother has returned. Why must the queen call a council about it?" He barely glanced at me.

"My brother Deiphobus," said Paris.

Now the surly man looked at me as if he were granting me a favor. "And you are?" he asked.

"The wife of Paris," I said.

Deiphobus laughed. "So he's finally got himself married! Found something better than that water nymph, eh? Where do you come from?" He waited, and when I said nothing, he said, "Didn't he tell you about the water nymph? It's very sad, she's pining away, but she really didn't belong in the palace. Now you, yes, you'll adapt well . . ."

I turned my back on the condescending man. I would have liked to see the expression on his face at that. From his manner, I would guess it did not happen often.

I found myself facing a pretty girl with large, fine dark eyes. Her hood hid her hair, but I could see traces of shiny dark curls around her cheeks. "Welcome home, Paris," she said, and her voice was as soft and pleasing as her eyes.

"Laodice," he said. "It is always good to see you. This is my sister, still unmarried."

"Not for want of Mother and Father's trying," she said. "Did you hear, they were speaking with someone from Thrace about it—can you imagine, Thrace! Those people with ugly topknots on their heads. Perhaps they all think they are kings, and want to wear turrets on their heads for crowns."

The poor girl, in the midst of marriage negotiations. How dreadful it always was.

More and more people gathered in the courtyard, and I could feel the massed might in such a large family. Priam presided over a clan, whereas poor Father had only his four children, and two of them women.

"How many brothers do you have?" I asked Paris.

"Nine full ones," he said. "And they say, thirty half-brothers. I am not sure of that. Father claims he has fifty sons but I think he just likes the sound of 'fifty sons.' He may not actually have them. He has some by his first wife and many others by various women about the court."

"And your mother does not find this difficult?"

"No. Why should she? It is custom."

That was another way the Trojans were unlike us, then. Our rulers might have bastards but they were not paraded out in pride, or accepted by the true wife. Priam must have been quite a desirable man in his prime. Even now he was impressive in his forceful strength.

There was a rustling and people parted to make way for Priam and Hecuba. Two torchbearers preceded them, and the flaming tips bobbed along, showing us where they walked. When they reached the middle of the courtyard they stopped, and a space opened up around them.

They had added cloaks to their attire, in deference to the night's chill. Hecuba had covered her head and thrust her hands inside her cloak, yet she still shivered.

"My dear children," said Priam, holding up his hands. "All of you are dear to me." As his deep voice rang out, the gathering fell silent. "I take pride in you all, and would not lose a single hair from the head of any of my offspring. Yea, rather than that, I would sacrifice my life."

Feet began to shuffle. What was the king leading up to?

"Were any of you in danger, I would set out to rescue and ransom you, though you be held in the farthest regions, to the west to the Hesperides, or the north from whence the fine amber comes and the daylight never ends."

More foot-shuffling. Had someone been captured?

"My dear son Paris, one of my eldest, yet my newest-known, has returned to Troy after a perilous journey. He went amongst the Greeks, those treacherous people!" He looked around, his head held high, his eyes searching the crowd. "Do not argue the point!" he cried. "They took away my sister and have yet to release her. Dishonor! Who can trust a Greek?"

Hecuba reached out to touch his sleeve, as if to moderate him, but he had decided on his approach and was not to be deflected.

"In his journey, Paris happened upon the court of King Menelaus of Sparta. You have heard of him, have you not? The brother of Agamemnon." He pushed off his head covering and cupped his ear. "Oh, let me not hear that you are ignorant of that dreadful house, with its unspeakable curse? Cursed thrice, in three generations! They have such things upon them as cannabalism, incest, murder of children by parents, oh! let us not even name the abominations! And into this . . . nest . . . strode Paris, innocent of what he was entering into. And there he rescued the wife of Menelaus, who longed to be delivered from the curse of that family, a family she had been forced to marry into!"

Oh, he had imagination and nerve. What a clever approach! I could almost congratulate him, except that it was all lies.

"This poor princess has sought our protection against the foul family she flees. What pure soul would not wish to be delivered from its vileness? She has thrown herself upon our mercy. We must protect her, in the name of decency and all the gods, who abhor murder and corruption."

He left his place and walked toward me. He held out his hands and took mine, drawing me into the empty space in the midst of the courtyard. "This is Helen, Helen of Sparta. She wishes to repudiate her former marriage and become the wife of Paris. Will we accept her as one of us?"

His strong arm encircled me.

"Hold your head up so they can look at you," he ordered me, his voice rough and nothing like the smooth, placating one he had used at full volume.

I obeyed, and looked out at the gathering. Beyond the scraping of feet and a few coughs, they were silent.

Priam jabbed me in the ribs in a manner that no one could see. "Speak!" he hissed in my ear. "Only you can win them now."

I was in sore need of the help of the gods. But there was no time to send up a prayer. The crowd was looking expectantly at me.

"Sons and daughters of Priam," I began, weakly, to gain a moment. "I have long dreamed of standing on the heights of Troy, to have my cloak blown free by the famous winds of your city. In faraway Sparta we heard of your glories and as a child I hoped to behold them myself someday."

Where had that come from? I had thought little of Troy, and certainly never as a child. I plunged ahead.

"Now I have come, not in the way I would have imagined, but the gods lead us on surprising paths. I, who was a queen, am a stranger in a foreign city. I come to lay aside the life I lived elsewhere. By my side is my companion in the new life, Paris, who also lived another life before coming to you. We have been born anew; we are no longer who we were earlier, but stand on the rim of a new world. Pray grant us entry."

I knew these thoughts came from a god, for they were not mine. But they described our plight well. We stood before the gates of Troy, knocking. We could enter only hand in hand, for our new selves had been created by one another, springing from our own desires and destiny.

The silence slid into sighs and murmurs of approval. Priam cried, "Do you grant her entrance?"

The family cried out, "Yes! Yes!"

"What new name do you take for yourself, daughter?" asked Priam. "Paris took the name Alexandros—although we still may call him Paris."

A new name . . . had I ever longed for a new name?

"Swan," I finally said.

"As befits your lovely long white neck." Hecuba was suddenly beside Priam. Her voice sounded more like the caw of a raven. Did she know about the swan story? Was she being deliberately provocative? "For that, we may call you Cycna, my dear."

"She and Paris have declared themselves to be a new couple entering upon a new world. Once Troy itself was new, and into it came the Pallas Athena, our protective statue, which rained down upon us from heaven. Let them pledge themselves to their new life before her, the patron of all Troy!" Priam cried. "Follow us out to her temple." He whispered an aside to some of the servants, then turned back to the crowd. "Afterward we will celebrate."

Paris took my hand. "They accept us," he whispered. "They have allowed us in. That was brilliant, what you said. It won them over. However did you think of it? We had never talked about it."

"It came to me," I said quietly. "It is true."

Beyond the courtyard, we were surrounded by the people of Troy and all private conversation was obliged to cease. The torchbearers took their places beside us, and we passed through the great gate of the palace, and approached the temple I had seen earlier.

In the dim light it was hard for me to see, but the stones seemed to be white—limestone or marble. We entered into the darkness of the building, and now I wished there were more than two torchbearers. I could not see to the end—the dark recess seemed to stretch on forever, a great swallowing blackness.

Ahead of us Priam and Hecuba walked slowly, but not hesitantly. They knew their way. I tried to follow them exactly.

A hint of a sweet scent came to me from the void. It was a flower, a flower I had known, but what was it? The scent was light and teasing as a whisper. A white flower . . . that was all I could remember.

Suddenly Priam and Hecuba stopped and bowed. The flickering torches showed a life-sized statue of a female with glaring eyes. Her right hand held a spear, and her left a distaff and spindle. This Athena was crudely made and had no grace about her—a strange thing, since the statue was made by the goddess herself.

"Our great protector, the Pallas Athena, now looks down upon you, child." Priam took my hand, led me close to the statue, and addressed the goddess. "Great one, she has come to Troy seeking a safe haven. Grant it to her. And confer your blessings on the union between my son and this new daughter of Troy." Paris took his place beside me.

Suddenly I saw the white flowers at the base of the statue; their perfume enveloped me. But the statue had no feet. She had no legs, either.

"Before taking Paris as your husband, and Troy as your city, you must renounce your former ones," said Priam. "Is there something from Sparta that you can offer up here to Athena?"

I knew what I longed to be free of. All along the voyage I had thought of flinging it into the sea, but the waste of that had stayed my hand. Now I could separate myself from it. I did not know why I had brought it in the first place, except that in my leaving I had not thought clearly.

"Yes . . . Father," I said. "But I must send my advisor to get it."

"Advisor?"

"Yes, the wisest man in Sparta, whom I brought with me."

Hecuba turned her dark eyes upon me. "No word of a wise man of Sparta has ever reached our ears," she said.

"He was a privately wise man, great queen, not a public one." I whispered to one of the king's attendants to go fetch the man Gelanor and tell him to bring . . .

"Let us continue our ceremony," said Priam. He turned back to the Pallas Athena. "You who came to us from the heavens, to my grandfather Ilus, the founder of Ilium, of Troy, and without whose protection we would perish, send us a sign that you accept the woman Helen, also called in her new life Cycna, amongst us. We know the sign may not appear at this moment, and that we must be alert for it. But you will not fail us. And while we wait, we will welcome her and join her hands with those of Paris." He turned slowly back to me, just as Gelanor entered the temple and made his way to us. He held a box in his outstretched arms, which he placed in Priam's.

Priam opened it, to see the heavy gold marriage chain of Menelaus within. In the torchlight the gold shone almost red. I could see his eyes widen.

"Great king," I said, "this Spartan gold was hung around my neck on the day Menelaus made me his. I gladly and freely relinquish it. Do what you will with it. It binds me no longer."

I could see Priam fighting within himself to muster the high-mindedness to give it to the goddess. He took it out and fondled it, on the pretext of inspecting its links. Finally he raised it aloft and said, "By this token of your former life, you have proved that you hand your past to us. Your present and your future will be in Troy." Slowly he knelt and placed it before Athena. Then he turned again to us and clasped his hand on top of Paris's and mine. It was done, then, and done publicly.

"They are joined," he said, and a polite ripple of murmurs buzzed in the temple, echoing slightly against the stones. Then he looked at Gelanor. "And do you give this wise man to Troy as well?" he asked.

"You must ask him," I demurred.

Gelanor made no answer. He merely looked at me and said, "I have now seen you safely to Troy, as I promised."

Instead of feeling safe, I felt a great hostility from the goddess Athena. It wafted out from her statue as surely as the scent of the flowers. But what had I ever done to her to incur her enmity?

❖ XXXII ❖

We were to leave the temple, but I dreaded turning my back on the goddess in her displeasure. If we were not to turn our backs on earthly kings, how much less would the gods tolerate it? But how could I refuse to follow Priam and Hecuba as they made their stately way out? Paris clasped my hand and in its warmth I felt safe, but at the same time the intensity of Athena's displeasure increased. I could sense, rather than see, Gelanor behind me, impatient to leave me in the hands of the Trojans.

In the short time we had been gone, the main courtyard—not the inner one around which the sons and daughters had their apartments—had been transformed into a place of feasting. The altar was cleansed and an ox stood placidly by waiting to be sacrificed, its horns gilded, its proud head held high. Several priests flanked it, and already the roasting fires were lit. The beast looked on the flames that would consume it, but without knowledge, just as we may pass the place where our bones will lie, and linger upon it to pick flowers.

"Helen, this is my eldest son, Hector." Priam turned me to face a dark-haired man. "Hector, this is the choice of your brother Paris for his bride."

"Oh, Father, why do you introduce him so modestly?" said Paris. "Eldest son is the least of it. Why not say, *my joy, my pride, the strength of Troy? The glory of the—*"

"Elder brother will do," said Hector. He had a pleasant voice, neither too loud nor silkily soft, either of which often mar an otherwise appealing man. In his face I saw no resemblance to Priam or Hecuba or to his brother. "Welcome to Troy," he said. But in those three words I heard shadows of others unsaid. "I see that the goddess has accepted you as one of us."

It was premature, but polite, to assume so.

"I am grateful," I said. The longer I looked at him, the more appealing he was, in that he lacked any displeasing features. He was without blemish. Even his ears were exactly the right size, as perfectly shaped as if they were cast from a mold.

"See, you cannot help staring at him!" Paris chided me. "You have fallen under his spell, like everyone in Troy." Did he mean this, or was he teasing?

"Brother, you are the one people call godlike," said Hector. Now he smiled, and the smile transformed his face. Where he had been appealing, he was now masterful. "Paris and his golden hair." He laughed, but kindly.

"Ah, but men won't follow me," said Paris.

"Only women." Hector shrugged his shoulders—shoulders that I now noticed were very broad. "Lady, we knew the only woman he could end up with was one prettier than himself, and there were none until you."

"I meant into battle," said Paris quietly. So he had been stung. The lightness had left his voice.

"We've had no battles since you came to Troy," said Hector. "So you cannot know how you would fare leading men into battle."

"Oh, I could lead them—but would they follow?"

"That, little brother, is something you must wait to find out. But not too soon, not too soon—it is quiet in the lands around Troy, and that is as pleasant as the late afternoon when the sun warms the hillsides."

"Hector's favorite time of day." Suddenly someone was standing beside him—a tall woman, almost as tall as Hector himself. *Athena!* flashed through my mind. But an Athena who stood lovely and serene, not the strange one I had just come from.

"Andromache, my wife." Hector encircled her with his arm.

"Welcome to Troy," she said. "I, too, came from another city. I am from Thebe, where my father is king of the Kilikes."

"It is near Plakos, a spur on the southern flanks of Mount Ida. Andromache is used to woods and mountains. When she longs for them overmuch, we betake ourselves to our side of Ida. There lie woods, springs, and slopes enough for anyone." Hector pulled her close to him. "Are there not?"

"The woods of home are always different," said Andromache. "Perhaps because they are home. Surely the trees are the very same."

"I, too, come from a place with mountains and woods," I said. "The peaks of Taygetus are high and often snow-crowned, and the slopes are covered in pines and oaks."

"I have found everything I wish in Troy," Andromache said. "May you do so as well." She laughed. Her laugh was like one of the mountain brooks. "Although it is so very flat!"

A great bellow split the night. It was the loudest I had ever heard, and I cringed. The ox was being sacrificed.

There was a scurrying around the makeshift altar. The priests would have to attend to all the horrid details—the blood, the steaming entrails, the flailing, the carving. Even from our safe distance, I could smell the blood. I felt dizzy, and put my hand to my mouth.

"Catch her, Paris, catch her." The voice was like the sound of chariot wheels running over gravel. "She would appear to have a squeamish disposition."

"Aesacus." Paris turned to him. "My half-brother," he said. The chill in his voice was not well disguised.

A small man stood before me, his face all but hidden beneath the ample folds of his hooded mantle. Paris yanked it back. A short-cropped head, close-set dark eyes, and a lined face confronted me.

With slow dignity, the man pulled his hood back in place. "Please, dear brother, it is cold tonight. Do not vent your hostility upon my poor head."

"My elder brother by Priam's first wife," Paris muttered.

"Oh, why stop there?" He turned to me, and false-confided, "Why does he not tell you all? My brother—half-brother—is too kind. That must come from his mother Hecuba, although, the gods know, she is rarely kind—rather than from our mutual father." He smiled and adjusted his hood. Now I could see his face. It reminded me of some night creature, wedge-shaped and alert.

I waited. I did not have long to wait.

"I have the gift of prophecy."

Not another one. So Priam had spoken truly. Troy was full of prophets.

"Yes?" I responded.

"Hecuba had her dream . . . that dream in which she brought forth a fire-brand that destroyed Troy. It was I who told her what it meant." He leaned forward and whispered in my ear. "This is our chance to test the gods and their dire prophecies. How do we know any of them are true?" He stepped forward and took Paris's face in his hands. "The gods commanded us to destroy you. Someone disobeyed, and now you stand before us, tall and straight and glorious. The gods rewrite their instructions all the time. Why should we follow their first orders?"

Scowling, Paris jerked his hands away. "Stop it, Aesacus. You have had too much wine."

He shrugged and smoothed the folds of his cloak. "Yes, perhaps. They are serving the best tonight, in your honor. I make it a point to take large portions of good things. As with the gods—when they give you fine things you should help yourself quickly, before they change their minds."

Gelanor glided up to us as Aesacus slipped away. A faint smile played on his face and he sighed. "Now my conscience is at peace," he said. "I can leave you, with no nagging worries about your welfare."

"Must you leave?" asked Paris. "Why hurry away?"

Gelanor laughed. "Already much time has passed since I left Sparta. More time will pass before I reach it again. I dare not linger."

"Oh, but linger a few days. To scurry off in haste might be insulting to the Trojans."

Again he laughed. "I doubt any Trojan gives a cow's udder whether I stay or go."

"That's not so. You heard the king asking if you intended to stay. He would welcome you." I would not beg him, but oh! how I wished to persuade him. But I knew that he was usually proof against my persuasions.

"There is nothing useful for me to do here, and you know I live only in my usefulness. I set you a task: within the next few days convince me there is need for me in Troy and I will stay awhile. But only for a while. Troy can never be home to me." The dull tone of his voice made the words thud.

"Do not be hasty," I said.

"I am not. I know myself. Do you know yourself?"

"Everyone is so gloomy!" cried Paris. "Stop this talk of gods and omens and knowing yourself. Can we not just drink our wine and embrace?"

"For some people, that serves well enough," Gelanor said.

The flames were leaping in the courtyard as the ox meat was roasting, fat sizzling as it dripped onto the fire, sending clouds of smoke swirling and disappearing into the night sky. People crowded around, eager for the first bites. In their wait, they consumed more and more wine, making their heads swirl like the smoke. The din increased, as if the crowd had grown.

Paris put his arm around me and steered me away. "I must show you something," he whispered.

We left the crowded courtyard behind and he guided me to the main building, across the megaron, and to the staircase hidden in one corner of it. It was eerily quiet here, all the people having been drawn off into the courtyard. We climbed up the wooden steps slowly, I holding my gown so I would not trip on it. At once we emerged onto a flat roof overlooking all of Troy and the Plain of Troy, like the bow of a ship riding high above them. The vastness of it was startling.

"Come," Paris said, taking my hand. He led me to the edge of the roof, where a waist-high wall protected us. The wind blew strongly, and I clung to the top of the wall.

"There it lies—all of Troy, and the territory around her," said Paris. The wind snatched his words away.

I leaned over the wall and looked at the city, encircling the palace like petals of a rose. On this highest point, there was only the palace and the temple of Athena; on the other three sides, falling away beneath them, were rings of houses and terraces stretching to the walls, those guardian walls standing sharp and knife-edged in the starlight. Flickering torches, like little dots, marked out their course. Dim and dark, large towers reared up along the perimeter.

Below the steep north side a flat plain stretched to the sea, where the starlight caught on the waves and showed us the swift-running water.

"You cannot see it now, with no moon, but there are two rivers down below—the Scamander and the Simoïs," said Paris. "The Scamander runs all year long, but the Simoïs dries up in the heat of summer. We pasture our horses there in the sweet meadows—our famous horses of Troy."

The meadows must have been just springing, for a delicious scent rode the next gust of wind. I inhaled deeply. "This is truly an enchanted land," I said. I looked out over all of it—the sleeping city, the grand homes, the strong walls, the neat lower town, the fertile plain. I walked over to another side of the roof and peered down at the courtyard, filled with noise, smoke, and people.

"Must we return there?" I asked him. From above, it looked like a field of writhing serpents.

"No. We need do nothing we do not wish to. You have been presented to the family and the Trojans, and all ceremony observed. Now you are free. *We* are free."

Could that be true? Standing there on the highest place in Troy, feeling the wind rushing past us, clean and fresh, I believed so. I clasped Paris's hand. In that moment, I felt as young as Persephone and as lovely as Aphrodite. Aphrodite then flew to me with the winds, enveloped me, entwined me. I felt her warmth all around me, soft as a cloud.

I have brought you here, my child. Obey me, revel in me, exalt me. I turned to Paris. "Let us go back to your chambers," I whispered. The wind snatched my words away, bore them southward over the city. I pressed closer to him, repeating them.

"Yes," he murmured.

Across the rooftop, down the stairs in haste, skirting the loud courtyard, we entered our private courtyard from another doorway, running through its emptiness. To Paris's doorway, flinging it open. The large receiving room, the connecting chambers, greeted us silently. As we rushed through them, the only sound was our footsteps on the colored stone.

The door shut behind us; we were alone in that innermost bedchamber. The little brazier had not been lit. I would have liked a fire, if only for its golden flames and its sweet scent. But now nothing mattered but being with Paris—no fire, no crackling, soothing sound, nothing but the two of us.

There were no wolf skins spread here, no bulwark against the cold. The apartments of Troy were not made of heavy stone boulders, to lock in the cold long past winter as in Mycenae, but of the finest clay and cedar beams— delicate, dainty. Spring would already come to these chambers when winter still lingered in Sparta.

I wanted only to hold Paris, to embrace him and the life in him, the life he offered me. Lying with him side by side, I could not help tracing his face with my fingers, as if I would memorize every plane and facet of it. And I have, I have . . . I can feel it even now, as I remember . . . But then, with his face beneath my fingertips, I was aware only of the warmth and the deliciousness.

"Paris," I said, "now I am truly yours. I have laid my fortune—what will become of me—at your feet. I have followed you from my world to yours. Nay, more than that—I have disclaimed mine, incurred the wrath of my family and land. I have placed my hand in yours, between just us in privacy, and before the goddess who guards your city. May she guard us as diligently!"

Paris leaned over me and kissed me, his soft lips drowning my thoughts, all save my longing for him. "She will . . . she will . . ."

I had felt her enmity, but now it was washed away in hope. Did the gods not bend their favor to those who honored them? And now I cared for nothing but Paris. The strong swelling arms of Paris, the divine face of Paris, the urgent and insistent body of Paris.

They speak of an Isle of the Blessed. A place where living people are snatched away so they never die, and live out their eternal lives in bliss, wandering in this magic isle far from everything we know upon this earth. Paris and I flew to that isle; we were transported to a realm where we could touch one another for eternity, where we would never change or age, where passion would never slake nor the sun rise to shatter a night of love.

There was no time in the chamber. It stretched out and made one hour two, like a supple piece of leather. Whatever we wanted, whatever we did, we could savor, repeat, as many times as we wished, a bard's favorite passages recited again upon request.

We slept, finally. And then the sun found its way into the chamber. We had not thought to bar the window; when it is deeply night, we do not think of the dawn.

Paris lifted himself on one elbow. "Stupid intrusive sun!" he muttered. "How dare it invade our privacy?" He staggered over to the window and tried to bar the light. But there were no shutters strong enough, and the sunlight could not be kept out.

"I was never bothered by the sunlight before," he admitted. "I was always up with it."

The light showed his body to perfection; its early morning slant caressed its hollows and swells. "The sun brings me a daylight Paris," I said. "So I cannot be angry with it."

Each hour, each minute, was ours. None was our enemy. Each laid its own gifts at our feet.

❖ XXXIII ❖

But we had to emerge from our Isle of the Blessed, Paris's chamber. Outside, the world of Troy waited, in the form of a summons to come to the king and queen.

Dressed, dismissing the night as best I could from playing about my thoughts, I stood before them in the privacy of their palace chamber. Priam looked weary; his hands clutched the side of his chair as if he feared falling. Hecuba, seated beside him, was unreadable.

"The ceremony was observed correctly," Priam finally said. "And people seemed to join in the celebration freely enough."

"As well as we could discern," said Hecuba. Her words were soft and measured.

"But we must know what will happen. We talked bravely enough last night, but the gods are another matter—and what will the Greeks do when they believe I spoke them false?"

"Father, you are agitated. I tell you, nothing will happen. Nothing ever has, in such instances. People forget. The only person harmed, after all, is Menelaus, and he has no army."

I was startled. I had never heard Paris speak so analytically. But he was right. Menelaus had no army. Paris was wrong in something else, though: the person most harmed was Hermione. My Hermione. I felt a cold sorrow at thinking of it.

"I must know," Priam muttered. "I must know. I am sending Calchas, my seer, to the oracle in Delphi."

"Father, why?" cried Paris.

"Because we do not know what wrath you have brought down upon us!' said Hecuba. "Should we not know the price we are expected to pay?"

"What of a Herophile Sibyl? Is one not nearby?" asked Paris.

"Bah. They are not so reliable."

Clytemnestra had said the opposite. "I am pleased to hear that," I said, "as one foretold that I would bring great bloodshed to Greece."

Priam started. "What? What was prophesied?"

"It was when I was but a child. I can still remember her hands clasping my head and making the ugly prophecies. She said . . ." I had tried to block them out of my mind; now I tried hard to call them back. "'She will be the ruin of Asia, the ruin of Europe, and because of her a great war will be fought, and many Greeks will die.'"

Perhaps I should not have spoken, but it was too late. "My father was afraid of this prophecy. So he made my suitors—and there were many, from all over Greece—swear an oath to uphold my choice of husband. He thought thereby to avert the curse."

"Aghhh!" Priam lurched forward, catching his head in his hands. "Oh, oh! He thought only that Greeks would fight one another, not that Greeks would fight far afield, would fight in another land. Greek blood can be spilled in many ways—he foresaw only one!" He glared at me. "What chance that that oath will prove binding?"

I thought of the suitors and their selfish concerns. Once I had chosen another, they had lost interest. It was ten years ago. "Very little," I said. "The leaders of the various Greeks are much too concerned with their own worries. They will hardly risk themselves to rescue a rival's wife—regardless of the oath Father made them swear upon the severed parts of a horse, all those years ago."

"But we must still consult the oracle," said Priam. It was my first taste of his stubbornness.

"Yes," said Hecuba. "We dare not neglect to do this."

Priam stood. "You must speak to Calchas yourself," he said, looking at me. "It is important that he know you when he stands before the oracle."

"Why?" said Paris. "If the oracle does not know her, what difference whether Calchas does?"

"Stop the questioning!" Priam's eyes, bright within their surrounding wrinkles, blazed. "There have already been too many questions—along with too many questionable actions."

"Do as your father commands," said Hecuba, rising to stand beside him. "We shall summon you when Calchas arrives."

They made their way past us, heads held stiffly on rigid necks.

"Am I ten years old," fumed Paris, "to be dismissed and ordered about thus?"

"Evidently yes, in their eyes."

"The air of disapproval they exhale is stupefying. Let us leave this—this enclosure fit only for tamed beasts!"

I looked up at the gold-leaf cedar beams overhead and the delicate frescoes splashing the walls with vibrant-hued flowers. "I think no beast ever guzzled feed in such a stable." I laughed.

"No, better still, they spend their days in the freedom of sweet high meadows of the mountain," he said. "I should know. I tended them most of my life. Let us leave the city! Come, and I'll show you the glory of Troy—our horses!"

"But—if we are not here when Calchas arrives—"

"Let him wait! Father did not say when he would come." Paris laughed. "The horses are calling. Am I not to show you all of Troy, as you are now a Trojan? Take your mantle, and your sturdy sandals."

Paris sent orders to ready a chariot for us, and we made our way back down through the city to the south gate. I looked carefully at the terraced houses—some two-story and quite large—and the clean-swept streets that wound gradually down from the heights of the citadel, keenly curious to know the Trojans and how they lived. They were equally curious, watching us as we passed.

When we reached the broad inner passageway hugging the circle of the walls, a fine chariot was awaiting us, the gilded spokes of its wheels winking in the sun. Two dun-colored horses were in the traces. Paris stroked the neck of one.

"Want to see your cousins?" he asked it, ruffling its mane.

We stepped into the chariot; the massive gates stood wide open to the morning. Paris drove out and into the lower city, where carts and wagons and chariots cut a broad swath to reach the Plain of Troy. Instead of the reticence of the upper city, cries of welcome resounded from the lower. People thronged the street, pressing so close to us the chariot had trouble passing.

"Helen! Paris!" they cried. Flowers, fruits, dyed clay-bead necklaces pelted us, and some landed in the chariot. "We adore you! We worship you!"

Paris turned to me. "Now you see how the true Trojans feel," he said.

A man leapt up in front of the chariot and lunged, grasping it. For an instant he hung over the rails, his face pushed up to ours. "The most beautiful woman in the world!" he proclaimed. "It's true! And now she's ours!" He swung himself around by one arm, hanging off the chariot. "She's ours! She's a *Trojan*!"

Was he drunk? He fell off the chariot and rolled in the dust, as supple as a tumbler, then picked himself up and laughed. Had wine loosened his limbs thus? No matter. He was cheering, cheering for *us*.

"Helen! Helen!" they cried.

I raised my arms, and indicated the man standing beside me. "Paris!" I answered them. "Paris, my love!"

A roar went up, as we gathered speed and left the last of the lower city behind.

"They love you," said Paris, as soon as it was safe to slow down. "Did you not hear them roar? As loud as a Syrian lion?"

"I have never heard a Syrian lion," I said. "I must take your word for it." We threw our heads back and laughed in the bracing air. Before us stretched a wide level plain, covered with new spring grass and wildflowers. But I saw no horses.

"The horses graze nearer the flanks of the mountains in high summer," said Paris. "But just now they are still on the plain. Look more closely."

I squinted and then was able to make out herds of animals, placidly moving about the green expanse. "I think I see them," I finally said.

"They number some two hundred," said Paris. "Some are quite wild, and require a long taming process. Hector is superb at that, so one of his nicknames is Breaker of Horses."

"And you?" I asked.

"I am also good, but I have reaped no nickname."

Did he resent this? "Show me," I said, to bury my own question.

We made our way out to where the nearest herd was pasturing. It was a difficult passage, as the chariot tracks dwindled away. Some fifty horses were eating and looked up warily when we approached.

Paris stepped down from the chariot, moving in measured steps. I followed him. "Careful not to startle them," he said. "These are almost wild."

Some of the horses snorted and moved away from us. Others stood their ground but with nostrils flared. Most of them were a dull dun color with black mane and tail—the same colors, I had been told, as the wild horses in Thrace.

Paris made his way over to one, sidling up to it. Tentatively he put out his hand, but the horse moved away, retreating and staring back at him with wide dark eyes.

"This one is truly unbroken," he said. He left it and approached another. It merely watched him with placid curiosity as he came closer. Slowly he extended his arm and touched the horse's neck, and although it made a flapping noise of exhalation from its nostrils, it stood its ground.

"Have you ever been ridden?" Paris whispered. He came closer and began stroking the horse on its back and sides. Still the horse did not move. "I think yes, you have." It was not much of a leap to get onto the horse's back; none of these horses were very large.

The horse shivered and then started galloping from a standstill. Paris clung to its mane, wrapping his long legs around its flanks. The horse thundered across the plain, its tail streaming out, its head extended in a flat line. Then it started to buck. The horse was not tame after all; clearly no one had ridden it before.

I watched in helpless fear as the horse twisted and arched its back. All I saw were its hooves and its tail as it tried to dislodge its unwelcome passenger. Once—twice—thrice—that dreadful arch shadowed itself against the bright green grass. Then the figures separated, and Paris flew through the air. The horse galloped off.

I ran as fast as I could to him. The ground was rough, and I kept tripping on clods of dirt and clumps of weeds.

Paris was lying on his back, framed by wildflowers and grass. His arms were flung out on either side of him, and his head lay at a frightening angle. He did not move.

"Oh!" I rushed to him and cradled his head. Still no movement. Was he breathing? I scarcely breathed myself as I laid my palm on his chest and felt a slight rise and fall.

His eyes were closed, and I gazed down at him, frightened. What if he never opened them? What if—

Just then he groaned and his eyes fluttered open. For an instant they were unfocused, then he saw me. "I was wrong," he said. "This horse had never been ridden." He lay still. "Is anything broken, I wonder?" Slowly he sat up and flexed and tested his arms. Then he moved his legs, shaking his feet and then drawing up his knees. Finally he leaned far over and arched his back. "It hurts, but it all moves," he said. "Even Hector would have had trouble with that horse." He shook his head.

"You stayed on him a long way," I said.

"He was swift and a pleasure to ride—for a while." He looked about. "I must remember that horse. I will reclaim him for myself. He had a black spot just behind his right ear. Someday we shall ride together again." He stood up, and cried out in pain. "In the meantime, I shall mend, and the horse shall forget."

"Let me bring the chariot over," I said, steadying him. "Do not try to walk." Before he could protest, I hurried back to the chariot, where the horses were patiently waiting. Leaping in, I urged them forward over the bumpy ground; the wheels shuddered but rolled through the grass. Paris climbed in, wincing a bit as he gripped the rail. I started to turn the horses around, but he shook his head.

"No, I have more places to show you," he said. "Look! The sun is climbing in a perfect sky, and the day is young. It is too early to retreat. Here, I'll show you—there's a path alongside the Scamander, just where you see that line of trees. We can follow it down to the sea."

The chariot fought its way through the meadow until we reached the smooth path he spoke of, shaded by pink-flowering tamarisk trees. The Scamander, not as large as the Eurotas, flowed swiftly. I assumed it was fed with the melting snow from Mount Ida. Did not the snows linger there until almost midsummer?

"Indeed they do," said Paris. "I have seen snowbanks there right beside the blooming crocus and hyacinths. But the Scamander's water doesn't come from snow. Its source is two streams that bubble up almost side by side—one very hot and the other very cold! They are on the other side of Troy. The women have their washing troughs there."

"Why, that's impossible! A hot stream and a cold one—no, it cannot be." I laughed. "Or is it part of the magic of Troy, a place unlike any other?"

"Just so," said Paris. "And I will show them to you and dispel your doubts. Later. Just now we are heading in another direction, the direction of the Hellespont."

The chariots made its way along the smooth path toward the shining sea. When we reached the beach we stepped out of the chariot. Paris was hobbling, but he insisted it was of no import, and he led me down to the wide beach, gray and littered with seashells. The roar of the sea filled our ears.

"Look! Look over there!" He pointed to a dark line across the sea, beyond the bay where we now stood. "The opposite shore is so close, and yet so difficult to reach."

I could see the low hills, framed by the choppy reflections in the water. "Because of the currents?"

"Yes. They run so swiftly, and there are two of them—one on the surface and one underneath. Both have ferocious pulls. The main, upper current sweeps you westward, out to sea. It is so relentless that if you wish to cross at the narrowest point, you must cast off far downstream. It is impossible to cross directly. And if you miss your landing point, you are doomed. Well, doomed to explore the Black Sea if you are pulled the other way by the undercurrent. Perhaps that is not a bad thing."

"They say the Black Sea is rich with goods men covet," I said. At that moment I could not name them, though.

"Yes, silver, gold, timber, amber, linen, and many other things; they pass in and out of the Hellespont in good sailing weather."

"Who has those trading rights?"

He looked startled. "Anyone who can get there," he said. "There is no one to grant or deny trading rights. Who would have the power to do so?"

"I have heard that you Trojans hold ships to pay a toll."

"The farther away, the stranger the tale," he said. "By the time it reaches Sparta, it is twisted indeed. We have no means of actually holding ships," he said. "How would we do that? There exists no way to erect a barrier across this passage. As it is, the winds aid us. If they blow in the wrong direction, a ship must pull up here"—he indicated the beach—"and wait it out. Then they run out of water. So they must come to us, because we *do* have the means of guarding the Scamander. In that way I suppose you could say we 'exact' tolls, but the gods decide who gets delayed, not us. Of course, they decide to aid us most of the time!"

"I am afraid that this tale—true or not—may spur the Greeks to come here, claiming they must rescue me, but truly to seize this toll station which they believe exists." I could imagine Agamemnon forging such a plan, convincing his ignorant followers that this was imperative.

"They will come, then, to take something that does not exist. The Greeks are free to travel the Hellespont whenever they wish. It is Poseidon, not us, who determines their success."

"But what, then, does give Troy its wealth?"

"Many caravans coming from the East converge here," said Paris. "They reach the Hellespont and can go no farther on land. They must either transfer their goods to ships and ferry them across, or load them onto camels and swing far eastward for a further long land journey. So they prefer to sell as many goods as they can here, and people come from many quarters to buy. We host this gathering, each summer, and grow rich from the cruelty of the seas in hindering land travel beyond us. And then there are our famous Trojan-bred horses—which you have just seen."

"But surely it is not only that!" I thought of the dazzling palace atop Troy, of the great walls, dressed in shining stone, thick and yet decorative with offsets which allowed the play of shadows at different times of day, the clean, wide streets.

"No, not just that," said Paris. "It is the fruit of being isolated, far from the strife that tears apart other cities in the thick of things, and of having a wise ruler."

"But—can that be enough?"

"Think," he said. "Think of the peace and security of being apart, undisturbed. Think of the difference between a ruling family of wisdom and one of folly. Add to that the peculiarities of our location, making the trade fair a necessity, and yes . . . that accounts for most of it."

"So it is an absence of evil things, coupled with two lucky things, that makes Troy legendary," I said.

"Yes," Paris answered. "Simple things have complicated implications." He wrapped his arms around me. "People always underestimate the importance of simple things. Or assume that an almost-wise ruler is the same as a wise one. Yet it makes a tremendous difference who is on a throne."

"And after Priam—who rules?"

"Hector," he said. "We can all be happy that in this case the eldest is the best man for the position. The gods have been good to us in that way—in many ways, truly."

The wind whipped my covering from my head, blowing it swiftly away, and the brisk sea air tore my hair loose from its restraints. "I would not like to sail here," I said, clutching the strands of flying hair.

"Few ships do like it," said Paris. "Well, shall we leave this place? Have you seen enough? Let us turn our gaze to Mount Ida, in the opposite direction." Taking the reins from me, bracing his feet, he turned the chariot around to face Troy. It lay spread out on the flanks of its cliff, the lower city gradually thinning out, like a foamy wave spending itself on a beach, the higher city within its walls tightly self-contained and compact.

Far away I could see a great mass topped in white. "Is that Mount Ida?" I asked. "It looks too far to go today."

"Yes, it is. We should plan a special trip there. But look!" He guided my head to gaze toward the faraway peak. "Zeus lives there. Or so they say. I myself have never seen him. And the highest top is disappointing—an ugly expanse of stone-strewn ground with no life. Thus many things are best appreciated from afar. But its lower slopes are glorious—they call it 'many-fountained Ida,' and so it is. One stream after another rushes down, with green glens and flowering meadows everywhere. I will take you there, and show you my foster father and the place where I was raised."

Would he also show me the spot where they had left him out to die? Was it an open space where the wild beasts could find him more easily, and the sun burn him quickly? I clutched him to me. To think that this came so close to happening.

"What is it?" he asked. "Do you see something I do not?"

Perhaps, I thought. But it is in the past. And before us I see only the grandeur of Ida and the splendor of Troy.

We wheeled the chariot this way and that, searching out first one path and then another, rumbling all around Troy. As we circled it, I could see that Troy reared highest on the side facing the sea, where its sheer rock cliff rose from the plain. On the other sides the slope was gentler; on the south it was almost level. That was the way we had first entered Troy, at the huge covered gateway. I remembered how nervous I had been . . . was it only two days ago?

"It must have a name," I said.

"It's the Dardanian Gate," he said. "The southern one that leads to Aeneas's country, and right to Mount Ida—Zeus' doorstep." He laughed. "Sometimes we call it the Market Gate, since it's the busiest one. But why don't you ask about the one everyone asks about—the one beside the famous Great Tower of Ilium?"

"Very well, then. Tell me."

"It's the Scaean Gate. It's the one warriors use when they leave the city."

"Why only that one?"

"Oh, it's just tradition. Although it is the fastest way for a chariot to reach the plain. That's why"—he pulled me toward him as a confidant—"we took it just now. We weren't supposed to, but . . ."

The tower. The Great Tower. Why had it not struck me before? It loomed over the others like a giant.

" 'The topless towers of Ilium,' " I said.

"What?" Paris looked at me quizzically. "What do you mean, topless towers?"

"I don't know . . . the phrase came into my mind." And not for the first time. *And burnt the topless towers of Ilium.* Now there were more, other words, coming from someplace far away, the way they did sometimes. "Nothing." I shook my head, clearing it of what was crowding in—bright images of flame, and cries, and smoke. Yet the tower stood calm, solid, in the bright sunshine, birds flying over it.

"You are troubled," he said. "About the king and queen. Please, do not be."

Let him think it was that. I did not know, I could not explain, what I had just seen, flashing for an instant, in my mind. "This Calchas—"

"A self-important seer," said Paris. "I told you, Troy is full of them." He turned the horses toward the eastern side of the city, where the wall turned in upon itself, creating a protected, almost hidden gate.

"We're most proud of the walls here," he said. "These are the newest ones, with the best stonework. The ones over on the west side are the oldest and the weakest, and we keep meaning to strengthen them, but—the council of elders is, well, elderly. You know how stingy elders can be. If it isn't needed in their time, they won't bother with it."

"But can the king not do as he likes?" It seemed curious to me if he could not.

"Certainly. But he listens overmuch to them. He is old himself, you know." He laughed and flicked the horses on faster. The chariot jounced and swayed.

The sun was almost directly overhead, making the delicate insets in the wall invisible. "These walls change appearance according to the time of day," cried Paris. "They are prettiest at sunrise, when the shadows lie deepest."

Another great tower was around the bend, just beyond the eastern gate. "It's our water tower," said Paris. "Our main well is deep inside it, down a flight of steps cut in the rock. No one can ever cut us off from our water supply; we do not have to leave the city to get it."

"But what of those in the lower town?"

"They have the springs, and the Scamander," he said.

"But could an enemy not seize those?"

"Yes," he admitted. "But those people could flee to the surrounding countryside for safety. We have allies all around us—the Dardanians, the Phrygians ready to provide help."

"But what if the enemy attacked those allies first?"

"Why must you be so gloomy? No one is that determined. Armies come, they strike quickly, they retreat. Armies do not stay in the field. They cannot. That would require food and discipline beyond anyone's imagining. And the Trojan winter would send them packing. It is nasty here in winter— damp, cold, howling winds, sometimes even snow." He slowed the horses and turned to me. "But it is coming up upon summer—must you dwell on winter?"

But it is coming up upon summer—must you dwell on winter? In those few words, Paris described himself. And even now, when I think of him, I think of summer and the warmth he carried with him like an enveloping mantle wherever he went. There are always flowering fields, butterflies, and sweet winds surrounding him in my mind. How long a winter has my life been without him!

Paris brought the chariot to a halt. "Where to, my love? We have been all around the walls now." The dust settled around us.

All around the walls. A roar arose in my ears and I could hear thundering, the thundering of hooves, hear a chariot, hear cries of woe from the walls . . . but what? Why? And then, replacing the hooves, footsteps, fast runners, but how many? More than one, that was all I knew.

Stop! I took my head in my hands. Stop!

"What is wrong?" said Paris.

"Nothing!" I answered defiantly. "Nothing!" I looked out. The walls stood silently, nothing circling them but us.

"I brought wine, cheese, and figs," he said. "Let us sit in the shade by the banks of the Scamander and refresh ourselves."

It was growing dark when we returned to the city through the Dardanian Gate; the great doors were closed and we had to request passage. Ordinarily no one was allowed in after sunset, and already the stars glowed in the dome of the sky.

Waiting for us in Paris's apartments was a messenger from Priam. "Report at once to the king!" he barked.

We betook ourselves there, not changing our clothes; we did wash the dust from our faces and feet. We entered the king's council chamber to find Priam and several men pacing about. As soon as they saw us, they whirled around.

"So you come at last!" Priam said, glaring at Paris. "Did I not tell you to wait upon our pleasure? How dare you leave the city and keep us waiting?"

Paris neither apologized nor argued. Instead, he shrugged and smiled. "Dear Father, the day was lovely, and beckoning. I did not reckon on our little journey lasting so long."

A discreet throat-clearing from a portly man indicated his skepticism. But he awaited the king's response; he would take his cue from that.

"No, you do not reckon on anything. Dear son." He smiled. "But come. Enough time has been wasted. Here is Calchas, and I intend to dispatch him to the oracle to probe what the fates have in store for us."

The plump man stepped forward and bobbed his balding head. He had eyes like a bird—alert and searching. There was something about his face that indicated deliberate blandness, an effort to make itself unreadable.

"I will make every effort to go and return as swiftly as possible," he said. His manner was itself like olive oil—smooth and unctuous. "And of what must I inquire?"

"Nothing less than the future of Troy," said Priam. "We have here a queen of Sparta. We have admitted her to our city, acknowledged her marriage to a prince of Troy. But what will come of this? It is a simple question."

"I fear it may not have a simple answer. What if the oracle—"

"Make her give a clear answer! Keep questioning her! Do not let her hide behind whirling words!"

"My esteemed king, if I may give my opinion?" A small man, his remaining hair dark, stepped forward.

"Yes, what is it, Pandarus?"

"As Calchas's brother, I understand the difficulty of what you are asking him to do. You want him to cross the seas, go all the way to the oracle, avoid the Greeks, and then return. Do you realize—"

"Yes, I do! He is a seer! If he cannot help us now, what good is he?" said Priam. He glared at the others. "Only those who have something pertinent to say should speak! It is late enough already; my patience draws thin."

An elegantly dressed man made his way to Priam's side. His full head of hair was silver, and his older face still handsome. "It seems to me, great king, that all this is unnecessary. Why send Calchas on a perilous journey? We know the answer now. It is not an answer we want, so we seek another. But the Pythia, the prophetess of Apollo, will say the same: Helen must return to Greece."

"Antenor," said Priam. "I cannot argue your wisdom. This is the easy, the obvious, answer. But might more not be at play here—forces we cannot determine? Therefore we must seek the counsel of the gods themselves. This is no ordinary situation, subject to ordinary common sense."

Antenor drew himself up. "With all respect, great king, I find that when common sense is ignored, tragedy follows. Perhaps we look too hard for hidden meanings and exceptions. The truth is, a Greek queen has stolen away— been stolen away—to Troy. The Greeks are a nasty, warlike people. We know that Agamemnon has been bristling with war talk, and war weapons, for years. They do not need a strong reason to attack us. A flimsy one will do, when a man seeks war. Therefore I say: Send Helen back. Send her back, before it is too late!"

Another man came forward; this one was thick-bodied and broad-faced. His walk was one that bespoke a former warrior. "Are the walls of Troy too weak to withstand the pitiful assaults of a few foreigners?" he cried. "What are we talking about here? A few hundred miserable men, forced by Agamemnon to cross the seas to Troy? Huddling on the seashore, hiding in the shadows of their ships? Why are we cowering before even the *thought* of this—something that has little chance of coming to pass?"

Priam nodded to him. "You speak true, Antimachus." He looked around at the others, still silent. "We tremble before shadows. We need the oracle to tell us truly what is to come. Calchas, go. As soon as possible."

The others stirred and murmured, but had nothing to add. Either they would second Antenor's advice to send me back, or champion Antimachus's provocative stand.

Calchas stood before Paris and me, and bowed. "I will listen intently to what the Pythia says," he told us. His face was still unreadable. Would he truly do his best? "I will convey her exact words back to you, and to your king." He looked around as if he were searching for something. "With your permission, my king, I will take my son, Hyllus, with me. It would be good if he learned what the life of a seer entails, and to behold the greatest prophet of all—perhaps it will inspire him."

Annoyance crossed Priam's lined face. "I do not see the purpose in that," he said. "Taking a youth with you will slow you."

"No, no, it is the other way around!" Calchas smiled assuringly. "As we all know, it is age that drags, not youth."

"Oh, very well!" Priam waved impatiently. "Just go, as soon as you can strap your traveling boots about your ankles."

"Shall I take a torch and begin now?"

A tolerant laugh rippled through the chamber. Calchas said, "Pandarus, fetch Hyllus here so that he might receive the king's blessing."

Before Priam could forbid him, Pandarus had tripped from the room, smirking. In an instant—obviously the boy had been waiting outside—he returned with a tall gangly youth and dragged him up to Calchas. The boy kept his eyes downcast, but they were almost obscured by his long hair flopping across his forehead.

"Hyllus wishes your blessing before he departs for Delphi with me," said Calchas.

"Am *I* a priest?" snorted Priam. "Is he a mute? Can he not speak for himself? And let him look me in the eye, instead of out from under a waterfall of hair!"

Calchas grabbed the boy's hair and yanked it back. A jagged scar, like a staircase, revealed its livid stamp. So that was why he kept his forehead masked.

"Forgive me, son," said Priam. "May the gods heal the memory of your wound that your skin holds. And may you journey safely."

Father and son bowed, then Calchas took Hyllus's hand and they made a dignified retreat from the chamber. After they had gone, Priam turned an angry eye on Pandarus. "Your amusement at this lad's scar was cruel. But what can you know of scars, you who have never lifted your arm in battle?"

Pandarus raised one eyebrow before submissively nodding his head. "My apologies, great king."

"May we go now?" Antimachus bellowed. "It grows late."

"Indeed, yes. All of you may depart." Priam waved them away. "You as well." He was looking at Paris and me.

Morning sun spilling into our bedchamber; we had slept late again. I awoke before Paris; I was learning that whatever he did, he wished to prolong, so that he always overlapped the allotment of hours. Liking to stay up late, he outlasted the night's welcome; now, being tired, he overslept, treading on the hospitality of the day.

He rolled over, rubbing his eyes. "In our new palace, we must have sturdy shutters to keep our sleeping chamber dark." He sat up. "And today is the day we can begin planning it. I shall call in builders—"

"So soon?"

"Why become fond of these rooms, when you shall only have to leave them? I do not want you to feel that life with me means always leaving something."

A fleeting picture of the palace in Sparta flashed into my mind, but I quashed it. "But obviously Priam is displeased with the idea," I said. "Perhaps it seems an affront."

"Nonetheless we shall proceed," Paris insisted.

"You mean *you* will proceed," I said.

"It is for you," he said. "A proper housing for a mortal so fair that no housing can do her justice."

"You make me sound like a god, which I am not, or a lump of stone or gold, which I also am not."

"Oh, stop quibbling!" cried Paris. "Let me do this! Let me build something, present something of worth to Troy. This fair palace will stand long after we are gone; others will live there, and marvel at it, and invoke our names in gratitude."

Paris almost skipped about the streets of Troy searching for his site; I, his builder, Gelanor, and Evadne followed more sedately. There was little unbuilt space in Troy; the houses were packed together, one wall against the other, as the streets wound upward toward the summit. Upon the summit, Priam's palace—with its huge adjoining apartments, storerooms, and workshops—Hector's palace, and the temple of Athena claimed the choice spots, overlooking the plain and the shining sea.

"I want to be up here!" said Paris. "Up here, where the winds blow fresh and strong."

"It seems that others have come first," said Gelanor. It was almost the first thing he had said. In all this time, I had not been able to speak with him at length, privately. Was he still bent on leaving?

"Others came first in my father's household, but I have taken my true place. So shall I, here, alongside him." Paris pointed to a surprisingly modest house perched near Priam's palace at the summit. "Let us pay this man for his land and build here."

"There is not enough ground to build anything much larger than what is already there," said the builder. "It might be smaller than your present apartments."

"But the location is perfect!" Paris looked dashed.

"Perhaps you could build upward," said Gelanor.

"Upward?" said the builder.

"Two stories are commonplace," said Gelanor. "Has anyone ever tried three stories?"

"It wouldn't hold—the weight would be too great—the middle floor would be oppressive—I don't think—" the builder said.

"But has anyone tried it?" Gelanor asked. "I am not being argumentative, but it would be helpful to know. Men are always reaching to try new things."

"In days to come, there will be a hundred stories," Evadne suddenly said. "Or more. Shall it begin here?"

The builder turned to Paris. "Am I to help you, or do you insist on listening to these Greeks, who admit they are ignorant of building?"

Paris turned and looked at me. "My dearest, your companions . . . perhaps they should hold their questions."

"No," I said. Gelanor had never failed me with his probing mind. The question he raised was an intriguing one. "There is no land left here for the wide palace you envision. Perhaps it is time for another vision. Or we can seek another location, lower in the city, and build in the traditional fashion."

Thwarted, Paris turned back to Gelanor. "Do you really think there could be a building with three stories?"

"Perhaps. If there can be two, there can be three. Or even four."

"But if we were to build this, it would loom over the other buildings here on the summit," I said. "Would that not cause ill feeling?" Above all, I did not want that with the Trojans.

"That is why I would recommend only three stories," said Gelanor. "Although four would be a challenge . . ."

"This is absurd! The upper stories would collapse the building and kill all those beneath!" The builder threw up his hands. "I cannot condone this. I cannot be a party to it. If anything happened to you—the king would have me executed. No, I will not!"

Gelanor smiled at Paris. "It seems you must make a choice. Be safe and choose another, less lovely site, or be bold and build here, trying a new type of dwelling. Of course, the price for failure is high."

"I want a palace here!" Paris's face was set.

"You'll find another builder, then!" the builder proclaimed.

Paris looked angry. "Very well." He turned to Gelanor. "Can you linger here in Troy a bit longer and oversee this? If it is successful, you will become renowned throughout the world!"

"And if it fails?" Gelanor seemed amused, not frightened.

"Then, as a Greek, you can flee Priam's wrath when Helen and I lie beneath the rubble."

"I could never flee my own sorrow," he said. "So I shall make sure it does not fail."

"I leave you to your folly!" cried the builder. "I shall attend your funeral rites. They will have to drape your mangled bodies. You will have created your own earthquake! Deliberately!" He shook his head and made his way back down the paved, slanting street.

"People are always afraid," said Gelanor. "But desperate wants create desperate acts of courage. And, my prince, building such a palace is an act of courage."

"You will stay to direct the building?" I asked.

Gelanor slid his eyes over to me. "How could I not?" he said. "You have won again. You set out that bait—"

"I set out no bait!" I said. "I argued with Paris that the whole idea of leaving the king's palace is provocative. We hardly need that."

"Oh, the lengths you go to to keep me!"

"You conceited man!" I said.

"Stop it, you two," said Paris. "If I did not know better, I would say you sound like lovers!"

Gelanor laughed again, more heartily. Finally he said, "Well, you do know better."

"Gelanor rarely laughs, so this proves how preposterous the idea is," I said.

Suddenly Hector strode out of his doorway and looked at us in surprise. "Little brother!" he said. "And the most beauteous Helen." He crossed over to us quickly, a man who did not hesitate. "What are you about, this glorious morning?"

"I am looking to become your neighbor as well as your brother," Paris said. "I shall build my palace here. Beside yours."

Hector raised one eyebrow. "There is already a house here, the house of Oicles the horse breeder."

"I shall buy him off," said Paris airily, making a gesture of dismissal.

"I am pleased to see that you are modest, my dear newfound brother," said Hector. "For any palace here must perforce be a miniature one, as there is no space. But it can still be exquisite."

"It will be large," said Paris. "I have a plan to make it so."

"Unless you have recourse to magic arts, I fail to see how that can be."

"Wait." Paris cast a knowing glance at Gelanor. "My magician!"

"The wisest man in Greece," Hector recalled. "I await this with interest."

"Where are you off to?" Paris asked. "Down to the horses?"

"Yes," said Hector. "I need to inspect the breeding pens. A request has come in from Cyzicus for a number of mares and one fine stallion. I will make a selection this morning."

"I showed Helen the herds out grazing yesterday. We did not visit the pens closer to the city."

"Horses are our joy," said Hector.

Paris did not relate being thrown, I noticed.

"Andromache loves horses," Hector continued. "She is quite knowledgeable about them. Are you?"

"Not yet," I said.

"Ah!" Suddenly slender hands grasped Hector's shoulders from behind, the fingers looking like tendrils. He whirled around.

"Cassandra!" I saw his arm encircle whoever it was and turn her toward us.

A flat face stared back at us, framed by lank red hair. I had never seen a paler face—even her eyebrows were invisible. Her eyes were blue, protected by deep lids that rendered them both expressionless and placid.

"I see with whom you stroll," she said. Her voice was as flat as her face. "I had heard of their arrival. But I heard it in my head first." She stared at him. "Your house will fall," she said. "It will tumble."

"Do you refer to the building of my new palace?" said Paris.

"No. It will stand as long as the others. But it will topple, consumed. Along with the others, in the flames."

And burnt the topless towers of Ilium. I shuddered. That awful phrase again, that phrase that had come to me, unasked-for, from my own store of prophecy.

"That must be generations from now," I said. I looked out at the magnificent buildings and the tranquil green countryside with its horses grazing. "As you know—as I certainly know, having had my own visions—time is not specified in the messages we receive."

Cassandra looked at me as at a vile thing. "You are the cause of the flames," she said.

"Oh, stop it," said Paris. "Please, dear sister."

Hector cleared his throat. "I must to the horses," he said. "Helen, call upon Andromache when you can. She would welcome the opportunity to tell you everything about our famous horses. She loves them so." Then he was gone in a rustle of mantle and a tramp of sandals.

We were left confronting the hostile Cassandra. She glared at us, then lifted her chin and evaluated me.

"Yes, it's true," she muttered. "A face to cause a war. And it will."

"No wonder Father locked you up," Paris said. "I shall tell him to again."

" 'Because of her a great war will be fought and many Greeks will die,' " she recited. "And how many Trojans?"

How had she come by that phrase—the bloodcurdling one of the Sibyl? "Cassandra," I finally said, "the shadows of the possible future must not poison our thoughts."

"The shadows of the future have already ruined my life!" she cried.

"That is because you allowed them to drown out your present," said Paris. "You live only in what has not yet happened, and in that sense you do not live at all, since the future always recedes before us." He reached out to her. "Both of us, sister, have been robbed of much of our past. But if we let our prophecies rob of us our present, we are fools, and have only ourselves to blame. Come with me—come with me, into the present. Into this morning, here, sunny and warm. Live here, sister! Live with us! The truth is, you can live nowhere else."

To my surprise, she began to cry, big tears spilling out around her guarded eyes. She made no sound at all, she just stood stricken. Finally she mumbled, "You are right. I cannot go on like this, always living in some other time, hearing other voices, never voices of my own time or place." She touched his shoulder gently. "I do not want to go down to Hades without having walked in the sun—my own sun, not an image or a dream-sun."

"Then stifle your prophecies, and when they come thick and fast, turn your back. Come, take my hand."

Just as he had with me: *take my hand*—and made me leap, wild and bold, into a new world.

Cassandra put her pale one into his, closing her eyes and breathing deep. "I am afraid," she said. "I have never lived—here—before."

"It is more interesting than the world of shadows and fancies," said Paris. "Just look at what your own eyes show you, and drink in what is before you. If you do that, you might find that Helen is a woman you would care to know, not a sign or an image."

"But who is Helen?" she asked. "*Is* she more than an idea or ideal?"

Paris laughed, and put my hand in hers. "You cannot hold an idea."

I lived; I was real; I had come to Troy to take her hand in mine.

❖ XXXV ❖

Yes. I came to Troy, and I began to make my home in Troy.

Evadne and I searched for a place for the sacred snake. "We must find a home for your snake," she said. "He will feel unwelcome here if we delay much longer." We found a small room beneath the main chambers with a trickling spring diverted into a pool. It was secluded and quiet, a perfect abode for the serpent.

It was a simple matter to have an altar built, and a place to set out the honey cakes and milk for him. When it was ready, I asked Paris to come and help release him. After all, we had first spoken privately in his presence, had declared our love in the household shrine where he lived.

Together we loosened the sack holding him, and let him slither out. He paused, regarding us—did I imagine it, or was he solemn?—and then slowly made his way across the slippery floor to a dark recess.

"Bless us," Evadne implored. "We need your blessing. We are in a new land where only you are of our old home."

"This is your third home," I said. "You came with me from Epidaurus, then to Sparta, now here in Troy. But to change is to ever renew. As you shed your skin, you live forever young. Teach us to do the same. And look after Hermione, even from afar."

Paris knelt down and spoke to him where he waited, coiled, watching him. "You gave me a sign in Sparta. You bound me to Helen, your mistress. Now we are in my city, and we look to you. Keep us bound. Protect our home."

The snake flicked his tongue out; then he disappeared with a start into the darkness.

Day after day the workmen came; Paris's new palace rose on the summit of Troy. I sought out Andromache, and found her sympathetic to me, a foreigner, as she was one, too. She had been wedded to Hector from her father's home on Plakos; more than anything she longed for a child.

As she spoke of her longing, the image of my lost Hermione loomed before me; I ached for my own child. Sometimes it was so intense I had to retreat to the secluded underground chamber with the altar, and cry out to the gods, before the sacred snake there.

Andromache confided that she had sought all the remedies, made all the proper sacrifices to the gods.

"Yet I am barren!" she murmured. "Day after day, these chambers echo with only adult voices." She gestured toward her vast halls, her spacious chambers.

"You are young—" I would begin. Always she would cut me off.

"Young! You know better than that! I am past twenty, by my reckoning. Is that young?"

"I am past twenty-five," I would reply.

"And? I see no children with Paris. You had your daughter at sixteen. And now—nothing!"

I would wince. Yes, that was true. And I longed for a child with Paris.

"The gods cannot deny Hector a child," I would say. It was an unsatisfactory answer, but the only one I could give. As I had come to know him, I thought Hector one of the finest men the gods had ever fashioned. Not because he was a warrior, not because of his bearing, but because he was the sort of man who would always judge fairly, who saw and considered everything before him.

"The gods can do anything they like," she would say. "You know that, Helen." She would smile gently. "You are next of kin to them."

"You mean that old swan story?" I would laugh.

"Not just from an amusing story, but your whole manner. I think there are some of us closer to the heavens than others."

Such talk made me uncomfortable, as it always had. "Is it not time for the sweets?" I would ask her. "Your attendant is late."

Summer came to Troy, warm sweet winds replacing the relentless sweep of the chill blasts. The grass on the plain sprang bright and green, and the Scamander shrank to a gurgling placid stream. The other river on the plain, the Simoïs, transformed itself into a series of pools as its sources dried up in the heat. It was always cool up on the heights of the city, though, and the workmen were able to continue building our palace without slowing their efforts. They said it would be ready for us by the time the days grew short again. The furnishings and decorations would come later, of course. The workmen grunted as they indicated that artists always took a long time, and were unreliable in any case. The third story had not yet risen; Gelanor was still building his clay and stick models and adding weights to it to see how it would fare. For a time he had spoken of a fourth story, but lately he had not mentioned it. Perhaps his model had collapsed when he fashioned its fourth story.

As I was mixing two types of dried meadow herbs to make a sweet-smelling potpourri for our chambers, Paris burst in and cried, "See what's coming into Troy!" His face was flushed with excitement and he grabbed my hands so quickly I dropped the herbs onto the floor.

"Never mind the mess! Let's go see before it gets too crowded!" Pulling me along, he rushed down the main street and toward the Dardanian Gate, where a big throng was already gathered. Someone was trying to pry the doors even farther open, so that a large object outside, groaning on a lurching platform, could be wedged in through the gate.

The crowd was already so thick we could hardly move, so Paris said, "Up into the guard tower, where we can look down on it." We scrambled up the ladder to the platform where the archers and guards manned the tower, and from its window I could see a long golden statue. Its body was that of a lion, but it had the head of a woman.

"Straight from Egypt," a swarthy little man with monkey arms was crying. "And what will you pay for it? I'll not haul it a step farther unless someone is willing to buy it! I'm a fool to have brought it all this way on the promise of a man who, evidently, does not exist!"

"Was his name, by any chance, Pandarus?" someone yelled.

The statue's owner shook his head.

"Pandarus likes such things. Or perhaps it was Antenor?"

At the sound of "Antenor" the crowd roared. I remembered the man had been elegantly dressed, so I was not surprised when someone else called out, "Oh, Antenor would never want anything so vulgar and outsized."

"Vulgar?" its owner cried. "This is a statue from a palace of a pharaoh!"

"Stolen, I'll warrant." I saw Deiphobus run his hands along it, careless of dirtying it.

"If it is, the owner will not follow it here." The man winked. "Now, which lucky Trojan will take possession of it?"

"It's a sphinx, you know," a dried husk of an old man said. "Sometimes they ask riddles, sometimes they tell the future. The one Oedipus encountered killed people. Perhaps you must be an Egyptian to safely own one."

"Troy needs a sphinx!" a guardsman bellowed. "All great cities need a sphinx, and are we not the greatest city of all?"

"Yes, indeed!" the owner jumped in. "Along the Nile, there's a city that has a whole avenue of sphinxes. You should not be outdone by—"

"I'll warrant it has one less now!" Deiphobus said. His tone was always nasty, even when he tried to disguise it as a joke.

"We could set it up in the open space beside the lower well. And we'll plant flowers around it, yes, and have a fountain running, and people can sit in the shade—"

"Troy deserves it!" A woman cried out.

"How could we have gone so long without one?" Another wondered.

"You see?" The owner shrugged. "Now, don't fight over it, but who's to be the proud owner?"

"Troy will." Priam suddenly appeared by its side. "I, its king, will give this to the city of Troy as a gift." He patted its back. "We must continually make Troy more beautiful." He motioned to the workmen standing idly by the cart. "You can get it through here, even if it's narrow. And take it to the square, as you heard."

The owner almost rubbed his hands, but stopped himself with a twitch. "Very good, sir. But may I say, why only one? I can get you another. You know what they say—one statue is a lonely one, but two is a collection."

Hector appeared and, putting his arm around Priam, gave the merchant a look. "Don't press your luck, my friend."

Laughing and skipping, the crowd fell in behind the sphinx and helped push it along. Someone brought out wine, even though it was early, and a boy started piping. We descended from the tower and followed the crowd to the paved area, watching as the sphinx was settled into its temporary place.

"I do believe my courtyard will now look bare without its own sphinx," said Pandarus, who had arrived late on the scene.

"Confess. Confess. You were the one who ordered it, weren't you?" Hector teased him.

Pandarus gave a look of mock horror. "Oh, no, not me! My weakness is furniture with inlays, as you well know."

"As well my back knows," Hector said. "Hideously uncomfortable things!"

"Inlaid furniture?" The merchant must have had superhuman hearing. "I have lovely stools and tables still on my ship. Just down there!" He pointed toward the landing place. "I can fetch them in an instant!"

When Pandarus said, "Inlaid with what?" Hector groaned.

"Now you are finished!" he said.

"Ivory, or mother-of-pearl. Whichever you prefer, sir, I have them both!"

"Ummm . . ."

"Bring your wares up here!" someone in the crowd shouted. "Let's see them all!"

"Yes, bring them all!"

"I'll need help," the merchant said, "to carry so much."

Like children, the Trojans rushed out to his ship and soon returned laden with boxes and bags and carts. They spread them out on the smooth pavement of the square and let the merchant announce each thing and offer it. All the while they were gleefully commenting and bidding against one another.

Wool carpets—alabaster vials—dog collars studded with carnelian—woven sun hats—painted vases—ivory hair combs: all were snatched up by the eager crowd. Larger items like the inlaid furniture, which was truly exquisite, went more slowly. True to his word, the merchant had other statues with him, but smaller ones and no more sphinxes. These disappeared into houses and courtyards. Occasionally a spouse could be heard saying, "Dear, perhaps we should wait for the trade fair, and see what's offered there . . ."

Paris whispered in my ear, "Shall we get something for our new palace?"

"No," I said. "How can we furnish what exists only in a dream?" I was unsure about the safety of the new dwelling and buying something for it seemed premature.

The crowd gleefully turned from the merchant's dwindling store of goods and began to chant, "Greek treasure! Greek treasure!"

The puzzled man said, "I do have a few jars from Mycenae, with exceptionally nice handles," and began pawing through one of the carts.

But the people cried out, "We have our own Greek treasure, the best there is! Helen, the queen of Sparta!"

"What did we pay for her?" one man yelled.

"Nothing! She was free! A gift to Troy!"

"I'll drink to that!" Wineskins were passed over shoulders.

I saw Priam frowning, over by the sphinx, as he heard the cries.

In the privacy of our apartments, Paris looked around wistfully and said, "I thought his hearth stools most attractive. We will have so many hearths in our new home."

The Trojans seemed to favor much richer surroundings than we had in Sparta. Even Paris, for all his simple upbringing in a herdsman's hut, wanted them. Perhaps it was something in the blood. "Your father was most . . . generous." I wanted to say *extravagant* but did not wish to criticize.

"He sees himself as father of Troy, and wants his children to be happy."

How indulgent. The thought of Father and his stinginess flashed through my mind. Father . . . what had he done when he awoke that morning and I was gone? Had he . . . was there any possibility he had summoned the suitors, tried to rally them? And Mother . . . and Hermione . . . I ached to hold them both, and they were so far away, unreachable. I had rejected Idomeneus because I did not want to be separated from my family by a sea, and now I was.

"You look sad," said Paris, coming over to me.

"I was thinking of my family, and especially my daughter."

"We knew it would be difficult," he said.

"I did not know how difficult, and how painful," I admitted. It is impossible to experience loss in advance. "Paris, would you like a child?"

"Yes, of course. Our child. But it could never be Hermione. Each child is different, as all of Father's are. I am not Deiphobus, nor Deiphobus, Hector."

"I know that!" His answer, meant to be soothing, increased my pain. "But it could bring us joy." Joy that would exist side by side with loss.

"Then let us hope the gods send us a son or daughter," he said.

Forgive me, Hermione, I begged her in my mind. I do not seek to replace you, for I know that is impossible. I seek only to find a way to remain a mother.

The next morning I received a summons, disguised as an invitation, to join Hecuba and her daughters in the women's quarters of the palace. I was apprehensive at the same time as I was flattered, pleased to be included. The queen had never called upon me nor invited me to call upon her since I had arrived in Troy. I said as much to Paris.

"Be careful what you promise her," he said. "She may want something."

My suspicions were confirmed, then, although that took the pleasure from the invitation. "I shall be on my guard," I assured him.

Hecuba was already surrounded by her daughters when I arrived at the specified time; obviously they had gathered earlier. She was standing in their midst and I instantly thought of the proud Niobe and her seven lovely daughters. The tallest was not her own daughter but Andromache, who was as stately and graceful as a tall poplar. But all the rest were hers, and they clustered around her like flowers of the field, differing greatly in coloring but all with clear complexions and shining eyes. There was one I had not seen before, younger than the others, about the same age as . . . Hermione. Envy of Hecuba swept over me, but I forced myself to smile and ask the little one, "What is your name? I haven't seen you before."

"Philomena," she said politely.

"My youngest daughter," Hecuba said. "She has seen ten Trojan winters. One with snow!" She gestured around her. "You know the rest?"

Some better than others, but none well. Creusa was rarely apart from Aeneas, so the times I saw him I also saw her. Cassandra, with her red hair, was easy to recognize. Laodice—the one who had spoken of marriage—yes, I remembered her, but I had seen little of her since that first night in the courtyard. There was another girl whose looks were unusual but memorable. Her nose was too large, her lips too thin and straight, her forehead too broad, but somehow all these elements came together in a haunting face not easily forgotten—one I would remember when more perfect ones had faded from my memory. Just as I was thinking that, Hecuba encircled her shoulders protectively and kissed her cheek. "Polyxena," she said. "Just twelve."

The last, a slender dark girl with haunting beauty, introduced as Ilona, merely stared and said little. I could not tell if her quietness was from shyness or hostility. In the beginning, it is impossible to know.

The girls fell away from their mother's side, like a colorful knot untying itself. I noticed how they all wore a different color, and I marveled at the array of choices in Troy. A table to one side was listing under bolts of cloth with more colors.

"Now that you are a daughter of Troy, it is only fitting that you should join with the others," said Hecuba, assessing me. "I have been remiss not to have included you earlier."

"It was lonely, being the only one not born of Hecuba. Although, of course, she has been like a mother to me," Andromache hastened to add.

"It is time some of my other sons married," said Hecuba, shaking her head. "And some of my other daughters, as well. Only Creusa, alone of all my dear ones, has been so fortunate as to wed. We will remedy that. That is what we are here for." She turned to me. "You had that suitors' contest, the one you . . . told me about. Do you think we should have such a one in Troy?" Her eyes were searching, inquisitive.

I looked around at her daughters. What a dreadful thing to endure! "No," I said. "Such a contest is tedious, embarrassing, and expensive."

"And then you ran off with someone who didn't even come to the contest." Laodice giggled. "Isn't that funny?"

Hecuba gave her a cold look. "*Funny* is not the word I should choose."

"Oh, but I think it's wonderful—and brave!" Laodice kept on, despite her mother.

"I hope you are not planning to do the same thing," Hecuba said.

"I might, if you persist in your idea about marrying me to a Thracian. Mother, I don't want to leave Troy. Don't send me there!"

"It's true, Trojans usually marry each other," said Creusa. "Even Aeneas can pass for a Trojan, he's so closely related to us."

"Oh, yes, Dardanians don't count as foreigners. Laodice, would you consider someone from Dardania?"

"It's better than Thrace, but it's still not Troy."

"What's wrong with all of you?" said Hecuba. "When I was younger than you, Laodice, I left Phrygia to come here as Priam's bride. I didn't snivel about leaving my mother and father. Why, even my boys don't seem to want to marry!"

"It's just too merry here in the children's quarters—I mean, the apartments," said Laodice.

"Yes, it is! Don't leave us!" said little Philomena.

"Whatever shall I do with you?" said Hecuba. "At least Hector finally married, and now Paris . . . Helen, you tell them. You did not shrink from marriage when the time came."

I looked around at the faces, wanting to say something pleasing, but I was not sure what that something would be. So all I could do was speak honestly. "I did not wish to leave home, either, and so I chose . . . perhaps partly, anyway . . . someone who would not take me away."

"Well, that wasn't Paris!" Ilona spoke, and her voice revealed that, after all, she was hostile. One question answered.

"No," I agreed. "That was not Paris. I chose my first husband, but the gods chose my second."

"Let's choose my wedding gown first," said Laodice, pointing to the cloth. "Perhaps if I've already selected the attire . . ."

Chattering, the girls turned with relief to the material, while Hecuba waited beside me.

"You don't wish to give an opinion?" she asked.

"Laodice looks good in any color, so she cannot make a wrong choice."

Hecuba shrugged. "You speak more for yourself than for her. She cannot wear red, or brown."

No matter what I said, she would argue with it or refute it. It was wearisome. Why had she truly invited me?

"Now that we are family," she said, "it is good for the girls to get to know you better." She paused. "Things that are forbidden become more alluring. I fear that already Laodice admires you more than is good for her. While I cannot reject the wife of Paris, I would be less than honest if I pretended I wished any of my daughters to imitate you."

"Honesty is such a virtue," I said, letting the sting remain in my voice. *So is kindness,* I wanted to add, *and sometimes they war with one another. Out of kindness I will restrict the honest answer I could give about you and your ways.*

"We understand each other," she said.

In truth, we did not. I still could not read the depths of her character, and I felt that she knew little of me, and did not wish to.

"Are you with child yet?" she suddenly asked.

"What do you mean, 'yet'?"

"I meant that I had assumed that was behind your hasty flight and rush away from Sparta."

"If that were so, you could see it for yourself by now." Truly, the woman was offensive in her bluntness and assumptions.

"Pity," she said. "Give Paris a son, or he'll be sorry he ever ran off with you." She nodded smugly. "I know."

"You know very little about him," I said. "In fact, you barely know him at all."

"It's you who doesn't know him," she said. "The gods blind us that way."

"Mother!" cried Laodice, rushing over with a pale yellow bolt of linen. She held it up under her chin. "This is the one! Now all we have to do is find a man to go with it!"

❖ XXXVI ❖

At last the time of the great trade gathering on the Plain of Troy drew near. For a few weeks at the end of summer thousands came to the meadows at the foot of the citadel before the seas closed again for the winter. They came from Babylon, from Tyre and Sidon, from Egypt, from Arabia and Ethiopia. They spread out their goods for all to see and buy, and for a short glorious time Troy was the center of the world.

Do you want to hire a tutor in Accadian? Surely there will be someone there who is expert in that tongue. Do you want to buy a length of cloth so light it floats? It will be there. What of a delicacy made of whipped almond paste? It will be there, you may be sure of it. And for each day's transactions, Priam took a fee. His agents were everywhere, noting the merchants and collecting his due. People paid gladly, for the site was so situated that they could never find a better. Here at the crossroads of Europe and Asia, East and West, Troy sat as queen of the world.

Paris and I strolled through the grounds late one afternoon, when the sun's shadows were already slanting. All around us a cacophony of languages rose, and I reveled in it. Unknown tongues made me invisible; I passed through them like a shade of the underworld. I saw the tempting and curious products spread out on bright cloths: chunks of unworked mottled amber, heaps of wool carpets, sweet-scented curling bark, dried octopus, axes of a dull-colored metal, lumps of raw frankincense, bags of rare turquoise from the desert of Egypt.

Then, suddenly, as we were inspecting a litter of baby leopards for sale by a merchant from Nubia, I heard the sound of Greek. Spartan Greek. Its sweet melody, its cadences, wafted across the air like the spices spread out on a nearby blanket. Spartan Greek! I clutched Paris's hand and dragged him away from the leopards, following the sound like a child drawn by a flute.

"Spartans!" I said. "There are Spartans here!"

"Perhaps you should not go," said Paris. "Or if you must, cover your face."

Oh, yes. Of course. I had become careless about that, as I was so free amongst the Trojans.

We approached the merchants. There were three of them. The oldest, thinnest one was clearly the leader. He directed the others in replenishing the wares, and bossed the bargaining. I saw jars of dried wild olives from the foothills of Taygetus, a local delicacy, and the distinctive honey from Eurotas's meadows. Instantly I was hungry for them. They also had some finely worked gold earrings. I probably knew the craftsman who had fashioned them.

I edged closer and nudged Paris to barter for some of the honey. The less I spoke, the better. As he offered Paris different-sized jars, I heard the other two— one young, heavy, and one with a beard like a he-goat's—say they had arrived late because most of the Greek ships had been commandeered by Menelaus and Agamemnon; ordinary merchants had been stripped of their vessels.

"Yes, there is hardly a ship in Greece," said the burly one. "This one I had hidden around the lee side of the island off Gytheum, otherwise it would have been taken."

"Taken for what?" Paris asked.

They looked at us, wide-eyed. "Why, for the great fleet Agamemnon is assembling. He has called on all of Greece to supply men and arms and ships. Families draw lots; they are required only to send one son, and that is hard enough. Some would rather pay their fine to keep their son and be out of it."

"But . . . for what reason is he assembling this . . . this army on water?"

"What, do you live in a cocoon here? Because the sister of Agamemnon's wife has been stolen by a Trojan. Or so they say. Others say she went away willingly enough. But long ago there was some sort of oath sworn about this woman, or her marriage, or something. In any case, Agamemnon has called on all the men who swore the oath, as well as many others. He means to fight the abductors and recover the woman." The man laughed. "What woman would be worth all that? None, I say. But if she comes with a city like Troy, then there'll be a lasting prize from it all. So we want to trade here as fast as we can, then leave."

His words stunned me. Why had we heard nothing of this? Agamemnon!

"Is this a secret?" Paris asked.

"Hardly," said the man. "But plans still unfinished are often not reported—what is there to report, after all? Many a plan comes to nothing." He flopped out his rugs of rough wool, still smelling like sheep. "I think what fired them on was the death of the lady's mother. She killed herself out of shame—hanged herself in her bedchamber. The old king and Menelaus were so sorrowed, so shamed themselves, that they must do something."

"The queen—the queen of Sparta—killed herself?" I could barely say the words, forgetting I meant not to speak.

"The old queen—the former queen. The present queen, that's her daughter, that's the one run away to Troy."

Mother! I would have stuffed my fist into my mouth to stop myself from crying out, but no sound would come.

"Will they attack directly? No embassy first, no attempts to solve this by diplomacy?" Paris asked the practical question.

"I heard that they already sent an embassy and that Priam lied. So perhaps the time for embassies is past. I don't know. I'm only a merchant, and thankful Menelaus didn't seize my boat. That woman—the queen—why are they in such a pother about her? Let her go, I say. A faithless woman isn't worth a spit."

I felt myself about to faint. I sagged against Paris. He supported me and I heard him saying, "The sun. She is with child," before leading me away.

"In this heat, she should not cover her face like that," the merchant said. "But I know some of you people from the East are used to it."

I staggered along, leaning against Paris. Mother. Mother had killed herself! An army was coming! "I must . . . please, Paris, take me back to our chambers!" I was not sure I could even walk that far; hot and cold shivers and shakes had overtaken me. My legs buckled.

"I will hold you," he said. We made our slow way out of the thronging merchant area and through the dry clumps of grass in the open field. The walls of Troy seemed a long way off.

Trembling and weak, I sank down. I would only rest; I would rise again shortly. I bowed my head and stared at the ground and swaying weeds around me. They rustled a little, making dry little rubbing sounds. Then I saw a slight movement at their base, although I could not discern what it was. I stared harder and still saw nothing; all the colors blended. Then, suddenly, it moved again and I saw the tortoise, its brown and yellow markings now visible against the green grass. It was like one of Hermione's. Hermione. Hermione . . .

I gave a moan and felt pain beyond any that I had ever felt before. It ripped through me. And all the while the tortoise was regarding me with curious black eyes, free of all judgment. They grew larger and larger until they filled my vision; then I saw nothing more and darkness took me away.

"What happened to her?" Gelanor was asking. I heard his voice from far away. I could not move. Was I dead? Was my spirit just hovering above my body, listening before it flitted away? I could not open my eyes; my arms lay at my side like carved wood. I could utter no sound.

"We were walking through the fields." Paris's voice rose with a tremulous quaver of fear. "She sat down to rest. She fainted."

"Is she with child?" Evadne spoke.

"No. I told the merchants that, but it isn't true. She was—we were—desperate to get away."

"Why?" Gelanor again.

Because we heard about Agamemnon, I tried to say. But nothing came out. *Menelaus. My mother! My mother!*

"Some merchants there—at the fair—they told us—they told us—dreadful things!" Paris's voice rose to a shriek.

"Calm yourself!" Gelanor was shaking a prince of Troy. "Gather your thoughts. Whatever it was, we can confront it."

"An army. That's what we will have to confront!" Paris cried. "Agamemnon has gathered an army, and commandeered ships, and Menelaus has enforced the oath Helen's suitors took, and they are coming, coming to Troy!" His voice rose so high he sounded like a eunuch.

"When?" Gelanor's voice was sharp.

"I don't know—they didn't say—"

"Why didn't you find out?"

Because they were saying other things as well, coming at us like a flock of birds, filling the sky, and each one streaked past, and then they were telling me about my mother—Why could I not speak? Was I . . . could I truly be . . . dead?

"I don't know—I don't know—we couldn't think—"

"When you ran away with Helen, did you not think something like this might happen?" Gelanor pressed. "Had you not even considered it?"

"Priam did, but I thought he was wrong, as wrong as he was about Hesione. This has never happened before! Why should it be happening now?"

"There has never been a Helen, a Menelaus, and an Agamemnon before. A queen never ran away from her realm with another man before, either. What will happen now, no one can say."

"Helen! Helen!" Paris was leaning over me. "Wake up. Oh, wake up!"

"Let her rest." Evadne was firm. "She will wake when she can face what has stricken her. The body retreats when the mind has borne too much." Soft fingertips were caressing my forehead. Then a cool cloth was dabbed on my wrists. She lifted my heavy arms and crossed them over my breast.

But I was awake. I was awake! I wanted to scream, but silence muffled me. Far from being granted surcease from my troubling thoughts, I was held prisoner by them.

Mother. Mother had hanged herself! I could not keep the hideous picture from my mind. Mother, a rope around her neck, swaying and turning, her little feet drooping from under her gown. What color gown? She had always favored white, like the feathers, perhaps in memory of the feathers . . . was this gown white? She hung in the air like a wraith, her head lolling to one side . . . all memories, white and otherwise, gone, drained from her . . .

I shrieked, an earsplitting roar, as my throat was freed from the grip of paralysis. "No! No!" I flung myself up, lunging to a sitting position. My eyes opened and I saw them staring at me. Then Paris sprang forward to embrace me.

"My dearest," he murmured. "Would that I could say it was not true, that you awaken but from a black dream."

"We must tell Priam." Gelanor was grim. "Immediately. With your leave, I'll go to him."

Priam, alarmed, sent for the merchants. But no one could find them. Paris then led his father to the spot where they had been, only to find it empty. Trampled grass betrayed the site of the vanished booth. None of the surrounding merchants knew where the Spartans had gone, or whether they planned to return. Priam sent soldiers to scour the area, including the beach, but they found nothing.

"The escape route is too easy," one of the soldiers said. "It takes no time to get from the fair-fields to the shoreline, and then to cast off. They are probably already making out to sea."

"Why did they run away?" said Priam. "Why?"

"Someone must have told them who we were," said Paris. "They must have realized that behind the veil was Helen, and they were afraid."

"Of what? Punishment?" bellowed Priam. "*They* didn't run off with her!"

"People are not as clear-thinking as that," said Gelanor. "Whenever people scent trouble, like a hare scenting a hound, they flee."

"So!" Hecuba strode into the room. "It has begun!"

"Nothing has begun yet," said Priam. "We must make sure nothing does. I shall send an embassy—"

"They said that the time was past for that," I remembered. My voice was still faint. "When, in all good faith, you told the envoys who came to Troy that you knew nothing of Paris and me, it was apparently regarded on the other side as a—a deliberate falsehood."

"Just as I said!" he cried. "Just as I feared. What did I say, Paris, as soon as you returned to Troy with your prize? I said you had made a liar of me." He paused. "But not a deliberate one."

"They think otherwise," said Paris gently.

"Indeed, how can they not?" Hecuba spoke low. "We must send another embassy. We must call a council. Helen must—"

"No!" Paris cried. "Do not even speak the words! Helen will not return! I will never let her go. Never. Understand that, Mother. Understand that, Father. We will flee Troy to the mountains, but she will never leave my side."

"The mountains!" scoffed Priam. "And what will you do when they come for you there, to hunt you down like a stag? At least the walls of Troy provide some protection."

A dreadful, looming guilt soaked me. Mother was dead, dead of shame over me. Now they were talking of walls and being hunted down and fleeing and killing.

"Paris." I rose and took his hand. "Already my mother has sacrificed her life. There should be no other sacrifices, except by me. I should be the one to require a price, but paid by myself." I trembled as I said it. Returning there would be dreadful, except for coming back to my Hermione. But for the rest—

"Nobly spoken, Helen, spoken like a queen." Hecuba's voice was warm, warmer than I had ever heard it. At last I had earned an approval of sorts from her—because I was willing to leave.

"I should . . . I should . . ." I could hardly frame the words.

Paris clapped his hand over my lips. "Do not speak them! Words have a life of their own, and those words must never come from us. No. I would die first!"

"Perhaps Helen would not," said Hecuba. "Do not choose death for others without their consent."

Before I could speak, Paris cried again, "I choose death for myself, then! I will die before I surrender Helen."

"And so you shall," said Evadne. "And so you shall." Her voice was cold, like the little trickling stream that flowed where the snake had its abode.

"I'll call a council," Priam muttered, turning toward the door.

❧ XXXVII ❧

The fair was to continue for a long while, until the sailing season drew to its natural close. Priam was resolute that no murmurs of trouble should ripple the calm of the fair, from whence he derived so much wealth. Troy would need all the wealth she could amass.

Gelanor persuaded him to send spies out amongst the booths and traders to garner bits and scraps of information, which he deemed more important than any booty. The true wealth of spies was secrets and knowledge, he said. Priam's spies—not very subtle ones, in Gelanor's view—fanned out and listened everywhere, slipping in between blankets and booths and pretending to compare the taste of dried date cakes from Thebes to those of Memphis, to examine the carved ivory combs of Sumer, to leer over the potions of mandrake and toad sweat to enhance desire. All the while they were trying to draw the merchants into conversation about what was happening to the west. Each day they would return and lay their findings before Priam, like a carpet.

Tantalizingly little was learned, for all that. They confirmed that a call had gone out through the Peloponnese to supply ships and men for an overseas venture. This was to be led by Agamemnon, as brother of the wronged Menelaus. Some princes whose realms lay inland and therefore had no ships were to be given them by Agamemnon. My old suitors were honoring their promise to Father upon the bloody carcass of the horse in the glen. Ajax was coming, along with his brother Teucer. Nestor and his two sons had responded to the summons. Odysseus had been tricked into joining the expedition, after feigning madness to avoid it. King Cinyras of Cyprus had angered Agamemnon by promising fifty ships and then sending one, along with forty-nine clay model ones.

"They do not wish to participate, then," said Priam. "They have to be forced to, and even then they try to evade it."

"Nonetheless, a great number have flocked to the call." Hector frowned. "A warrior tends to lose his reluctance once he puts on his helmet."

"We don't know the number of ships, nor where they are gathering, nor when they sail," lamented Priam.

"Obviously they cannot sail before next spring," said Hector. "The seas will close before long. They will not come then, only to arrive in time to camp on the Plain of Troy and endure a winter. Though I wish they would! Oh, how I wish they would!" He looked around at his listeners—Priam, Hecuba, Paris, and I. "We could smash them easily then, with supplies and shelter on our side."

On our side. But I did not wish Menelaus, or Idomeneus of Crete, or any other men I knew, to be killed. Where was my "side"?

"They would never be that foolish," said Priam. "We must credit them with some strategy and foresight. No, they will arrive in the spring. But how many?"

"Dear Priam, I can tell you only of the number of men my father forced to swear the oath," I said. "There were forty of them. Each would, of course, command different numbers of warriors."

"Forty." Priam squirmed on his chair. "Say each brought two ships"—he held up his hands—"I know this is a low estimate, but let us begin there. Two ships, forty leaders, that means eighty ships. Fifty fighters in each ship means four thousand warriors."

"We can easily defeat four thousand warriors," said Hector.

"But if they brought ten ships each, now there would be twenty thousand warriors."

"We have our allies to call upon," said Hector. "The Lycians, the Thracians, the Carians, and more farther to the east and south. Even the Amazons, formidable warriors. Or should I say 'warrioresses'?"

"They fight better than men," said Priam. "We can rely on them, and their strong right sword arms."

Gelanor—who seemed to be a shadow everywhere now—spoke softly. "How can an army of twenty thousand sustain itself in the field?" he asked. "They would be in hostile territory, and every day twenty thousand men would need food. Where is it coming from?"

"They would raid our allies. Destroy them first, before moving in on us." Hector shook his head. "We would have to take measures to deny them this . . . this privilege."

"Strengthen the allies," said Gelanor. "And do it now, before the enemy arrives."

"Someone needs to visit them and ascertain their supplies," said Priam. He nodded at Hector. "But I shall still send envoys west. It is preferable to settle disputes by tongues than by sword arms."

"Agamemnon hates tongues," I said. "Ever since I have known him, he has looked longingly at his store of weapons. He amassed them before he had any cause." I looked around at them, people already dear to me. "And now I am that cause. It grieves me greatly."

Those four words did not begin to convey the lowering sorrow and guilt I felt at providing my vicious brother-in-law with a reason to bring out those arms he had looked so hungrily upon at that gathering in Mycenae, with his strutting warriors encircling him.

Now Agamemnon's eyes were measuring the Hellespont, the rich trade beyond it, the booths and wares of the great gathering every year on the Plain of Troy. Fewer merchants came to Mycenae; fewer goods fell into Agamemnon's grasp, so he must go pirating. He must raid and plunder abroad to satisfy his lust and his reputation. And he would use the honor of Helen as his figurehead to cleave the seas to come to Troy.

While the men scattered about the countryside to visit our allies, the women within Troy gathered in their chambers to draw closer to one another. The days were growing shorter and the merchants had departed, leaving the plain empty, waiting for winter to turn it back into a spongy swamp as the Scamander and the Simoïs flooded their banks.

Although I was hesitant at first, I found myself welcome at these gatherings, the other women taking their lead from Andromache. Just as Hector was preeminent among men, so was his wife preeminent among women. She honored our early, hesitant friendship and no woman dared defy her and behave otherwise. Still, I felt that only Andromache felt any true warmth toward me.

"Helen, we must procure a proper loom for you," Andromache said when we women were gathered in the great chamber of her palace. Through the western window the shadow of my own, rising beside it, slanted across the floor. It would rise higher still. Gelanor had succeeded in designing four stories. It would rear above all of Troy and command a higher view of the plain and the Hellespont and the Aegean than any other building. Now I feared what we would soon see from that height.

"I had a small loom at Sparta," I said. I had been a good weaver, but my designs, as well as my imagination, had been limited by the size of my loom.

"You need a large one," Andromache said. "We perfected them here in Troy. We weave stories, tales, and for that we needed special looms."

Stories. Tales. We women could be bards, then, telling our urgent truths in wools of scarlet, violet, black, and white, instead of words.

"How long will it take for a craftsman to build me one?" I asked. I was eager to begin.

"Not long," said Andromache. "They are quite simple, really."

"We weave all winter," Creusa said. "When the cruel winds sweep across Troy, there is little else to do."

"We find ourselves with a world before us," said Andromache. "We lose ourselves in it, in the scenes we create with our wool, and when we look up, it is spring again."

"Spring!" Laodice sighed. "Already I long for it." She turned to me. "Winter can seem so long."

What would this spring bring them? Not the glorious springing hyacinths and violets they cherished, but Agamemnon and his ugly ships.

"Yes," I said. "Yes, it can." But might it, this year, last forever!

As the other women prepared to depart, Andromache motioned me to stay. In spite of the braziers, it grew cold in the chamber once they had left.

"I know we worry about what is coming," she said, drawing her mantle closer around her shoulders.

"Yes," I said. I dared not say more.

"And being cut off from my family, far to the south, I worry for them, too. My mother—"

I longed to tell her. I wanted to speak to her as a friend and not to guard my words. Did I dare?

"Andromache—I must tell you—my Mother! Oh, Andromache, she has killed herself!"

Did she step back, or was that only my fancy? Her face clouded. "Helen," was all she said, and embraced me. "How can you bear this sorrow?"

"I cannot," I said. "I have not borne it, only writhed within it."

"Who told you this?"

"I heard it . . . at the fair."

"And kept it inside yourself all this time?"

"Paris heard, too. She killed herself because of us. So we cannot comfort one another."

Tears spilled down her cheeks. "Oh, Helen."

I reached over and brushed away the tears. "Still we go on. We must." I felt I must end this talk; it stabbed me like a dagger. "Perhaps it is only in new life that we can find joy. And as to that . . . ?"

She shook her head. "Nothing. And you?"

I smiled. "As you."

"Shall we go to Mount Ida?" she asked.

"I do not understand."

"There's a festival of fertility there in the autumn. It is ancient and untamed, and only women may come. Male intruders are torn limb from limb. But for the desperate . . ." She smiled. "The desperate are brave. Come with me, Helen! There is no one else who has my needs, or would understand."

It was impossible to go to the flanks of Mount Ida in secret; it took the better part of a day to trundle there in a cart, swaying to and fro. Paris and Hector insisted on driving us there. They were worried about our safety, but Andromache told Hector we need have no fear, since we came in the true spirit of the festival.

We had our torches—great resin-soaked pine branches—and wore thick hooded cloaks; our sandals were the sturdiest to be fashioned.

"To tramp about the mountain in the darkness . . ." Hector frowned. "And in the company of strangers. I like it not."

"You'll like a son well enough," said Andromache. "What is a night on a mountain to obtain him? A small price."

"Where are these people you should join?" Paris craned his neck, searching the looming woods.

"Around this bend, where the hot springs gush," said Andromache. "That is what I have been told."

"Ida is covered with hot springs," said Hector. "Hot springs, cold springs. That is why they call it 'many-fountained Ida.' "

"It is the spring that faces toward Troy. The first one we shall come to."

The late afternoon sun was sending fingers through the stand of pines ahead, stabbing between the trunks. A chill breeze sprang up; we had passed the point when days and nights were equal, and now the time when Persephone would descend to the darkness drew near. I shivered and Paris drew his arm tighter around me.

"You need not do this," he whispered close to my ear. "If we have no sons or daughters, it is perhaps our lot."

I shook my head. "I know that. I shall accept the will of the gods. But I must ask them first."

"Here." Hector reined in the horses. A group of women were gathered around a stream just ahead of us. Every one of them carried a pine torch or a wand wreathed in ivy, and wore a cloak of animal skins.

We disembarked from the cart—after reassuring our men once more that all would be well—and made our way over to the group of women. I heard the cart turning to head back to Troy, but I did not look to see. Instead I kept my eyes on what lay ahead.

Light was fading rapidly. It was hard to make out the faces; they blurred before my eyes. Young, old, middling—there seemed to be all sorts. Was there a leader? Yes, an older woman with a shock of white hair that spilled out from under her hood, at odds with her obsidian-black eyes. Or was she old? Her skin was unlined.

"We'll wait only a bit more," she said. "Then we must climb the mountain. We must be halfway up before dark." She lifted her unlit torch aloft. "The path becomes rocky and steep, and we must make our way across it by torchlight. The torches will last only half the night. So let us not waste them on the first part of the climb."

"And when we come to the place . . . ?" a young woman—her voice betrayed her youth—asked timidly.

"You shall know it. And you must never speak of it afterward. What you see here must remain here. When you lie on your funeral pyre, the things you saw must be burned along with your body." She flung back her hood and revealed her strong-featured, blunt face. "Do you understand, my daughters?"

"Yes, Mother," they all answered.

Mother who? She must be the keeper of the mysteries, but no one spoke her name.

"Come," she said, and turned to enter the woods.

She marched straight through the pines. We followed; as soon as we were amongst the tall trees, the light grew dim. Overhead the branches wove themselves loosely across the sky. We were silent as we walked swiftly behind the Mother, trying to get as far up the mountain as possible before lighting our torches.

I glanced over at Andromache, admiring her fine strong profile. She and Hector were well matched. If only they could have a child, what a marvel that child could be! If only this . . . this ceremony—whatever it was—could bestow a child on them, and on Paris and me. Just then she looked at me and smiled in complicity.

The climb was hard. Soon I was breathing fast and sweat covered my face and neck. I threw off the hood to let the cooling air rush around me; it was dim enough now to conceal my face. My feet began to slip on the loose stones and pebbles on the path. Once I stumbled and Andromache caught my arm.

We emerged out onto a flat plateau. The plain, now far beneath us, swam in an indistinct blue haze. The sun had set, sending up a few last feeble rays from beneath the horizon.

"Let us light our torches," said the Mother. She knelt down and laid a clump of dried moss on a rock, then twirled a stick against a piece of wood to create first smoke, then a flame. She dipped the end of her own torch into it, then, when it had caught, motioned to one woman to come up and light hers. She touched her torch to the lit one.

"Now light the others, light your sisters'," the Mother said.

The woman began to move amongst us, touching her torch to ours until all were alight, all flamed, and the air around us grew bright even as the light faded in the west.

"When we reach the summit, embrace what is there," she said. "I can tell you no more, except to say that she who does not fling herself into the riches of our rite will reap no benefit. Hold nothing back."

The flaring torches, their new-lit tips sputtering and jumping, made the air around us alive with capricious spirits. Overhead the pines swayed and groaned, bending like dancers.

"Higher, higher," the Mother exhorted us. "Do not linger here." We streamed after her, a snake of bobbing lights.

The path grew much steeper and narrower. We had to scramble up, holding our torches in one hand and using the other to grasp roots and rocks as we skirted ravines falling away to one side. It grew blacker and blacker. The moon was dark now and hid her face. The stars shone more brightly, but starlight cannot keep one from stumbling.

Around a great sheer face of rock we came out upon a narrow path that wound to a summit where a tumble of stones, twisted pines clinging amongst them, crowned the mountain. The wind was whistling past us, whipping at our cloaks.

"Play, my daughters, my sisters," the Mother said. Several women pulled cymbals, flutes, and small drums from under their fawn-skin cloaks, and began to play. It was soft at first, barely rising above the wind and the cries of the night birds that were circling the summit.

It was music I had never heard before. The sweet low flute was pierced by the strident bronze cymbals, and the throbbing of the goatskin drums created a tide of sound that ebbed and rose, ebbed and rose.

Some of the women planted their torches in the ground, making a wide circle, and began to move, swaying and bending, clapping and humming. The wind carried their hair streaming out behind them, and they stepped faster as the music grew louder and more insistent. Now the drums were strongest and drowned everything out, now the flute screamed above the drums, and now both were shocked into retreat by the cymbals.

"Come!" Andromache took my hand and we joined the circle of dancers. We were almost the last to do so, and already the pace was quick. Around and around we traced the path that circled the heap of rock at the summit. Someone planted a torch on the very tip of the pile.

"Do not look at your feet but at this torch," she cried. "Keep your eyes upon it!"

I lifted my eyes and focused them on the wavering flame. I could sense the women before me and behind me, but now I was held on the tether of the flame upon the summit, it was my master.

The flute speeded up its piping, and we moved faster; now we needed to trip and jump. Suddenly one of the women broke from the group and started turning, her cloak flying out behind her. Faster and faster she whirled, letting her arms propel her, whirling her. Others broke away and started turning, flinging their arms out and their heads back. The circle of dance broke into swirling leaves. The women began to utter shrill cries of jubilation and excitement, competing with the music.

"Turn, turn, turn!" cried the Mother. "Close your eyes now, embrace the god!"

What god? Who was this who they worshipped in dance and fire?

Suddenly grapes were arcing through the air, landing all around us. We stepped on them and the ground grew slippery, the scent of sweet juice enveloping our senses.

"Drink his gift!" A big pouch, a drinking skin, was flung onto a rock. "Drink the gift of wine, wine that brings gladness and joy and release!"

We rushed to the wineskin and gulped the wine in draughts, wanting to get our fill before yielding our place to another. Wine dribbled down our faces and onto our gowns, but the Mother assured us, "Every drop is a blessing. Never wash it away, and now you may ask the god for his other blessing—fertility. He is the god of wet things that grow."

Still I did not know what god she meant, and she never named him. I saw Andromache looking down at the stains on her gown, touching them.

The women spun away from the wineskin, their dancing wilder. I twirled with them, feeling my head grow dizzy and my thoughts loosen. Loosen . . . float away . . . I drifted in a sea of movement, cut free from everything else.

Time ceased. I know not how long I turned and turned, only that I was in a trance. I barely heard the shrieks when a cage with a pig was opened. I was knocked down by a hoard of women running after it, shouting and screaming. They were like a pack of dogs, their faces twisted and their teeth bared.

The music had stopped, and now the guttural cries of the women resounded in the air. I heard them rise to a shrieking scream and then stop. They had disappeared down a pathway on the other side of the mountain.

Andromache and I and several others who had been left behind by the pack followed them. What we saw when we reached the little glen was unbelievable, shocking: a circle of women covered with blood, blood up to their elbows, tearing at the carcass of the pig, ripping it into pieces. And then—one woman grabbed a piece of the raw meat and began eating it, staining her face and neck with blood. Her eyes looked slanted and dark like an animal's.

Andromache and the other women in our group shrank back, not seized by whatever madness had taken these women, and watched in horror as they devoured the pig raw, making hideous swallowing noises, gulping not only its flesh but its blood.

How had they even killed it? By tearing it with their bare hands? This seemed impossible, yet it had happened.

So this was why it must never be spoken of. What else was to come here on the mountaintop? We had to leave before whatever it was took place. Might it even be sacrifice of one of us? I clutched Andromache's hand and said, "We must escape! Even though it is dark, we cannot wait for light, we must find our way down! Even if we get lost, I would rather be amongst true animals than these human beasts!"

"Oh, Helen, forgive me for bringing us here, I did not know—!"

Together we turned and stole away, hoping no one would see us. I tried to remember the paths we had taken on the ascent, but I knew we would be lost sooner or later. Better later, was all I could hope.

The wind howled and tore at us as we slipped and slid down the steep path, being careful to lean away from the yawning ravines on one side. As we got lower, the trees suddenly grew thick again around us, and the dangerous ravines disappeared, but now the path was not so clear and the forest enveloped us. We could hear the cry of wild dogs and a thousand other sounds of night creatures surrounding us. Paris's teasing about lions no longer seemed a joke.

Andromache clutched at my arm as we threaded our way through the dark forest, stumbling over tree roots and loose stones, slipping on old leaves and needles underfoot.

"Ida is enormous," I whispered, marveling. This one mountain seemed as vast as the entire range of the Taygetus at home.

At home . . . at home . . . I was frantic to return safely to Troy . . . was that home now? My sister Clytemnestra was now a shadowy figure, wife of my enemy, Agamemnon, whereas Andromache was my companion, a fellow outsider who had been brought to Troy. How complicated my allegiances and loyalties had grown, like a monstrous and many-tendriled plant.

We grew weary, stumbling along. Sometimes we sat to rest, but not for long. The nearby howls of animals and the batting of wings had us back on our feet quickly. But at last the darkness lessened on the eastern side of the forest, and we knew we were delivered from the hand of night.

The sunrise was glorious. The light burst on us and filled the sky. At once everything around us was revealed. We were upon the lower flanks of the mountain, where it dwindled to gentle humps and dips. Ahead of us we could see open meadows, deep green.

"Thanks be to . . . whatever gods watch over you," Andromache said. "For me, it is Hestia."

"For me . . ." I could not say *Aphrodite,* it was too embarrassing. "It is Persephone."

"The goddess of death?" Andromache took my hand. "I would not have thought it. She has few devotees, though, so she must appreciate you."

"She is much more than the queen of Hades," I said. "She loves life, as we do. That is why it was so difficult for her to leave it." It took a dark night of wandering for me to appreciate even more her joy when she came back to the light and air of the upper earth.

Paris and Hector were waiting for us on the far side of the meadow. They had waited all night. Their faces revealed their relief upon seeing us, and they pulled us up into the chariot to make for Troy.

"What happened there?" asked Hector.

"We cannot divulge it," Andromache said. "But perhaps it will reward us with what we most desire." She looked down at her wine-stained gown. "It is a pledge," she said.

❖ XXXVIII ❖

Our house was rising. It thrust itself up through the fog that was Troy in winter as if it were seeking the vanished sun, boldly claiming it for its own.

We were meeting on a cold day with the artists who would make our walls sing with beauty. They would design and paint scenes of our choosing—we would select the story to be told, they would tell it.

"I don't want the usual," said Paris. "Warriors prancing about, or hunters tripping after their prey. Or more labors of Heracles." He had wrapped himself in a thick robe to ward off the chill, but still he shivered. The wind was moaning outside, seeking entrance into our chamber.

The painter and his apprentice looked eager to comply. When Paris offered no suggestions, the painter said, "May we have your preferences, then?"

"You are the artist!" said Paris. "It is up to you to think of what I might want."

"But, my prince, once it is painted on the walls it cannot be erased. We would never proceed without knowing what it is you wish to see. We could make sketches first on pottery." The artist shrugged. "But we would still like some guidance."

"Paris," I said. "Could we possibly have the springs and glens of Mount Ida? They were so magnificent. And since this is all within our own will and whim, may we show the wildflowers? I know they bloom only for a short time, but on our walls they could bloom forever. And when we are wrapped in wool and surrounded by fog, we could look upon them and all but smell the perfume."

He nodded. "That would be an unusual decoration. No people at all. But, my love, let it be as you wish."

We had been choosing plasterers and tilers and gilders and timberers and hearth-men for what seemed forever. Paris wanted rafters gleaming in gold, wanted marble thresholds and cedar-lined chambers. Each decision seemed to occupy a full day.

But the days were increasingly dark and dreary, and we were glad of a diversion. Let us immerse ourselves in the color of rafter paint and thickness of the wood for the inner doors. Let us shut out the murmurs from the streets of Troy and the rumors that curled, smokelike, under our thresholds: rumors that spoke of the Greeks and their fleet, a fleet gathering at Aulis—in winter, a thing unheard-of.

We were shut in upon ourselves. Mist swirled through the streets, making it impossible to see more than a few feet ahead of us as we measured our steps to the temple at the summit or made our way down to the gates.

Evadne came to me before a late winter dawn had truly passed into daylight, so shaken she knelt by my side. She had risen from a dream that began at dusk and held her captive all night. "I must speak of it," she said. "I must, to purge myself of the knowledge. I cannot carry it within myself in secret."

"Speak, then. But first, take some nourishment." She looked ravaged.

"No," she said. "I am too poisoned within."

Then she told it, in hesitant whispers—what she had seen on the shores of Greece, at a place called Aulis. That was where Agamemnon had gathered his gigantic fleet, ready to sail for Troy.

"And it was huge, my lady," she said. "The ships darkened the water, with their black-tarred hulls, spreading across the whole bay."

I shuddered. He had succeeded, then, in raising his full army. The other kings did not deny him, like the wily king of Cyprus.

The winds blew steadily from the east, trapping them in the bay day after day, until their supplies dwindled and they began to quarrel. Then Calchas, the Trojan priest who had been sent to Delphi by Priam, appeared in her dream, advising Agamemnon what to do.

"He had become one of them," she said. "He stood at Agamemnon's right hand. But he did such evil that Priam can be thankful he no longer serves in Troy. He advised him that Artemis was holding them prisoners by the contrary wind, and that she demanded a sacrifice from him. He must kill his oldest daughter, Iphigenia, on an altar."

I felt my heart jump. "A human sacrifice? But we do not—"

"That is what Agamemnon said. He refused."

Yes. Of course he would.

"But it was no use. The winds kept blowing, and the men began crying for Agamemnon to do it, threatening to mutiny if he did not. And so he . . . sent for Iphigenia, pretending—oh, heaping shame upon shame—that she was to marry Achilles. That she should bring a wedding gown. She did."

"But Achilles . . ." My mouth was so dry I could hardly speak. How was he there?

"He was not a party to it. He knew nothing of it. Iphigenia asked to see him, of course, and then she was told the truth."

I shut my eyes. What did she do? "Did she beg? Protest? Fight?" I could not begin to imagine what she would have done in this hopeless horror. She had always been a quiet child, but that did not mean she would not struggle.

"She did all of those things. Begging availed her nothing. Protesting and arguing fell on Agamemnon's hardened heart. Her fight was quickly subdued. So, when all had failed, she turned the other way, gave herself willingly. She asked to be allowed to pray privately to her patron gods, and to dress herself in the wedding robes. She looked sorrowfully at her father and told him she was a willing sacrifice for Greek honor."

Greek honor! No, Agamemnon's honor!

"They came for her and escorted her out of the tent and to the altar, where, like a sacrificial animal—"

I shrieked, unable to hear more.

She sat silently. Finally she said, "Artemis kept the bargain. The fleet has sailed. It is on its way."

For a long time we sat unmoving. The chamber lightened and the feeble rays of the winter sun finally entered through the window.

"I must go," she said, rising.

"Are you delivered of the evil vision now?" I asked. "Are you Evadne again, free of it?"

"Yes, but it is a dreadful burden to be delivered of. Now it will live in others, in everyone in Troy."

After she left, I sat, stunned, by myself. I could not even tell Paris. Not yet. I could not bear to tell him what my family had done to itself. The curse on our houses was coming true. Mother dead—Iphigenia murdered by her father. I needed to mourn Iphigenia in quiet and in solitude. And to reach out, somehow, to my bereaved sister, who had endured the unendurable, with my mind and spirit, and hope she could feel it.

Within a few days, all of Troy knew the Greek fleet was on the sea. It was impossible that the whole world did not know; the news traveled faster than the ships themselves.

Calchas was another matter. He had sent a private message to Priam about his new allegiance. Priam called a conference about him, lamenting his defection.

"He sent us a message," said Helenus. "He did not desert, he merely—"

"Do not dress it in other words," cried Priam. "We sent him out as a loyal Trojan, to ascertain what our future held. Instead, he has bolted and allied himself with the Greeks."

Cassandra knelt. "Perhaps, Father, he received some information from the seer at Delphi that sent him on this course."

"Then why should he not have reported it to us first?" cried Priam.

"I think that is obvious," said Hector, stepping forward. "He was told that he must go to the Greeks. Why he was told that, we cannot know."

"That they would be victorious?" Deiphobus raised his voice. "I cannot imagine what else it could have been. What else would send him scuttling to the other side?" Now he, too, edged close to Priam in a possessive way.

"Cowardice? Or even loyalty? Suppose the oracle foretold the downfall of the Greeks. Might he have received instructions to go cast himself upon them, give them false readings?" Helenus said. "Perhaps he is amongst them to mislead them." His voice was, as always, low and faintly insidious.

"Wishful thinking, Helenus. Should it be true, we will rejoice, but for now we must look on it more glumly, seeing only the worst. To look for the best and refuse to consider the worst is a crime against ourselves," said Antenor. He made it sound like a crime against good manners as well.

"What of his brother, Pandarus? Might he have received some word?" Paris asked.

Priam twisted up his face. He was reluctant to consider anything Paris might suggest. "Yes, send for him," he finally said, nodding to a messenger.

"Perhaps we have worried overmuch about omens," said Hector. "I, for one, feel that to keep alert and strong is the best omen for success. Or victory. Calchas would still be here if we had not gone a-wailing after oracles and omens. Then we would have no need to worry about what he told the Greeks."

"Already you, and others, speak of victory," noted Antenor. "To speak of victory is to invoke the specter of defeat, its twin."

"Oracles—defeat—you sound like frightened children," snorted Hector.

A stir. Pandarus was brought in, swatting aside the insistent arm of his accompanying servant. "Begone!" He flicked him away. Then he turned to Priam and smiled broadly. "Most esteemed king," he said. "For what honor have you called me away from my melancholy supper?"

"You have never had a melancholy moment in your life," said Hector.

"I do try to avoid them," he admitted. "But into every life . . ." He sighed and shrugged. "In what way might my simple thoughts be of benefit to this august company?" He ran his hand over his balding head.

"Just this. Have you knowledge of your brother, Calchas? Have you any word from him?"

Pandarus looked genuinely surprised. "No, my lord. Not since he left our shores some time ago. Why—have you?"

"Yes!" said Priam. "He has gone over to the Greeks, and has given them favorable prophecies regarding the outcome of an attack on us."

"I—I—cannot imagine that!" he finally muttered. His jaunty manner had vanished. "I cannot question his loyalty."

"Begin to question it now!" bellowed Priam. "When actions do not square with words, trust the actions. Choose what you see people do, not what you imagine they would like to do. He is sailing with the Greeks. They are preparing to descend on Troy even as these words leave my lips."

"But, good sir, it is too early to sail." He looked around as if to garner nods and agreements.

"Not for them, apparently," said Hector. "They will be here soon enough, buoyed up by whatever your brother has told them."

"But . . . what can I do?" he said. "I will not see him. I can only say that if he has joined them, it was because he was forced to. He never would have done so by his own will. He is loyal, sir. He is loyal!"

"Unless we capture him, we shall never know," said Deiphobus with a nasty slant to his mouth.

"And what of that boy he took with him, that he insisted on taking? Has anyone seen him?" Deiphobus asked.

"No, no, I swear!" Pandarus held up his hands. "If I do, I shall bring him to you immediately!"

"There was something odd about the request," mused Priam. "I was suspicious even then. It served no purpose."

"I agree, it served no purpose. How could it?" Pandarus cried. "He is only a lad." He swallowed. "*Was* a lad. But let us consider the most obvious explanation. Youth wants adventure, wants to sail to lands far away. The old are content to stay where they are and savor what is at hand, but youth wants to rove. I think his desire was innocent, and my brother merely sought to let him indulge it."

Priam grunted. "Perhaps." He cleared his throat. "We need to post lookouts, not only in our own vicinity but up and down the coast."

Yes. Paris and I had not landed at Troy but farther south. They could land anywhere. It was a very long coastline.

"And we must alert our allies, order them to report any landings to us. For now, we can come and go as we wish. Let us bring in large stores of food and goods. Enough to last a year or more. No siege can last longer than that. When the winter winds blow again, the Greeks will go home."

"You speak of a siege?" asked Hector. "Surely we must meet them in battle?"

"Perhaps," said Priam. "But I am thinking of all the Trojans, not just of you warriors. The Greek contingent will have only men, only fighters, whereas we have a city full of artisans, laborers, women, children, livestock, all that makes Troy, Troy. We fight for it all: the smallest item that is dear to us, the sword of our grandfather, the necklace of our great-grandmother, the cradle of our firstborn. They left all that safe behind them; they are unencumbered by goods and by memories, whereas we must defend all—life, property, everything we love."

"You speak again of fighting," said Antenor. "Perhaps it will not come to that. Surely they will send an embassy and we can discuss terms."

"If you think for a moment of asking me to return Helen, the answer is again no!" Paris cried, leaping into the middle of the floor. "She is my heart, my mind, my own hand. I cannot give her up. If they kill me, then I will be gone with the shades into Hades, and care not. But I cannot live without her!"

"But we can," said Hector. "Must we all suffer because she is your heart, your mind, your own hand? Surely that is unfair."

Hector had dared to say what everyone surely must be thinking.

Paris did not immediately respond. Instead he made his way out into the center of the chamber, slowly and deliberately. A silence flapped down like one of Athena's owls. It lighted on my own shoulder and I could no more have spoken than if my own tongue were cut out. I could only look on, and listen.

Paris smiled. That smile was so glorious, and he never seemed to begrudge it, even to those hostile to him. "You speak wisely, Hector. I am fortunate to have a brother both honest and brave." He turned in a circle, facing each of his interrogators, looking each in the eye. Finally he spoke.

"Dear friends and family," he said. "I bow my head before your very just observations. It is true, the root of your possible trials seems to lie with me. Had I not brought Helen of Sparta here to Troy, you would not face the threat of this army. But sometimes we must bow our necks to the will of the gods, no matter how perverse or mysterious they may seem. I was selected for the task that has set all this in motion, and there was no way I could evade it. I have not spoken of it before—there was no need to. It seemed as a dream. But Zeus forced me to settle a dispute between his daughters and his wife. Not that I was worthy! Perhaps he chose me for no particular reason at all. I tried to demur, but it was no use. Have *you* ever tried to balk the gods? I tell you, it cannot be done!"

The company just continued staring at him. They shot looks at one another, as if to say, *Is he mad?*

Paris cleared his throat. "The goddesses—Zeus's wife, his daughter Athena, and Aphrodite, all came to me at Mount Ida and forced me to choose between them."

Deiphobus scowled. "In what way? And to what end?" he scoffed.

"I was to choose the fairest," Paris said.

"Ah, that's no contest," said Antenor. "Neither Hera nor Athena is noted for her special beauty, although of course all gods are beautiful."

"Ah, you make my mistake," said Paris. "I had always assumed that each god or person was jealous of his excellencies and dismissive of his weaker areas. After all, who can be perfect in all things?"

"Just so," said Priam. "Son, why have you not told us of this?"

"It seemed a private matter," said Paris. "Alas, now I see that when dealing with the gods, there is no private matter. Nor do they have weaknesses—or acknowledge them. The militant Athena, preeminent in ordered warfare, longed to be declared most beautiful as well. And so the goddesses sought to bribe me. Me, a mortal, whom they could wipe out with a swipe of their hand. And I chose Aphrodite, and now Hera and Athena seem to have a mighty grudge and have taken all of Troy as liable for the judgment of poor Paris."

"Oh!" Priam reeled to a chair. "Oh, my son, what a dreadful burden to fall upon you. But still I do not see where this has led to our present difficulties."

"The goddesses Athena and Hera are hostile," Paris said. "They make Troy me, and me Troy. They wish to punish me."

"But what of Aphrodite?" Antenor asked.

"Alas, she is not much help in battle," said Paris.

A great murmuring broke out between them. No one seemed to notice that he had not explained exactly how Aphrodite had brought about our present plight. No one asked him what the goddesses had bribed him with.

"The goddesses have put us in this position," said Paris. "I was but their tool."

"Then we must undo their doing," said Aesacus, who had kept quiet until now. I remembered him from the earlier council gathering in which sending Calchas was discussed—a little weasel of a man with stubble and bright eyes. "I have found that, unlike people, gods are easily distracted and bought off. A little flattery and sacrifice will make them forget quickly." He managed to look both sarcastic and weary at the same time.

"In this case there is no way to appease them," said Paris. "The judgment is over."

"No judgment is final, unless the parties are dead," said Hector. "You must return to the site and propitiate them."

"But they won't be there any longer."

"They can travel anywhere they like, and they will, as soon as they hear about the retrial."

"But I would not decide differently!"

"Pretend to have reconsidered. Say something that will flatter them. They like that." Aesacus again.

❖ XXXIX ❖

As soon as we were safe in the deepest alcove of our chamber, I pulled Paris toward me and whispered—no, even softer than a whisper, I breathed—my request directly into his ear: "You must tell me of that day on Mount Ida." I sought to keep any human or divine ears from overhearing.

He turned his face toward mine and in the golden light from the oil lamps I could read, rather than hear, his reply. "When I was still a herdsman, I was dozing near a pool in the twilight. The cattle had wandered away, but it was too early yet to fetch them back. I was lying there, just as—" He broke away and flung himself down on the bed. "Just like this." He stretched his arms out above his head and wallowed luxuriantly. "I was dreaming—drowsy warm dreams, and the little violets under my head were like a fragrant bolster—and then . . ." I settled beside him on the bed; his voice had risen too loud. "I thought it was a vision, but three female figures stood around me, enveloped in a green shade. I could see through them, but it did not seem odd. I sat up." He rose, enacting it. "And I whispered, 'What do you want of me?' and they bade me rise and to take off my sandals. I did. Then they beckoned me to follow them. I walked over the cool grass, which felt like polished marble, and they drew me toward the pool, secluded and overhung with branches."

He sat up on his knees. "It was then I became frightened. Kneeling on the ground, feeling the pebbles under my shins, suddenly coming wide awake, I knew this was no dream. And as I looked at the . . . figures . . . I knew them to be no mortals, but gods. I started to shake all over."

Sweat sprang out on his forehead. I thought of my mother and what had happened to her. It is not easy, coming suddenly upon a god. "Did you . . . did you even think of running away?"

"No, I knew better. I thought they would strike me dead. I knew they would. Their eyes . . . there was something so deadly about their eyes, for all their smiles and compliments."

"You saw their faces?" I had always thought that to gaze directly on a god was sure death.

"Better than that—I saw them naked!" He started to laugh, nervous gusts of laughter in the remembering. "They forced me to look at them." He was sputtering now. "Yes, they disrobed before me and sought my . . . my evaluation of their comparative beauty!"

"But . . . why?" Perhaps it all *had* been a dream.

"I don't know why, I only know they said I must choose between them for the fairest."

"You said they offered you bribes," I coaxed.

"Yes."

I waited for him to tell me what they were. But he only hung his head. I asked him directly.

"I don't—I don't remember," he said miserably.

"How could you not remember?"

"I told you, it was like a dream. Do you remember dreams? Some of them, perhaps, but little details become blurred, melt into something else. The harder you try to catch hold of them, the more they recede."

"Are you certain you could find that place again?"

"I think so. I know the mountain very well."

"Stand there again, and it will come back to you. That is the difference between dreams and real places. You cannot reenter a dream, but you can go back to a place."

"But why should we go back there? I don't want to." I half expected him to say, like a trembling child, *I won't!*

"You must remember what it was you did to offend Hera and Athena, if ever we have any chance of placating them. It goes back to what they offered you, and how you responded. Aesacus is right."

"It's too late."

"No, no. If they have sent an army against us, should we not try to find out why, and repair it?"

"I don't want to go back there. What if they . . . take it all back?"

"Take what back?"

"The thing they gave me. That *she* gave me."

"I thought you didn't remember what that was."

"I don't. I don't!"

I took his face in my hands, tried to wipe away the frantic fear on it. "Paris, Paris. We must go back, for the sake of Troy. And while we are there, you must show me the herdsman's hut where you grew up. I want to meet your foster parents. I want to see where you spent your childhood. We can do it all on the same day, the pleasant with the frightening. Will you show me?"

"Yes," he mumbled.

"Do you promise?"

"Yes." He looked as if he were about to be whipped.

Ida, again. In the bright, cold sunlight it felt nothing like itself during that murky wild night when last I was on the mountain. We were not going toward that peak where the women's rites had been carried out, but on to another spur of Ida. The mountain had so many little peaks and flanks and spurs that it was like a mother lion suckling many cubs.

The moment we set foot on Ida, Paris changed.

"Here's where I used to run—over there is where I built a treehouse—and there's where I made a fort of boulders—and look, in that dale is where Agelaus and Deione raised me. I see no smoke rising—they aren't home. We can return at sunset, see if they are back. And I'll show you the place where they found me. Where I was lying on a wolf skin."

"Please do not."

"Oh, but it's a sacred place, at least to me. Where I passed from one life to another."

"We came here so that you might show me that other place where you passed into another life—and brought danger to Troy."

"Oh, yes . . ." The lightness left his voice. "That place."

"You said you knew exactly where it was. Let us go there and get it over with."

He turned abruptly and headed in the opposite direction. Clearly he had wished to go there last, if at all. We traversed gentle dips and valleys, going from shaded stands of pine to vine-choked hollows filled with thick shrubs then out again, climbing higher. The path up the mountain twisted and turned, loose gravel falling on either side.

Suddenly we reached an open space, a meadow sloping gently downhill. Tall dark cypresses guarded its edges, and I could see a sparkling stream running through it on its way through the thicket on one side.

"Here. It was here." Paris stopped and extended one arm. "I was sleeping here, beneath this tree. This very one." He sought out an old oak whose thick trunk cast a wide shadow. "Yes, and here is the stone I pillowed myself on." Gingerly he knelt down beside it, ran his hands over it. "I was lying thus . . ." He stretched himself out. "There were more leaves above me then, but otherwise it is the same." He closed his eyes to imitate the sleeping. "And then I heard them—I saw them . . ."

There was nothing there but the sound of the wind passing through the branches.

"I think there was someone else with them—yes, a male—Hermes. How could I have forgotten? It was he who told me I must decide between the goddesses. He said he could not help me, I must make the decision by myself. He said"—low laugh—"that my looks and my knowledge of love affairs qualified me to judge. Then I stood up, and they led me . . ." He looked around, casting his gaze in all directions. "There! There, into that grove."

"Then let us go there," I said.

The grove surrounded a deep pool, filled by a spring-fed stream falling from rocks above. In summer, when the rains and melting snows were gone, it probably vanished. Like the goddesses themselves. But now it spread itself out in dark wide ripples, its center reflecting the sky, its edges shadowed. A hush hovered over it. I could hear the splash of the water as it entered the pool at one far end.

"They bade me sit on this rock." He sank down on it. "Then they stood before me. They were frightening. First of all, they were larger than humans. The arm of Athena was as big as a ship's mast. I need have no illusions about what that arm could do to me. Hermes explained, as if he were talking to a simpleton, that Zeus had appointed me to choose the fairest of them. He would give them some prize or other, I believe it was a golden apple engraved with the words, 'To the fairest,' once I decided." He shook his head. "Perhaps it *was* a dream. Why would goddesses care about an engraved golden apple? They could make their own. And why would they care what a herdsman said? They hardly consider mortals, any mortals, of any importance. It made no sense. But I did not question it, I was so frightened of my safety. I only wanted to escape with my life." He coughed. "I told Hermes I would divide the apple between them. He said that was impossible, that I must decide. My heart was racing. Well I knew that a person may make conditions before an action, but never afterward. I begged the losers not to be vexed with me, as I am only a simple mortal, and prone to error. Hermes assured me they agreed with my request."

"But clearly they did not!"

"The gods are not to be trusted. We know that. That is why I sought protection—not that it availed me any."

"But you gazed upon them. Tell me about them, what they looked like."

"I hardly noticed," he admitted. "If you saw a gigantic mastiff, its jaws dripping with foam, about to spring, would you notice its coat?"

"And they disrobed?"

"Hermes suggested it. So the first was Hera. She looked well enough, but then her attempts at bribery were pathetic. She sought to dangle riches and territory before me." He paused. "Then came Athena. She had insisted that Aphrodite remove her magic belt, which caused all who saw her to fall in love with her." He laughed. "Aphrodite agreed, if Athena would remove her helmet. She said Athena looked hideous in it. She was right. Athena was . . . almost attractive without it."

"And what did she offer you?"

"Oh, more territory and victories, things I care not about." He shrugged—too quickly. Then he went to the edge of the pool and, kneeling, dipped his hand into it.

"Aphrodite, then," I coaxed him.

He sank back on his haunches. "That lady knows how to please a man." He smiled.

"Yes, she is known for that."

"The first thing she told me was that I was the handsomest man in the region and was wasting myself in cattle-herding. She said I was meant for better things. She promised them to me."

"She promised you a place in Troy? But of course she already knew of your true birth." Oh, how quickly I rushed to supply the answer! Would that I had waited for him to speak first.

"Yes, that is exactly what she promised," he said, smiling. "Just that." He flipped some water over at me, spraying my face. "And it was soon after that that I went to Troy and the truth of my parentage was revealed. I must thank her for that. Because of her, I became a prince of Troy."

"You were already that."

"But it was Aphrodite who revealed it to my mother and father."

"Then it was worth it to choose her. It changed your life in a manner you desired."

"Yes, yes."

"I thought you did not remember what they promised you."

A fleeting look of alarm crossed his face. "Coming here has revived my memories. As I hoped."

"As *I* hoped. Now we must propitiate the losers, so they call off their vengeance on Troy."

"Yes, yes, of course." He dug into his sack and brought out two painted vases celebrating their charms, along with homage acknowledging their beauty with exquisite necklaces of carnelian and amethyst strung with gold beads. He laid them reverently on a flat stone, invoking their presence.

Holding up his hands, he cried, "Great goddesses of Olympus, Hera of Argos and gray-eyed, aegis-bearing daughter of Zeus, sublime Athena, look with favor on these gifts I bring you, and have mercy on Troy." Then he offered more things to fire their hearts: spread out upon the rock were models of ships and walled cities, as if Paris could deliver them! "All these are yours

{ 324 }

to command. You promised to abide by my pitiful decision, but I am only an ignorant mortal. My weak opinion should weigh nothing in the scales of the immortals."

He knelt before the makeshift altar.

There was utter silence. Did they even hear him? They were most likely occupied with other matters, all as frivolous as an engraved apple. I clamped my thoughts shut, lest they read them.

"You threaten Troy, which never did you harm. I am not Troy. I was not even acknowledged by Troy when I was summoned to award the golden apple. Do not blame innocent people for my failings."

More silence.

"Call off the Greeks! Beseech Zeus, call off the havoc of war!"

No sound but the rustle of the thicket and the gurgle of the waterfall.

"Then . . . Aphrodite, save us!" he cried. "Do not let us perish!"

Aphrodite: the goddess who, leading us by invisible traces, had brought us together. She was not trustworthy, but now she was all we had. Our petition to the others had been ignored, and Troy must suffer. I gave a cry. Was there nothing we could do? But what could we promise to the losers, Hera and Athena? It was they who had the power to bestow gifts, not us.

I reached out to Paris and took his hand, drawing him up. "Come," I said. "This is as it is." I felt both sad and defiant. "We must stand up to it, bear it, whatever may come. The gods can buckle our knees and crush our shoulders, yet there is a majesty in being destroyed by them—but by their hands alone. Meanwhile, we stand on our feet. This is our last petition to them, to hateful Hera and Athena." I cast my glance across the skies. Sometimes the gods even admired those they destroyed, if they were worthy adversaries. "You made your choice, Paris. Now we must accept the consequences."

"You would do that alongside me?" He sounded incredulous.

"Of course. Without you there is nothing of me." I clasped his hand. It was cold, like a jar left outside in the night.

"Helen." He leaned toward me, his eyes asking a hundred questions.

"I thought never to see you again." A clear, sharp voice rang across the glen. I jerked my head around to see a woman standing on the far side of the pool. She was young, slender, robed. Paris's hand trembled in mine. I felt a slight movement as if he would withdraw it, but he did not; instead, he squeezed it tighter.

"Oenone," he cried.

"Oh, yes. Oenone." She was striding forward, coming toward us. Her steps were brisk, kicking out her closed mantle around her; inside it I could see a rose-colored gown. The closer she got, the clearer I could see her lovely face. Paris stood rooted as if he were a tree. He clutched my hand.

"So this is the one you left me for." She was within a few paces of us before she stopped. "Oh, I have heard of her." She flipped back her hood. Long honey-streaked hair tumbled out. "She's not so superlatively beautiful as they say. So why, Paris?" Her voice was loud and challenging. I wanted to answer it, but it was not my place. Let Paris speak.

"I love her," he finally said.

"Love her, or love the fact that she is daughter of Zeus?" The bold woman circled us. "You carved our names together on the forest trees. You said you would be mine forever. Then suddenly you were gone!" She brought her arm out in a swift gesture. "Gone, and gone to *her*." She thrust her face up into mine. "Tell me, lady, what trick did you use to win him? When he came to your husband's court, why did you throw yourself before him?"

I did not, I started to say. But why should I defend myself? Best to say nothing.

"A married woman," she hissed. "Did you know special things to lure him? Or was it just the melody of the forbidden? I know Paris, he likes the forbidden. That is why he went to Troy that day. It was forbidden. Mark yourself, lady, and now that you are no longer forbidden, but come with a price—watch for him to flit away!"

Why did Paris not speak?

"Begone, Oenone. You are wearisome. It is over between us." Now Paris did speak, but his words were drooping, weak ones.

"So you think. Have you forgotten my gifts of healing?" She pulled herself away, glared at us.

"What of them? I am not in need of them."

"Ah, but you will be. I see ahead, I see it. You will suffer a grievous wound and be brought to me here—*she* has no powers of healing—but in that day I will turn my back on you and send you back to Troy to die."

If she sought by this to win him to her side again, she was ignorant of men. "Such is your love, then," I spoke. "A shallow one, that smarts only with your own pride. This is not love."

"Curses on you!" she spat. "Source of all his doom, and you dare to call me names!"

"I only know that if I truly love someone, I would never withhold vital aid to him, regardless of what he had done. But perhaps that is because I am a mother, and know other dimensions of love."

"A mother who has left her child—abandoned her for her lover! What right have you to speak to me of love?"

Ah, well she knew how to wound me. "Perhaps I understand love even better because of that. I have suffered."

"And I have not?" she glared at Paris. "Speak to me, you coward. Do not let your lover speak for you."

"Oenone, I have told you, it is over between us."

"Because you have gone on to a higher station—prince of Troy, lover of a queen."

"It was my destiny." His voice was faint, reluctant. "I was already a prince of Troy, and not to claim it would have been cowardly. And Helen is my other self, my soul. Meant for me since the beginning."

"Let that other self save you, then, when the time comes!" she cried. She turned, then stopped and looked back at us. "I had prayed to see you just once more. The gods brought you here, whispered in my ear where I could find you. Bitter finding! I leave you to her, and in those final hours, even she will beg me to save you." She flung back her head. "But I won't, my lady. Your pitiful supplications will be balm to me, but they will avail you nothing. Rejoice in your short time together!" In a swirl of her cloak she was gone. The foliage swallowed her up as she slipped away.

"Paris," I said, shaken. "You had not told me of her." Now I remembered Deiphobus's sneering remark about a water nymph Paris had left. "Perhaps it is best. Now I know everything: the hard test the goddesses put before you, the woman you had loved before me. You know Menelaus, I now know Oenone. I have looked upon her face." He looked so distraught I sought to reassure him. "There should be no secrets between us."

Fool that I was, I thought I knew all. I still did not know the final secret of Aphrodite's promise, how she had dangled me as a prize.

At the rumors of the Greek fleet, Troy seemed to swell with pride and excitement. Too long slumbering peacefully, too long prepared with high walls, stout towers, and stores of weaponry, it welcomed the exhilaration of coming action. Awakening from its golden haze, it stirred like a lion eager to hunt. Evidently these desires had been pent up for a generation, and the young hailed Paris and me when we walked among them on the streets, crying out that they would defend their "Greek treasure" to the death. But the way they laughed, with their flashing teeth, it was clear they did not think it was they who would die. They would strike such terror into their enemy that the enemy would flee—not before a fierce battle or two, however. The Trojans did not want to be robbed of a great battle, in which the end was a foregone conclusion. What else could it be? Everyone knew the Greeks quarreled and fought amongst themselves and were a ragtag bunch, who had never mustered a proper army. One Trojan was worth ten Greeks, became their song.

The workshops were humming, the artisans and smiths of Troy busier than ever, and trade was brisk. People flocked in to Troy to get goods and trade their own. A market sprang up around the new sphinx in the open courtyard, and it was thronged from dawn to dusk. Then Priam insisted that they leave so the gates could be closed for the night. But every morning the people were there again, and it seemed the numbers grew.

The women of Troy enjoyed the market coming to them, and being able to shop without leaving their city. Husbands forbade them to indulge themselves with trinkets and tidbits, but their lectures went unheeded.

Strangely, it was a happy time in Troy.

In addition, Troy began fortifying itself. Workmen oiled the pivots of the great gates; carpenters hewed new bolts to secure the doors. Stonemasons added a fresh parapet of clay bricks atop the stone walls. The ditch surrounding the lower town was deepened, and a further row of stakes were set bristling in back of the one already there. Priam himself went down and addressed the people living in the lower town, warning that trouble might be coming. He was careful to avoid the word *war*. Or even *siege*.

The steps to the covered well beside Athena's temple were refaced and the well dredged; new buckets were set out and fresh ropes were provided for hauling water. Busiest were the merchants who had the responsibility of laying in food supplies. They fanned out across the region and returned with wagonloads of grain and oil. These were transferred into huge sunken stone storage jars. Just seeing them there, buried in rows up to their necks, their lids sealed with tar, gave Trojans a sense of security, but also added to the holiday mood.

There was no further word on Agamemnon and his fleet.

Exactly how many of them? Who were the commanders? We would not know that until they set foot on our side of the Aegean and we could send spies amongst them. Already Priam was recruiting these spies, largely young men with no family obligations. He called upon Gelanor to help train them, but Gelanor told him he would have to include volunteers of varying ages.

"The point of a spy is to blend in perfectly," he said. "A spy should be the most forgettable person possible—so that later if someone is asked to describe him, he will scratch his head and say, 'I cannot recall.' Handsome men, swaggering men, men with scars and red hair, cannot be spies. But we need older men and even some women."

"Women?" Priam's thick eyebrows rose.

"Yes, women. Does not every army have a flock of women, called by the less-than-flattering name 'camp followers'? What else is a spy but a camp follower? Who better to blend in?"

"You mean . . . prostitutes?" Priam twisted up his mouth.

"He who scorns a prostitute scorns himself," said Gelanor.

Priam drew himself up. "What, sir, do you mean by that?"

"I mean only that those who look too high overlook important things," he said. "Who has better access to generals than prostitutes? Who overhears secrets muttered in the dark? Some of the most loyal defenders of a city have been prostitutes." He coughed discreetly. "There should be a public monument recognizing their contributions."

"All right, find them! Train them! That is, train them in retrieving information."

"And older men, too—you will need them. Pitiful, broken things, lamenting the cruel fate that deprived them of limbs or livelihood. They hang on the edges of armies and are employed for menial tasks. The more bitter they are, the less anyone suspects them." He paused. "Surely you have such at Troy?"

"It has been a great long while since we had a war at Troy," Priam said.

"Men are broken by things other than war," said Gelanor. "We must find them."

"How many do you think we will need?" Priam asked.

"Allowing for desertion, execution, and failure, I would say . . . at least two hundred. Then we might be left with a hundred."

Priam nodded. "You shall have them, sir, you shall have them."

Training spies seemed ominous. Gelanor assured me it was not. He said there were always amateur spies; these were usually caught and killed, so did it not make sense to learn from those mistakes?

"You make it sound as if these people are weapons like bows or swords, always needing improvement," I said.

"They *are* weapons," he said. "Perhaps the most deadly we have. After all, knowledge of the enemy's thinking and position determines the action against it."

Now he had hit upon it. "How can these people from Greece ever be our enemies? We are Greeks. I cannot think of them as enemies."

"Then you should learn to," he said. "Your brother-in-law has assembled an armada of soldiers to invade Troy and retrieve you. Do you wish to go with him?"

"No," I said quietly.

"Then it will not be peaceful. Oh, they will send an embassy, which will be rebuffed. Then the fighting will start. Agamemnon would be gravely disappointed if it did *not* start. So would the Trojans, I sense. So we need to know exactly how many men he has, and what tactics he plans."

"Yes, I understand that."

"It may save lives."

"Trojan lives."

"That should be your only concern."

Oh, but how could it be? I had kinsmen and neighbors amongst the Greeks. Possibly even my own brothers! How could I care only for Trojan lives? "But what of you—you are a Greek, these are your people too," I cried.

"That is my sorrow," he replied. "And the price I pay for not having left Troy immediately, as I wished."

"Can you change loyalties so completely, even if your heart is partly elsewhere?"

"I try not to think of that," he said. "My task is to outsmart Agamemnon and disarm him before he does any harm. So that is why I will select and send out spies, and teach them every trick I know to ferret out Agamemnon's plans." He smiled. "Helen, I know you will not wish to be known in ages hence as the cause of a war."

"Never!" I agreed.

"But again, we both know that down the ages knowledge fades and only a few memories remain, and the memory of the beautiful Helen as a cause of war between Greeks and Trojans may linger. Unless that war is prevented."

Winter came and went. The seas opened. But the horizon remained clear. Down on the plain, the Trojans were training, seemingly thousands of warriors exercising in the thin sunlight, practicing archery and sword-thrusting, charging up barricades and ditches set before them by their commanders. Drivers raced chariots across the expanse, and the horse pens were transformed into stockades to protect their precious wards. Meanwhile, the smithies were turning out swords, shields, and armor by the cartload, and craftsmen were preparing new chariots as quickly as possible, the wainwrights fashioning eight-spoked wheels, the leather workers creating the floors, others fashioning the soft, pliant willow rushes gathered by the riverbanks into guardrails.

Representatives of Trojan allies came to promise aid to Priam. I met many of these ambassadors, and I must confess that aside from differing headgear they all seemed similar, although of course they spoke different tongues. The only truly unusual ones—and the ones I was keen to see—were the Amazons of Asia. They sent a chieftain, along with a contingent of soldiers, to assure Priam of aid should the need arise.

Because I occupied a place in Troy outside of any normal protocol, when I wished to see someone, it was entirely within my prerogative. I hurried off to Priam's megaron as soon as I received word that the Amazon ambassador had arrived.

By the time I entered, she had already presented her credentials to Priam. They were conferring about the number of warriors she would be able to provide in the hour of need. I slipped in and slid along the wall, staring at her.

She was very tall, and outfitted in fighting gear, although not armor as I knew it. She wore a linen corselet and a helmet, but other than that was unprotected. Her long hair was drawn back in a braid. Her arm was like a column of marble—smooth and impenetrable. I saw her hands, fingering her sword—broad with stubby fingers. At my movement—although I had tried to be quiet—she swung around and confronted me, grasping her sword.

"Peace, Elate," said Priam. "This is Helen. There is no need to draw on her."

The Amazon pushed back her helmet a bit to get a clearer look at me. An expression of disdain flitted across her face. "No, I think not!"

I walked over to her. "I am your friend, not your enemy." I smiled. "I must confess everyone is curious about Amazons. Is it true that you have no men in your villages?"

"Oh, we have them for a little while. They are useful for some things. I think, lady, you know what those things are."

I nodded and laughed nervously.

"But beyond that, we do not need them," she said. "We find them a nuisance."

Now I did truly laugh. That amused her.

"Now, come, Helen, have you never felt the same? Would you not like them to vanish after they have fulfilled their purpose? So much simpler."

I found myself unable to answer, I was so overcome with laughter.

"Some of them," I said. Certainly not all.

"No men are worth the bother they cause," she said. "Begging your pardon, Your Majesty." She all but winked at Priam. "Well, I can guarantee a force of some hundred warriors, like these." She motioned to her bodyguards, all of them tall and muscular. "Trained since childhood to fight and shoot," she said. "A hundred Amazons are worth a thousand men."

"Why would you come all this distance to protect Troy?" I asked her. Her homeland was far away.

"We want no Greeks here," she said. "Let them stay on their side of the sea. My lady, although you are indeed lovely to look on, no one is fooled by their wavering cries of needing to retrieve you as a matter of honor. They want a foothold in our region. We want to deny it them."

"Then we welcome your help," said Priam.

Elate shot a look at me. "I don't doubt that your husband wants you back and is a lovelorn creature." She snorted at the thought of it. "But as for the rest of them—they just want the pluckings of this land." Now she smiled. "I hope I do not disillusion you."

"No," I said. "No."

* * *

The white storks returned from their winter journey, and were now wading through the marshes. The sky sang a clean blue song. All the signs of spring that would give us joy were now signs that our land was open to invasion. The passage was easy now, beckoning.

As swiftly as the returning birds flew, rumors flapped alongside them. *There are ships on the horizon. No, those were only waves. They've landed far to the south of us, at Larissa. A great mass is coming from Thrace. My son saw them with his own eyes, when he went to the hot and cold springs on the mountainside, there they were, spread out on the plain below him. They say there are two of them, coming on a special embassy. What two? I don't know, but they both have red-gold hair. Lots of Greeks have that. It could be anyone. Has Priam received any word? No.*

As the days passed, I grew increasingly on edge. Then one day I received a baffling summons to come to the queen's apartments as soon as possible. There was no explanation and no formal greeting, just a command.

I still was not used to no longer being queen, but having to obey one. In Sparta I had thought the queenship sat lightly on me and had not changed me, but now I knew that once a woman is queen, even briefly, she is queen forever, in her own heart. Still, Hecuba rarely summoned me at all, so in one way this was a good sign.

When I reached the outer chambers I saw all her daughters waiting nervously, flitting and milling about. Priam had twelve daughters, but they were not all by Hecuba. I saw no strangers amongst them, so these were all Hecuba's. Laodice came up to me, her great dark eyes shining. "I wanted you to come!" she said. "Won't Mother be surprised?"

"Yes, she will," said Ilona, gliding up to us. "She will be even more surprised when she hears that you pretended to be her and summoned Helen."

So it was not Hecuba after all. I felt a keen disappointment at that. Still, at least the princesses accepted me, particularly Laodice. There are stories of men sitting motionless in the forest attempting to win the trust of a wild animal. I felt like that with the royal family of Troy.

"It is Mother's birthday!" Laodice said. "And we have planned something to please her and surprise her."

"You know it is impossible to surprise Mother," said Creusa. "She knows everything."

"She didn't know about this," said Laodice stubbornly. "Come, we can decorate the chamber now; she's gone to the rooms where the robes are kept, and she always takes a while there."

They festooned the chamber with green garlands and meadow flowers, and Ilona busied herself hunched over a large tray. There was little for me to do and my task was not to appear as awkward as I felt. I watched the youngests, Philomena and Polyxena, playing tag with one another, then settling down to a game played with bone knuckles. They were children one moment and young women the next. They reminded me of Iphigenia and Hermione playing together, and such a heavy weight of sadness fell over me I had to turn away. Iphigenia would play no more, and Hermione . . . what was she doing, this very moment? Oh, if only I could see her—just for an instant.

"You look sad!" Cassandra stood before me accusingly. "What for?" she barked.

"You look angry," I replied. "What for?"

"She's always angry," said Laodice, rushing to my defense. "No one listens to her, that's why."

Andromache joined us, and just then Ilona said, "She's coming! Quiet!"

I heard soft footsteps approaching the chamber; then Hecuba stepped in. She looked about in surprise, but a frown rather than a smile settled on her face. "What is this, my daughters?" she asked

"We are here to honor you on this day of your birth sixty years ago."

"Bah!" she said. "What is that to me?"

"Well, Mother, it is something to us and we wish to honor you." Creusa lifted her chin in the stubbornness she took care to hide from Aeneas.

Hecuba walked erect into the middle of the chamber. She moved like one who was ageless, with neither the springiness of youth nor the shuffle of decline. She looked around at the eight of us and her face softened. "All here, then," she said. "And the wives of my sons. The only two that have managed to marry so far, shame to the others!" Finally she smiled. "I am blessed in my daughters, from my eldest, dear Creusa, to my baby, Philomena."

"We are more blessed in having such a mother," said Ilona.

"And we, newly adopted into Priam's great family, are also blessed." Andromache encircled me with her arm, speaking for me.

"Now that we have finished with the honey, what shall we have for a real meal?" Hecuba said briskly. "What have you for me?"

"A game," said Ilona.

Hecuba waved her hand. "Games. I hate games!"

"Not athletic contests, Mother, but a game of the mind," Laodice said.

"Something you excel at," said Creusa.

"Oh, my, the flattery is so thick I wonder the chamber is not swarming with flies!" said Hecuba.

"We each have put a trinket on this tray," said Ilona. "All except Helen, that is." She smiled a deadly sweet smile at me.

"I had no opportunity to bring anything," I said. "This was as much a surprise to me as to you . . . Mother." I still found it very difficult to call her that.

"Yes, I am to be your mother now," she said. "Since you have lost yours to an unfortunate . . . unfortunate . . ." It was unlike her to stumble for a word.

"Impulsive act," said Cassandra flatly.

"Brave, but misguided," said Andromache quickly.

Everyone knew, now, about my mother, what she had done and why she had done it. That was my torment and my grief, no longer private but everyone's property.

"You may call me daughter," I said. I wanted us to leave speaking of my mother, before I wept in front of them.

"So, what is this?" Hecuba peered down at a tray covered with a soft cloth.

"You are to look at the things underneath while we count to ten, then we cover it up again."

"What's the point in that?"

"To test your memory and make sure you are not like some of Father's councillors, who are so befuddled with age they cannot remember which door they have just come out of."

"I remember everything, my darlings, so don't think you can put anything over on me. It would be just like you to add or subtract something from the tray so that I'd begin to doubt my senses. I warn you, it won't work." She whisked off the cloth herself and said, "Start counting!"

I saw her keen eyes moving over the tray, scrutinizing each object. Before Laodice could get to ten, Hecuba said airily, "Take it away!"

"So soon?" Ilona was incredulous.

"I haven't been queen of Troy for nigh on forty years without being able to remember every item that crosses my path and every word spoken." She shook her head. "Some I would rather have forgotten."

"Very well, then, Mother, recite them. Any one you forget, you may not keep."

She closed her eyes. "I can still see every one, where it was lying on the tray. You will have to explain the significance of them once I name them. There was a clump of little dried berries in a bowl. They looked like raisins but were not. That was in the upper left corner. Next to that was some sort of grass, tied up in a little bundle. Then in the middle there was a folded packet of something very blue. And a little box next to it, made of ebony with spiral lines radiating out from the middle. A very long white feather . . ." I shuddered at the word. But then she went on to say, "fluffy, floating. And an enormous egg, so big it must be from the gods. And then there was a bracelet of bronze, an arrow tip, a pair of earrings, also bronze . . ." She went on to name several other items, quite ordinary ones. When she finished, she opened her eyes. "Well?"

Ilona was staring down at the tray. "You have missed nothing."

"There, there, don't be so disappointed. Now, which ones are my gifts, and which one of you chose them, and what is their significance?"

"I gave you the herb grass, Mother," said little Philomena. "I gathered it myself in the fields, and it will soothe you and give you good dreams if you put it in water and let it steep in the sun and drink it slowly."

"Thank you, my pet. I need more good dreams."

"I gave you the cherries, Mother," Polyxena said.

"Whatever are cherries?"

"A fruit that grows far inland, beyond even the Black Sea. I found them in a booth at the fair. They are sweet, and, the merchant told me, red when they are fresh."

"Beyond the Black Sea! I have heard there is another sea, a bit smaller, farther to the east, but I don't know its name, or even if it has a name," Hecuba said. "Thank you." Ilona handed her the little bowl and she popped a dried cherry into her mouth. "Tasty," she said.

"I gave you the ostrich feather," said Ilona. "They say the pharaoh in Egypt uses fans of ostrich feathers, and I thought the queen of Troy deserved one as well."

"And to go with it, I gave you the ostrich egg." Creusa picked it up and twirled it. "It is indeed beyond the size of any other bird's, even an eagle's or a crane's."

Or a swan's, I thought. *I've seen the eggshell, it's blue, hyacinthine blue . . .*

"I don't suppose it will hatch," Hecuba said. "What is that folded blue item?"

"It's a cloth from even farther east than the cherries," said Laodice. She unfolded it and flicked it through the air, where it floated as lightly as the plumes of the ostrich feather. It looked like a blue mist, transparent and wafting. "I was told it was silk. Oh, Mother, if I might have a wedding gown of this!"

Everyone laughed. Laodice was consumed with wedding plans, even with no fiancé.

Hecuba fingered it in wonder. "Marvelous," she murmured.

"And Mother . . ." Cassandra stepped over to hand her the little ebony box.

"A box. I must have a hundred of them, but this is still very attractive."

"Look inside it." In her eagerness, Cassandra almost grabbed the box away to get the lid open faster.

Hecuba drew out a round bluish stone.

"It has a star inside," said Cassandra. "Look, if you hold it this way . . ." She tilted it. "See, a six-pointed one."

"What stone is it?"

"I don't know its name, but the man told me it was a powerful talisman, so powerful it protects the wearer even after being passed on to someone else. Mother, may it protect you."

Cassandra the seer giving her mother something to protect her—what did Cassandra see?

"Thank you, my dears." She looked around at her six. "It seems you have given the merchants at our last trade fair much business."

Was it my imagination, or did she emphasize *last* in an ominous way?

She turned to Andromache and me. "Now, what have you for me?"

Andromache fluttered, then said, "We were invited at the same time as you, it seems, so we had no time to prepare something. But let us—"

"There is only one gift I want from the two of you," she said. "Children! Give me grandchildren!"

Self-contained as she always was, Andromache did not respond except with a tepid, "It is one I would gladly bestow, if I could."

Before anyone else could cover the hurtful moment, the doors to the hall flew open and Priam strode in, surrounded by a pack of nervous, jumping hounds. "To my queen, the mother of Troy!" he cried, spreading his arms.

"You know you are not to bring those animals in here!" Hecuba said, backing away. "I've told you, I won't tolerate it!" As she spoke, one of the dogs grabbed a corner of her rug and started chewing it. "Out!" she cried.

Priam bent down and nuzzled the dog, pulling it away from the rug. It obeyed him, wagging its tail wildly. "Oh, be kind, my dear. On this special day all creatures wish to pay homage to you. See?"

Just behind him trooped in all their sons, followed by the elders of Troy. Suddenly the chamber was filled to bursting. Hector, resplendent in a white robe, stepped forward to embrace his mother, and the brothers then followed in order: Deiphobus, wearing a leather tunic and his usual sardonic look; Paris, attired in the Eastern-style trousers he usually wore only in private, with a panther skin draped over one shoulder; Helenus, his black seer's robe adorned with silver stars; Troilus, still wearing the tunic of youth; the four who were just names to me—Hipponous, Antiphus, Pammon, and Polites—and the very youngest, Polydorus, his cheeks flushed with the excitement of a party and his part in it. He walked solemnly over to Philomena and took her hand, leading her up to Hecuba.

He bowed, and, eyes tightly squeezed shut to help him remember his words, recited, "We, your youngest son and youngest daughter, salute our mother on this special year of her life."

Hecuba's lip trembled a bit, but she stifled it. "Thank you, my dearests, the last son and daughter I gave Priam. All the living children that I have given him are here today, from the youngest to the oldest. We are most blessed."

"And," said Priam, "we have many old friends who have made the journey through our years together by our side, and they greet you as well." He waved toward the group of councilors standing eagerly by.

"Thymoetes!" One-eyed from an ancient battle with the Mysians, the old man bowed.

"Lampius!" So rotund his wrinkles were plumped out from within, he nodded gravely. Had he bowed, he would have toppled over.

"Clytius!" His toothless gums flashed pink as he greeted the queen.

"Hicetaon!" His face and form bore vestiges of the marvel he had been in youth. But the features had softened and melted, the muscles withered, the hair thinned. Staring out from this ruined vista were dark puzzled eyes—puzzled to find their owner in this state.

"Now let us include Zeus in our commemoration," Priam said. "*My* Zeus."

Indulgently, the family followed him out into the main courtyard, where they gathered every few days as he called upon them to sacrifice before his strange wooden figure of Zeus. He felt that this image was his personal protector, and he was fiercely loyal to it. I found it unsettling, with its three eyes and wild, twining hair, but I knew that each man's god must speak to him alone and none should question why.

As the large family stood around the altar, I could not help comparing it to my own back in Sparta. Even when we were all together, there had been only six of us. Father had no circle of comrades and councilors who had been with him all the years. Our lives in Sparta seemed barren in comparison to Priam's. Barren of people, but also barren of the luxuries that Trojans seemed to feel were necessities. From what I had seen so far, they denied themselves nothing. Perhaps they even thought it unhealthy to do so! I was still not sure if I envied their comfort or disapproved of it.

"We pledge ourselves to you, Zeus, and know you will continue to protect us as you have all along." Priam was addressing the image.

Now that the forbidden guest, the coming trouble, had been mentioned, Hector cried, "Whatever comes, I can defend Troy with only my brothers and the husbands of my sisters!" He looked around. "What say you to that, my brothers? Are you ready to follow me, to defend the walls of our father's city?"

"The walls of the city belong to Apollo," said Helenus. "He built part of them, and he will protect them."

"No, *we'll* protect them!" cried Deiphobus. "All of us! With our swords." He turned to Paris beside him. "And you, of course, you'll rely on your bow. You can hide up in the tower with the city archers."

Paris glared at him. His prowess with the bow kept haunting him; it was considered a lesser form of fighting. "My arm is as good as yours, and I can use the sword whenever I choose. I just have another skill you don't, and it's the bow. Practice on it a bit. Maybe I can help you learn."

"Will I have to put on trousers as well?"

Everyone roared with laughter.

"Try them sometime," said Paris. "They are very practical."

"If you want to look like some Easterner, or a common laborer."

"I was a common laborer, which is also practical, more than anything you've ever done. You claim to be a warrior, but when there's no war, it's a useless occupation!"

"My sons! Stop this squabbling! You sound ten years old!" Hecuba's sharp voice silenced them. "It is good that one of my sons, at least, has spent time with the common people. They are, after all, most of our subjects, and we should know them better."

"But as for this war . . . or conflict . . ." Old Hicetaon stood trembling. "Helen, if I may ask you"—suddenly all eyes turned upon me; I was the only one, after all, who personally knew the men in the ships—"do you think they will be willing to go away if we bribe them . . . I mean, make payments? You know them all."

Should I speak the truth and shatter the happy occasion? There was no other way, not now. "The leader, Agamemnon, already has much gold, cattle, and lands. But he has never fought, nor led, in a big war. It is this he seeks. He has hungered for it ever since I have known him. He has even sacrificed his own child for it. He will not give it up for gold, for that is not the novelty for him." There it was, and I had not shrunk from telling it.

"Cease your fretful fears!" Helenus held up his hands. The sleeves on his glittering robe swayed as he moved. "There are prophecies about Troy, and they must all be met before we are in danger of falling."

"So tell them to us!" barked Deiphobus, sounding almost like one of Priam's dogs. "Don't keep them a secret!"

"Yes, son," said Priam. "Speak."

"To start with, there's the one that as long as the Pallas Athena is here in Troy, we are protected."

"Of course she'll stay here!" cried Troilus. "She isn't about to run away!"

"She hasn't any legs." Philomena giggled. My thought exactly, but I could never have said it out loud.

"Another is that someone must come and attack Troy with the arrows of Heracles."

"Helen—isn't there a Greek with those arrows?" Hector asked.

"Yes, so I've heard," I said. "His name is Philoctetes. But I don't know if he would have joined Agamemnon."

"Then there is something about Thracian horses drinking from the Sca- mander River. If they drink from it, then Troy is protected."

"Thracian horses drink from the Scamander all the time," said Paris. "The imported ones we are rearing on the plain."

"I think these Thracian horses have to be brought by actual Thracians, not tended by Trojans."

"The traders who bring them during the fair—they must water them from the Scamander." Troilus said. "They don't go all the way to the spring- house near the temple of Apollo where the water is purest. I take my horses there, but they don't."

"The Simoïs is closer. I think they go there," said Antenor. I had not seen him join the group, so quietly had he come in. He had a young man with him, whom I guessed to be his son. Oddly, with so elegant a father, his son was very rumpled. Perhaps he was trying to be an anti-Antenor. If we cannot surpass our parents, we become their opposites.

"We have control over that prophecy," said Deiphobus. "If any Thracians land with horses, we'll make them go to the Scamander. What else?"

"The son of Achilles must come."

"The son? Achilles doesn't have a son," I said.

"Not that anyone knows of," said Paris. "There could be one."

"Do bastards count?" asked Thymoetes, narrowing his one good eye.

"I don't know," Helenus admitted. "I will have to find the precise wording of the prophecy."

"Is that all of them?" asked Hector. "I think we are protected against them."

"There's one more," said Priam, "but I shall not speak it aloud here in public. It is enough that I remember it, and I know what must be done to prevent its being fulfilled."

❖ XLI ❖

Troy waited, as the spring advanced and the ships must surely be making their way to our shores. It was the dreadful time of waiting before an action, when all preparations have been made and anything further is but nervous repetition, when the body and mind long for the release of action. Still each bright day brought nothing on the seas and no advance parties from the land side. There were rumors—but then there are always rumors—that some embassy was on its way from the Greeks. How many emissaries, and when they would come, or if the rumor was even true, no one knew.

In the streets of Troy, people were tense with waiting, and they no longer smiled as they passed me. Some seemed suddenly to look away, drawing their mantles closer about them and pressing against their side of the walls.

At the great well where women passed up and down the steps in a graceful ascent and descent, like a dance before a god, they began giving me wide berth.

As I picked my way carefully down the smooth steps one bright morning, I noticed that the women around me disappeared, and I was alone as I descended deeper and the natural light from the opening above grew dim. The steps echoed as I trod them; usually the many footfalls inside made a sort of music.

The torches in their wall-sockets flickered and the water far below reflected the bright red and gold flames. It was still; it always was, as the water flowed in gently from a calm spring.

At last I reached the bottom where I could dip my jug into it—I need not fetch water, but I found it relaxing and I liked being able to say to Paris I provided the drinking water for the ewers in our inmost chamber; I always flavored them with petals of roses. As I did so—as the jug disrupted the calm surface and created new ripples on it—suddenly, even the faint light from above was cut off. I heard a loud clunk as the wooden cover was dropped into place overhead. Suddenly there was no light at all save that from the guttering torches. They leapt and protested as if gasping for air.

Clutching my jug, I climbed slowly up to the top. The well cover was securely in place. I pushed on it and found it impossible to lift. Something must be weighing it down. Or a bolt must be holding it.

Someone had locked me down here.

Why? Who? And how could I escape? I started pounding on the wood, but it muffled my fists. I cried out. Surely my voice must carry through the wood, but no one answered, no one raised the imprisoning lid.

I sank down on one of the steps. The stone was cold and damp. I felt my heart pounding at the thought of being held here below the ground.

But I forced myself to think clearly. This was a public well, the main one near the temple of Athena. People needed to use it. It could not be cut off for long, with no explanation. Therefore whoever had locked me in foresaw only a short time for me to be held here utterly invisible. But what was happening of such importance for only a few hours? And why must I be invisible?

There must be someone I should not see—or who must not see me. The Greeks. Had an embassy come? Why should I be hidden away? What were they afraid of? Surely not that I would decide to return to the Greeks? Everyone, except Paris, would rejoice at that.

But . . . perhaps not. There were those in Troy who wanted this war, and did not want anything to hinder its progression.

Or could it be that someone did not want the Greeks to glimpse me, for fear they would try to rescue me then and there? Or perhaps . . . Oh, this was futile. There were many reasons why someone would want to prevent me from seeing the Greeks, and the Greeks from seeing me.

The damp seeped into my gown and I started to shiver. My feverish response had died away, too, and now the cold sweat soaked me and made my teeth chatter. I hunched myself up on a step and pulled my mantle as tightly as I could about me, but it was a thin one; after all, spring was here.

I seemed to wait there forever. In a muffled way, I heard people come to the well and mutter when they saw it covered. Gradually light faded from around the cracks, and by that I knew night was coming on. Hours, long hours, passed. From my filled jug I had water to drink, but my stomach cried out for food. Far below me the torches guttered and burned out, their fuel consumed. Utter darkness enveloped me.

Only the faint streaks of light coming in through the well cover told me morning had come. By that time I was slumped against the wall and shivering uncontrollably. Why had no one complained about the covered well? But then—my heart sank in remembering it—there were other wells in Troy. Perhaps someone had spread word that this well had poisoned water. In that case they would keep it closed for a long time.

As the day crept on, I suddenly heard, even through the stifling wood, a great hue and cry: screams, yells, and war cries. Then it died away. Desperate, I began pounding on the cover. But no one heard it; perhaps no one was nearby. I kept hitting the cover and crying out so loudly I hurt my own ears. I should have done this straightaway; I was much weaker now and less likely to be heard. But now I was panicked. I knew I could not endure another night here.

Suddenly the cover was wrenched off and the frantic face of Paris peered down at me. "Oh, my dearest!" he cried, then burst into tears. "Who has done this to you?" He leapt down and stood beside me. "Are you all right? Can you climb out? No, never mind, I will carry you." Over my protests, he bent down, picked me up, and carried me out into the daylight. Never had the light of the sun seemed more beautiful to me.

A crowd of curious faces surrounded us. Silently they gave way so Paris could carry me through the circle.

"What happened?" I said. "I was fetching water when suddenly the lid of the well closed above me. Was it an accident?"

"No accident," he said. "Menelaus and Odysseus have been here. Clearly someone did not wish you to see them, or them to see you."

Menelaus! Here! "Truly?"

"Yes," he said. "Menelaus demanded that you appear and tell him, in person, that you were here of your own free will. He said that without hearing it from your own lips, he would never believe that his loyal and loving wife was not held a prisoner. Priam sent for you, but when his men returned alone, Odysseus accused him of making a mockery of the embassy, and said this proved that you were a prisoner whom they dared not produce."

"Why did *you* not speak out?" I expected him to say that he had, but the sight of his face drove Menelaus into a fury.

"I was not there," he said. "Someone drugged my wine and I fell into a stupor that lasted all day. Priam sent for me, and his men could not rouse me. I have no memory of this. But they returned to the council saying I was drunk on my bed."

"Oh, all the gods!" Our enemy was both bold and clever. Now Paris was a dissipated weakling in the eyes of the Greeks.

"Then, at some point, Deiphobus grew so angry at their insult to Priam's honor that he rushed at the Greeks with his sword. Antimachus shouted that the best action would be to kill Menelaus and Odysseus and throw their bodies over the wall—"

"No!" My heart started pounding as I pictured it.

"The rest of the chamber backed Deiphobus. Except Antenor—he cried out, saying that although he was a true witness that you were here of your own choice, nonetheless honor demanded that you be returned peacefully to Menelaus. Then the council attacked *him*. He and the Greeks had to flee to his house for safety. Menelaus and Odysseus left early this morning, under heavy guard."

They would never forgive this insult. And they would believe I was part of it, that I deliberately flaunted them, avoiding them and refusing to speak to them, or else that I was indeed a prisoner—both reasons for war. Menelaus . . . Menelaus would want personal vengeance on me and on Paris.

"Menelaus is a gentle man, but this affront is personal," I said. "He will believe both I and the Trojans spurn him and want war. Nothing could be further from the truth!"

"Our enemy has gained a brilliant victory. I do not know who laid me low. And you have no idea who closed the well?"

"No. I was far below, down at the water level. I never saw the person, not even the hands."

"Still, it should not be too hard to identify him. Or her."

"Why do you say that? We have many enemies." The enormity of that simple statement stung.

"But very few in Troy who hate us enough to wish death on their fellow Trojans. I tell you, it will be clear enough who is behind this."

We needed to find out, but when the moment came I would hate to look at his or her face and *know*.

And Paris might be wrong. It might not be hatred of us that occasioned this, but pure lust for war.

❖ XLII ❖

Gelanor," Paris said, "I respect your eyes and ears. You know of the incident at the well. What are your thoughts?"

We were pacing in our antechamber. The smell of fresh plaster still lingered, so new was our home. Evadne had joined us. I now had two Trojan handmaids, Scarphe and Leuce, but I had dismissed them for the day so they would not hear our conversation, so much had mistrust and apprehension crept into my mind.

Gelanor cast that measuring eye on me. "I am new to Troy. I am only just learning the stories behind the faces and the names."

Paris shook his head. "Nonetheless, sometimes an outsider sees things a native overlooks."

"Well, then . . ."

I expected Gelanor to start naming Trojans one after the other and analyzing the probability that he or she was the culprit, dissecting the motives. Instead he said, "I think spies have penetrated our walls." He paused. "They are disguised as Trojans. There is a possibility that they *are* Trojans, disaffected ones, but it is less likely."

"Spies!" breathed Paris.

"I would assume that they are outsiders, masters of disguise," said Gelanor. "It is true, it is always preferable to corrupt a true Trojan. That way one need not worry about accents, explanations of how the person came to Troy, telltale mistakes that give him away. But it is difficult to find that someone unless you have an opportunity to freely meet the enemy and make your approach. The only open contact many strangers have with Trojans is at the trade market, and that is long over."

"Could someone impersonate a Trojan convincingly—to other Trojans?" I asked. I knew that in my case, the accent was different, many words were different, there were things at every turn that would signal I was not a Trojan.

"Believe me, they can," said Gelanor. "That is their job, like a farmer yoking oxen and a smith forging metals. They can forge a person who does not exist."

"But how can they keep it up?" asked Paris. "Children play such games, but they tire of it by nightfall."

Gelanor smiled. His smile was always both reassuring and somehow oddly distant, as if he were amused by it. "They come to believe it themselves," he said. "They embrace it entirely, and the old self fades away."

"I see a face," said Evadne suddenly. "A young face." Then she sighed. "But that is all I see."

We asked witnesses more about Menelaus and Odysseus. What did they say, how did they look? Men present at the council meeting said that the chamber was filled to overflowing, that people lined the walls. Menelaus was soft-spoken, persuasive. His person was comely, and his appeal rational. He said that Paris had violated the most basic law of hospitality, coming under his roof with the pretense of friendship and stealing his wife away in his absence. He claimed that I had been taken against my will—raped, even.

"No!" I cried out.

"But what else can the Greeks think?" said our informant, a young council member. "It is necessary for their pride for them to believe that." He paused "Menelaus also said that Paris had stolen vast amounts of gold and treasure from Sparta."

"That is not true!" cried Paris. "I took nothing. Helen took only things of her own—things we are nevertheless more than willing to return."

Menelaus—lying! Had Odysseus put him up to this, to make his case stronger?

"I swear before all the gods that is untrue," I said. Even as the words left my mouth, I knew the ears they needed to fall upon were long gone. Our enemy had seen to that. My testimony would have set things straight. Now it would never be heard.

"A great pity, then, that you could not swear it before the council," the man said quietly, "After Menelaus spoke, Odysseus took over. He is the most persuasive speaker ever born. Oh, it is not obvious at first. When first he rises to speak, he seems negligible, his words far from nimble. But then they pile up, and form drifts of words, words that bury you. He spoke of the disgraceful behavior of Paris, of Priam, of all of Troy. He spoke of the longing of Menelaus for his beloved wife. He spoke of the deceit and effrontery in holding her here against her will. He warned us that punishment is our due. Priam insisted in the strongest terms that they were wrong, that it was impossible for Paris to have taken you away against your will, as he had only one ship, not a fleet. Menelaus just sneered. 'Lies from Trojans,' he said. 'What else can we expect from these despicable people?' Odysseus slapped his chest. 'We will meet you in armor on the Plain of Troy,' he said. Then he added that Agamemnon, leader of the Greeks, demanded not only the person of Helen and her treasure, but large amounts of gold to cover the expenses the Greeks had already incurred in their quest to recover her. Otherwise they would level Troy to the ground."

"There was a riot," prompted Gelanor. "I'm afraid it proved their point about the Trojans being dangerous and barbaric, outside the normal rules of conduct—the sort of people who steal wives."

"Who started that hue and cry?" asked Paris.

"I don't know. It seemed to come from the back of the room," said the man.

"So there are several of them," said Gelanor. "Drugging Paris, confining Helen, and spying in the council chamber. We must look for many."

A suspenseful calm descended on Troy after the tumult with the Greek visitors. It was as if the two men were gods, or strangers from an unknown world, whose existence, to the shock of the Trojans, had now been confirmed.

I was shaken as well. Menelaus had been here, walking these streets. But the two halves of my life were separate, utterly sundered. So I believed and so I wished. How could they now come together? I was not sure what I would have felt, seeing his face again.

Nervously, a group of women decided to leave the city to go to the washing troughs as usual. This time they went with armed guards; several of the royal women wanted to join them, not to wash clothes but to soak their newly woven tapestries to blend the colors. Much weaving was done in the palace and there was a small cartload of it waiting for the next step in its processing, which could only be done at the troughs. My own weaving was stalled, I felt. I wanted it to tell a story, an important one, but the old stories had lost their pull for me, and so I had begun nothing. Perhaps seeing the designs and works of others would help me.

The day was fair and promised to be hot for the first time in the new summer. Trundling out of the Dardanian Gate, the carts carrying the laundry and tapestries rolled down the incline. The women laughed and walked beside them; boys eager for play patted the horses and leapt up on the carts, jumping from one to the other. A fine sweet breeze blew in from the countryside.

One of the boys standing on the highest pile of laundry suddenly cried out, "Look! Look!" and pointed toward the sea, which was visible from where we were.

"What is it?" the guard nearest him asked.

"Can't you see? Black things out there!"

Grunting, the guard climbed up on the nearest cart, after ordering everyone to stop. He shaded his eyes, squinting. For several long moments he said nothing. Then he shouted, "Ships! Ships! Back into the city!"

The big carts turned laboriously around and headed back to the gate, their loads of wash and tapestries quaking.

"Shut the gate tight!" barked the guards, after the last cart had rumbled through. We women hurried, tight-lipped, to the ramparts on the northern side of the city to see what was happening. When we got there, we found people lined up six deep, staring out to sea. We pushed through them to find our men, and then, standing beside them, we saw what they were seeing.

Spread out upon the sea, a great dark web of ships drew toward us, making a pattern like that on a loom, a tapestry telling its own dreadful tale. The ships were as numerous as flies clustering around a spilled pool of sticky wine—swarming, jostling for place, hungry.

"How many?" Andromache, standing beside me, was still out of breath from our dash to get there.

"Hundreds," said Hector, staring grimly out. "The lookouts at Sigeum and Aesyetes's tomb on the headlands have just come in, reporting that there are hundreds."

"A thousand," said Deiphobus, next to him. "At least a thousand."

"That is impossible," said Hector. "There simply cannot be a thousand of them."

"Can you count, man?" snapped Deiphobus. "One . . . two . . . three . . ."

"They move too swiftly and are too far away to be accurately counted," insisted Hector.

Deiphobus sneered. "You will admit, dear brother, that there are a great many of them?"

"Yes, I grant you that. I see it gladdens your heart."

"Indeed it does. I am eager to engage them."

"Hector . . ." Andromache touched his shoulder. "Look at them." Again she pointed out to sea, shuddering.

"The more, the better!" cried Deiphobus. "The more to perish. No army of that size can maintain itself in the field. They will starve to death, and the more of them, the faster it will happen. They must count on a quick strike, a quick victory, before the problems of living in an alien land bear in upon them. But they are fools. The walls of Troy are impregnable. They cannot assault us here. All they can do is mill and mass upon the plain. Perhaps," he said smugly, "a few of us may venture out to give them battle. But it will be an individual or two." He whirled around and looked at me. "Here it is. The face that has called forth all those ships. One ship for each hair of your head, each eyelash, each finger and toe. Let them wreck themselves on the rocks of our walls! We have more stones than you have golden hairs on your head!" He swung away, a little smile of pleasure playing about his lips.

I turned and fled. I could not stand and watch the hideous black line of ships come closer. *One ship for each hair of your head, each eyelash, each finger and toe.* Let it not be so. But it was so. The forty suitors had grown into an army. *My* forty suitors, come to fulfill their promise.

The streets of Troy were thronged with people, pushing and jostling. I looked into their faces and they did not seem frightened, but acted like children being presented with a new toy. The ships had come to play with them!

I rushed through them and up into my palace. Hurrying up to the roof terrace, I had my own private view of the approaching ships. If I had somehow believed that they would have vanished, I was disappointed of that miracle.

I descended to the household shrine and sat quietly, hoping that if I were absolutely still my heart would stop pounding so violently. I could barely catch my breath, and was gasping for air.

Soon the calm of the place soothed me—that and the fact that it was underground and in another world from the one above. Slowly, silently, the sacred serpent glided from his dark abode and waited by my feet. He raised his head as if expecting me to impart wisdom to him, rather than the other way around.

But I had no wisdom. Everything we had counted on had turned out to be wrong. That Menelaus would not pursue me. That the suitors would not honor their oath. That Agamemnon could not gather a large army, and even if he did, men would not follow his bullying command. All wrong, all wrong.

Evadne had seen it in her vision, people had spotted the fleet on its way here, but seeing it making for our shores was altogether different.

The vast number of ships—how could Troy withstand them? What if— unthinkable thought—Troy fell? Yes, unthinkable thought, but all the earlier possibilities had been unthinkable, too, and yet the ships were here.

Because of her a great war will be fought, and many will Greeks die.

But if many Greeks died, so would many Trojans. And all because I had chosen to run away with Paris.

I started the familiar song that I had sung to others—it was *not* on account of me, Agamemnon had just been searching for an opening for war. But I need not pipe that music to myself. *I* had given him the excuse.

A mixture of panic and guilt surged through me, gripping me so hard, each breath hurt. These men—they were coming to assault my new family, new home. But amongst them could there be my old family? Were my brothers there? Were Castor and Polydeuces in Menelaus's ships? Was Father? But no, they could not have all left Sparta. Someone had to remain behind to rule.

Oh, let not my brothers be there!

The snake slid over my foot, caressing it with his cool belly.

Tell me, tell me! I begged him. But his dark eyes gave no answer.

Night fell, but in the last fading of the twilight, before the darkness of night blended with the darkness of the ships, we could see how much closer they had come to our shores. Tomorrow they would land.

Priam called an emergency council meeting, sending us our summons by torchlight. Soon we were crowded into his megaron, the poor light making it hard to recognize faces. Priam, in his agitation, did not wait for everyone to arrive before he began speaking.

"We all know why we are here," he said, skipping the usual niceties. "The Greeks are bearing down upon us! By sunrise they will be here! Our lookouts have reported the number of ships to be well over five hundred. We cannot count, of course, until they have landed and tied up. This is our last unmolested night." He stopped to catch his breath. I saw his hands were trembling, but he clenched his fists to cover it up. He gestured to his elders, motioning for them to come to his side. Thymoetes, Lampius, Clytius, and Hicetaon appeared, taking their places beside him, while Hecuba stepped back, disappearing into shadows.

"Antimachus. Antenor."

They came forward.

"My sons."

Paris left my side and went to stand beside his brothers.

"You are what stands between our enemies and our citizens, our women and children." He looked around at all of them, letting his eyes linger on each face. "Troy has never faced such an attack. But I know it is safe in your wisdom and strength. Let the lookouts speak first, tell us what we are facing."

The lookouts, both young soldiers posted at Sigeum and Aesyetes's tomb, stepped forward. "We think, sir, that there are more than seventy-five hundred ships but possibly fewer than a thousand. So let us take five hundred as an estimate."

At that, Priam cried out and clasped his head between both hands. "Five hundred! Even if there are only five hundred, and in each ship there are only fifty men, still it is . . . twenty-five thousand men! And if it's the worst it can be, a thousand ships, with a hundred men each, it's—a hundred thousand of them!"

"Yes, sir," the lookout said.

Priam slowly lowered his hands and held his head high. "Very well. It is what it is. What—and I ask you all—in your considered opinion, should be our first action?"

"That's obvious!" said Antimachus. "Attack them on the beach when they are attempting to land. Catch them at their most vulnerable. How many do we have at full-trained battle strength?"

"We have near seven thousand," said Hector. "The best in Troy."

"Then we are outnumbered at least five to one?" cried Antenor.

"This does not count the allies, who will soon even out the numbers," said Hector. "I'll lead them!"

Priam nodded. "Of course. And Deiphobus and Aeneas will bring up the second rank."

"And I?" said Paris.

"We don't need archers on this mission," said Deiphobus. "Stay back and guard the walls." The flickering light hid the pleasure on his face, but I could hear it in his voice.

"And I," Troilus cried.

"You'll stay inside, away from the walls," said Priam. "Along with little Polydorus and Polites."

"And I?" Hicetaon asked. "My armor has been burnished, the leather bindings replaced, and it's as supple as ever."

"But you are not," said Priam firmly.

"I can still thrust and slash with the best of them." His eyes narrowed in his wrinkled face.

"But you can't run. You're as slow as a hobbled donkey."

"That's not true! Who told you that?"

"I've seen you try." Now Priam's voice grew gentle. "We are of an age, and our swift days are past." *My javelin arm is still strong, and once I could have raced any one of these lads into the ground.* The old athlete. Had he begged to join Menelaus, too? Had Menelaus shaken his head apologetically and turned him away?

Lampius looked at me and shook his head. "There she is, her beauty frighteningly like that of the immortal gods. But no matter her loveliness, it would be better for Troy had she never come!"

"It is done, Lampius, and cannot be undone," Priam told him. "It was willed by the gods."

How accepting they all were of this. How different from Greeks, who never embraced their fate until they had first tried unsuccessfully to trick it.

"At first light, then, to the ships!" cried Hector. "We will arm and prepare all night!"

A great roar of excitement swept the hall, filling it like smoke.

When we were alone together in our chamber, Paris stood with his back to me, staring out toward the dark sea. "We know they are there," he said. "Just knowing makes everything different."

I turned him around to face me. "I feared this day might come," I said.

"You *said* you feared this day might come, but did you really?"

"No, I did not want to," I admitted. "Do you remember the waterfall on Cythera? The long one, where we stood at the top and looked down, and could barely hear the water splashing far below? I feel as if we are holding hands, jumping off into it together, and we cannot see the bottom. Oh, Paris, I am so fearful of what harm may come to Troy, and on our account."

"Then the prophecy would have come true, about my causing the destruction of Troy," he said. "In which case, once they decided to let me live, harm to Troy was inevitable. Therefore we need not punish ourselves for it."

"You hold it so lightly, then?"

"No, I do not, but neither do I bear the entire burden for it."

"I feel suffocated in omens and prophecies. When we ran away together, we thought we were fighting our way out of that net. Now I see the net is bigger than I imagined."

"Fighting . . . the real fighting is about to begin. I was stung tonight when I was forbidden to join my brothers on the beach attack. 'Stay back and guard the walls'—!"

"It was not the king who spoke thus, but Deiphobus." The sly and malicious Deiphobus.

"The king did not contradict him, nor reprimand him."

"Perhaps—"

"I must learn to fight better in the usual way. I'll have new armor made. They'll not hold me back!"

"Perhaps this is the only fight there will be. Perhaps they'll give the Greeks such a thrashing they'll pull up their freshly dropped anchors and head home."

"Menelaus is a stubborn man," said Paris. "It will take more than one skirmish to send him packing."

No one slept that night, and before the dawn was even hinted in the east, Paris was gathering up his bow, arrows, and quiver and stealing out of the room. He assumed I slept; I pretended to, so he would not feel the need to assure me all would be well. The moment he was gone, I leapt up and threw on some clothes, my heart pounding, my hands shaking so badly I had to clasp them together to stop the trembling.

Standing with all the other Trojans at the high northern wall, I watched our men streaking across the plain toward the Hellespont, the place where the ships would have landed. Paris was somewhere inside one of the guard towers and there was a part of me so thankful he was not among those rushing headlong toward the Greeks. The other part of me, the Paris part, felt his anger and shame at being ordered to stay in Troy.

Night fell and the men were not back, and we could see and hear nothing. It was not until near sunset the next day that the army returned, wearing a fine coat of dust on their armor, sweat smearing their bodies, with litters carrying the dead. They had attacked the Greeks just as they were landing, and Hector had killed the first man to step ashore—a good omen, although he disdained omens. But the rest of the Greek company put up a fierce fight, and although they were driven back almost into the sea, they managed to attack and burn many ships of the Trojan fleet anchored at the mouth of the Scamander.

No sooner had the gates closed behind our men than the Greeks followed them across the plain, as if they could not wait to behold Troy. Our high, polished walls and stout gates repelled them, and they withdrew under a hail of arrows and stones hurled from the ramparts.

Their futile march across the plain allowed us to see how large their army was. It filled the basin between the two rivers, and from our heights, it looked like a blanket, a moving blanket. There was an occasional flash of light from a shield angled to catch the sun, and the clank of their armor made a dull music as they marched.

I recognized no one amongst the leaders, but their helmets obscured their faces and the light was fading in any case. In armor all men look alike.

❖ XLIII ❖

War. We were at war. How chilling to utter those words, to realize them. Inside our chamber it was safe, with all the pretty playthings enjoyed in peace scattered about—lyres, mirrors, gaming boards of ivory. Outside, the streets were bustling with grim evidence of war—soldiers, of course, but also boys carrying baskets brimming with arrows, men leading donkeys staggering under the weight of stones to be thrown from the parapets, taking them to be piled up at stations around the walls, women rushing toward the safe southern gate to take their washing to the troughs outside before it was too late. The horse-keepers were leading their animals to the springhouse and watering troughs before penning them up behind the first barricade in the lower town. And everywhere the traditional horsehair crests atop the war helmets were waving, as men swaggered down the streets enjoying the narrow vision from behind their eye slits.

The mood in Troy was defiant. The Trojans gloried in the strength of their walls—the strongest and highest anywhere in the world, they said—and in their brave warriors.

The prospect of many young men losing their lives filled me with dread. When I voiced my sadness, Deiphobus just laughed in that dismissive way he had. I had disliked Deiphobus from the beginning and the feeling was growing. "You think overmuch of the men and little of the needs of the army. An army needs to win. It does not care about the individual soldier."

"But the land that gathers the army must care about its people."

"Perhaps it should, but it does not." He pointedly put on his helmet. Now his face was encircled with bronze; only his tight lips showed beneath it. "You choose an odd time to be tender-hearted, lady," he said. "You are the cause of all this. You should revel in it. You cannot undo it, so you should embrace it."

"I would have done everything I could to stop it, but some unknown enemy prevented me."

He laughed, and the laugh echoed oddly within the bronze of the helmet. "Oh, Helen, do not seek to shift your guilt that way." He fastened the strap under his chin. "It is only a pity that it is Paris you chose . . . but women are fickle, and nothing is forever."

I turned away, but only because I was speechless. There could be no clever retort, no response, to such an insult.

The Plain of Troy was empty. After their first heady dash across the flats to our walls, where they spent themselves like foaming but futile waves, the Greeks withdrew.

A walled city was difficult to assault. Did not Agamemnon know this better than anyone, snug behind his walls at Mycenae? He must search his mind, think of how someone might exploit Mycenae's weaknesses to be victorious, and then translate that into a plan for Troy.

The odd suspension of activity unnerved the Trojans, as the enemy had seemingly melted away. Our spies reported that they had beached their ships in rows upon the shore, with the last row bobbing in the water, held by stone anchors at their bows and cables at their sterns. We had succeeded in placing a number of spies in their midst already, and the wave of Gelanor-trained prostitutes were soon to follow. He thought that we should allow the lust of the men to grow outsized before we provided for their relief.

"They are milling around down by the shore," said one of the spies. "The ships have been drawn up in a special order, with the warrior known as Achilles on one end, a huge chunk of a man called Ajax on the other, and one known as Odysseus in the middle."

"So those are the real leaders," said Priam. "And where, in all this, is Agamemnon? And his brother Menelaus?"

"Tucked away somewhere along the row," said the spy. "But you are right, Achilles, Odysseus, and Ajax seem to be the tent poles. Achilles is reputed to be a warrior of supernatural prowess, Odysseus is clever and devious, and Ajax is simply huge and immovable."

Achilles! But he had been on Scyros, disguised as a girl. How came he here to Troy? "How can Achilles be such a great warrior?" I cried. "As for the other two, Ajax is dumb as a well bucket, and Odysseus fights with his wits rather than his sword."

"Achilles is lauded as their foremost warrior," insisted the spy. "I do not know on what basis they have decided this."

"Sometimes one just knows," said Priam. He shook his head. "I have heard that Achilles has a goddess mother. We cannot match that. We in Troy are mortals. All are born of a human father and a human mother."

"That will assure that defeating him adds even more to our glory," said Hector, who strode into the room. He looked around at all of us. "Huddling like a group of old women at a well? That is what it looks like." He ripped his helmet off and tossed it into a corner, where it clanged mournfully, as if protesting. "I do not give much credence to the 'son of a goddess' whispers. There is agreement on Olympus that the gods will not rescue their offspring, lest they challenge fate, so what difference can it make?" He laughed, a glorious ringing laugh. "I pit the sons of man against the sons of a god any day," he said. "We have no unrealistic ideas of being rescued, and that inspires a man to fight at the top of his powers."

Paris and I had returned to our palace when we were summoned by Antenor to meet him at his house. It was located midway down the slope of the city, a fine dwelling with latticed windows. Inside, it was spacious and airy; there were few objects to clutter the surroundings. He ushered us in and then led us to a smaller chamber, shutting the door behind us.

"My dear prince and princess," he said, pulling at the place where his brooch held his deep brown mantle in place. As always, it was impeccable and did not need adjusting. But he was most concerned about his appearance—he liked being known as the most tasteful man in Troy. "I now gaze upon that face which Menelaus and Odysseus longed to."

I spread my hands. "As you know, we were forcibly prevented from being present when they arrived in Troy."

Antenor came close and dropped his voice to a whisper. "Nonetheless, they left something for you." He turned and clasped a small box, then handed it to me. "It is safe. I examined it."

I lifted the carved lid slowly. Inside lay an ornamental piece of jewelry—a deep red stone held by bright shining gold. It was meant to be worn as a brooch, or as a pendant, strung on a golden loop. I ran my finger over the smooth stone.

"Menelaus said to give it to you," said Antenor. "He wished you to have it."

At once, it struck me as odd. Why would Menelaus present me with a jewel, when he claimed I had plundered his palace? And it did not resemble anything he might have fancied; his taste in jewels ran to the heavy and ostentatious.

Still, perhaps it was a sign that his heart was not entirely hardened toward me. There might be hope, some means of sending a message, arranging another meeting.

I drew it out of the box, but Paris grabbed my wrist. "Don't put it on! Don't even touch it! It might be poisoned. Or cursed."

Slowly I laid it back on its wrappings. I hated to think that, but I must be cautious. "What exactly did he say when he gave it to you?" I asked Antenor.

Antenor smoothed his silver hair. "He said, in a choking voice, 'For Helen, my wife, that she may count the cost of her love.'"

"All the more reason not to wear it," said Paris. "He seeks to steal you back silently by way of this—this toy."

"That cannot be," I said. But it looked so paltry, compared to the treasures of Troy, as it lay there in its little box, I was touched. Stop this! I told myself sternly. "How was he? How did he appear?" I asked Antenor. That was of more concern to me than his gift.

"Worn down and weary," said Antenor. He stopped short of saying, *His heart was broken.* "He kept looking toward the door of the council chamber, expecting you. When you did not appear, when the messengers returned saying that you were nowhere to be found, he crumpled up."

"What do you mean, 'crumpled up'?" demanded Paris.

"He seemed to grow smaller even as I watched him. Soon he was the size of Odysseus."

This was painful to hear. My hatred of the enemy who had locked me up churned inside me. "He needs to be told—I should explain—perhaps if I went there, to the ships—"

"No!" Both Paris and Antenor cried in unison. "The time for that is past," said Antenor. "Even if they captured you and sailed away with you back to Sparta, it is too late. The rest of the Greeks would stay here and attack us nonetheless. They did not come all this way for nothing, and—begging your pardon, my lady—I see now they did not come all this way just to retrieve you. Menelaus would be content with that, the rest would not. This expedition was a monumental expense. They must recoup their costs."

"Better they should turn and leave, for Troy will never recompense their losses!" cried Paris.

"Take the jewel," said Antenor. "I want it out of my house." He thrust the box at me, and despite Paris's warning, I took it.

For a time it was quiet. The great Plain of Troy was empty and in our innocence it would be easy to think all was the same, and venture down there to play and sport as before. But the shoreline had changed; instead of a clear line where the sea met the sand, dark rows of ships now lay.

After a time—it was midsummer now—groups of soldiers began moving across the green fields and encamping. At first there were only a few of them, and Priam sent out men to harass and attack them, driving some back, but then more came, and soon they formed a semicircle around the northern side of Troy, the side overlooking the Hellespont. As their numbers grew, they started trying to block our gates and prevent anyone from entering or leaving Troy. But they left the southern side of the city unguarded, and Trojans were still able to come and go freely from those gates. They fanned out, bringing in more wood, torches, and grain, and taking the time to construct a shield over the drain conduit, so that no one could sneak into the city that way.

Aeneas took advantage of the lull to return to his kingdom of Dardania, which lay to the immediate east of us. He gave formal notice to Priam, promising to return swiftly if he was needed, but felt he should guard his own people now.

"For when the Greeks grow bored and weary of trying to subdue Troy by siege, and their morale suffers and their supplies dwindle, they will seek victims elsewhere. They will turn their eyes toward Dardania and Adrasteia and Phrygia," he said as he took his leave of Paris and me. "Priam was unhappy that I must take your sister Creusa away with me, but she *is* my wife," he told Paris. "And my father Anchises must be anxious about me."

"As you wish," said Paris. He was pacing in the megaron of our palace, around and around the cold hearth in its center. "But, oh, my friend, my cousin, I shall miss you!" He embraced Aeneas, holding him close for a moment, then letting him go. Their two profiles, clean and sharp, mirrored one another's.

"And I, you," Aeneas said quietly.

Aeneas, gone. I, too, would miss him, as I had first beheld him along with Paris, and that moment was forever seared into my mind, the two of them part and parcel of my fate.

Paris was eager to have his armor fitted. He had ordered a new suit of it, and the armor smiths visited him in his chambers, bringing linen versions of what would later be forged in bronze. "I want a breastplate with a raised design showing the walls of Troy," he said. They measured his chest and arms and shoulders, cooing about his fine proportions. Then they began to demur about the time it would take to complete the armor and the quality of the bronze. They complained about the purity of the tin they had received from the far north, and said it was not up to the usual standard. Paris also wanted greaves for his shins and a thicker helmet of bronze, with a chin strap of pliant leather. "And on top of it all I shall wear my panther skin," he pronounced. "It is my special insignia."

The craftsmen bowed and retreated, while Paris fretted. "I do not think it will be ready in time," he said. "I should have attended to this earlier."

"No battles have yet occurred, except for the skirmish when they first landed," I reminded him. "I am sure your armor will be ready in good time. But pray you may never have to use it. Then we can hang it in our halls and show our children their father's glorious armor."

He sighed. Our children . . . would there ever be any? But we seldom spoke of it now, as our disappointment deepened and hopes faded. "Perhaps it will be necessary that I fight Menelaus for you. Man to man. I have it in my mind to do so. Why should these armies clash and kill, when it is really just a duel between two men?"

"No, you must not!" It was not that I feared he would be injured, oh, no, I could not even think that—but if Menelaus won, even if Paris was spared, I would have to go with him. I would have to let him claim me, hold me, touch me, take me away. His hands would be on my shoulders, stroking my face, he would take me to his bed, his cold, dead bed.

"Why, do you have so little faith in me?" he asked. His face showed a drained white hurt.

"It is not that," I said. "But the gods are deceitful, and may betray you."

Evadne and I sat quietly in the inmost chamber. I always found her calming, wise. My other attendants were cheerful and chattering, but served mainly to distract me. As always, she carried her hedgehog skin and a bag of uncarded wool, and as she sank down on her stool she drew out the tangled, matted wool and began drawing it across the hedgehog bristles, stretching out its fibers. Her arms spread wide, the dun-colored wool grew into long strands, and a great peace descended on us.

"Paris is out, my lady?" she asked finally.

"Yes. He has gone to inspect his store of arrows and have more made." Some thought anyone who killed from afar was a coward, not daring to stand up and face his enemy. "Hector says that the best omen is to fight for one's country, to die for it. It seems to me that the best omen is to make the soldiers on the other side die for *their* country." Even if it *was* with arrows.

Evadne laughed. "It would be better if women determined the course of war," she said. "It would then proceed on common sense." She drew out another gob of unworked wool, dark and messy.

"Paris spoke of a duel between him and Menelaus."

"That is sensible," she said. "After all, it is really between the two of them. No need to involve thousands."

"But I cannot go with Menelaus!" I cried. "Even if he won, I would run away!"

I swung around and shoved the box with the brooch toward Evadne. "He had the audacity to bring me this!" I said. "A jewel! Surely he did not expect me to wear it!" I took it out and swung it between my fingers.

"Oh, do not!" she said. She reached out and touched it lightly. "There is more to it than just a pretty gem." She shook her head. "Where did he acquire it? And why would he give you a gift?"

I put the brooch back in its box. As I drew my fingers away, I noticed that my fingertips were slightly red. I wiped them on a cloth, but the cloth stayed white.

"It weeps," said Evadne in wonder. "Perhaps as Menelaus himself."

"Tears are not red, " I said. "This is something else."

Priam's store of weapons was growing. He had two supply depots for them—one in the lower city, where larger items such as chariot parts, shields, unfinished wood shafts for spears, and breastplates could be stored, and another in the upper city, to house the spears, swords, daggers, bows, arrows, and quivers. Large piles of rocks were heaped up inside the walls to throw down upon the enemy, should he attempt to storm them.

Antimachus, the truculent old warrior, seemed to relish the idea of the enemy daring to attack our walls. "Their pitiful scaling ladders will be death traps for them," he said, and snorted, striding back and forth before a pile of rocks. His nostrils flared in his sunburnt face. "In order to climb, they have to place them close to the base of the walls and climb straight up, wearing armor. Oh, I've heard of the shield straps that allow them to sling their shields over their backs, turning themselves into turtles, but it's so clumsy that half of them will lose their balance and fall. The rest—we'll take care of the rest!" He bent down and picked up a large rock, so easily it might have been made of wool. His forearm bulged with muscle, the veins standing out. He laughed, and heaved the stone over the wall. A moment later a loud thud signaled its landing.

"And, most exalted king, whom will you deploy to lead the soldiers when the fighting is done on the plain?" he asked Priam, overseeing his defenses.

"Oh, that I could lead them myself!" said Priam. He seemed younger since the Greeks had landed; he drew vigor from the coming war. "I would put a fear into them, into all of them, even their Achilles and Agamemnon!" He exhaled, said goodbye to his dream. "But Hector will be the supreme commander." Priam indicated the doorway of the palace. "Come, let us go inside." He did not wish to speak of what he knew in the streets. A rumble of disappointment arose in the watching crowd that had followed him and his party from the walls.

Once in the courtyard, Priam ordered us to take our places according to our station. Soldiers were to stand on his left, his sons and their families in the center, and councilors and advisors on his right. "I value all your opinions, but it is easier for me, at my age"—he made a little bow, as if inviting contradiction—"to know from what quarter attacks are coming."

No one argued; no one said, *What do you mean, 'at my age'—why, you are a warrior still!* He waited, but finally he had to continue. "My clever advisor, the man who came with Helen to Troy, has succeeded in placing spies amongst the Greeks."

I looked around the company, but Gelanor was nowhere to be seen. I whispered to Paris that we must summon him, and Paris sent someone to find him.

"It seems the ships are drawn up in several lines, some pulled far up on the beach, and the late-comers still bobbing in the water. There are far too many of them to be beached at once. They are using the ships as a sort of headquarters, with each end secured by their strongest fighters."

"We knew of their positions from the beginning," scoffed Deiphobus. "What is new about that?"

"If a battle is coming, best to meet it prepared," maintained Priam. "Every morsel of knowledge about the enemy is invaluable, old or new."

After the gathering dispersed, Priam shuffled toward his altar. "Oh, Zeus," he murmured, "give me strength." He knelt down and clasped the pedestal holding the peculiar wooden three-eyed Zeus, closed his eyes, and prayed.

Paris, Hector, Deiphobus, and Gelanor—late arrived—and I were the only ones still lingering.

"There is more we can do," said Gelanor. "Priam has spoken only of the offensive—troops, commanders, weapons. But we as the attacked must also fight defensively. We live here, and have advantages an army camping on foreign shores does not."

"What," asked Hector, "beyond the bravery and strength of our warriors?"

Gelanor looked at him oddly, almost pityingly. "Oh, there is so much more. Is your aim to win this war, or is it to be noble? They are not the same."

"Let us win it," said Priam, returning from his appeal to Zeus. "We can dress it in nobility later. After the victory."

Gelanor reached out and touched Priam's shoulder. "Your age does beget wisdom," he said. "Very well, then. There are many things we can do to defend ourselves. We must harness nature." He looked pointedly at Deiphobus and Hector. "I know you disdain anything but swelling muscles wielding a spear, and the human spirit driving that spear," he said. "But our friends amongst the animals and the plants are eager to lend us a hand. We must not insult them by ignoring them." He suddenly whipped out an arrow. "An arrow can carry death. Guaranteed death. If it is dipped in snake poison, it can dispatch the foe forthwith.

"And there are other things we can employ. Rocks to drop on the ladder climber, you say? What of heated sand, that penetrates between all the layers of a warrior's armor? Do you have an alarm system here in Troy, to signal breach of your lines? Why not? I know of many." He shrugged. "You are not prepared."

"Sir—show us how!" I was startled at Priam's naked appeal. But his only concern was for Troy, not his pride.

"The things I mentioned are but child's play," said Gelanor. "Obvious things. But there are others—do you know of poisonous garments?"

"Do you mean, smeared with poison?" asked Priam.

Gelanor laughed. "No, not that. I mean, garments that have rubbed up against victims of the plague or other diseases. They have the power to impart the disease to healthy people."

"No!" I cried. I could not permit such to be used against my own countrymen.

"You prefer the arrows of Apollo, then?" For the first time, I beheld Gelanor's hardness. "They strike here, there, to no purpose for either side? The cruel god of plague? If a man must die of plague, why should it not be for a purpose?" He looked hard at me. "Shall we not harness Apollo as well?"

Priam looked horrified. "You speak blasphemy."

"Even thinking of harnessing a god for your purpose is a challenge to the god." Now Hector joined his father. "Please, take it back."

Gelanor laughed. "Very well. Dread archer, god of the silver bow, I meant no disrespect." He squinted toward the sun. "Look down on us here. And guide us to your temple."

"We don't need to be guided to it, there is one right here in Troy," said Deiphobus.

"Not that one," said Gelanor. "I hear there is another one some distance from Troy, one called Apollo Smintheum. *That* is the one I wish to inspect."

"The temple with the sacred white mice?" Priam asked.

"Indeed," said Gelanor. "I believe that temple may hold answers for us."

* * *

Later in the day, having ascertained that no Greeks were anywhere south of us, our group set out from the Dardanian Gate, trundling along in a cart, guarded by soldiers. But it was glorious to escape the confines of the city and venture out into the countryside. As Troy dwindled behind us, I looked back to see the shining walls and proud towers, and at its summit the palace Paris and I had built, the highest thing in Troy. It flaunted itself there, proclaiming our love and our presence.

"Let Agamemnon see *that*," I whispered into Paris's ear. "It will drive him mad." If he noticed I did not say *Menelaus,* he gave no sign of it. *Menelaus* was a word we avoided, out of mutual embarrassment.

After much jouncing and bumping, we reached the temple in midafternoon, when the strong sun turned the stone pillars pure white. A sacred grove surrounded the building, and the trees stood silent in the heavy, windless air. At first the building seemed deserted; midafternoon was no time for visitors. But as we mounted the high steps to the building, we saw a dark-robed priest waiting for us, hands clasped.

Immediately Priam spoke, as leader of the Trojans. "Good priest, we come here to do honor to the aspect of Apollo who reigns here." He inclined his head slightly.

"We welcome your presence," the priest said. "We have heard of the arrival of the Greek army besieging Troy." He approached me, fixing his eyes on me. "Is this the cause of it all? The illustrious Helen?"

Rather than let Hector speak for me, I said, "Yes. I am Helen. I bring my friend from Sparta, as well as my husband and his brothers and their father."

"Ah, then," he said. He continued staring at me. "Perhaps you should cover your face here, lest Apollo . . ." His voice trailed off. He did not need to enumerate all the women and men Apollo had taken a fancy to and pursued mercilessly, to their doom. Yes, Daphne had escaped, but only by turning herself into a tree—hardly a satisfactory solution. I had no desire to become a tree. "Very well," I said, drawing out a thin veil.

"I understand that you keep sacred white mice here," said Gelanor. He was looking about. "And other things?"

The priest demurred. "The mice, yes, they are here behind the holy statue. Do you know the story? A swarm of mice once ate the leather bindings of the shields and swords of an enemy army, so we honor them to this day."

"And other things, yes?" Gelanor persisted.

"Other things. We keep them safe, protected, in the underground chamber."

He led us behind the statue of Apollo to a dark enclosure. The odor immediately announced that vermin were there. Even sacred vermin stink. I coughed, discreetly, I hoped.

The cages were swarming with mice, tumbling over one another, fighting for space.

"What if you let them loose?" asked Gelanor.

"They are only symbolic," the priest said. "True, mice have chewed through essential armor on the eve of a battle. But we have no power to direct them. So, in answer to your question—if we opened the cages now, the mice would swarm away and likely destroy the fields around us. They attack whatever is at hand."

"Then, I beg you, contain them," said Priam.

"Show us the other things in the arsenal," said Hector. "We need to know."

Making rumbling noises of discontent, the priest called for a torch. A resinous pine branch was thrust into his hand from one of the lesser priests. "Very well, then, let us descend." He turned and led us down a set of damp steps. "They are ancient," he said. "I do not know what they can teach you."

Once below ground, we discovered it was dank and fetid, so different from the sunny aspects of the upper temple. Rough unhewn walls resolved themselves out of our wavering vision. I could hear the drip of some cavernous stream far below. Green mold covered the stones, and silence enveloped us.

"Here is one thing," the priest finally said, approaching a locked wooden chest. "They say that in a time of plague the garments of a king and queen were removed for safekeeping, after they died of the disease." He started to force the lid open.

"No, do not," said Gelanor. "Leave it locked. I do not need to see them, as long as you swear they are there, preserved."

"I so swear!" the priest said.

"Very well, then," said Gelanor. "What else do you have here? It may be of great importance someday in the defense of Troy."

The priest looked startled. "I—there are more clothes, dedicated after their owners died of a dread disease. They are locked up, untouched. Some of the diseases struck quickly, in the noonday of a man's life. Others preferred to wait until twilight, until the person was weakened and the attack was not so obvious. But all sudden plagues are attributed to Apollo, and thus the leavings were brought here."

"What would you say if I told you that taking out the garments, shaking them, holding them up to you, would cause you to fall victim to the same disease?" asked Gelanor.

"I would say, then, that they must be kept securely locked. As they now are."

"Just so." Gelanor nodded. "But if ever we send you word to dispatch them to Troy, you will know things are desperate."

"Yes." The priest nodded.

"Let us seek the daylight again," said Hector. "This is too oppressive." He turned and left us standing in the dank dark. After a moment we followed him up to the temple. The clear air, the blue sky, sang to us.

That is, until we saw the huddled figure before the statue of Apollo. He seemed but a heap of rags, a heap that heaved and sighed and cried.

"What is this?" cried the priest, hastening over to him. He extended his hand, placing it softly on the pulsing heap. At length a head emerged; the shoulders straightened and then the man stood forth.

It was no man, but a boy. He shook his head and stammered, "F-forgive me, but I sought sanctuary here. Troy was besieged. I only knew to come here!"

"Who are you? What is your name, son?" Priam shuffled toward him.

"I am Hyllus, son of Calchas. I do not share his treason. I abjure my father. Only let me return to Troy, my home!"

Priam walked toward him, but before he acknowledged him, he pulled the boy's hair off his forehead. A bright red jagged scar stared out at Priam.

"I see that you are indeed Calchas's son," breathed Priam. "But how came you here?"

The boy cringed, then drew himself up. "When my father went to Delphi, the oracle ordered him to side with the Greeks. He did so. But I could not. Have you ever met these Greeks? They quarrel constantly, and were not even pleased to welcome my father. What is it they said? *I love treachery, but I hate traitors!* As if there could be one without the other. And my father was not a traitor, but was ordered to join the Greeks by the Pythia. Who could disobey? One must bow before the oracle. But I could not follow my father. The oracle spoke not to me. And I knew right from wrong. It was wrong, unless one received special instructions from the gods, to desert one's city. And so, I beg you, bring me back. Let me return to Troy."

Priam's eyes were filled with tears; Hector's as well.

"How do we know that you are truly Calchas's son?" It was Gelanor who spoke those words. "Are we content to rely on this lad's words?"

"We do not need words, we can see for ourselves." Priam pointed to the scar.

❖ XLIV ❖

We made our way back to Troy, the boy riding with us. He said very little, and kept his eyes down. Soon the temple was just a bright white spot in a green dale. I smiled when I thought of the priest and his smelly mice; my snake would doubtless enjoy an opportunity to sport amongst such delicious creatures. Gelanor seemed preoccupied; I knew he was thinking about the potent garments contained in the coffers and wondering how, and in what dire circumstances, he might use them. It would be a grim choice, if ever it came to that.

Hector and Deiphobus were clasping the rails of the wagon, standing shoulder to wide shoulder. I could hear their murmuring words above the groan and rumble of the cart wheels. Hector was worried about the weakness of a stretch of western wall; Deiphobus was more concerned about the Greek leaders, particularly Achilles. He had not been seen since the landing. What was he doing? Could he have been injured in the landing? Deiphobus's voice rose in hope.

I felt should tell them of my strange encounter with Achilles. I had thought much on it since that time in Scyros. I stood up and touched Hector's shoulder. "When Paris and I were on our way here, we stopped at the island of Scyros," I told him. "I recognized Achilles there, disguised as a girl at the king's court."

Hector frowned. "Are you sure?" The hesitation in his deep voice showed that he thought it my imagination.

"Yes, absolutely. I had seen him as a child a few years before, and I would know him anywhere. But I could not question him then, and now I do not understand how he comes to be here with the army."

"A girl? He was wearing the clothes of a *girl*?" Deiphobus snorted.

"Yes, I swear it!" Neither of them believed me.

Paris now joined in. "I don't remember your telling me about that. Surely you would have."

"I fail to see what difference it makes," said Priam, looking up from under his thick eyebrows. "He's here now, that's all that matters."

"But don't you see—perhaps he is deranged!" I said.

"I know what happened." A quiet voice rose from the back of the wagon. "I can tell you." The boy spoke. "Helen speaks true. Achilles was sent to Scyros by his mother to protect him. She did not want him to go to Troy—he was her only son and still very young. But the Greeks were determined to have him, and so they tracked him down there on the island. Then, rather than fighting with him—for if truth be told even those seasoned warriors were afraid to—they tricked him into revealing himself." Hyllus's eyes, soft and brown, looked up at the men for approval.

"Come here, son," said Deiphobus, hauling him over. The boy was smashed against his shoulder. "Tell us of this trick."

Hector turned around and riveted his attention on Hyllus as he cleared his throat.

"It was very clever," the boy said. "Odysseus is still bragging about it. He and Diomedes landed on the island to pay a visit to the king, spying to find Achilles. But after several days of feasting and games and all the rest, there was no sign of Achilles. So they returned to their ship and brought gifts for the king's daughters—and he has many, many of them—mirrors, and veils, and bracelets and earrings. And half hidden under them was a fine shield and a spear. While the girls were cooing over the gifts and Odysseus was arranging them, Diomedes from outside the palace clanged bronze and screamed war cries as if they were being attacked. The girls shrieked and fled; Achilles swooped down on the shield and spear and rushed to defend them."

"Clever indeed," muttered Priam.

"Oh, in camp they imitate Achilles throwing off his veil and mantle and ripping the brooch from his shoulder, and it never fails to win a laugh."

"Yes, so I imagine," said Hector. "Alas, Helen, he is not deranged. So we face a well-trained adversary, one eager to be here. And as for Odysseus, I hope he does not turn his cleverness on us."

"This Achilles . . ." Deiphobus now turned back to gripping the sides of the wagon. "Why is everyone in such a state about him? He's only one man. Hardly a man at all, more a boy."

Hyllus shrugged. "I don't know, I only know he was the focus of much talk. Perhaps they needed to create a Heracles for this venture, and it is always easiest to create a wonder out of someone unknown."

Gelanor laughed. "Very astute, lad," he said, observing him closely. "You seem to know a great deal." His laughter died away.

"We are already familiar with the abilities of the rest," said Hector. "Agamemnon is a fierce fighter but lacks the courage that inspires loyalty in followers. Diomedes is a good junior soldier but cannot lead. The large Ajax of Salamis fights well hand to hand but cannot think; furthermore, his great bulk makes him immobile. The small Ajax of Locria is small in every way—a mean-spirited and brutal man who likes to torment his victims. His only virtue as a warrior is his swift running, so he can pursue a foe. Idomeneus is a famous spear man and fights well enough, but his age means he cannot run fast; he has to take a stand wherever he is. And Menelaus is not a fighter of the first rank. He is too softhearted." He turned and looked at me. "Begging your pardon, Helen," he said.

"Why do you apologize? I do not make claims for his skills on the battle-field." Nor for anything else, I thought.

"You are trembling." Paris sat down beside me, pried one of my hands loose, and took it in his. "Please, do not fear what is coming. We will be safe."

"I am not afraid," I said. But I was.

The great Dardanian Gate, already shut for the night, groaned open for us and we arrived safe behind the walls. Nothing had happened that day; no sign of any enemy movement or attack. The besieging tents were still fixed in their half circle, but their ineffective positions did not threaten Troy. Hecuba wel-comed Priam back and I saw a near-smile on her face, for the first time in a great while. We would, perhaps, be safe. This would pass; the Greeks would fold their tents after the summer, hoist their sails, declare some sort of victory to please their vanity, and be gone. Paris would never get to wear his new ar-mor, and the rations horded in Troy would furnish many a fine banquet. We would drain the amphoras and sing rounds of song to celebrate our freedom, so easily won. Only the young warriors, so eager to try themselves on the field, would be disappointed.

* * *

Many days passed in this fashion, with Priam holding council with his old fellow warriors, sitting out in the sunshine of the portico and chattering like birds, spending more time reliving the battles of their youth than planning the pending one. In their midst, Priam seemed to shed his wrinkles, and even his hair was less gray; he nuzzled his pack of pet dogs who crowded around in hopes of scraps, wagging their tails wildly.

So far people could come and go freely to the springs and to Mount Ida, and Troilus was able to water his horses at the springhouse near the Temple of Thymbraean Apollo. Everything to the north was cut off, of course, making the lower branches of the Scamander out of bounds. This ended the tidy profits the Trojans customarily made from stranded ships in need of water, but it could not be helped. Hector decided to send a party east toward Dardanos and Abydos to see if there were any Greek incursions there. He selected a small band of men and they plotted a way through the foothills and forests, using pathways known only to hunters. In the meantime, the prostitute spies were providing us with amusing, if not strategic, information about the Greeks in camp.

It seemed that Agamemnon had already built himself a wooden hut and packed it with women. He spent most of his time inside with them, only emerging with shaking knees and dazed face to review his troops or eat. A foulmouthed common soldier, Thersites, led the ranks in reviling him behind his back. Everyone laughed at this, but it made my heart burn to think of him indulging himself while Clytemnestra waited back in Mycenae, grieving for their daughter. The dog-faced swine!

Menelaus stalked around the camp scowling and muttering; none of the ladies had ever seen him smile. Odysseus, on the other hand, was full of cheer and compliments for everyone, and eager to give the ladies a good turn in the bed. But somehow he was always missing his goods when it came time to pay. And Idomeneus kept an elaborate table with entertainment and wine aplenty, as gracious as if he had been holding court back in Crete. His lovemaking was equally refined, if a trifle slow due to his age. He always paid extravagantly. The Ajaxes—great and little—were not recommended. One was too large, the other too small, and both were stingy. Diomedes was probably the best of the lot in terms of skill and gusto, they all agreed.

Gelanor busied himself studying how our "plant and animal friends," as he had styled them, might help in the war effort. Always knowledgeable about poisons in Greece, he bent his efforts to learn about local ones he could use for arrows and smoke. There were certain types of plants so poisonous that honey made from their blossoms and smoke from their branches was fatal. Of course, the problem in using smoke was that it could waft back and hurt the people directing it. The use of poisons required the utmost care. It was important to construct quivers with lids to protect the archer from poison tips, or perhaps to make a pouch to hold the poison and dip the arrows into it at the last possible moment. The same went for attack animals—bombs of scorpions or wasps that could be lobbed into enemy camps, or mad dogs let loose: these were all weapons of last resort, as they were so hard to control. The only exception to this was a mixture of soils and ground rocks that ignited when the sun heated them. Very useful in smearing on the enemy's tents or wagons, but that meant one first had to be near enough to do it, and that was unlikely.

"And to think a simple bow is considered to be cheating a bit," I said to Gelanor. "That seems heroic compared to these things—smoke that clouds the air, scorpions raining from the sky, plague garments."

"Please! Let us call them 'the arrows of Apollo.' I believe that is the polite name for plague."

"As you like," I said. "So Apollo's temples hoard the diseases of war, and Athena's the weaponry of war?"

"Yes. Each god has his own arsenal. And Ares is somewhere in between—his war is not disciplined like Athena's but accompanied by panic and fear, such as plague spreads."

My smile faded. "Oh, Gelanor, I hope we never have to use any of these things."

"As do I. Still, it is comforting to have them on hand."

Our men set out eastward on a sun-filled, perfect day. It was a day to go galloping across the fields, had these days been normal. The men slipped away through the east gate, gliding through its complicated, mazelike exit, waving back at us as we stood on the walls, and making their way across the fields, vanishing into the woods.

"I am worried about Aeneas and Creusa in Dardania," said Hecuba, watching from the walls. "I cannot help wishing that they had remained in Troy."

"Mother, you know well enough that Aeneas is king of Dardania. He needs to be with his people," said Hector. His voice was reassuring. Masterful and strong, there was something innately steadying about the way he spoke. "I do not think any Greeks have ventured beyond their beachhead here. But we are sending a party to ascertain this."

"The Greeks are too quiet," said Priam suddenly, on Hector's other side. "I don't like it."

Hector laughed, a hearty roar. "That is because you and your old comrades want to get out there and fight."

Priam turned and looked at him. "No. I am not an old fool, Hector. Do not take me for one. I meant what I said. The Greeks are too quiet. They did not come all this way to sit in idleness before their tents and amuse themselves with prostitutes."

"Perhaps the battle looked more inviting back in rocky Greece," said Hector. "The thing one sees in the mind is never the same as the thing one actually beholds."

"I do not like it," repeated Priam.

Days passed. The men should have returned. The glorious summer days continued, mocking us by letting us gaze down on the empty, inviting Plain of Troy. The trade fair should open soon, but now it could not. More income for Troy suddenly vanished. And this was much more substantial than the loss from the water rights. The very presence of the Greeks, with no fighting at all, was beginning to take a toll.

After fifteen days, Hector finally said he would send a scouting party to see what had happened. Before they could be equipped, a survivor of the first party crawled out of the woods and collapsed on the field nearest Troy. We saw him lying there, and sent a wagon to rescue him.

Grim-faced, litter-bearers bore him through the streets of Troy to his home. The physicians worked frantically to save his life. He had been beaten and stabbed; one leg was broken and its bone protruded through his ankle. As one doctor left the house, he shook his head. The leg was already turning black with rot. Just as the man lapsed into delirium, Hector questioned him. Tossing and feverish, barely able to form words, he said their party had been ambushed.

"It was as if they knew exactly where we would be," he whispered. "They were waiting for us."

"Who? Who?"

"Greeks," he said. "That was their language, the special Greek they use over there. Not our Greek." He winced, grabbing at his painful ankle. "They took delight in slaying us. Oeax—they cut him down first. Before Hileus could move, they speared him from behind. They were all over. Everywhere."

"How many?" asked Hector.

The man's head lolled.

"Try. Try. We need to know!" said Paris.

"Many. Ten. Twenty. I don't know!" His voice rose to a scream, then ceased. His mouth fell open.

The physician bent down and put his ear to the man's chest. "Dead," he finally said. "So. The massacre was complete."

Hector was distraught. Somehow the enemy had known of our movements. Now the ventures out to Mount Ida and the springs did not seem so inviting.

"How can we win, if the Greeks know our movements?"

"Perhaps they just stumbled upon our party," said Troilus.

"No, the survivor said they were waiting, ready for them," said Deiphobus.

"Perhaps one of their seers told them," said another man. "That Calchas, for example!"

"No, my father cannot discern things like that!" The thin voice of Hyllus rose from a back corner where he had been standing. "He can only interpret omens, bird flights and entrails and such."

"They are bottling us up in here," Hector muttered, when we had gathered in his megaron with his friends. This was not a regular council; no elders were present, and Priam was not included. This was talk only amongst the younger warriors. He did not sit in the chair of honor but paced back and forth, his square jaw set. His normally smooth voice was edged with anger and something else. "Slowly they will strangle us."

"We can no longer send out unarmed parties," Deiphobus said. "There must be protection at all times."

A murmur rose as everyone discussed this. Young Troilus spoke up and said he thought the nearby springhouse, being so close to the Temple of Thymbraean Apollo—which the Greeks were bound to honor as neutral territory—should still be safe, and he intended to continue using it to water his horses. He did not want to place demands on the water supply within the walls when there was such plentiful water just beyond them. Several men lamented the loss of the trade fair, saying that merchants were all cowards and this proved it. They turned tail and ran at the slightest hint of trouble.

"Hint?" said Helenus, brushing his thick hair back from his forehead. "I would say this is much more than a hint. Why, there's not even anywhere for the ships to beach; the Greeks have taken the entire shoreline." As usual, he was soft-spoken, but his words carried great thought. He never seemed to speak without having thoroughly weighed his ideas.

"Then they'll go elsewhere," lamented Hector. "Farther to the south. And we'll lose everything."

"Yes, that could happen, if the war is not over by this time next year," said Helenus.

It was growing late, and through the open doors of the megaron we could see the light failing. The wives and women joined us; as I have said, I was present at many gatherings where women ordinarily were excluded. Now Andromache entered, followed by her sisters-in-law Laodice and Cassandra, and the wives of the other men. Musicians streamed after them, and torchbearers.

"You have let it get dark around you," said Andromache, sounding as lighthearted as she could. "Men!" She slid up beside Hector. "Now leave your talk of war, and let us enjoy wine and song."

❧ XLV ❧

T he wine did not really clear our heads of troubles, but it masked them under a soft haze, blurring around the edges of our cares. Andromache tried gamely to re-create the camaraderie of other gatherings in the time before the coming of the Greeks. But the enemy had penetrated into the very chamber itself.

Paris and I walked slowly and dispiritedly back to our home. Then, thinking of Paris, of my love for him, I slid under the smooth linen sheet, feeling its cool caress under my back, and held out my arms to him.

"Come, my love," I said. "Let us mock the enemy."

The sun sent his first probes into our bedroom, but the stout shutters Paris had designed repelled them. Then, as the sun rose higher, he beat down mercilessly on the Plain of Troy, making the withered ground send back heat waves, so that the sea wavered before our eyes when we leaned over the walls and tried to sight the shoreline. It was very still; the usual north wind had dropped away, leaving us held under a heavy hand of air.

Paris and I were trying to make out the Greek camp, but the heat waves, dancing and distorting everything, made us unsure what we were seeing. Just then Priam and Hecuba joined us, leading an elderly blind man by the elbows to the edge of the wall. Priam spoke to the blind man and then stepped back. The man grasped the edge of the parapet and stared out, unseeing, across the plain. Then he raised one thin, flapping-skinned arm. "Hear me, stones!" He ran his other hand along the top of the wall. "Hear me, great wall! Hear me, high towers! I bless you and bind you to protect Troy."

A rumble of voices from the watching Trojans repeated the words. Then he held his arm out over the wall. "Hear me, soil of the plain! Hear me, the sounding sea! Hear me, you enemy hoards! I place today a binding curse upon you, if you think to harm Troy or touch its people. Your tongues will dry up and cleave to the roof of your mouths, your soil will harden and never let grass spring forth upon it again, your waves will turn to poison." He clapped his hands loudly. "Thus do I curse the enemy of Troy, and all things which might give them aid."

A roar of approval filled the heavy air, and Priam embraced the man. They then sought the shade indoors.

Hector strode over to us and shook his head. "They say a blind man has the power to put binding curses on an enemy, if he speaks from the city walls. I, for one, do not believe it, but I would be pleased if it were so."

"Eh." Aesacus had come up behind him. "People believe too many of these things. It's all nonsense." He was a weedy little man—the sort who usually believed in magic and forces stronger than himself, if only because he could use help. But, surprisingly, Aesacus sneered at such crutches.

Hector was squinting out across the plain. "In any case, I believe it came too late to hobble the Greeks. They have already set out."

Was that a haze of dust rising from near the ships?

"No," I murmured, looking where he indicated. But I did see something stirring, although I could not tell what.

"Arm yourselves!" Hector cried to the men on the wall. "Arm! I will call the rest," he told Paris.

Paris turned to me quickly. "My armor. It is time."

Must it be? Must he put it on at last? I wanted it to lie, the bronze slowly turning green, the leather stiffening, locked away in its chest forever.

"Yes," he said. "Come with me. Quickly."

We hurried toward our home and without looking back Paris mounted the steps inside to the highest room, the one that overlooked all of Troy and its plain. There, far below us, I could now see the army moving toward the city. Paris's new armor was stored here, and he yanked it out and shook it. It clanked, its metal pieces settling against one another.

"Here, help me," he barked, quite unlike himself. "Hurry." He had summoned his attendant, but the boy had not appeared. "I cannot wait." Trembling, I fastened the buckles and the straps, performing the rites of a war companion. Bit by bit the Paris I knew disappeared behind a wall of bronze and leather.

He was so young. No, you cannot go, I cried inside. I remembered, oh, so long ago, when I was choosing a husband from the suitors, I had ruled out anyone younger. I had said he would defer too much to me, and would know less than I. Now I knew that was false, and his youth was so precious I could not bear to sacrifice it, no matter the reason, before its time. It shone like a star. Now its light was dimmed beneath his helmet.

"Do not go," I heard myself saying. But I did not think he would hear.

The newly unknown man before me waited a moment before answering. "You of all people should not say that," was all he said. He bent over and gave me a metallic embrace.

The Greeks were in full attack, marching resolutely toward the walls of Troy. They seemed to fill the whole plain, swarming like insects, and as they marched, their armor, from a distance, made a dry rustling sound like the rubbing of locusts' legs.

"Man your positions," said Priam, directing the older men to take their stations by the piles of stones; the younger archers were to mount the towers ready for enemies approaching within bowshot.

The soldiers filed out through the Scaean Gate, under the gaze of the Great Tower of Ilium, bristling with archers. Still the Greeks came on and on. Now they were yelling and charging toward the walls, screaming and bellowing.

"Helen, get back!" Hecuba grabbed my shoulder and tried to pull me away. "We must leave the walls!"

Priam had fallen back, gathering his old councilors around him, shrinking away. "It lies with the young now," he said, hurrying toward the summit, where he could watch from his rooftop.

The Trojans charged out, rushing from the entrance, but they were badly outnumbered by the locustlike Greeks. I cringed watching them; bravery gives glory, but it cannot prevail over overwhelming odds. I got away from Hecuba and returned to the walls; I could not bear to leave. Down below me I saw the company of Trojans but not Paris amongst them. From the towers the defenders were firing covering arrows to keep the attackers at bay; from far back in the Greek ranks slingers were launching stones over our walls. They arced through the sky and then fell sharply just inside the walls, causing damage that an arrow, with a different path of flight, could not. Trojans groaned and fell where they stood, felled by the flying stones.

A company of Greeks approached the Great Tower and Scaean Gate, but there was something curiously slow about them. The Trojans rallied and sent volleys of arrows toward them, but the Greeks never came close enough to be hit. On the eastern side of the city I could hear cries; the walls were under assault there, too.

Just then a bloodcurdling cry rang out from close at hand, and I heard shrieks from everyone around me. A grinning face appeared over the wall, and a man leapt over. He was quickly subdued, but others swarmed after him.

"The western wall!" one of the guards cried. "They are at the western wall!"

At least ten Greek soldiers clambered over the side of the western wall before being slain by the waiting Trojans. But behind them were hundreds, eagerly finding hand- and footholds on the loose stones of the weakest stretch of the walls of Troy. A roar of excitement welled up from the ground.

I climbed up on a pile of stones and peered down below, from a point of safety. The Trojans had turned to fight the Greeks at the base of the western wall, trying to drive them back. Our defenders from above were flinging stones on the adversaries, while our warriors battled them hand to hand.

Gelanor came running with a covered cart, trundling it through the street. "Here! Here!" he cried. A group of guards surrounded him and they hustled toward the wall. They yanked the cover off to reveal a pile of sand, which they began scooping up with clay pots and dumping over the side of the wall. Heated sand—heated blistering hot, so that it would sting and scald between the chinks of armor. As it hit its victims, howls resounded all the way up to the heavens.

Gradually the Greeks fell back, leaving the western wall. I could make out some of the Trojans now, could see Hector striding beside the big oak that grew near the Scaean Gate. With the retreat of the Greeks, the Trojans scattered. I still could not see Paris.

Suddenly I saw a figure running toward the oak, making for Hector. He moved at an astonishing speed, bounding and leaping like an animal, even though fully armored. Almost before Hector could sight him, he was bearing down upon him, brandishing a formidable spear. Hector turned and fell back to gain his footing, the other man almost on top of him. The man threw his spear and missed by a hair's breadth, rushed to retrieve it and aim again. In that instant Hector dodged and moved and was able to escape the next throw, which went wide. Now the assailant was without a spear, and he grabbed for his sword, advancing on Hector. Hector raised his shield and then, straining at full height, cast his own spear. It whizzed past the man's helmet, so close it surely must have made a whisper in his ear as it passed. For an instant the man turned to see where it fell so he could capture it, and in that pause Hector escaped, making for the Scaean Gate, hastily opened for him. It clanged shut after he was inside, just as his adversary beat his fists upon it and cried out, "Coward! Coward!" The fists must have been made of metal, they battered the thick wooden doors so. Later I saw that they had actually dented them— a series of depressions in the bronze-sheathed wood showed where the knotted fists had struck.

Hector, eyes bulging, yanked off his helmet. His face was streaming with sweat, his chest heaving. "I see now," he muttered, "what they say of him is true."

"Who? Who?" I asked one of the guards surrounding Hector.

"Achilles," the guard said. "That demon was Achilles."

"They say he can outrun even a stag," said Hector. "I had heard it, but thought it was just an expression. Now I know it is not. He is beyond any human warrior I have ever seen."

"Coward! Coward!" The words were still ringing.

Hector shook his head as if to shut them out. "No man has ever called me that," he muttered.

"Nor are you," said Priam, who had come rushing from the summit, his robes flapping out behind him.

I peered down over the wall to see where Achilles was. His cries and poundings had ceased, and he was turning away from the gate, shouldering his spear. Beneath the plates that shielded his cheeks and the long nose guard, I saw his thin lips drawn in a tight line. His armor was splendid, decorated with scenes worked in the breastplate and shield. No one else had anything remotely like it; even his greaves winked silver from their clasps. This was the boy who had insisted on racing the tired Menelaus up the hill, the boy hiding his muscled arms under a girl's tunic on Scyros. So he was still, at the age of eighteen or so, a swift runner, but it seemed he was running only to carry out the bidding of Menelaus. Just then he jerked his head up and saw me.

"Helen!" he shouted. "So you are indeed there in Troy! Do you come out to watch your kin? To gloat at us? See, men, here she is!" Achilles motioned to his cohorts, pointing at me.

"I told you not to stand at the walls!" Hecuba jerked me back. "You can cause great harm by being visible!"

That had been my curse all my life.

"We must make sure you are safe," said Hecuba crisply. "It is our duty to protect you."

Our warriors were pouring back into the city; the encounter was over. They were welcomed with shouts and roars of approval. Later the old councilors and the commanders would confer about the mistakes made, the weak points in the Trojan defense, and how to correct them. But for now, it was enough that the men had returned safely and the attack on the western wall had been repelled. Several Greek soldiers lay dead at the bottom of the wall, crushed by stones flung on them or killed by toppling to the ground.

There was no official celebration, but spirits were high and that night many bands of young men, fresh from their first brief foray out in war, caroused through the streets, singing and drinking. Paris and I could hear their voices echoing from wall to wall in the streets, but we shuddered in our chamber. Paris had been only too glad to shed his armor, which now lay in a heap in the wooden trunk, and kept saying, "They mean it. They mean it. They are here to fight a war." He acted as though he only just now believed it.

"Where were you? I did not see you," I said. I had asked him to lie flat on the bed, so that I could soothe his back with scented oil. Several torches flickered on the walls, but still the light was poor and the room shadowy.

"You should not have been looking," he said. It was hard to hear his words with his face down. "It was dangerous."

"So your mother told me," I said. "Nonetheless, I was able to watch for a while, before I had to draw back."

{ 379 }

"I was on the eastern side of the city. They had attacked that gate as well," he murmured. "Ah, that feels delightful." I was massaging the muscles under his shoulder blades, kneading the tenseness out of them. "I fear nonetheless I shall be sore tomorrow, as I'm not used to heaving a heavy shield about. It strained my left arm."

"Did you see . . . ?"

"I recognized no one. They were all strangers to me." He stretched and arched his back. "It is odd, how they knew about the weakness in the western wall," he mused. "Ordinarily one would not expect an attack there, as it is so close to the Scaean Gate and the Great Tower. Not unless they somehow knew of the vulnerability there."

"As if someone told them," I said.

"It is not visible from the other side," he said. "No one would have reason to suspect it is thin and weak there. Perhaps a seer—"

"Or perhaps something less than a seer, just an ordinary traitor," I said. "Were any Trojans captured today?"

"None that I know of," said Paris.

"Good. For a man does not have to be a traitor to tell what he knows, if he is tortured enough."

Paris slid out from under my hands and sat up. "Torture? Do your countrymen torture captives?"

"They claim they do not, but why, then, do the prisoners we capture often kill themselves?"

"Let no Trojan fall into their hands, then," he finally said.

The Greek commander, Agamemnon, did not hesitate to sacrifice his own daughter, so he was hardly likely to treat enemy prisoners gently. No one should fall into his hands. What a pity my sister had.

❖ XLVI ❖

We shall proceed regardless!" Hecuba announced her decision to Priam and dared him to countermand her order. "Our daughter shall not be robbed of her day by the Greeks."

In the days just before the assault, Laodice had at last found her bridegroom: Helicaon, the son of Antenor. Priam and Antenor had made the arrangements, and Laodice was giddy with relief. She was now eighteen years old and seemed to have longed for marriage the entire time I had been in Troy. Helicaon was a winsome, if perpetually disheveled young man. She probably had visions of transforming him into a replica of his fastidious father.

But all that was before the battle around our walls, was before more Trojan blood had been spent, before our wounded hobbled through the streets. Thus Hecuba's resolution was a surprise.

"But the people . . ." Priam said. "Might it not seem a mockery to them, after our losses?"

"No! It will serve to show them we in Troy do not buckle or break under our losses."

Laodice turned to me. "Helen, you shall help me choose my gown, select my jewels." Her eyes still held that reverence that I wished would abate, as it caused jealousy in the family.

Jewels . . . I thought of the strange jewel Menelaus had bequeathed to me, with its threatening message. *For Helen, my wife, that she may count the cost of her love.*

Love of whom? Himself? Paris? In any case, I had left the brooch in its box.

"Yes, yes, of course," I said. "But Ilona has exquisite taste in jewels. I am sure she—"

"I want *your* help," she said stubbornly.

Now at high noon we stood in Priam's courtyard to begin the betrothal ceremony. Outside, we could hear the shouts of the people, who sounded even more defiant than Hecuba. They cheered for the brave king and queen and their celebration in the face of danger.

In Troy, the betrothal was the most binding and solemn ceremony, rather than the wedding. And they had other special rituals as well: seven flowers from seven hillsides, seven wines from seven vineyards, seven waters from seven sacred springs. All these were mixed and handed around in a confusing medley of chants and gestures that comprised the Trojan bond of commitment.

Rather than the fragrant, floating gowns they usually wore, the women were attired in coarse, undyed wool. This was Laodice's own touch.

{ 381 }

"This is a war wedding and we must dress accordingly," she had said. She also asked the men to wear the tunics and cloaks they used in the field. So we were a dull-hued group, the only bright colors the red of Cassandra's and Helenus's hair and the glow of amethyst, amber, and gold on necks, ears, and arms.

Everyone was there. There must have been well over a hundred people, since the elders, councilmen, cousins, and half-siblings were included. I wondered about the bastards and other wives of Priam. In all the time I had been here, I still had never formally met them, so that even if they were here today, I would never recognize them. I assumed Hecuba would not tolerate the presence of the other wives, at least not on this day, but their sons might be another matter.

"As you share with us the joy of our betrothal, we share with you the pain of your casualties," said Helicaon. "We do not hold it lightly." He himself had been out in the field, but returned safe from the fray.

"Let us contribute!" cried Troilus, from the thick of the crowd. "Let us sacrifice for the cause!" He strode forward and grabbed a bread basket off the feast table, dumping the loaves out. "Men and women of Troy! Your gold and jewels!" He peeled off a gleaming arm bracelet and threw it in the basket. Someone else snatched the basket and tossed a ring into it. More baskets followed, and soon they were heaped full of treasure, the women competing to see who could strip off necklaces and earrings the fastest.

Paris pulled off his arm cuff and added it to the collection. I wondered if I should slip away and get the brooch from Menelaus. It would be an ironic use for it.

"To them it is a game." Hector spoke quietly next to me. "They do not understand. Not yet." He sounded weary. "But we do, do we not, Helen?"

I stepped back so that we would be less likely to be overheard. Paris was talking eagerly to Helenus and did not notice.

"I am not sure I know what you mean," I whispered.

"You know the men who have come here, what they are capable of. I know the man I faced outside—Achilles. Now I dread what I know must come."

"Troy can rely on your courage," I said. Even as I said them, the words sounded a sop to a child.

"You disappoint me," he said. "Do not mouth token, pretty words. You know the truth." He looked sadly at the excited crowd, reveling in their light and voluntary sacrifices. "Let them have their hour of play. The other hours will follow soon enough."

Laodice looked blissfully up at Helicaon, her future settled at last. There are certain women who cannot rest until they are married; there are others who cannot rest until they are free. Helicaon seemed unaware that he had just delivered Laodice from her restlessness, and stood grinning from having too much wine, swaying a bit.

Deiphobus drifted by, arm in arm with the old councilor Clytius. Together they cast lascivious eyes at me, the exact same look, one eye surrounded by wrinkles and the other not. Deiphobus always made me shudder.

The treasure baskets were listing under their contents, the flower garlands were drooping, and the wine was running low. The celebration drew to its natural close, and people were drifting away, when we heard a tumult outside. A huge crowd was surging up toward the portico, gesturing and crying out that someone had a message for Helen.

"Bring him in, then!" said Priam, addressing them from the portico.

"He's not in the city, he stands outside the walls and calls for Helen, queen of Sparta."

"Bid him deliver his message and be gone, then," said Priam. "On my daughter's betrothal day, I'll not—"

"He'll speak only to Helen. If she does not appear on the walls, tomorrow he'll lob fiery arrows into the city."

"Shoot him!"

"We can't, he's protected by a gigantic shield that's as tall as he is and half circular like a tower."

Ajax! Ajax had come before the walls of Troy to speak to me. But Ajax was not a man of words, or even of thoughts.

"I'll go," I said. I did not wish to have Laodice's day, even the very end of it, interrupted or spoiled.

"Not alone," said Paris, stepping beside me.

When we reached the walls near the Scaean Gate, I saw the Ajax shield down on the field, looking like a little fortress. I stood on the broad top of the wall and cried out, "Helen, princess of Troy, is here. Speak!"

"I speak only to Helen, queen of Sparta!" A dreadfully familiar voice rang out from behind the shield.

"Then you have come in vain, for there is no such woman here."

"Oh, I think there is, lady, and I think she is speaking now." Agamemnon stepped out from behind the shield.

His stocky, truculent body, his cocked, arrogant head—I had hoped never to see them again. Time had done nothing to make them less repulsive to me. A horrid laugh followed his words.

"The queen of Sparta is no more," I insisted, keeping my voice steady. Hordes of Trojans were lined up along the walls listening, but Agamemnon stood alone on the plain.

"Indeed not, for she killed herself from shame over you."

But I already knew that, and he could not add to my sorrow. I did not answer.

"And the present queen of Sparta is killing herself of shame as well," he bellowed.

Still I did not answer, but stood as still as possible, as if by not moving I could dismiss him.

"Do you wonder if your brothers are out there in my army? Coming for you? Do you think they'll rescue you when Menelaus seeks his revenge? Well, lady, look no more for them, for they rest beneath the earth of Sparta!"

I felt myself move, now, felt as if I would tumble from the walls. Paris steadied me.

"Your mother is dead, your brothers are dead, your daughter has been taken away to Mycenae, and your husband hates you and means to destroy you. So think upon what you have wrought for the sake of that slight man standing by your side!"

Instead of answering him, I turned to the archers in the tower. "Shoot him if you can, for the coward hides behind the shield of another and greater warrior, cowering like a dog!"

At that Agamemnon bellowed again, but ducked his head behind the shield. A roar of laughter came from the watching Trojans.

"See how he slinks and trembles," said Paris, grabbing a bow from one of the wall archers and quickly fitting it with an arrow. He sent it flying, where it glanced off the edge of the Ajax shield with a hollow ring. Agamemnon shrank down to avoid it.

Paris sent a second arrow hurtling toward the shield, where it stuck in the thick bullhide, trembling.

Just then a chariot raced up, driven by a ferocious charioteer. Agamemnon jumped into it, securing the shield behind him; the chariot rumbled away, its wheels sending up swirls of dust. The shield faced us like a wall. Paris attempted to shoot high, so that the flight-arc of the arrow would over-reach the shield and land inside it, but they were too far away.

"A coward's address, and a coward's retreat," cried Paris to the crowd. "Such is the mettle of the high commander of the enemy army."

The crowd laughed hysterically and cheered.

But, alone in our quarters, I wept. My brothers, my dear brothers gone . . . How? How had they died? Together, in an accident or battle? Separately, from illness?

"It may not be true," said Paris, knowing why I wept without my saying a word. "He is a liar, we know that. He said what was most calculated to wound you."

"It is true about my mother," I said.

"He may have compounded truths with lies. After all, he lured his own daughter to her doom with a lie about marrying Achilles."

And could it be true about Hermione? Sent to Mycenae? "Hermione . . ."

"Your sister loves her, and it may be better for her to be with a woman who will speak kindly of you," said Paris. "Helen, you have paid dearly for coming with me. Would you take it back, knowing what you now know?" He drew me close to him, as easily as pulling a feather. I felt as insubstantial as one.

"No," I said. "If I were standing with you in the moonlight in the court-yard in Sparta again, and Aeneas had gone to ready the chariots, and I could say, *No, depart without me*—I would not. Rather I would say, even more strongly, *Let us mount the chariots and be gone.*"

"The road was rough and dangerous from that first descent," he said. "We have, it seems, been pursued and fleeing ever since."

But the memories were warm ones. "Cranae—the islands—into the gates of Troy—I thought we were safe at last." Now the warmth was replaced by a spreading chill, as if Troy were suddenly enveloped by a creeping mist.

"We are safe," he assured me.

I did not, would not tell him that Hector felt otherwise.

That night, unable to sleep, pictures of Polydeuces and Castor careening through my mind, I stole away from our bed. One never feels more awake and sleepless than lying alert beside a slumbering companion.

I roamed the chambers, coming at last to the one where my empty loom stood. Now, suddenly, I knew the pattern I would create upon it. I would show both sides of my life, make them one by weaving them into one design. Until I had confronted Agamemnon on the walls, I had thought my old life was no longer a part of me. Now I knew that I would forever be Helen of Sparta as well as Helen of Troy. Within Helen there could be many Helens. Only by admitting the Spartan Helen into my presence again could she be rendered harmless.

I would—I was absorbed as I sketched out the design in my mind— make the outer borders of the tapestry Sparta, encircled on the outer rim by the Eurotas, using gray-blue thread. The inner circle, a clear and brighter blue, would be the sea between Sparta and Troy, and the heart of the weaving would be Troy, with its citadel in the center. And hovering at the rim of these worlds would be Persephone and Aphrodite, who held me in their watch.

I must not forget. I must capture it all now, for in the morning it would fade, and it was so clear now. I fumbled for the pieces of broken pottery we kept for such use, and in the dim light of a dying oil lamp I traced out the design, the design that would knit the broken pieces of Helen into a whole.

Sunlight and a gentle touch on my shoulder woke me. Paris was standing beside me in the early morning.

"I am here," he said. He did not say, *Do not grieve,* or *Put it from your mind.* He knew me so perfectly he knew that would be impossible.

❖ XLVII ❖

For the following days, all was quiet. The Greeks disappeared behind their line of ships—where our spies reported they were building a defensive wall— and it would have been easy to pretend they were not there. But the days of pretending were over.

Priam called many assemblies, and let everyone speak freely. One or two voices were raised questioning what the Greeks seemed to be aware of. How did they know about the party en route to Dardanos? How did they know about the weak spots in the western wall? Spies must have penetrated.

Priam directed workmen to strengthen the western wall immediately. We had been spared a dreadful fate that would have been due to our earlier neglect.

Everyone agreed that the heated sand had worked impressively well, and that the archers in the towers had taken a toll on the enemy. Gelanor reported that his work on insect bombs was proceeding well. He expected to have clay and straw containers full of bees, wasps, scorpions, and stinging ants ready to fling at the adversary soon.

Achilles had made a frightening appearance as he descended on the field with fury. His speed was especially startling: he seemed almost to run without ever touching the earth, skimming above it, disdaining it. But Hector pointed out that it would be easy to ascribe outlandish characteristics to anyone who behaved unpredictably. The truth was that after a few encounters even the supposedly unpredictable became a known thing. Achilles was fast; we knew that now. He could not surprise us with it again.

Priam's council diverged in their advice about future preparations. Everyone agreed that we had acquitted ourselves well in our first encounter, but the true test was yet to come. At what point should we send for the allies? Now we were outnumbered by the Greeks but the allies would almost even things out. However, sending for them would require feeding and housing them, swelling the numbers within our walls. Were we ready for that?

Priam's sons began to quarrel amongst themselves. Hector was resolute that we should fight each battle as fate presented it, but not before its time. Deiphobus wanted to lead an attack on the Greeks before they finished building their defensive wall, to take the battle to them. Helenus advised caution, to respond only to direct provocation and perhaps negotiate before that. Young Troilus was eager to join the fighting, although Priam had forbidden him to. He was too young, his father said. He was the joy of the old age of his mother. And he needed to be protected, because . . . because of a prophecy about him which Priam kept a secret. Troilus, standing up in the assembly one day, challenged his father to reveal this prophecy that seemed to bar him from participating in the war. Priam refused. He said our enemies already knew too much, and as for himself, he would hold the prophecy close to his heart. Troilus had declared that that was unacceptable. Unacceptable or not, his father replied, that was the way it must be.

In the gloomy half-light of our megaron, in the time of year when to light the fire would make the chamber so hot it would drive us out, we spread ourselves around its dead hearth. I had ordered some stands of incense to provide a feeling of closeness without heat, and had had armloads of meadow flowers arranged in vases at the four corners of the great hearth, guarding each of the pillars. Paris was languishing on his chair; this idleness was killing him. He needed to be able to come and go, fight or not fight. Troilus sprawled at his feet.

"I wish I were you," he said, brushing his long straight hair off his forehead. "You were born just enough ahead of me that you are free."

Paris laughed. "The lament of the younger," he said. "No one wants to be the younger, but in the end the younger is the best off."

"I cannot see how that could be so," muttered Troilus. "There is nothing enviable about being younger. They always come last."

"Or first. The young ones always have a special place."

"Bah." Troilus set his wine cup down. "There is nothing special about it."

"I am the youngest," I said. "I always liked being youngest. I could watch my brothers and my sister and chart a different course. In a sense, they tried out different clothes for me and found which ones fit."

"None of their clothes—or lives—would have fit you," said Troilus. "That is hardly a fair test."

"Troilus," said Paris. "Keep yourself safe here. Why should you endanger yourself on account of my—my—actions?" Was he about to say *folly*?

"Your actions are now beyond you. They involve us all."

A heavy silence descended. Troilus was right.

Hyllus entered the megaron. He waved at us; he came and went cheerfully, in spite of the fact that his father was hated here and his kinsfolk seemed to regard him as an evil omen. He joined us at the dead ashes of the hearth; indeed, he started drawing patterns in them with a stick.

"Do you know the prophecy about me?" Troilus looked imploringly at Paris.

"Yes," said Paris.

"Will you reveal it to me?"

"No. It is a dreary one, and would sadden you."

"Nothing would sadden me more than having to flounder about blindly under the net of a prophecy I know not, but which others know all too well. Is it not an insult to me? Why should others know it and I, the focus of it, know it not?"

"Often if someone knows a prophecy he for some reason brings it about," said Paris.

"Let me be free of it!" cried Troilus, leaping up. "I promise to avoid it, but first I must know it!" His freckled face grew red with anguish.

"Very well, then," said Paris. "The prophecy is that if Troilus reaches the age of twenty, Troy will never fall."

Troilus smiled. "Ah! I am fourteen already. So I should refrain from joining the fighting for another six years."

"Yes," said Paris. "Is that so very much to ask?"

"I want to fight! Must I wait six years?"

"If you do not want to be the cause of your city's downfall," said Paris.

"That is not fair!" he wailed. "I am not even a soldier yet. Why should the city's fate rest on me?"

"No reason," I could not resist saying, as a person teased and dangled by the gods. "The gods do not use reason in making their vile demands upon us."

Troilus propped himself on his elbows, sprawling out before the hearth. His legs were very long, and he was still growing. He might turn out to be the tallest of all Priam's sons. "We used to train the horses together," he said to Paris. "Now it isn't even safe to ride out on the plain," he lamented. "All I can do is take the horses for a bit of exercise by the springhouse. Hardly any sport at all. I hate my life!"

"Never say that," said Paris. "It is evil to say that." He paused, then leaned over and ruffled Troilus's hair. "Troilus, be patient. This war cannot last long. As others have said, the Greeks will tire of camping by our seashore and go home by winter. Their attempts at a siege are pitiful; we still come and go from the side of Troy facing Mount Ida. It is not so bad."

Troilus sighed. "I suppose not, but still I hate it!"

His words were so common for a young person I could not help but laugh. They all say they hate their lives, when what they really mean is that they cannot wait to step from the chamber of childhood into the arena of adulthood.

After Troilus left—as a youngster he still lived in the palace of his parents, not having his own apartments yet—I set down my wine and embraced Paris from behind as he sat in his chair. He was only three years older than Troilus but seemed a completely different creature. Perhaps it was due to his responsibilities as a herdsman long before he came to the palace, when he had had to defend his herds with his life. Perhaps it was due to his grace in forgiving his father and mother for casting him out. Whatever it was, for all his seventeen years he was a man. And more of a man than Achilles, with his bulging muscles and special armor, although they were within a year or so of age.

I turned his head around, slowly, to face mine. My love for him seemed boundless. He was the true treasure of Troy. He should succeed Priam as king. Of all Priam's sons, he was the only one who had faced true adversity. I knew this was the voice of love speaking in my heart, but so be it.

"Paris, my dearest," I murmured, taking his face in my hands.

He laughed nervously, glancing at Hyllus—so silent we hardly knew he was there.

"I shall say good night," said Hyllus, jumping up, embarrassed. Quickly he scurried out of the chamber, bowing before he left, stumbling on the doorstep.

"Farewell," said Paris, nodding toward him. He laughed. "Now our observer is gone," he said. "He is so quiet, one forgets about him."

His words stirred a thought in me, but it was unformed. "Perhaps that is the purpose," I said. I was uncomfortable in his presence, yet he seemed harmless. Perhaps I did not like any unnecessary persons about.

"He is a sad boy," said Paris. "He has abuse heaped on him because of his father, whose actions are hardly his fault."

I swung around and sat on his lap. "Do you know what your most noble trait is?" I asked him, kissing his cheeks, first one, then the other. "Your feeling for others."

He laughed. "That is hardly one of the known virtues of a warrior."

"I am not speaking of a warrior, but of the virtue of a man."

Safe within our lovely chamber, we clung together. There had been no question as to which bedchamber to seek. In defiance of custom, we had only one: ours. Unlike other Trojan palaces, there was no prince and princess's bedchambers, but only a single lovers' retreat. The builders had complied with our odd request and we had never regretted it.

"My love, had we those extra suite of chambers, we would never use them," said Paris. "An unnecessary expense!"

"I cannot bear to be apart from you," I whispered in his ear. It was true. Paris illuminated my world, he lighted the corners of myself that had lain dark.

"Nor I, you," he murmured. "And we need never be parted."

To think that had I listened to reason, I might be still in Sparta and he here—I unable to reach out and touch him, unable to hear his voice, unable to see those glorious eyes, so young and shining and filled with joy.

"Paris," I murmured. "Let them vanish."

"Who?" he asked, his lips beneath mine.

"All our enemies," I said.

"Then that is everyone," he said. "But I care not. They are all misguided, or jealous, or meddlers, or stupid. Our love will live long after they have gone to dust."

I embraced him. It was for this I loved him. He was so jubilantly, so joyously of the moment. And the moment was all we—anyone—truly had: a succession of moments, a triumphal march of them, to create a life beyond compare.

Troy remained quiet. The Greeks had seemingly melted away after that first encounter. It was beguiling to think that they were refitting their ships to depart, that the danger was past. Still the Trojans guarded the ramparts, and the strengthening of the western wall went forward.

Inside the walls, in the heat of summer, we curdled like milk held too long. In the stifling houses quarrels brewed and then exploded out into the streets—personal quarrels that had nothing to do with the Greeks. People pent up too long in one another's company, unless they be lovers, soon find it unbearable. The only people who thrived on the stillness were the old councilors, who shuffled through the streets every day to Priam's council chamber, invigorated by a standstill that allowed them to play at war. When there is no action, all men are warriors.

There comes a day each summer that whispers perfection, says, *Remember me*, and you do, deep in the winter. The sky is achingly blue, the wind kindly, the warmth pervasive and lulling. On such days you lean on a windowsill and surrender to the sun on your face, eyes closed. Sometimes this day comes early in the season, sometimes at its very end. This day in Troy visited us just as the crones had begun to speak of autumn.

I had been showing several women my loom and the emerging pattern. Evadne had glided amongst us, showing us different qualities of the wools—how one was thick and wiry and used to best advantage to depict water or grass, another so fine and thin it could show hair or slender fingers. Andromache was there, and the sisters Laodice and Ilona. Polyxena was missing; near to Troilus in age, they kept company much of the time, although lately Hyllus had invited himself to be with them more than they liked. Still, they did not want to hurt his feelings, so they often included him.

Cassandra was not interested in weaving, nor in women's matters, and I never expected her to be there, but I missed little Polyxena, especially since she had helped me select the scarlet wool. I wondered where she was, but on such a lovely day she would naturally be out-of-doors.

We found ourselves drawn to the window, leaving the looms. We, too, should go outdoors, or at least into the streets of Troy. I was longing to walk once more in the countryside, but that must wait. Below us the city lay, fawn-colored and quiet in the noonday sun.

"Ladies, let us go to the highest path, the one circling the temple, and taste the sweet wind," I said. "On such a day—"

A piercing cry, seemingly from one of the courtyards, shattered the calm. It sounded as if someone had been impaled, had had a stake passed through his body. It rose to a scream, then whimpered away and vanished, as though the breath were sucked out into a final gasp.

A horrible accident! Some child had fallen on his father's spear, or tumbled from a rooftop and crashed onto a stone step. Now another wail. It was the mother, shrieking all the louder in the silence surrounding her child. I grabbed Andromache's upper arm, as if that would make it not so, undo whatever had happened.

Without a word, we all rushed for the steps. The screaming kept on, and now more voices joined the first one. Outside, we looked around at the empty streets—people were usually inside at noonday. Now that we were at the ground level, the voices seemed to be coming from lower down in the city, near the east gate. We hurried down, passing side streets and curious people, now drawn out to see what had happened.

"Here, it's here!" said Laodice, turning the corner where the street led down to the east gate. Now the sound had changed to a roar. We rounded the last house shielding us from the open space around the gate, and beheld Hecuba screaming, her hands on her face, kneeling by a still form, its legs splayed awkwardly. Bending over the person was little Polyxena, her rounded back shaking with sobs. Hyllus stood by, white-faced. Even as we approached, the crowd swelled, and high keening filled the air. Paris and Hector appeared, pushing people out of the way to get to their mother. I saw Hector bend down and look, then swiftly embrace Hecuba and try to turn her face away. Paris clasped Polyxena and tried to comfort her.

Priam shoved his way through, parting the crowd, running the last few steps. His deep pain and anger was in the roar with which he met the fallen body. As he fell to his knees, we caught a glimpse of the face—that of Troilus—turned to the sky, his fair hair gleaming like gold under the sun.

I stumbled toward him, closing and opening my eyes, hoping each time that when I opened them the sight would vanish, or Troilus would move. But he did not. His arms were flung out on either side, and Paris, weeping, straightened his legs and arranged them neatly. He clasped the feet and kissed them, then made a precious bundle of them and lay over them—as if he could warm them back into life.

A dull red stain covered the front of his tunic. He had been speared, or stabbed. This was no accident.

Polyxena gave mournful gasps as she fought for breath, and words tumbled out—*he did it, he was waiting*—

Laodice embraced her. "Peace, peace," she murmured. "Breathe slowly. Slowly. There, there."

"Who has done this?" Hector's voice was as cold as the waters of the Styx.

"It was that man, that Greek—" Hyllus stood trembling. "We went to the springhouse to water the horses, and—"

"All three of you?" barked Hector. "Troilus took his sister? I thought we had forbidden even Troilus to go!"

Polyxena's voice rose faintly. "I wanted to go. I m-made him take me. I am so tired of staying inside the walls."

"You disobeyed." Hecuba could barely form words, she was still shaking so hard. "Both of you. You knew you were not to go outside. And now . . ." She sank to her knees again and fell across Troilus, covering his bloody chest.

"What man are you talking about?" Hector asked. "At the springhouse?"

"That fierce one. He was waiting for us, hiding on one side of the springhouse. I filled a water jar, and Troilus was just leading his horses to the trough when he—he sprang out at us. He leapt like a panther, and Troilus dropped the reins of the horses and ran, but he caught him up and—" She burst into tears again, shaking her head.

"That man? That fierce man?" Hector looked around. "Does no one know his name? Or do you know it and dare not speak it?"

Oh, let it not be Menelaus!

"It was Achilles," whispered Hyllus. Then he sank to his knees and, trembling, tenderly wiped the forehead of his slain friend.

Overhead the perfect summer day looked down on the sacrifice, on the young man who loved horses and meadows and was cheated of all his summers to come, and even the rest of this day.

The streets of Troy were silent in the dawn as we walked by the litter bearing the body of Troilus to the funeral bier. They would hold the customary rites outside the city walls, and woe be to any Greek who sought to interrupt them.

"We will kill them to a man," said Hector, his deep voice so low it sounded like the rumbling of carts over stones. A full contingent of armed men accompanied us, protecting us on all sides. They had already guarded the building of the great funeral pyre, which used some of our precious wood stored for winter, and as we approached it I could see it rearing up against the sky. Such a big mound for the slight young man.

With all solemnity, he was taken gently from the litter and placed on the rough platform waiting on top. They folded his arms over his chest and arranged his robe. I saw his poor white feet, those feet that had rushed down the streets of Troy to be the first to greet Paris upon his return, sticking stiffly out from the platform, which was too short for him.

It had been two days since his death. He had lain on a ceremonial bed, surrounded by ritual mourners singing funeral dirges for the first day. Those singers formed a procession to accompany the litter to the pyre, but now they melted away, their task done. The real mourning would be done by those of us who loved him, and it would not follow a ritual, but come and go in waves.

The sacrificial sheep and dogs were slain at the pyre, their bodies laid around its base, their blood poured out. Then a basket was passed amongst us, and we put the locks of hair we had cut earlier into it, so that they might be placed on the pyre as well. Jars filled with honey and oil were set around the pyre. And I myself had brought something to add to the pyre, to be consumed as an offering and a penitence.

Priam, shrouded and tall, approached the pyre. He threw back his hood; the just-setting sun illuminated his lined face. His so wrinkled, Troilus's so smooth—death was greedy, to want to consume only the fairest.

"I call upon all the gods to avenge this cruel death," he said. "I beg the lord and lady of the underworld to receive him kindly. Be gentle with him.

He is not—he is not used to the dark." His voice broke, and he turned away quickly to take the burning torch and thrust it into the wood to start the fire.

Hecuba took his hand, then, and drew him away, and together, embracing, they watched the flames catch and the wood crackle. The fire burned quickly, high, and hot. It overcame the sun and blotted it out.

"Now his soul is released," said Paris. "It is freed from his body." He wept. "But it had no wish to be freed! It was happy where it was!"

The pyre would burn all night. In the morning we would go and extinguish the last of the smoldering fire with wine. Then, when the embers cooled, the bones would be collected and placed in an urn; the urn would be buried in the sacred tomb. In normal times there would be funeral games held in his honor. But these were not normal times.

As we made our way back through the city, I saw red spots on the front of my bodice—drops that gleamed wetly. I touched one and my finger came away slick with what looked like blood. I tasted it and it was salty and metallic like blood. But had I cut myself? Then I remembered. The brooch! I had worn the hateful stone that Menelaus gave me, meaning to fling it into Troilus's funeral pyre to rid myself of it and as a symbol that I repudiated the Greeks and their deed. Instead, overcome with sorrow about Troilus, I had forgotten, and now I still wore it.

I touched it, expecting to find it had a sharp edge that had pricked me. There was nothing, but it was slippery with the blood. The blood seemed—but that was impossible—to be oozing from the stone itself.

Returning to the palace and parting from the others, I quickly sought my chambers and stripped off the gown. Evadne would know how to remove the stains on the white wool. Evadne knew all such things. I would ask her, and—as I held the gown up to examine it, I could not see the stains. I turned the gown around, inside out. They were gone, and the wool as white as new.

How could they vanish like that? I had felt the sticky stains, I had even tasted them. The brooch had been wet—

The cursed brooch! Paris was right, it was evil! Menelaus had given it to me for some fell purpose of his own.

As I was smoothing out the gown, studying it in bewilderment, Evadne slipped in.

"That brooch—I was fool enough to wear it—I never should have touched it—but I wanted to have it consumed in flames, destroy it—"

She clasped my hands and held them in hers, removing them from the gown I was still stroking. "Or destroy Menelaus?" she asked. "Destroy him in your own mind, purge him out of it?"

"He isn't in my mind—"

"But he is in your past."

"Yes, of course, I know that!" What was her point?

"And in your present."

"He's here in Troy, yes." Her words seemed absolutely aimless. "And this is the present. But he is not in *my* present, nor in my mind."

"He is in your future."

"No, that is impossible."

"It is written. And I see it. The brooch sees it."

I thrust the brooch into her hand, pushing it there. "Nothing is written unless I write it," I said. "Take the foul thing, confine it in its box."

But in not ordering her to destroy it, did I not thereby confirm her words?

Troilus was holding a banquet—his funeral banquet. His bones had been gathered and placed in the urn and conveyed in yet another solemn procession through the streets of Troy to his hastily erected tomb. Now his spirit would preside as host at a feast on the third day after his death, as Trojan custom decreed.

Because he was too young to have his own quarters, the banquet must be held in his father's palace, which carried its own sorrow—he had never grown old enough to leave the house of his mother and father.

As we filed into the great chamber, we must first be purified; Theano, the priestess of Athena, poured sacred water over our hands and washed away our inherent contamination from the funeral. Then we were directed to take our flower garlands. A basket of them was placed near the door. Paris and I bent to take them. The leaves and bright summer meadow flowers, gathered at peril outside the walls, seemed a fitting tribute for the boy who had lost his life in those very meadows.

Priam was waiting to receive us. The fire was out in his hearth, but the solemn scent of myrrh, perfume of the dead, filled the air. By his side Hecuba stood rigidly, looking as lifeless and wooden as the Pallas Athena statue in the temple.

All their children came to the feast. The ranking Trojans came, too. Priam beckoned us all to the long table, where we would sit according to rank. It was a rough wood one—or rather, several joined together, as no table existed that could serve so many people. He stood not at the place of honor but rather to one side.

"I call upon my son Troilus to join us," said Priam. His normally robust voice was faint. "Son, come from the fields of Asphodel, come from the shadows of Hades, which you have not yet passed so deeply into. We await you." He indicated the empty chair at the place of honor.

A profound and heavy presence filled the room. Priam closed his eyes. When he opened them, he held out his hands and said, "My dear family, and my most esteemed Trojans —I, Troilus, bid you seat yourselves as my guests."

In silence, we took our places. Slaves came bearing platters of fresh-roasted kid. Others followed with wine and pitchers of water to thin it. The funeral dish containing fruits and nuts and roasted asphodel roots was brought in. We would take it to the tomb later.

Slowly people began to talk, although guardedly.

"The memory of Troilus will live forever," said Antenor, a few places down from me. His voice was soothing.

"Troilus would have grown up to be as great a warrior as Hector," said Panthous, the nervous councilor who knew more about the engineering of gates than of any other matter.

"Troilus was unsurpassed," said Antimachus, smiling. He raised his cup to him.

"To the glory of Troilus!" cried Deiphobus, waving his arm and downing a cup of wine—not his first, all too obviously.

"We must not speak ill of him," said Paris to me. "He is present here, hence we can only praise him." Suddenly he stood up and looked up and down the table. "You speak of the future of Troilus, what he would have been. But I say that is not necessary. He was perfect as he was. My younger brother, and I loved him." He sat back down and tears swam in his eyes.

"You speak true." The high, distinctive voice of Hecuba. "There is no need to invoke what he might have been. Had the gods permitted it, we would have been content to have him forever as he was—a boy enveloped in sun and gladness."

But the gods had not permitted it, I cried to myself. They never do.

The final dish was brought out, figs and pomegranate—precious offerings from our limited stores.

Priam rose again, raised his helping. "Pomegranates are sacred to you, O dread lords of the realms of death. We offer you this sacrifice from our very substance, which cannot easily be replenished."

We all partook of the dish, the sweetness of the figs muting the astringent sting of the pomegranates.

Priam took a smoking brazier and walked slowly around the great table. "Troilus, tears blind me, and I am loath to let you leave us. I would keep you here forever. But that would be cruel. We must release you to your new home, the home where we will join you. We will come to you, but you will not return to us. And so we must relinquish you to the gods below. Farewell, my dear son." He wiped his hooded eyes with his bended arm and set the brazier down.

Still silent, we followed Priam and Hecuba out of the palace into the street as they bore offerings to Troilus. Torches lit our way, and I was unable to see Priam placing the tributes on the tomb, so many people were crowding around it.

The ceremony over, Hector suddenly addressed the company. "I bid you welcome to my home," he said. "All is in readiness. I wish us to gather to further honor my lost brother."

Now, the shade of Troilus no longer actually amongst us, we hurried to Hector's palace. Torches were blazing, servants were waiting to provide more substantial food, and wine was to flow unchecked. We removed our funeral garlands and laid them in the basket provided.

Life thronged Hector's chambers, replacing the death pacing Priam's. We are still here, the company promised themselves. We are here to defend Troy, to rout our enemies. We must do whatever is required of us, but we must prevail. We cannot fail. We fight to protect our very lives, our survival, indeed, our very existence. The unspoken chorus was this: We have never had to defend ourselves thus, not in this fashion. Can we truly do this? Are we able?

❧ XLVIII ❧

Hector had prepared for the company; as the heir and Troilus's oldest brother, it was his obligation. His palace was as he himself: traditional and strong. Before we had built ours, his was the finest on the citadel. It still would be considered in the best taste.

"Tastes change," Hector had said diplomatically when he first beheld ours. Andromache told me privately she liked it, and wished they might have a chamber or two without the dreary decorative warriors marching across the walls. Now she beckoned us into the megaron—one like every other megaron I had ever stood in.

Show me a man's wife, a man's chariot, and a man's house, and I can tell you everything about him, Gelanor had once claimed. Now I looked at Andromache and the megaron and thought, Yes, they reflect Hector: conventional but always tasteful. Hector would never be embarrassed by a wife's behavior—he would not choose a wife capable of it.

"We gather here in remembrance of our dear Troilus," said Hector, holding his hands aloft. "A funeral feast requires special foods and time-honored rituals, and we have duly performed those. Now we gather together to comfort one another on our loss, in whatever manner deeply calls to us." He indicated the slaves bearing cups, wine, and food. "These will be at the table for us to partake of as we wish."

Everyone moved toward the table, although none of us were likely to be hungry.

Paris saw Polyxena standing momentarily alone and, tugging on my hand, drew near to her. She was standing very quietly, clutching a goblet—but more as something to hold than because she wished to drink the wine—and staring blankly at the company.

"Polyxena," said Paris, attempting to embrace her. "You saw what no one, least of all you, should have seen. It should have fallen on broader and older shoulders."

"In a dreadful way I am thankful I was there, although it will scar my memories forever." Her voice was so soft I could barely hear it, but it drew me closer to her.

"I should have been with him," Paris said. "I should have been in your place."

She smiled, a very slight curve of her lips. "But why in the world would you have been? Troilus and I were companions and spent much time together. It was natural that I was the one there."

"As you say," said Paris. "But I grieve for it."

"Do you think that, had you been there, you could have prevented it?" Her sweet voice twined itself around the words. "I tell you, he was waiting for Troilus. He meant to cut him down. It was a mission, not a chance happening.

Somehow he knew we would be there . . ." Her voice trailed off. "And to what purpose?" she suddenly cried. "As if Troilus were any threat to anyone!"

A shadowy presence appeared by our sides, as if drawn by our voices. It was Helenus, the peculiar twin of Cassandra. He had the same red hair, the same pale white skin, the same flat pitiless eyes. "I hear you speaking of Troilus," he said. Even his voice, no doubt meant to be soothing and beguiling, sounded more like the soft sound a snake makes as it slides over rocks and pebbles—dry, rustling, menacing. Did he cultivate it as part of his stance as a seer?

"It is natural we speak of him," Paris said. "This gathering is in his honor, and we have just interred his bones."

"But I heard you ask something—or do my ears fail me?—about why Achilles would have determined to kill Troilus. There is—there was—this prophecy—"

"Do not speak it!" Paris clamped down on Helenus's shoulder. "It is over."

"Fulfilled," said Helenus sadly. He breathed out heavily. "Luckily there are others. All must be fulfilled before Troy falls. Troy cannot fall unless the son of Achilles joins the expedition. After that—"

"So one is fulfilled, then," interrupted Polyxena.

Helenus pursed his lips. "Yes, one. But still more stand between us and defeat. The arrows of Heracles, kept by Philoctetes, must be used against us, but Philoctetes has been left behind on the island of Lemnos because of an infected snakebite—thanks to the gods. *He* is not any immediate danger."

"What are the others?" asked Paris.

Suddenly the garrulous Helenus glanced around, alarmed. "Perhaps I should not say. I trust you, but how did Achilles know about Troilus and the prophecy? It was a very private matter. I fear we have an informer in our very midst."

"Whisper in my ear, then," said Paris.

Helenus leaned over, brushing back his limp red hair, and murmured into Paris's ear. I saw Paris frown. "I think these things will never come to pass," he said. I knew I could ask him later in private what they were.

The chamber was now humming with voices; they sounded like the swarming of bees on a warm summer's day. Somewhere outside our walls people could still lie under a tree and listen to real bees. I wondered if Aeneas and his family could. He had been wise to leave Troy and return home to Dardania; they were still free in his land.

A group of the older councilors and warriors were knotted together at the end of the table, and Paris made his way over to them, pulling me along. It was the old war mastiffs, Antimachus, Pandarus, Aesacus, and Panthous. I saw that Antenor, as one who advised peace and negotiations, was at the far corner of the chamber, excluded—or had he excluded himself?

"And I tell you, we need to smash them where they sit, smash them in place. Set fire to their ships!" Antimachus was loud; no worry about spies on his part. "The moon will be full soon and we will have ample light. I say, strike!"

Two sets eager for the full moon: lovers and soldiers. The flooding light could serve many purposes.

Pandarus demurred. "How many could we take on a raiding mission? It is true, we might be able to score some surprise strikes, set fire to a few ships, but then we would be trapped in their camp."

Antimachus snorted. "Send a group, then, that does not expect to return, but can wreak havoc before they are cut down." His feet were already spread wide in a defiant stance. "A well-timed raid can reverse everything," he said. "Let us recruit a band of brave men willing to undertake this. They may save us from further war."

"You will never be able to persuade Priam," said Aesacus.

"Hector, then," said Antimachus. "Let us approach him."

"Priam is still king. It is he who must direct the strategy."

"Strategy is not the province of old men." Antimachus glared at the faces surrounding him as he tiptoed close to treason.

"Old men have sight we may not have," said Pandarus, pulling back from the rim. "We must honor that."

Antimachus shrugged. "Then I want you to remember this, in the days to come: Antimachus advised a quick and preemptive attack, to break their will and spirit." He held up his wide hands. "Anything else is letting the enemy dictate the terms of fighting. It gives them the advantage. You know that siege warfare is ruinously expensive. Our neighbors to the east are experts in it. They use engineers, sappers, battering rams. That is an active siege. The Greeks have not those means. They will resort to a passive siege—encircling us and starving us out. Already their presence has chased away the trade vessels that plied the Hellespont, and ended our trade fair. Do you wish to perish by such lackluster means? Fade away, defeated by a dull army that did nothing but camp in our fields? I say, smash them! And smash them *now*. They will turn tail and run home."

There was murmuring amongst them. His words made sense. Indeed, they were the essence of clever strategic planning. But he was not supreme commander. Hector was, and Hector in turn was subject to Priam. Paris reminded him of this.

"Hector relies altogether too much on individual prowess and bravery," said Antimachus. "I tell you, that is not the way to win wars. It is by outthinking the enemy, anticipating, and then attacking him—fairly or not—in his weakness, with your strength. There are those who say there is no glory in that. I say: Where is the glory in fighting bravely for a lost cause? Use your heads, men, as well as your sword arms!"

Panthous shuffled forward. "I have been working on some new triggering mechanisms for our gates," he told Antimachus. "When the enemy trips them, then the hot sand will pour down."

Antimachus actually laughed. "If the enemy gets inside the gates, it is a bit late. We need to go to *their* gates first. But I thank you, Panthous, for your efforts."

Panthous, in his bumbling fashion, looked perplexed. "But this is an innovative and clever plan," he protested.

"A plan for the timid, cowering behind their walls!" said Antimachus. "You are like a cart with a pair of dull, trained oxen, trained to stay within their old trodden path." He looked around. "Such may be forgivable in a dull beast, with no thought or reason, but for a king, and a people—" He turned abruptly away. His rough words did not disguise his acute distress, his fear.

Hector strode over, just as Antimachus was leaving. "What is it, my good soldiers? I hear dissent."

His very presence, his noble face, seemed to belie the concerns that Antimachus had raised. "What is it?" he pressed.

"Nothing, my lord," said Panthous, spreading his hands wide. "We were but speaking of the dreary fact that the Greeks have chased away the merchants that usually throng our shores this time of year." He laughed. "A minor annoyance, and next year they will be back in force."

Hector smiled and rocked back on his heels, crossing his muscled arms. "Let us hope so, Panthous. Let us hope so."

Exhausted, Paris and I almost crawled onto our bed at home. The entire day had been so filled with pain that I felt buffeted. Had my body absorbed the blows rather than my heart, I would have been covered in bruises. As it was,

I could hardly move. Paris lay flat on his back beside me, staring up at the ceiling.

"It is over," I finally said. He did not reply. "This day has finally closed."

"It will never close," he said. "Troilus will always be missing from our lives." His voice was dull and flat.

"I meant . . . that the worst of it has passed. The funeral, and the feast, where he had to act as host. I *felt* him there in the room, did you?"

"Yes. He was there. And I wanted to pluck him from the air and force him to take fleshly form again. Helen—I killed him. I cannot endure that knowledge."

"Achilles killed him, Paris. Not you."

Paris's eyes filled with tears. "Troilus. Hector told me that when Troilus was a baby, one of his earliest memories was of Hecuba holding him, as he reached out and pulled her hair." He smiled in spite of himself. "She smacked his little hand. She hated it if anyone messed her hair. She still does."

The picture of Troilus as a laughing, happy baby was like a stab. "Paris—if only we had had a child, a boy, like Troilus . . ." Now I ached for that lost son.

"Are you mad?" His voice went from soft to harsh, and he sat up. "So he could get killed, too? Have we not already killed enough people? I tell you, I killed Troilus! For if I had not . . . done what I have done, Achilles would not be here!"

"It is what *we* have done," I said. "Not you alone, but us together. And . . ." Suddenly I felt bereft, unfairly attacked. "My mother killed herself! And my brothers—who knows how they died? I have had more losses than you! And my daughter, I've lost her—"

"We said we were willing to pay the price."

"But you, apparently, weren't!" There, I had said it. He was content with my losses, but now that Troilus was sacrificed, it was a different story.

"I don't think we can ever know a price until we are confronted with it. But now, in this world we have brought about, to have a child, to even think of it . . ." He shook his head. "Oh, Helen, I am sick with grief!"

"I know," I said. "As am I."

"We should be the ones to die, not others. I could more easily die myself."

"Perhaps we will," I said. As if that were any comfort.

As I walked along the ramparts with Gelanor, we spoke of the death of Troilus and Paris's continued gloom. Paris's happy manner had vanished, as if it had only existed in company with Troilus's. Certainly they were the only ones of Priam's sons with glad laughter and flashing smiles, and now Troilus had taken Paris's with him to the underworld. Even Paris's voice had changed, so that when he spoke from another room I did not recognize it. I told Gelanor that Paris was especially haunted by the thought that Troilus had been killed because of the prophecy. Gelanor asked who had known about the prophecy, and I said very few, it was not commonly spoken of. Gelanor thought that the ambush of the party to Dardanos and the obvious knowledge of the weak spot in our western walls, as well as the targeting of Troilus, all pointed to uncanny lucky guesses—too lucky, in fact. He suspected spies. But how had they penetrated our walls?

"Who comes and goes freely? Who is likely to be present when private matters are discussed? Did you speak of the prophecy about Troilus at any time?"

I tried to remember. "Priam refused to speak of it publicly," I said. "As for the scouting party to Dardanos and the weak wall, many people would have known about those things as well."

We turned to look out over the walls; we were looking down over the south slope, where the lower city spread out below us. In the midday sun, the palisade fence and ditch were barely visible, casting no shadows at noon. Far away the faint blue of Mount Ida beckoned. Mount Ida. Oenone. I put her out of my mind.

"These people must be protected," Gelanor said. "They must not be betrayed unto death by a spy—or several spies. I thought I was the spymaster, and now I see I have a rival. Someone in the Greek camp challenges me." He drew his shoulders back. "It is these lives we play for. We must win."

I did not wish to return to the palace, and Paris. These days he sat inside, burnishing his armor, polishing his shield, and evermore refitting his greaves. I would come upon him practicing his sword thrusts, and once I found him stringing his huge bow, his face knotted in the sweaty effort. He meant to fight, and all else had paled before him. He would look up, embarrassed, but there being no place to hide armor or a bow, he had to stand and stare at me defiantly. I would pass silently across the corridor and leave him to his exercises.

I could avoid him and seek the chamber where my loom was waiting. The great picture I was weaving enveloped me and when I began guiding the shuttle across the warp in the pattern I had designed, it was as if I myself had stepped into the story. With great care I wove the blue wool depicting the Eurotas, making it encircle the whole tapestry, as it had encircled my own life as a child. I could see the swans on it again, and the great swan I had beheld that vivid day with Clytemnestra.

Mother. I had begun her outline, but got no further. An outline: that was what she was to me now. And her outline had shimmered and faded and fled, because of me, because of my flight.

Hermione. I had not yet begun her picture on the tapestry. Should I keep her still a child, still with her turtles? The turtles she chose over me.

But no, I must not think that. She asked how long you would be gone, I told myself, and you did not tell her. She thought you were coming back.

I had not thought it would come to this. But then, I did not think. Aphrodite did my thinking. Now she had withdrawn and stranded me here. With Paris, who fretted and wept and regretted his part in this, and had little thought of me. There was no one else here for me. Gelanor, yes, and Evadne, but them I would have had in Sparta.

And you, I thought, brushing the loom, caressing the growing pattern there. You speak to me, you console me. I touched the purple threads with my forehead.

I began avoiding Paris. Or was he avoiding me? We passed one another in the hallways of the palace, smiling, murmuring regrets about having to be at the armorer's or the goldsmith's, or attend upon Hecuba, or inspect horses. Now the wisdom of separate quarters for men and women came home to me; at night we could not pass one another but must light, like weary moths, in the same room. Still it was possible to slide past one another and, even in the same bed, to awaken, backs to one another, one looking east and the other west.

It began to echo my life with Menelaus: the surface politeness, the unruffled demeanor, the cool untouched middle of the bed. And yet it was not the same. I had not been mad for Menelaus, and passion had been absent from the beginning. With Paris now I was ill at ease; his changed manner had left me nervous about causing him distress. Any thoughtless mention of the name Troilus, any accidental humming of a tune connected, in any way, with Troilus, or a thousand other things that had some private meaning to Paris in regards to Troilus, would plunge him into despair—or anger. He was holding me up in the balance with Troilus on the other side, and it seemed that there were days when I weighed lighter than Troilus, when he would have exchanged me for him. Thus the false smiles as we passed one another in silence.

There were no Trojans to whom I could express my unhappiness. Gelanor and Evadne were the only ones to whom I could flee, who could read what was happening without my saying the words, for they had come with me, they had made the journey with me here.

Evadne had rooms in my palace and Gelanor had been given a tidy little house by Priam midway down in the city. Priam liked knowing that he could call upon Gelanor for ideas whenever he liked; lately I had had to compete with the king for Gelanor's time.

On a day when Paris had been particularly distant and sunk in gloom, Evadne and I hurried down to Gelanor's. His little house was crammed full of objects that had caught his eye and taken his fancy: boxes of butterflies, bits and pieces of rocks, bronze spearheads, bows in various stages of assembly, seashells, pots of paint, horse bridles with metal mouthpieces. They were arranged in neat rows on shelves, to be sure, but still it struck me that this was the room little boys dreamed of. My brothers had collected things and brought them home, but Mother had had their rooms purged regularly as messy and unworthy of princes.

He emerged from an alcove, walking with his arms extended stiffly in front of him. "Greetings," he said. Blood was dripping off his forearms. What sort of accident had he encountered?

"Oh, let me help!" I rushed to him, ready to daub the wounds and bandage them.

Laughing, he pushed me away. "Nay, let them be." He waved his arms to dry the blood. "I cut them myself."

"Are you mad?" Evadne said. "What fool cuts himself?"

"A fool intent on seeing if a scar can be willfully induced to mimic a known one," Gelanor said. "Now . . ." He pulled a clay pot down from a shelf running across one wall and wrenched its lid off. "This will do for one of them. Get me that gray jar on the table there. And the little bowl beside it."

I brought them to him, and he lined them up with the first pot. Carefully he dipped his fingers in each container and rubbed the contents into the oozing cuts on his forearm, wincing as he did so.

"Can I create a scar as I wish?" he asked. "We shall see. This one"—he indicated the gray jar—"has clay from the banks of the Scamander. The others are ash from a hearth fire and soil from a field of barley. All common enough, all easily gathered by anyone."

"But what if the wounds fester?" Evadne cried. "What if your arm becomes withered?"

"I have not finished," Gelanor said. He reached behind him for a pitcher of wine, and poured it slowly over the wounds. "This will seal in the dirt and protect the wound from festering."

All this begged the question: why was he doing this?

"Ah, my lady, you see how far I am willing to go to protect you and yours in Troy." He raised his eyebrow in that teasing way I hated. "You know the trite saying, I would give my right arm? Well, here I prove it!" He held up his bloody, smeared arm.

"You prove nothing but that you have taken leave of your senses," I said. "I fail to see how this has anything to do with Troy, or me."

Now his face changed, in that sudden way he had. "Oh, you are wrong," he said. "Tell me what you know of scars, and of their importance."

That was easy. "I know that they are with us for life. If we fall on our knees as children, the scar holds a testimony of that spill for the rest of our lives. Warriors speak proudly of their scars as the proof of their battles."

"Ah. You said the word: *proof*. We rely on scars for proof that a man is who he says he is. How many tales are there of a man returning to claim his heritage and having to prove himself by his scars? Usually, in these stories, an old nurse or his mother or someone recognizes them. Oh, yes, they say, little Ajax was bitten by a wolf on his leg, I remember it . . . welcome home, Ajax. But what if a scar can be duplicated? Especially a very unusual one? And that clears the way for an imposter to gain trust. I am not sure it is possible, but I intend to find out." He stopped for breath. "Someone in Troy is a spy, a spy placed very high. He listens to our most private conversations. He comes and goes in our homes without arousing suspicion. I have my idea as to who it is. Now I need to prove it."

"But who?"

"Look at what has been known that should not have been, ask yourself who was present to hear it. It is a very clearly marked trail, if you have eyes to see. But the person is young and did not think to cover his tracks better."

"Who? Who?" I asked.

"Not now," said Gelanor. "It is best no one knows my suspicions until I am sure. After all, why besmirch someone who may yet be innocent?"

Evadne and I left him, shaking our heads. I worried about him; I knew he had not wanted to come here, and now he was trapped. Had his frustration and anger led him to these strange actions?

"Evadne," I said, "if only you could see who it is!"

She shook her head. "I have tried, my lady. But the vision is granted only as the gods allow. I cannot command it. They have revealed nothing nearby; they seem to delight in the faraway and the future. And even there they have disclosed nothing of late. Perhaps my springs have dried up."

My own gift of seeing—nay, of *knowing*—seemed also to have waned. It had been so strong in Sparta when first I returned from Epidaurus. "Perhaps we should consult the household snake, which you so lovingly brought from Sparta," I said. He was, after all, connected with my gift. "Let us visit him."

We could safely go there without encountering Paris. He never came to the little chamber we had allotted to the snake, though the snake had once bound us together, in that strange and wild night, when first we met alone . . . No, I would not think of that now!

"Well met, my lady." I was wrested from my thoughts by the voice of Deiphobus. I abandoned the snake in my mind and turned to face him. He was planted in our pathway, standing, hands on hips, leering down at me. "Ah, such a sight as your fair face makes the morning blush."

"It is long past morning," I said, holding my gown to step past him on the steep path. I tried not to look at him.

"Oh, is the sun overhead?" He refused to budge, and gazed at the sky. "But Phoebus has not yet whipped his horses to the highest zenith," he said. "You are mistaken." He leaned forward, whispered in my ear, "I hear you like all these old tales, my lady—Phoebus and suchlike. I understand this; it befits the daughter of a swan, after all, to believe such things. Did your mother save any feathers?" He chuckled.

I could not help myself: I drew back and struck his face. "Let us pass!" I said. "Or, by all the gods, the king will hear of this." I shoved him.

Instead of giving way, he leaned forward and grabbed my forearm in a hard grip. "You cannot walk amongst us and expect to escape our desires," he hissed. "That is all you do—create desire. Never think there is any other worth to you."

I flung off his arm and pushed him as far away as I could.

And he was my husband's brother! Had he no shame? No restraint? I wanted to tell myself that it was his bitterness about Troy and its dangers that had sparked his words. But I had seen the lust in his eyes from the beginning.

The snake. The snake—cool and impassive in his grotto. I must seek him as an antidote to all this ugliness. Shuddering, I took Evadne's arm and pulled her through the streets, perhaps faster than she would have liked. But I desperately needed the snake and his solace, his wisdom.

There was an entrance to the chamber on the ground floor. Together Evadne and I descended the stairs into the underground chamber. It was always lit with oil lamps; an acolyte brought the milk and honey cakes for the creature at dawn. Daily bouquets of dried herbs kept the air fresh.

Still, it seemed dark as we entered the chamber, after the brilliant light outside. It took a long time for my eyes to adjust and for forms to resolve themselves, stop quivering, and stand still. Once they had, I would pray before the altar and lure my beloved snake out so I could see him, whisper my desperate concerns to him.

The dark slowly dissolved. The polished stone floor came into view, its squares gleaming in the light of the oil lamps. I breathed deeply, smelling the sweet herbs in the urns beside the altar. Evadne sat beside me, only her breathing betraying her presence.

Then, as the room swam into view, there was something ropelike lying just before the altar. It was not arranged as a deliberate offering would be. I felt a chill in my heart as I saw it.

Was this innocent, or something very evil indeed?

Evadne's eyes could not see it. "Stay here," I said, trying to make my voice as normal as possible.

I crept up on it, and as I drew closer, I saw the horrible truth: my snake lay dead, killed. The cuts—I cannot describe them, I do not wish to see them ever again.

I fell to my knees, raised my hands, and screamed. Screamed to the heavens, screamed to the gods, begged them to restore life to my snake, my guardian.

Silence, and stillness. The pale body of the snake lay stretched before me.

* * *

I forgot the Paris I had avoided and rushed upstairs seeking the Paris I loved, fleeing the horrid sight in the grotto. Panting, I reached the uppermost floor; as I thought, he was there, surrounded by his weapons and armor. He looked up as I stumbled through the door, slowly raising his eyes to me.

"What is it?" His voice was chill, but I did not care. I cared only about the attack on me—on us.

"Paris—Paris!" I flung myself in his arms, seeking the warmth that was lacking in his voice. It would be there in his embrace. But no, his body was as lifeless as the snake's. He stepped away from me.

"What?" he repeated, but his tone shouted, *I do not care.*

"Paris—someone has killed the snake! Someone came into this house and struck him, and destroyed our—our—first companion!"

Now at last his face came alive. His lips quivered. "The snake?"

"Yes. Go see. It will rend your heart." I took his hand and led him to the entrance of the chamber, but drew back before entering. I could not look upon it again. I heard Paris's footsteps, heard him murmuring to Evadne, heard the two of them come out of the little room, while I waited, head bowed.

Paris's hand touched my shoulder gently. "We grieve together."

I looked into his eyes. I thought I saw—but the light was dim—the old Paris looking back at me.

❖ L ❖

The streets of Troy seethed with agitated crowds, crowds filled with restless desire to burst out of the walls and pursue the Greeks, take action, any action, while at the same time bracing to defend themselves. Winter was drawing on. The soldiers wanted to strike a blow before the Greeks departed—as depart they must, as the sailing season closed; older councilors warned that it was wise to let nature do their work for them. But there is no glory in winter sending an enemy home while a warrior's bronze lies unused, losing its luster, in his storeroom.

Our household priest gave the snake a ritual burial and there was some comfort in that. We did not replace him—how could we? There could be no others for us. I would incorporate him in my weaving, give him life again there in the limited way that memorials can give life, but he was gone, and with him, one of the most precious parts of my past.

Paris seemed to rally as time passed after the loss of Troilus. He still did not laugh as he used to, but he stopped lying on his couch and brooding, and even acted lovingly toward me at times. But it was only at times, and I could never predict when those times would be. At first, especially after the slaughter in the grotto, I was grateful for what seemed the rebirth of his love. But as it came and went, disappearing and reappearing like the moon on a windswept and cloudy night, I felt myself withdrawing bit by bit, to a place where he could neither reach nor disappoint me. It was safer thus.

Then the refugees began flooding into Troy. It came as a shock—one autumn day, across the empty plain where the trade fair should have been, a mob of people fled toward our gates. Standing on our flat rooftop I could see the crowds streaming across the meadows, but could not make out even whether they were armed or not. The sentries on the walls and towers yelled out at them and they cried back that they were from Dardanos and Arisbe and Perkote and their villages were being raided by the Greeks; they begged for protection.

Priam and Hector dispatched officers to set up camps around the outer defenses of the city where they could stay and be attended to. There were mainly women, children, and old men. The young men had been killed, they said, the livestock raided, many women taken captive and force-marched to the Greek camp. Then their homes were set afire or demolished.

Hector stood looking out at the people. "There are hundreds," he said quietly. "So the enemy has made massive raids. There is more to this than just wishing for supplies for their homeward journey." He leaned forward on the ramparts, gazing out like a bird of prey. The wind, chill from the sea, ruffled his hair.

"They mean to stay the winter." Standing beside him was the truculent Antimachus. He sounded incredulous. Had this taken the experienced war planner by surprise?

"This is most unlooked for," said Hector. "We did not reckon on this. So they have attacked the nearby towns. I heard one of the women saying they had raided the islands of Tenedos and Imbros as well. That is grim. How far afield will they go?"

"There is a limit as to how far they can raid," Antimachus assured him.

"What do our spies say?" Paris joined them on the wall. I had not known Paris's whereabouts this morning; I had left him sleeping.

"They will be returning as soon as it is safe," said Hector. "Then we shall know more. In the meantime, we must somehow feed these people. Inform the quartermasters. Set up a grain supply for them."

Antimachus cleared his throat. "But we cannot deplete our own stores for them."

"We must do something," said Hector. "It is because of Troy that they have lost their homes."

I was grateful to him for leaving me out of it. Hector never blamed me for the sorrows I had brought with me. He alone of the Trojans seemed to accept me as faultless and as much a plaything of the gods as they were.

But for the rest of his family, the death of Troilus had been a turning point, as it had been with Paris. Up until then they had tried to make me one of them; when their own true brother and son had perished, they realized that Helen could never truly be a part of their family. I would always be an outsider, a foreigner, a stranger, and the person who would fulfill the overhanging curse embodied in Paris. We had become the instruments of one another's, and Troy's, destruction.

The people—the ones who had cheered me as their "Greek treasure" not long ago—cast baleful looks at me as I passed them on the streets, shunning me as if I carried a curse. Perhaps I did. As I wandered through the city, through the squares and the small byways, past the tomb of Troilus, I looked at all the little ways people trimmed their lives with beauty: the little pots with herbs at the doorsteps, the painted shutters, the woven rush seats of their stools. Sometimes swaggering warriors would push past me, overturning the stools or breaking the pots. Already things were being destroyed in Troy, and the Greeks were still outside.

Just when the dread sacrifice I would have to make settled itself in my mind, I cannot say. I only know that one morning when the sun was barely painting the sides of the houses I looked at them and thought I would always be seeing them, and by the time twilight had come and torches were flickering against those same walls I knew I must banish myself. I must save Troy from myself. I must return to the Greeks—even though I vowed to die there by my own hand.

How nightmarish it is to plan to end one's life, to leave all that is dear. I must leave Paris, so that he could live. And Priam, and Hector, and my only friend amongst the women, Andromache, and . . . Evadne and Gelanor. As I sat enumerating them, I was saddened to realize that I could count so few here in Troy who would be even the least sorrowed by my loss, even though I had lived for some time amongst them.

I resolved to do this, and then set a time of thirty days in which to wait, to be sure that this was what I must do. It was not something to be undertaken on a whim.

During those thirty days I saw Troy differently, through faraway eyes, bidding it farewell already. I heard the thunderings in the council chamber about the raids; I saw the milling and despair of the refugees who were living in makeshift camps near the walls; I could smell the burning villages surrounding us. In vain I cast about searching for some sign that I should stay, but there was none. Everywhere I turned, I could see only improvement if I suddenly disappeared and the war was halted.

And Paris? He was better, now, grieving less over Troilus, but how would he cope if someone else dear to him was killed? And there *would* be further deaths. Paris himself would, perhaps, even follow them. So to give him life, I must leave.

How odd it was to hug such a secret to myself, to pass amongst them like a ghost already gone, but no one yet could discern that I was a ghost. I savored the times I sat before the hearth talking to Hector and Andromache, cherished the attention old Priam lavished on me, because those times were soon to be no more.

As for Paris, I could now forgive him anything—his moodiness, his coldness, his unpredictability. Those things were set against the shining gold of his entire person. I had caused these shadows, now I would lift them, and he would revert back to the Paris he was before. Only I would not see it.

Iphigenia, so it was said, at the last moment stopped struggling and laid down her life so that the Greeks might sail for Troy. Could I do less, if by my actions I could protect my new countrymen from those very Greeks?

Paris suspected nothing. I was surprised—not pleasantly—to find how easily I could play a part. After the first days when the very thought of leaving Troy stung me in the heart, that heart hardened and I could bear it. I felt that my own pain counted so little in the scales against the pain awaiting others if I did not go, I must not even consider it.

When to go, how to go? The wall was well guarded even at night. The stretches between each tower, manned with keen-eyed guards, were easily visible. Only in the few days when there was no moon did the flanks of the wall lie in darkness, and even so, soldiers would be alert for every sound. Someone trying to scale the walls would quickly be discovered. Was it even possible to get up or down them? They were as high as five or six men and faced with smooth stone that allowed no foot- or handhold.

Well, then, what of the watercourses? We had two wells inside the walls, so there was no weak spot in the defenses for the water supply. Wastewater flowed down through a large drainage channel and then out at the base of the southern walls, but that had been fitted with a grid to prevent anything larger than a sewer rat from passing through it.

Perhaps, then, I could pass out during the day to attend to some task and then fail to return in the evening. But I would never be permitted out without guards, and in any case there were no tasks considered worth the risk these days, not after Troilus. If I responded to a bogus request from the Greeks for an audience? Again, the Trojans would never let me accept what they would consider a transparent ploy to kidnap me back.

I dared not enlist any help in this plan, for I knew I would be betrayed. I was back to my first thought: that somehow I would have to descend over the walls undetected, with no accomplices.

As the term of the self-imposed thirty days drew to a close, my resolve almost collapsed, quite unexpectedly. I was trudging uphill to the palace when I was suddenly overcome with a desire to grasp onto a post and never let it go, as if some malevolent force were trying to pull me away, as if it had not, all along, been me myself. I wished never to leave Troy, I wished to cling to every pillar and stone so nothing could part us. But I knew the only way those pillars and stones could remain was if I left them.

Ahead of me, the palace seemed lovelier than ever before. Paris was waiting inside. That night he was in one of his good moods; the old Paris held court. He greeted me effusively, telling me that we would have guests that evening who would please me. He bustled around eagerly, setting up little braziers against the chill so we could be seated in a smaller room than the drafty megaron. As always with him, it was not what he did but his joy in doing it that was the truly pleasurable thing.

"Your second winter in Troy," he said. "That qualifies you as a true Trojan."

Was this why he was celebrating? The dear man, who could make the ordinary so special. Helen's second winter! I took his head in my hands and kissed him. "I love you," I said, laughing. At the same time my heart felt like a heavy stone in my breast.

Hector and Andromache were the guests he had prepared for; they stepped across the little space separating our palaces and entered. I noticed they had dressed as if the visit entailed a formal journey, rather than a short few steps. It was their way of showing their brother that they treated his invitation with respect. They were like that, Hector and Andromache: thoughtful and proper. Gravely they divested themselves of their cloaks and joined us. Hector was attired in a warm wool wrap as well as wool leggings, and Andromache was wearing a long garment of the sort I had never seen before. It was blue and had tiers of yellow fringes all around the skirt. She told me it was a fashion from Crete, where flounced and beaded skirts were worn everywhere. It flattered her, as she was tall enough that the skirt could fall like a column to her feet.

"Come, come." Paris ushered them toward inlaid chairs with matching footstools.

Hector took his seat and leaned back. Even in relaxation he looked poised to leap up. "Yes, dear brother? What is this occasion?" The unspoken question: *What is so important to have called us here for a social evening in the midst of this war?*

I, the shade, sat impassively. I, the shade, soon to pass away. I had secured my rope—long enough, I thought, to reach to the base of the northern wall—had bundled up my sturdy sandals and dark cloak beside it. I had selected the northern wall as the one least watched, as it was so high the guards assumed no Greek would attack from that side. There was no lower city around it, nothing but open fields. It was near the palaces, but the temple of Athena, dark and unguarded close by at night, meant I could approach it without being sighted.

"I merely wanted to see you in private," said Paris. "We have met on the walls, at the funeral, at Father's palace, and at war councils, but have seen little of each other as men."

"I fear that is the way of war," said Hector stiffly.

"Then I long for the day when peace will come again and permit us to be normal," said Andromache. She leaned forward on her chair. "We have a secret—but it is a secret I must tell you, Helen. You were with me on Mount Ida. We—I am with child!"

Shade though I was, I leapt from my chair to embrace her, dizzy with joy for her. "Oh, Andromache!" She had so longed for this. And now I would not be with her to see the face of her newborn. But no one must know that, and it did not subtract from my happiness for her.

"A son of Hector!" said Paris. "At last!"

"We do not know if it is a son," Hector said, but the slow smile around his lips showed how pleased he was even to be thinking of it.

"Son or daughter, the child will bring great pride to Troy," said Paris.

Andromache bowed her head. "I will petition the gods every day for a safe delivery. Helen, will you be with me?"

"Yes," I said, without thinking. I hated to lie, and seeing her eyes lighten with pleasure made the guilt even worse.

The rest of the evening passed as a dream, a dream in which I was an outsider. I heard the conversation, even participated in it. They discussed the mysterious person who had locked me in the well, and drugged Paris, and killed our snake. No one had been apprehended, and they concluded it was a person who disliked us personally. That left most of Troy as suspects.

They fretted over the increasing aggressiveness of the Greeks in attacking the surrounding countryside. Andromache was worried about her family in Plakos, but Hector assured her they were out of reach, as they were so far south, beyond the Smintheum near Thebe. They spoke of measures to curb the raids, but only I knew of the measure I planned to unleash. If Helen surrendered, that would end it all.

Every time I looked at Paris, I had to look away. How could I leave him?

Afterward he remarked, "You seemed sad."

I rushed to assure him I was not. All I wanted was to spend one last night with him in our bed, with hours to hold him. Tomorrow night was the dark of the moon. That was when I must make my escape.

Never had Paris looked more precious than when he stood, happy and ignorant, by the side of the bed, gazing at me. All I wanted was to live with him, be happy with him, and grow old with him. But no, Agamemnon had made sure that could not happen. His vile excursion here to terrorize innocent people would get me back, but only for a little while. No one would embrace me but the grave.

But for now, I lived and wanted and touched. I embraced Paris, holding him as close as possible, and as we made love, slowly and several times, I savored each caress, each sensation, each murmur. I knew how little time we had left together and I was determined to wring from it every drop of sweetness it could give me.

❖ LI ❖

The following day—my last in Troy—I rose early. I did not want to miss a moment to savor it, painful as it would be. Paris slept on, and I leaned over to kiss his cheek, clutching my robe around me.

Like a sleepwalker, I went out onto the streets of Troy. I meant to walk all the streets, to memorize them, to look at every detail. Peering over the walls, I saw that the Greeks were still camping halfway across the plain. When I scrambled down over the northern wall, I must make my way toward one of the tents. What matter who took me into custody? Soon enough Menelaus would dig his fingers into my shoulders.

Should I wear the dreadful brooch he had left for me? I vowed to fling it back at him, and so I must. Just to make it all the more difficult, the day, even though it was late autumn, was perfect, with a clear cloudless sky and a brisk—but not sweeping—wind. Troy, Troy! I wept inwardly. How lovely you are!

The sun swung overhead, started its downward slant. Priam, Hecuba—should I bid them farewell in my mind by seeing them once more? But no, it might arouse suspicion. This must seem an ordinary day.

When shadows fell and the city pulled back into itself, a purple-blue peace descended on it. There had been no attacks that day, no reports of raids elsewhere. All was peaceful.

Paris and I had a quiet supper, saying very little. I cast surreptitious glances at him, trying to memorize his face. When he looked up and caught me, puzzled, I looked hurriedly away.

Paris slept soundly beside me. I waited until I heard his breathing become deep and regular. Then I sat up slowly, testing him to see if he would rouse. He did not. I slipped my shoes on and rose from the bed. The movement still did not disturb him. I wanted to kiss him, but I did not dare to risk it. You have said your goodbyes, I told myself sternly. It is over. You must go.

I pulled on a stolen pair of Paris's trousers—deemed effete Eastern dress, which he wore only in privacy—to make my descent easier. Who ever heard of someone in a gown sliding down a rope? This would enable me to wrap my legs around it.

I stole away. I could not look back. I slunk out of the palace, not by the main door, which was guarded, but out through the kitchen and back quarters. I had hidden my rope and dark cloak there, just to one side of a grain storage jar. They were still there—no one had discovered them.

Tucking them under my arm, I crept as quietly as possible toward the great darkened temple of Athena. No priests or priestesses were on duty, and all the columns were shadowed and empty. Just beyond the temple was the highest point in Troy, the great bastion and lookout on the northeastern side. But I did not mean to descend here, as I would be easily seen from the tower. A bit farther to the west and I would be invisible.

I had already secured a large rock that would serve as an anchor for my rope. I looped the rope around it and strung it over the side of the wall. All was silent. The sky overhead was utterly dark, the moon having fled, abandoning the heavens for a few days.

I tested the rope. It seemed strong enough. I lowered it over the wall, and looked down to see how far it fell. I heard a dull thud as it hit the ground—far below. Very far below. I sucked in my breath and took the rope between my hands. It was bristly and rough, and immediately its fibers cut into my hand. But no matter.

I approached the side of the wall. It was high. It would require that I clamber over it. Thank the gods for Paris's trousers. I grabbed the rocks and hauled myself over, wishing my arms stronger. I prayed I would not lose my grip and crash to the ground. But what matter? I would die a little early, but I had planned to die nonetheless.

I began to slide down the rope. I bounced against the hard stones of the wall, which were shiny and unyielding. Already I was bruised, but so be it. Bounce, hit, jounce. I swung back and forth on the rope, hitting the wall time and again. I knew this created noise, but I hoped no one could hear.

It was utterly dark. No one would be able to see me, suspended there on the rope. I was halfway down. The ground below loomed into my vision. It was covered with brush and scrub. Something to break my fall, I thought. For my arms were aching and I did not know how much longer I could hold on. The ground opened up before me.

I fell. I landed heavily on my back, missing all the cushioning of the bushes and hitting hard rock. A pain ripped through me. For a moment I did not think I could move, but I willed myself to. You are here, you must walk, you must reach your goal, I told myself.

Gingerly I rolled over and tested my legs to be sure they would still obey. They trembled a bit but held me up. On to Menelaus, then. On to Menelaus. I staggered down the small incline. Somewhere, not so far away, were the Greek tents. I stumbled over the rough ground. Troy was high behind me. The great northern wall looked like a sheet of bronze, high and impenetrable. It was gone. Troy was gone for me. Before me were the mean little tents of the Greeks, sheltering mean little men.

Mindlessly, I pushed forward to a place I did not wish to go, commanding my legs to carry me.

"Stop right there!" A harsh voice rent the air. It must be a Greek sentry. Now I would give myself up. Wearily I turned to face the speaker.

Someone grasped my arm painfully. Let him. What matter? I did not care how I was batted around, smacked, misused. It would be over soon enough. A torch was thrust up into my face. I winced and turned away.

"By all the gods!" An angry voice.

Yes, it is Helen. Take me, punish me, convey me to Menelaus. Get on with it. I was suddenly anxious to have it take place. Put it in motion, let it run its course.

"Helen!" Antimachus stuck his face up into mine. "What is this?"

Antimachus! I shrank back.

"A traitor, then?" he cried. "Slinking off to join the Greeks?" He pulled painfully on my arm.

"No, it is not so!" I cried.

"I see a rope. I see an escape. I see escape clothes." He stared at my trousers.

I drew myself up. "I wished to sacrifice myself for Troy," I said. "This was the only way. If I were returned, they would have no more cause of war."

"You stupid little fool!" I thought he would break my arm off in squeezing it. "That is not why they are here!"

"That may be, but it is their excuse. I meant to remove that excuse from them."

"So you were ready to go back to Menelaus, snuggle up to him in bed?"

The thought made me gag. "No. I would have ended myself before that happened."

He snorted in disbelief. "So, who knows of this?"

"No one," I said.

"So you told no one? I do not believe a woman capable of that."

"Believe what you like. It is true."

"So only you and I know of this?"

"Yes."

"You are going back to Troy, my lady, and right into the bed of your husband, and no one must ever be the wiser."

"It must end!" I cried. "Only I have the power to make it end."

"It is too late," said Antimachus. "No human can end it now."

He got me back into Troy through the tiny gate at the base of the northeastern tower. He forced me to cover my face and head with my cloak so that the guards would not recognize me, and hugged and leered at me so they would think I was a prostitute. He enjoyed doing this, I could tell. The city still lay quiet in the hush of night, and my palace was close by. He shoved me toward the door, after hissing, "Your secret and mine, lady."

I had no choice. I had to go back in. But I held my head high and indicated to him that I would choose the entrance, not him. I wanted to go back as I had come; I did not want to alert the guards at the front door.

Through the porch and vestibule, then up the stairs to our chamber, where the wind was sighing softly through the pattern in our wooden shutters. Paris still sleeping, one bare arm trailing to the floor, his face turned away. It was all as I had left it, and I felt like a soldier returning to a home he thought never to see again. Now, as Antimachus had said, the war itself would dictate its own course, and I was powerless to steer it or change it.

I was just bending to pull off the trousers when Paris suddenly sat up and stared at me. I froze, hoping he would lie back down and think this only a dream, have no memory of it later. I held my breath. But he cried out, "What are you doing?"

When I did not answer, he reached for his brass bell to call a guard. I rushed to him and muffled it, twisting it out of his hand. He fell back onto the pillows. "Helen! Helen!" he cried, clutching at the trousers.

I threw myself across him and stifled his cries with my hand. "Be quiet,"

I warned him. I must think of some harmless tale to tell him, but nothing came to mind. And I was weary of the effort of lying, and had no cleverness left. I would have to tell him all.

"Why are you wearing my trousers?" he whispered when I took my hand off his mouth.

"I was trying to escape from Troy," I confessed.

As I had feared, he let out a wail. "Leave?" he cried.

"Only because I believed it was the only way to stop the war and prevent more deaths." I leaned back, my knees underneath me, rocking nervously back and forth. I did not need to tell him that I had thrown my life into the bargain as well.

"And what of my happiness? You know I cannot live without you!" He stopped my rocking and clutched me to him. "How could you abandon me like that?"

"That was the most difficult part. I—I barely had the courage to do it," I stammered.

"I wouldn't call it courage, I would call it cruelty."

"I was cruel to us so that others would not have to suffer."

"But you are here. You did not leave after all. Why?" He was longing for me to say I changed my mind, not that I had actually done it but been intercepted.

"Antimachus caught me. The man must never sleep. He was patrolling the base of the northern tower."

Paris gave a howl of pain. "You were already out of the city!"

"Yes."

"You betrayed me. You left me. Without even a farewell. And you expect me to forgive you?"

"No, I do not expect that. I feared it was a price I would have to pay."

"But you were willing to pay it!"

"Yes, I told you." Oh, this was so dreadful! Oh, if only he could have been spared this knowledge.

"You like leaving your husbands at night, I see. You were sneaking away from me as you snuck away from Menelaus. I can never trust you again!"

"That is my punishment," I said. I did not blame him. I knew how it looked. I would have felt the same.

He jumped up from the bed and gathered his blankets. "I cannot share a bed with you," he muttered, descending the steps and leaving me alone in the darkness. I heard his footsteps padding across the vestibule below and then they were swallowed up in silence.

Shaking all over, I lowered myself down onto the bed, where I lay rigidly until day stole into the chamber. I had been ready to give all this up, but I was deeply thankful I was waking up to these walls instead of the walls of Menelaus's tent. And I was also thankful that I could continue to draw my breath without thinking that each one was numbered.

Paris had disappeared by the time I was dressed and came down in the morning. The attendants indicated that he had gone out "to see about the war." Yes, the war would provide all the opportunities he needed to lose himself and avoid me. At least it would keep our separation from being known. But I must keep the attendants from suspecting. I must find an excuse for Paris having his own sleeping quarters. Perhaps it could have something to do with the cold, or braziers, or noise—all mere reasons of comfort, with no hint of a quarrel. I would have sought out the solitude and peace of the household shrine, taking comfort from the wisdom of the snake, but now the empty chamber deepened my gloom.

I was bruised all over; my whole body felt tender from banging myself against the wall. It was all I could do not to limp, and I was thankful that in this cold weather I was well swathed by thick wool cloaks and wraps. I called Evadne and together we set out to see Gelanor. Perhaps he knew the turn the war was now likely to take. I could tell him of my thwarted plan and ask his advice. He never judged; or, rather, he did judge but he never censured.

We caught him just as he was leaving his house, hurrying toward the central storage depot of weapons. Nonetheless, he looked pleased to postpone his errand; he put his sacks down gently. "My scorpion bombs," he said. "Let us not disturb them! I was just about to test them out. But they will keep. You look troubled," he said abruptly. "What is it?"

I would have thrown myself in his arms for comfort, but that was unthinkable. "Oh, Gelanor. Everything is as wrong as it can be!"

"Everything? Surely not." He stepped back and cocked his head. Usually this gesture was charming, but now it annoyed me in its cool detachment.

"Yes, yes, it is!"

He turned and unlocked his door and ushered us in. It was useless to keep walking in the streets. I sank down on a stool, grateful to ease my aching muscles. "You move as if you are a hundred years old," he said.

"I feel it," I moaned. "I am battered all over." Before he could ask questions, I held up my hands. "Let me tell you direct. I tried to leave Troy, to turn myself over to the Greeks."

Both he and Evadne drew in their breaths with a whistle.

"It was the most vile thing I have ever asked of myself. But I had passed through the streets of Troy, had seen the frightened refugees, the angry Trojans, heard the toll of the attacks on the villages, seen Troilus—oh, I could not bear the responsibility for all this, and more yet to come. The burden was greater than any one person could carry. If I went to the Greeks, that would end it. I had to. Only I could do this, and only I would do it, do what thousands of soldiers could not."

"How deluded," Gelanor said tartly. "And so you tried to climb over the walls and were promptly caught. What happened—did your gown catch on a stone?"

So even he underestimated me! I wanted to smack him. Why did everyone assume I was so hapless, so stupid?

"As a matter of fact, no, for I was wearing trousers!"

He burst out laughing.

"Stop laughing!" I ordered him. "I didn't wear them for your amusement, but to allow me to climb better."

"Trousers!" He could barely catch his breath, and wheezed, holding his sides. Finally he gasped and said, "Since you were caught, I assume they did not protect you."

"I was caught later, by that hateful Antimachus, who was lurking outside the walls. What he was doing, I don't know. I only know that suddenly there he was."

"Perhaps he's a spy," mused Gelanor. "Perhaps you caught him as he was going to the Greeks himself, and he had to make a show of discovering you. Antimachus . . . who would suspect him? A perfect spy, then."

Could it possibly be true? Our most stridently warlike general? But it was he who had baited the Greeks and been the loudest in refusing to consider handing me back. Could it be . . . ? "No!"

Watching my face intently, Gelanor went on, as if talking to himself. "That is why I say that you are deluded. It is in the interests of many people on both sides for there to be a war between the Greeks and the Trojans. Only Menelaus has the pure purpose of recovering you. For him, the war would end if you returned. But the others would fight on, and you would have turned yourself over to Menelaus in a vain sacrifice."

Evadne leaned forward. "I understand why the Greeks might want this war, but not any Trojans."

"I know you have lost your eyesight, but you must have lost your hearing as well," said Gelanor. "In the beginning the streets resounded with the cries of young men eager to go to battle. It must be in the nature of youth to want to take up arms. Now, if Antimachus could help assure that the war would take place, he would indeed be a friend of some of the Trojans and all of the Greeks. Not necessarily in collusion with them, but certainly working toward the same aim: to have spears flying and skulls split open. He clearly has a keen appetite for it."

Evadne shook her head. "But as the deaths have mounted, the Trojans are losing that appetite."

"True," said Gelanor. "But I think I will have an announcement soon that will revive it."

Being Gelanor, of course, he refused to tell us what it was. At the same time I was relieved that he did not pursue my lament that everything was as bad as it could be. He assumed I meant only my thwarted escape.

But Evadne had not forgotten. On our way back to the palace, she asked me and I told her about Paris.

❖ LII ❖

The private war between Paris and me was swallowed up in the wider war raging around us. Not only were we never alone—for the palace was filled with our allies who had fled from the butchering raids—but everything in our lives was suspended while the war swelled like a monstrous spider and ingested our days and nights. No one noticed on what floor Paris slept, or, if they did, they assumed it was done to accommodate our allies. My chamber was now shared with several princesses and ladies from Phrygia and their younger brothers and cousins found rest in Paris's new quarters.

Aeneas and his family arrived, and then, most ominously, a stream of frightened and wounded people from Lyrnessus near the home of Andromache far to the south, babbling about a massacre. At first there were only incoherent recountings about a sudden attack by a contingent of warriors, named something like *Myr—Myr—* They meant the *Myrmidons,* then. Achilles's contingent. So he had taken his men and raided that far afield. Then they told more stories about the towns around them being attacked, the killing and looting and burning. The men were all dead, they said, except the youngest and the oldest and the crippled, and many women were carried off as prizes and slaves. Achilles had so many rounded up it was like a herd of cattle. One emaciated woman, her bleeding feet being rubbed with ointment by my workers, muttered that if he took his turn with all those women, he would be an old man before he was finished and there would be no war. She shuddered in thinking of falling into his hands.

Others told us that Assos had been raided as well, and the shrine of Apollo at Chryse had been violated and the old priest's daughter carried off, "like Hades did Persephone," one said. But what of the king of Thebes? What had happened to him, and his queen, and his sons and daughters?

Then we heard: killed, all of them. In one day, all of Andromache's family had been slain by Achilles himself. Her father King Etion had been killed in his courtyard, hacked down as he clutched the altar of his god, and he became the sacrifice before the stones where he himself had sacrificed for so many years. The seven brothers, peacefully tending their cattle and white sheep on the hills, were taken by surprise and died fighting the Myrmidons, but for each of them Achilles had driven in the bronze that killed them, and they fell in the meadows on the mountain flanks.

I rushed over to Hector's palace through the throngs in the vestibule and courtyard to be with Andromache. Hector was just leaving the chamber when I arrived, and he was grim-faced. He was thankful I was there, he said, for she needed me, and they feared for the child with this shock. He could not linger now, he must be out on the ramparts.

Andromache was lying on her couch and looked dead herself. Her face was wan as unworked wool and her eyes, though open, seemed to be staring sightlessly. I touched her arm and it felt cold. I covered her more completely with blankets and asked that a brazier be brought closer. I rubbed her wrists and whispered her name. At length, very slowly, she turned her head and looked at me, and the look in her eyes froze me. There seemed almost to be no life there, and what little remained was pure sorrow.

"Helen," she whispered. "I am slain."

I took her hands and blew on them to warm them, to fan the flame of life. "No, you are here, and safe." I kissed her cold forehead. "Safe within these walls of Troy, safe behind the shield of Hector, your husband."

"Not only my husband but now my father and brother and mother as well," she said, her voice so faint I had to lean over to hear it. "He is my only family now."

"Not your only family," I said. "You and Hector will soon have a child."

"It will never live. Even if I live to bear it, Achilles will cut it down. And he will then honor it in death, a death he created. Do you know what he did?" She sat up, shakily, on her elbows, and stared wide-eyed like a hunted animal. "He gave my father a proper funeral." Deep from within her throat a ghoulish laugh burst out, grew louder. "He dressed him properly in his royal robes and laid him respectfully on a pyre and then made his Myrmidons build a burial mound and even"—now her coughing, gasping laughter sounded demented—"had them plant a grove of elm trees around it. To make a sacred site. Oh, that is what the ceremonious warrior will do to Hector and to our child. He kills, then he bows before what he has killed to do it honor."

"Achilles is mortal," I said. "Mortals die as easily by accidents of nature as in battle. He cannot go on killing forever. I will say, he will never enter the gates of Troy."

"You may say so, but it is only wishing."

"Andromache, you waited so long for this child and desired it above all things. Now if you do not fight to put this sorrow from you, Achilles will have killed it without striking a blow, without ever coming near you. I say, take your strength from your father and your brothers—they left it for you. Take it up and put it on like a helmet, and be as strong as all of them put together. And rise up and give Troy this child." I paused. Was she hearing any of this? "Perhaps he will avenge your family. Why assume he will die at Achilles's hand? It could just as likely be the other way, and what a glorious revenge that would be."

She sank back down again on the couch, closing her eyes. "I will think of them," she murmured. "I will call each of them by name, and take their courage where they left it lying. It must not be left in the meadow, discarded like an old cloak." She gave my hand a weak squeeze. "Thank you, Helen, for letting me see what they left behind for me."

Shaken, I made sure that her attendants would tell me if there were any changes, and then I left the palace, where full-scale keening and mourning resounded in the public chambers I hurriedly passed. Outside, the crowds were surging through the streets like a herd of frightened cattle running madly from a lion. Unlike cattle in a meadow, there was no place for them to go, and so they rushed here and there, back and forth from one side of the city to the other, bound in by the walls.

They bellowed and cried out for Priam to come and address them. The old king should show himself, they demanded, else they would regard Hector as king instead. These shrill challenges brought Priam out onto his rooftop, which served as a podium for him to address the crowds. I could see the strain on his face, could see it in his eyes, hear it in the slight hesitation between words as he picked his way between them like a horse with a tender hoof treading a pebbled path.

Troy was in no danger, he assured them. Troy's strength was shown by the fact that the enemy had not attacked her directly but was trying to sap her strength by attacking her friends.

"Then why does Troy not come to the aid of her friends?" a loud voice called. "Why does the friendship go only one way? The Dardanians and the Adrasteians must suffer for Troy, but Troy does not suffer for them!" A roar came from what presumably were the Dardanians and Adrasteians.

"You agreed to fight alongside us," said Priam, raising his voice to be heard. "And for reward," he added.

"We did not agree to have our towns attacked," another voice called. "We agreed to send soldiers to fight, not have foreign soldiers descend on us and loot and kill."

"We thought it was Troy that would be attacked, not us!" a quavering old man cried.

"Oh, so you were pleased enough if it was us!" Deiphobus suddenly appeared beside his father on the rooftop.

"Troy has high walls and towers," the voices in the crowd cried. "She is built for it. We are not!"

"Ptah!" Deiphobus waved dismissively. "Now you are here, partaking of our hospitality."

"Son, you speak out of turn." Priam laid a strong hand on Deiphobus's shoulder. "You do not speak for the king, nor for the honorable people of Troy." Speaking louder, he approached the edge of the roof and held out his hands to the crowd. "We are grieved by your misfortune, and admit we did not anticipate it. What may we do to assure you of this?"

"Cattle! Gold!" yelled one man.

"Cattle cannot bring back my mother," cried another.

"Good people, come into my palace tonight. It will be open, and I will feed you all and we shall talk." It was not Priam who spoke this invitation, but Paris, who had appeared on the rooftop near Deiphobus.

A groan rippled through the crowd, until someone shouted, "It's him! It's the cause of it all! Paris! My fellows, your homes lie smoldering and your herds taken and your fathers dead because of *him*!"

Priam yanked Paris back, his face dark with anger. "I am shamed by my sons, who speak before they think," he said, looking first at Paris and then at Deiphobus. "No, it is to my palace you must come. Tonight. The doors will be thrown open for you."

Rumbling, the crowd dispersed, placated. I saw now how dangerous Troy could become in an instant once people were agitated. They were confined, like beasts in a cage, packed too close together, and everyone knew that several beasts in the same cage were prone to fighting. Now Troy was swamped with foreigners, volatile as dry tinder, and swarming with the wounded, Trojan and non-Trojan.

So Paris wanted to throw open the gates of our home to them? He must have taken leave of his senses. Or else his deep and lingering sorrow over Troilus made him think he could make amends this way. I was selfishly relieved that Priam had put a stop to it.

But I pitied Hecuba tonight.

With no time whatsoever to prepare, the king and queen of Troy must welcome hundreds of guests into their private domain. It would cost them dearly, depleting precious stores needed for the continuing siege. But we were at that stage of war when courtesies still could outweigh necessities.

The courtyard was blazing with torches—I had expected no less. Several oxen were roasting—again, as expected. Jugs of wine stood like little soldiers, five abreast and six lines deep, on long tables. Heaps of bread—hastily baked that afternoon—and baskets of precious dried figs and dates were spread out lavishly beside bowls of olives and apples.

I was alone. Paris had been nowhere to be found in our palace, and I knew that meant he did not wish to be found. Not only did he not care to share my bed, he did not care even to share my arm for a public occasion. He had meant what he said. He was finished with me. Paris and Helen were no more.

As I weaved my way through the crowd, seeing their wounds and knowing their losses, guilt and sorrow descended on me like a rain-sodden mantle. Guilt because they had suffered for nothing; if Paris and Helen were no more, then all their losses were for nothing—Troy need not have been attacked. And sorrow for myself, grief that Paris no longer loved me.

He had brought me giddy happiness, fulfillment, freedom. That made it all the harder to go back to the gray world without him, a world as gray as the flat Plain of Troy in winter, as gray as the rolling sea breaking against the pebbled shore of Gytheum. I had wanted to taste the flavors of ordinary life, had prayed to be released from my position as a near-goddess. Now I had my wish. Ordinary women were cast aside, ordinary women every day heard their husbands say, "I do not love you any longer." Ordinary women went into a room alone. Ordinary women looked around that room for the face of one who would only turn away.

Welcome to the land of the ordinary, Helen. Do you like it? A voice was whispering low in my ear, but no, it was not in my ear but in my mind. A voice I knew too well. *I did not think you would.*

"I have not had time to accustom myself to it yet," I told her. "In time, I shall."

I can make all things glow again, she said. *I can change Paris back in an instant.*

Now I would have rounded on her, had she been visible. "We must now make our own way," I told her. But there was a part of me that longed to say, *Yes, yes, cast your spell and make him mine again.* But I would not belittle either of us in that manner.

As you wish, she said mockingly. Her light laugh echoed in my head.

The room seemed louder than ever, now that the hush and audience with the goddess in my head was over. I was overwhelmed by the noise of the milling people, the shoving and jostling to get near pieces of roasted ox being sliced and handed out. It was true, Priam had to welcome them in to honor their suffering, but it was a pity all he could do was provide earthly food and drink, when what they needed was something on another plane.

Deiphobus was looming just ahead, bobbing through the crowd. I turned aside. I had no wish to speak to him, even to acknowledge him. When the heart is sick, one does not encourage the carrion crows. In turning away from him, I bumped into that self-effacing lad Hyllus, who bowed and stuttered and smoothed at his cheeks. He made a few gasping compliments before melting away. I was alone in the crowd, pushed and shoved and heaved here and there. There was no one for me to talk to, unless I insisted on forcing someone to talk.

Alone in Troy. And yet, except for Paris, I had always been alone in Troy. Now he had withdrawn and left me stranded, a stranger amongst strangers.

I would leave, slip away to my own home. I turned to do so. I only wanted to be alone, truly alone. I saw Gelanor at one end of the chamber and turned on my heel. He would seek out my company. But I wanted no company now, I felt only the burning need to escape.

He saw me! His face changed and he started to come toward me, but I pretended I did not see him and wended my way through the people. I was almost clear—I could feel the cool air from outside flowing between the pillars—when I heard him addressing the company.

At first I thought it could not be. Only the king, only the royal family could address the guests in the chamber. But no, it was his voice. Slowly the buzzing stopped, and all heads turned in his direction.

He was standing next to Priam. Priam's arm was encircling his shoulder, giving royal sanction to whatever he would say. Priam was looking at him almost tenderly.

Gelanor spoke at length about the mysterious spy who had wormed his way into the innermost bastion of Troy. This spy, he said, had knowledge that only someone free to come and go, to listen and pass amongst us, would have. He—or she—had known of the scouting party to Dardanos and Abydos. He had known of the weak portion of the wall.

"And he knew of the prophecy about Troilus," he said. "He knew only because it was spoken in his presence. Troilus trusted him; Troilus died for that trust."

Now it was so silent it seemed the room was empty. I could not even hear any breathing.

"We call upon Hyllus to come forward." Priam extended his arm: a royal command.

Nothing happened. No one stirred. Then, suddenly, there was a scrambling in the back of the room. Then a cry, and two strong men were dragging Hyllus forward. They flung him in a heap at Priam's feet.

"Stand up." Priam's voice was cold as the snows that fall somewhere high on the peaks of Ida.

Still the bundle of clothes that were Hyllus shook and shivered at Priam's feet. Two soldiers hauled him up.

Gelanor stepped forward and pulled away the waterfall of hair that hid Hyllus's forehead, exposing the jagged scar. Roughly the soldiers turned him to face the people.

"A scar," mused Gelanor. But I knew it was no idle musing. "A scar is always proof that someone is who he says he is. A thousand stories and songs attest to this. Enough to lull us, would you not agree? Enough so that when young Hyllus—or whoever he might be—returned to us lamenting his father Calchas's defection, we merely noted that he had his disfiguring forehead scar and welcomed him back. So much had been made of that scar before he departed! And from the moment that boy entered into our gates, the enemy had mysterious knowledge of our whereabouts and concerns. How many deaths followed? Enough that I wanted to learn how distinctive a scar can be." He held up his forearms. "Here is what I have learned. Scars can be duplicated. It is easy. Here are the distinguishing scars on my arms—all created by me." The sleeves of his mantle fell away and three scars revealed themselves. Now I knew the purpose of his experiment with the clay and the ash and the soil.

"This young man duplicated the scars of Hyllus. Where is Hyllus? Murdered, perhaps. In any case, this person is not Hyllus, but a clever impersonator sent by the Greeks. He was sent here to play upon our desires, upon our wishes that both the father and the son had not betrayed Troy. But where is Hyllus's mother? She has been strangely silent. She would have known this imposter was not her son. But"—Gelanor walked directly over to him—"you avoided your 'mother,' did you not? You said you did not spend time at home. Small wonder!"

Hyllus now began to blabber. "Ask my mother! Ask her! You shall see! My mother knows!"

"Fetch the wife of Calchas, the mother of Hyllus." Priam's command was quiet but sharp.

"While we wait, let us continue the questioning," said Gelanor. "We would like to know how you conveyed your findings back to your friends in the Greek camp. Going openly yourself would have been too obvious. Either you sent someone else or you devised signals in advance. You don't seem clever enough to have created a code yourself, if I may say so. Perhaps you will tell us who it was? And what it was?" His polite tone was as insulting as a slap.

Hyllus closed his eyes and shook his head, to indicate ignorance and sorrow at the misunderstanding.

"No, I did not think so," said Gelanor. "You will continue the playacting until the end. Very well, for the end is near."

Hyllus's mother was brought forward. Hyllus made a great show of embracing her. I could not see whether the embrace was warmly returned or merely endured. "Mother! Tell them, Mother! They are making a dreadful accusation, saying that I am an imposter."

She looked at him searchingly. She reached out and touched his cheek, running the back of her hand lightly along it. "My son . . ."

The room came alive with murmurs.

"Yes, Mother!" he said, tears trickling down his face, his mouth starting to quiver. "Thank you, Mother!"

". . . I do not know," she said, twisting her hands together, her face contorted as well. "I do not know . . ." She turned to Priam, her eyes desperate. "There are days when I think, yes, it is he, Hyllus—days when he turns and makes a gesture and it could only be him. But when I first beheld him, I did not know him for Hyllus." Turning this way and that, between Priam and Hyllus, she was distraught. "It was not my son. It was someone else. It frightened me—as if he had died and this was a shade, a pale visitor. As the days went on, the paleness disappeared and color came into him and he took on the life of Hyllus."

"How could you have done this?" Priam was shocked. "How could you have received him—this ghost?"

"Because . . . because I could not know, for certain."

"A mother not know her own child?" Hecuba spoke for the first time, from her place near Priam. Yes, Hecuba, the mother who had cast out her own son!

"It had been some time since I had seen him . . . people change . . ." She looked miserable. "And you know the longing of a mother for a lost child. There is a part of you that will accept back any morsel you can get, even if it is not complete. Part of you that will settle for a copy, if the copy is a good one."

"Even if it is false through and through?" Gelanor sounded outraged.

"This boy was not a piece of Hyllus, he had not a shred of Hyllus in him. He was no more Hyllus than I am! Would you have called me 'son'?"

"No. Because there is no way I could have convinced myself that you are Hyllus, no matter how I longed to. This boy made it easy." She took his hands, then dropped them in farewell. "Now it is doubly hard. I lose Hyllus twice."

"Mother!" the boy cried out, extending his arms.

"If you truly knew me for your mother, you would not be so cruel as to torture me any further," she said, stepping back, her arms still at her side. "This proves what I wish were not so."

"Take him away!" said Priam. "Hold him in chains, and mind that he does not escape. Before he is executed, we must know what he knows."

The two soldiers grabbed him and, locking his arms behind his back, pushed him through the crowd, which had grown nasty.

"Let us kill him!" yelled one man. "Think of the deaths he has caused!"

"All in good time," said Gelanor. "There may still be some deaths we can prevent, if we know what this spy and his friends have planned."

"Mother!" the boy wailed from the back of the room, then we heard the soldiers strike him and silence him. Calchas's wife, weeping, stumbled from her questioners and disappeared into the crowd.

Suddenly the room erupted into wails and cries of mourning for all the death caused by this war. Priam's attempt at solace and reconciliation had only gathered large numbers of war victims together in one room, where their grief and anguish could multiply tenfold. Women screamed and raised their hands, children sent pitiful shrieks like dagger stabs through the night. They overturned the tables and shattered the wine containers, scattered the food, turning the chamber into a slippery deck.

"My friends—" Priam held up his hands, imploring them. But his voice was lost in the melee.

"I will end this!" One voice rose above the others, cutting through them like the sweet high notes of a flute rise above the throb of drums. "I began it, and by all the gods, I shall end it!"

Paris! But how could he end it? There was no turning back.

He had taken his place beside Priam and in the flickering light I had never seen him look so glorious—but was that only because he had withdrawn himself from me? He was no longer mine, therefore his beauty increased?

He held his arms up, his fine hands reaching for the sky. He held his head high, his chin lifted, but I could see his eyes searching the crowd. When he saw me, he looked away. "I brought us to this," he said. "I plunged headlong into the realm of the unknown, and now I have dashed us all upon the rocks. But the ship—the ship of Troy has not foundered. And my good fellows, you know what we do when a ship seems to be endangered or cursed—we lighten the load, we throw the cursed object overboard. So I shall. I am that cursed object."

I could not believe what I was hearing. Was he to kill himself? No, rather than let that happen, I would fasten my arms around him and entwine him for the rest of his life, I would be his hated chain.

"Two men call themselves the husband of Helen, daughter of Tyndareus of Sparta." Slowly he turned his head to look over the entire gathering, and his eyes darted across all the faces. I was thankful he had not said *daughter of Zeus.* "Menelaus of the House of Atreus in Greece, and I, Prince Paris of Troy. This is a private quarrel, which the brother of Menelaus has chosen to make an occasion of war. This man, Agamemnon, was a warlord without a war until I appeared in his vision. But I say, it is still a matter between two men—between the man Helen chose as husband in a contest her father arranged many years ago, and the man she chose for herself. It is Agamemnon's doing that anyone else should suffer for it. Let us thrash it out for ourselves. I challenge Menelaus to a duel. Let him meet me on the plain before the walls of Troy." He lowered his arms at last. "The fight will be to the death. And may the gods anoint the best man."

I expected Priam to object, Hecuba to cry out. Instead they stood silent. For the longest time the great crowd in the room did nothing, then they began to chant and sway, and praise Paris for his bravery. They surged forward and enveloped him, then hoisted him on their shoulders.

"Paris! Paris! Paris!" they cried.

They buoyed him along; he bounced and gestured, but he did not look at me.

Deep night. I sat alone in my inmost chamber, barring it to all. I heard Gelanor asking to be admitted and my attendant sending him away. I heard Evadne beg to come in, and being turned away. I was utterly alone, and so must it be.

The stillness of the winter night stalked the chamber, letting Paris's words echo in the cold. At dawn they would fight. And this time tomorrow, who would lie quiet and breathless?

I knew it would be Paris. Menelaus was stronger and more skilled in fighting. Furthermore, he was driven by anger and desire, fueled with the need for revenge, whereas Paris had lost his spirit some time ago; it had fled with Troilus. Menelaus would be fighting a man already dead. This time tomorrow night, Paris and Troilus would be walking together through the gray fields of asphodel. And I would be standing a widow on the banks of the deep black Styx, seeing their shades but unable to cross. Menelaus would proclaim victory and I would have to return to him as his wife, the mother of his child.

Dark. Dark. The sky was still dark as a squid's ink. There was no dawn. Not yet.

Dawn finally came, the rooks and crows cawing deeply to welcome it, their rasps sounding like funeral drums. The sun rose triumphant in the eastern sky. Down on the plain there was movement. The Greeks were on their way; dust from the chariot wheels rose in pale puffs. Below my window I could hear and see the rustlings of the Trojans as they readied for the spectacle. Someone was preparing Paris for his contest. It should have been me, but I knew he would have turned away, despising the sight of me, knowing he was probably going to die for a woman he no longer loved.

I longed to see him as he set out, but I could not trust myself not to fling myself into his arms, dismaying him and harming his ability to fight. No, I must remain here. Only after he had departed would I be able to see him, far below on the plain, only when it was too late.

I changed my clothes, putting on a warm mantle, and went up to the rooftop to watch. I saw the great line of the Greek soldiers drawn up, and a contingent of Trojans marching forward to meet them in the rosy half-light of dawn, and then heard, faintly, cheers as the Scaean Gate of Troy swung open and Priam and Hector emerged in their chariot, then, behind them, Paris in his. Yet a third followed, bearing a herald and sacrificial offerings. In this formal challenge, a ceremonial treaty had to be proclaimed and terms stated.

They milled about as they met, and I longed to be able to see and hear all that was happening. A whisper close behind me, and I turned to see Evadne standing there. How had she come up here, into these most private quarters?

"Helen, you called me," she said softly. Then I saw the curve of her neck and the flash of her eyes, and I knew her for who she was: not Evadne. Thus Aphrodite likes to mock us, thinking us blind and stupid.

"Indeed I did," I said, pretending to believe her disguise. "Today I feel as blind as you," I said sadly. "I wish I could see what was happening on that dreadful plain below. And hear the words being spoken."

"Because my eyesight has faded, I have learned to see far in a different way," she said. I could not have told her voice from Evadne's true one. "Shut your eyelids tightly until you see wheeling colors and spots, then open them again. Focus on what you want to see far away, and it will show itself to you."

Dutifully I followed the instructions, still pretending, humoring the goddess. When I opened my eyes again, it was as if I stood on the plain beside the men. I could even see puffs of smoke from the horses' nostrils rising in the chill dawn air.

Priam stepped from his chariot and approached Agamemnon. The two men stopped a length apart—the long shadows of early morning showed them nearly the same in height, but Agamemnon's shadow was twice as thick as Priam's. The heralds brought out the sacrificial lambs, mixed wine in a gleaming bowl, and poured water over the kings' hands. They nodded to one another, then Agamemnon cut hair from the lambs' heads; the heralds distributed it to the captains on both sides. Then he raised his hands and prayed in that braying voice I had always hated. He called upon Zeus, and the sun, and the rivers and the earth, and the powers of the underworld to witness their oaths and to see that they were kept. "If Paris kills Menelaus," he cried, "allow him to keep Helen and all the wealth she took with her, and we will depart from the shores of Troy. But if Menelaus slays Paris, the Trojans must surrender Helen and her treasure. Furthermore—they must compensate all of us for our expense in coming here! Yes, pay us back, on such a scale that all future generations shall remember it. And if they do not, I will keep my army here and destroy Troy."

To my surprise, Priam agreed. Could he not see that no amount of recompense would satisfy Agamemnon, and that he had just given him permission to sack Troy? And as for the wealth he claimed I had brought, that was a lie.

"No!" I cried, but I was far away.

Agamemnon drew out his great sword, and cut the throats of the lambs. Next he poured wine into two cups; he took one and gave the other to Priam, and they poured it out onto the ground. Then, in one voice, the Trojans and the Greeks chanted a curse: *May the brains of anyone breaking this treaty be dashed out upon the ground, yes, and the brains of their children, too, and may their wives be taken slaves by foreigners.*

Trembling, Priam muttered that he must return to Troy. "I cannot bear to stay here so close and see my son Paris suffer. My only comfort is that the gods already have chosen which man will win, and all that follows has already happened." Stiffly, he turned and got into his chariot. But not before he—and I—heard both armies pray that Paris should die.

"Let the man who brought all these troubles upon us perish," they implored the gods. "Let him go down to the House of Hades, and give us peace!"

Could any father, or wife, hear a worse prayer? And what fools they were, if they thought that would truly bring peace to them. Agamemnon wanted the treasures of Troy, and these did not include me.

Now the puffs of dust traced a line as Priam returned to Troy, and the gates swung open once again to admit him.

"He takes his place at the walls," said the Evadne-spirit. "I propose that we join him." Her lips—oddly supple and missing the purse-string wrinkles usually there—was curved into a sly smile. I wanted to object, but I recognized the command.

A large crowd of onlookers had gathered in the area just above the Scaean Gate, and I could see Priam's gray head surrounded by his family and councilors. As I passed through their ranks, I heard them muttering. Old Panthous, who usually fretted himself over irrelevant mechanical devices, turned baleful, red-rimmed eyes on me. Beside him the elegant Antenor looked at me reproachfully.

My place was beside Priam and Hecuba, no matter how painful that must be for us all. Priam turned to welcome me. His words were kind, but I saw the blank terror in his eyes. He said that he did not blame me; no, he blamed the gods. Hecuba said nothing. She looked at me with narrowed eyes, and her daughters beside her kept staring straight down on the plain to watch their brother go to his doom, even a doom he had brought upon himself.

Hector remained by Paris's side, and he and Odysseus measured out the combat ground. The two contestants stood watching. Menelaus, who in all my time in Troy had produced so much anger in me, was standing before the Greek army, his feet planted in just that awkward way I remembered so well. My heart went out in pity for him. He, also, was still suffering for me.

Paris was looking down at the ground, his head bowed. A sacrifice. He did not expect to live.

Hector stood between them, shaking the lots in his helmet, turning his head away. The lot for the right to cast the first spear-throw leapt out. The gods had chosen Paris.

Both men drew on their helmets and their faces vanished beneath the bronze. Menelaus took up his round shield and, striding to the middle of the measured piece of ground, staked out his place. Paris drew back the long-shafted spear and hurled it through the air. It struck Menelaus's shield with a loud noise but did not penetrate all the way through; for an instant it protruded in a straight line and then the bronze tip bent under the weight and the spear sank. Menelaus wrenched it out with one hand, tossing it aside, then drew back his own and threw at Paris. The hateful goddess enabled me to hear his muttered words, calling on all the powers to see that he killed Paris, to grant him revenge. He added spitefully that our children's children should still shudder at the thought of wronging such a kindly host as he, Menelaus. Selfish words, and they snapped me back from my pity of him.

Hatred gave his throw strength and the spear penetrated the shield of Paris, tearing through to rend his tunic. But he had swerved in time to avoid real injury. While he was reeling and trying to regain his balance, Menelaus rushed on him, brandishing his sword, and brought it down hard on Paris's helmet. The force knocked him to his knees. But instead of piercing the helmet, the silver-mounted blade broke into pieces and fell as glittering metal rain around the kneeling Paris.

Menelaus yelled and raised his hands to the sky, then lunged at Paris and grabbed him by the crest of his helmet. His fury gave him the strength of Heracles and he swung Paris off the ground in an arc, then started dragging him toward the line of Greeks. No more bothering with spears and swords; he would kill him with his bare hands.

Writhing, Paris clawed at the strap of his helmet; he was being choked to death. A groan went up from the walls as we watched helplessly. Paris's feet were trailing in the dust, and his arms were tearing at the helmet.

One moment the newly risen sun was casting its golden light on the contest ground, and in the next a dull mist was creeping across the plain, reaching odd fingers toward the dust-enveloped combatants. Just before it reached them, I saw the strap of Paris's helmet snap and he scramble to his feet. Menelaus held an empty helmet. He stared at it, then threw it back into the lines of his army. He turned on Paris, looking for a way to kill him. Then suddenly both men vanished.

The mist enveloped us, too. I could not even see Priam, near as he was. But I heard the soft, sweet voice of my companion. "Back to your palace," it murmured. "Paris awaits you in your fragrant bedroom, in all his radiant beauty. Go, join him in the inlaid bed."

This was too much to endure, even though I was mortal and she who taunted me immortal. "No!" I said. "Menelaus has defeated Paris down on the plain. You torment me. I will not be mocked by an empty room."

Before she answered, I felt a cold fear spreading through me. "If you provoke me again, I shall hate you as I've loved you," she hissed. "Oh, yes, you sit and feel sorry for yourself when you have had my favor! If I withdraw it, you will look back on that sorrow as bliss." She waited a moment. "Now do as I say. Go to your palace and seek the bedchamber of Paris. *Now*."

I fell away, leaving the Trojans at the wall. No one missed me, no one watched me go. The mist saw to that.

My legs heavy as wood, I trudged uphill toward the palace. There would be no one there. The only Paris waiting would be the one I carried in my mind, while the real one lay slain. No chance ever to repair what had sundered us, either in this life or the pale underworld. There we would wander in the darkness, cold water seeping around the stones where the hopeless dead gathered, passing one another, unable to think or speak.

The palace loomed ahead, surrounded by emptiness. Everyone was down on the walls, and the summit of Troy was deserted. The doors stood open. Odd, when they were always shut fast. There were no guards inside, no attendants, none of the people who had thronged our quarters for so long. My feet sounded very loud as I walked across the floor. I trudged up the stairs, to silence. Up more stairs, ascending into stillness. I did not want to mount the final steps or to enter the bedroom. I looked back; there was no one behind me. "Evadne" had vanished, as I knew she would.

On I went, reaching out to the big handles on the door, pulling them toward me, drawing the heavy portals open. I stepped in, and saw the movement on the bed. Paris was lying there, as provocatively as a faun stretched out on a flowering riverbank. Startled, he sat up, clutching a cover to himself, blinking as those suddenly awakened from sleep do.

What was he doing here? Where was his armor? Why was he lying naked in the bed? How could he have been asleep? I stared at him, speechless.

"Helen," he said, and his voice had not a tang of the old, ugly nuance to it. "Helen." He sounded like a lost, bewildered child.

Suddenly we were not alone. Aphrodite, not bothering now with the likeness of Evadne, fluttered near. She brandished a chair and set it down beside the bed.

"Sit!" she ordered me.

I sank down onto it. I did not look at her, though. I saw only Paris.

"I saw you on the plain . . ." I began.

"I—yes, I was being dragged by Menelaus, and then suddenly I was free. My head snapped back and the helmet was off, and I scrambled away. Just before that, I knew I was going to die. And I did not want to, in spite of all my brave words the night before. I would die and you would go back to Menelaus."

"You did not understand," I said, "that I never would have gone with him."

"But you had tried to once before! You climbed over the walls to make your way to him!"

"To end the war and to make my way to Hades, not to Menelaus. Are there no daggers? Are there no poisons? Oh, there are means aplenty to take ourselves to Hades. Rope was good enough for my mother, after all!"

"I wronged you, Helen. You left the palace—or was it a prison?—in Sparta. I had no right to put you back into it. And dying in that duel would have done so." Now he was sitting up and I could see he was not naked but wearing a tunic of the finest spun wool, shot through with silver threads—not the undertunic of a warrior. "I was crawling away from Menelaus, giddy with surprise that somehow I had been released, hearing the roar of the Greeks in the lines behind me, but crawling to nowhere, as there was no safety. The duel must go on, until one or the other of us was dead. And then, as I scampered through what seemed a forest of legs and flung myself over the sandaled feet, suddenly I was here, here in this chamber, and, overcome with sleep, I lay down. And when I looked up, there you were."

"And she as well." I glanced over at the smiling Aphrodite.

"Who?" asked Paris. He could not see her.

"Our friend. Our enemy. With the gods, it is one and the same."

He looked at me, all the old trust and yearning and splendor in his youthful face. "Helen, I beg you to forgive me. I love you beyond any words to express it. I cannot live knowing that there is any shadow of a cloud between us."

"But you have cast that shadow!" My sun, Paris, had gone behind a gray blank cloud and my world had gone cold.

"Sorrow at the deaths around us, deaths that I—not you!—have caused, weighed me down so heavily I could barely breathe, or even look up. I wanted only for that to end, and I tried to end it the only way I could see. But Helen—oh, Helen!" He rose from the fragrant bed and embraced me. I felt the warmth and strength in those arms, which had hung limply at his side whenever I was near since the deaths began.

His kiss was sweeter than any I had ever tasted before. Was it only because I had been denied them for so long, or had Aphrodite increased that sweetness? I looked around the room from the corners of my eyes, but I saw nothing. She had vanished. This, then, was entirely our own love and our own desire. I clasped him to me and vowed that I would never let anything sunder us again.

We hid in our private quarters—some later said we cowered. But that is not true; we were just once again removed from all the rest of the world, as long ago. The day, which had started so sternly and passed so slowly, now leapt like a deer through its hours.

Then Hector strode in, flinging the doors open with no ceremony. He looked around eagerly, but when his eyes lighted on us, he scowled.

"No!" he cried, his voice breaking with disbelief. "It cannot be! You cannot be here. They said you ran—I did not believe them—I knew you better than that, but here you are. The shame of it, the disgrace to our father's house!" He rushed to Paris and yanked him up, pulling him off his feet. I thought he would shake him to death. "I came here to prove them wrong, and instead of finding your chamber empty, I find you here." He hurled Paris to the floor. "How did you do it, you slinking coward? How did you slither away, in plain sight of everyone? Oh, you must have had the escape route all planned when you issued your mock challenge. But what was the point? If Menelaus lived, you still had not won. Or were you and Helen planning to run away, like you did from Sparta?"

I had never heard so many words from the reserved Hector, not in all the time I had been in Troy. Paris wrapped his arms around his head to shield himself from the coming kicks. From his muffled mouth came a plea that Hector listen. Hector's legs were trembling—aching to kick Paris as he would a stuck door. His right foot was pulling back. Then it stopped. "Very well. Speak, then. Defend yourself with words. You, who cannot defend your honor with arms."

Slowly Paris lifted his head and drew himself up. His face was ashen and his eyes desperate. "I—I cannot," he stammered. "I cannot defend myself, for I know not what happened. I fought Menelaus—you know that. You know that in spite of his sword breaking to pieces and his spear failing to wound me, he was strangling me as he dragged me in the dust. Did I run then? No, I could not breathe. But suddenly I was free—I know not how. And I crawled away, and when I stood up, I was here."

"What nonsense!" Hector cried. "You betray my own good sense, to insult me with such a lie."

"It is true, I swear it, all I can say is that the gods—"

"Lies! Stop involving the gods, when it was your own duplicity that did it! Yes, you planned it all—"

"Hector," I said, "think! Even if Paris had planned such a secret escape—which he did not—his plans could not have rescued him from the death that Menelaus was dragging him toward: a death outside the rules of a duel! Menelaus had lost the duel, so he resorted to this strongman's trick. But such tricks work, all the more sadness for honest men. Only a god could have saved Paris then. And a god did. It is clear."

"No, it is not clear!" Hector roared.

"Hector, it is clear to anyone who looks at it as a stranger would, rather than a wronged brother," said Paris. "I did not ask for the help. I was prepared to pay the price; indeed, I thought I had paid it. But I will not refuse a gift from the gods, particularly when the gift is my own life."

"Why they love your life so, I cannot imagine!" Hector cried. "How many times have you been slated to die, and they rescue you?"

"A man cannot die before his time," said Paris. "You know our destiny is determined at birth and no man can change his. Even the gods, though they could, do not. I was destined to live at least through today. And Helen is right—Menelaus cheated by trying to kill me that way, so the gods were justified in preventing him from it."

Hector gave an ugly laugh. "Agamemnon has proclaimed Menelaus the winner. What did you expect? And then someone from Troy shot an arrow at the Greeks—by accident, I think—and Agamemnon used that as an excuse to start the fighting again. Can you hear the battle noises from the Plain of Troy—or is the air in your chamber too rarefied for such sounds to carry up here?"

I rushed to the window. I could hear rumbling noise, faint and wavering like heat waves, from somewhere far away. Then the unmistakable sound of metal hitting metal. Paris came and stood beside me. He gripped the sill.

"We are all powerless to stop it," he said plaintively to Hector. "Too many people want to fight."

Hector shook his head. "Foolish boy! This is all on your head."

"No," Paris said. "I refuse to accept that! There were—and still are—people within Troy who want this war as badly as any of the Greeks. Who was it prevented Helen and me from seeing Menelaus and Odysseus when they came? We never found out. True, the spy impersonating Hyllus was unmasked, but he must have had accomplices, and they go free. Hyllus could not have been everywhere, doing everything. Someone killed our sacred household snake to frighten us. Who was it? Helen tried to end it by going to the Greeks herself, but was stopped by Antimachus. Ask him what he was doing outside the walls at night!"

Hector started. Clearly he had not known about this. Antimachus had kept our secret. "Helen tried to go to the Greeks?"

"Yes, to end this. Antimachus caught me."

"Caught you—where?"

"Outside the walls."

Hector's eyes bulged in disbelief. "You escaped over the walls?"

"Yes. I was a good piece away already before the prowling Antimachus grabbed me."

I could tell by his face that Hector did not accept my story.

"Very well, then," I said, "ask him yourself. See how surprised he is that you know!"

"I shall," said Hector sternly. "But if it is true, he has been adamant about wanting to keep you here, and bait the Greeks with you. Whereas Antenor has most sensibly tried to avert the war." A particularly jarring clash down below came to our ears. "But it is too late now."

"That is what I just said," Paris reminded him. "It goes forward now and there is no stopping it. Those of us who tried have been cast aside."

"I must return to the battle," said Hector. "Lest it be said I, too, am a coward." He swung around, so quickly his tunic flew out behind him.

"I am not a coward!" yelled Paris. "Stop calling me one!"

"It is not I who call you that, but every man on that field who saw you flee."

"I didn't flee! I just told you—"

Hector was gone, his footsteps dying away.

"Paris, from today onward we are branded as cowards and villains," I said, turning to him. "We know the truth, but there is no convincing others."

"We must! We must! We must clear our names."

Now he seemed what Hector had just called him—foolish boy. No, not foolish so much as naïvely hopeful.

"There must be a sacrifice." My niece Iphigenia had been the one for the Greeks. This was more subtle, but we would be the Trojan sacrifices. "People demand sacrifices. It is part of war."

"I thought the fallen warriors and the sacked cities were the sacrifices of war."

"For something within the human heart, more is demanded." I felt drained.

Paris smiled. "You upset yourself in defending me. Such a fierce champion! It must be true what they say about women—they are more deadly than men. At least the Amazons will fight for Troy."

"Then let us call them now. We will need them."

"We call them?"

"Yes. Before it is too late."

"I do not have the authority to call them. It has to be Priam—"

"He will dither and dally until we are so penned up by the Greeks they cannot reach us. You call them. Are you not a prince of Troy?"

"But it has to be the king who makes these decisions."

"Make this one on your own. Then see if they do not look at Paris differently."

I was ready to declare my own war on Troy. I was done with bowing to her self-defeating rules and demands.

❖ LIV ❖

The Amazons are on their way," said Paris. We were in our uppermost chamber, polishing his armor, when he suddenly looked up and told me. In the evenings we took refuge up here; the lower floors were still teeming with our foreign "guests," but here, as in a hawk's nest, we were far away. The fighting had come close to the walls of Troy at times, but there had been no attempt to storm them, and the war had become an everyday affair.

We had learned to shape our lives around the coldness we found in Troy, a coldness that had nothing to do with winter. That had passed, and even another summer was passing, the sun still strong and yellow and warming on the bricks, but winter in the faces of the people. Hector and Andromache's baby had come—the longed-for son—but I had not been invited to see him except in secret, when all other family members had left, even though I felt that by accompanying Andromache to the rites at Mount Ida I had, in some way, helped in his conception.

Andromache said as much, but, sighing, she covered the baby's head and took him from my arms. "It grieves me," she whispered, cradling him against her body. "I feel as though you are his aunt more than any of the others, but . . ."

"Leave it unsaid," I answered. Someone might be listening. I had grown used to spies everywhere.

She asked after my weaving.

"I devote more and more time to it," I told her. "It seems to grow of its own accord, take on new meanings and directions. I am using purple wool for the background. The gray-blue borders are my old life, the inner area Troy and her history, but the heart of it is still empty, still forming."

"The fate of Troy has yet to be written," she said. "Someday you will fill it in, and the gaps will close."

What I did not say was that I was driven more and more to the weaving; as the rest of my life shrank, it expanded, took on a life of its own—or perhaps it created its own life, as art does.

"Paris has been fighting well," she said, to cheer me. "Hector welcomes his help."

I smiled, appreciating her effort to cheer me up. Paris, true to his dedication, had put aside his bow and was learning to fight skillfully day after day on the plain with spear and sword. "Yes," I said. "Hector complimented him yesterday, saying that he fought as well as any man." I did not say how difficult it was for him to make himself go out day after day, nor how frantic with worry I was as the wounded stumbled back in at sundown and the dead were carried on the shoulders of the able. In the lower city the casualties were lying on blankets, tended by our physicians and women. Gelanor and Evadne were busy aiding them, and Gelanor had compounded some salves that speeded the healing, but only for those destined to recover; for the more severely injured, we still were at the mercy of the gods. I was thankful that plague had not struck yet. People believed it was caused by an angry Apollo's arrows, but Gelanor said it also appeared whenever there were too many people crowded together. Perhaps the arrow-god just waits until his targets are conveniently packed close, he had said.

"The Amazons are coming," I said. It felt right to inform her; she had confided in me, and was the only member of the family still to be my friend. "Paris sent for them, and he has a message that they are on their way."

She frowned. "Paris sent for them? Without permission?"

"Without whose permission? Hector's?" Hector did not rule here, not yet.

"The king's," she said. "Did Priam give his consent?"

"He gave his consent when he asked them to be his allies," I said. "He will wait too late, that is his way."

"So you are directing the war now?" Her voice was suddenly as cold as the rest of the family's. "I cannot think it was Paris who urged this action."

"And why not?" I burst out. "Why does no one credit him with any command? It was he alone of Priam's sons who was raised beyond the sheltering walls of Troy, in the wilds, where he had to survive on his wits and his strength."

She smiled indulgently. "Helen, let us not pretend. It is touching that you are so solicitous of Paris and his abilities—" She paused. "But it is a mistake to insult Priam this way."

"We meant no insult."

"He will take it as one." She took a deep breath, to reset the mood. "Now tell me, when will the Amazons come? We will welcome them with a great to-do. Perhaps I can even sit down and talk to the famous Penthesileia, their leader. I saw her ambassador—or should it be ambassadress?—when she came to declare herself Troy's ally. What a woman!"

"She was indeed formidable," I remembered. "I cannot imagine anyone more stalwart or fierce. But their commander must be . . ." I would have said *must be a female Achilles,* but I must not speak that name.

That evening I took refuge in my weaving. It was more and more my beloved companion and my solace. I loved the feeling of the slight rasp of the thread against my fingers, the unique smell of the wool, and the lingering softness it bestowed on the hands that touched it—all this apart from the rapture of losing myself in the story I was telling in the pattern. I thought of weavings folded away in trunks in the treasure rooms of palaces; I wondered if, in years far away, anyone would take mine out to remember us here.

I barred no one from my weaving chamber; still, almost no one chose to come in. I was used to being quite alone. But one cool day Gelanor strode in, a bit out of breath from the many stairs. I was pleased. I had seen little of him of late. He had to be the busiest man in Troy, tending to the wounded and ill in the lower city, running his spy circle, preparing his various weapons to be put into action if the enemy came close enough to the walls. I hardly knew what to inquire about first. He spared me the choice by announcing, "I have news from Greece."

Greece! And I had just been there, in my mind, at least.

"The seas are closing for winter, but one boat managed to get through," he said. "I thought it well to know what was happening at home, so I had sent people to inquire. Not spies!" He held up his hands. "I assumed there were no secrets there. I was wrong." I would have spoken then, but he plunged ahead. "Your sister Clytemnestra—she has taken a lover, and together they rule Mycenae. Should Agamemnon return, he will find his way barred."

Clytemnestra! A surge of pride washed through me. Her husband had trampled upon her, sacrificed their child. Instead of meekly bowing her head, she had turned elsewhere. So in chasing after his greedy dreams, Agamemnon had made a second sacrifice he did not intend.

"Who?" I asked. It was of no matter, I thought.

"Aegisthus," he said.

All part of the curse of the House of Atreus! Aegisthus was but the last generation of it, having had his heritage taken away by Atreus. And there was another, different curse, the one Aphrodite had laid on my father, saying that his daughters would be husband-forsakers. So now they fulfilled one another.

I gave a great whoop of laughter. It was all too fitting. "I hope he is handsome?"

Gelanor pursed up his lips. "I know not, my lady. That was not important to my informant. Shall I dispatch another?"

"No," I said. "May my sister have joy of him, whatever he looks like."

"The Greeks, in sailing away and staying gone for so long, have hatched many troubles for themselves. Thrones are not tanned hides; they do not keep."

"What of home? What of Sparta?"

"Your father, Tyndareus, manfully holds the place. But he does not know who will follow. Your brothers . . . It was true what Agamemnon said."

"Oh." I had half believed it; now I knew. "What of Hermione?"

"Tyndareus has sent her to Clytemnestra."

"Also as Agamemnon said." Oh, why could not these have been lies? He lied so much. "Why has he done this?"

"Perhaps he did not feel he could provide for her, there being no woman in the Spartan palace for her. So he sent her to her aunt's in Mycenae."

"Where she will learn of adultery and treachery!" Oh, my dear daughter!

Gelanor gave one of his strategic coughs. "Adultery and treachery . . . if I may say so, my dearest Helen, lessons begin at home."

"I never committed treason!"

He laughed, and I joined him. There was no other response possible.

"But enough of Greece," he said. "My spies here have been busy lads and girls inside that palisade protecting the enemy camp, and you will be most interested in what they report."

"Should you not tell Priam?" I felt I owed him this respect.

"I tried," he said. "He waved me away. It seems I am too closely allied with you and Paris, and some of his advisors wish to bar me from the king's presence."

"Should you not tell Hector, then?"

"Hector, in his nobility, also wants no information that might deflect him from his chosen course."

"But only a fool refuses to take new knowledge!"

"Sometimes nobility transforms a man into a fool." He said this with sadness. "Down in the Greek camp, dissension has broken out. It seems that Agamemnon insulted Achilles by taking away a woman he won in one of his nasty raids. The woman Agamemnon had taken for himself was the daughter of a priest of Apollo, and you know what havoc Apollo can cause when he is angered—yes, plague has broken out among the Greeks. So the woman must be returned, and Agamemnon must have another, else his loins will ache. So he grabbed Achilles's prize as a substitute."

Who cared what these squabbling men did? They were loathsome.

"I can see by your face that you do not understand our great good fortune in this," he said.

"I hear you say *our* fortune. Have you become so entirely Trojan, then?"

"No. I still long for home, but my home and my people have nothing to do with the likes of Agamemnon and Achilles. If they perish, all the better for common Greeks. Our good fortune is that Achilles now refuses to fight under Agamemnon. He first threatened to sail away, but now is content to sulk in his tent. 'Someday you'll want me!' he says. 'And in that day . . .'"

"It shows how entirely selfish he is. For if the day comes when they are desperate, it means many of his countrymen have been killed."

"Surely you are not surprised that he is besotted with his own importance," said Gelanor.

"No, he has been since childhood," I said. "He allowed that his cousin Patroclus existed, but no one else. One could hope he would have grown out of it, but I see he has not."

"He has forbidden Patroclus to fight as well. And my best spy, who has ingratiated himself with Patroclus, told me that Achilles stormed and yelled and called upon his goddess mother to make sure that the Greeks were soundly thrashed, to punish Agamemnon for insulting the pride of the great Achilles."

"I wonder if she will obey her darling son," I said.

"Perhaps she has already. For Hector and the company are arming for an assault on the Greek camp. Something put it into their heads, after all these months of sticking close to the walls of Troy. Who can say it was not the goddess?"

Eager to breathe some fresh air, I walked with Gelanor out into the courtyard as he left. My palace rooms, shut up in winter, seemed suddenly stale and sealed; the herbs we burned to perfume the air only made it worse. But as I stepped outside, my mantle was almost ripped from me. Suddenly it was very cold, and a fierce wind was howling, its fingers tearing at my hair and clothes. Tiny pinpricks of chill landed on my nose, my cheeks, my brow. It was something I had not felt in a long time.

"Snow!" I cried, looking up at the sky, where swirls of white were covering the stars.

Gelanor grunted. "Chariot wheels will clog and there'll be no fighting for a while."

"Hecuba told me it snowed in Troy, but I didn't believe her."

"You should always believe Hecuba!" He laughed. "This is going to bury us!" Bundling himself up, he hurried away, down toward his house. "I hope I have enough wood at hand," he muttered.

I stayed out in the courtyard for a few moments, relishing the sting of the cold and the roar of the wind. We had seen storms like this attacking the Taygetus Mountains back in Sparta, when they disappeared behind a mist of cloud and the next day sparkled an intense white from the new snow. And Mycenae turned into a palace of ice, so Clytemnestra had told me. Clytemnestra . . . the next time it happened, would she fold herself up into the arms of her lover and delight in thinking of Agamemnon shivering in his tent?

Now the Plain of Troy would turn white, the top of our walls would turn white, and all the streets of Troy would be muffled beneath a thick white blanket.

Paris came stamping in later, dusting snow off his mantle. I kissed the flakes from his nose and chin, lifting them delicately away with my tongue. They were an icy treat.

"Everything is closing down," he said. "The gates are shut tight and you can be sure no one will be going in or out of the city for a while. No more battles."

"If only that were final, not just a respite," I said.

"Someday it will be," he said. "There will come a day when the battles will cease and the plain will be empty . . . empty except for our fine Trojan horses—who can graze there once again—and for the trade fair, which will be bigger than ever."

He sank down on a stool and reached across a table for a dried date, which he popped into his mouth. "I should not be profligate with these, I know our stores are running low . . ." He sighed. "All the way from Egypt you came," he addressed a second fig waiting its turn in his hand. "From that placid place where the Nile runs through a flat desert and the only mountains are man-made ones, pointed things built of stone." He ate it. "A strange place. A very strange place, so I am told." Suddenly his eyes changed, and he got a faraway look. "Helen . . ." He took my hands, grasped them tightly. "When this war is over, when it's all done, let's leave Troy. Let's go to Egypt. I could set up a trading center there for Troy, act as Father's agent. If Troy could have some of the profits from a direct trade with Egypt, and we managed it ourselves instead of using Egyptian middlemen—"

"But . . . you are a prince of Troy! Does a prince become a merchant?"

"True, I am a prince, but I shall never reign here. Hector will inherit, and after him there's Deiphobus."

"That lecherous ape!"

Paris laughed. "Father seems to think highly of him. As concerns fighting, that is, and with Father that is all that counts."

Then Priam is a fool, I wanted to snap, but I knew that Paris was touchy on this subject. "When the war is over, he may value other traits," was all I said.

"I cannot wait for that day. Oh, Helen, let us go make our lives elsewhere. I was wrong to bring us back to Troy. I know it now. We can never be anything here but curiosities . . . curiosities rejected by our families. And every Trojan death will be laid at our feet—rightly, I fear. Oh, I never should have come back!" His eyes pled with mine. "Listen to me. Let us just go and be free people in another land."

It was a mad dream, I knew that. But a tempting one for us, locked in tonight by the falling snow and the cessation of everyday life. Let us play our little game, for just a little while. "Very well, then. Where shall we go?"

His face had a dreamy look. "We'll sail from here, along the coast by Rhodes and Cyprus, but we won't stop there. Oh, unless you want to?"

"No, let us make our way quickly to our final destination."

"Egypt," he said. "I've always wanted to go there. There are so many places I want to see, and so far I've seen nothing but Troy and Mount Ida and a bit of Greece. My life of exploration was interrupted when I found you—but now we can do all the things I would have done alone. We will sail up the Nile—it has seven mouths, I'm told. We'll choose one and follow it as it goes deep into Egypt. It will get hotter and hotter . . . there will be no winter . . . and we'll visit their huge stone mountains."

"But wouldn't you want your trading colony to be nearer the sea?"

"Oh, yes, of course, but I want to explore Egypt first. And I want to do it secretly. We already have other names—Alexandros and Cycna, remember? So we'll call ourselves that. No one will know."

I laughed at the happy realization that to him, now, I was just Helen, and my face was just the face he saw every day. But the world might recognize Helen, unless I went back to the hateful veiling. But perhaps not. Perhaps my face had changed in the years since I left Sparta. I hoped so.

"Their king has an odd name, or title."

"Yes, pharaoh," Paris said. "And they marry their sisters. And worship gods with animal heads. But"—he bent forward and whispered—"they do unspeakable things to dead bodies. They gut them and salt them and wrap them up in linen. They think they will come back to life someday."

"I shall take care not to die there," I said. "Where do they put these bodies?" I imagined they must keep them in their homes, to have them always at hand.

"They construct elaborate tombs," said Paris. "But we can't get inside them. They are all sealed up." He poured himself some wine and tilted it thoughtfully in his cup. "Farther up the Nile there is a vast city where the priests have a temple that is bigger than Troy. It has statues five times the size of a man. We must go there. As soon as this war is over."

Outside, the snow fell, smothering Troy, holding the war at bay, but not ending it.

As I moved through the room in the hush, Paris whispered, "I know as well as you it cannot be."

❖ LV ❖

The snow must have been under the command of Ares, for it did not stay long, and soon the streets of Troy resounded with the thump of warriors' feet as they marched out toward the Scaean Gate to attack the Greeks. Reinforcements were on their way to Troy—the Paphlagonians and Thracians and the Lycians, under the command of the renowned Sarpedon, as well as the Amazons. Paris was welcomed at Hector's side, and together the brothers swept down the main street and mounted their chariots. Other brothers—Deiphobus, Aesacus, and Helenus—were right behind them. I saw Antimachus striding quickly, leaping into his chariot just beyond the gate.

I dreaded to see Paris go. His hasty and guilt-ridden training with the sword and shield—were they adequate? I had urged him to take his bow, the weapon he excelled at, but he scoffed at me. He was determined to prove himself in the arena that other Trojans honored. But he was many years behind them in practice. On the slopes of Mount Ida where he grew up, herdsmen did not fight with spears and swords against wild beasts—only a fool would, and that fool would soon perish.

On across the plain. The Greeks were advancing to meet them. So orderly and measured. Then they all vanished into a dark mass as they clashed. We could see nothing.

Night. Darkness fell and only stragglers had staggered in, beating on the gates for admittance. They told of a melee, of Aeneas being wounded, but no other warrior of note.

Oh, thank all the gods! Paris was safe.

Later they all came back, wearily carrying their injured. More men to lie on blankets in the lower city, to be tended as best we could. Aeneas was hobbling, leaning on two men, his shoulder a red stain. Diomedes had done it.

Paris stumbled in, beside Deiphobus. He was panting and mud-covered, but Deiphobus was laughing, fresh as a newly unfurled flower. "Here's your husband, lady," he said, pushing him toward me. "Restore him, as you know best." He gave a smirk, then peeled off to continue trooping up to Priam's palace, where they would all be welcomed with wine and food and, better than that, would be honored.

"What happened?" I clutched Paris, feeling the sweat-soaked corselet under my hand.

"They were waiting for us," he said. But his voice rang with pride. "We gave them a good thrashing."

"Did you drive them back to the ships?"

He looked at me oddly. "No, that we did not." He was still breathing heavily, his chest heaving. "But perhaps we would have had the light not failed."

Hector exhorted all the Trojan women to supplicate the Pallas Athena with gifts and prayers. Hecuba, holding the finest-woven bolt of cloth from her treasure chamber as offering, led the princesses in solemn procession at dawn. Behind them came the wives and daughters of the commanders and councilors. I was not invited. My presence would upset the ladies and disrupt the mood. I watched them from my high window as they shuffled into the temple beneath us.

Later that morning Paris and I went to see the wounded in the lower city, lying in painful rows waiting for aid. Many women were tending them, and I saw the pots of unguents Gelanor had prepared standing at the head of each row. Aeneas, a highborn warrior, would not be among them, but these were the men who bore the true brunt of the fighting.

"Today's fighting went well, as far as it was allowed to. They must stop these pauses!" Gelanor said.

"You only say that because you want to try out your insect bombs," I said.

"I do confess, I think I have perfected them. And the plague-ridden garments in the temple can serve as a last defense."

Paris looked at the row of tossing, groaning men. "Tomorrow at this time—" He squared his shoulders. "I must go arm. We are to fight again. Hector will lead us out shortly."

I had betaken myself to the guard tower, so that I might watch them depart. I found it empty—curious, but perhaps the archers only manned it when a battle was in progress and there was a chance the enemy would approach. Or perhaps the guards were changing their watch.

Down below I could hear the gathering troops. They were waiting for Hector. Just then someone entered the guard tower. I could not see who—I could only discern that he wore the crested helmet of a soldier. I shrank back into a corner to watch. Then I saw that the soldier was not alone—a woman was with him, a woman carrying a baby. But the poor light obscured their features. The woman held out the child to him. The child cried and shrank away, and the man took off his helmet and laid it aside.

"There, there," he said, and I recognized the voice. It was Hector.

"He is frightened of the horsehair crest." The familiar voice of Andromache. "To have a soldier for a father is always to be fearful." She clutched his arm. "Hector, do not leave us!"

I saw his backlit profile move in a startled jolt. "Woman, what can you be thinking?" His voice, always deep and measured, was sorrowfully puzzled.

"You are all I have now," she said. "My father, my brothers, all dead, killed by the vile Achilles. You are my only family. I beg you, do not go out there! Lest he kill you as well! And I have nothing! And your dear son, Astyanax, be left fatherless!"

"If I desert my men, then all will lose heart, and Troy fall," he said. He stepped away from her, as if to protect himself.

"How can one man be the sole protection of an entire city?" she cried. "There are hundreds, thousands of others here. But they are not the heir of Troy, the son of Priam, the father of my son."

"If the heir of Priam shirks, then why should anyone fight?" Hector spoke slowly. His very deliberate framing of his words betrayed how deeply he had thought about it. "Oh, Andromache!" Now he clasped her to himself. "You have barely touched upon it." He bowed his head. "If Troy falls . . ."

Andromache made an inchoate sound of distress and buried herself deeper against Hector's breast.

"What I cannot bear is the thought that you will be led away captive, or that our son will perish. The only consolation is that I will be dead by then, buried, and cannot see or hear the cries as Troy dies."

"But then . . . why must you go forth? If there is no hope, why go?"

He shook his head as if to clear it. "Because I can think both things at once. Troy needs me—Troy is doomed. May my son grow up to be a greater warrior than I—my son will die. I have no god or goddess mother or father. I am entirely mortal and the gods do not strive to protect me. So I must fight as a man alone and uncovered. But that is what I was born to do." He slowly pulled away from Andromache and held up little Astyanax. Now the child laughed and gurgled, touching his father's face.

"Here. Take him." He thrust him back at Andromache and slid his helmet on. "Farewell."

Brutal in his abruptness, he turned on his heel and left. Perhaps that was the only way he could force himself to do it.

Andromache stood weeping, holding Astyanax, who joined in, wailing.

I did not want her to see I was there and had witnessed all that passed between her and Hector. Such private moments should remain private. Slowly, holding my breath, I crept toward the door. She was not looking; her head was bent over her son's, her eyes squeezed shut. I did not know how long I could keep so silent; my lungs were bursting, but I dared not breathe. Gradually I edged outside and tiptoed down the ladder. At the bottom, I gasped for air.

"Helen!"

Too late I saw the helmet and recognized it; a muscular arm hooked around me and pulled me behind the ladder.

"How long were you listening?" Hector was angry.

"I was there first," I said, realizing I sounded like a child justifying myself. "I thought I was alone. I meant to be alone—my presence disturbs people now. But I need to watch, to know what is happening, as much—no, more than they!"

His arm relaxed and he released me. "It is best that of all people, it was you who overheard me." He spoke in a low voice. "Things are not as simple to you as they are to others, who have never seen the other side."

"Alas, that I have seen what I have seen."

"We have both seen many things from the beginning that others are blind to. That is why I can entreat you: take care of Andromache and my son when the time comes." Before I could protest, he said, "As I said—and you heard—the unbearable part is knowing what will happen to her when—if— Troy falls. But you will survive, you can protect her."

"I will be the first to reap the fury of the Greeks when they storm us. If they do." I was careful to add the *if*.

"No. They will spare you. You are one of them, and they will want to take you back as their prize of war."

"No!" I cried. "I'd rather die!"

"But you won't," he said flatly. "You are strong. You are a survivor. And if she clings to you, Andromache will be spared, and my son as well."

"Please, Hector!" I laid my fingers across his mouth. "Do not speak these words. They carry their own power. Do not make it happen."

"I need to know I have your promise," he said, removing my hand. "Then I can fight content."

"Very well, then, I promise. But I promise a future that may never come about."

"That is enough for me," he said. "Take Andromache with you wherever you go." He stepped out from the shadow of the ladder and fastened the strap of his helmet. "I must wait no longer," he said, and fell in with his marching men on their way out of the city.

LVI

Hector survived that day's battle, and reentered the city to great acclaim. Then he vanished into his house, where I knew Andromache embraced him, ignorant that he had consigned her to me for safekeeping.

I was greatly disturbed over his charge: both to look after her, and that I would, regardless of what happened, survive. *You are a survivor,* he had said, making it sound an ugly thing. A survivor was a rodent—was there not the adage about abandoning sinking ships?—who scavenged for himself, utterly without pride or morals, who lived only for himself. Was it the opposite of being noble? What was it Gelanor had said about Hector, that he was too noble and that was no way to win wars?

Were Gelanor and I two of a kind, he with his insect bombs and heated sand, and I with my instinct for self-preservation? But surely Hector was wrong. Had self-preservation been utmost in my mind, I never would have run away from Sparta.

Yes, he was wrong. He had to be.

Several days passed—an informal truce. Then word reached me that Antenor had suggested that tired old idea that Helen be returned to the Greeks. Before he could air this publicly, I knew I should call upon him.

On official business, no one could refuse to see the notorious Helen. I knew Antenor would not turn me away, no matter his private feelings. When I was announced at the door, I was told the councilor would see me straightaway. He came in, trailing his long robe. His face wore a smile, as assumed as his emblems of office.

"My dear princess," he said, inclining his head.

"Esteemed councilor," I said.

"Come, let us speak privately." He swept out his arm expansively, a signal to his servants that this meeting must not be disturbed. I followed him back into shadowy quarters.

The room was not large, but each object in it was chosen with an eye to pleasure. There was a shapely clay vase with a dark octopus design resting on the floor, and several cups of pure gold were displayed on shallow shelves jutting from the walls. The chairs were draped with deep-dyed fabrics from

Sidon and even the stools had carved feet, inlaid with ivory. Two bronze incense burners were smoking.

Antenor nodded toward them. "One holds dried cypress, the other hyssop," he said. "I find either by itself to be too strong, but when they are blended"—he stepped forward and fanned the smoke—"what a marriage!" He inhaled deeply. Only then did he turn to me. "To what do I owe this honor?"

"You know well enough," I said, settling myself on one of the chairs—oddly uncomfortable despite their drapings. "Your suggestion that once again I be returned to the Greeks. Surely you are aware that my return is no longer enough to avert the war." Should I tell him of my own attempt? No.

"And why do you say this?" he asked.

"The only one who cares about that is my former husband, Menelaus," I said. "As for the others, they will not rest until they have plundered Troy and taken her riches."

He was observing me with a curious stare. Did he not understand? "I heard Agamemnon speak of Troy long ago. He wanted to come here. Returning me will not dissuade him."

Antenor leaned back and crossed his arms. "Are you afraid to return to them?"

This was too much! "No! I was prepared to do so. But wiser heads convinced me it was to no purpose. And I listened. The Greeks did not come all this way for Helen. I am not so deluded as to think so."

He looked at me as if he didn't know whether I could be trusted. I looked back at him. The long-ago hints of my mother to my father about a Trojan visitor during his absence began to circle in my head.

He was handsome, comely. The sort a queen might welcome, after a long stretch of loneliness. His hair, the way it grew in a whorl from his crown, was like mine.

"You are a wise woman," he finally said.

"I have inherited it," I answered.

"From whom?"

"I know not, but whoever it is, I should honor him."

"Indeed, one should honor one's ancestors." He nodded. "So there will be no proposal to the Greeks. Very well. Now, my friend—"

"Are you my friend? If so, I am glad of it. Friends often stretch a long way back and I understand you once visited Sparta and saw my mother and father."

He spread his hands. "Your father was away. Fighting the Hippocoon. But your gracious mother welcomed me. She ushered me into the palace—a glorious place high above the plain and the meandering Eurotas. I remember we—"

"Undoubtedly you were entertained in the proper fashion," I suggested.

He gave what passed with him as a frown—he was so polite he never truly frowned. "But before that she took me for a long walk beside the Eurotas, which was in spate from the melting winter snows. Delightful river! And there were the most stately swans there, larger than any I had ever seen. One of them chased us! I do believe . . . oh, forgive me, Helen, if I fumble in searching for it . . . he had the most magnificent feathers, unlike any I had ever seen—blindingly white . . ." He got up and rifled through a small patterned wooden box. "It is here somewhere, I know it . . ." At length he grabbed a feather and waved it. "Here! Here is that feather!" He placed it in my hand.

It lay there, gleaming. It was the very same sort of feather I had seen in Mother's jar. Its brightness, after so many years, was not dimmed. Was it the swan she treasured, then, or the memory of the man who had seen it with her? Who, in truth, was my father?

Time passed in an uneven fashion. Just when it seemed something momentous was about to happen—a pivotal battle, an inciting decision—time froze and we felt motionless, suspended in a sea of inaction.

But that was an illusion. All the while time was rushing by, faster than it seemed. Was the natural world a reliable marker? Were the trees growing normally, or were they the playthings of the gods who guard the passage of the seasons, as we were? Could I look at them and say with confidence that yes, this is a year's growth, therefore a year has passed? It seemed the Greeks had been at Troy for a long time; other days it was as if they had just come. We watched the seasons change but it seemed there were no true changes: the Greeks waited, and waited, and waited, and so did we.

On a cold, clear night, Gelanor came to the palace. A half-moon was shining forlornly on the patchy, lumpy ground stretching between us and the Greek camp. Nothing moved down there. The sea beyond it gleamed faintly. The waves always captured whatever light there was and twinkled it back.

"Hector and I have been training a spy he is particularly impressed with," he said. "His name is Dolon—of course, that's not his real name, who would know what that is? He's to reconnoiter the Greek camp, pass into the walls."

"I thought you already had people there," Paris said.

"I do. But Hector does not, and it is important to him to train someone. I think . . . Dolon is perhaps not the man I would have chosen. But no matter," he quickly said.

"No one is listening," I assured him. "There are no spies here—unless you sent them, you spymaster. Why are you hesitant about Dolon?"

He twisted his mouth—something he always did when thinking. "Dolon has a vanity about him . . . the enemy can use that. If they appeal to it, his caution will flee. A good spy has no vanity. Why should he? His identity is false in the first place."

"Some men may find it impossible to lay their identity down, walk away from it," said Paris.

"Such men should not be spies," said Gelanor. "Vanity has betrayed more spies than informants."

As the cold wind whispered through the trees outside, we let the wine warm us, savoring our quiet time together. I see us now, as a painter might have seen us: Gelanor sitting calmly on a stool, Paris young and glowing, me, so happy with my loved ones beside me, their faces so close I could reach out and touch them with my fingertips.

Once again, both armies readied themselves for battle. The Trojans marched out through the Scaean Gate as usual, although the company seemed larger to me this time. Perhaps more of the common soldiers had joined in. We had word that the Thracians were nearby and would reach us in the next few days. Close behind them the Lycians were coming, the Carians, and the Mysians. The Amazons, coming the farthest distance, would be last.

This was the largest battle joined so far. It was as if the Greeks finally had realized they were here to fight—after so many seasons of sitting on the seashore or making tentative little forays into the field—and they were willing to do so. We could see the demarcation line where the armies met—at first it was in the middle of the plain, then as the day drew on it moved back, closer to the Greek camp. Then darkness fell.

No one returned to Troy. Our warriors were camping out in the field. From my rooftop I could see the pricks of light from the fires, spread out on the plain. They were close to the Greek lines. The Greeks must have drawn back behind their defensive palisade wall, cowering there. Onward, Trojans! How well had they done today?

* * *

Oh, they had done marvelously well, and my Paris magnificently! He had wounded and disabled Machaon, their physician, and Eurypylus, the highborn son of Euaemon, and best of all, Diomedes, the bragging, swaggering upstart who had wounded Aeneas in an earlier battle. The only possible disappointment was that he had done it with his bow, and Diomedes taunted him for it, but what matter? Diomedes said it clutching himself, teeth clenched for the pain. Better than that, Agamemnon was wounded, as were Menelaus and Odysseus—not seriously, but their best fighters were taken out of the action. Meanwhile Achilles and his Patroclus held themselves aloof from the fighting, so they might just as well be wounded—or dead.

Menelaus, wounded. How badly? Where? I did not understand myself, but I winced in picturing it, and even prayed that he was not in pain. Now he had paid a price for his pursuit of me, but knowing that was no balm to me. I did not feel that way about Agamemnon; no pain could ever compensate for that which he had wreaked upon his own daughter and his wife. I hoped he was howling in agony, clutching whatever part of him was wounded; I hoped that Menelaus had been given a sleeping draught and would awaken calm and mending. As for Odysseus—let his wound incapacitate that mind of his, unhinge it so he thought only of remedies for his pain and not plans against the Trojans.

But we received news that Dolon had been intercepted on his way into the Greek camp—intercepted by Odysseus and Diomedes before the battle where they sustained their wounds—and tricked into revealing the site of the Thracians, who were camped in the fields approaching Troy. Odysseus and his party not only murdered Dolon, they killed Rhesus, the Thracian leader, stole their fine-bred horses, and pranced their way back to their camp.

It became clear to me in that moment that Odysseus had been the most dangerous foe the Trojans had. Not because he was the greatest warrior—he was not—but because he could strike from under a rock, like a venomous snake. Agamemnon, Menelaus, Idomeneus, the sons of Nestor—those men rode out in their chariots, fought with sword and shield, fell or retreated. But Odysseus—he was like a covered pit lined with sharpened stakes, his true, deadly nature disguised.

Evadne came to me, stealing in silently while I stood on the balcony watching the fires on the plain. Before I realized it, she was standing beside me. I was happy to see her; her very presence was reassuring.

"You cannot see them, but there are hundreds of little flickering fires down below. The Trojan forces are camping close to the Greek lines." That was before I knew of the attack on Dolon.

"That is good, my lady, but I do fear for the morrow. Something bad has already happened, I feel it."

"Not to Paris!" I cried, as if saying it would make it not so. "Tell me."

"Not Paris, no, I would feel that more strongly. But then, there are always bad things in war." Now she sought to undo her frightening words. "My powers have been stirring again. There was a time, after the serpent—when I received few messages. Perhaps that is because there were no messages to receive. But you understand how it shakes one to have revelations suddenly stop."

Yes, I did. I had received few leadings; my impressions of things yet to come were mere whispers, the pictures faded and wavering. The snake had taken that with him, or so I believed.

"The battle will turn now," she said. "Things will happen very quickly, after so long when nothing happened. Are we ready, my lady? Ready for whatever is to come?"

"No," I said. "I am not ready for anything, save for the Greeks to board their ships and return home."

"I see that, but I see you on the ships with them. I see Andromache on a Greek ship, and Cassandra."

"No. Your vision fails you. You have just said that you do not see Paris!"

"The visions are incomplete, they come as patches and pieces."

"Until they are joined and whole, do not speak of them." But too late— she had, she had.

I lay down on my bed, rigid. Evadne had departed; the palace was silent. The bed I shared with Paris seemed huge without him, as if I were on the deck of a ship. A ship . . . why think of ships now? Because of what Evadne had said? I would never board a ship with Greeks, that I vowed. If the day came that she foresaw, it would mean that Hector's horror had come true, and what he had dreaded for Andromache had come to pass. It would mean Paris was dead.

I turned on the flat mattress. All the pillows of sweetest lambs' fleece were of no comfort. I could barely draw my breath. I was frightened; no, beyond fright. As I lay there, a slight movement fluttered in the far corner of the room.

I sat bolt upright. Coming toward me was a hunched-over slave, who came and knelt before me. "My mistress Andromache sends me to you. She cannot sleep. She said, if you also cannot, please come to her."

A strange summons. Yet I welcomed it. We were two women keeping watch for our men in the night. "I will come. Pray wait for me."

It did not take long for me to slip into my gown. Silently I followed her into Hector's palace, through the courtyard and up to the private chambers. The sleepy guards on duty turned half-open eyes upon us. Andromache was waiting, standing on her rooftop balcony and staring at the campfires.

"Soon they will sputter and die down," she said, not even turning to acknowledge me. "Then the day will come. The day of battle."

"Yes, my friend. And I am honored that you knew I also would be lying awake, and sent for me." I took my place by her side. "Where are they, do you suppose? At this fire, at that one?"

"We can never know. Would Paris and Hector even share the same fire? There are so many companies."

"Our men will fight to the best of their abilities, as the gods allow." That was all we could be certain of.

"But what if the enemies storm the city, take us by surprise?" she said.

"It is impossible to take a city by surprise, not a city as big as Troy. The assault on the walls must needs make a great commotion. We will have enough warning. Will we have enough courage, that is the question. It can never be easy to die." I took a breath. "But we will have the example of our husbands to call us. We will follow them, or we would not be worthy wives."

She embraced me, trembling. "You do truly love him," she said. "I tried to tell them all, Hector, the king, Hecuba, but they—"

So they—the Trojans—had not believed even that! Why else would I have come here, destroying everything else in my life? I was so disappointed in them all that I could barely form the words. "Yes, my lady. I love him above my own life." I waited an instant. "As you love Hector."

Waiting in my bedchamber when I returned was a little pouch with a barbed arrow wrapped within it. The messenger, a boy who had had no sleep that night, murmured, "Prince Paris sends it, and tells you that its brothers have struck true. You need have no shame."

I thanked him and dismissed him. I sat in the growing light and caressed the unused arrow. I need never be ashamed of Paris.

LVII

I saw the dawn come up and knew that the armies would be stirring, if indeed they had slept at all. Suddenly trumpets sounded, and criers, their quavering voices riding on the chill air, shouted that Priam would address the city down by the wide space by the walls.

The old king—looking even older now—flanked by Hecuba and his very last son, Polydorus, who barely came up to Priam's stooping shoulders, held up his hands for silence. He spoke of the successful push toward the Greek camp and named the allies who had joined us: the Dardanians, under the command of Aeneas; the Paeonians and the Carians, with their crooked bows; the Paphlagonians and the Lycians, under the joint command of the noble Sarpedon and his cousin Glaucus. The Thracians, and their famous white horses, were already in the field with their king, Rhesus. In addition, the Amazons and, also, a company of Ethiopians were rumored to be on their way. At this point the allies outnumbered the Trojans. Thus, in order to feed and equip them, it would be necessary to sell Trojan treasures to the Phrygians and the Maeonians. His shoulders drooped even lower as he announced this.

As he was speaking, a guard came forward and whispered something to him. He stopped and blinked, then turned back to us. "It seems," he said, "that our friend and ally, King Rhesus, has been slain while he slept in the field, his men killed, and his horses stolen." He dragged each word out like a lame leg. "There will be other deaths." He drew himself up, raised his chin. "That is what war is. Death and surprises. When you go to gather the bodies of fallen comrades, I forbid any of you to cry. It is too disheartening. Cry, if cry you must, within the privacy of your own chamber."

The war was everywhere now—in the voices of the shopkeepers and horse-boys and stonecutters, in the eyes of the foreigners, refugees who jammed our streets, in the quick grabs of thieving children and the glazed look of old widows. The food sacks had vanished from the vendors, wine was a private, hoarded commodity, and goats were kept out of sight lest they be taken. Fuel was meager, or many more altar fires would have been sending their smoke skyward in offerings. No one wanted to use up their meat or their wood that way, so only voices, which were free, could supplicate the gods. Most able-bodied men had taken to the field, and only the children and the infirm and the women were left to walk the streets. The young had lost their eagerness for war, bewailing the day it had ever started. And the stealing of the Thracian horses had further dispirited the Trojans: they knew the prophecy that Troy would never fall once these horses had drunk from Scamander water, and they had not reached the Scamander. There remained only the hope that the unknowing Greeks might allow them to do so later. Otherwise two of the five prophecies leading to the fall of Troy would have been fulfilled.

The sun shone strong on that day, the day that changed the course of the war. We could see little from where we were, save the swirls of dust. Sometimes the din of battle would carry on the winds, but that told us nothing. Nonetheless, the remaining Trojans lined up on the walls, straining to see, to hear.

Evadne and I returned to my chambers. She bade me lie down, and I obeyed. She lit incense, letting its musky sweet smoke curl about the room, in no hurry to slip out the windows.

"We can see better from here," she said. "Without our eyes."

"I can no longer see faraway things," I said.

"Yes, you can," she whispered, stroking my closed lids. "Do you truly believe it was Aphrodite who brought you down to the plain when Paris faced Menelaus?" She laughed softly. "It was your own vision. The goddess sought, as usual, to confuse you. Now let yourself fly there."

I breathed the dense scent of the sandalwood and camphor. I felt my arms go limp, felt myself float above the couch.

Evadne took my hand. "I am with you. We go together. When we are there, open your eyes."

When she told me, I opened my lids. Or thought I did. Or did I dream? I did not see the walls of the familiar chamber but stood next to Paris, who was dirty and tired. He was muttering as he fumbled with a strap for his armor. Hector was stamping nearby, ordering the men about. Antimachus was there, too, patrolling, directing the arrangement of chariots. They were worried about being able to cross the deep ditch in front of the palisade wall guarding the enemy camp and the ships. It was exactly the same sort of defense we had at Troy around the lower city, and it was designed as ours was: to stop the chariots.

Hector was yelling, saying that they would never retreat until they had driven the ships out to sea. He gave the command, too early it seemed to me, but in battle to be too late is fatal. The chariots charged. They were unable to cross the barrier.

Hector left his chariot and assaulted the gates and wall before him on foot, with his bare strength, flanked by Aeneas and Paris. The Lycians were right beside him, and the first to reach the gate. Later Hector was described as being "like a god," and perhaps he was. He threw an enormous boulder at the gate, and its wood shuddered and gave way, its bolts broke, and the Trojans poured in, war cries resounding.

Now they were in the very Greek camp itself. Like ants in an anthill taken by surprise, the Greeks scattered, running here, there, everywhere. Some took refuge on the ships, others rushed for their huts, still others rallied and attacked. Agamemnon, Menelaus, and Odysseus were nowhere to be seen; the wounded leaders hid themselves.

The fighting was so confusing and hot that I only saw flashes of different moments. Hector and others set fire to some of the ships, making a pretty blaze. Ajax—the large one, not his smaller comrade—stood his ground on a ship's deck and held Hector at bay. He brandished a bronze-tipped pike twice the normal length—but then, he was almost twice the size of a normal man—and challenged Hector. Hector managed to feint and strike off the end of Ajax's pike, so it became merely an unwieldy pole.

Taunts tainted the air on both sides, so that a deaf man would have the advantage, hearing none of it.

Now Odysseus appeared, squealing like a woman with hot water poured on her arm. But he could do little, because of his wounds.

"Take to the sea, cowards!" a Trojan cried, he and his men charging toward the ships.

But gradually the assault faltered. The ships did not flee, and only a few were actually on fire. Mysteriously the tide of battle turned and the Trojans began falling back. Paris was safe, as were the other commanders. But as they were retreating, Ajax leapt from his ship and grabbed one of the huge boulders used to secure them. He hurled it at Hector, and it struck true, knocking him flat. His comrades swarmed around him and pulled him away, safe beyond the ditch. He was unconscious and spitting blood.

Night fell. I saw, dimly, the curtain of darkness fluttering around me, but still I did not move. To move was to disrupt the vision, and I might never be able to rekindle it. I was not hungry, nor was I tired, but floated where those things were of no concern.

Paris was lying down, pillowing his head on his arms, his helmet beside him. His greaves were off, as was his breastplate, but he kept on his heavy linen corselet. His eyes stared dully; he looked stunned, and kept turning toward Hector. His sword and his bow were carefully laid side by side. Beside him Deiphobus was rubbing his arms with oil and boasting about the day's kill. He glanced over at the stricken Hector, but there was none of Paris's sadness about his face. He coveted Hector's place as commander. How nakedly this showed, in the firelight, when he thought no one saw.

Antimachus was striding about the camp, encouraging his men. In such a time an Antimachus was what was needed. All men have their place.

In the dawn everything changed again. Achilles appeared, striding out in his armor. Achilles! What had become of his quarrel, his refusal to fight? Confused, the Trojans fell back. Hector stirred, recovering himself just in time to see Achilles lowering over the trench. "It is prudent to pull back," he said. The arrival of Achilles changed all tactics. True, he was only one man, but there were so many prophecies and legends about him that he must be treated as more than one.

The very presence of Achilles and his fresh troops infused new courage into the weary Greeks, and now they attacked with vigor. Suddenly the Trojans' measured regrouping turned into a rush toward the city walls. The chariots careened madly and the men on foot ran as fast as they were able. The Greeks pursued, catching up to the slower ones, and gave battle.

Achilles led. Achilles caught up with the Lycians and attacked Sarpedon, their leader. The men faced one another, cast spears. Sarpedon fell, and Achilles exulted. A fierce fight broke out for the body of Sarpedon, but it seemed to disappear and no one saw where it went.

Emboldened, the Greeks rushed toward the city, and a company of them tried to scale the walls, again targeting the weaker section. But our repairs held. Now, their prey close enough at last, Gelanor's men lobbed the scorpion bombs into their midst; the clay containers burst and released their stinging, biting contents. The men fell off the ladders and crawled and beat their way back from the walls, screaming.

And then, his golden armor gleaming, Achilles assaulted the walls himself, as if he would climb them with his bare hands. Running fast and leaping as high as his strong legs would spring him, he reached almost halfway up the steep slanted sides, then slid back. A hail of arrows sought him, but he was too close to the wall for them to strike. Stones dropped, more scorpion bombs, but three times Achilles almost mounted the wall, screaming like an eagle in flight. Later someone even claimed that his fingertips curled around the top, and then that he was pushed back, as if by an invisible bronze shield. Yelling, he tumbled back to the ground, landing heavily on his knees.

Then he was surrounded by Trojans, and he disappeared in their midst; in an instant he staggered out, wounded and reeling. He was assaulted from behind by a nameless soldier. Then Hector suddenly blocked his path, raised his spear, and felled him.

He lay flopping and flailing on the ground. Hector, taking his spoils, yanked off the helmet, held it high. Then he tossed it aside, bent over. It was the armor of Achilles, but underneath was Patroclus. It was Patroclus he had killed. And I heard Patroclus murmuring the words, "You, too, will die soon. Destiny and death hover over you, death by the hands of Achilles, the shining son of Peleus."

Hector grunted and yanked his spear out of the lifeless body. He gave no sign that he had heard, or heeded, the words. He looked up at the walls, where his countrymen were calling out to him, urging him and his men to come inside. "I've work to do first," he called. He began stripping the golden armor from the dead man, pulling off the finely carved breastplate and throwing it atop the shield, tossing the greaves beside it, setting the helmet like a beacon above them. These were the trappings of a king, the famous armor given by the gods to Achilles's father, and a worthy prize. Hector called for a cart, and the prize was thrown in. Now the corpse of the fallen Patroclus lay bloody and naked. Before Hector and his men could add it to the wagon to ride beside the armor, Menelaus and another man rushed out from the Greeks and began fighting Hector for it. Each side grabbed a limb and fought like jackals over a carcass, pulling, jerking, growling. I was surprised at the ferocity of Menelaus with his wounds. At length the Greeks won control of the corpse and bore it back to their camp, guarded by the two Ajaxes.

"Inside, inside!" the people were chanting on the walls. "Celebrate your great victory!"

"When the battle is finished, when the Greeks depart," cried Hector. He insisted on staying out in the field himself with his men. But the rest he allowed to return for the night. Perhaps he did not want to face Andromache, knowing he would not have the strength for a second parting.

The Scaean Gate creaked open as the guards pulled back the heavy doors, and the soldiers stumbled in, dust-covered and dragging. Their families, eagerly awaiting them, rushed them off to warm baths and food, while those without families went to the soldiers' mess. Behind them the wounded were carried through the city and taken to the growing quarter on the other side where the sick, maimed, and dying were laid out in rows, tended day and night by women and physicians.

Andromache had hidden herself away in her chamber, weaving. She did not come out on the ramparts or wait for Hector except in privacy. Some thought it pride, but I knew it was fear.

"Awaken, my lady." Evadne was whispering to me. "Awaken, he comes."

But I had never been asleep in the true sense. I was suspended like smoke somewhere between waking and sleep, between here and elsewhere. Coming back was difficult, like being pulled by a long rope down to the ground. I fought to stay where I was, but the pull was too strong.

"Helen." Standing by the couch was Paris, very much as I had seen him in my vision. He was dirtier now, his armor bore dents and ugly deep scratches, but his person was safe. "We fought well! Oh, how can you have slept through it all?"

I sat up. How could I tell him that I had seen it all? And would that ruin his recounting it for me? "Had you not returned, I would never have awakened. Better that way," I said. I touched his hair, the gold dimmed with dust and sweat.

"We fought all the way into the Greek camp." He pulled off his breastplate. Hector and Aeneas and I led the charge through the gate—Hector smashed it wide open with a boulder. Then we set fire to the ships!"

"Glorious!" I said.

"We spent the night in the field. We thought to continue at first light and burn the rest of the ships, but it was not to be."

"But we saw smoke . . ."

"Only smoke from the night before. But almost as the sun rose, Achilles appeared, leading fresh troops. We could not get close enough to set more ships aflame."

"Achilles . . ." Oh, I could not tell him what I had seen. I must hear it all afresh, and hearing it from Paris would make it new for me. "I thought he was sulking, refusing to fight."

"Perhaps—so we thought—he had been singed by our fires, angry that we had come so close, shocked that we had wounded the leaders. Or perhaps he saw his chance, since Agamemnon was down. In any case, there he was, rallying the Greeks, and gradually they pushed us back."

"He had the power to put fresh heart into them."

"Fresh legs, in any case. The Myrmidons had not fought yet, sitting out their time with their leader, so they were eager to fight. He led them right up to the walls of Troy—surely you saw *that*?"

"Oh, yes, but the crowd was so thick. Tell me."

"He tried to climb the walls himself. His fury and his speed almost drove him over the top. But Antimachus was yelling that something was wrong. Anyone who had seen Achilles run could see that this man was slower. And his spear-throws did not go as far as they should. So when Hector killed him—"

"Easily," I said. "Easily?"

"Too easily. It should not have been the surprise it was to Hector to find that it was Patroclus, not Achilles, inside the armor."

"Did he truly have no idea?"

"He was caught up in the fighting, and fooled by the armor. So, yes, it was a shock. He took the armor and it's here now, displayed in Priam's palace."

"I heard it said that no one but Achilles could wear it, it was so heavy and unwieldy, but clearly that was not so."

"Hector means to wear it. Tomorrow we go forth to fight again," said Paris. "But that is tomorrow."

I embraced him, holding him close even with his sweat-soaked corselet next to me. Aphrodite forgive me, but the sweat of a lover smells better than any of her perfumes. I do not think I have ever seen him look more lovely; perhaps it is true that war is a man's ornament as jewelry is a woman's.

Hector sleeping out in the field. Patroclus lying dead in the Greek camp. Paris in my arms high in our palace. I wondered, fleetingly, how Achilles was passing this night. I could not know that he was awaiting a new suit of armor, hastily made by the gods, so that he could come and destroy us all in the morning.

LVIII

Before dawn, so that I am not sure Paris slept at all, he was up and readying himself for battle. I watched his dark outline moving in the chamber. He bent over and kissed me, thinking me asleep. I sat up and embraced him, trying to keep the fear and urgency from tingling down my arms.

"Today will be the day," he murmured. "I feel it."

"As do I," I said, wanting our victory, dreading the destruction.

Hector and his men were waiting on the field near the Greek lines, and in the fresh new light their fellow soldiers poured through the gate to rejoin them, chariot spokes catching the sun, winking at those of us watching from the walls. Numbers swelled on the field until it was covered. The area near Troy was empty; everyone was near the ships.

We were too far away to see, but I knew I could remedy that. I went to my chamber and called for Evadne. She would know what to do, how to take me there.

I was at the very front of the lines. I saw Hector—his face looking suddenly much older, his helmet hastily cleaned of its grime but no longer shining—striding amongst the men. He greeted Paris and Aeneas as they joined him, and was giving instructions to his soldiers when suddenly, in the red blaze of the rising sun, Achilles stood on the crest of the defensive trench and cried out. His voice was so loud it blared like a trumpet, his face contorted and his lips quivering. He screamed at the Trojans that he was here to avenge the death of Patroclus, and meant to kill Hector. Somehow he had had new armor made overnight, and it shone like a mirror.

At the sound of his name, Hector flinched almost imperceptibly. Only someone placed as I was could have seen it; surely Achilles did not. Before Hector could retort with a speech of his own, his men were drawing back. The vicious face, the thunderous voice, and the stories about Achilles as an invincible warrior did their work. The Trojans began to flee.

Yes, flee. They turned tail and began a disorderly retreat back toward Troy. In vain Hector and Paris ordered them to stand their ground.

"You fight a man, not a god!" cried Hector. "Stand firm!" But all around him the men were falling back anyway.

"He is mortal, one spear can cut him down!" shouted Paris. "Do not melt away!"

But in vain. The retreat turned into a rout. The Trojans panicked and ran toward the walls of their city. Their allies, surrounding them in the field, were no braver.

Antenor lost two sons, cut down by the pursuing Greeks. Deiphobus, running alongside Hector, panted, "We must all take refuge in the city!"

"No!" cried Hector. "Never!"

The Trojan forces separated. One side, led by Deiphobus, made directly for the city; the others were cut off by the surging Scamander River. Achilles, roaring like the river itself, came upon Aeneas and attacked him. Aeneas stumbled and fell, but somehow managed to escape the killing wrath of Achilles. The enraged Greek warrior had to turn his attention to the Trojans trapped by the river. Suddenly he came upon a young boy—far too young to be there at all—and cut him down, as if he wanted to make up for Aeneas. It was Polydorus, the little son of Priam. He must have slipped through the gates with the soldiers, disobeying his father, running away to battle. He crumpled and fell headlong into the river. Achilles plunged after him, pursuing the flailing Trojans, sword arm swinging, and killed many before being caught in a mighty wave of water, almost drowning. Bedraggled and more infuriated than ever, he hauled himself up on a bank.

"Kill! Kill!" he screamed, slashing at the air around him. "Let my arm grow weary with the killing!"

The Trojans quivered as if enchanted and unmanned.

"There is nothing magic about him!" I cried. "Take action!" But I was mumbling in my dream-mind and my cries reached no one, not even Paris.

Paris! Where was Paris? I did not see him. Oh, let him be safe!

The Scamander was choked with bodies; they swirled and spun in the muddy water, catching on branches. But Achilles was beyond the river now. Those men he killed had done nothing to sate him. It was Hector he sought, Hector he hungered for.

"Hector! Hector!" he screamed. His voice had lost strength, and he rasped, but somehow that was more menacing. He moved like a beast of prey, flying over the terrain, scattering the entire Trojan army across the plains ahead. Oh, the shame! To flee before one man!

Priam, leaning over the walls, gave the orders for the gates to be opened, and the guards pulled at them. Trojans poured in, in disarray and panic.

The entire army had been routed! All the commanders fled, the braggart Antimachus, and Helenus and Deiphobus and Aeneas himself, and Paris. Oh, thank the gods, Paris was safe!

At that knowledge, I stirred on the couch. "Evadne," I said. Could she even hear me? Was my voice a normal one?

"Yes, my lady?"

"Undo this," I said. "Paris is back. I must watch with him."

I know not what she did, but my vision faded and all I saw was my own chamber. I was weak and limp, as if I had been on the battlefield myself.

"Go, my lady," she said. She touched my hand and pulled me up, slowly. My feet smarted as they touched the cool floor.

Like a dreamwalker, I made my way down the broad street to the walls. He was stumbling through the gates when I saw him and rushed to him. "Paris, Paris!" I threw my arms around him. "Achilles," he murmured. "He turned everything."

"He is only a man," I said.

"He holds Hector responsible for the death of Patroclus," panted Paris, trying to catch his breath. "It is a private quarrel."

"It is a war! There are thousands of men on the field," I said.

"But to him, there were only three: himself, Patroclus, and Hector. Or, I should say, only one—himself. He has made the entire war about himself, insults to his honor, and so on."

I had a wild temptation to say, *For once, it isn't about Helen?* But I would not voice those flippant words, not at this moment.

"*He* has killed his friend, and that's what torments him. He made him wear his armor and impersonate him, sent him out to his doom, because his own pride refused to let him fight. So who has killed Patroclus, truly? The sword of Hector, or the pride of Achilles? Achilles knows the truth."

"He betrayed his friend, then."

"Yes, and now he seeks to assuage his guilt by attacking Hector, but it can never be assuaged. Nothing can change or erase it."

"You are here, you are safe," I said. Gods forgive me, Andromache forgive me, but that was my chief concern.

Paris turned away, looking over the ramparts. The field was empty now. Hector stood alone. From a distance, Achilles approached. He had ceased running and was walking slowly and deliberately, inexorably. I could see the front flap of his armor lifting as his thighs moved.

"Hector!" Priam called. "Come inside. Do not face that man! Do not! You are our glory and our defense! Oh, think of me, your father!" He then launched into a recitation of all the dreadful things that would befall him if Troy fell—how he would be dishonored and mutilated, torn by dogs in his nakedness.

Hecuba, standing beside him, suddenly lurched forward. She ripped open her gown and displayed her withered, sagging breasts. "Hector! Hector!" she called. "Honor these breasts, the breasts of your mother, which nourished you! I beg you, come inside! Do not face that man!"

Hector looked up. "Mother, cover yourself!" he ordered. He turned back. Achilles was within spear range.

Hector stared at him a moment. Troy's greatest warrior stood his ground, legs planted firmly apart, head up. Then, suddenly, unexpectedly, he bolted and ran.

He ran faster than I could imagine. He tore around the walls of Troy. We could not circle the inside walls quickly enough to keep pace with him, keep him in our view, as Achilles chased him. What was he thinking? That our archers would shoot Achilles down? But Achilles was too close to the base of the walls for that, and no arrows could reach him. And he was too close to Hector the entire time. He was right behind him, as happens in the worst dream when we run and run and the *thing*, whatever it is, shadows us, trips our heels.

Three times Hector circled the walls of Troy. He could not shake Achilles. Then, at last, he stopped and faced him. He seemed to see someone beside him. I heard him, faintly, speak to Deiphobus. But Deiphobus was inside the walls with all the rest. I saw Deiphobus leaning over the ramparts, his usually smug face showing anguish.

"No, brother! No, it is not I! He fools you, a cruel god fools you!" he cried.

Could Hector even hear him, far below?

"Here I stand, Achilles!" cried Hector. "I run no more! But before we move, I swear to you, if I kill you I will keep your armor but not your body. Your comrades shall have it, to honor it. Swear the same to me!"

A silence, then a dreadful laugh. "You wear my armor already! So when I kill you, I'll take it back, and have two sets at once. But as for a pact, an honor between us? No, lions make no pacts with men, they tear them apart. Wolves and lambs do not part in peace. One must die. And so with you and I."

He took one small step forward and hurled his spear, but missed. Hector yelled, "So the godlike Achilles has missed his mark!" He threw at Achilles and his spear struck the shield but did not pierce it—how could it, made by a god?—and he called for Deiphobus to bring him a second weapon. Then Hector turned around and saw there was no one there, glanced up and saw his brother inside the walls. "Athena . . . you bitch, goddess-enemy of Troy, you have betrayed me."

Athena, hating Troy, loving Achilles, had impersonated Deiphobus and then left Hector naked on the field. He knew what it meant. His doom, his destiny, was there by his side, breathing death upon him. "Ahh!" Hector reached for his sword and lunged toward Achilles, swinging at him with all the wildness of hopeless rage and grief.

Achilles stood coolly, watching him come, then cried out, "I know my own armor, where it is weak!" and plunged his spear into a place near the collarbone, in the neck, as Hector rushed upon him.

For an instant Hector hung there in the air, speared, then he toppled to the ground and lay on his back, arms sprawled. Achilles jumped over him and cried, "The birds and dogs will have their fill of you."

Hector still moved; he was not dead. His arms scrabbled on each side and his chest heaved. From inside the helmet his voice carried faintly. "I beg you, in the name of your mother and father, to spare my corpse and let my countrymen bury me with honor. Take a ransom for me, ransom of bronze and gold, but give me to them." His words faded away, his strength gone.

Achilles laughed again, more loudly, as if he had imbibed the ebbing power of Hector. "Beg me not, you fawning dog, and do not mention the name of my mother or father! Ransom? Nothing could ransom you, not even if Priam weighed out your weight in solid gold!"

Still Hector had some speech left. "So . . . no heart to you, hear my curse. Paris and Apollo will destroy you at the Scaean Gate. Mark it." Then all speech stopped.

Then—so shameful it was excruciating to watch, and utterly without honor—Achilles cut the ankles of Hector, threaded them through, and dragged his body back to the Greek camp behind his chariot, laughing hysterically all the while. The poor dead Hector bounced behind the chariot, raising a cloud of dust.

I buried myself against Paris. "No, no!" I cried.

Priam screamed, and Hecuba stood like a statue. Someone went to fetch Andromache. She had been waiting within their chambers, drawing a hot bath for Hector. So many times had he gone out to battle, so many times had she welcomed him home. She had not wanted to watch at the walls, as if she believed that keeping the same ritual every day in their chambers would protect him from harm. But now, called, she came to the walls in time to see the dust cloud of Achilles's chariot making for the Greek camp.

"Achilles has slain him," Priam told her. "My son, your husband, has fallen."

She gasped and clutched at her cheeks, then fainted and tumbled down, her headdress and veil becoming dislodged and rolling on the ground beneath her. Just so her life with Hector, as he had so grimly foreseen, had been tumbled into the dust. Laodice and others crowded around her. But now I knew I must speak. "Let me attend her," I insisted. My promise to Hector had come to claim me.

I oversaw her conveyance back into her rooms—already glaringly empty because Hector would never stride into them again, singing and calling and embracing her. Astyanax wailed from his crib, piercing cries.

But we could not be concerned with him now. He would not remember this day, and there was mercy in that. Already Andromache had fallen into a fever, or a wildness of mind. "Hector! Hector!" she called. "Hector, come to me!"

"Calm yourself." I attempted to comfort her. "Hector has fallen defending you. He gave you his love up until the last instant. He thinks of you now."

"I must see him!" she cried. "I must prepare him—oh, I cannot—no, I cannot live without him. I will see to his funeral, then I shall join him."

"Yes. The funeral. It may take time. Arrangements—"

"I shall—I shall—" she struggled to get up.

Now the dreadful news. "Achilles has taken his body. We cannot have a funeral until we retrieve it."

She gave a cry of anguish and fell, weeping, upon her couch.

"But we will retrieve it. We *will*."

Night fell, and the plain before Troy remained empty. Priam sent men out under cover of darkness to try to retrieve the bodies of the fallen, repeating his orders not to weep. But the men disobeyed, their tears shielded by the veil of night. So many bodies could not be found; the vanquished at the Scamander had washed out to sea, others were lying forlorn in marsh grass. One body that was found was that of the twelve-year-old Polydorus, Priam's adored last son. I was told that when he beheld it, he stared long and hard at it, finally saying, "He is hand in hand with Hector now." He kept his own orders not to show tears in public.

But Polydorus was not hand in hand with Hector, for Hector could not pass over into Hades until he had had proper funeral rites, and his naked corpse was lying untended before Achilles's tent.

Gelanor was the man of the hour; only his spies could know what was happening within the Greek camp, and they had to keep hidden lest they betray themselves. They could not run messengers to us, and so we waited to hear, waited in agony. At last, one man dared to come to us and reported that the night before, Achilles had held a funeral feast for Patroclus. "Patroclus ordered it," the man whispered. "His ghost came to Achilles and demanded burial. He begged Achilles to set him free to pass over. He had lain unburied for three days, while Achilles dragged the body of Hector around him. As if that would please Patroclus! But nothing appeases the dead except being allowed to pass unhindered into the realm of the underworld." So this very morning Achilles had constructed the funeral pyre and, along with it, reflecting his own cruelty, he had killed twelve young Trojan captives as well as hunting dogs and horses, and carefully arranged their limp bodies around the pyre as offerings. For what? His own guilt at his friend's death? It could be none other than that. The smoke had ascended to heaven, and then funeral games were announced.

"Funeral games?" said Priam wearily. "He is having funeral games?" The very words bespoke superficiality. That was what Achilles was made of—outward show.

"Yes, the usual chariot racing, running, boxing, wrestling, javelin throwing."

Priam gave a howl of pain. "Games! While my Hector lies dishonored, naked and desecrated!"

Then someone dared to ask—who were participating in these games? The answer: Diomedes, Antilochus the son of Nestor, Idomeneus of Crete, the two Ajaxes, Odysseus, Teucer the archer, Agamemnon, and—oh, the shame of it—Menelaus!, and most of the other commanders. Menelaus, Odysseus, and

Agamemnon had healed speedily, then. But better if their wounds had kept them from this dishonor.

"But now it is over," said Priam. "Patroclus is sent on his way, and Hector can be returned to us."

Paris leaned forward, his face blank, trying to mask his pain. "Remember he rejected Hector's plea for honorable rites. He said that . . ." He shook his head. No need to repeat his threat about the birds of prey and the scavenger dogs. We all knew it.

Priam leapt up, his stoop gone, surging with his old vigor. "I will go myself, retrieve him!" He bolted from the room like a madman. He succeeded in rushing through the gates—on his own word, they had to be opened—but once out on the plain, Paris caught up with him and restrained him, laying strong hands on his father's person. Right behind him was Deiphobus, determined not to be outdone. Already the jockeying had begun for position among the king's remaining sons. And beside him, Helenus of the red hair and the flat eyes contended for notice. Paris shook them all off and brought his father back within the gates.

Now the third night fell since Hector's death, and the weeping and lamentation within Troy could be heard even within our chambers high above the city. I turned to my weaving. It would calm me, steady me. Hands shaking, standing before my loom, I tried to draw the wool through my tapestry, but it stuck and I turned away in tears.

Paris stood beside me. "I swear here and before you that I will avenge Hector," he said. "I will kill Achilles."

Hector had said so, with his dying breath. Paris had heard it, and taken it as his sworn task. But how could this be?

"I do not care what means I must use to kill him, I don't care about honor and custom, I only care that he dies. If it is to be by a contaminated robe, or by an arrow dipped in poison, what matter? The noble Hector faced him in fairness and he died. I *will* kill Achilles. He shall fall by my hand." He took my hands, kissed them. "Do you understand what I say? I will kill him. If I die, and if anyone calls me dishonorable for the way in which I did it, do I have your promise that you will never be ashamed of me?"

I stared at him. "It is impossible that I should ever be ashamed of you."

"It seems that you and I brought death with us to Troy," he said. "Do we face it with strength or do we cower and hide?" He clasped me to him. "Helen, I want to live with you until old age snatches us, drags us from one another. But this war—"

The war that we brought, I thought. We cannot leave Priam and Andromache and Troilus to pay our price.

"Our war," I said. "It is only fitting that we fall in it."

"Then you truly understand."

"I understand that we have brought this upon our heads and the heads of others. Oh, Paris, we should have sailed far from Troy, as we spoke of . . ." If only we had turned the sail of that ship.

"We did not. We are here. Here we must take our stand."

The night passed slowly. In the morning, I arose and saw a long red stain marking the stones beneath one of my jewel cases. I knew what it was before I examined it: the weeping brooch of Menelaus was crying its blood-tears for the dead. It would be in vain to call for a cloth to scrub it, for the stain would never fade until this war ended, as Menelaus had intended.

The next few days seemed not to be days at all but perpetual night. When I remember them all I see is torches and shadows and night guards, bats and murk and dark corners. It seemed the sun would never shine again. Hector was dead, and Troy plunged into eternal night.

It had been eight nights since the funeral fires had blazed for Patroclus. The games had been played, and the bones of Patroclus had been gathered and placed in a golden urn. Yet the hatred of Achilles fed on itself and grew, rather than extinguishing itself like the pyre. Priam had collapsed in his palace, sleepless and half mad. He knew that Achilles was dishonoring the body of Hector by keeping him lashed to his chariot and driving around the funeral mound with glee. Eight days! The state of the noble form would have fallen into corruption, out in the open where all men could see it.

Priam's messengers were turned away and his offer of ransom for the body were laughed at. "I told Hector himself that I wouldn't ransom his body even for his weight in gold, no bronze, only pure gold. Even twenty times his weight! The birds will have at it, and what's left over is for the dogs." A wild screaming laugh had resounded off the messenger's helmet, and Achilles had rushed over to his chariot and driven it off, with Hector trailing behind. "Look your fill!" he had screamed, lashing his horses.

Paris and Deiphobus had tried to go to bargain with Achilles, but Priam forbade them. "And do not disobey, like your two dead brothers!" he said. "No one but I shall go."

The pleas of Hecuba, the begging of Andromache, the warnings of Helenus, did nothing to dissuade him. Priam would divest himself of all his kingly trappings and go in supplication to Achilles. "If he kills me, so be it. I am dead already, since I must do what no one else has ever had to endure— kiss the hand of the man who has killed my sons. So let me die hereafter."

On the ninth night, he set forth by himself, driving a large mule wagon. The gates were pulled open for him and the wagon descended down onto the plain, making its way along the path through the fields and across the ford of the Scamander. He had two torches mounted on each side of the wagon, and we saw their blazing tips grow fainter and fainter and then vanish in the night. He had driven himself straight into the heart of the foe.

❦ LIX ❦

Will he return?" Paris fretted as we sat, paced, sat again. "He should have let me go, as I asked. I would have gotten close enough to Achilles to kill him. That was my plan. Now . . ." he spread his hands in despair.

"It would have been dishonorable to go on a peaceful embassy and then kill him," I said. "That is something the Assyrians would do, not a Trojan."

Paris gave a snort. "Dishonorable? Is there any revenge that could sink to the dishonor he has done to Hector?"

Hector, the most noble of Trojans, did not deserve such a death or its aftermath. "Hector was betrayed," I said. "He thought Deiphobus was beside him. He turned to him. But it was some god in human costume, and that god deserted him. What perfidy." My heart was heavy in thinking of it. "I hate them all!" I cried. "All the gods. Can they not behave as decent human beings do? Is that asking too much?"

Standing behind me, Paris put his arms around my shoulders. "They say—wiser men than I—that the gods do nothing but what would happen naturally. They may prod us, they may resort to dreams or visions, but in the end we could ignore them and nothing would change. Hector was doomed to die by the hand of Achilles, as Achilles was a stronger fighter." Gently he turned me to face him. "And I was doomed—or privileged—to love you. The promise of Aphrodite had nothing to do with it."

I remembered the warm rose-scented bower of Aphrodite. Could I honestly say she did not change my eyes so that I saw Paris differently when I first beheld him than I would have done without her? Looking at him now, I could not believe I would not always have loved him, no matter when or how I had first seen him. If I had seen him in a meadow taming horses . . . if I had seen him standing at the prow of his ship sailing for Sparta . . . if I had seen him tending his cattle . . . At this last thought I smiled. "In my heart I know you are right."

"But my father—I cannot bear to think of him in the presence of that man!" He let me go and bolted to the edge of the rooftop, where he could look over the plain to the Greek camp. There was nothing there. No movement, no flares. Priam had been swallowed up in the night.

Early in the morning a small dust cloud marked the progress of a wheeled vehicle. We could not see what it was, but Cassandra shouted from the walls that her father returned, and before long Priam's wagon came into view, with the old king driving.

He was safe! He was safe! But then, behind him, came another, fast-moving dust cloud, and yet another one behind that. Achilles had followed in his chariot. He outpaced Priam and pulled up before our walls, wheeling his mount around.

"I will release the body of Hector!" he cried. "But only for a ransom of his weight in gold. Your old king did not bring enough. More is needed!" Now the second wagon rumbled into view. It held some device which servants unloaded, and then—the horror of it—someone hoisted the body of Hector onto one side of it.

He was still Hector—uncorrupted, his face and form preserved—by the gods?

"Gold to balance the weight of Hector!" Achilles screamed. "His body is heavy, even without my armor that he stole! I got it back, but I no longer need it. I have new armor, forged in one night to protect me. The gods love me! The gods love me!" he screamed.

"Now," muttered Paris. "Now I kill him." But his deadly bow and arrows were lying harmless back in the palace. He started to go fetch them.

I touched his arm. "It is too late," I said. "Stay."

Priam climbed slowly down from his wagon. Even from where I stood I could see the anguish on his face. "Release my son! Release him!" he cried. "You agreed to release him. Last night, you swore you would. Keep your word!"

"Only with enough gold, old man. You brought too little. Do you not know how much your son weighs? Did you not even figure on the armor? I shall count it, add Trojan gold for every bit of my armor."

"He is not wearing armor now!" yelled Deiphobus.

"No, he wouldn't, would he? The dead do not wear armor!" He pointed at the empty pan of the huge scale. "Gold in here! Let us see if you can afford this corpse!"

"Oh, Trojans! Help redeem your prince!" cried Priam. There was a long, agonizing pause, while Priam stood with bare, bowed head, until attendants came through the gate with armloads of gold. They heaped it up in the pan, but the body of Hector on the opposite pan did not budge.

"More gold!" cried Priam. "Oh, I beg you!"

In a sad procession, people came out onto the field, offering plates and cups and what jewelry they had left—small things. They heaped it all onto the pan. Hector moved a little, but not enough.

"My son, my son!" Priam wept. "Oh, redeem him!"

But the rest of the Trojan gold had been spent, and replenishments from the sale of our treasures to the Phrygians had not yet been realized.

"Yes, Father." A small clear voice sounded from the wall. "I will give what I have." Polyxena leaned over the wall and threw bracelets and earrings to her father waiting below. He clasped them in his shaking hands and placed them on the pan, and it began to move. Slowly the body of Hector rose and the pan with the gold dropped.

Achilles was staring at her, dumbstruck. "A noble princess," he said. The pan continued to rise until Hector was higher than the heap of gold. "Very well." He sounded angry. "Take him!" With a jerk of the reins, he drove off, back to the Greeks.

With a cry, the Trojans rushed out of the city and surrounded Priam and the body of Hector on the wagon, and, with exultation, escorted them back in to safety.

The funeral of Hector. Now we could have it. Not only the funeral of Hector, but the brutal Achilles had agreed to a twelve-day truce in which each side could gather their dead and hold funeral rites.

Hector's funeral pyre was built on the southern side of Troy, beyond the lower city, on the side that faced Mount Ida. We did not want the Greeks to see the flames. All around it were scattered the pyres of other fallen warriors. The entire city would do homage to Hector and then the private funerals would follow.

As was the custom, the pyre was lit late in the day. From early morning the rites had been under way—the solemn procession with the washed and anointed Hector borne on a funeral cart surrounded by mourners singing dirges and weeping. All night long he had lain in ceremonial repose until the whispers about how untouched and perfect he appeared reached a humming buzz. So many days dead and yet he looked as if he merely slept. Eight days of being dragged behind a chariot and not a scratch or a bruise upon him. But the gods do what they will—had not Paris and I spoken of just this?

I looked down the row of royal mourners and felt the huge gap that Hector left. Priam, his eyes dim with grief, was old and broken, Hecuba devastated. She had lost her dearest child. Deiphobus was not the warrior Hector was, no, nor the man, either. Helenus, the next eldest, was a slinking and elusive man. Polites was still a child. Paris was clearly the most gifted and should take his place alongside Priam as his new heir, but Priam showed little interest in him. There was Aeneas and his family, but they were not in direct line for the throne. As for the others dutifully standing with us—Antimachus, Antenor and his son Helicaon, Aesacus, and Glaucus—were they any match for our adversary? Our enemy had lost no valuable man except Patroclus. After all this fighting, no one lost but him! Whereas we had lost Sarpedon, and Rhesus, and now Hector.

Three women were to speak laments over the body of Hector: his widow, his mother, and I. I knew not why I was chosen, but Antenor had whispered to me that I was last. Andromache stepped forward and clasped Hector's hands where he still lay on the wagon, and spoke of all she was bereft of—her life with her husband, their days to come, and the loss to Troy. But her loss was bitterest of all, for she was cheated of his last words, something he might have murmured in their bed that she could cherish all her life.

Her face looking whiter and deader than Hector's, she stepped back and wrapped herself in a dark hooded mantle. Hecuba crept forward. Hunched over, trembling, she reached out and stroked Hector's forehead. "I loved you best of all my sons!" she cried. "And you were not the first that Achilles took from me. But all the days of your life, the gods loved you, and I can see they have not deserted you now. They have returned you to me as fresh as the first time I held you in my arms." I waited for her to say more—how can a mother ever say all she feels at such a time? But perhaps because it was impossible, she clamped her mouth shut and stepped aside.

A long pause. Now I must speak. But what could I say, and what right did I have to speak, compared to Andromache and Hecuba?

No one else moved. I took a step, then another, approaching Hector. How stern and immutable his face was, his mouth set in a straight line, his eyes closed. It seemed impossible that he, with all his strength, was gone from us, yet he had foreseen it. He had used that strength in gentleness amongst us.

I raised my head and spoke, but only to Hector. "You, my dear Hector, I loved the best of all my Trojan brothers, nearest to my own brothers far away. You alone were kind to me at all times, making a shelter for me from the stones and stares of others. Hector, it was your born nobility that made you courteous and kind, and allowed you to welcome such a stranger as I. Now, without you, the winds blow cold in Troy."

Too late, I thought I should have sung innocuous praises to Hector and said nothing of myself and him. But I was Helen, notorious Helen, and the war that had brought him to lie on this bier was ignited by me. It would have been cowardly to let that pass in silence, disrespectful to Hector.

I stepped back and the ritual continued—the hair cutting, the offerings and blood libations poured on the great pyre, the chanting, the call of, "Hector! Hector!" by Antenor before he touched the torch to the wood.

As the fire consuming Hector blazed, other fires were lit, and the whole plain became a field of bonfires, lighting the night skies and sending sparks swirling heavenward.

The next morning, gray-cloaked Trojans gathered the bones of their men from the smoking ashes of many fires. Priam insisted on doing it himself, clambering over the remains of the fire, stepping carefully to avoid the glowing coals. Paris, Deiphobus, and Helenus stood by to receive them. As the most prominent, they could stand side by side and look at one another out of the corners of their eyes, knowing themselves as rivals. Lesser children of Hecuba—Polites, the boy who kept signal watch outside the walls, Pammon, and Antiphus—stood behind them, flanked by the seer Aesacus, child of Priam's first wife. He still had sons, but as he gathered the white bones of Hector it was clear he had lost his only true child, the child of his deepest heart. All around the giant pyre of Hector other families were gathering their sad relics. The sky was gray as the ashes, as if to be clear and bright would have slain them all with cruelty.

Though our stores were low, Priam gave orders for a funeral feast. Nothing would be spared to send Hector in style and splendor to the gods.

Hector's feast was held in his expansive hall, directly after the bones had been gathered. Even with the large crowd, without Hector it seemed empty. As if to confirm the words I had spoken over him, the rest of the family did not address me, but talked only to one another. Andromache was seated, like a queen—and here she was indeed queen of the dead—and others knelt before her, kissing one hand. With the other she held Astyanax. Hector's helmet lay at her feet. Priam announced that they would build a shrine to it.

"In ages to come, men will honor Hector," he promised her. "They will stand in awe of this helmet that once graced his head." He stooped and picked it up. "How strong a neck, to have carried this weight," he sighed.

I clasped Paris's hand. Priam had living sons and he must now open his eyes to them. He must!

The old king was still mumbling and setting the helmet back in its place with trembling hands when with a rustle someone pushed forward to stand before him. He stopped caressing the helmet and let his eyes move slowly to the sandaled feet and then up the muscled legs. His head tilted back and he rose to see a comely woman of immense strength. Laughing, she picked up the helmet as easily as if it were made of fine cloth, and put it on.

"Take it off!" Priam ordered her. "Sacrilege!"

She just laughed again and plucked it off, handing it back to him; he sagged with the weight. "Mine is heavier," she said, shrugging. "How fortunate you do not have to lift it." She spun hers, which she had been holding easily in her other hand.

Priam stared at her, as did we all. He was forming the words *Who are you?* when he suddenly realized. "Penthesileia!"

"None other," she replied. "And my warriors." She gestured to the entrance, where a company of women were standing—we could just glimpse them. "Come, my companions!" At that, they marched in, sandals tromping. "There are more, of course. These are my officers."

"You had such a distance to come," said Paris, stepping over to Penthesileia. "I sent for you, never hoping you could be here so soon."

"Not soon enough, I am sorrowed to see," she said. "I am grieved that you have lost Hector." She sighed. "I had looked forward to fighting along-side him."

Priam took a deep breath, most likely to prevent himself from saying, *No one is fit to fight alongside Hector. Hector is always in front. The others follow—even the Amazon queen and commander, daughter of Ares himself.* Instead he just said, "He would have welcomed it." On hearing his words, Andromache rose and left the chamber.

Her warriors crowded in, surrounding Penthesileia. All were as tall as men; all had youthful skin sheathing muscles that did not bulge as men's did but swelled with smooth power beneath. They were carrying shields and armor that were as heavy as Hector's, but they did not droop under them, standing proudly erect.

"I pray you, put your burdensome armor down." It was Paris who spoke, taking Hector's place. "We welcome you as allies, and you will be fighting no one in this hall."

"Women, do so," Penthesileia ordered them. They obeyed. Now, much lighter, they turned to meet us.

"You have traveled from a land to the east," stated Priam flatly. "I remember your warriors, when the battle beyond Phrygia was joined in my youth."

"We are even better fighters now," said Penthesileia. "We train with superior weapons, and we begin our training earlier. All girls at the age of seven must report for testing on the field. We select only the most promising from the start. The strength and ability to be a warrior is present from the beginning. It is given, not bestowed by the will. Then the joyful part begins! Riding, swordsmanship—or, in our case, swordswomanship—spearing. Oh, it makes the heart sing!"

Her warriors all nodded. My eyes traveled down their tunics and I saw nothing that would indicate they had cut off their right breasts to enable their fighting arms better to slash, as hearsay had it.

"Achilles," hissed Penthesileia. "It is time to end his scourge."

They lodged with us. I would not have the Amazons stay elsewhere. Paris had summoned them, and we would find room for them, despite the refugees crowded into our open spaces, sleeping on the floor. Our new guests seemed relieved to escape the sorrow and darkness of Hector's chambers, and once they were with us, they smiled and laughed and celebrated their long journey, recounting its perils and tediousness.

"Such a journey—one is either fighting for one's life or bored to death. It is either furious and fast or so slow one feels buried by the sands," Penthesileia said, putting down her goblet still half filled with good wine. She looked hard at Paris. "We were pleased to answer your plea and come." Now her voice grew from its quiet timbre to a militant tone. "Achilles must be stopped." She held up her hands to ward off any interruptions. "It is disgraceful that he could rout an entire army. No man has that power. You Trojans gave it to him."

"He is the son of a goddess," said Paris, almost timidly.

"Oh?" Penthesileia glared at him. "And I am the daughter of Ares, the war god himself. What goddess does he come from?" she snapped her fingers. "Thetis! An almost-unknown sea nymph. We must put all this aside. He has ridden a wave of fear and unearned reputation to your shores. Prophecies, legends—all foolishness. What was the word of your Hector about omens? 'Fight for your country—that is the best and only omen.' You have been unnerved by that man. He is just a man. I shall kill him," she said matter-of-factly. "The great Hector was cut down. But one such victory does not make an invincible warrior. Do not give him that power over you. Someone here will kill him. If not I, then one of you." She looked around at the company. "Achilles will lie in the dust, choking and fighting for breath, and you will see—and believe—that he is mortal. Then you will cease to fear him, but you should fling that fear away before he lies sprawled and dead. Do it now!"

Paris retired to our bedchamber, and we found sleeping accommodations for the company of Penthesileia's warriors. I could not help thinking there were not many of them, but she assured me these were the commanders, and the regular soldiers were fending for themselves in the regular quarters with other soldiers. "We need no special treatment!" she all but bellowed.

I waited for Paris to retire to sleep. I wanted so badly to talk privately to Penthesileia. There is a time when we need to shed ourselves of our men and speak from the heart to other women.

I admired her so much I worried that I would not be able to find words to speak to her. I myself hated grovelers. (*Oh, my Helen, you rob me of vision! I cannot speak, I am struck dumb!*) Such people are tiresome, and I did not wish to join their company. But she and the other Amazons had made themselves feared as warriors throughout the world, and hearsay had it that they tolerated no men in their villages. I remembered speaking to the Amazon ambassador, and we had exchanged lighthearted jests about the value of men, but now I burned with curiosity about Penthesileia and her life.

I was in luck. She was still up, staring moodily into the brazier fire, her strong arms hanging loosely over her knees. She looked up sharply at the (I thought) silence of my approach.

"Who's there?" she called, reaching for her sword. She had not divested herself of it, keeping it strapped by her side even at darkest night.

"Only Helen," I assured her, stepping out into the dim firelight.

" 'Only Helen!' " she exclaimed, relaxing her grip on her sword. "The immortal Helen! Let us finally study the faces of one another."

I seated myself on a stool beside her. In the dim light I leaned forward to truly see her. "I have so long admired you," I said.

"And I have for so long wished to glimpse you. They have a saying in my land, *Her face caused a fleet of ships to sail the Aegean.* So let me look at it." She grasped my chin and stared at me, turning my face this way and that. "Well," she said. "Perhaps it could be true. If I were a man, I could pronounce it true or not. As it is, I cannot say. I do see a crease here and there." She released my face.

"As have I." Lately in the polished bronze mirror in my chamber I had thought I had seen tiny lines, creases, but in the poor wavering reflection I could not be sure.

"You need not worry, I shall not tell anyone!" She laughed. "Although perhaps if they knew, down at the Greek lines, they would sail home. *Helen has little lines around her eyes!* they might shout, and hoist their sails. Then my job would be done by time itself."

What she spoke of had worried me. Not because I feared to age as mortals did, but did it disprove the claim that Zeus was my father? And if he was not, what mortal was? I thought of the refined Antenor and his visit to Sparta and just as quickly shut that door.

"Forget me. How do you live in your land, without men? Are there no men at all?"

"We do have some men," she said. "They arrive with the hunting seasons. We bed down with them—you know of what I speak—and it is pleasurable, but nothing to bind us, any more than the buzzing of wine in our heads would make us servants to wine." She looked hard at me. "For to subjugate ourselves for a pleasure would be slavery," she said. "Or to subjugate ourselves for any-thing else. We need children. Men are useful for that. But once they have done that duty, what use do we have for them?" She looked genuinely puzzled.

"Do not children need fathers?" My question seemed pitifully weak.

"What for?"

"To teach them—"

"To teach them what?"

"How to be men, how to behave as men." I had had a daughter, but I knew sons needed fathers. I thought of poor Astyanax.

"But we have no boys, so no need for fathers," she said briskly.

"What do you do with the boys?" I had to ask, although I suspected the answer.

"We expose them on the mountainside to perish, of course," she said. "Who needs boys?"

Early the next morning I watched her arm. She let me stand with her atten-dants and even hand her her greaves, which she quickly fastened with silver ankle clips on her shapely calves. Unlike Hector, she seemed to relish all tasks on the battlefield. "You are brave," I said. I thought of all the things I had wished to ask her, about who her mother was, how Ares had intertwined him-self with her, how she had risen to be queen. Even about the breasts.

She saw me watching closely as she put on her breastplate. "We keep our breasts," she said quickly. "As you know from your own life, many stories arise when someone is different. I know *you* did not truly hatch from an egg, my lady!"

Stories. I wondered what Hermione had been taught about me, what sort of a young woman she was growing into. Would that she had had a guide as stalwart as Penthesileia. Did Clytemnestra serve for this?

"Return safely," I said, touching her arm.

She looked at me with surprise. "That is not the goal," she said. "Defeating Achilles is."

The Greek camp had been quiet for the funerals, but when the Amazons left the city, making for the ships, they stirred. Soon we could see the line of the Greek soldiers advancing to meet Penthesileia and her warriors, and then the dust that announced their clash.

In the busy fighting, she and her women routed the Greeks and drove Achilles himself from the field. Their return through the city gates was jubilant. All of Troy met them, rejoicing for the first time in months. They had come at our darkest hour and infused new strength into us.

"They were taken by surprise," she told Paris and me in private. "But next time it will not be so. We will not have that advantage."

"Achilles—" Paris began.

"I knew him by his armor, but otherwise he did not seem any more formidable than any other warrior," said Penthesileia. "He fought little. Then he returned to his lines."

So she had not yet taken his measure. He had watched, then retired. The engagement was yet to come. My apprehension returned in full force.

There were two more battles, each bravely led by Penthesileia. Both times the Greeks were driven back, even with Achilles mustering his Myrmidons to resist them. Penthesileia met him on foot and they exchanged blows, but Achilles seemingly melted away and she could not find him.

The spirits of Troy rose higher, and at each triumphal return the cries of delight rang to the heavens.

The Amazons took one day of rest to repair weapons and armor and replace horses lost in the fighting. Paris offered them the best in his stable, including his favorite, named Ocypete, "swift wing," for Penthesileia. She leapt up onto his back in one motion, testing him in a gallop around the walls. Pronouncing herself pleased with his performance, she gratefully accepted him.

This time all the Trojan forces would join the Amazons and the allies. Our commanders would take the field alongside Penthesileia: Paris, Helenus, Deiphobus, Helicaon, Glaucus of the Lycians. I helped Paris arm as I had many times before, hearing him vow that Achilles would not leave the field alive.

The day was cloudless and warm; summer was on its way. How many summers had passed in this war? It seemed we had been pent up within the walls for years—was time enchanted, expanding or shrinking in some mysterious way? The lines around my eyes and the tiny creases on my hands—did they testify to an unnatural passage of time?

I saw the vast assembled forces on the plain, making for the Greeks. This time I had no need of Evadne's help to see it. Paris would be my eyes and ears when he returned. I stood trembling, watching him depart. I felt I could see him even in the midst of a thousand.

From inside the Trojan walls, all battles looked the same; only if they were fought right under our battlements could we detect what was happening. I felt no alarm as I watched the dust moving and finally lock with the other cloud of dust as the armies engaged. Even from where I stood I could hear the clash of arms, the unmistakable ring of bronze against bronze, and the cries of the wounded, sounding the same whether the victim was Trojan or Greek.

It went on forever. The freshness of the early morning blended into the clarity of midday when the shadows are short, and then the sun was slanting its rays across the plain as it set. Light lingered for a little while, and still the armies fought on.

Gradually the dimness deepened, night creeping out to cover the plain. Frantic with worry, I rushed down to the walls, as if that would bestow some knowledge of the outcome. I cared not for the hostile stares of the Trojans. I cared for nothing but the safety of Paris and of Penthesileia

The crowd was moaning and swaying. So much depended on this battle; so many hopes had been set upon it. They could not endure another defeat; their trampled spirits could not surmount it.

The stars were fully visible; true night had come. No army could fight at night. They would be returning. The battle was over.

Torches finally flickered from the field. Still we could see nothing. Only as they approached the gates was the extent of the Trojan force revealed. All had returned.

My heart leapt up. They were safe. They had prevailed! I leaned over the battlements, the better to see. Why were they so glum? Tiredness, I thought hurriedly. Exhaustion. Even a victorious soldier cannot smile if he has given his all.

Then I saw the horse with a body slung across it. I saw the legs I had admired in Penthesileia's chamber only a few days ago. Her feet swayed and swung in the loose way of the feet of the dead.

I clapped my hand over my mouth and shrieked. No! I rushed to help open the gates, and stood back as Paris, leading the horse with its dreadful burden, was the first through them.

He was safe! She was dead! My heart was torn both in rejoicing and in mourning.

He looked over at me, his eyes dull.

"Paris!" I hurried to his side, embraced him. I tried not to look at Penthesileia, but her body draped across the horse commanded me to see.

"At least we saved her body," he said, reaching out to touch it as if to make sure.

I was walking alongside him, but the noise of the crowd made it difficult to hear. "Will you take her to the palace?" I asked.

"Yes. We will lay her out there." His face had a frozen look.

Behind him the other commanders were marching.

"So long a battle—did you score any successes?"

"Penthesileia killed many Greeks. She fought so bravely that . . ." He turned away, his eyes filling with tears.

Priam met them halfway up to the citadel. He betrayed no emotion, his face like the wooden Zeus in his courtyard. "My sons," was all he said, welcoming them all back. "A great warrior." He nodded toward Penthesileia. "All the rites, of course . . ." He turned away.

Her countrymen took her body to prepare it. It would lie in state in our hall. The Amazons did not build funeral pyres, but rather buried their dead in stone-lined tombs after a three-day mourning period.

Safely within our rooms, Paris removed his armor and sank down on a stool. The dusty arms did not even gleam in the lamplight, as if they mourned with us. Carefully I measured out a cup of wine, preparing it with spices and grated cheese as he liked, diluting it with clear water from Mount Ida's springs. I let him lift it and drink, and waited until it had begun its blessed healing of the mind. He drained it and set it down, then stared oddly at the wall as if he were seeing something horrible.

"Now you must tell me," I said.

"No! No, I cannot live it again!" His voice trembled as if in terror.

"I must know!" I said. "Please, please—!"

"More wine," he said. "I cannot speak until more is soothed within me."

Only when he had finished the second cup did he speak. "We fought well," he whispered. "There were so many of us, with the Amazons and all the allies. It was like . . . like the beginning of the war, when we were strong. Penthesileia fought fiercely and killed many of their leaders. When they fell, the Greeks drew back and regrouped. But it seemed to invigorate Achilles. Perhaps only killing can stir his blood. If his own are killed, it drives him into a fury; if he kills, it sets off a fever within him for more killing."

He stood up and began to walk about the room. I saw cuts on his legs and started to get a bowl and cloth to clean them, but he waved me away, annoyed. "What matter these little cuts?" he cried. "Achilles came charging out of the Greek lines and pursued her. She drew him out onto the plain, where they would be alone and could have room to maneuver. She managed to drive him back and put him on the defensive. The great Achilles, retreating and shrinking away! But her success made her overbold; she came too close to her enemy with her shield open, leaving a tiny part of her body unprotected. Perhaps the horse gave her too much courage. She spurred him to run Achilles down, thinking to cut him to pieces under the hooves—for even Achilles cannot withstand the weight of a horse or its sharp hooves." He shook his head. "The horse reared up like a wave of Poseidon, and Achilles swerved. But he kept his spear poised, and as she passed, he—he thrust it into that place on her side the shield did not cover. She slumped forward and the horse stopped. Horribly, slowly, Achilles approached the animal, speaking sweetly to it to calm it and keep it from bolting. Then, just as calmly, he reached out, took hold of the spear, and pulled her off the horse. She hit the ground with a thud." He winced in remembering it, and I winced as well, picturing it.

"He crowed with victory and went to take his trophy, the armor. He pulled the helmet off and then cried out as he saw her face for the first time and realized it was a woman. He kept kneeling and holding her head; she was still alive and trying to speak. He stared at her dumbly, held there as if under a spell. Then—and this is so unlike Achilles—he let her head down gently. Then he removed the armor, almost tenderly. He kept hovering over the body."

I encircled his shoulders with my hands, which were trembling. "Do you think he did not know the Amazons had come?"

"Unless the Greeks have very good spies, how could they know? And it is true, in armor they look like men. As he was kneeling before her, a disgusting little man came up and taunted him, saying she was a whore and best left to the birds and dogs, and was Achilles to make love to a corpse? Achilles turned on him. I have never seen such anger. Suddenly I knew what the

Trojans trapped at the river had encountered, and what Hector had faced. His anger was like fire, like lightning. He snarled at the man, snarled like a beast, and then with one blow of his hand he hit the man's face, knocking out all his teeth, and then again, smashing his skull. The man fell, a bloody-faced pulp, alongside Penthesileia, deader than she was, as she still faintly stirred.

"Ignoring the man as if he were carrion, Achilles fell back to his knees and stayed with Penthesileia until she died. Then he turned to us—he had not hindered our approach—and said, 'Take her. Give her all honors. And take the armor.'"

"Why didn't you kill him then?" I said. He had been within range, easy to hit.

"I—I was too stunned," he said. "And it seemed a dishonorable thing to do at that time, as if it would insult Penthesileia."

"Insult her? It was what she wanted, what she had come to do. Oh, it would have been justice at that moment."

"It seemed wrong to slay a man who was perhaps for the first time showing kindness." He shook his head. "It sounds foolish, and now I regret it. I was carried away by noble feelings. A mistake."

"The gods rarely give us a second chance," I said. As soon as I said the words, I wanted to take them back. It was done. He had missed his opportunity, failed to fulfill his vow. But he did not need me to tell him that.

❧ LXI ❧

A silence fell over Troy after the death of Penthesileia, as if a giant voluminous shroud had dropped from the sky to cover us all. We spoke in whispers, so it seemed; we treaded quietly in soft-soled shoes through the streets, empty of the clatter of carts and horses. Only wheeling crows dared to make raucous noises. The pallor of doom was upon us; by bringing us hope that was so quickly extinguished, Penthesileia had shattered Troy as much as an enemy could have.

Locked in the crumbling box that was Troy, stripped of its grandeur as so much was sold off or hidden, we had little hope of reinforcements now. Our allies from far and near could send no more fighters. The Amazons, the Thracians and the Lycians had lost their commanders, and all of them many soldiers. We would have to fight on with what was left to us.

In the Greek camp, the wounds of Agamemnon, Odysseus, Machaon, and Diomedes had presumably healed and they had returned to the field. We had killed many soldiers, but somehow their ranks seemed as large as ever, as if they regenerated like sown dragon's teeth.

Days passed, months, seasons, each seeming longer and longer as our spirits sank lower. The world was static, and we were held in a black grip of timelessness, captives in our own refuge. It protected us; it entombed us.

Then, like a sudden bolt of lightning, another ally arrived: Memnon, a prince from Ethiopia, and his contingent of shining black warriors. It had taken him all this time to travel here, and why he had come, to throw his lot in with faraway Troy, was a mystery. But we asked no questions, only welcomed him with glad cries.

Like Penthesileia, like Achilles, like Aeneas, like Sarpedon, he was the son of an immortal. (So many children of gods fighting around Troy, for yet another child of a god.) His story was more interesting than theirs, though, as his mother was the goddess of dawn. She it was who had fallen in love with a mortal and asked Zeus to grant him immortal life; Zeus, cruel as he was (for well he knew what she had forgotten to ask), granted it but did not stay his aging. He grew older and weaker until Dawn had to shut him up in a room, where his piteous chirps, coming from his withered old throat, sounded like a dying cricket.

But their son was absolutely splendid—a glowing warrior with a soul of courtesy. Too much like Hector, perhaps . . .

Our joy was short-lived. As he had killed the others, Achilles slew Memnon on the field. It was said each man's goddess mother hovered just behind him, striving to protect him. Perhaps they each canceled the power of the other. In any case, Achilles once again broke our hearts and even the heart of a goddess.

Another funeral, another time of mourning. I did not think Troy could have become more despondent, but she did. At this last feat of Achilles, Paris became obsessed with killing him, berating himself for his missed opportunity when Penthesileia fell. He cursed himself for his hesitation and scruples, calling himself weak and womanish, all the names his enemies flung at him. In vain I sought to soothe him, to remind him that to show momentary mercy was not to be weak, but that this mercy had been misplaced. Achilles himself had never shown mercy except in that one instance, and it was that which had confused Paris. But would he be an Achilles? Who would want to be such a man, a man whose heart was that of a ravening wolf? Still Paris claimed that that was what he intended to become, a man as merciless as Achilles, if that would serve his purpose. To kill Achilles, he must become Achilles.

A golden, still day in autumn, and suddenly a glistening army of Greeks rushed toward our walls. Did they mean this as the final attack on a weakened foe? Their chariots raised whorls of dust on the plain, their soldiers were massed like hordes of devouring rats. And out in front—Achilles and Agamemnon in their chariots.

I watched from the high tower as they came closer. Inside the walls the Trojans were massing under the command of Deiphobus and the few remaining allies under Glaucus of Lycia. Priam was standing over them, giving them his hopeless blessing—hopeless because he had no hope they could prevail.

Agamemnon. I squinted, trying to bring his face into focus, but all I could see were the dark shadows of his eyes, and the grim slash that was his mouth. Leading his Myrmidons on the left flank, Achilles turned his head this way and that, looking at Troy as if it were a carcass to be dismembered. His armor gleamed—Priam later described it as bright and ominous as the Dog Star—and caught the sun as he bounced across the bumpy plain in his chariot.

Paris had been standing beside me in the tower lookout. He had refused to join the troops led by Deiphobus. He knew what he must do.

"They will fight. *I* will employ the best means of killing," he had said. At last he was at peace with his difference from his brothers. Now he stroked his bow, the finest in Troy. He looked down at the approaching enemy. "It is time," he said. He touched my shoulder lightly. I turned to him.

"May the gods guide your arrow," I said.

Trembling, I took my place in the tower with the guards. All I could do now was look. Should I have clasped Paris to me, taken what might have proved a last embrace? But selfishly, I rejoiced in the knowledge that the wife of an archer need not do that. An archer might miss his target, but that did not mean certain death.

Agamemnon wheeled his chariot around and threw the reins over to his charioteer. He jumped out and stood, beating on his shield, yelling insults. But, tellingly, he looked to Achilles to actually do something.

Obligingly, as if to offer a target, Deiphobus and his men rushed out, war cries resounding. Now the Myrmidons surged forward to engage them. Achilles dismounted and advanced on foot. His every step betrayed his utter disdain for his enemy. He even bared his vulnerable spot, craning his neck above his protective armor and making a show of scouting for adversaries.

"Come out, come out!" he called. "What, is there nobody? Was Hector all you had? Oh, pitiful Troy, to have only one champion!"

He strutted up to the very gate—closed now—and called out, "All shut up, are you? Huddling, cowering! We shall break you down soon enough; we shall lay every defender in the dust and trample you!"

Paris darted out from the base of the tower where he had lain in wait. "Die, liar!" was all he said. Before Achilles could wheel around, before he even saw him, Paris let loose an arrow that struck him in the exposed part of his body.

The expression on Achilles's face—I shall never forget it. It was not anger, not fear, not even surprise. It went beyond that, to utter astonishment. He clawed at his throat, silenced, while Agamemnon gaped.

He fell forward, and Paris fired another arrow, this time into the back of his unprotected calf. Then another, into his heel, crippling him.

Achilles writhed on the ground. He was whimpering and crying, clawing at the dust. His companions rushed forward, but they were useless to do anything besides ward off more arrows.

No more were needed. The first one in the neck had severed his life's blood, which poured on into the dust.

It did not take long. He died quickly. Too quickly, for one who had killed so many. On the walls, we stared in disbelief at the still, sprawled figure, expecting it to leap up and taunt us. But it did not.

The usual battle ensued over his corpse. The hulking Ajax carried it off, after spearing Glaucus, who had attempted to secure it for the Trojans. Ajax wounded Aeneas as well, and hit Paris with a huge rock, knocking him to his knees. Odysseus appeared from nowhere and fought to cover Ajax as he retreated; they managed to secure the armor and take it back to their camp. The Greek army retreated with them, and soon the plain was empty, save for the carpet of corpses littering it, fallen like leaves.

Troy threw open the great doors of the gate, but everyone was so stunned by what had happened that silence greeted Paris as he drove Hector's horses inside. The slayer of Achilles received no tumultuous cheers, betraying the fact that the Trojans as well as the Greeks had thought him invulnerable and had never truly considered the possibility, had never dared to dream that he might ever lie dead at a Trojan hand. The unthinkable had happened and they could only stare dumbly.

I alone rushed forward; I leapt into his chariot and embraced him, my head spinning. He was safe. He had killed Achilles. I was more thankful for the first than for the second. Even I could not comprehend that our scourge was gone.

"I am in awe," I whispered. "You have delivered Troy!"

He tightened his arm around me. He seemed unable to speak. Perhaps he had stunned himself. He looked out, searching the crowd, watching for Priam and Hecuba.

"They are most likely in the palace," I said, reading his thoughts. "With all the sorrows, Priam does not stand at the walls any longer to witness the carnage on the field."

"But someone must have told him!" said Paris. "Surely he knows by now."

Indeed they must have. But I needed to think of something to soothe him, he was so raw and longing for a word from the stern Priam, a word of praise which he had surely earned. "Age has weakened him and sorrow has taken its toll. He and Hecuba await you, I am sure, at the palace, where you may speak in private."

Suddenly on all sides of the chariot surrounding us the people came to life. They began waving and stamping and cheering. There were no flowers to shower on Paris—how could anyone gather them when the fields had become dangerous?—but their glad songs and cries were just as sweet and beautiful.

"Paris! Paris!"

"You are greater than Hector!"

At that he answered, "No, for Hector was our finest warrior."

"Who killed Achilles?" they shot back. "The finest warrior is the one who kills our greatest enemy, not one who is killed by him!"

"He'll attack us no more. He's gone, he's dead—where is the body?" a man called.

"Dragged away! They'll sing to it and bow to it and have games for it, but all the while it's rotting and the worms, his lowly enemies, are feasting on him!" Paris's words were so savage I was taken aback. "I hate him for what he has done," he hissed to me. "Even if I watched the worms twining and coiling within him, it would not be enough."

Yes, we all hated him that much. I remembered the insolent little boy at the suitors' contest. I had wanted to slap him even then. Perhaps if someone had, he would not have grown into a killing maniac. But then I remembered the boy I had seen at Scyros, forced to play the girl because of his protective mother. Then he had been wistful, winsome. He had been held back from his destiny and had strained against it. Well, now he had pursued it to its furthest end.

The chariot wound its way up the wide road running through Troy and toward its summit; the horses had to make their way slowly through the crowds, which grew larger the higher we went. At Priam's great palace Paris stepped out and said, "I go now to lay my victory before the king. There will be celebrations afterward, of that I am sure. Go home and raise prayers of thanks that our great enemy is gone."

"We shall raise prayers of thanks for *you*!" they cried.

How long had Paris waited to hear those words?

"We must thank the gods," he finally said.

"Thank them for *you*!" they repeated. He smiled, drinking in the words he had waited years to hear.

"I thank them for my life," he said. "And *I* thank them for you."

Then he ducked inside the gates of the palace, pulling me with him. We ran through the courtyard, and then, with a nod to the guards, into the sanctuary of the palace itself.

All was eerily quiet. No one from the family thronged the courtyard, although Priam's daughters and remaining sons and sons-in-law lived there. Where had they hidden themselves?

Paris barged into the royal chambers, crying out for Priam.

"Father! Father! Have you not heard? Have you not beheld the fighting?"

Only an echoing silence answered. Then Paris began to scream, "You watched from the walls when Hector was slain! Watched and leaned forward to call out to him! And yet, when I, and Deiphobus, and Helenus were on the field, you hid yourself. I killed Achilles! I killed him! Not your precious Hector, nor your baby Polites, nor Troilus, but I, Paris, your castaway! And now can you not even greet me!"

More silence and darkness.

"As you put me out on Mount Ida, so now I turn my back on you!" he cried. "I would not restore Achilles to life, I would not undo what I have done, but now I taste the full measure of an ungrateful father and what that means. Henceforth, old man, I have nothing to do with you!"

"Paris!" I clutched his arm. "Pray, do not speak in haste."

He turned to look at me, the dim light barely showing his eyes. "In haste? These words are a lifetime in coming."

As he turned to go, Priam tottered at the head of the steps leading to his private apartment. "Pray, wait!" His voice, usually strong, now sounded old and quavering. Stiffly, he descended the stairs and came to Paris across the polished floor. Behind him, Hecuba made her way. Shuffling forward, he held out his hands. "Son." He embraced Paris, clutching him to himself. Then he stepped back.

"You have avenged Hector," he said. "I kneel before you." Before he could bow, Paris took his arm. "No. It was bad enough you had to kneel to that butcher Achilles. Never kneel to your own son."

Priam straightened himself, looked Paris in the eye. "You are truly noble," he said. "Perhaps the noblest of all. How could I not have seen it?"

"It never had a chance to show itself until now," said Hecuba. "But my Paris was strong enough to wait until his time came around."

"I could have died waiting for that time, and would you have noticed?" cried Paris.

"A man must prove himself. The gods choose the hour." She looked at him, her gaze unwavering.

"You are not a natural mother," he said.

"Then you do not know mothers," she replied. "Or rather, mothers of kings and princes. They are different."

He brushed her aside. "In my life, I would have preferred one of those other mothers."

"Perhaps I would have preferred different sons—or a different husband who did not already have children by a first wife—what we prefer is of no account." Hecuba stared at him. "Do you not, even now, understand this?" Then she smiled, held out her arms. "I salute you, I rejoice that you have killed our greatest enemy. I care not how he was killed, by spear or by arrow, only that his heart is stilled and he raises his arm no more." She inclined her head. "Hail, Paris, prince of princes. You are my dear son."

"At last," he said, draped across our bed. "After all these years, she finally proclaims me her dear son."

I hated seeing him lying like that. It was too much as Penthesileia's body had lain, slung across the horse. "Get up," I said. "Please, I want to see your face."

And indeed, I never tired of looking at it. But it was older. No longer a boy's. He had spoken of waiting all the years for words from Hecuba. The war . . . the war had gone on forever, stretching out like eternity, and within it, inside the walls of Troy, time seemed to have stayed still, holding its breath. But outside those walls, it had rushed on, and suddenly its passage stared us in the face. No wonder Priam seemed so stooped and feeble, no wonder Hecuba was worn away with grief. And Paris grown bitter with waiting.

"You have killed Achilles," I said, still marveling at it, hoping that now his vexation would subside at last. "You have performed the bravest feat in Troy! You are her hero, her savior!"

"He lay there, gasping out his last," said Paris, relishing the memory. "The great man, the son of a goddess, the man who made Hector turn tail and run around the walls of Troy, and then who dragged him—"

"Oh, do not think on it!"

"And who ambushed and killed sweet Troilus! *I* killed him! I robbed him of his life, I stilled his sword arm. Can anyone imagine how that felt?" He gave a nervous laugh. "Even I cannot recount how it felt. I was astounded, disbelieving, and now it seems like a dream. Helen!" he grasped my arm. "I saw him wheeze, and gasp, and pitch forward, and saw his color change, and saw the dark blood gushing out. And then he did not rise. He did not drag himself upright. I knew then he was doomed. He was dying; he was dead: Achilles."

"Glory to you," I said, stroking his hair. Slowly I clasped him to me, half expecting to feel not flesh but cold stone, as if he had already been turned into a victory monument. "Now they will surely write songs and poems about us," I said. "Your eternal fame is assured."

His hands trembled a bit on my back. "You were the only one who believed in me, who saw what was there."

Yes, long ago I had told myself, *Everything he learns will make him more and more outstanding among men, until there is no touching him.* "When first we set out, I loved seeing the young you beside me and knowing the man you would grow into," I said.

"But my mother did not! Never did!"

"A wife has a different loyalty. I chose you. A mother cannot choose her children. And she has other children, whereas I had only one husband."

"Some still say you have two, even now," he said. Was he asking a question, or merely arguing?

"People talk and say foolish things. My loyalty was and is only to you. Ah, but my child and my husband were pulling me apart." I had gone with the husband, but my heart still sought my child. Child no longer, though. The years that were aging us were turning her into a woman.

"You have had a long wait for vindication," I said. "But I never doubted it would come."

❖ LXII ❖

Beaten, like a cur that has been whipped, the Greeks slunk back behind their lines. They vanished from the plain, and never was an empty expanse lovelier to behold in all its stark nakedness. The Greek tents, the Greek campfires, no longer flapped in the wind or winked at night, insulting our eyes.

Troy rallied. Her spirits rose; the wounded stopped arriving on litters and the ones already being treated within the walls began to recover. Repairs were made to weakened sections of the walls, and forays out into the countryside for supplies were safe again, for the moment.

Priam ordered a day to honor Paris, and, after riding through the streets in his shining armor, to shrill cries of acclaim, Paris ended at the temple of Athena high in the citadel. Entering the sacred spot, he dedicated his victory to the city's protective goddess, the Pallas Athena. Standing behind him, I did not think the goddess looked any more welcoming than she had that first time I had beheld her, that fearsome time when I was trying to win the acceptance of Priam and Hecuba. Athena was a stern goddess, touchy and prone to change sides in a moment. I, for one, did not trust her to protect Troy anymore than she had protected Hector.

Afterward there was the customary feast and celebration in Priam's palace. The tables were more sumptuously arrayed than usual. Our food supplies having been replenished, we had fresh venison and pork and delightful stuffed cheese, as well as good wine from Thrace. There were even sweets of plump figs and grapes in a dark spiced syrup.

Deiphobus and Helenus smiled when they spoke but glowered when they stood unobserved—as they thought—in the shadows. Paris had now eclipsed them; Paris was to be Hector's successor.

I delighted in taunting Deiphobus. I had always disliked him—he combined crudeness with gloating, and there was something inherently dishonest about him. I would never have trusted him to carry out even the most impersonal, unimportant task without trying to secure some benefit to himself. He fancied himself irresistible to women, too. They say confidence is a gift of the gods. I say ill-placed confidence is the gods' jest on a fool.

True to form, he sidled up to me. "My lady Helen," he began, "your Paris has indeed scored a mighty blow against the Greeks. Their Achilles has fallen. We all breathe easier." As if to underscore his point, he moved closer to me and sighed.

"Are you troubled by a chest disorder, my lord?" I asked. "Your breathing sounds labored—perhaps you have an illness. You should see a physician."

"I always find myself short of breath around you." He stared hungrily.

"The best remedy, then, is for you to keep a long, safe distance between us. Let me help you!" I turned and walked away. I held my back straight, but I was insulted. I felt assaulted, as assaulted as the walls of Troy when the Greeks had stormed them.

I hurried toward Paris, who was standing beside one of the shields in Priam's hall, admiring it. All around us in the hall, torches blazed. People were circling around the tables, eating. War talk blazoned forth. Wherever Paris strode, people fell away as if he were a god. Even if he did not savor it, I would. Every smitten face, every awkward bow, every stammered compliment—yes, I would sup full on this food. I had waited too long for it—for others to see in him what I had seen from the beginning, from that moment when I had first beheld him in Sparta.

Our commanders were now confident that the danger had passed. Antimachus gave a stirring speech down by the city gates a few days later, to the effect that the Greeks had received such a telling blow they were mortally affected. Gelanor's spies confirmed it—they reported that spirits were so low in the Greek camp, preparations were under way for withdrawal. The ships were being readied, and the soldiers were eager to depart.

Encouraged, Priam sent his son Helenus to speak with them, arrange terms for ending the war. In his expansive mood, he was even willing to draw up a treaty of peace between the Trojans and the Greeks. They responded by holding Helenus captive.

Everyone was stunned. The celebratory mood was shattered. Priam was reeling as if from a sword strike: another of his sons in the hands of the Greeks! He was shocked into collapse, and Hecuba tended him in the palace, speaking for him. "Get my son back!" she said. "Get my son back!" It had a dreadfully familiar ring.

Helenus did not return. Cassandra grieved for him, burning lumps of figwort and resin incense, sending her pleas to heaven and toward her brother.

"We are linked," she said. For once her expressionless blue eyes showed life, as if Helenus had bestowed his on her when he was captured. "I feel his mind, I feel his thoughts. Oh, to fall into their hands! They will not release him, I know it." She turned to Paris—she always ignored me—and flung herself on him, crying, "I see it all!"

Gently he took her hands. "And what do you see, dear sister?"

"I tremble to disclose it," she murmured. She shook her head as if to clear it, and her lank red hair flew all about, finally settling like dead snakes on her shoulders and back. "He will betray us."

"What?" Paris cried. "How?"

Her voice was dull and so soft I had to strain to hear her. "He knows all the prophecies—as do I—concerning the fall of Troy. The ones left to be fulfilled."

Afterward, in the privacy of our upper chambers, we spoke further about them, these prophecies daring the Greeks to fulfill them.

"Two prophecies have been fulfilled, and there are three left," he said. "It has been a long time since the second one, involving the Thracian horses, but there is no time limit on a prophecy. Of all things, it has the most patience. Now we must worry about the arrows of Heracles."

"The arrows of Heracles—Philoctetes has them."

"Yes, when Heracles was dying, he gave his bow and arrows to a lad who was willing—when no one else would step up to the task—to light his funeral pyre and end his misery. That was Philoctetes as a boy. Now the Greeks will bring him here, feel bound to retrieve him from the island, along with his bow and arrows."

"What matter?" I asked quickly—too quickly. "You are the premier bowman of the war."

"These arrows never miss, so it is said," Paris corrected me. "And they are deadly, since Heracles dipped them in the slain Hydra's blood. They cause a man's blood to boil, and his flesh to melt, and there is no remedy. Oh, if Philoctetes comes here—"

"Perhaps he won't," I said. "Perhaps he is dead of his wound. He has resided alone on the island since the start of the war."

"Even if he is, they will find the bow and arrows," said Paris. "Someone else will wield them. And fulfill the prophecy."

"Troy will fall because one man has a deadly bow and arrows? Troy is bigger than that!"

Paris looked at me almost pityingly. "The prophecy is not concerned with the size of Troy, nor who is slain," he said. "It matters only that the bow and arrows of Heracles, given to Philoctetes, come to Troy. That is all the prophecy specified. Perhaps it would count if the arrows were fired into the wall!"

"Let them do so," I hissed. Oh, enough of prophecies, of the war, of suspense.

It was night. Paris was standing with his back to me, looking out the window into the deep, star-filled night. The gentle curve of his white wool robe seemed to glow in the dim light of the chamber. I rushed to him and embraced him from behind. The wool, soft as a baby's cheek, slid under my fingers. I held him tight, my arms enclosing him. Slowly he turned to me. He had that smile that was only a hint of a smile on his lips.

"You almost knock me over," he said. "But it is a sweet assault. Dear Helen." He reached out and took a lock of my hair in his fingers and smoothed it against his palm.

As we lay on our bed together, I traced his face more than I was wont. Visitations, god-induced encounters, visions—however fleeting, they are real when they occur. Children result from them—I myself, if Mother entertained the swan as she would have it, rather than Antenor in an ordinary, ugly way—O let me not think upon that! I must believe that it had all happened, that Troy was real, that Aphrodite as she appeared in the cave was real.

Tales were filled with women who consorted with ghost lovers and spirits and gods. So be it. The vision fled in the morning light. But in the night it was real enough: perhaps the only reality. A reality that followed them into their old age, that faded last of all. When their memories dimmed and their husbands and children were sucked up into the mist of oblivion, that one divine encounter lived on.

"Paris," I whispered, "let us have one more divine encounter."

"One more?"

"Yes, and perhaps this one will grant us the child we long for. I have never given up hope."

"Nor I," he said.

He slept, I kept from sleep. Dreams were cheap. I wanted to be able to reach out and stroke his cheek, to bend my head and listen to his breathing as he slept.

The chamber was still, unearthly still. I did not hear the call of birds outside, nor the stir of air puffing against our curtains. On the floor the late-rising waning moon traced its light and brought the shadows of the windows to dance across the floor.

I lay safe and happy and drowsy in the circle of Paris's strong arms. I knew such things were not proof against danger, but deep down we feel that they are—that a warrior's arms bestow immunity from harm.

Then it came: the hateful vision. I had questioned whether my second sight, the one conferred on me by the sacred snakes, was still alive. Oh, this answered me, but I would have wished the vision never to have come.

Paris lay dead. He had been slain but I did not see by whom—only that it was by an arrow.

I screamed and bolted upright. Immediately Paris was awake as well. "What is it?" Muddled with sleep, he clutched at my shoulders. "A bad dream," he muttered. "Turn on your other side. That way the dream will not continue."

This was no dream, and it went on, stamping itself on my heart, and I saw it all: Paris lying white and unmoving. The fall of Troy—the high towers toppling. Slaughter and blood running in the streets. A great wooden . . . something. Disarming, misleading. The Greeks conquer.

In pain, I tumbled from the bed.

Paris slept on, and I crept back near him, trembling. I dared not touch him for fear of waking him; if he waked, he would surely see what I had seen. But I needed to be beside him, to protect him in the futile way a wife feels she can protect her husband from all evil.

❖ LXIII ❖

It was true. After many months, the Greeks were stirring again, rousing themselves like a bear from its den after a winter's sleep. Our spies soon told us why: Philoctetes had indeed arrived from his island exile, and Odysseus and Diomedes had fetched the son of Achilles from his mother, the princess Deïdameia, in Scyros. She had been reluctant to let him go, but when they had come upon him he was practicing with spear and sword, driving a chariot, and was eager to come to Troy and leave the placid safety of his mother's court. Perhaps she had wept and bewailed the loss of Achilles from her life too ardently and for too long. The young do not tolerate that. They want to be doing, not reminiscing. So the Greeks were busy trying to bring about the three prophecies which either Calchas or Helenus had revealed.

Philoctetes was far from well; his wound still festered and he was weak. He was being treated by Machaon but until he recovered he could not fight.

"But you wounded Machaon!" I said to Paris.

"Not mortally, obviously," he said glumly. "My arrows are not the potent ones of Heracles."

"I do not understand about the arrows of Heracles," I said, more to distract myself from the horrid vision I had had of Paris wounded and dead than to ask a question. "If Philoctetes has had them since he was a boy, and he used them to hunt food for years on the island, how many can remain? A quiver does not hold many arrows!"

"Perhaps he has a little vial of Hydra poison to dip new arrowheads in," said Paris. "That way he could keep replenishing the store of lethal arrows."

"There is nothing in the story to say that Heracles collected the poison of the dying Hydra," I said. "Only that he washed his arrow tips in her blood. He must have stuck them under her spouting neck—"

Paris smiled. "My dear Helen, you are too literal. You should know—being the subject of them—that stories twist what truly happened. We do not know what passed between Heracles and the Hydra in her cave. Any more than anyone knows what passed between us on Cranae."

At that memory he made me smile, as he knew he could. "Only we know that," I said. Oh, the precious memory!

"Nonetheless, your point is well taken," he said. "There will be no flying arrows until Philoctetes recovers, and who knows when that will be?"

It was summer again. Truly time seemed bent and folded, for it had been autumn only—days?—before. But the trees and their broad, dark leaves, the continual winds from northeast, all shouted that it was summer. Let the gods do what they would. They wanted it to be summer: therefore it was summer.

We sweltered in Troy—proof enough that it was true summer. The sun beat down on the stones of the city with such intensity that the heat penetrated the soles of our sandals and came near to blistering our feet. To wear armor in such heat was deadly in itself, causing our soldiers to collapse and crumple as they practiced in the drilling field to the south of the city. But they were a ragtag band; so many able-bodied men had lost their lives, and now the ranks of the soldiers were swelled with the too-young and the too-old. Little boys who had been forbidden to fight, shriveled old men whose grandchildren sternly told them not to go, now could take up arms. In vain Priam ordered them only to man the walls and attend to the warriors. Let the wounded do that, they retorted, hobbling out to try to protect Troy.

Seeing the pitiful men trying to defend Troy, women wanted to join in as well. They did not aspire to fight like the Amazons, but they could do as well as the old men and little boys, they said. Theano tried to dissuade them, but they argued that no priestess of Athena could do that, as Athena herself was a goddess of warfare. So they served as lookouts on the walls, ready to lob insect bombs and heated sand down below if needed.

Troy itself had become as shabby as its army. Stones had been pried from the once-proud streets to mend damaged walls, and the fountains were dry. The sphinx down in the lower marketplace was awash in trash and dust around its base. Men came there to sell their belongings in order to get food, which was running low—the grains were moldy and the fine wines sour. Clothes were soiled and stained; no one could squander precious water within the city for laundry, and the springs outside were unreachable. Our brief respite of relief had passed, and the Greeks were besieging us again.

Sometime in all this, I consulted with Antenor, who was still trying to arrange some sort of honorable settlement to the war.

"But we have waited too late," he said. "The Greeks sense that we are desperate, and now they need only to keep doing what they are doing—and wait."

"Antenor—what do you think will happen? Truly?"

"I would like to think that we hang on in here until the Greeks give up. But that would take either a decisive defeat, a catastrophic incident, such as a massive plague, or bitter quarrels between their leaders. Thus far, the loss of Achilles has not stopped them, nor the plague that visited them earlier, and as for bitter quarrels—that is all they have done since before they left Greece."

"And otherwise?"

"You know what happens to defeated cities. They are always put to the torch, razed to the ground."

That vision, that horrible vision I had had of fire, and the Greeks . . . and the towers—that odd phrase that had come to me long ago. I shut my eyes, yet the vision was not outside me but inside.

"I cannot comprehend it," I said.

He waved his hands as if to dismiss the whole subject, then settled them quietly on the table before him. Quietly, when he was looking across the room, I laid mine beside his. They were a very close match.

The enemy was on the march. How strange that this day does not resonate in my memory, preserve itself sharply. Instead, it fades and blurs in its normalcy. I rose at the usual time. I watched Paris as he opened his eyes, as always feeling that strange little jolt of unbelief and excitement as I beheld him.

When he comes into a room, you give a little gasp, deep inside, far inside, someone once said when trying to describe what it meant to love. And it was true: when I looked at Paris, I felt it as if for the first time. As when I first beheld him in my hall in Sparta.

We took our early breakfast together, a simple meal of barley gruel and cheese. He said he must attend the morning meeting at Antimachus's headquarters. Still I thought little of it; it was too ordinary.

Paris returned and said he must arm. Spies reported that the Greeks were ready to mount an assault, and Philoctetes had been healed of his debilitating wound. Still I made light of it. I walled off the image of the wounded Paris, as if walling it off would destroy it. I helped to fasten his armor on him. I tied the fastenings of the linen undercorselet myself, and fetched his sword and his quiver. His young attendant did the rest: presented the breastplate, the greaves, the helmet, the bow. Together we stood back and admired him in his militant glory.

I leaned forward and ran my fingers over his lips, barely exposed by the cheekplates of the helmet. They were soft and curved.

"Go," I whispered. "Though I would keep you here." Oh, I was so very weary of these thoughts and deeds, but resigned to them, like a ritual, thinking they would continue this way forever: Paris arming, me bidding him farewell. Though others fell around us, we never would. This was eternal—his going forth, my staying.

"This I know full well," he said. This time he put his hand on my shoulder. When they ask me, *Was anything different?* I can only say, *This time he put his hand on my shoulder.* But of what moment was that? It was just a gesture, a careless gesture. Afterward we search for messages, meanings, as if the departed knew in advance what would happen and wanted to leave something behind for us.

He rode out through the warriors' gate, the Scaean Gate. He stood proudly in his chariot, facing the enemy, his face turned toward them. They advanced in groups, chariots and soldiers, spears bristling. They seemed to spread out across the entire plain, far too numerous after all their casualties.

The flanks of the two armies met and clashed; bellowing war cries resounded even up to where we stood on the walls. I had taken my place beside the women of Troy; I no longer slunk back and hid in the shadows. Hector had fallen and my Paris was now the foremost son of Priam.

The women on either side of me did not acknowledge me, but kept their gazes straight ahead, stick-straight. I felt their hostility seeping into me. I had killed their dear ones. In their place, I would have felt the same way. Yet to honor Paris I must stand beside them.

There were cries and yells as one confrontation gave way to another, and still another, but the armies held fast, locked together on the plain. Slashing swords caught the sun and came to us as winks of light; spears twisted and turned in their flight and, spinning, streaked like meteors. But who was winning?

Gradually the Trojans fell back, dogged foot by foot, giving ground. Then, suddenly, the lines broke and they rushed for the gates, the Greeks in heated pursuit. The Trojan army turned into a mob pouring into the city. Where was Paris? Some time ago I had seen him abandon the cumbersome chariot and fight his way into the melee. Now he disappeared, while his compatriots rushed back through the safety of the gates.

The Trojan ranks thinned, and it almost seemed they bleated like a herd of frightened goats as they pushed and shoved through the gates, the weak and ill-trained soldiers crumpling before the assault. Then the gates swung closed, groaning in the sockets, and bolts were shot to secure them. The seasoned Trojans who had chosen to remain and fight the Greeks were cut off from retreat. They fought on alone, as Hector had done before them. Now I saw Paris by himself, wheeling around to face three Greeks who were advancing on him. No matter which way he turned, his back was exposed to an enemy.

I could not help myself. I leaned forward, screamed, "Paris, no! Paris, come inside!"

He could not hear me; even if he could, he would not have fled like a coward. He rushed upon one of the Greeks, sword raised, spear at the ready. He looked so formidable, the image seared itself on my mind—this is a true warrior, the noblest of Trojans.

As he raised his sword against the nameless Greek and felled him, a chariot wheeled up, and a bowman took aim, sending an arrow flying toward Paris. It grazed only his forearm, and he fought on, slaying his second opponent. Next he turned to the third man rushing at him from the right side, and slashed him as well. Only then did he look for his adversary in the chariot, but the man had wheeled away out of range. Paris glanced down at his arm and rubbed it, shaking it as if to test it. Then he wrenched his spear from the fallen Greek and turned to help another Trojan who was battling two Greeks.

The Greeks on the front lines found themselves deserted as their compatriots withdrew behind them. Slowly they melted back, and the victorious remaining Trojans wearily returned to the city, proudly and slowly, not routed like their fellows who sheepishly cheered them as they entered.

"It is nothing," Paris said jubilantly, waving his arm as the crowds greeted him. The wound was slight; it was barely bleeding. "A child's wound," he said, laughing, removing his helmet and waving it. But after the salutations, the celebrations, the goblets raised in tribute, the child's wound began to throb, at first only a tingle.

In the privacy of our chamber, after he had removed the rest of his dusty armor and called for water to wash, he examined the wound. Angry red streaks now surrounded it, and it felt hot to the touch. When I laid a finger near the swelling open cut, he gave a cry of pain, so sharp it frightened me. He gasped and grasped his elbow, as if to stop the pain there. "It feels like liquid fire," he said.

"Shall I call a physician?" I asked.

"No, no." He attempted to laugh. "There are many truly wounded men they must see to. It was a nasty battle."

In the dim light I could not be sure, but it seemed the wounded forearm was turning purple, and as I watched, the skin stretched and became shiny and taut. At the same time, sweat broke out all over his face and he suddenly muttered, "I feel dizzy—sick—" and he gave a shudder and turned his head away.

Despite his reluctance, I cried out for an attendant to summon a physician. While we waited, the arm swelled even more, until it looked like it would burst, and then the discoloration seeped down into the fingers and over the shoulder onto his chest. Now his lips started chattering and his limbs began contracting, making him writhe like a fish landed on dry land.

"My stomach is eaten away," he moaned, clutching it. "It is consuming me!" The physician arrived and stared down at him, pulling away the clothes to see his abdomen. But there was no mark on it. Then he laid his hand on Paris's forehead and jerked it away.

"He is on fire!"

Fire . . . burning . . . entrails consumed . . . Oh, had that been Philoctetes in the chariot who had struck him? The Hydra's poison was said to smite its victim just so.

"Who struck you?"

"This arrow—it came out of nowhere," he said. "I do not—" he gasped and clenched his jaw in pain. "I do not know who loosed it. I did not see the man's face."

If indeed it was Philoctetes, let him not know. The will can be as potent as the gods, and unless he believed it was from Philoctetes, it might not prove dangerous.

"Rest, my love," I said. "Our foremost physician is here to attend you."

He gave a smile, contorted by a grimace as the pain tore through him. "Whenever it is said that the foremost physician will attend you, it means the situation is serious."

I forced myself to smile. "Or it means you are a prince of Troy, and entitled to the foremost physician even for a scratch."

He grasped the shoulder of my gown with surprising strength, using his other arm. "Do not lie to me, Helen. You above all, do not lie to me. I cannot bear it!"

I looked down upon him, not wanting to feel that I was so doing—that I, strong and well, gazed upon a stricken Paris. "Paris, you are wounded. But wounds are commonplace in war. You yourself wounded Machaon, but he has recovered. So has Odysseus."

"Not all wounds are the same," he gasped out, clutching his swollen arm.

"Don't touch it!" ordered the physician, grabbing his hand. "Here, I have a draught that should help—"

"I am afraid to take it until I know what has caused this. It might make it worse." Paris could barely get the words out through his clenched lips.

"An antidote!" I cried. "Is there no antidote?"

The physician spoke quietly to me over Paris's head. "There can be no antidote until we know what it is. The prince is right. The wrong antidote can intensify the venom's strength."

"Venom. Is that what you think this is?"

"Clearly the arrow was poisoned," he said. "But with what?"

The Hydra's blood, I thought. But I would not say it.

Suddenly Paris opened his eyes. Had he heard us? He looked at me, sadly, slowly, shaking his head. "Helen." He coughed. "So many years—I want them all, I brought you here so we might have them—no, it cannot be—" His head lolled to one side, but not before he breathed, "All ended, over . . . we will visit Egypt . . ." His eyes glazed, the eyes that had still been bright when he had just said, "Helen." Now they faded.

But he could not be dead. No, he could not. It could not end like this, so quickly, so simply, with the droop of a head and fixed eyes. This love was to be eternal. Not ended.

He still breathed. The poison had closed his eyes—now I was sure it was the Hydra's poison; nothing else could have made a surface wound so potent—but not stilled his heart.

"Help! Help!" I cried, cradling his head. Someone must know how to reverse this. It was a poison, and all poisons had antidotes.

In those final hours, even she will beg me to save you. The words flitted and played in my memory, like sunlight chasing shadows. Someone who knew about poisons. Someone who had loved Paris. Someone who knew the day would come when she held the keys to life and death for him. Someone who hated me.

Oenone.

❖ LXIV ❖

I must go to her. Where was she? Even if Paris knew, he could barely speak. He was writhing on the bed, by turns arching his back and falling back limply onto the blanket, clawing at his chest.

"My blood is bubbling inside, like a cauldron," he muttered, rousing, his unseeing eyes rolling backward. He grimaced so hard his face contorted.

"My prince, if you can take an infusion of leaves of dittany of Crete . . ." The physician was bending over him.

"Oenone," I whispered in his ear, his burning ear. "Where does she live?"

He turned, his eyes opening to slits. "Mount Ida," he said. "Not the spur near the hot springs." He drew in his breath. "The one nearest the long waterfall."

But there were hot springs all around Mount Ida, and many waterfalls, some seasonal with melting snow, others year-round. "Dearest, is this waterfall called by any name?"

He only gave a grunt and a shudder, turning away and squeezing the coverlet.

It was night, but I could not wait for dawn. The poison was spreading too quickly. I ordered two chariots and my heavy mantle, as well as torches and guards. Then I rushed across to Hector's palace, stepping over the displaced people sleeping on the ground around it. The doors were shut fast, but I beat on them, crying out to be admitted. One of them creaked open and I tumbled in, calling, "Andromache! Andromache!" to the startled guard.

One of her personal attendants appeared, clearly displeased. Her mistress had retreated to her chamber; she made ready for sleep.

"I must speak to her!" I threw back my hood so she could see it was Helen. An order from me, presumed future queen of Troy, could not be ignored. The woman glided away, her torch disappearing with her.

Every beat of my heart reminded me that time was passing, slipping away. It must not have been long, but it seemed a day before Andromache appeared, clutching a robe around her.

"What is it, Helen?" The tone was one she would use with an annoying child.

"We have to go to Mount Ida!" I cried. "I need you to come with me! Please, Andromache, I cannot go alone. As I once went with you, please help me now!"

"Now?" She jerked her head around, looking out into the darkness. "That is impossible. We must wait until we can see. Even if we weren't surrounded by Greeks, it would be dangerous. Do you not remember we got lost coming down from it in the darkness?"

Her face was hard to read in the poor light, but there was little welcome for me on it. The death of Hector had sundered us forever, it seemed. But she had to come, she had to! She knew the way we had gone, I lunged forward and clutched at her robe, tugging her almost off her feet.

"Andromache! I must get to a place on Mount Ida, find someone there, even in the dark. It can't wait. Paris has been poisoned—an arrow, I think—and the only hope of curing it lies in finding this woman—this woman who knows such secrets—else he will be die before daylight . . ." I felt as if I was losing strength even as I begged, for she stood unmoving and all this time I was not beside Paris, I was pouring my heart out to this stone.

"What woman?"

"Someone named Oenone, someone Paris knows, who has magic means of healing wounds. I must find her and bring her to him. Without her, he will die! Oh, I am sure of it!"

"Does no one else know how to find her? Do *you* know where she lives?"

"I've seen her—I've been near where she lives, in a grove of trees on . . ." It was coming back to me now. The place where Paris had taken me; if I were just put on the beginning of the correct path, I would be able to retrace my way step by step.

"If we are captured—"

"I have no choice!" I cried. "If I am captured, I will have less regret than if I stay safely here and just watch the poison take him." Take hold of yourself, I thought. That is true for you, but not for Andromache. If she is hurt or captured, you will have injured an innocent person—whom you promised Hector to protect—in your pursuit to save Paris. "I understand why you cannot come," I finally said. I would have to go alone. "Forgive my selfishness in asking."

Now I had no hope of succeeding, yet I must make the attempt. The attempt was all I could offer Paris, but I gladly gave it.

"You are wrong," she said. "I will come." She gestured for her traveling cloak and heavy shoes. "Perhaps in grappling directly with death, I will be delivered from this house of half death hunched in shadows where I have lived alone without Hector. In any case, I am ready to die. I did not know until this moment how ready." She took my arm. "Let us go, and may the Greeks look the other way as we pass."

Our chariot rolled through the lower city, or what was left of it. As the Greek attacks had grown longer and fiercer, the frightened people had abandoned the lower slopes, fearing its protection of rock-cut ditch and wooden fence was not enough. They now, along with all the refugees, huddled in the inner city, making the streets a continual boil of bodies. As we exited from the southern gate, I saw that they were right to have fled—the Greeks had begun filling in the trench and tearing down the palisade, exposing the lower flanks of Troy.

But we saw no telltale torches in the gentle sloping fields on the southern side of the city, no smell of horses. This night the Greeks were not there. I clutched the side of the chariot as we bounced along, and held fast to Andromache with my other hand. I could feel her bracing and swaying beside me. But it was a long while until she slid her arm around me and I felt it as an embrace rather than only a means to steady herself.

Oh, I had missed Andromache sorely, the one woman I had considered a true friend in Troy. But now the balm of her gentle presence was lost in the pounding of my heart and the panic spreading throughout me. With every pace of the horses we were leaving Paris farther behind, and my soul cried out to be by his side in this hour, not trundling toward Mount Ida in a vain search for a woman who hated him.

Our guards and driver warned that the road would become rough as we reached the foothills of the mountain. I begged Andromache to try to remember the place where Paris and Hector had driven us. Paris and Hector. Oh, let me not think on that, on those lost days! If only we could dismount there, we had the best chance of threading our way to the right place. We tried to direct the drivers, but the task became even harder in the dark when we could see only the largest landmarks; the wavering torches were of little help in thrusting away the night.

"I think that is the hot spring," said Andromache, peering out into the blackness. I could see nothing, but I did hear a gurgling and rushing. "It had a stone seat beside it, remember?"

"Yes, vaguely," I said. "I think so . . ." I laughed—how could I laugh now? It was insane. "My main memory is of the priestess, or the Wolf-Mother, or whoever she was."

Now Andromache laughed, too. "I am grateful to her," she said. "Whatever she did, it was potent. Now I have Astyanax. My little boy . . ."

A fearful jolt almost threw us from the chariot as one of the wheels struck a rock and the other lurched into a hole. "We can go no farther, my ladies," our charioteer said. "We must dismount now."

Dark surrounded us, as if we had stepped off into an abyss. Andromache and I stumbled and clung to one another blindly. Somewhere up there she was waiting.

Slowly, testing our steps as our feet slid along, we began the climb, holding small torches. We could feel the path by its bare trodden ground, and were careful to keep upon it. Far to our right we heard the swish of a stream, tumbling over its rocks, blending with the whisper of trees as wind passed over their crowns. How agonizingly slow it was to shuffle along like this.

The pebbles beneath my feet . . . the murmur of a thousand night creatures surrounding us . . . the dizzying feel of the ascent . . . I found myself studying these things as if they truly mattered, keeping at bay the terrifying thought of Paris and his wound.

Light leaked from the eastern corner of the sky after a great long time. Like a fog clearing, or a cloak slowly withdrawn, the darkness receded and left the mountain exposed.

We were standing near a place where the path opened onto a wide, grassy meadow—a halting spot for those seeking the highest height, the seat of Zeus. It looked vaguely familiar. But would not any green meadow look the same?

I grasped Andromache's arm. "This looks like the place where we saw her. But she does not live here. She only happened upon us here. She roams the mountain, coming and going at will. Paris called her a nymph—but what sort? Wood, water, sea? Not the sea, so wood or water—" I put my hand over my own mouth. "Helen, you are babbling." Babbling . . . babbling . . . I think that Paris said she was of the water. Was that why he said to seek her near the waterfall, a particular waterfall? *The long waterfall . . .*

"Past here . . ." On our left was the tree-guarded pool where Paris had judged the immortals, where Oenone had suddenly appeared. It looked innocent enough now, its surface reflecting the coming sunrise in iridescent colors. We passed it, and went toward the left, where I hoped the long waterfall was.

Rocks and boulders began to dot the meadow, until the grass gave way to hard stony ground. We skirted it and then I heard the faint splashing sound of water ahead of us. I reached out and took Andromache's hand. Behind us the guards were snorting, their forbearance for my quest almost gone.

Behind that curtain of tall trees the water lay. I approached it fearfully, not daring to name which water it might be and whether we had found our landmark. We slipped between the trunks of the screening trees and beheld a wide dark pool, and above it, a waterfall, thin as a skewer, plunging straight down a cliff so steep we could not see its top.

"We have found it," I breathed to Andromache. "Now we are near her."

As if she had not heard me, Andromache walked toward the water, then knelt and dipped her hand in it. "It is bitter cold," she said, letting it stream out from between her fingers. "It is cold enough to numb all pain."

Was that what she sought, a substance strong enough to dull her pain? But nothing I then knew of was that powerful. I joined her by the edge of the water.

"Has your pain not lessened even a bit?" I asked.

"No. If anything it has grown. When first I lost Hector, it was a stunning blow, so enormous the sky and its light were blotted out. But now the sky has cleared again, and I can see all the little hollows and empty places in life he left behind. One big thing or a thousand small ones—which is more painful?" Her face was stark.

I did not know. I did not wish to find out. Oenone! We must find her.

I threw a rock out into the deep pool and saw it swallowed up; some ripples spread out, but they were feeble. Then, suddenly, the water wavered and something hovered just under the surface, white and floating.

We drew back. Before we could retreat farther, a column shot out of the water, and the face and form of Oenone took shape. In shock, we both jumped back, and we both fell.

As we watched, she grew to her full height, but she seemed to be borne up by the water, her feet supported just below the surface. Then she moved, striding across the water like a dragonfly, and stepped out onto the shore in her bare feet. Water dripped from off her garments, which floated about her as if they were dry. Her hair, too, was not wet but tumbled in full curls about her shoulders.

"Oenone?" I whispered.

Instead of answering me, she said in a cold, distant voice, "Are you surprised to see from whence I come? You knew my father was a river god and that I am a water nymph."

I picked myself up from the ground, rubbing my scuffed knees. "I knew little about you," I said.

"Ah, so Paris did not speak of me." Her voice was growing stronger now.

"He did." Oh, let her not be angered! "And I am always awed when I see an epiphany, a manifestation of the gods. You did what no human could do—rise out of a watery realm."

She laughed, but it was not a pleasant laugh. "Why, do you mean you cannot ride up to your father Zeus in a chariot drawn by swans? Perhaps it is not true, then. Perhaps you are merely a mortal with unusual beauty. I suppose we shall find out when it comes your time to die."

"Let us not speak of me, but—"

"Of Paris, yes. Indeed, let us speak of him." She walked slowly from the edge of the water and stood beside me. Andromache moved away, looking on with frightened eyes.

I stood still and faced her. "Paris has been wounded. It may be by an earthly poisoned arrow—they can be lethal enough, smeared with snake venom—or it may have been one of Heracles's arrows, dipped in the poison of the Hydra. He was only grazed by it, but now it has taken possession of his body. His blood boils, he says. The wound is ugly, changing before our eyes as we beheld it. First it was red, then purple, then swelled, and his body was consumed by it."

"Most likely it is an arrow with the poison of the Hydra," she said, as if it were no matter to her. "A very bad piece of luck."

I grabbed her arm—it felt solid enough, not insubstantial as it had appeared beneath the water. "Help him! Reverse it! You must have an antidote. You have special knowledge of these matters!"

She seemed unconcerned. "He spoke of me, you say?" She sounded dreamy. "What did he say?"

Flatter her, I thought. Think of something. Anything.

"He spoke of your time together." I must say more than that! "He spoke of what a happy time it was, one of the happiest he had known."

She rounded on me. "What a liar you are! Had it been so happy, he never would have deserted me."

"Men do odd things." I shrugged. "They do not always have their own best interests at heart."

"You are right there, Helen of Sparta, wife of Menelaus. It was not in his best interest to bring you here, even if there were no Oenone. But I told you when I saw you both that time by the pool, there would come a day when you would need me, beg me to help, and I would turn my back on you. Now that day has come."

I stretched out my arms to her. I did not care if I abased myself. I would lie on the ground, kiss her feet if need be. "Have mercy on Paris! Do not condemn him to death!" I begged.

She stepped away, lifted her chin. "If he dies, he dies," she said. Her voice was so cold, colder even than the water from whence she had arisen, I knew it was not indifference but revenge. She wanted him to die.

"If he dies, it is because you let him," I said.

"If he dies, it is because he turned his back on me and said he had no need of me. Now he does. He miscalculated in his choice, so it seems."

"Be merciful!" I said. "Lay aside your own hurt and pride and stretch out your hand to Paris now."

"Never!" she said. "He cared little enough for me when he left me to go to Troy!"

So he had left her long before he had met me. Her cruelty, entwined with bruised self-love, was staggering. "Once death has come, there is no undoing it," I said. "Oh, be merciful now, and lay your grievances before Paris when he recovers."

She stepped over to me and grabbed my hair, jerking my face up to hers.

I saw two yellow-flecked eyes looking directly into mine. "No mercy," she said. "Let the man die!" She twirled two strands of my hair in her fingers, twisting them painfully. "My only regret is that I will not be there to see it."

"Come with us, then, and behold it for yourself. No one will prevent you. Come, we return now to Troy." I smacked her hands, and she dropped my hair. What matter now if I offended her? I wanted to kill her. But nymphs do not die. "What, are you afraid?" I taunted her, the vicious woman. "Afraid to look upon your own decision?"

"You call me coward?" she said. "You dare to call me coward?"

"A coward of the worst sort," I said.

She raised her arm, struck me. I struck back, sending her reeling into the water. I saw her arms flailing for the instant before the waters rescued her, whisked her away into the deep.

The waters roiled a moment, then calmed. I watched the churning and turmoil as she disappeared. Our journey had been in vain. She had flung mercy away.

We had wasted treasured time in coming here. The nighttime jouncing in the chariot, the stumbling ascent of the mountain, the rush to find Oenone— all wasted! Better to have stood by Paris, sponging his brow, keeping watch beside him. Better to have sent for every physician within a day's ride, better to try Gelanor and his wild ideas. Better anything than this!

❖ LXV ❖

I cursed myself for having been led on this fruitless journey. Our way down the flanks of the mountain was swift because we could see. Our stomachs were crying out for food, the guards accompanying us were grumbling, but even so we were able to make good time. Soon we were on the flat ground and heading for Troy. The walls, bathed in the glow of the afternoon sun, beckoned us toward them.

From a distance Troy looked as she always had: gleaming and invincible. Her citadel, crowning the heights, was just barely visible. I could see our palace, and Hector's, and Priam's, and the temple of Athena. What I could not see was what was happening inside them. From the outside they were lovely as ever; their vulnerability would not be apparent, not until they shimmered in flames and fell.

The southern gate was open. Another lull in fighting was allowing Trojans to leave the city, fanning out into the woods to gather herbs and firewood, pasture horses, and replenish supplies.

I rushed inside the gates, eager to be with my love, and learned his state from the guards soon enough: he was just clinging to life.

I clutched Andromache's shoulder. "I cannot bear it, I cannot withstand it," I cried.

"Yes, you can," she said. "If the gods will it so—Oh, the hatred of them!—then you must."

"As you have?"

"Yes. As I have."

I began to run up the steep road to the citadel, beyond the fallen houses in the lower city, one part of me seeing that they were deserted, that their owners had fled, but all I saw, truly, was Paris. Paris. Paris. With my own will, I would make him live. It was impossible that he would die. That he could die. It could not be.

Andromache and I had held hands all the way up to the citadel, but then we drew apart as we stood between her palace and mine. I faced her, she who had lost everything in her life, I who still stood on the brink. "Come inside with me," I urged her.

She brought her hand up to her mouth. "Forgive me, Helen, I cannot." She bit down on her fist. "I cannot witness it again."

"I understand." And I did.

"Go now," she said. "It may yet all be right."

Slowly I mounted the steps. As I approached the chamber, the musky smell of sick-masking incense enveloped me. Then the unmistakable sounds of helpless people scurrying.

I stood in the doorway and saw the shutters were drawn; I marched across the room to fling them open. Yes, I would open the shutters, Paris would sit up and thank me, turning his face to the sun. So I bestowed restorative power upon the shutters; it was a token of my desperation. The sickroom attendants winced at the stab of light. It showed the incense smoke curling grayish blue in the air. Still I had not dared to look at Paris. Now I could wait no longer. From where I stood, behind him at the window, I could see his rigid arms extended on either side of the bed, like poles. They were so stiff they could not bend at the elbow, and they were horribly swollen, to the size of gourds. His hands were black and so distended I could not see the separate fingers.

With a cry, I dropped to my knees beside him and looked upon his face at last. What I saw was no longer Paris, but a purplish bruised visage that had once been a face. Even his hair was no longer his: the bright gold was muddy, hanging in clumps like rotted weeds. His eyes were swallowed up in the puff of their sockets, his skin was purple deepening to black. Even his lips, cracked and open, were black, with red fissures running through them.

"Helen . . ." His voice, so faint I had to lean over to hear it, was still his. "She said no?"

"She did, may her body dissolve into slime," I said. "But we do not need her. I am here now; I was foolish to seek help from another. I can—"

What could I do? Call on my father Zeus? *Was* he my father?

"—call for help far above what she could do. Oh, my dearest, I should have done that straightaway!"

He tried to move his arm, to touch my hand. But it would not obey him; it remained as stiff and unresponsive as a stick.

"Wait," I said. I bent over to kiss his forehead. Instead of being hot, it was as cold as Oenone's pool. It sent waves of fear through me. I rushed from the chamber. I could not supplicate Zeus here.

I sought the privacy of an inner room—difficult to find, with all the soldiers and refugees crammed into our palace. No large space remained. At length I found an empty chamber, but it was one used to store provisions, not a lovely and airy room such as Zeus in his majesty deserved.

I had snatched up two of the censers with their incense, and now I set them with shaking hands on the floor. I stretched myself out before them, feeling the cold stone under my cheek, under my chest, my legs.

Zeus, son of Chronos, if you are indeed my father, take pity on me. I lie here before you utterly abject, begging for the life of my husband, Paris. You can save him. You can restore him to health. You, mightiest of the gods, can make or undo anything you desire. Oh, grant me this wish!

I felt nothing, no response. Did that mean . . . there was no Zeus? That he was not my father? That I had not addressed him properly?

I know not the proper words to use, but see into my heart! See my true submission. If it is possible . . . let me die instead of him. Yes, transfer this affliction onto me! You allowed Alcestis to take the place of her husband. Allow me!

Still silence. Did he not hear, or was it just that he willed himself to reject my plea, as if he had not heard?

Let me die instead of Paris! I rose to my knees, addressed him out loud. "Let me take Paris's place in the chamber of death," I said. "Let me exchange my life for his."

Silence. I fell back to my knees and blew on the censers, frantic to coax more smoke out of them, as if that would command the attention of Zeus.

"Please, Father," I said. "Hear my supplication."

Then I heard—did I hear it as a sound, or only words whispered in the secret inner recess of myself?—his voice. *My child, I hear you, but it cannot be. I cannot reverse fate, a man's destiny. We gods cannot interfere with that. We could, but at the same time we cannot, as it would destroy the order of things. Your Paris is slated to die, and die he must. I am grieved, my child, but I cannot stop it, no more than I could stop the death of my son Sarpedon on the field before Troy. I wept for him, as you shall weep for Paris.*

"You called me child," I said.

You are my child. The only mortal woman I acknowledge as my daughter. And you shall not die.

"Without Paris, I do not wish to live," I told him.

You have no choice. You will live, because your blood decrees it. We will welcome you amongst us when the time comes.

"I shall make a poor goddess," I said, "grieving always for my lost Paris."

Many of us grieve, but I shall share a truth with you: still it is good to be a god.

The voice ceased. I had failed. Zeus had rejected my plea, as had Oenone. That was all I cared about. I rushed from the chamber—more wasted time!—and ran to Paris.

I clasped his head in my hands. I could feel the sweat on his brow, but I touched him gently, lest I cause him pain. His swollen eyelids opened and he looked at me.

"What did—what happened?" he murmured.

"I was promised that you shall recover. Yes, from this moment on, new strength will flood into your limbs and the poison will recede." I hated lying, but I could not speak the hideous truth. I stroked his arm, with its skin stretched so tight that if I scratched it with my nails it might burst. "All this shall recede," I said. "Your arm will be yours again."

He smiled—or rather, his lips attempted to move. "He listened to you."

"Yes. He will spare us. For I would not live without you, and so the Hydra's poison would fell me as well." As it felt like it was already doing.

"Helen." He gave a great sigh. I saw how his whole body had darkened in the short time I had been away from his side. No, not so soon! "You were ever faithful. I did not deserve you."

"None of that, now!" I told him. "No such foolishness. I was yours from the beginning. I am only thankful your ship came when it did. I do not think I could have waited a moment longer."

"Hold my hand," he said.

I took it—the swollen remnant of what had been Paris. *O the gods! Aphrodite, could you not bend yourself to attend on us now?* "Yes, my dearest. I shall never release it, until you stand strong again and leave your bed."

"It is so dark in here," he said, agitated. "Dark, dark! And a tunnel is sucking my feet away, making me slide down it."

"No, my love, you are lying here wrapped in finest linens." Linens that were sweat-soaked. "You are safe."

Then he was gone. No last words, no farewells, nothing left for me. He was whisked away down that tunnel he had spoken of—not in fear, but in wonder.

Paris was dead, and I a widow. But that meant nothing—although it was soon to—beside the enormity that Paris had ceased to be.

I closed his eyes, gently touching his eyelids. How many times had I stroked them, kissed them? Oh, I could not bear to think upon it.

I turned to the chamber attendants and managed to say, "Prince Paris is dead. His spirit has departed. Prepare him."

I could remain no longer in our chamber. I stumbled out.

I sought the privacy of the little chamber where my attendants slept. There was no one there. I fell down on the pallet. Tears would not come. Nothing came but a great desolation. Paris was gone. The world had ended for me.

I had spoken true to Zeus. I had no wish to live. Life ceased for me with the last breath of Paris. And he had had no words for me, only nonsense about dark tunnels. It was meaningful to him, but not to me.

He had not known those would be his last words. Perhaps we never know. While we are robust and in the prime of life, we imagine our deathbeds, the wisdom we mean to impart, and the precious words, like jewels on a necklace, that we intend to bequeath to those around us. But it is rarely to be. We perish quickly on the battlefield, or in an accident, or in a lingering illness that will not announce its schedule for our destruction. And so our words perish with us, and those left behind are condemned to clutch at memories, at what they imagine we wished to say.

I could feel sorrow, but not the finality of it. It was too great to be comprehended. I forced myself up from the pallet and ran blindly to Andromache, my one other companion who had faced this.

She was waiting for me in her chamber. She had made a forced attempt to weave, but her shuttle lay idle beside her on a stool. As I stumbled in, she rose and extended her arms. I fell into them, feeling her embrace.

"Paris has joined Hector," I said.

"They are embracing, even as we, those left behind, are also embracing. If we had eyes to see, we might behold them," she said. She stroked my hair. "With sorrow I welcome you as my sister."

The funeral of Paris: a high mountain of wood, Paris lying respectfully draped on his bier to cover the horror of what the poison had wrought upon him, official mourners weeping and keening through the streets of Troy. By the side of the funeral pyre his mother and father stood, as wooden as the fagots under their son. The remaining brothers formed a flank around them. All of Troy, so it seemed, had deserted the city and now stood on the southern plain where the funeral was to take place.

But there had been so many funerals, and tears were dried up. Troilus, Hector, innumerable private losses, made Paris a latecomer. Always there was the feeling that Paris had brought all this about, and without him the other deaths need not have taken place.

They were right. Without that fateful glance in Sparta, none of this would have happened. For that reason I had been willing to take his place. But adamantine Zeus would not permit it.

The oldest brother left to speak words was Deiphobus. His speech was brief, commending Paris to the gods. Priam spoke, touching on the sorrow of having found his son only to lose him. Hecuba wept.

The wood was torched. There were no sacrifices scattered amongst the fagots—no slain horses, dogs, or hostages. Paris would not have wanted that, and I had insisted on his wishes. The flames leapt upward, licking toward Paris. I shuddered, trying not to think of the pain when the fire reached him. He knows no pain any longer, I told myself. But I did not believe it. We feel pain forever, even after we are dead. I watched the fire reach him. I turned away; I could not look. But I could smell it. The smell changed when fire encountered something new.

"No, no! Stop!" someone cried. Still I cringed and did not turn back to the fire.

"Stop her!"

Now I did turn back, and I saw Oenone rushing toward the fire, her garments streaming. "Forgive me! Forgive me!" she was crying. Before anyone could take hold of her, she flung herself into the flames. With a shriek she was immolated. The flames leapt up as they fed on her. Nymphs cannot die. But it seems they can, if they so wish.

"A woman has thrown herself in," the guards were crying.

"Not a woman, but a nymph," I said. "Of her own free will. You cannot save her, she will have vanished into her elements." I was stunned by her wild act of love and in some deep part of me wondered why I had not thought to do the same.

I looked at Priam and Hecuba, expecting them to solace me. But they turned away. I was alone.

❖ LXVI ❖

When I returned to our—my—chamber, it had been cleared of all the sickbed detritus, swept clean. No incense or perfume lingered in the air, and bright sunshine played in the empty room. Paris's armor, still dusty from his last battle, was piled in a corner.

Tomorrow when the pyre cooled they would collect his bones, put them in a golden urn. Then the bones would be placed in his family tomb, and afterward there would be dispirited funeral games. And then it would be back to war, back to dreary war for the Trojans.

And for me? I could think of no life for me at all. There was nothing waiting but sublime emptiness, as empty as this room.

The rest of the day I stumbled about in my quarters, barely able to see for the tears that would suddenly well up, blurring everything. Attendants brought trays of food, but I waved them away. I admitted no one to the rooms. Sometimes I fell on the bed, dizzy while the room rotated around me. Other times I got up and addressed myself to absurd tasks like sorting through different balls of wool, dividing them into big piles, rearranging them, finding containers to store them in. Everywhere I looked I seemed to see something of Paris, except when I bent my head over the wool balls or, for some reason, removed my jewelry from its box and laid out the necklaces, bracelets, and earrings each in their separate rows. Then I put them all back in the same place. As long as I was bent over this task, I could not see the face of Paris.

And how could I ever restore the face I had loved for so long, and erase the one that had usurped it in his last hours? The hideous swollen one had blotted out the gentle one. The poisoned arrows of Heracles had stolen not only the life of Paris from me, but his face as well.

In my numbness and bewilderment I found myself dragging his clothes and possessions out of their chests, putting them on the floor. With trembling hands I arranged and smoothed the clothes, preparing them for a visitation that would not come. I could not even feel foolish; I wanted him to appear so badly, I believed I could will it. With all my power I called out to him, raising my arms and falling down upon the clothes, the clothes that still smelled like him.

"Helen, get up!"

I swam up through what I thought were the fogs of Hades; it was dark and I could not see where I went. I clutched at cloth beneath my fingers. I was lying flat.

Wavering light came toward me. Someone set an oil lamp down. A face bent over me. "Helen, get up! Oh, for shame!" Evadne cradled my head. "For shame, that they left you here alone." She smoothed my hair. "You are deserted!"

I looked into her deep eyes. "Yes," I said. Paris had deserted me. She spoke true, there was no other truth for me.

"I mean your attendants!" she said. "How dare they?"

"I sent them away," I assured her. "I wanted no one here. No one, not even you."

"It is dangerous for you to be alone now," she said, rubbing my forehead.

As if I cared if anyone killed me. I gave a feeble laugh. They would be doing me a favor.

"I meant it is dangerous for your spirits to suffer alone," she said.

"There is no other way," I said. "I suffer alone even in your presence; no one can share it with me."

"Someone can be present." She was stubborn.

"Why waste their time? There is nothing they can do." Slowly I picked myself up. "Go, Evadne. I want no company." I was eager for darkness.

The funeral games. I shall not even describe them, for does it matter whose horses won the chariot race, whose javelin went farthest, whose legs propelled him fastest? One thing was certain: the Trojans were weary, even when they were rested, and their performances were slow and clumsy. War had worn them down, as the steady tunneling of rodents will collapse a foundation. I awarded prizes from Paris's armor and weapons. In my chambers, they would be only another thing to grieve me. I could not pass his helmet without imagining him still wearing it. Some eager Trojan boy won it; let him revere and keep it.

The first, most elaborate funeral banquet proceeded according to protocol. Paris presided, as Troilus had presided at his. Now at Paris's I heard the echoes of his words at Troilus's. All the losses melded together, one great cry of grief for Troy, a private one for me. Paris's favorite foods were served—roasted kid and honey cakes, and equally honeyed, unctuous words were uttered over them. No one bleated out the insults that were bubbling inside.

Of all the people gathered, only Priam, Hecuba, and I felt true grief. The others just painted themselves with grieving colors. Priam's voice trembled as he spoke of finding his lost son only to lose him again, and Hecuba bemoaned the years that had separated them, when they were both still walking in the sunlight.

"What I would give to have those years restored," she whispered. I had to strain to hear her. "We were both here, but could not reach one another. In my folly of sending him away, I robbed myself. Now I have all the time in the world to lament."

I could say nothing. My throat was clutched by an invisible hand that made it ache. I merely stood and bowed my head.

The bones and ashes were ceremonially conveyed to the tomb, libations left, the lid opened and closed. Paris inside. Vital Paris—how could he rest content there? But we know nothing of the dead, what they want, what they feel. We only know they are profoundly different from us. Even those we love are changed into something we cannot fathom.

As we trod through the streets afterward in our sad procession, Priam fell back to walk beside me. Deiphobus, as the foremost surviving son, took his place beside Hecuba.

How stooped and frail Priam had grown! I remembered the sunlit day I had first encountered him, how muscular and strong he was, even at his age. But that day was with Paris. Paris beside me, Paris proudly presenting me, Paris protecting me! "Helen . . ." Even his voice was thin, old-man thin.

"Yes, Father," I answered.

He fumbled for my hand. He must have something momentous to say.

"Some would say the war is now over," he said. "Paris, who violated the sacred laws of hospitality—although we all recognize that love-madness can overturn peaceful laws—has relinquished you. You are now his widow. We must make our way without him."

I stiffened. Now he was going to ask me to make the sacrifice of returning to the Greeks, to Menelaus. What else could it be? It was the only sensible response. Troy would be saved, as its original reason for punishment was removed.

He was finding it difficult to frame his words. I would help him. "Dear Father," I said, "you need not force yourself to say the hateful words. I will do whatever lies in my power to save Troy. I will return to the Greeks." How could he know, after all, that a dead person did not care what she did, where she went? There is no abasement when you are dead. And I had died with Paris. "I will go to Menelaus, bow before him, and then the Greeks will have to leave the Trojan plain." I cared nothing for what happened to me. Let Menelaus kill me. Then I could join Paris, and be spared Menelaus.

"No, there is another way," he said. "You must marry Deiphobus."

I jerked my hand away. "No! I am Paris's forever." The words poured forth before I had a single thought.

"It will put heart into the resistance," he said.

"The best resistance is for me to end the war. Its pretext is gone."

"Deiphobus demands this." He forced the words out.

"As a price for what?" Surely he had no basis for demands.

"As a price for defending Troy."

"So he would turn traitor if he cannot have Helen?" I could not keep the disdain from my voice. "What sort of son have you sired?" And to think they dared call Paris coward, ignoble!

His reply was abject. "I sired many sons, but few, it seems, who are heroes."

I started to make a sharp retort, then I heard the failure in his words. To have so many sons, and so few in whom one could have pride. "I cannot wed Deiphobus," I said.

"You must," he insisted.

On both sides of us now, in the falling twilight, people were lining the street, leaning forward and calling out. We could speak no further, and I believed my silence would serve as adequate refusal.

I sat in our bedchamber. The megaron was still occupied by the foreign allies and refugees; most of them had dutifully attended the funeral games, and I was grateful to them.

In accordance with my wishes, I had been left alone. No attendants fluttered about, no family members kept me company. The chamber seemed, somehow, more deserted now, as if the shade of Paris had obeyed the mourning ritual and duly fled into his tomb. I had expected to return to this retreat and find him waiting for me here, but he had melted away.

I circled the chamber like one of Priam's hunting dogs seeking a place to lie down. Only there would be no resting place for me again, no matter how many times I lay down. I sank to one of the chairs, and stared out in the darkness.

If only we had had a child . . . if only he had left something behind to indelibly recall him . . .

If only I could speak to him, see him once more.

I rose, went to our bed. I stretched myself out on it, hoping for surcease. But not for sleep, only for utter oblivion. Should I do as my mother did, knot a length of rope around my neck and let them find me swinging in the dawn? Never see another moonrise, never see another noonday, be spared the entire black road stretching out before me?

I could feel my breathing, feel my chest rising and falling.

In—out. In—out. Soft as a whisper, but it meant I lived and Paris did not. The chamber was dark, dark. The doings of the day closed in on me, swirled me away. *A tunnel is sucking my feet away, making me slide down it.*

Paris, I follow! I follow, I fall down the tunnel with you.

Long, black, close sides in the tunnel. So close I can claw at them. It is over, then. It is over, and without the ugliness of dagger or rope. Helen is gone.

I land, softly. Still it is dark. I pick myself up, my legs trembling, and see nothing. Something brushes against my legs and I reach down to touch it. Asphodel. The flower of the fields of the dead. I am here at last.

These are the new-dead souls, awaiting passage. Mother, Troilus, Hector, have all passed over. But Paris . . . Paris must still be here.

All I see is a great confusion of souls, their mouths open as they gesture for libations to succor and feed them, their arms reaching. They are pale, as pale as the asphodels surrounding them, and waving like those flowers on their thin stalks before a strong wind.

I see no face here I recognize, and I wave them away, deflecting them like darting, swooping bats. Then, out of the gray murk, a pale shadow approaches, his face like that of Paris. The original face of Paris, not the horrid one of the death chamber.

I cannot help myself—I gasp with the delight of seeing him again, knowing that we are together.

"You have come." His voice is odd, soft, obscured as if it came from deep inside a cave.

"I am here. Nothing can part us." I reach out my arms to him, but they pass through him.

Sadness stains his face. "You are still of the daylight above," he says, as if it were a betrayal.

"No, I tell you, I have lain down in darkness and was taken here."

"But when the light comes, you will rise."

"Not if you teach me otherwise, how to avoid it."

"By your own hand, wife, by your own hand. You have the strength."

This is not the Paris I have known. Has death, then, so changed him? "Paris, I cannot live in your absence. My life has fled with you," I said.

"Then do what you must to truly enter here, rather than cheating by clutching life to yourself."

"Why are you still here, on this farther shore of Hades?" I burst out. "The funeral rites, they should have released you."

"I was waiting for you." He looks at me. "You are here. But you have not had the courage to truly follow me."

This wraith, this accusatory shade, is not truly Paris. Now I feel, more

{ 532 }

deeply than ever before, that Paris is gone forever. Death has changed him into a stranger. *Paris is no more.*

"Get away from me!" I cry. "You are not Paris, but some other vision. One I do not wish to see."

I scramble away, in such haste that I trip and fall into the stiff stalks of asphodels. They are real enough. Why, oh, why, is not Paris?

The journey back was instantaneous. I blinked and was back in my chamber, lying rigid on the bed, shaking and muttering. An unutterable misery descended on me. I had fled from Paris. I had beheld him, but I had fled.

No, I had fled from what he had become, pacing that sterile dark shore. *Paris is gone.* Those three words, embodying all the truth I needed to know, pranced, jumped, jeered at me: *Paris is gone.*

I heard my own breath. I was alive. Helen was alive. Helen must soldier on, alone. That is what living is—to soldier on. There is no virtue, no solace in the afterworld, thus no merit in hurrying there. And Paris, the Paris that I had loved, was not even waiting for me there.

It was still dark. We were a long way from dawn; I lay waiting for the light to steal in, solacing myself with the knowledge that no light, no matter how feeble, ever penetrated down into Hades. I must learn to treasure the light.

"Helen." It was Evadne again, bending over me, a robe fluttering in her hands, ready to envelope me. "Helen." I could hear the fear in her voice. I was lying so still.

"Yes, dear friend," I said, sitting up to reassure her. She smothered me with the robe, as if I were so delicate I would perish in the chamber air. I wanted to tell her I had journeyed to the boundary of the underworld, had seen Paris. But she would say it was only a dream.

"Helen, they are waiting. Everyone—Priam and Hecuba and others."

Ah. It was the *others* that I dreaded, one other in particular.

"Gelanor begs to be admitted as well."

"Admit him first." I forced myself up off the bed. My legs felt weak. "But not before I have dressed and taken some food." I was not hungry, but I needed strength.

Wearing my robes of mourning, with no jewelry or adornments, my hair bound and covered to be invisible, I welcomed a somber Gelanor.

Uncharacteristically, he bent and took my hand, kissing it. Then he straightened and looked at me.

"It is over, then," he said. "I mourn your sorrow. Although—I will not pretend—in the beginning I thought coming to Troy ill-advised, what is done is done, and if it brought you happiness, then for yourself you chose wisely."

"Gelanor—I cannot believe he is gone!" I burst out.

"It is the hardest thing on earth, to be severed from those we love. May he find peace."

He has not! I wanted to cry, but Gelanor would also say I had but dreamed last night.

"Priam wants me to marry Deiphobus! That sweating, leering man. As if I could ever—"

"You must," he said bluntly. "Close your eyes, hold your nose, extend your hand, and pretend to acquiesce."

How could he desert me like this? "No!"

"You are a prisoner of Troy now," he said. "You came here freely enough, but now you are a prisoner and they can do with you as they like. And what they like is to reward the sole remaining warrior son of Priam, so that he will soldier on."

Soldier on . . . we all would be soldiering on, then: nothing but a slog through mud and rocks and steep barren hills for the remainder of our lives.

"How could they expect me to allow him to touch me?"

"Prisoners allow all things."

I began to weep. How could I ever treasure the light that shone itself on this? Perhaps Hades was preferable after all.

"Helen, do not. I cannot bear it." Gelanor's voice was gentle. "You persuaded me to come here, and now I must behold . . ." He shook his head. "There is something you can do, if gentler means fail. I will prepare it for Evadne to give you." He looked glum. Did he mean poison? "If Troy prevails, if the Greeks sail home— I have heard that a contest over the arms of Achilles ended in a fight between Odysseus and Ajax. The arms were awarded to Odysseus; Ajax went mad and then killed himself. The Greeks are at a breaking point, as we are. I shall send my last weapon amongst them—the plague shirts. That may prove the final blow that sends them home. I will have them delivered in bundles tied up as treasure. You know how greedy they are. They will fall on them, rip them open, and then . . ." He gave a grim smile. "Agamemnon will probably be the first to tear the largest package apart. He will claim he has the right, as overlord and commander."

I would like to see that man felled in a mass of boils and welts. He had sacrificed his daughter, torn her from my sister's side. But even the most agonizing and humiliating death would not repay that.

"May it happen as you envision." Thus I gave him permission to loose this cruel weapon.

"In the meantime, you must placate them here. It will be brief. Keep yourself from Deiphobus, say you have taken a vow—are you not allowed a certain number of days for mourning?—and before he can claim you, the Greeks will have run from these shores."

"And then? Will I not still be bound to Deiphobus?"

"Only briefly, as I said. For when the Greeks are gone, you are no longer anyone's prisoner."

"Yes," I said, nodding. I had led us down this road, and now there was no turning back.

❖ LXVII ❖

I bowed my head in false obedience to Priam. I would never truly embrace Deiphobus, but by this action I could rally the spirits of Troy. Priam walked haltingly over to me.

"We will proclaim the forthcoming wedding," he wheezed.

"Not until my forty days of mourning for Paris have passed," I reminded him.

"Yes, my daughter," he said. Hecuba, by his side, looked at me sadly. She had lost Hector and Paris because of me, and now I was to wed one of her last remaining sons. She knew the dowry I brought was death.

The forty days passed too quickly, and they paralleled that of the dying year. The cold gathered in the stones of the city and worked their way into our bones. The color faded, like a sunset, from the fields as they awaited the stillness of winter.

Deiphobus did not bother with courting, presenting gifts, or calling. He was content to wait until I would fall into his hands like a late-season fruit—or so he believed. While he waited, I kept mourning for Paris, conjuring his image in my mind all throughout the day. But I did not attempt to follow him beyond this world again.

The wedding. Should I even dignify it by that grand word? Deiphobus led me from my palace to the open space between Hector's palace and mine. The wind was brisk, lifting our cloaks. Crows were calling one to another. They were the only birds abroad these blustery days. Their raucous, deep voices sounded like bickering merchants in trade booths. (Trade booths, days of peace. Would I ever hear such merchants again?)

My face was covered by a dark mourning veil. Deiphobus raised it, peering at me. Triumphantly, he flung it back. "Your period of mourning is ended!" he announced.

Had I seen his face in a market or on a street, he would have passed for handsome. He even resembled Paris a bit in the way his hair, shot through with gold, grew on his head. But there the resemblance ended.

"My mourning will never end," I said as loud as I could.

"But now you will embark on a new life. You will board the ship that is my life voyage."

"Is that so, my prince? I understood that you were to move to my palace."

Deiphobus, eager to escape from the courtyard of Priam's sons, expected to move into my home.

"It is symbolic," he muttered. "I did not mean our actual dwelling place, but our station in life."

"I see. Then I am to take it you will be my guest and the guest of your departed brother?"

"No. I shall be your lord and husband. Where I exert this privilege is unimportant." His mouth was a straight ugly line. I could not bring myself to respond.

The ceremony dragged forward—the vows, ritual phrases, ceremonial gestures. I fulfilled my obligations in lifeless fashion. We exchanged gifts. He crowned me. There were no living flowers in the fields now, so he used dried, dead ones. He grasped my wrist in the age-old assertion of marriage.

At the banquet, unable to eat, I watched others feast. My heart longed for Paris. I would never, could never, celebrate the attempt of others to sever us.

* * *

In the chamber—the very one I had shared with Paris—we retired after the tedious day. He was eager. He threw off his cloak and approached me, arms outstretched. I brushed him aside, dissembling. It was too much for me. My womanly modesty had been overtaxed. I bade him forgive me. Then, before he could protest, I bolted myself in the inner chamber I had prepared.

Let him wait.

The next morning, when Evadne came to me, my shut door, the draped cloak of Deiphobus, and his sandals in the outer room told all the story. She held out a covered jar. "I see, then, that you will need this. Gelanor had hoped it would not be necessary."

I took the jar and peered into it. A short thorn-covered branch lay curled within it. I drew it out.

"Careful—do not allow the thorns to prick you."

I held it by the end of its stem. "Poison?" I said. This was not what I wanted—I had no stomach for murdering Deiphobus.

"Of a sort," she said. "But a selective one. It kills only his . . . ability. Not his military ability, I must add. It will disable only the one that threatens you."

"Oh." Gelanor had refined his skills impressively. "Does it affect women as well as men?"

"I would not take the chance, my lady. That is why I warned you."

She seated herself on a chair next to my bed. "When he comes near," she said, "you must draw the thorns across his bare skin. The smallest scratch will suffice."

"Is the damage lasting, or does the ability revive?"

"I believe it is lasting."

For the next few nights he kept away from my chamber. But every night he crept closer, until the night came when he pushed on the door and stood possessively on its threshold as it slowly swung open.

The disgrace of being barred from Helen's bedchamber was clear in the belligerent expression on his face.

"Wife." He held out his arms and advanced toward me.

I turned away, retreating farther into the chamber, luring him after me. Avidly, he shut the door. It thudded into place on its hinges, and he dropped the bolt into place. "Now," he said, "we begin our life together."

When I reached the darkest part of the room, I stopped. He kept walking toward me, and when he reached me, he embraced me. I shuddered at his touch—it sent little wriggling snakes of aversion all over my body.

"Are you cold, my sweet?" He sounded solicitous. "Let us draw closer to the brazier." In a corner a round stone brazier was glowing faintly with its coals.

"No. I am not cold." I stood where I was and commanded my body to stop its quivering.

"Oh, Helen," he murmured dazedly, running his hands across my shoulders and back. "My wife, my beauty."

I stood stiffly, letting him fire himself to such a peak that he would lose his ability to notice anything else. Soon he seemed utterly lost in the web of his own desire and anticipation. He shuffled toward the bed, that beckoning goal. Trying to keep his dignity, he first knelt on it, then attempted to draw me after him. He would not fall on it like an unbridled, impassioned youth. I let myself follow him.

Safely—as he assumed—on the bed, he reached out for me. He plunged his thick and clumsy fingers into my hair, and for a moment I pitied him and would have left the thorn lying on its table, making do with ordinary ways of keeping him at bay. But he started kissing and biting my neck, lunging his thick body at me, and muttering insults about Paris. All these days in Troy, to have lived with the cowardly Paris . . . but now all was remedied. I should have been with him, Deiphobus, from the beginning.

"From that first night in my father's courtyard, I knew," he breathed. He started sliding my gown from my shoulders, pressing up against me.

"Pray, remove your tunic," I teased him.

"I need only raise it," he said, panting.

"That is what shepherds do in the fields," I said. "It is not worthy of a prince of Troy. Is not your body that of a warrior? Then why hide it?"

"I offer it to you," he said eagerly, sitting up and stripping off his tunic, leaving his shoulders bare.

Now! I reached over and plucked the stem of thorns. I dangled it before him. "This came from Sparta, my home. Our customs differ from yours. Yet I must honor them or feel that our union is not complete."

"Do what you must," he murmured, not knowing what he said.

"Very well." I placed the branch carefully on his shoulder and drew it slowly down across his back. The little thorns dug in; tiny punctures wept a little blood, thin lines down his back.

"If this makes you mine, and me yours, it is but a trifle." He sighed with pleasure.

"There," I said, laying the branch aside. How long would it take to work? I must divert him for a little while. "Husband," I said solemnly, "there is another ritual we observe in Sparta. We must intone the hymn to Hera as protector of marriage, and invoke her blessing."

"Very well." A trace of impatience mixed in his voice, but the night was long and he could postpone his pleasure for a few moments, if by so doing he gained stature in his wife's eyes.

I had never memorized the entire prayer to Hera, which left me free to improvise and add verse after verse, which I hoped sounded authentic: ". . . the fruits of the earth and the great expanse of ocean, / and Poseidon and all his forces, grant us safe passage . . ."

How much time had passed? I had no way of knowing. The coals in the brazier were dying, but that was no measure. It depended too much on the quantity and quality of the coals.

". . . and all Olympians—"

"Must retire at last to Olympus," he finished for me, firmly.

Now it had come to this. He pulled off my gown—as he had the right to do—and gaped at my nakedness. Incoherent, he threw himself on me.

A rush of sounds came from his mouth like bounding stags, but they were a confused mass of compliments and desire. He grabbed at my belly, cupped my thighs, my breasts, his stout fingers demanding a response. I tried to pretend, but my tepid flutterings were lost in his rush to consummate the union. He would conquer Helen, make her his at last.

O let the drug have worked its disabling strength on him!

"Oh! Oh!" he was crying out in pleasure—but it was a pleasure that could not go beyond those limits.

I let loose a silent cry of thanks to the gods, and to Gelanor. I was spared.

Bewilderment flooded him, then anger, then embarrassment. He fell away from me. He started to say something, then checked himself. He wondered if I knew what had happened.

The pretense must only last a bit longer. Whatever served best to send him away and keep him from my bed: I would feign ignorance, and in so doing make his disappointment greater.

"Deiphobus," I whispered. I stroked his cheek. I forced myself to gaze upon him dreamily in what little light there was. "Thank you."

❖ LXVIII ❖

What the Trojans thought of my "marriage," I have no idea. Most likely they cared very little. Their appetite for and interest in my doings, or in any member of the royal family's behavior, had shriveled like their bellies with the deprivations of the siege.

I was safe from the predations of Deiphobus. A few times he made half-hearted attempts to overcome his mysterious malady—bolstering himself with drink, or inflaming himself with lascivious songs—but when the result continued the same, he slunk away. Before long I could leave my bedchamber door open with no fear of his trespassing.

I worked at my loom, sadly completing the great pattern that had been empty and awaiting its final story. The edges, with Sparta, had been finished long ago, and within that, Paris and our voyage, but the center, with Troy, now must be filled in.

The once proud and shining city was threadbare, stripped. The artworks had long ago been sold to raise money, the fountains were silent and filled with dust, the streets teeming with injured soldiers and widows and refugees, beggars and urchins. The fine horses were gone, and only a few bedraggled donkeys staggered under their packs. The lower city, which had formed an apron to the south below the main city, had been overrun by the Greeks, who trashed and burned the houses and workshops, stealing horses and wrecking gardens.

The shining, sloping walls of Troy still held, and the towers still reared proudly over the enemy. They were impervious to the burning arrows and the stones the invaders aimed at them. As long as the walls of Troy held, Troy would stand.

But oh! the walls guarded nothing but misery, encircled only pain and grief. From the outside it looked stout and snug, but inside all was abject. The only consolation lay in knowing our enemy could not see through the walls to what lay beyond.

Of course, there were spies, always spies, on both sides. Doubtless the Greeks had hints of how badly things were going in Troy. They may even have heard about my "marriage" and undoubtedly they knew which of Troy's best warriors survived—Deiphobus, and Aeneas, and Antimachus—and which were lost. They would have guessed that Priam and Hecuba were sunk in mourning and that the councils of war had deteriorated into laments and hopeless plans, and that Troy floundered, leaderless.

But they, too, had lost leaders—Achilles, and Ajax, their two best warriors. Our spies told us that the survivors were disheartened and weary, and that to their eyes, the walls of Troy seemed untouched despite their years of effort. And then, a dreadful visitation of plague had ripped through their ranks. They prayed and asked the gods from whence it had come, and how had they offended.

But it had not come from a god, so they received no answer. It had come from Gelanor's mock treasure bundle, stuffed with the shirts from the temple of Apollo.

"They have been reading entrails and bird flights like madmen," Gelanor said. "But therein does not lie the answer they seek." He was leaning over the wall, staring across the plain to the Greek camp. His voice echoed a grim satisfaction, tinged with sorrow. "It has worked as I thought it would." He sighed. "As I hoped it would. But what an evil hope, to kill my countrymen."

I looked at him—so much older and worn than when I had first seen him. What had I done to him, to this honorable friend? My own journey had corrupted an upright man, to the point where he could poison his countrymen and call it a good day's work. The sun was setting, and in the coming shadows I knew we were part of that darkness.

It was left to the daughters of Priam and Hecuba to provide solace to their parents: Creusa, the wife of Aeneas, Polyxena, Laodice, Ilona, and Cassandra. They had been spared the arrows and spears of the Greeks, but if the city fell, they would suffer worse than their dead brothers. In a conquered city, there were only two fates for women: the young ones would be raped and taken away into slavery, the old ones, deemed useless, killed outright. No one survived the sack of a city—not even the city itself. Achilles, the most ferocious ravisher, was gone and would not stride through our streets as he did through the home city of Andromache, destroying everything before him. But there were others—lesser imitators of their hero. They could mimic his cruelty easily enough, if they could not match his strength and prowess. Thus do cowards always.

Our only hope was that the Greeks, exhausted and demoralized, might bow before the seeming invincibility of our massive walls and go home. As I said, they could not see through them, could not know how near the end we really were.

I awoke crying. In the night I had had a strange vision, clear as a crystal splintering the sunlight. Even as I tried to grasp it, to retain it so I could convey it to others, it was fading, jumping, wavering, wriggling like shudders under the skin. I had seen something made of wood, huge, looming. I had seen it once before, even less clearly. But what was it? The image swam away from me. It harbored death. And I had also seen—could this be true?—Odysseus walking the streets of Troy, disguised. Taking our measure.

He was wearing beggar's rags. Had I seen such a person? But the streets of Troy were filled with beggars now. If Odysseus had managed to sneak in, he could have lost himself amongst them easily enough. And why would he have come? Had they no spies?

Later he was to claim that I saw him, recognized him, helped him. But that is a lie. That man tells nothing but lies, whatever will serve his purpose. I pity Penelope, who waited for such a man!

I cried because this hulking wooden thing—whatever it was, I had seen it but fleetingly—signaled the doom of Troy.

I sat up. Daylight was nudging the shutters. The room around me was unchanged. Frescoes in red and blue showed the same serene flowers and birds. The polished floors gleamed, reflecting the fresh daylight. It seemed eternal, fixed. But the dream had shown it was all too vulnerable, living only on the sufferance of time.

It could not vanish, it must abide. But that was an illusion. Everything vanished—Mother, Paris, my own youth. Why should this room be different? Why should Troy itself be different?

"They are gone!" Evadne burst into the room, her spindly arms suddenly surging with strength as she flung the doors open. They flew out on either side of her, banging against the wall. The vases in their niches shuddered, trembled, but did not fall. "The Greeks have gone!"

The dream . . . it must be tied in with the dream . . . I leapt up out of bed. "Did they leave anything behind?"

She shook her head. "What matter what they left? They themselves are gone. Our sentries saw ship after ship sailing away, and then a brave lad confirmed it by going to their camp. It was deserted! And the spies report that they were so weakened by that mysterious plague they had not the manpower to continue the fight." Her words rushed joyfully like a long-dammed stream suddenly free to tumble where it would.

"Did they leave anything behind?" I repeated. I hated my own dampening words, but it was all that mattered.

She inclined her head. "Dress yourself, my lady, and I shall tell you. I see your second sight did not vanish with the serpent."

There was a horse, constructed of wood. From the camp a survivor had stumbled forth, claiming to have escaped the Greeks and their intended sacrifice of him by hiding in the forest. His name was Sinon, so he said. He told a pretty tale of their reasons for constructing the horse and leaving it behind.

It was all lies. I knew it was all lies; my special knowledge told me. Yet the Trojans were so willing to believe him.

There are those who hold that Trojans were far nobler than Greeks. They cite the fact that no sons of Troy claimed kinship with the gods, but fought as mortal men, their fates in their own hands, with no hope of Olympian reprieve. They speak of the high-mindedness of Priam in honoring the choice and marriage of his son Paris, refusing to surrender me, even though a more worldly king would have trussed me up and delivered me to the Greek camp, averting trouble.

But a noble nature can blind a man to the motives of those who are not as he is, rendering himself helpless before them. Priam and his advisers did not practice deep duplicity, and credited their enemies with the nature they themselves possessed.

Priam eagerly questioned Sinon and satisfied himself with his answers. His bruises, his cuts, argued for his veracity. Yet a clever enemy is willing to disguise himself in any way he deems efficacious. That never seemed to occur to Priam, in spite of the example of Hyllus. Hector would not do such a thing, therefore no one else would stoop to it.

What if . . . what if . . . the Greeks had selected him to be their persuader, their spokesman, and he had undergone a few beatings and buffetings to make himself credible? I asked Priam to let me question him, as someone knowledgeable about Greeks and the Grecian language. He refused.

Instead, he embraced the story Sinon told him. Here it is: The Greeks, eaten up by plague and realizing the walls of Troy were impregnable, had taken their leave of our shores after fruitless years of fighting. They had placated Athena—she who had urged their voyage here for her revenge on Paris and must be mollified before a return trip—with a horse of wood. Horses were special to Athena, and she must therefore look with favor upon it. Some seer of theirs had said that if the horse were carried into Troy itself, then Troy would stand forever, so they had purposely made it so large it would be difficult to drag through the gate and up to the temple of Athena. That way they could satisfy the goddess without endangering their own reputation, for if Troy stood untouched forever, then they had failed.

"It is not like the Greeks to do this," said Antimachus, circling the horse. I had dressed myself and come down, passing out the gates to inspect the large structure.

There was something wrong. We both sensed it. A big wooden thing . . .

He swung around and looked at me, knitting his brows. Tapping smartly on the horse with a rod, he muttered, "I like it not."

If three Antimachuses had stood on one another's shoulders, the top one would have been able to reach out and touch the horse's head. If five Antimachuses had stretched themselves in a line on the ground, they would have extended from one tip of the platform to another. The horse rested on a flat bed with logs underneath to make for easy rolling. It was made of green wood, hastily fashioned together. Its legs were tree trunks and the round part of its body bulged as if it were a pregnant mare. For eyes, it had two seashells. They looked down, unseeing.

Cautious at first, a few curious people ventured out and inspected it. But soon hordes of Trojans streamed out and swarmed around the object, jabbering with glee. Pent up inside the walls for so long, their only excitement the daily ingress of the mangled and dead, this toy delighted them, as the sphinx had long ago. They stroked its legs and boys tried to clamber up to sit astride it. Women wove garlands of flowers to drape its neck, and tossed them up to their sons to festoon it. Pipers played flutes and people began dancing around it, crying with relief. It was over. The war was over.

Priam and Hecuba emerged from the city and stood before it. Priam had arrayed himself in his most kingly robes, and Hecuba, still in black, wrapped herself in her cloak. Priam walked around it studiously, his dark eyes sweeping over it, taking in every detail—the fashioning of the planks, the size, the ugly white staring eyes. Then he turned back to regard the Scaean Gate.

"It will just pass under it," he said, measuring them both with his eyes.

Again, that chill: it rippled over me, like wind stirring a barley field. *It was constructed to do just that! It cannot fit just by chance.*

"We shall take it into our city, to protect us and fulfill the prophecy. Troy cannot fall if the horse passes through our walls." His voice rose, almost to its former strength.

No, this was wrong! "Dear father." I stepped forward. "How do we know that is the prophecy? Sinon told us. But he is a Greek. Other than his words, we have no knowledge of what the horse betokens. And how comes it that they have fashioned it the exact size to pass through the gate? Surely they would have made it bigger if their true intent was to assure it remained outside Troy? As it is, they have invited you to bring it in. Think upon this."

Instead of answering, Priam stood dumbly staring up at the horse.

Hecuba answered for him. "Do you, who brought all this upon us, now presume to warn us?"

"I have lost the dearest thing in the world to me, but my loyalty is still to Troy," I replied. "It always has been."

She flung back her hood. "You lost one person. We have lost many, including the one you loved. Our very city was threatened. You know the fate of vanquished cities—to be wiped from the face of the earth, left a smoldering mound of ashes. This was what the Greeks intended for us—because of you and Paris. Thousands of deaths for one kiss. If they had won, you would have switched your loyalty back to them quickly enough."

"Do you not yet know me?" I cried. It was as if she had struck me.

"Into the city, into the city!" the people were chanting, swaying in the morning sunlight. "Drag it in!" And their cries drowned out Hecuba's reply as she turned away.

Suddenly Cassandra plucked at her mother's arm. I had not seen her earlier, even though her red hair gleamed like a jewel amongst all the dull colors. "Helen speaks true," she said. "There is evil here. Do not let it contaminate our city. Leave it here, out on the plain."

"Daughter of Priam, we all know of your frailty," a man in the crowd yelled. "Go, stop speaking madness."

Laocoön, an outsized priest, came puffing toward us, two of his sons trotting to keep up with him. "Stop! Stop!" he cried. "Test it first!" He brandished a thrusting spear and flung it at the horse's flanks, where it stuck and swayed. "Find something to penetrate it!" he cried. He looked around wildly.

"Deiphobus? You have a bigger throwing spear. Let me have it. Let me pierce this horse's hide and make the Greeks inside yell."

Deiphobus shook his head. "I have no magic spear, old man. Mine has a head like yours. But you may use it."

The priest grabbed it and threw it at the horse's rounded belly. It made a hollow sound as it struck.

I had not seen Deiphobus in days. As I said, he kept well away from my chamber, lest he suffer further embarrassments. He looked at me for an instant, then turned away. At this charged moment, I wanted to go to him, whisper in his ear, *Some wishes are better left unpursued. The granting of them only leads to more misery.* But I did not. I stood rooted where I was.

"Let us build a fire under it if we cannot pierce it!" Laocoön cried. "This platform is handy. It will hold a pile of wood. Torch it, and send the Greeks hidden inside scrambling out to save their lives!" He walked backward, entreating the crowd. The people stared back at him, silent. "Oh, you fools!" He looked around. "At least test the thing before you bring it in!" But the crowd kept clapping and calling out, "A horse for Troy! A horse for Troy!"

Then, before our horrified eyes, a huge serpent shot out of the plain, reared up, and coiled itself around Laocoön and his sons, strangling them and then dragging them off toward the sea. No one moved to help them. Their wavering cries resounded across the fields.

"Athena!" cried the credulous people. "Athena has punished him for his blasphemy! This proves that she wants us to take the horse into Troy."

"It proves nothing other than that Athena has a vested interest in seeing you take the horse into Troy," cried Cassandra. She was brave. I admired her as she stepped forward, daring Athena to strike again. "Oh, foolish Trojans! Whose goddess is Athena? Does she not watch over Odysseus? Over Achilles? Is she not the protective goddess of Athens, city of Greeks? Why would she wish good upon Troy?"

"We have a temple to her here!" one man yelled back. "Her special statue is here!"

"Every city has a temple to Athena and a statue," she answered. "It proves nothing. Athena, like all the gods, adopts certain humans, humors and pampers them beyond reason. She is insulted if you do not have a temple, but having one means nothing to her."

"Priam, your daughter is mad!" someone called out. "Stifle her!"

Cassandra twisted around and screamed at him, "You cannot mute the truth!"

"Cassandra, dear." Priam came to her and encircled her with his arm.

"Troy deserves her doom, then!" said Cassandra. "I leave it to you. I shall perish with you! But I see my end, whereas you are blind." She pushed off his arm and tore toward the city, her gown streaming.

❖ LXIX ❖

It was midmorning. The stubborn townsfolk threw ropes around the horse's neck and affixed a loop to the platform to enable them to drag the horse toward the south gate. Even so, it was very slow. The horse was heavy—too heavy, perhaps, for it to be empty?—and the rollers slid out from under the platform. Several times the horse lurched and almost slid off its carrier. Each time it was saved, righted, and sent on its ponderous way. When it approached the south gate, Priam insisted on a little ceremony to bless its entrance into the city. The doors were pulled back as far as they would go, like stretching a grin, and all the people together had to shove as well as pull to get it through. The top of the horse's head cleared the lintel by only a hand span.

Oh, how thorough the Greeks were. How well they had figured.

Priam blessed it as it jerked through the gate, calling upon it to begin the era of plenty for Troy.

Heaving it up to the citadel proved more difficult. The street angled upward and soon the pulling stopped; it required shoving. The entire apparatus was very heavy, and only the determination of the Trojans was able to budge it on the steepest stretches. The sun went down with it stuck halfway up, the temple within sight but still far away.

They could not leave the horse where it was; it would roll back, crashing back through the gate. So they strained themselves shoving it, grunting and groaning. No horse or ox could pull the structure, as it was impossible to hitch any animals to it; only the muscles of determined men could do so. Thus Troy strained to accomplish her own doom.

* * *

It was late before the horse arrived at the temple of Athena, coming to rest on a paved expanse of ground alongside it. My and Hector's palaces overlooked it.

From my chamber I could see the people of Troy throwing flowers upon the platform of the horse, could hear the music of the flute players and singers extolling the horse. Below me wine-bearers had brought out Troy's last remaining amphoras of wine, and they were sloshing it about with abandon. Drunken men and women reeled away, dancing—and falling—around the horse. Giggling, they got up, weaving their unsteady way about it.

As I gazed down upon it from the height of my window, the horse looked like a child's toy, even to the ropes dangling from the platform. I had seen clay and wooden wagons, laden with sweets or dolls, being pulled along by children on just such strings. The top of the horse did not show any dent or outline of a door. But it had to be hollow inside.

A late-rising moon was struggling to surmount the walls, and when it finally burst over them it flooded the city with unearthly, cold light, making the torches look bright yellow. The sudden glare of extra light fired the revelers, as if the heavens themselves had joined the celebrations. Sleepers stirred and tumbled out of their houses, gleefully parading in their nightclothes. Vendors—long vanished from the streets of Troy—suddenly set up stalls, and jugglers and acrobats thronged the summit of the citadel, weaving in and out amongst the crowd, performing for free.

Up on the actual platform of the horse, lovers swarmed and embraced, and little boys competed to see who could climb up its legs the fastest. Someone started a throwing contest for empty amphoras, smashing them down the streets, rousting even more people out of their houses.

"Troy is free—Troy is free—Troy is free—" lines of people started chanting as they swayed, holding hands, up and down the streets and around the horse, tottering, falling, laughing, crying.

The horse. The horse. Now it was inside the city, lodged in our very midst. Apollo, as builder of the city walls, promised divine protection for those walls, but neglected to offer the same promise for the city itself. Usually if walls stood stoutly, nothing could penetrate them. But not so in this case.

It seemed to me that I could almost see inside the horse, and what I saw were dark, hunched shadows that moved ever so slightly. It was like looking through a cloud, discerning something dimly. The special sight of the serpents had not deserted me.

I put on my long trailing robe and forced myself down to where the horse was. The crowd was very thick and I hated the push and warm closeness of the masses of people. One of my guards cleared a path for me, so that I could step up onto the platform. Flickering torches showed the seams of the boards used to seal up the horse's rounded belly. I could not see any opening, but in the darkness it was hard to tell.

How many men could this device hold? How many moving shadows had I seen? There was not much room in it, and the men would have to be crouched in uncomfortable positions, but perhaps as many as six might be inside. But that would be enough—enough to open the city gates, so that hundreds could pour in. But that meant they would have to reach the gates undetected, after the crowd thinned and vanished, and Troy drifted into sleep.

The wood had been too thick to be pierced by spears, and the people of Troy would not hear of setting fire to it, especially now that it was within the city.

What else could be used to pass into the horse to test and disable it? Sound—blare of trumpets, music, or voices. Voices. How long had it been since the Greeks had heard the voices of their wives and mothers and children? What would hearing them again do to them?

Who was likely to be inside? Would it be the men of rank, or men deemed unimportant and easily sacrificed if they were discovered? But one man I knew would be there: Odysseus. It was against his nature to send others and wait to hear what had happened, to hold still and miss out on a daring raid. He would be in there, and possibly Menelaus and Agamemnon. I could sound like Clytemnestra, and like Penelope—who was, after all, my cousin—and for Menelaus my own voice would be enough. The lesser Ajax might be in there, but I had no idea of any of his loved ones; he was said to be a cruel and vicious man, but that does not mean some fool of a woman did not love him.

I approached the horse, stood by its side. My guard yelled and held up his hands, calling for silence. The music stopped and the loud noises of the crowd died away. I banged on the belly of the horse to catch the ears of whoever was inside. I believed now that men were there; I would not speak to empty air. I filled my lungs and, holding my breath for a moment, willed myself to become Clytemnestra, remembering her voice.

"My dear Agamemnon, my lord and master"—that should please him— "I long for your return, to stand by my side once more. I cannot endure this separation; I think I shall go mad." All the time I was speaking, I circled the horse. The crowd hung on my words, puzzled. "Oh, come to me!"

I thought I heard a creaking from inside the horse, but it was impossible to tell. Just the shifting of people on the platform could cause the structure to groan. "Wait no longer!" I begged. "I am here. I have followed you to Troy."

The sound inside had stopped.

"Odysseus, I know you are there." My voice changed, becoming higher and lighter. "I know you all too well, husband of mine. The years on rocky Ithaca have been so hard I cannot tell you of them. There are men who think to persuade me that you have perished here at Troy, and who want to force me to wed. So I have fled here. If you are nearby, show yourself to me. Otherwise I shall mourn you as gone. I know that if you yet live, you will be here. So close to me at this moment!"

The utter stillness in the horse told me that the men were holding their breaths, trying not to move a flicker. I signaled to my guard and he smacked the horse with his spear. My hope that this would startle them into betraying themselves was disappointed.

Now for Menelaus—if he was within. He was the most likely to crumble. "Menelaus, dear husband! It is I, Helen. Forgive me, take me back! I fall at your feet and supplicate you. I long to see your face again, the face that has haunted me for all these years, years of longing. I wear the lovely jewel you gave me!" Oh, let the shade of Paris be truly far away in Hades, lest he hear these lies.

Now I could detect the slightest little murmur of sound, less even than the scrambling of mice, from within the horse. (But what if it were mice? That was possible. Was I singing only to rodents?) But no trapdoor was flung open, no Menelaus jumped down to confront me.

Three more times I circled the horse, calling on the three men. But I failed to stir them, if indeed they were in there. Sadly, I turned away.

"Continue your carousing," I told the people. "Make as much noise as you like." Immediately they sprang back to life, as if they had been turned briefly into statues and now were released to move again.

My palace echoed as I returned to my chambers. I must be the only person in Troy to stay inside, alone, on this night, I thought. I stood at my highest window and looked out toward the shore and the deserted Greek camp. In the moonlight I thought I could see movement on the water, but it was only waves. The Greek ships would be out of sight already if they had sailed two days ago.

I wished with all my being that Paris stood here beside me. It would never feel normal to be without him, even if I lived to a wintry old age. If only I had kept his helmet after all. How foolish of me to give it away. How blinded with grief I was, not thinking at all. Now it was as if I had given Paris himself away, for anything he had touched or been proud of was part of him.

Down below they were still dancing around the horse, drinking and yelling. Was this truly the end of the Trojan War? All those lives lost, and then, in the end, nothing but a wooden horse for a prize? I had been right—it was a toy, a mocking toy that we were left holding. What would Paris have said about it? This stupid thing cheapened us, made us and our love seem a toy as well. Perhaps there was no one in it at all, and it was nothing more than a parting insult from the Greeks.

I sat alone watching the moonlight creep across the floor, rigid and seized with grief. I do not know how long I sat there, but later I realized that the noise below had died away. I went to the window and looked down, to see the last of the revelers stumbling away, tripping over discarded garlands. A boy with a flute was weaving his steps around the horse's legs, playing a few plaintive notes, and then he, too, left, and the horse stood alone in the moonlight.

It was the very deadest time of night—long past midnight, when all creatures are normally sleeping. I, too, must try to sleep. But instead I went to the box where I kept the brooch from Menelaus and fastened it upon my shoulder. I had told him I wore it. Perhaps I thought by doing so, I would induce Menelaus—if indeed he was within the horse—to come forth. Perhaps this object would have some power to draw him, just as the helmet would have kept Paris nearer to me.

I lay down on my bed, feeling too tired even for sleep. I heard the heavy footsteps of Deiphobus coming toward my chamber, hesitating at the threshold, then turning away. He did not come in anymore, but often I had heard him approach and then withdraw. He went into the chamber where he kept his bed and lay down. Soon his loud breathing told me he was sound asleep. He never had trouble sleeping. His thoughts were simple and he was utterly free, like a three-year-old, of any troubling questions to wrack his mind.

As I lay quietly, something still prevented me from sleep. Now I know it was my guardian, the god appointed to keep me safe. Aphrodite? Did she still care for me? Or had she vanished with Paris? Persephone, my childhood allegiance? I had neglected her, but perhaps she did not neglect me. Awake, I heard a soft sound down by the horse. It was muffled, but it sounded like a creak, followed by a thud. I flung off my covers and flew to the window, where I beheld the outlines of forms descending on ropes from the horse's belly, little lumps like beads on a necklace, but beads that moved.

Yes. The horse had carried men inside it. Even as I clutched the windowsill, I saw them land on the platform and then steal away, down the main street. They were headed for the gates—to fling them open.

"Stop!" I cried. "Stop! Guards!"

One of the men halted and looked up at me. The moonlight hit his face underneath his cap. It was Odysseus.

"Silence!" he hissed. "We are here to rescue you!" His voice carried up to where I leaned from the window.

"You are here to kill!" I shot back. "Guards! Guards!" I yelled.

But all the guards had deserted their posts, drunk and sleeping in the shadows of what they assumed was safety.

"Her first! Her first!" A voice I knew well reached me. Menelaus had slithered down the rope and stood beside Odysseus, pointing at the window. "Get her! Get her! Forget the gates!"

Fool that I was, to have betrayed my station. Why had I not kept silent?

"She is yours," said Odysseus. "None of us may lay hands on her." With that, he leapt from the platform and rushed down the main street. Behind him, the others, descending from the horse, their legs wrapped around the dangling rope, slid quickly and followed him.

Menelaus made for the palace. I must withdraw, hide myself. All I could think was, I cannot be taken by him! The thought of seeing him, confronting him, was revolting. Menelaus did not know Troy. I could hide somewhere— where? Menelaus! For so long he had been but a name, an old memory. Now he stalked the streets of Troy, he was within our very sacred precincts.

And oh! he was quick. I had forgotten the young runner who had competed for me. Before I could descend the stairs, he was rushing up them. But he turned right instead of left, coming into the room where Deiphobus slept.

I had to get away. Where was he? As I glanced into the chamber I saw him approaching Deiphobus, saw him yank his head up by the hair. Wide startled eyes looked at Menelaus.

"You are Deiphobus?" Menelaus asked as if he were meeting him in a council chamber.

Deiphobus tried to grab his sword rather than answering. Menelaus ran him through, thrusting a sword clean through his throat. "Answer first," he spat. "Only an enemy reaches for a weapon before responding." He jerked the body off the couch, where it fell with a loud thud. It rolled over once and then sprawled in an embarrassing position, legs wide open, tunic hiked up.

I ran down the stairs. Menelaus spun on his heels, sighting me. "Helen!" he called. "Helen!"

I fled, down the stairs and out of the palace, the beautiful palace Paris and I had built together. He was here; Menelaus was here, killing. He would kill me as well. Let it be at some site worthy of the deed. I ran across the open courtyard and into the temple of Athena. But even as I did, I knew this temple would not shelter me. From the first moment I had beheld her primitive and ugly image on that first day in Troy, I had felt her animosity. But I rushed to her nonetheless.

I took hold of the base of her statue, babbling supplications. At its feet I saw the gold marriage chain I had offered her long ago. It was neatly coiled and even had fresh flowers twined about it.

Heavy behind me I heard Menelaus's footsteps. There was a rasp as he drew his sword from its sheath. I bent my head and clutched the wood of Athena's statue. I would meet death like one of the sacrificial animals, dedicating myself. But all I could see was the face of Paris. It was he I would die for. I was glad to do so. *Paris, I come!* I trembled and waited.

Instead, cruel fingers twisted themselves in my hair.

"A quick killing is too easy for you," the voice was saying. "Speak first, before you die."

I was hauled to my feet, my hands pried from the altar. I kept my eyes shut. I wanted to see only the face of Paris.

"Open your eyes, you coward, you adulteress, you bitch." A finger forced itself into the corner of one eye, digging in. He meant to blind me, gouging out my eye while pretending he only wanted me to see.

I opened my eyes to see his face set in hatred.

"Oh, I have imagined this moment for so many years," he hissed. His hot breath raked my face. "Now it has come to pass. I see your face again. I have power over you. You will pay."

"Take your payment, then," I said. "And be quick about it."

"You dare to order me? Oh, your effrontery exceeds even what I had imagined, all these years." He grabbed my hair again. "You should be begging me for your life." He forced me down on my knees. "Beg! Beg me!"

My knees ground into the stone floor of the temple "I beg the opposite," I said. "Kill me."

He laughed. "I know that trick. Ask the opposite. It is an old one, my lady. It will not work. You shall die."

"Good." I waited. "Strike, then."

His eyes lifted over my head and saw the gold chain on the altar. He stared, disbelieving. "My marriage gift!" he sputtered. "You disdained it so deeply. But why should I think a gold chain would be held in higher esteem than your vows?" Now, infuriated, he drew back his sword. It hovered in the air.

Let it be over. Let me join all those I loved, who had fled or been snatched from this world betimes. Mother . . . Troilus . . . Hector . . . most of all, Paris . . . Now. It would happen. Be done. Life flit away, down to the dark regions. The transition is the worst terrain to traverse, but the journey is brief.

Paris, I come! I held out my arms to him.

There was a gasp and a clatter as something fell to the ground. I stared as Menelaus's sword hit, jounced, and skidded across the floor. As I raised my arms, my gown had gaped.

"How could you, how could you, how dare you show yourself, you shameless . . ." And then Menelaus was blathering, sweeping me toward him. "Cover yourself!" The brooch—his brooch—holding the shoulders of my gown had been ripped open by his rough handling of me, and he had glimpsed my breasts. He started weeping.

"Stop it!" I commanded him. "Kill me. Now!"

But all he did was bury his head in his hands and cry, loudly. "My wife, my dearest . . ."

Oh, this was torture! Was there no honorable end to it?

I looked down, and the front of my gown was covered in blood, seeping out from the cursed brooch.

"Stop the killing!" I took his hands away. "Look at me. Call off your countrymen from their mission. Let Troy go. Let it live. Then . . . I shall go with you and be your wife again."

Was it truly I who spoke those shocking, unthinkable words? But all was lost, and Paris gone. If by sacrificing myself I could save others, what matter?

"It is too late," he said. "They will sate their hatred of Troy."

Now I knew why the brooch spouted blood; it was blood yet to come.

"You gave me this." I pointed to it.

"With each drop that oozes from it, know you caused it," he said. "Is that not fitting?"

"It is the Greeks who have caused the bloodshed," I said.

"You shall lie in my bed again, covered with blood or no," he said. "I gladly smear myself with it, if I can smear myself with the scent of you along with it." He shoved me out the door and into the open air, then dragged me back into the palace. "Blood and Helen are inextricably intertwined."

❖ LXX ❖

Once back inside, he recoiled at the realization he was standing in Paris's domain. He jerked me against himself and steered me from the room, bending my left arm painfully behind me. And just so, I left the bedchamber I had shared with Paris, never to behold it again. "There's work to do in Troy," he muttered.

"More killing?" I trembled to ask. The wet ooze of the brooch felt cold against my skin.

"Killing the likes of which no one has ever seen, for Troy is larger and richer than any other city." We were descending the steps, Menelaus stumbling in the unfamiliar darkness. But he kept his tight grip on my arm, propelling me downward.

All was silent in the halls below; people slept in a drunken stupor, garlands still twined about their necks. Some wore half-smiles, others lolled gape-mouthed. Menelaus steered me through them, stepping around them.

I pushed them with my foot, crying, "Awake! Awake! Troy is betrayed!"

"You—!" Menelaus spun me by my arm, turning me toward him, slapping my face. Warm blood trickled from my nose. "Another sound, and . . ." he drew back his fist.

The sleepers were stirring. "Raise the cry! The Greeks are in the streets!" I cried, before he hit me so hard I spun to the floor, landing on my knees.

But I was free. Shielded by the mounds of people, I crawled away, lost in their arms and legs while Menelaus turned and turned helplessly in the dull light, seeking me. I gave thanks, now, for all these strangers. *Xenia,* the laws of hospitality that Paris had outraged under Menelaus's roof, now saved me. Our uninvited guests were my salvation.

They were roused, and leapt to their feet. "Greeks? Greeks here?" they cried.

"They came from the horse," I shouted. "From the belly of the horse! To the gates. Guard the gates!"

At the sound of my voice, Menelaus gave a roar and charged toward its origin. But again darkness and the crowd saved me. I ducked down and, borne along with the surge toward the street, emerged from the palace safely.

The horse stood on the paving stones, the trapdoor in its belly hanging open, escape ropes dangling down. It was empty now, its deadly cargo discharged. The Greeks had rushed elsewhere; only Menelaus had been distracted by seeing me. The streets were still, hushed as if lying under an enchantment. I hurried toward the walls, and as I careened down, I saw people slumped in doorways sleeping off their wine, murmuring in pleasure at some foggy dream. I tried to shake as many awake as I could, but some were still so drunk they could barely move.

There could not have been more than ten men in the horse, and their task must have been to steal through the streets and open the gates. Their fellows—who had never sailed away at all, but hidden someplace nearby—would then come streaming in, with the full strength of their army.

But if the gates could hold, then the Trojans could make short work of the few Greeks—bottle them up in Troy, corner them, slay them. The gates must stay closed! I rushed down the streets, the cold night air slapping my face, stinging where Menelaus had hit it.

Looming ahead of me was the Scaean Gate, flanked by the Great Tower. It was ominously dark and quiet. I saw no sentries on duty. Had they, too, drunk themselves into oblivion around the horse? Oh, the sorrow for Troy if they had.

The huge wooden bolt was still in place, resting in its socket. But there was no one to protect it. Oh, let the tower beside it be manned! But my thumps on the door echoed mournfully, and no one opened it.

The tower where Hector had stood, bidding Andromache to be brave. For the first time I was thankful Hector was gone, and could not see this shameful moment, the moment his fellow Trojans had deserted their posts.

What matter, then, that Hector was so brave, if a city could be lost through carelessness?

"Helen." Someone stepped out of the darkness. But it was not a Trojan. He would have called me "Princess Helen." This was a Greek, who called me roughly by name. Other Greeks were already here. They had not been delayed like Menelaus.

It was Ajax, the nasty little Ajax. "No need to knock. No knocking can rouse them. They were in a stupor; we have made that stupor eternal." He advanced toward me, his narrow face twisted in a semblance of a smile. Then suddenly he lunged toward me, grabbing me. "This prize is for Menelaus," he breathed, so close I could smell it. "Hold her here," he ordered one of the others.

An overmuscled young man clamped his hands on my shoulders. "With pleasure," he said. "Who could not hold Helen with the greatest pleasure?"

Ajax laughed. "Take your pleasure of her, who's to know? Nothing she says will be believed. Menelaus knows she is a liar."

The soldier led me away. I heard the scrambling of Greeks behind me, their groans as they slid the bolt back. The gate began to creak as they pulled it open.

Open. Open. Troy was doomed! I cried out, but the soldier shook me. "It is too late," he said. "And you could not have stopped it."

Unlike Menelaus and Ajax, he was comically respectful of me. His hands trembled as they held me, and he seemed hesitant to push me.

"What is your name?" I asked.

"Why should you care?" he replied. Ah! He was flattered that I wanted to know.

"So I may reward you for your gentleness, if ever I have the power."

"You never will," he said brusquely. "Your power is eclipsed. It falls with Troy."

"But if it does not?" Press him, Helen, I told myself. Press him. He may become your only friend among the Greeks.

"It has," he persisted. "When the dumb Trojans brought the horse inside the walls, your power passed away."

"That is for Menelaus to say."

"Menelaus hates you," he said. "He means to kill you. He told us so. And when I hand you over to him, he will do so."

I forced myself to laugh. Laughter was so alien to this moment that it startled him. "I have already seen Menelaus. He did not slay me." I turned my face so the faint light would illuminate it, show my nose. "He smacked me. But he took me back. He will not harm me." I took a deep breath. "He wants me."

"My name is Leos," he finally said.

"Very well, Leos. I shall remember you when I return to Sparta." Return to Sparta! May that never come to pass!

"I thank you, my lady."

He was so young. Young as Paris had been, young as I had been. Gone forever to me, that innocence and that excitement. Nothing left now but cunning, strategy, perseverance: the gifts of age and disillusionment.

He left me unguarded, releasing me by the wall, smiling at me. He thought me secure enough, beaten. He turned his attention to the gates, which the invaders were straining to open.

I watched helplessly as it swung open. The outside told all the tale: the entire Greek army was streaming across the plain, making for Troy.

The invaders were turning to their comrades, eager to welcome them. I slunk away, hugging the wall, and then made for the citadel using the winding outer streets. I fleetingly hoped the young soldier—what was his name?—Leos would not be punished for his dereliction. But this was war.

The citadel was still deceptively quiet, still under a spell. Nothing had yet happened here, though the empty horse reared mockingly above us. But down below, I could hear the shouts and cries as the Greeks poured into Troy.

There was no sign of Menelaus. He had evidently hurried to his men at the walls, letting me go. Why did no one rouse? What sorcery was this? The hall of the palace was empty of its sleepers, but where had they gone?

I ran into Andromache's palace and shouted, "Awake! Awake! The Greeks are in Troy!" But I heard nothing.

I rushed down the streets, banging on each door. I nudged the drunken sleepers. But it was no use. Troy slumbered on, determined to make its last night ordinary; it could not comprehend that the end had come.

The end of the world. The end of the world of Troy.

Evadne. Gelanor. I must find them, save them. We could flee together. Evadne had had a little chamber in the palace, but when I looked for her there, it was empty. Gelanor's house halfway down the winding street—I banged on the door, forced it open, but he was not there. Oh, where had they gone?

Then the clamor began. Clamor—no, it was more than clamor. It was the very death cries of Troy. Wails and screams floated up to the citadel. The Greeks were in the city near the gates, slaughtering everything in their path. They were hungry. For so many long years they had endured exile and frustration. Now all that burst forth, exploded as they stormed into Troy.

Sacker of cities: the honorific of Achilles. But like all neat titles, it failed to convey the depth and essence of it. The Greeks would sack Troy, and Troy would cease to exist. That was what sacking meant. The smoldering ruins were the last token, after the treasures had been taken, the women raped and sold into slavery, the men slain, the children run through with swords. It was a final judgment, the ultimate punishment that wiped the very name of the city from history. And who was this judge, who had the power to decide the fate of a great city like Troy? Ah, better not to ask. For the judge was flawed, bribed, venal, petty. No true judge at all. We require more of our human judges than we do of our godly ones.

I had no fear. The worst had already befallen me, and now all I could hope to do was lessen, in any small way, the fate awaiting the—still sleeping?—Trojans. I went from door to door, banging, shouting. Finally, almost all at once, the people sprang to life, flung open the doors, looked wildly about, heard the din far below. The soldiers—where were the soldiers? I sought Antimachus in his headquarters, halfway down the city. The farther I descended, the louder the noises and the nearer the danger, like the pounding of surf far below a rock. Antimachus was groggily shaking his head, staggering to shake off the sleep. He stared at me, muttering, "Thrashed by Deiphobus?"

"No, by Menelaus! The Greeks are here, they've killed Deiphobus and are in the city. Where are your men?"

"In the barracks."

The barracks were by the lower city. They were already fighting, or being slaughtered, then. "Your guards, then? Where are they?"

He rushed to call them out, turning only to shout at me, "Hide yourself. Find a place of safety."

I laughed hysterically. The entire city would be a tinderbox—where in a kiln could one hide? Only the well, with its steep steps descending to the water, might offer any refuge. And if the buildings around it collapsed and blocked its entrance, then I would be trapped down there to die like a starving rat. I tore away from him and sought Antenor. There was no hope for any of us, but it is better to meet your enemy on your feet than sleeping.

He was up, armed, and his wife Theano was dressed for traveling. "Laocoön was right, the horse was filled with evil," he said. "Oh, Helen!" He shook his head when he beheld my bruised face. "You must flee with Theano," he said.

"It is impossible," I said. "The guards deserted their posts. All the gates are shut fast except the Scaean one, and I saw how many Greeks it took to open it. We women could not do it."

Antenor twitched. "You saw it? You have been there?"

"I knew it! She signaled to them. She—"

"Silence, Theano!" Antenor glared at her. "There are those who always held you would betray Troy to the Greeks, but I never believed that."

"There are those who said the same of you, since you were conciliatory to them and harbored Menelaus and Odysseus on their ill-fated embassy here," I answered. "In my case it is not true, nor, I believe, is it in yours. I saw what I saw at the gate because Menelaus came looking for me when he left the horse, and captured me, but I escaped and ran to the gate. The citadel is still quiet—but they will seek it out as soon as they can. I know not where Priam or any of the royal family is—their palace was silent and I dared not linger and penetrate inside."

Antenor sighed. "May your guardian goddess protect you," he finally said. "We have no other hope. Theano, gather up the other women. Perhaps if you are all in one group they will spare you."

The proud priestess sneered. "Make it easy for them, having us all together waiting for them?"

I left the quarreling couple; nothing further for me to do with them now. I would not join her group. Now the streets were ringing with noise and filling with panicked people. All of Troy had awakened at once, awakened to horror.

I saw Aeneas running up the street toward his house. "Aeneas! Aeneas!" I cried, but he did not hear me. Behind him, like a wave, came a company of Greeks, screaming and slashing, cutting down everyone around them to clear the street. The dead fell heavily, and far from clearing the street, their bodies blocked it. The Greeks leapt over them, pursuing the others who had fled toward the citadel. The force of the crowd pressed me against a wall, almost flattening me. Those of us wedged against the sides were overlooked by the bloodlusting soldiers seeking the treasures of the palaces above.

Gelanor. I was near Gelanor's house again, and vainly I tried to fight my way back to his door and see if this time I could find him, but I could not force my way through the crowd. Instead I was carried along with it, floating in it like a piece of dust. I did not see Menelaus again, nor any Greek I recognized, just dozens of regular soldiers.

Long habits of deference halted the crowd at the entrance to Priam's palace and the upper citadel; even panic and mayhem could not loosen the iron grip of custom. Some of them surged up to the horse, where they had earlier frolicked away their lives; others ran into the temple of Athena, hoping for sanctuary. The festal greens recently hung on the temple to celebrate the Trojan victory over the Greeks welcomed them.

Then, suddenly, the Greeks were upon them. With screams and war cries they plunged toward the people, and the crowds fled into the temple. I ran with them, though I had been cornered by Menelaus there. The goddess gave no protection to any of them; all the confines of the temple did was box them up to make them easier to kill. Where hymns of praise had resounded off the walls, now screams and thuds and clashing metal echoed.

The soldiers made short work of the terrified, confused people, and their sacrifice to Athena covered the floor of her temple. Because I had been squeezed into one corner, behind a screen, they did not see me, but I peered out through the holes in the wooden screen to see the horror. When it grew eerily quiet, except for the laughs and brays of the soldiers, the altar cleared away and I saw Cassandra clinging to the base of the statue, weeping and trembling.

"No, no!" she was crying, as a man wrenched her away, pulling the sacred Pallas Athena with her. The princess and the statue fell heavily to the floor; the desecrated statue rolled a few feet away, and the man kicked it, lunging on Cassandra, tearing at her clothes, and raping her as she screamed for help. He did not stop; he finished his work as his fellow soldiers stood by watching, then he rose and, hugging her across her middle, dragged her from the altar and out the temple door. As he passed, I saw his face. It was little Ajax, laughing like a madman.

Screaming now myself, I bolted from my hiding place and tore out the door after them. Off to one side I glimpsed the affronted Pallas Athena lying abandoned on the floor. I should have righted her, but instead I fled to Priam's palace.

❖ LXXI ❖

The outer courtyard was now a bobbing mass of people, dark shapes bouncing up and down, eerily lit by the torches the Greeks carried, a grotesque version of a nighttime festivity. Instead of flutes and singing, there were screams and keening; instead of wine, there were sprays of bright blood; instead of acrobats, there was the writhing of people desperate to escape. Dogs rushed through the crowd, howling and biting, and horses, loosened from their pens, careened about, trampling the dead and crushing the living. I thought to hear resounding crashes as the gods joined in, Poseidon roaring, waves tearing at the base of Troy, Zeus sending his lethal lightning. But there was nothing but the sound of human anguish.

Priam's palace! Enveloped in a sea of people, its guards valiantly protected the doors against the people beating against them, trying to force their way in, as if their king would save them. The Greeks pursued them, cutting them down with spear and sword. Up on the roof, guards pried loose the tiles and hurled them down on their assailants; they felled some, but most of the Greeks laughed at the ineffectual missiles.

Behind me I heard yells as Trojans turned on the Greeks near the temple. I saw—but just barely, as it was so dark and I was now across the courtyard— some Greeks trying to climb back inside the horse. Unable to pull themselves up the ropes quickly enough, they were slain by the Trojans and fell heavily to the base of the horse.

Now the soldiers were ramming themselves against the palace door; the guards had been overwhelmed. The door strained and even the wood bulged, but it held. Then a Greek soldier pushed in front of all the others and halted them. "Cease!" he screamed. His voice broke—indeed, it sounded as if it had barely taken on an adult timbre. "I will open this door!"

He turned and held out his arms, and the soldiers obeyed.

In the mayhem, I was astonished that anyone would even hear, let alone obey. He was tall, but slight, confirming my impression of extreme youth. He was wearing a helmet that obscured his face, but his neck was slender and his torso long, with almost gangling arms and legs. He held a gigantic shield, worked with intricate art. The carvings caught the meager light and revealed their fine workmanship. This was the shield of someone confident it would never be captured, for who else would carry such a valuable thing into battle?

Achilles. The shield of Achilles. Suddenly I knew to whom it now belonged. This was Neoptolemus, his son. The youngling. Now the last of the prophecies was fulfilled for the fall of Troy.

"Yield, old man!" he was screaming.

How old are you, lad? I asked him, silently. Fifteen at most? It can be no more than that.

He grabbed some flaming torches from the soldiers and lobbed them up onto the roof, hitting several defenders, who fled their places.

"Smash it again!" he directed his soldiers. They obligingly rushed against the door and this time it groaned and splintered.

"Let me, let me!" Neoptolemus jumped at the door and wrenched it off its hinges, although the real work had been done by others. "I conquer!" he yelled. "Stay here!" he commanded the men. "I go inside alone. Let the glory be mine!"

He must have had loyal guardsmen, for they held back the other Greeks while he strode inside. He seemed concerned only that another warrior would steal his glory; the terrified, heedless crowd, me along with them, streamed in unhindered.

The first thing that struck me was how quiet the inner courtyard was. The rows of potted trees and flowers were still set in orderly lines, still proclaiming that life was peaceful. The doors of the apartments belonging to Priam's sons and daughters were closed, it is true, but they were still intact, their brass ornamentation polished, now reflecting the torches of those who came to destroy them.

I tore myself out of the crowd and ran ahead of them. I almost caught up to Neoptolemus, but I did not want him to see me and turn on me. So I slunk along behind him, hugging the shadows.

At the far end of the courtyard, at the altar of the three-eyed Zeus, I saw a gathering of people. I sank down behind one of the potted trees and looked through their branches to see who it was. Behind me I heard the rush of people pressing forward.

Hecuba. She was standing at the altar, embracing her daughters, huddled on either side of her. Polyxena was there, and Laodice, and Ilona. Hecuba's black eyes darted around the courtyard searching for adversaries, bracing for them.

Neoptolemus leapt forward, landing almost at their feet. He pulled off his helmet and peered at them. "You must be Hecuba," he said, thrusting his face up into hers. "And you—who might you be?" Quick as a lizard's tongue, he flicked out his sword and poised it on Polyxena's throat.

"Polyxena," she cried.

"My father fancied you," he said. "Perhaps he'll have you yet." His high-whining youngster's voice was bloodcurdling in its ignorant remorselessness. "And you?" he said to the others. Trembling, they gave their names.

Just then Priam rushed up, fully armed. He had been fumbling in the shadows, strapping on his breastplate and his sword, and now he lunged at Neoptolemus, missing him.

"Old man!" Neoptolemus sounded delighted. "Attacking me! You must be King Priam! How foolish, to think you could oppose me!"

"You are a cruel and inept child," said Priam. "A poor wavering reflection of your father. I met him, we talked as men together. He would spare the old and the weak. Look into your heart to see him. Be worthy of him." He circled Neoptolemus.

Neoptolemus gave a nasty laugh as he turned, keeping Priam within his sights. "My father had one leading trait—to win, to cover himself in glory, to vanquish his enemies."

Priam stopped, faced him. "It is no glory to vanquish enemies that are aged or helpless."

"An enemy is an enemy. Many poisonous snakes are small and seemingly helpless."

"Men are not snakes."

"Are they not, then? Men are worse. A snake kills only when it is threatened, when someone steps across its path or disturbs its burrow—but men?"

Priam then drew himself up to his full height, and he became, for that instant, the Priam I had first seen. "Are you not doing just that? And may I not defend it as a poisonous snake might? Yet that does not mean I am dangerous and must be destroyed. Have mercy on my nest, my wife, my children."

Neoptolemus just laughed. "Supplicate your gods, take your farewell."

Just then one of Priam's sons darted out from near where I was crouched hiding. "Die, you Greek!" he cried. His voice was even higher than Neoptolemus's.

It was Polites, Priam's next youngest son after Polydorus. Neoptolemus swung around and ran him through with a sword: two children, one killing the other. The child lay limp on the floor; Priam slipped in his blood as he rushed to attack Neoptolemus with his bare hands, a wavering war cry resounding from his old throat. Clutching, Priam tightened his grip on the young man's neck, holding him fast as he toppled backward. For an instant they rolled and tussled together, Priam's face contorted with the effort of squeezing so hard.

But then Neoptolemus rose like an inexorable force, drawing Priam with him. With one arm he held Priam fast, with the other he drew back his sword. "Farewell, old man!" he said with mock affection as he swung his sword and sliced off Priam's head. It flew off, rolling away, while the body slumped beside the Zeus altar, spouting blood. The head came to rest looking upward, eyes wide with horror, staring at the rivulets of its own blood trickling down the monument.

Hecuba rushed at Neoptolemus and tried to claw his eyes out, but she was even weaker than Priam and he flung her aside easily, so that she hit her head on the altar base and lay stretched out beside her husband. Polyxena fell to her knees and embraced her mother and father. Neoptolemus bent down and pulled her up, jerking her head back by the hair.

"Which one are you, did you say?" he hissed. "Old Priam had so many sons and daughters, did he even name them? Well, what of it? To what avail his fifty sons, his twelve daughters? Not one will resound to the ages with the fame of Peleus's one son, my father. Nor of me, my father's only son!"

"Pitiful braggart!" Polyxena cried. "No one will remember your name. No one can even pronounce it. Even mine will ring longer and louder than yours."

Grinning like an old skull, Neoptolemus pinned her arms. "Oh, I'll see to that!" He signaled to one of his men to truss her up. "To the ships!" he ordered.

The body of Polites lay in a pool of blood. Priam's was spreading, still seeping from his neck; it reached out to his son's like fingers and the two touched and blended, becoming one.

I dared not move. There was nothing I could do to help Hecuba and her daughters until Neoptolemus left them. If he saw me, he might capture me and send me to the ships, too. The leaves of the bush I was hiding behind trembled. Had it not been dark and had Neoptolemus been more wary, he would have seen me. As it was, I crouched and prayed for him to be gone.

In that odd moment I felt a brushing against my shoulder, a smoothing of my hair. I am betrayed! They have discovered me! I thought, terrified. But the touch was gentle. I looked up and saw a shadowy form. I could not be sure of what I saw, and as I reached out my hand, it passed through air. But the touch had been real.

My child. The voice whispered in my ear, even while the courtyard was filled with yelling. Somehow I heard it above—or below—the ugly sounds around me.

Yes, I said in my mind. I am here. Your servant is here.

Not my servant but my child.

My father? Zeus?

A soft laugh. *Only in a manner of speaking are you my child. I adopted you. Aeneas is the child of my body, but you are the child of my essence, my being.*

"Aphrodite?" I whispered.

Yes. I am here to gainsay your safety. I have already directed Aeneas to leave Troy, now I guide you. Leave this place of killing, find your way to the ships. You two alone will survive the fall of Troy without hurt. I vouchsafe my own!

I will not go to the Greeks, I said again in my mind. I will not go to the ships!

Dear child, in a short time all of Troy will buckle, blaze, and fall. If you hope to live, you must flee its walls. If you choose to die, so be it. Mortals always have that choice. Sometimes they embrace it. I do not understand this, but they are free to do so.

Hecuba was muttering, rolling over, bringing herself to her elbows in the lake of blood. Laodice pulled her up, clasping her mother to her. She turned her mother's head so she would not see what she had lain beside, and shielded her eyes.

The warriors came pouring in; Neoptolemus's orders had held them back only a short time. They fell on everything in sight, swinging at the potted plants and the benches as if they were enemy soldiers. Hecuba, the altar, and her daughters vanished beneath the surge of people.

I crawled away, still shielded by the plants. I saw some of them blazing, some urns overturned, and knew that Andromache's prized assemblage was gone. But her heart must have left them for greater matters long ago.

By the time I reached it, the outer courtyard was already piled with looted goods: upended three-legged tables, bronze cauldrons, wooden chests, ivory game boards, bedsteads. I half crawled, half scurried between the stacks of booty and fled the palace. Gasping, I stood at the gates and saw the conflagration before me.

The citadel was on fire. Hector's palace flamed, as did mine and the temple of Athena. Even the horse had caught fire. The flames licked up its sturdy legs and crackled around its belly—the belly that had delivered death to Troy.

I rushed down the street leading down into the city. These houses were still intact, but the street was filled with screaming people.

"This way, this way!" one man called, trying to direct the crowd. "Proceed in an orderly fashion!" His eyes were dull, unseeing of what was truly happening.

A well-dressed woman came out of her house, adjusting her veil. "What is all this confusion?" she asked, puzzled. "Good people, return to your beds." She turned and said, "You should not miss your sleep. It is not good to be awake when the sky is dark." Smoothly, she turned and went back inside. "I have tried my best," she said. Her eyes were fixed, uncomprehending. A shrill laugh followed her, floating on the air.

I was almost pushed down as I rushed through the street. I heard a scream as someone leapt from the top of the temple and landed in a pit of flame. Athena had not saved him or her. Why should I think Aphrodite could save me?

More people leapt off the walls and vanished into the darkness and flames. A Trojan strode down the street, shoving others with his shield, but he was dead already, completely unresponsive to what was happening around him. No sound or cry caught his attention. Step by step he advanced, like a statue.

I looked back to see a trio of people leaping directly into the flames from one of the towers, singing, holding hands. Were they one family, or fast friends? The singing stopped, replaced by screams as they hit the fire. It flared up briefly as it digested them. Then it collapsed in a ball.

"Down here, down here." Two men were directing people toward the lower city. "Take the gate out, and make for Mount Ida." They bowed to me. "Good evening, my lady," they said, smiling.

"Flee!" I cried. "Abandon this!"

"Someone must direct," one of them said. "It is important."

"You will die!" I cried.

"We will all die," he said. "It is only a question of how, and with what honor."

"The Greeks will grant you no honor," I said, hurrying past them.

"It is not for them to grant it," he said. "We must grant it to ourselves." He turned his head. "Down here, down here," he continued directing those behind me. Thus the honor and civilization of Troy flickered bravely in its last moments before it was extinguished forever.

Farther down in the city, the houses still untorched, people were running in terror. Some were on their roofs, flinging tiles. Others were making a last stand, fighting madly against the Greek soldiers and whatever else stood in their way. Some used objects as weapons, rushing out of their houses swinging furniture, goblets, firewood to strike at their enemies. The Greeks easily parried them aside and slew them, swinging madly, lopping off limbs and heads, whatever they could reach. The maimed crawled away and were trampled, and the headless ones lay spurting in the street, making the stones slippery.

The flames rose higher on the citadel, and from this great distance, over the walls, I could see the fire reflected in the strait, the water turned sunset-red. But now the flames were starting in the middle part of the city as well, and people were staggering out of their houses, choking from dust mixed with smoke, only to be slain as soon as they emerged. The buildings, much smaller and flimsier than those of stone on the summit, began collapsing almost immediately, and wails from within told what was happening to those hiding inside. The flickering red flames bathed the brick walls of these modest houses in a bloody hue, as if they glowed from within.

I must leave the city, I must escape! But I was being pounded and pushed from all sides, carried along with a crowd that was dashing itself against walls and houses like one of Poseidon's mighty waves. The noise was overwhelming. We think of fire as a quiet thing, but it created a great roaring sound like a sea dragon, and the groans of collapsing buildings drowned out even the cries of the wounded.

Down, down, into the lower rings of the inner city. I was borne along past a dwelling that looked as if nothing had befallen it. Its outer door was holding fast, and there were as yet no singe marks upon it. Suddenly it jerked open and an elegantly dressed woman emerged, holding her mantle daintily, keeping it from dragging in the street dirt. She looked this way and that, wrinkling up her nose. Then she lurched out into the crowd and disappeared. She clearly was in a state of utter shock.

Did she have children inside? Had she left them? I had a glimpse of the dark deep interior, but could see nothing. I tore away from the imprisonment of the bodies around me, bearing me along like a helpless piece of floating wood, and tumbled into the house. I landed on my knees in the forecourt, and could see nothing. But I could smell the smoke. There was a fire in the back; the house was not unscathed after all.

"Is anyone here?" I called in my best Trojan dialect. "I am here to help!" If there were children inside, they might be sheltering under a table or cowering under their beds, thinking they could hide from the fire or the soldiers. "You must tell me. It is not safe to stay where you are!"

Now I was on my feet, stumbling blindly through the megaron, feeling the heat of the fire just outside the walls. All was yet dark within. "Are you here? Please, I come to help your mother!"

Just then I heard a faint scrambling. Then it stopped. It could be rats, or a pet dog. "Children!" I cried. "Please, call out to me! Help me to find you!"

Again there was a slight noise. But it could be anything, even the fire itself. Just then part of the roof collapsed, and a mass of bricks poured down in front of me, barely missing me. Dust rose in a choking cloud. The flames sucked loudly, happy to find an easier way to draw breath.

For a moment there was light—hideous light, coming from the fire. But I saw a body sprawled next to a table, its legs splayed out, the soles of its feet turned upward. It was a man. The woman's husband? He still clutched a bowl of wine, but its surface was clouded with dust and trickles of blood ran into it, mixing with the drink. Had he been entertaining friends when the horror of an earlier collapse fell upon them? Now in the shadows I saw other bodies.

"Would that it had been poison," I whispered. "It would have been kinder." Smoldering beams lay across the bodies where they had fallen from the collapsed roof. So the woman had survived, only to stumble dully out into the streets. But were there children?

"Are you there?" I called again, skirting the ruined chamber and penetrating farther back into the house. I dared not go much deeper, for the entire structure was unsafe.

A little squeak of a voice came to me, then a scurrying, and two little children crawled out in the dim light. "Mother! Mother!" they whimpered. I could not even tell if they were boys or girls, they were so hunched and begrimed. They clasped my legs.

"She is outside," I said. "Outside." I embraced them both and turned them toward the entrance. "Are any more of you hidden?"

"No," one of them sobbed. I hurried them in the direction of the door, but suddenly a great roar shook the building; the walls shuddered and fell inward. The children were torn from my hands, lost beneath the rubble. My hands were pinned beneath the gush of stones and I was trapped. The children were somewhere within it, but I could not see or hear them.

I did not think of myself, equally trapped but able to breathe and see. Instead I screamed for them. Then I felt a hand on my shoulder.

Aphrodite? She said I would survive the fall of Troy. Was she here to protect me? I turned and saw the face of Menelaus.

Menelaus! I dreaded him more than the fire!

"Here you are!" he cried. "Now I have you!" He was towering over me, delighting in his capture. "I saw you dash inside. And here I thought I had lost you." He yanked at my arms. "Firmly in here, I see." He looked up at the roof. "Ready to collapse, I also see." He knelt down and began digging at the rubble imprisoning me. Then he stopped and stood up. "You would have died like a dog in here had I not followed you in," he said.

"The children have already done so," I said. I wished it had been me instead. I could not believe Menelaus was here—a dreadful apparition. All I could think of was the two children, so close to escape and then dead. And I as well—so close and now dead in his grasp.

"They are better off so," he said brusquely. "A life of slavery is no life at all, and that is what they would have faced."

Now it was what I faced.

He grunted as he extracted my arms and hands. "We must flee!" He yanked me with him and we rushed from the house just as it collapsed in an explosion of dust and flames and wood and bricks.

Outside, the panic was raging around us. He grabbed me and pushed me ahead of him, propelling me down the winding street. "Outside this time, far from the walls, and to the ships." He was shaking his arm up and down in pain and I saw that blood was streaming from it. In extricating me he had injured himself.

While I had been inside the house, the conflagration had engulfed its neighbors, turning the buildings into funeral pyres flaring up by the hundreds. The unmistakable smell of human flesh now rode the air, familiar from funerals. People, then, had lain down on their beds drowsy with wine and awakened to a couch of fire. But they could hardly have lain serene like the draped corpses on their pyres.

"Faster, faster!" Menelaus shoved me, his broad hand spread out across my back, his arm behind it like a rod. He was still shaking the other one, and droplets of blood flew from it. In the sea of blood around us, they disappeared quickly.

Like a river in spate, the people were all rushing toward the gates, screaming and wailing. One man stood like a rock in the midst of them, looking longingly up the hill, trying to go in the opposite direction. We were swept past him; I heard him chanting, "I must go back, I must, I forgot to close the storeroom door." Then we were gone, past him.

The ground flattened out, and suddenly we were squeezed through the narrow passage just before the gates, then we burst outside. A sword hissed past my head, and Menelaus yelled, "You fool!" and hit a soldier who was stationed by the gate to kill people as they emerged.

"Oh, sorry, Your Grace," he said. "I did not see who you were."

"Fool!" Menelaus snapped again.

"But in the darkness they all look alike," the soldier said. "How's a man to tell who's Greek and who's Trojan?"

"You ought to know your own commander!" Menelaus yelled. "Now go back to the killing!"

Smartly, the man turned back to his task, attacking the helpless people as they poured through the gates; another soldier on the other side made sure none escaped. As the ground filled with bodies, they were dragged away so that the flow of the escapees was not hindered. Then they, too, would be pulled off as soon as they were dead.

"Along here!" Menelaus pointed with his sword to a path lit by flickering torches. In the shadows I could see lumps and I knew they were bodies. Behind me a roar filled the air; I turned to see Troy one flaming pillar, encircled by its collar of walls—molten glowing red with a black ring. The flames sang, keening on the air.

"Keep moving." Menelaus shook me.

"Turn and look," I told him. "At least behold what you have done."

Grunting, he turned. Then even he was silent, lost in awe at the crackle of the flames, the dying city.

The front of my gown was soaked in blood, clinging to my skin. With trembling fingers I wrenched off the brooch, its source, and handed it to Menelaus. "There is much more to come and I cannot be bathed in more blood." If the brooch were to weep drops of blood for each Trojan, the fields would be flooded.

He turned it over in his hand as if he did not recognize it. "And why not? You are the cause of the blood."

His attention was on the brooch. I turned to flee, but one arm shot out and his hand closed on me like a raptor's talon. "Not ever again, my lady," he said. "You shall never escape or flee me again." He tossed the brooch into the darkness. "It was to help you count the cost of your love. Now *you* look, and see what you have cost Troy. Its life. Now move." He shoved me forward.

It seemed a very long way to the shore where the ships were beached. Always behind me I could hear the convulsions of the city in its death throes; flames lit up the plain in throbbing flickers. Gradually the smell of the sea embraced us and overpowered the smell of the fire, and I could hear voices and see people milling beside tall dark shadows.

Menelaus gestured to someone and bellowed, "Tie her up and put her with the others. And mind you, use strong rope and a good knot. On second thought, make that a chain." He grinned at me, a horrid fixed curve on his mouth. "Like all snakes, she is good at escapes."

I was chained to a post like a wild animal, my wrists shackled and my feet bound. As dawn came, I saw there were others up and down the beach tethered like me. There was also a stockade fence confining other, presumably more docile prisoners. Even in this dim light I could see that there were no men at the stakes. So no Trojan men would be allowed to live; those not perishing directly in the flames would be killed.

As day lightened, the full horror surrounding me was gradually revealed. The fields were strewn with so many bodies it seemed impossible Troy could have held so many living. As far as my eye could see, telltale dark bulges and lumps lay unmoving. Each little dot, each mound, was someone who had been alive yesterday, before the horse was dragged into Troy. No crops had ever been so plentiful in the fields; no harvest ever so rich.

The seashore began to grow crowded as men returned from Troy, dragging spoils with them. They were singing, laughing gleefully. As they converged, singly and in groups, they heaved their takings onto a pile that grew as I watched. Swords, spears, armor, pedestals, curtains, lyres, inlaid tables, pottery, decorated boxes, bolts of linen, board games, pitchers, ladles, bronze mirrors, pipes, and medicines and ointments created a mountain of the remnants of Troy. Each piece seemed to cry out for its owner, the person who had played its strings, beheld her face in its reflection. Was my weaving there? Its center had been unfinished. Now most likely singed and scorched, the center was complete, the ending of the story told in its blackened threads.

Was Hector's armor there? No, something so famous would be like gold or jewels and claimed by Agamemnon. Paris's armor, his helmet? At the funeral games a Trojan had claimed them; now, if they were not melted, they were most likely buried in the pile of booty.

I saw groups of men swaying around another huge mound, putting offerings on it. This must be the tumulus of Achilles, the place where he and Patroclus were buried. Now their victorious countrymen were telling them about the fall of Troy, trying to share it with them by leaving them tokens of the spoils.

The mist and blue light of dawn were gone, replaced by sun and a brisk breeze. The waters of the Hellespont sparkled, clean and laughing, sweeping out to sea. Nothing floated on them. The dead instead were landbound, lying like boundary stones as far as the eye could see. Amongst them were the corpses of horses, the famous horses of Troy. The Greeks, knowing they could not transport them back, had slaughtered them, destroying more of Troy's riches. The orchards had been chopped down, too, as if the trees were their enemies. There must be nothing of worth left to Troy.

I struggled against my chains. I could not even shield my eyes, and the sun was glaring into them. The men were starting to file past me and gape, muttering and pointing.

It was all back. The staring, the lip-smacking—all I had left behind when I fled with Paris to freedom. Oh, I was back in the prison that enveloped me even without chains.

Soon Menelaus was standing in front of me, his legs spread, hands on his hips. I recognized his knees—strange the things that identify a person and never change. I did not want to look at his face, so I kept my eyes on his knees.

"Had enough?" he said. "Are you ready to behave?"

Now I could not endure even the sight of his knees. I shut my eyes.

"Get her up and into the tent," he barked, and I felt hands fumbling with my chains and freeing me. Standing up, I was dizzy. They spun me around and pushed me toward a tent, but not before I looked back at the black smoke streaming into the sky, marking the place where Troy had been.

The tent was filled with weeping women. None were old—all those had been left behind. These were young and strong enough to serve either bed or kitchen duty for their new masters—perhaps both. Some were sitting and staring unmoving at their laps; others were walking restlessly about. None seemed to really see anything; their eyes were dull and glazed.

Crouched in a corner were the princesses of Troy, in a place set aside for the high-ranking. I saw Cassandra, Laodice, Ilona, and Polyxena. As I approached them, I saw they were shielding their mother, who lay stretched and stiff on the ground. I tried to kneel down and touch her forehead, but they pushed me back.

"I saw what happened in the courtyard," I whispered. "But in the confusion I was swept out into the street. Blessings to your father, and to your brother."

Laodice said, "They had their proper pyre. The last funeral rites that Troy will ever offer."

Cassandra's eyes were fixed, staring ahead. I had seen what had befallen her, too, but I would say nothing. Perhaps the others did not know of it, and for others to know makes it more real.

"Creusa is dead," said Ilona. "We saw them attack her. Aeneas—no one has seen him. They were not together when she was slain."

Polyxena recounted, in her sweet voice, which made it all the more terrible, that her little sister Philomena had perished in the palace, Antimachus was dead, Aesacus was missing, and Panthous died trying to open one of his devices to rain down destruction on the Greeks, a device that crushed him instead. Antenor had survived, and his wife Theano, who was here in this tent.

"Deiphobus is dead," I told them. "Menelaus killed him in his bed."

"Helenus is here, but the Greeks will not allow him to speak to us."

"Why are we here?" I asked. "Why are they keeping us in here?"

"To auction us off." Cassandra suddenly came to life and spoke. "They will let the men bid on us. Then they take us back to Greece with them. But they won't do that for me. I am spoken for. I go with Agamemnon."

I drew a deep breath. Could this be true? Why would Agamemnon choose her? The virgin prophetess, now despoiled, not even pretty—why would the high commander choose her from all the women of Troy?

Fleeting within my mind I saw her at Mycenae, saw her with Clytemnestra, then saw . . . I blinked and it vanished, a scarlet flash. Greece was waiting. Greece had been waiting all these years, and it had not ceased to exist, but lurked like a beast to devour us all when we returned. It was all back, then, not just the staring of the men but the lowering walls of stone and soaring mountains and the families left alone all this time. The men, returning and trying to take up where they had left off, would find they could not, that time never permits that, time changes everything in a thousand subtle ways, so that even the walls they touch are not the same.

"You'll avenge us, then." From the floor Hecuba spoke. "The daughter of Priam will be the one to avenge him, not one of his many sons." A scraping sound like a scudding leaf was her laughter. "The gods are amused."

"Mother." Polyxena raised Hecuba up, embraced her.

"So we know who has perished, who still lives?" Hecuba asked.

"None of us lives," said Ilona.

Hecuba looked around her. "Where is Andromache?"

One by one her daughters shook their heads. "We have not seen her."

Nor had I.

They fed us barley gruel dished out from a common pot, and left us to sleep on the ground. We lay down, and passed the first night in which there was no Troy. Occasionally, when the wind shifted, I could smell ashes and smoke through the tent cloth. But the prevailing winds were from the north and they were clean.

Soldiers came in and separated the women, taking Priam's family and me outside and pushing us toward a substantial wooden house that stood at the end of the line of ships. Stools and benches had been set up outside it, filled with onlookers.

"This must be the auction," murmured Ilona, her head bowed. She did not look at the men squirming on their seats like little boys.

They would not auction me. Menelaus had claimed me. Or would he, in revenge, give me to a slave? No matter. He could not know that to me it was all the same. I had died with Paris, died in Troy. And a slave, whom I had never seen before, would be easier to endure than Menelaus, with his list of grievances.

They made us stand in a row. Then they made a show of putting Hecuba first, in recognition of her former status.

An old man rose to preside. Nestor! Now my eyes swept over the group of leaders from long ago and beheld them all once again: Agamemnon (the child-killer), Odysseus (the liar), Diomedes (another liar), little Ajax (the rapist), Calchas (the traitor): a band of merry malefactors. Others, guilty mainly by association with them, were Idomeneus (once a good man, now . . . ?), Menelaus, and Nestor himself.

Nestor held up his hands, so thin and wrinkled they looked like oak bark. He swiveled his scrawny neck and looked far into the distance. But his head was high and his eyes were still dark and proud. "Troy is gone," he said, looking to the place where it had been. Now the smoke was only wisps, rising forlornly into the sky. Even smoke dies, and when it does the erasure is complete. "What is left of it stands before you to dispose of as you will—the lovely women, and the spoils on the beach. It is fitting we meet here at the house of our greatest warrior, Achilles, to conduct this . . . dispersal of Trojan goods."

Trojan goods. That was all we were, then.

"And the queen of Troy must be first." He nodded to her. "Like you, my lady, I am old. Yet we hope for respect from those younger, in memory of what we were." He looked around. "Whose household will welcome her?"

Odysseus leapt up. "She comes with me. She shall live in Ithaca."

Hecuba made a strangled sound. "That rocky island, far on the west of Greece? Let my tomb be here instead."

"Penelope will welcome you," Odysseus insisted.

"How do you know Penelope even lives, let alone will welcome anyone—even you?" Cassandra suddenly cried. "You presume much! But that is your way."

Odysseus grunted, then gestured to Agamemnon. "Not to take this out of order, but she is yours, shut her up."

Agamemnon stood. It was the first time I had seen him close up, and separated from the others. The years had eroded him, like a bear whose coat is now motley and faded. He was still dangerous—he still had sharp claws and teeth and keen, covetous eyes, but he had passed the height of his strength. Perhaps that made him more vicious and therefore even more threatening. "As you say," he muttered. He jerked his hand and his guards seized Cassandra, dragging her into Achilles's house.

Embarrassed, Nestor continued. "And this fair daughter of Priam, Laodice?"

A man I did not recognize claimed her. Next came Ilona, and another unknown man asked for her.

"And now the former queen of Sparta." Menelaus's voice rang out. "Let us hear of her crimes before remanding her to her rightful owner. After all, we have all left our homes, fought, and suffered many years for her crime. Why? Because you are honorable men, and upheld your vows over the sacrificial horse so long ago, at great cost to yourselves. And now look at the horses strewn across the plain of Troy. This war began with a sacrificial horse and it has ended with many sacrificial horses—a great wooden one and herds of Trojan beauties." He strode over and stood eye to eye with me.

Had I ever looked into those eyes with love? Had it truly ever been so?

"Let me recite her abominations!" he said gleefully. "First, she—"

"Let me spare you the trouble," I said. I could not bear to listen to his rehearsed self-glorification. "Let me recite them, for I know well what you are going to say. This way I can answer them at the same time, and have the whole business over more quickly. For we know how it will end, with all this but a ceremony."

Had Menelaus ever truly known me, he would have expected just those words from me. But the poor man was rendered speechless, as I had intended. I stepped forward and stood before the whole company. A hundred eyes stared hungrily at me. "First, as Menelaus started to say, I stole away from my home in Sparta with the prince of Troy, Paris. I went willingly, I was not abducted—as some tried to claim. I did not take treasure with me—as others tried to claim—but a few goods of my rightful ownership, and only in my haste and confusion. I did not use them to enrich myself but dedicated them to Athena in Troy and gave the rest to Priam." I stopped to draw a breath. It was so quiet that that breath sounded very loud.

"The only crime I committed," I continued, "and which no one here has the power either to punish or to forgive, was leaving my daughter. For that crime I have grieved and only she can pronounce judgment upon me for it. When I face her, I will beg her forgiveness."

Now Menelaus came to life. "She will never forgive you! She hates you! She has told me many times how she despises you, and hopes that I kill you when finally I lay hands on you."

He probably spoke true. Menelaus had never been a liar, unless all these years with Odysseus had tainted him. "I will submit to whatever she decides," I said.

"You'll have no choice, you adulterous bitch!"

I looked past him to the audience. "I must ask why any man who calls himself a man would want an adulterous bitch for his wife." That made them laugh, as I knew it would. Menelaus could stand anything but being laughed at.

"I never said I wanted you for a wife, but for a prisoner. And that's how you shall return to Sparta."

I preferred being his prisoner to being his wife. But that did not make me safe from his attentions. "Does my father still live?" I had to know to what I was returning. There must be something there, something.

"Yes. Who do you think has been ruling all these years?"

"And what of Mycenae? And Pylos, and Ithaca?" All those kings away—who ruled in their places? Orestes and Telemachus had been only children at the time, and all the sons of Nestor had gone with him to Troy. What had happened in Greece while they were gone?

"We don't know!" cried Odysseus, sounding suddenly threatened. "Messages are few—the distance—we will not know, truly, until we land."

"So you'll sail with us and be surprised along with all of us at what awaits," said Menelaus. "Happy homecoming, you shameless whore."

I stepped to one side to address the men. "Again, I must ask you, what man of honor would want—"

Menelaus grabbed my shoulders and shook me so hard one of my hair bindings came off. "A whore in a bloodstained dress, stained with the blood of the men you have killed, a murderess as well as everything else. I shall tell you, lady, I shall tell you: a man bent on revenge!" Now he turned to face his men. "And I'll have it, I'll have it back in Greece, where she'll stand before the people who suffered because we all had to come here—"

"So you have become a liar after all!" I cried. "I have murdered no one. If thousands have lost their lives, they died for your pitiful hurt pride. And as for the blood on my gown, it is symbolic blood—a part of one drop for each ten lives. But see, it washes clean—I have tried it, and that is when I knew it was not true blood but magical blood—clean as your hands will never be! The true blood does not wash away!"

I watched his face stiffen with his struggle to control his anger. Finally, jerking his head down, he said, "Take her into the house with the others."

I was dragged into the dark interior of that structure, where I could just make out the huddled forms of the captive women. The house smelled musty, dank, and was poorly lit. As my eyes adjusted, I could see a bedstand and several sagging benches, along with chests. The only kept-up thing in the room was a pedestal with a tunic draped over it, a gold ring and knife laid carefully on top of it.

I heard gentle sobbing from the women; not desperate, not keening, just a tired sadness. Not enough life-force remained for them to grieve loudly. The fall of Troy had sucked it all away—or so I thought.

"This vile, stinking house! Kept as a shrine to Achilles!" Hecuba spat. "*He* lived here, therefore it is holy. And to think my Priam came here, sat here, to beg for the body of Hector. Oh, Priam! You looked upon these ugly walls, too!"

"What is this stupid thing?" the usually mild Laodice said, kicking at the pedestal.

"It is their way of worshiping him," said Cassandra. "This is his tunic. This must be his ring and knife."

"Ladies." A discreet male voice interrupted us. "Queens and princesses." How polite, to announce his presence and warn us, although whatever we said could hardly alter our fates.

He stepped forward. He was not young, although his voice was. "I am Philoctetes," he said. "I am sent here to . . ."

I heard nothing more. Philoctetes. The man who had killed Paris. He was of medium height, with a sturdy body, well-muscled arms, and a dignified stance.

I felt myself gasping for breath, trying to steady myself. Where were his arrows, his deadly arrows? His poison? His quiver? His bow? The arrow that he had aimed at Paris had only scratched him, but it was immeasurably deadly.

"Where are your weapons?" I asked. My voice was so low I thought I would have to repeat my words.

"Lady Helen," he said. "I can say nothing beyond war is war. At least I was an enemy. To meet death at the hands of an ally or companion is even worse. I know; *they* left me alone to perish. Only when they needed me did they come for me."

"The vile Greeks!" I cried. "Truth and honor are not among them!"

"But I was bound to them. I could not join the Trojans. And so—"

A wild idea entered my head. I would take one of his arrows, scratch myself with it, die as Paris had. "But your deadly gear," I said. "Where have you put it?"

"Safely away," he said. "The arrows of Heracles must be kept from harming innocent people."

If only I could lay my hands on them. And as for who was innocent—how could he determine that?

"Put such thoughts far from you, lady," he said. "Many seek those arrows to do much mischief. I regret the day I lit that pyre and inherited them from Heracles. What an intolerable burden he gave me."

❖ LXXIII ❖

I now realized that I would have to enchant one of my captors if I had any hope of escape. Could I do it with Philoctetes? But my being rebelled. I could not cajole my husband's murderer.

The door flew open, and Andromache stumbled in. Right behind her was Neoptolemus, shoving and laughing.

For the first time I could behold his face unobscured by a helmet. His eyes were a muddy color—in this dim light I could not discern whether they were brown or blue, but whatever they were, they were not vibrant. Like his body, his face was presentable, passable but forgettable. He had not inherited his father's fierce grandeur.

"My new slave!" he cried. "The widow of Hector!"

Andrómache turned on him. "I am too old for you," she said. Her voice was low.

"Yes!" I said, coming to her side. I encircled her shoulders in an embrace.

"I am here," I whispered. Then I turned to Neoptolemus. "You do not want a woman old enough to be your mother."

"What care I for that? I care more for who was upon her before I." Neoptolemus sneered. "I will wipe him from her memory. In that obliteration I have my glory."

"You have no glory, little boy," said Andromache. "You have killed my son and I despise you forever."

Astyanax! What had he done?

"He killed my son, Helen." There was no expression at all in her voice. She turned to me, ignoring Neoptolemus. "He took him from my arms and flung him from the walls of Troy—no! there were no walls of Troy left, he flung him from the smoldering heaps into a tumbled mass of stones, but death came just as surely." The words, dull and low, marched in orderly fashion from her lips.

"Astyanax!" I wept. Her beloved only son, so eagerly sought. The night on Mount Ida . . .

"The baby snake must die," said Neoptolemus. "It cannot live to slither into the ruins of Troy and start the Trojan menace all over again. The seed of Hector must be destroyed."

All heirs of Troy obliterated! But Aphrodite said Aeneas had escaped. No matter, we could not know. "Oh, sister." I embraced her and we sobbed together. For the first time I was glad Paris and I had no child. It would have perished as all else in Troy.

"You shall return to Greece with me," said Neoptolemus to Andromache. "Perhaps not as my main wife, for it is true, you are a bit old for me. Occasional relief or diversion in bed you shall grant me. But I think I deserve a princess of Greece. I think your daughter Hermione is more to my taste, lady Helen. I have already spoken to your husband about it and he has granted permission. I shall be your son-in-law." He chortled and leaned forward, kissing my cheek. "Mother!" he giggled.

I slapped his face; I could not help myself. "If my daughter is anything of mine, she will reject you."

He laughed. "But she may not be of you; she may be her father's child, or entirely of her own thinking." He drew himself up. "She may want the son of the mighty Achilles. Many women will."

"Then go find them, and spare my daughter."

"Your daughter may be amongst them," he said. "It is most likely." He laughed softly. "But I must speak not of what is likely, but required." He turned from Andromache and me as things of no import, and addressed the women who were gathered at the back of the house.

"My father has sought me out of late," he said. "He has spoken to me in dreams and portents."

"How odd!" I cried. "He did not know you as a baby, as a boy, and now he speaks to you!"

He whirled around to me. "The gods do not necessarily speak to their children until they please," he said.

"So Achilles is now a god?" I said. "Strange, when I first saw him he was but a nasty, meddlesome child."

"Shut your mouth, whore of Troy!" he cried.

"The surest answer from someone who has no answer." I spoke to the women. "Insults. But that is no true response, it is the desperation of those who have nothing else to call upon. What does your illustrious father—if indeed he *is* your father—command you?"

"He demands blood. He needs a sacrifice in order to let us sail from Troy."

"Whose?" Hecuba stepped forward. "It must, in all justice, be mine."

"No," said Neoptolemus. "It is your next youngest daughter's, Polyxena's."

"What?" Hecuba choked, clutching her throat. Suddenly she was not the withered old woman, shuffling toward death, she had affected to be. She seemed to grow even as I watched her, until she stood eye to eye with Neoptolemus. It was an illusion, of course, but even Neoptolemus felt it. He stepped back. "Why?"

"My father fancied her," he said.

"How could he? He had never seen her!"

"Yes, he had," said Neoptolemus. "He saw her at the springhouse."

Now Polyxena stepped forward, her eyes blazing. "The day he slew my brother Troilus? He remembers seeing me then? He should curse that day, and anything his eyes looked upon. I have, and I despise your father. Tell him that when he appears in your dreams!"

"Your feelings are of no matter. He will have your blood, lady, and have it spilled on his tomb. Then and only then will the war be over."

"Troy is a heap of ashes, its dead smothered under fallen stones and burning timbers, and he needs another killing to complete the war?" Her voice had faded, as if she had used all her strength in remembering Troilus.

"Who can fathom the desires and needs of the dead?" he said. I remembered the cold shade of Paris. "I resent it, too, my lady. Why should not having his son come to Troy be enough for him? Why does he need *you*?"

"Because he is a cruel and violent man," said Polyxena. "It is as simple as that. He murdered as long as he was able, now he recruits others to carry on murder in his name."

"Kill me!" I cried. "It is I Achilles should want as a blood-price. My husband killed him."

Neoptolemus gave a horrid little smile. "I've no doubt he lusts for you, that much is true. He sighed to have you walk by his side on the White Isle, where I am told he paces. But, *Mother,* I need you here."

With a choking cry of revulsion, I bent my head. I could barely stand to look upon him. So I did not see Polyxena shake off her mother's hands and stand before him.

"This will end the war? This will be the last killing?" she asked him.

"Yes," said Neoptolemus. That much I heard. "Then we will sail for home, abandon Trojan shores forever."

"And I shall have a tomb? A proper tomb?"

"Child, what are you thinking of?" Hecuba shrieked.

"I want a white marble tomb," she said. "Nowhere near Achilles." She paused. "And I want it to say that, as the innocent blood of a Greek princess sent the ships here, the innocent blood of a Trojan princess sent them home!"

"No, no!" cried Hecuba.

"Oh, Mother, cease!" Polyxena commanded her. "Do you think I wish to leave the land of my home? Go to be a slave, endure the sweaty fumblings of some vile Greek? Do you think it will be better for Andromache there than for me inside a white tomb?" She turned back to Neoptolemus. "I am sure you sweat and fumble, and I do not envy Andromache. Truly, I prefer the tomb."

Neoptolemus bit his lip at the insult, but did not strike her. "You shall have it." He looked to the door. "The preparations should take time, but we shall hurry them. By sundown, we will both have our wishes: you will be in a tomb and we will be readying our ships for home."

He left the house, and the women encircled Polyxena, weeping and lamenting. It was a grotesque reenactment of a wedding. They would attire her, dress her in her finest robes (if any remained from Troy), adorn her with the royal fillet, anoint her with scented oils, and whisper secrets in her ear. In marriage, those who had ventured into marriage long ago imparted their wisdom. But there was no one present who could help her, arm her, for the dark place where she was going.

Near sundown, two soldiers came for Polyxena. She had been dressed in white robes, a makeshift royal diadem, made of a linen strip torn from Hecuba's gown, tied around her head. There were no jewels, no gold. They were being counted in Agamemnon's tent, heaped up and inventoried. Even sacrificial cattle had their horns gilded, but she went unadorned to her slaying. Someone had brought a handful of meadow flowers and these were fashioned into a necklace and bracelet of sorts, yellow and red against her flesh.

"But we will accompany her on her journey," I insisted to the soldiers.

Hecuba, calm now, embraced Polyxena. "It is only for a short time," she said. "You spoke true. You are privileged to leave all this behind. Greet your father, greet Hector, greet Troilus, and tell them I will hurry to their sides."

Polyxena turned her head and kissed Hecuba's cheek. "I will, Mother. Now I take my leave of you all, whom I love." Tears traced themselves down her cheeks.

"Come!" The two soldiers grabbed both of her arms and steered her outside.

Hecuba and I followed, as did Andromache and Polyxena's sisters. No one stayed behind.

The tumulus of Achilles was only a short distance from the Greek ships. It reared toward the sky, its soil already covered with grass and flowers. Achilles had died long enough ago for the meadow to begin reclaiming it.

Someday this will be flat, I thought. Storms will beat upon it, wear it away, and shepherds will let their sheep feed on the grass. The tumulus of Achilles will shrink and shrivel and melt away. And Troy will be likewise. The mound where it was—I glanced toward the place, where now the smoke was barely rising—will disappear.

An altar had been set up before the tumulus—a heap of stones with a flat stone atop it. A fire was burning before it, as if that would cleanse the foul murder shortly to take place.

Lined up on one side were Agamemnon, Menelaus, and all of the Greek leaders. Of course they would be here to witness it. There was no bloodshed they did not wish to participate in, to relish.

Agamemnon spoke of appeasing the gods and needing a safe passage home. He spoke of the similar sacrifice he had offered to enable the ships to cross.

"And you've not yet paid for that sacrifice!" screamed Cassandra. "But you will!"

Agamemnon gave a discreet cough and soldiers apprehended her and hustled her away. Now I saw her twin, Helenus, bowing his head and looking ashamed, standing with his captors. I also saw Antenor, misery written on his face, and his wife Theano, standing before him.

They led Polyxena to the altar. "My tomb," she said. "It is all arranged?"

Antenor made a gesture. "Yes, my child. It is as near to Troy as possible. I have seen to that."

I expected her to castigate him as a traitor, cooperating with the Greeks. But she was past that. "I thank you," she said. "And you will tend it?"

"Someone will," he said. "I may not be allowed to remain here. But I promise it shall be tended."

"And not by the same person tending Achilles's mound here? I want no part of him. Hands that touch his tomb may not touch mine."

"Princess, I promise," he said. Sobs cut off his voice.

"Proceed!" ordered Neoptolemus. Several strapping soldiers stepped up.

"Need we so many?" asked Polyxena.

"To convey you," said Neoptolemus. He addressed the silent mound. "Father! As you have commanded, we have brought you the princess Polyxena. She will shed her blood here on your tomb. And you will then free us of your wrath!"

Why should he be wrathful? So the selfish, demanding child was demanding even in death. Or perhaps it was not Achilles himself, but the memory he had left behind in the minds of others that was so unreasonably demanding. We go one further in our idols, our gods, making them require things they would not think of.

Five men hoisted Polyxena aloft. She lay daintily in their arms, her ankles crossed modestly, her head back. She had bound her hair so that it would not impede their blades finding her throat. She had a dreamy look on her face, and had refused the blindfold.

They bore her to the altar. There they halted.

"You die to appease the gods!" cried one of the soldiers. I noticed— dreadful, the things you notice at such moments, odd splotches of calm—that no priest was present. Of course: the god demanding blood was Achilles, not any being of Olympus.

Another of the soldiers pulled on her bound hair to extend her neck. She closed her eyes. I could see her lips moving. She was speaking to someone, addressing someone, but no one could hear.

"Now!" A dagger came from nowhere, but did not hesitate; it slashed across her white throat and a gush of blood spurted up, hitting the soldier's chin, dripping off, bright scarlet.

She lay still. She did not struggle, or clutch at her throat, or convulse. Instead she was like a carved piece of ivory, utterly unmoving. Why did not her body rebel, heave, jerk? Had she commanded it to imitate the ivory?

Her eyes were closed and stayed closed. Her lips were curved into a placid smile. Slowly they laid their burden down, let her lie on the altar bleeding to death. Still she did not move, not even a twitch. It was as if she had died the instant the blade had touched her, died by her own stern admonition.

It was difficult to determine when she was dead. Gingerly they touched the soles of her feet with the point of the fatal dagger, and they did not curl upward. Someone put a feather in front of her nostrils to see if it stirred. It did not. Someone else laid a finger on her neck to test for a pulse.

At length Neoptolemus shouted, "It is done! My father is satisfied!"

Antenor stepped forward. "I shall convey the body to the waiting sepulcher, with all due respect." Now I could see, from the way her body draped on the litter, that she was truly dead.

Such courage. She was worthy of her warrior brothers. Her fame would last as long as Achilles or Patroclus or Hector's. Fortunate, blessed daughter of Troy!

Oh, what a world, when to die is deemed more noble than to live.

For the rest of us, less noble: we must grace a celebratory banquet for the departure of the Greeks.

"And now to the feast!" Agamemnon stood before the crowd like a ship's prow. "To speed us on our way!"

While we had been at the tumulus, soldiers had been readying the beach. For the high-ranking, makeshift tables had been set up, stools brought to allow worthy legs to rest. Resin-dipped torches, thrust into the sand, created a flickering yellow fence around the area. Huge fires were burning, several oxen—or something else?—roasting over them in varying stages of readiness. Amphoras of wine were lined up like trees in a forest, ready to be felled. Some youngsters were testing their flutes and older boys were plucking their lyres. The line of ships helped to cut off the worst of the wind.

Night was falling; the sun had set and even the glow on the horizon had faded. A few stars were already appearing. Had Polyxena gone there? Was she among the stars—she who had been with us when the sun had risen? There were stories about people being carried up to live with the stars, or being changed into a star. But we know too little of this.

The table of honor—inasmuch as it was a table—would seat Agamemnon, Odysseus, Menelaus, Nestor, Idomeneus, Diomedes, Philoctetes, and, shame of it all, Sinon, little Ajax, and Neoptolemus. Lesser men would be allowed to stand around it and share in the speeches and bantering. We captives were to stand farther back, serving as sauces for the meat, an appetite stimulant to help them digest their spoils. Had even the cattle come from Troy? Or were these men eating the flesh of the slain horses?

Mercifully the dim light softened the faces of the flushed Greek warriors. I could see Agamemnon's, turned red by the bonfire flames, his dark beard now streaked with white. As he talked and flashed his teeth, I could see that several were missing. Well, he was of that age. Nestor looked no older than he had when I first met him, but battle makes old men younger and young men older. Idomeneus—he seemed aged, and I had heard that he had lost his speed on the battlefield.

Agamemnon walked down the table, distributing goblets. "Gold of Troy!" he said. "It is fitting!" He pulled one after another out of a sack and handed them to his men. They were all different, collected from looted Trojan homes. Some might have been Priam's, but they might just as well have come from wealthy Trojan merchants. In his wake came servers pouring wine into them.

The oxen were carved with much shouting and glee. Huge hunks of steaming meat were put on the men's platters. None was offered to us, but we could not have eaten in any case. I looked on both sides of me, at Andromache, Laodice, Ilona, Hecuba. Their eyes were dull and their mouths set. They would endure: *perseverance,* that sad virtue of women.

"My men!" Agamemnon was crying. "Did we ever truly believe this day would come? Troy is destroyed. We are victorious. It has been many a long year. But I am grateful for you who stood the course. We have lost many, and those of us who remain must remember them. Without them we would not be here to speak these words. Now, as for the treasure—"

How quickly he got to that!

"—as we cannot give due reward to those who have perished, it is fitting that we divide them amongst ourselves in their honor. We have gold, we have jewels, we have fine carvings, and armor, and many other things, all . . . rescued . . . from Troy." At a nod from him, boys trotted out with litters heaped with booty. A large chest was laid at Agamemnon's feet. He lifted the lid. "These are the special treasures, which I will personally award." He bent down and scooped up a gold diadem. It must have belonged to Priam. "This is for you, brother." He gestured to Menelaus. "When you return to your throne in Sparta, you will wear diadems once again." Suddenly he broke off. "I know many kings have laid aside their diadems to fight here with me. Now you have your reward, and for the rest of your lives you can wear your diadems in peace."

Menelaus took the offered gold. Suddenly Hecuba screamed, "If you wear my husband's diadem, death fastens itself around your head as you fasten it."

Agamemnon scowled. "Lady, if you cannot keep silent, you must be removed."

Hecuba let out a hideous cackle. "Removed? As Priam was, as Astyanax was, as my daughter was just this afternoon?"

"If you had removed Paris as you intended, none of this would have come about." Menelaus glared at her. "You could have been spared all this. As for your warning . . ." Calmly he tied the diadem around his head. "It fits nicely."

"A circlet of death!" she cried. "Good. Now you can wait for it." She looked around at everyone. "When will it come? A sweet summer afternoon? A nasty, ill-howling winter's evening? You cannot guard against it. It will be ugly. Priam will see to that. And waiting for it will make it all the worse."

"Take her away," said Agamemnon.

As the soldiers moved toward her, she laughed. "I take myself away!" she said, and seemed to shrink and become shadowy. The soldiers lunged for her, but all they caught was a black dog, yelping and biting.

"Find her," said Agamemnon grimly.

"I wish to say that our brave men need to be saluted," said Idomeneus, standing up, trying to rescue the feast and divert attention. "Especially those who brought about the ruse of the horse and those who secreted themselves within it. Odysseus, you mastermind, you must claim the invention of the horse as your own."

Grinning, Odysseus stood and bowed his head. "It was clear Troy could not be taken by force. Its warriors were too fierce, its walls too strong. But guile can win where direct attacks fail."

"And Epeius," said Idomeneus. A short man stood up, eager to be acknowledged. "You constructed the horse."

"Indeed I did!" He grinned. "We went to Mount Ida for the wood, and if I may say so, we fashioned a lovely creation. And in a short time, too."

Agamemnon handed him a heap of golden things; I could not see what they were. "You deserve this and more," he said. "I am only sorry that I cannot lay all of the spoils of Troy before you, for they would not be here without your cunning."

Epeius bowed and retreated with his hands brimming.

"Sinon!" Agamemnon's voice boomed out. The monkeylike Sinon appeared. "All hinged on you and your performance. You were willing to undergo harsh, disfiguring punishment in order to convince the Trojans we had mistreated you—as indeed we had. You did not falter or stumble, but carried our mission through to success. To you"—Agamemnon thrust a set of armor in his hands—"you deserve so much more than this, but take this as a token."

Sinon looked down at his prize. "Thank you, my lord," he said. Undoubtedly he would demand more later, but, showman that he was, he would not spoil the moment.

"Now we salute those who, at great risk to themselves, hid inside the horse. Menelaus!" Menelaus stood. "Odysseus!" We raise our glasses in salute to you!" Then followed Diomedes, Machaon, Epeius, Neoptolemus, little Ajax.

Someone thrust a glass in my hand. A boy quickly followed, pouring wine. I turned mine out on the ground.

"To Epeius! To Sinon! To the horse!"

Everyone but the Trojan women drank.

Agamemnon laughed exultantly. "We are for Greece, then." He wiped his mouth. "Home again. Home. It is calling."

I saw Menelaus whisper in his ear. Agamemnon frowned, then turned to us.

"The gods are pleased enough. We have not offended."

No one ever found Hecuba. Privately I thought she had rushed into the surf and drowned herself. As the feast concluded—the torches were doused, the tables dismantled, the empty amphoras dragged to the water and abandoned—

we captive women were herded up and sent to our tent. Idomeneus suddenly appeared by my side.

"Helen," he said. "I have been here these many years yet have never beheld you, let alone spoken to you."

I looked at him, a kindly remnant of a vanished, ordered world. "Idomeneus. I am grateful for your good wishes."

"As I am for yours. Helen, I do not know what awaits you in Sparta. Only know that whatever it is, I am your friend. As I said long ago, in whatever age you reside, you are the supreme being. No other woman could command awe with gray hair." He looked me in the eye. "You are Helen, the never-diminished."

I shook my head. "I am Troy, and Troy is me, and Troy is gone. So Helen is more than diminished. There is no more Helen."

The fools that were taking me back to Greece did not understand that.

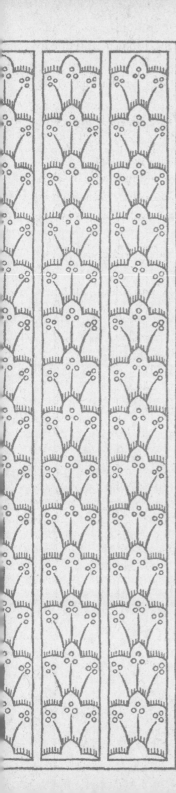

PART III

SPARTA

❖ LXXIV ❖

The wind was rising; it made the last flaming torches dance and snuffed the rest out. It sent showers of sparks into the sky, new red stars against the old white ones. Sand flew into my mouth, and the men began to gather up the stools and full amphoras and prize armor.

"At first light, men, we sail!" Agamemnon called to his men.

I saw Menelaus tug on his shoulder. Agamemnon shook him off.

"It wasn't only the temple little Ajax polluted, it was Cassandra as well," Menelaus warned him.

"You call Cassandra polluted?" Now I could hear clearly, and so could the men around them.

"What else can you call a woman who was raped?" Menelaus sounded as if he were glad of it.

"Don't you wish yours had been, instead of offering herself?"

"And do you know what yours has been doing, in your absence?" Menelaus taunted him. I did not think he had it in him.

"She wouldn't dare," said Agamemnon. "She can see—she has heard— what punishment I've wreaked on Troy, and on those who defied us."

"And how has she seen it, or even heard it?" Menelaus was turning himself on the sand, and I noticed that he seemed to limp, favoring his left side.

"The beacons are ready to be fired. But the biggest beacon—smell that?" He stood on tiptoe and inhaled deeply, putting his fleshy hands on his belly. "It's roasting Trojans!"

"The fire is out," said Menelaus. He was always so literal. But Agamemnon was right—Troy would burn forever.

"It was a good war," said Agamemnon. "For us. *I* am proud of it, even if you are not, little brother."

"I shall see you in Greece, then," said Menelaus. "In only a few days. We will return to what we left so long ago. We will reclaim what is waiting for us." Now he turned and made his way over to me, walking stiffly. Yes, he had an injury of some kind. I had not noticed it before. "Helen," he said. "Your last night on Trojan soil, wife. I shall leave you to your thoughts. Tomorrow we sail for home—Sparta. I have thirty-one ships left. Only thirty-one, after the sixty that first touched this beach all those years ago. That is the price I—and many other warriors—have had to pay for your folly."

I had nothing to say. I stared at him in the dull light, seeing only the changes in him, superimposed over the wavering image of him as a young man. His face was lined now, his lips set, and he moved in the gingerly fashion of one guarding a weakness, not like the young athlete of long ago. The war had taken a grave toll on his body.

I was taken back to the women's quarters in the damp and decaying Achilles house and given a pallet to lie upon. The others were silent, except for muffled weeping. The place where Polyxena had been was screamingly empty.

My last night in Troy. Menelaus had said it. This was the last time I would pillow my head on my arms and know that beneath lay Trojan soil. But Troy was a smoking mound, and when the sun rose I would have to behold those ugly streaks of smoke still sending their tendrils up into the sky, like beseeching fingers for a mercy that would not come.

Polyxena had been brave, the last Trojan to die. I would have changed places with her, or so I wanted to believe. But I did not know if I had that courage. And now I would go back to Sparta as a prisoner.

My promise to Hector! I had failed him. I had not been able to protect Andromache. *You are a survivor,* he had said. But that had not availed to save anyone else.

Evadne. Gelanor. Where were they? Had they perished in the conflagration? Oh, I should have let Gelanor return as he had wished! Instead, out of my own need and vanity, I had kept him in Troy. His death was my horror.

The brooch had wept blood, drops for the dead. I had killed so many. I felt their vexed ghosts crowding around me, prowling in the ruins of Troy. Because I had loved Paris, I had killed them, and him as well.

Is this what you wanted, Aphrodite? I asked her. But she did not answer. She had promised to save me, and she had done that. Beyond that, there were no answers.

* * *

I boarded the ship—as Evadne had foreseen, and I denied, so long ago. Menelaus was laughing, his head thrown back, standing at the stern as the shore was left behind. I did not stand and watch the land recede, nor behold the smudge and smoke from the noble ruin of what had once been Troy. I did not think I could bear it.

I had my own quarters; Menelaus did not come near them. He kept to himself, his own bed up near the bow, beside the captain's. I did not come to his, either. We barely spoke if we passed one another on the decks. Strange: this man who had been obsessed to possess me did not try, in any way, to act upon it. It was enough for him, apparently, that I was on his ship.

I felt dead. I even wondered if I might, perhaps, *be* dead and be unaware of it. Sometimes the dead do not know they are dead. But the stinging sea air, the dips and stomach-roiling tossing of the ship told me well enough that I was here, a prisoner on the ship making resolutely for Sparta.

What would I find when I returned? I only cared what I would see reflected in the eyes of Hermione.

We did not reach Sparta as planned. Instead, a great storm accosted the fleet, scattering us in all directions. Where Agamemnon went, we did not know; we lost sight of him. The ship carrying little Ajax sank; the gods punished him for his desecration of the Pallas Athena and her temple. Twenty-six of Menelaus's ships were lost, and we were driven helplessly before the wind for days. When we finally reached a shore, it was a flat and sandy coastline, fringed in palm trees. We had come to Egypt.

Egypt. We staggered forth to behold a strange warm world of green, brown, and blue: the three colors of Egypt. Green along the riverbanks and the irrigation canals, brown in all the rest: the sand, the murky Nile water, the mud-brick houses. And blue above it all, a vivid and cloudless sky.

Menelaus was immediately apprehended by soldiers of the Egyptian king—the pharaoh, who resided up the Nile in a place called Memphis. We had no choice but to go with them. Most of Menelaus's soldiers had been lost with the ships, and he did not have the means to resist.

The Nile was a broad, flat, slow-moving ribbon, very different from the Eurotas or the Scamander. The current was exactly balanced by the wind, which blew in the opposite direction at the same speed. If someone wished to sail down the Nile, he let it take him. If he wished to sail up it, he merely had to hoist a sail.

The pharaoh and his wife received us kindly, but made no pretense that we were anything other than his prisoners. They knew little of the war at Troy; Egypt was insulated against what went on elsewhere. They listened with polite curiosity as Menelaus attempted to explain about it. I noticed that he did not betray the reason it had started. Perhaps he felt it reflected too badly on him.

The pharaoh assigned us quarters together. Now I must sleep in the same room as Menelaus. I did not expect him to approach me, but I was taken aback when, as he stripped off his tunic, I saw the massive scar running from his thigh to his groin. Now I knew why he moved so carefully; he had lost part of his leg muscle.

"Staring, are you?" he snapped. "Look your fill. That's what your Trojans did to me. Crippled me!"

"You aren't crippled—" I started to say. He still moved, just not as a young man.

"You can't see the end of it!" His voice was savage. "Trace its path, and you shall see well enough where it ends!" He grabbed my hand and pulled me over to him, lifted up his undergarment. "*That's* what your Paris did to me. But he had already done it anyway, when you chose him."

"I am truly sorry," I said. I meant it. The ruins of Troy, the killing and destruction, left me with no appetite for any more sorrow or revenge. Menelaus's deficiency could not bring Paris back, could not make children sing again in the streets of Troy. All of it was useless waste.

"A bit late for that," he said. "A bit late. Have you not wondered why I have not sought your bed as is my right after all this time?"

"I heard you call Cassandra polluted, and I thought you felt the same about me." I had not tried to change his mind, either. It served my purpose well.

"It is hard to look at you and think that. It is harder to look at you and know I have this . . . this impediment." Ashamed, he covered the vivid scar and said, "Now you will tell everyone, tell them that Menelaus has lost his manhood—twice!"

"I shall tell no one anything," I said. "We are siblings in our misfortune, playthings of the gods. Neither of us has deserved what we got."

"You deserved it. You brought it about, for all of us."

Should I speak what was in my heart, even though it would hurt? "I meant, I did not deserve the glory, the beauty, and the love of Paris; nor did you deserve being branded a cuckold and a lesser warrior than your violent brother."

"Always Paris!" he cried. "Always he is here!" He put his hands on my head and squeezed. "If only I could squeeze him out, crush him out of your head."

I pulled myself away. "He is a part of me; you cannot."

He turned and flung himself on his bed, lying stiffly to accommodate his disability. "He paces Hades!" he muttered. "Why can he not find peace?" He coughed. "And leave *us* in peace?"

The pharaoh announced that we were to be transferred upriver to Thebes, where we would be more comfortable. What he meant was that we would be more remote, the better to hold us prisoners. But as far as we knew, he had not attempted to raise any ransom money for us, or even told anyone we were there.

We rode in a long ceremonial boat, gilded at its bow and stern, with a fragrant cedarwood canopy where we could watch the land slide by under our blessed shade. The sun baked the riverbanks, crocodiles languishing upon them, tails trailing in the cool water. It was several days' sail, but at sunset on the fourth day we saw huge temples on the left bank, glowing red in the dying light. They seemed to stretch out forever, row upon row of columns. From our boat I could hear deep, rumbling chanting from across the water, as priests performed their nightly rites.

A nervous official showed us the largest temple, after we had been settled into our quarters and received by the pharaoh's deputy. Across the Nile lay tombs, elaborate secret burial vaults. The pharaoh was already constructing his, even though he was still young, our guide told us. "For we must be prepared for that next world," he said solemnly.

We picked our way through the vast temple, where columns larger than any tree on earth supported stone roofs. There were statues so tall their heads almost touched the ceiling—some were of pharaohs and others of their strange gods with heads of crocodiles, jackals, or hawks, bigger even than the horse of Troy. All these were tended by robed priests and priestesses with shaven heads.

"Look." Menelaus pointed to one that had the head of a crocodile.

Farther up the Nile there is a vast city where the priests have a temple that is bigger than Troy. It has statues five times the size of a man. We must go there. As soon as this war is over. Paris. Paris had wanted to come here, and see these things, and—

Now I could not see them, not without him. I could not bear it. I turned and ran from the temple.

That night I dreamed of him. He was standing right beside me, sorrowed that he was not here. *I know as well as you it cannot be,* he said, repeating his words of long ago.

"Hush." Menelaus was sitting awkwardly on my bed, shaking me. His big hands were on my shoulders, but he did not caress me.

Paris faded, slipping away in the dark.

"I heard you cry out," said Menelaus. "It is but a dream."

He must have heard me cry *Paris,* and yes, Paris had been but a dream.

"I thank you," I said, touched that he would try to wake and comfort me, even though he must have heard me call his rival's name.

Even though I had fled from the temple the day before, when Menelaus was summoned to meet with some officials I returned to it. Painful as it was, I felt that somehow Paris was here, or rather, that even his glaring absence from a place he had longed to see somehow made me feel closer to him. I was wandering in the cool dimness—even at scorching midday—when a boy appeared, taking my arm and pulling me to one side of the temple. I could not understand him, but he seemed sure that I had come for some purpose, and that he knew what it was.

"Seer—very wise," he said, or rather, that was all I understood. I took my place in a little room in the vastness of the temple and waited. A woman came into the room. "Helen? I know of you."

How could I understand her? But I did. I was not sure what language she spoke, or how I knew it. I nodded. "Yes," I said.

"We are honored that you walk amongst us, if only for a short time." What age was she? I could not tell. "Now"—her voice turned brisk—"you have sought me out for what I can give, the famed elixir."

I had not sought her out, nor did I know of this elixir, but I would not contradict her. "Yes," I agreed.

"We in Egypt have long been masters of potions," she said. "We can make you young, old, astute, forgetful—"

"Oh, give me that one, for I would forget much!"

She smiled. "Only those who have lived intensely want this potion. Those who have not lived enough desire something else to make what they have done more meaningful, magnify it."

What if I told her? *I have caused a fearful war. I have caused thousands of deaths. I am in custody to the man I fled.* "Give me the elixir of forgetfulness!" I begged her. "Teach me to make it, so that I may replenish it as long as I live, for I shall have need of it forever!"

"It is very powerful," she said. "So powerful that should you see your mother and father and children slain before your eyes, you would feel no pain."

My mother had slain herself already, and what of Paris, dying? What of Troy, blazing? Was it truly strong enough to blot those out?

"I want it!" I said.

"As you wish," she said, and fell to her preparations. The vial she handed me was filled with a warm golden liquid. I drank it all, quickly, as instructed. I could feel little besides a warm tingling inside where the elixir was caressing my stomach.

"Only wait," she said. She began cleaning her implements, putting away her bottles and jars.

I reached out and touched her arm. "You promised to teach me," I reminded her.

While she took the bottles of syrup and dried grains and little pieces of bark and explained the proportions and the order in which they must be mixed, I felt a carelessness stealing through me, a lightness. I hoped I would remember what she was telling me, for suddenly it all seemed sublimely unimportant. Yet at the same time I knew it was vitally important.

Her delicate fingers stoppered the bottle. "Now think on those painful things," she whispered. "It is time to test it."

I took a deep breath and thought of Troy. I could see the flames and smell the smoke, even hear the cries of the doomed, but it was as if I were beholding a wall painting. It did not send stabs of pain through me. But those were buildings and people I did not know. Bracing myself, I thought of Paris. Oh, there was still grief there, still a piercing of the heart. "It is not enough!" I said. "Give me more."

She looked surprised. "You can still feel it? I fear more would be dangerous. Is the pain muted enough that you can endure it?"

I nodded. Perhaps it would be a betrayal of Paris were it to vanish altogether.

We remained in Egypt for seven years—impossible to believe, but that was how many times the Nile overflowed its banks, and that was how they measured years, so it was true. Who could have thought it would drag on for so long, who could have thought we could have endured it? But the elixir . . . the elixir gave me the power. It compressed and collapsed time, so that the seven years flitted away like seven days.

Menelaus was able to extricate himself from the pharaoh's grasp after many negotiations, and we were on our way, floating down the Nile, the sail folded away, the current hurrying us along toward the sea. The women carrying water jars down the steep banks stopped to look at us, as people always did when a boat passed by. They stood, tall and erect, watching as we left their world.

Menelaus took my hands. "It seemed to me that you belonged here, that you had stayed here all through the war. Yes, that the real Helen—you—had come to Egypt, where you waited for me. What went to Troy was not the true Helen but a double, a phantom. In that way, I hate to leave. This Helen who has been here with me, that is the Helen I competed for, the Helen whose loss I grieved." Thus he had found a way to live with it.

It seemed the opposite for me. The real Helen had gone to Troy, the Helen who had passed seven years here was a phantom, a ghost. Now that ghost would fade and disappear, and the real Helen must face Sparta at last.

❖ LXXV ❖

We landed at Gytheum. That was very hard. It had all begun there: that innocent day I had gone with Gelanor and encountered Aphrodite; the nine days later I sailed away with Paris. As we swung into the harbor, I cast a forlorn look at Cranae, riding tantalizingly in the waves, beckoning. Our night there . . . I felt waves of remembrance surging through me, more than remembrance, desire and longing. It was no more. All vanished, all come to this: a penitent, chastised return to Sparta for the erring, captive wife.

Menelaus mounted the gangplank and stepped ashore. He bent down and

poured a libation to the gods. "I thank you," he said, "for bringing me home."
He knelt for a long time, while the men waited to secure the ship.

"Come." He held out his hand to me. It was a command. I was to obey,
go back where I had been, take that place I had left so many years ago.

Night fell. We should have stayed in Gytheum, set out in the morning for
Sparta. Chariots were waiting, but they could have waited longer, until dawn.
Instead Menelaus mounted one and ordered, "To Sparta! I have waited a gen-
eration, I can wait no longer! Girls born the day I left are long since mothers!"
He held out his hand to me and I took my place by his side.

Going back. Going back, along the road I had thought never to travel
again. Menelaus encircled my waist with his arm. "Now it all begins again," he
whispered close in my ear. "Everything is erased. It is as if it never happened."

I looked at him, at his face covered with wrinkles, his thinning hair. "It
happened," I said. But I had no wish to make him unhappy. "What will we
find?" I murmured. "I am fearful."

"We cannot know," he said. He clutched the hand grip of the chariot and
stared straight ahead. The chariot lurched forward.

Cresting the last rise, we saw Sparta before us: Sparta, sleeping beside the Eurotas, calm and beautiful. The swift-flowing river caught the moonlight
sparkle and tossed it back at us, laughing. The citadel, the hilltop palace, was
easy to see from where we stood.

I clutched Menelaus's arm. "Let us wait here. It would be better to ascend
in daylight, when the palace is up and stirring."

He frowned. "Wait outside our own palace? How foolish!"

He flicked the reins and the horses moved forward, up the hill.

It was still dark when we reached the gates. The doors were fastened shut. I
saw that they were still the same red-painted wood ones I had left. Menelaus
called for the guards, and they, sleepy-eyed, swung open the gates, not really
caring who we were.

The grounds were quiet, the only sounds the crunching of our chariot
wheels. Everything was bathed in moonlight, the sinking moon painting all it
touched in cold white light.

You will return in moonlight. Yes, as I had left Sparta in moonlight, now I
returned to it in the same way, as foretold.

We dismounted. Before us it was utterly still, waiting.

I walked slowly toward the building where I had lived. It was horrible that it was still the same. It should not have been. All that had passed should have been reflected in its stones. But how could it have been?

We pushed the doors open and went inside. Nothing was altered. I and Menelaus might have left it yesterday. Silently I passed down through the corridors. I reached the bedroom. Moonlight shone in, touching the bed.

"Tomorrow we will see it all," said Menelaus. "We will see it, and know the worst. In daylight we can face it."

The moonlight was slanting, withdrawing its fingers from the chamber. Soon it would be dawn. I did not know if I could confront it. Where was Hermione, a grown woman now? I wanted to see her, embrace her; yet I did not want to. I knew she would hate me. How could she not?

The unkind sun came up. He would not spare us. We must behold Sparta. Menelaus, apprehensive but less so than I, dressed himself and made ready. I did not know what awaited me. I was soon to find out.

My father tottered out to see us; his guards had informed him of our arrival. At first I did not recognize him—he was a bent, crippled old man. He could not hold his head up but had to peer at us sideways.

"Daughter?" he said. His voice was thin and quavering.

"Yes, Father," I said, coming to him and taking his bony hands. Now that I was close, I saw that he was almost blind; a white film lay upon his eyes.

He embraced me, and it was like being embraced by an empty cocoon. "Daughter," he kept murmuring. Then he pulled back and squinted at me. "You are old!" he said. "Your hair is gray!"

I laughed, for the first time since I had entered this place. "Yes, Father. Much time has passed. Or perhaps it is your eyesight?"

"I don't see much these days, but I can see that silver is crowding out the gold in your hair. And—your face has lines."

"You see altogether too well, then." And my aging must be very visible, for him to see it. "Tell me, Father. Tell me what has passed."

"My dear child . . ." His dull eyes filled with tears. "So many deaths. They are all gone—your mother, your brothers. And your sister Clytemnestra is a murderess. She killed Agamemnon the moment he returned."

"What?" Menelaus cried. He swung around and grabbed Father.

"Agamemnon landed, with all his war booty and his . . . that woman he brought from Troy. Clytemnestra greeted him with all ceremony, pretending to be overjoyed at his return. The beacons had alerted her, and she knew he was coming. She ushered him inside with great fanfare. He went first to the warm bath she had prepared for him in a silver tub. Naked, unprotected, exulting in his return—she entangled him in a net and stabbed him to death!"

I felt a rush of . . . yes, pride. After all Agamemnon had done to her. It was justice for Iphigenia! Was this what I had passingly glimpsed in my vision?

"Now, Odysseus, he was just the opposite," said Father. "When he returned to Ithaca—"

Must we hear about Odysseus? Would that he had been stabbed as well!

"—he went in disguise, to see what had happened in the palace in his long absence. Wily man! For the palace was beset with enemies, although his wife had remained faithful. He had to kill them all before he could resume his rightful place. Agamemnon was not so foresighted. And so he lies in a tomb, whereas Odysseus reigns again in Ithaca."

"What of . . . the Trojan woman?" Menelaus asked.

"She was killed as well," said Father. "Before she even entered the palace."

Cassandra. Cassandra, another Trojan casualty.

"But who reigns in Mycenae, then?" Menelaus sounded desperate.

"My daughter Clytemnestra," he said. "My shame! And her lover, her cousin Aegisthus. Oh, the curse on my house has been fulfilled!"

"And the rest?" I asked him, not wanting to hear any more about the curse. "There were others, returning home. And Hermione?" I remembered the dreadful taunt of Neoptolemus, that he would have her.

"Oh, they came. That son of Achilles stormed in here and took Hermione against her will, forced her to marry him. But it was short-lived. The violent man attempted to steal treasure from Apollo's temple in Delphi, and was killed. Now people speak of 'the debt of Neoptolemus'—meaning that as you kill, so shall you be killed." Just as he had cruelly killed Priam at an altar, he himself had been struck down beside one.

"Hermione? Where is she?" I asked.

"Here. Here in the palace. She is a childless widow, with no hope of another marriage: her mother's notoriety and her husband's violence have stained her."

Hermione—in her thirties now, alone.

"I must warn you, she is not pleasant," said Father. "I hesitate to say this about my own grandchild, but much has befallen her." He took my arm. "Do not attempt to see her, not right away."

She was here, nearby. Only a few steps away. Yet I must wait. "Neoptolemus—did he not have another woman from Troy with him?" He had taken Andromache. What had become of her?

"Oh, yes, that tall woman. She escaped from him when he married Hermione, and ran off with someone—they went north."

Andromache. Safe. I had not been able to vouchsafe it myself, but now Hector could rest.

"My dear brothers?" I had to ask, had to hear it all.

"They fell together. They were preparing to join the Trojan folly. But the arrows of Apollo felled them first."

So Agamemnon had been right, with his cruel words. They were gone; we would not hunt or ride together, ever again. But I had not killed them. Almost alone of the men I knew, they had not perished in Troy. Persephone had been gracious, and did not call them because of me.

Suddenly I was so tired I could barely stand. The bright daylight swirled around me. I was back in the palace, but all was changed, and everyone was dead.

Menelaus collapsed on the bed with me. "I shall never clasp his arm again. And we quarreled when we parted."

It took me a moment to understand that he meant Agamemnon. "We are always tortured by our memory of the last time we were with anyone, what we said, what we did not say. With Mother—oh, Menelaus, how can any of us bear what the years have put upon us?" I thought longingly of the elixir and its mercy, but no, I needed to feel this.

"We cannot," he said. "That is why the aged are so stooped."

I needed to see it all. The palace, with all its rooms that called out to me, each with a memory. The megaron, where Clytemnestra and I had selected our husbands. The gates, the back one where Paris and I had run away, the other where Clytemnestra and I had stolen away that day, to the city. The great meadow, where Menelaus and I had first strolled as husband and wife, and where we had seen Gelanor. Gelanor . . . gone now, too. The woods where I had hunted with my brothers, and the riverbank where I had raced, and oh!

they were all still here, but the moments when they changed my life were gone, as vanished as Troy.

The Hermione tree had grown huge in the years since it was planted. Its leafy crown rustled quietly in the benevolent midsummer breeze. The horse mound, yes, that was where the evil had all begun. I must go to it, confront it, must stamp on its earth and curse it.

The mound lay a fair distance outside Sparta. I remembered how long it had taken us to reach it, my heart hammering and my whole being gripped by confusion and embarrassment. Now I retraced those steps, walking calmly, aware of everything I had missed before: the quiet valleys on either side, the dark woods, the heat of midday stilling the land.

Raise a mound to it, so that it remains a memorial to this day and this oath, Father had said. His voice had been loud and strong that day, not the cricket's song it was now reduced to.

I saw it up ahead. It was lumpy and uneven, but it was unmistakable.

Mounds—the tumulus of Achilles, the memorial of the horse. One led directly to the other. Hideous things, ugly on the landscape.

Closer to it, the earth was higher than I had thought. I climbed up one side, aslant, grabbing tufts of grass to pull myself up. Under here, under here the bones lay—oh, the men had kept their promise! I sat down on the top of it, remembering the men who had sworn. Father had thought to avert bloodshed, and instead he had induced it.

Omens. If I were beginning again, starting out in life, I would ignore all omens, neither heeding them nor trying to disable them. If we chose to pass them by, then perhaps they would lose their power, as old gods and goddesses, no longer worshiped, fade away and lose their grip on us.

How sweetly the wind blew over these grasses, caressing them. Like the grass at Troy, that the horses fed upon. Horses. Troy. Live ones and wooden ones. Troilus and his horses, Paris riding wild horses. Hector, breaker of horses. Dead ones littering the Plain of Troy. The mysterious little horses on the island of Scyros. The slaughtered horse, sleeping here.

I sank my head down on my knees, closed my eyes. I did not know what I had expected to find here, but it had not been this slumbering, drowsy mound. I must have dozed, for when I opened my eyes the tall, swaying grasses swam in my vision and a woman stood before me.

It was no one I knew. She was looking at me with narrowed eyes, bending down to see my face.

"Not so beautiful," she said.

Who was she? "Good," I said. "For that old song has grown wearisome, past its time."

"But I suppose there are some who would insist on pretending that it is still there." Her voice was hostile, and she kept staring at me.

I did not rise, and she sat down beside me, shading her eyes.

"I heard—we all did, here in Sparta—that Helen had returned."

So she was a woman from the town. "Yes, after many a journey."

"Twenty-four years it has been, to be exact." Her words were clipped, but there was something in them, something in the tilt of her head . . . I looked into her eyes. Brown eyes, staring back at me.

"Time has not passed in a normal fashion for me—the gods confused the years for all of us at Troy—but I trust your reckoning."

"Twenty-four years means your daughter is now thirty-three. Hermione, whom you left. Did you ever think of her?"

This townswoman was bold, to question me so. I was still, and again, queen of Sparta. "Every day," I said. "She was with me in Troy. She walked the streets with me, she warmed herself before Priam's fire, she trudged with me to Mount Ida."

"No, I did not." The words were bitten off, flung out.

Hermione? I could not think. "But—you are—?"

"Your abandoned daughter!" Now she leapt up, the better to look down upon me. "The one you ran away from! Left me here like a toy that is tossed aside! Yes, I am Hermione!"

I pulled myself up, not as quickly as she. "My dearest daughter, I—"

"Daughter? I am ashamed to be your daughter. The daughter of Helen of Troy! A byword for shame!"

I looked at her. There was nothing there I could recognize from the child I had left. This woman had brown hair, brown eyes, a face that was pretty but unremarkable, and wide feet, clad in sturdy shoes, peeking out beneath her gown.

"My shame is not your shame," I said.

"I come here often, to try to understand what began here."

"But you cannot," I said. "It is but an empty mound, its grasses sighing as the wind passes over it. You would have to hear your grandfather speak, see the men gathered." I reached out; I needed to touch her. She stepped away.

"How could you have left me?" she asked. "How could a mother have left her child? And to run away with that boy, he was only a few years older than I—"

"I did not leave you. I tried to take you with me. You did not want to come. You wanted to stay with your tortoises and your friends."

"I was nine years old! How could I comprehend what you were asking?"

"You could not." I took another step toward her, but again she drew back. "Paris knew that."

"Paris! Do not say that name! The name that robbed me of a mother, and drove my grandmother to end her life."

Once she had liked him. But now he was just a symbol of her loss. "Paris—"

"I said do not say that name!" Now she turned to go.

"Wait—" I reached out for her. "Please, do not leave!"

She whirled back, drew herself up, gathered her mantle around herself. "How many times have I wished to say that to you, to beg you? But you were out of earshot." She paused. "*Long* out of earshot."

"My mother . . ." I held out my hands. "Please, tell me."

"It was I who found her. Yes!"

As if I had been struck, I shrank back. This horror I had never imagined. I had thought it was one of her attendants, one of the guards. Not Father, not Hermione. "No—"

"Who did you think it was, then? Or did you not think of it? I came into her chamber early—she always liked to share a breakfast with me, and after you were gone, I had nowhere else to go. I went in there, even before the sun was up—and found her. She had been dead since night, so they told me, because she was so blue—and I took those cursed swan feathers and burned them up in the brazier, and if I could, I would have burned *you*!"

Now . . . now I must hold her. In spite of her pushing me away, I enveloped her in my arms, and I was sobbing. "That would have been justified," I said. "The swan—let him be gone from our lives." Oh, the glory of the gods and their brief visitations—not worth the sorrows that trail thereafter.

Hermione did not pull away, but let me embrace her. "Take me to her tomb," I said. "Let me leave an offering there."

The tombs lay in a partially natural cave, not far from the palace. A small grotto in the hillside had been enlarged to allow their carving. There were four of them: Mother's, Castor's, Polydeuces's, and an empty, waiting one for Father.

"I come here every day," said Hermione. "As my cousin Elektra comes to her father's grave, and vows to avenge him."

Little Elektra. But, of course, she would be a grown woman now. How could anyone mourn Agamemnon, least of all the sibling of the sister he had so mercilessly slain? "I am not sure what needs avenging," I said, hesitantly, not wanting to alienate Hermione.

"That mother who took a lover!" she said fiercely. "It seems to run in the family."

Now I could not help but smile. "It was a curse, a powerful one, visited on us. I see it has come true." But I did not want to talk about it. All I cared about, now, was my daughter. And the tombs of my dear mother and brothers.

"Here," she said, showing me the large stone box that was embedded in the cliff. A wilted wreath lay on top of it.

Mother. Oh, Mother. I draped myself over the cold stone. I had brought nothing—but no, that was not true. I had brought myself.

"I am here—Helen . . ." I murmured endearments as I pressed my lips against the sharp corner of the tomb. "Your Helen." I need not tell her what had passed since we had parted. I need not tell her of the time in Troy. I need not tell her of what had befallen me since. The dead are kind that way, they do not want a full recounting.

"And here, your brothers." Hermione was showing me the other tombs.

I knelt before them, asking them for guidance. "You always guided me before," I said. "You taught me so many things." I did not tell them I was grieved that they were gone; they knew that. We must not speak to the dead of things they already know. That insults them.

"A tomb waits for Father." She indicated it. "But after me—the line of Tyndareus will die. I am its last," Hermione said. Her voice was like a sad falling note.

"You cannot know that." She was still of childbearing age. "There will be another husband for you. Neoptolemus was not worthy. I saw the unspeakable things he did in Troy. You speak of my desecrating my own name, but he desecrated his father's, Achilles's. You are free, and now someone you love will come."

"As the daughter of Helen—" she began.

"You will be expected to be beautiful, and passionate. Are you?" Now I must be bold. I looked at her closely. Her face was pleasant, and her hair thick and shining.

She drew back, blushing. "Passionate . . . I do not know."

"You will not until the man you love holds you." I leaned forward. "With women, it is the man, and not the moment. That is the truth of it. With men it is the reverse."

I had seen my daughter, and we had made tentative steps toward reconciliation. The past would always be there; she would mistrust me for a long time, but she had, warily, admitted me into the forecourt of her life. It was more than I had dared to ask.

❖ LXXVI ❖

Afraid of frightening her away, like a butterfly alighting on a flower, I did not approach her too boldly in the days that followed. I let her go about her ways, although my eyes never tired of looking at her—but only when I could look secretly. Time. Time would bring all things about. I had to believe that.

And time I had in abundance. There was nothing stretching out before me, nothing to reach for or retreat from. I looked over the palace and the grounds—so modest compared to Troy's—and satisfied myself that they were well cared for. Little had changed—no new halls had been built, no new adornments had been added. Without Mother, Father had had no interest in such things. I wondered whether Father had ever thought of marrying again, but he told me, staring with his watery, filmy eyes, that no family would even consider marrying into the House of Tyndareus—as cursed, now, as that of Atreus.

"Then Menelaus and I make a suitable pair," I told him. "What of the Aetolian slave girl Menelaus left behind? I remember she was with child." I tried to make the question light and of no matter.

"She had twins. They are now grown men, still living in the palace. They were waiting all this time for both Menelaus and me to die before Hermione could have an heir. Well, they are now disappointed in their hopes of the throne. Let Menelaus award them something, send them away."

All these unfinished things I had left behind, now sprung back into life again. "I wish to see Clytemnestra," I said. "Have you seen her since— Does she ever come here?"

"No, daughter, and I could not go to her. I did not wish to leave Sparta in the hands of the twins with all those . . . upheavals. It did not seem wise."

"We could go together now. Menelaus will prevent any mischief."

He sighed. "I fear I am too fragile now. I could not endure the jolting of the chariot, nor the final climb up the mountain."

I noticed that Father asked me very little about Troy. He did not seem curious about it. Does curiosity flee with age, along with agility? Or was he, like Mother, awash with shame?

"I will make ready to go within a few days." I was longing to see Clytemnestra, share at last all that had passed in those long years.

Menelaus was not pleased; he tried to forbid me to go. My sister had murdered his brother and lived with another man. It came too close to home.

"I do not condone what she has done; I abhor it. But she is my only living sibling, and your brother committed a great crime against her. We need not carry it further. Only remember, as you loved your brother, despite his evils, so do I love my sister. If I do not go and see her again, it adds another wrong to the great weight of the war."

"I suppose you'll want to take Hermione? I won't have her around that woman!"

I had thought of it; had she not lived with Clytemnestra at one point? But I knew her response would be no. "I understand," I said. "I will go alone— except for the drivers and guards, of course."

He took my arm. "Be careful," he said.

"Do you think she would harm me?" How odd that he would hint that.

"You have not seen her in many years. You do not know what you will find."

"As was the case with you and me," I reminded him. He looked hangdog, as he often did. "I will be wary," I promised.

* * *

Going to Mycenae! To be there without the oppressive presence of the brothers, to be with Clytemnestra again! I did not think about Aegisthus; I did not make room for him in my mind. The day was clear and clean, and I had two chariots to carry myself and my attendants, and a slower wagon laden with gifts. I had scoured the palace for something to present; this was difficult, as there would be much the same things at Mycenae. There would be the same alabaster ointment jars, the same brown-painted handled jugs, the same fragrant scented robes. We rumbled down the steep incline and out onto the plain, dotted with plane trees and small orchards and fields of barley. No destruction here as in Troy, but the absence of men to tend things had caused a subtler ruin. Neglect stalked the land. Many of the men had not returned from Troy and it would be another generation before the land could flourish again.

Why, why had they gone? What persuasive power did Menelaus have? He must have promised them a quick resolution, glory, and spoils. None of it had happened; no one got spoils but the leaders and the few lucky ones who returned. Instead of enriching Sparta, the war had impoverished her.

My charioteer pointed to a grove of poplars by a stream. "There," he said. "Where Menelaus gathered the army."

He had spoken of it. What a cursed place, dooming all those who had convened around it with high spirits. I saw a large plane tree, a bit apart. That must be the one Menelaus had planted to commemorate the war. Seeing it gave me a chill. I thought of the oak of Troy, that other emblem of the war. There was nothing left of it.

Leaving the plain, we started climbing the hills, the chariots pulling out ahead of the heavier cart. Hawks soared overhead, playing in the sky.

We had to stop for the night, and we chose a little dale that seemed safe and sheltered. The birds were replaced in the sky by bats flitting out from their resting places, quick dark darts against the fading light. Safe, tired, I slept soundly. Tonight I did not need the elixir of forgetfulness.

At first light we were on our way again. But sometime in the night Menelaus's warning words had spread inside me like a stain, and now they colored everything I saw. I felt my apprehension growing as we drew nearer to Mycenae. Suddenly everything looked suspicious. The people who watched us from the fields looked sullen. The sky lost its hawks and became dimpled with clouds.

What would I find? Now it seemed naïve to think Clytemnestra and I would meet again as if nothing had changed. I should have sent messengers ahead to tell her I was coming. I should have given her an opportunity to prepare herself, or to refuse to see me. I gripped the handles of the chariot as we lurched along.

The men were laughing and joking. For them, the day was fair. I felt my heart thudding, as if I were being chased by a pack of dogs. Something hideously oppressive hovered over us, and they could not see it, could not feel it. But that vision of mine was revealing it, and it grew stronger the nearer we got to Mycenae.

Hurry, hurry! I wanted to urge them. Perhaps we could get there before it happened. It was important that we do so. That was why I had set out on this journey on this particular day. Now I knew it.

"Faster!" I suddenly said, startling my driver. "We need to go faster."

He smiled. "Oh, there's plenty of time, my lady. As it is we shall arrive well before dark."

"Too late, too late!" I said. "I tell you, hurry! Let the others follow, but let us go as quickly as the horses can pull us."

He looked at me quizzically. "It is not good for them. They'll overheat."

Was my fate always tied up with horses? "Forget the horses!" I cried. "Something worse will happen—is happening—if we do not get there in time!"

He started to argue, but I was his queen. "As you say," he grunted, and took his whip to them.

We tore up the hills, gravel flying out behind us. It was the closest I would ever come to flying, but my heart was not soaring. I was gripped by the blackest dread I had felt since the dream of Paris and the arrow.

Just over the next rise! I remembered the landscape well. Almost there, almost within sight of it. It was always invisible, tucked in its mountain gap, until you rounded that last bend, and then you could see it, stone fastness rising, blending into the mountainside.

Lathered, the horses tried to slow, but I begged the driver to keep their speed up. Everything looked in order, undisturbed. For an instant I felt both very foolish and very relieved.

Then, bursting from the gateway, a chariot rushed toward us. The horses were as wild-eyed as demons, and their driver was screaming and forcing them into a faster gallop. Behind him, on foot, people were pursuing; archers shot after him, but he was beyond bowshot range. Screams and yells carried across the hill.

"He'll run us down," my driver said. The narrow road would not permit two chariots. He attempted to get our chariot out of the way, but one of the wheels stuck in a rut, and we were only halfway clear when the fleeing chariot seemed to fly over a rise and make right for us. The charioteer tried to pull aside, but had to veer to one side and finally stop. He leapt from the chariot and took the reins, to guide his panting horse around us.

Blood covered his mantle and his forearms; his red hands had smeared the reins. "Stand aside!" he commanded us, pulling out a sword. "Do not look at me."

But I could not help it. He was young, well built, and under the blood his face might have been handsome. "Who are you?" I cried. "What have you done?" Somehow it was as if my special vision gave me the right to question him. But he could not know of that, only that I had disobeyed him.

He turned slitted eyes at me, started to say *Who are you?* when the thing I had always hated saved me. "Helen. You must be Helen. The cause of it all, of whatever I've done." But he did not plunge his sword into me.

"I have nothing to do with what you have done. I know not what it is."

"I've avenged my father. It's taken me many years, but I was only a child when he was murdered. A son must grow strong enough to take revenge, and that takes time." He jerked his horse past us, as if he spoke of fishing or the seasons.

Murdered . . . father . . . revenge . . .

"Oh, who have you killed?" I cried.

"My mother," he said.

It was Orestes, the baby son! "You have killed . . . your mother?" As horrible as the deed, almost equally horrible that he could speak of it calmly and proudly.

"It had to be done. Yes, and I killed her lover Aegisthus, too." He looked dazed, and I could see now that he was not proud or careless, but so stunned he hardly knew what he did. He jumped back into the body of his chariot, now cleared of ours. "Go clean up the mess," he said. "She's *your* sister. *My* sister hates her, and might desecrate the body." Yelling at his horses, he sped them into a gallop and disappeared in a cloud of dust.

I sagged against my driver. "So that is why I knew we must hurry." I knew my words sounded foolish, as they always do in such times. There are no words big enough. "And yet we were not in time."

The pursuing mob breasted the hill and confronted us. "You let him get away!" they screamed.

"We could not stop him," my driver said. They moved threateningly toward him, spears, bows, and swords drawn.

"Do not waste your time with us," I commanded them, "but continue after him. I am Helen, the queen's sister. Pray, let me pass, that I may tend to her."

Now they became more agitated and angry. "The cause of it all!" one man hissed. "Without you, he never would have gone away. Had he never gone away, then none of the rest of it would have happened."

"I am weary of this," I said. And in that moment I knew I had listened meekly to the last round of blame I ever would permit myself to endure. If this had not happened, then that would not. Yes. But how long, and how far back, could this be pursued? There was, in truth, no end to it. "Enough of it. I need to tend my fallen sister. Get out of my way." They fell away like leaves.

Now there was no need to hurry. We waited for the other chariot to catch up with us, and the cart with its useless gifts. Then we rolled toward the fortress-palace, going as far as we could on the road, as if there were safety within the chariots. But we had to abandon them as we reached the base of the citadel, which was hidden in a cleft between two mountains. A steep path led to the entrance gate, with its lions snarling down at us from the lintel. There had never been a time when I had passed beneath them with good feelings, but now all those other times seemed happy in comparison.

How quiet it was. No guards, no workers, and the gates were gaping open like a wound, exposing the inner flesh of the palace. We entered, seeing no one about. Had they all left, pursuing the murderer? Fearful, we kept ascending, until we reached the top where the palace sprawled. It had its own gate, also standing open, and we walked through it. There were the workshops and storage houses, but there was only one thing that drew us: the palace itself. I rushed ahead of them to enter it first, alone. The eerie quiet lay over it like a fog. Then, as my eyes grew used to the dim light inside, I saw huddled forms, whimpering and choking, around something.

This must be where she lay. I approached; not until I was standing beside them did the cloaked figures perceive me. "Is this the queen?" I asked.

One of them looked up, threw back her hood. "Who are you?" she whispered. Then she shook her head. "It cannot be, but I think it is Helen."

"It can be, and I am," I said.

"She thought you were dead," said the woman matter-of-factly. "Lost after Troy. Now it is the opposite—you live, she is dead."

"What has happened?" I needed to hear it from people who had loved her, not from her murderer. Oh, let a sympathetic telling of it sponge away the horror of what Orestes had so proudly recounted.

Others in the mourners' circle now spoke. "She was attacked and killed by her own son, in the act of welcoming him. He had been away for so many years, and had just returned, rejoicing her heart. But he had returned for only one reason, to kill her. He stabbed her when she reached out her arms to embrace him. The first thrust was true. She only had time to say, 'Orestes?' and then she fell. And here she lies. We covered her, but we did not touch her. To prepare her for burial, that is the task of the family. But there is no one here to do that duty."

"Elektra?" I asked. But I remembered Orestes's words.

"She will not perform the rites. She is even now sacrificing at her father's grave, telling him of the murder."

"But that is nothing new," another witness said. "She goes to her father's grave every morning and every evening. She pretends the purpose is to honor him, but in truth she only steeped herself in hatred and thoughts of bloody revenge. Day after day she kept him company, whipping herself into a black fury of malevolence. I truly think he himself could not hate Clytemnestra as much as his daughter did, on his behalf."

"It was she who summoned Orestes here so that he might be her arm and do the killing. Now it's he who will be pursued by the relentless Furies, but what is that to her? No, she'll not prepare her mother for the tomb," one woman said, finally answering my question.

"Then I shall," I said. "And willingly." I bent over to pull the cover away, dreading to see, yet I must begin. Slowly the cover slid past her head, past her shoulders, down to her waist. Her long hair covered her face, but the blood painted her from her shoulders to below the waist, and made a thick dark pool underneath her, a pool that her fingers clutched. "Oh." I flinched. Gently I tried to brush her hair away, but the ends of it were stuck in the blood. Finally I saw her face, eyes wide open and staring in surprise. Surprise at seeing Orestes at long last? Surprise at the pain of the knife? Surprise to be dying? Gently I closed the lids. Some warmth still lingered, but the cold stones would soon rob her body of the last of it.

"Two sad reunions," I told her. "Had ours been first, then perhaps the second might have had a better ending."

A shrill voice cut through the chamber. "Or ended with two deserved deaths rather than one." I swung around to see someone coming toward me, a young woman dressed in sad black robes like the others, but with a sneer on her face.

"Why, you must be Elektra, that gentle creature I have heard so much about." I was surprised at the sharpness of my own response. "Sweet, loving, and kind."

"Ask my father, he will tell you that is so. Ask *her* and she will say otherwise. It all depends on who is speaking." She was now close enough that I could see all her features—heavy and dark like Agamemnon's. For an instant I felt I was confronting him again.

"You and my mother are true sisters," she said. "Adulteresses and husband-leavers."

"As the curse on our father foretold," I said. "It is a grief to have daughters who are married many times, that I admit."

"Married?" she jeered. "Is that what you called it?" She drew herself up proudly. "I would like to wield a knife and send you to join her."

"But you are too much a coward for that," I said flatly. "You lurked and plotted and waited for years but had to send for your brother to do the deed. Bah, what a pitiful false warrior you are." I hoped to goad her into trying to strike me, for I was sure—in spite of her younger years—that I was stronger than she. I wanted to fight with her; my heart cried out for an immediate punishment for her, and I wanted to be the one to deliver it. It was not noble, but, gods help me, that was what went through my mind. And she, already furious, lunged at me. She was easy to overcome, and I flung her against the wall and pulled her head back by her hair. Panting, I said, "Your father would be ashamed of you now. You have no more strength than an old incontinent dog. But then, he was a blusterer, too. So perhaps he understands." I let her go before I might smash her head against the stone wall, committing another murder in the hall. I recognized, with shame, that I had used her in this way to attack her father, which I had long burned to do.

"Go!" I ordered her. "Leave us, so you do not vex your mother's ghost."

The attendants had sat speechless all this while, stunned. When Elektra picked herself up and fled from the room, they murmured, "Good. Now we can proceed."

"Where is the body of . . . *him*?" I asked.

"Outside," one of them said. "He was preparing a sacrifice of welcome. Orestes ran him through from the back with a spear, and he fell onto the altar."

I shuddered. "A fine pair, this brother and sister." The best of the children, then, was the one Agamemnon had had the folly to sacrifice, Iphigenia, leaving these two monsters. He had never been very intelligent. Or perhaps he felt Artemis deserved the best and he must offer it. I shook my head. No more thoughts of that man, nor of the war. They must not be allowed to pollute the rites of burial.

She already had a tomb, beside Agamemnon's. The idea of her resting beside him seemed wrong, but I told myself that she had had years to prepare another tomb for herself, so this must be her chosen place. As the attendants and I drew the shroud up over her face, I whispered a final goodbye. "Thank you for taking me to Sparta that day," I said. "Thank you for showing me a world outside our gates. I shall never forget." We scattered wildflowers over the shroud—some of the same ones I remembered from the fields that day—and then we had the melancholy task of sliding the heavy stone lid in place. We strained to do it, but in the end it moved under our own strength and we did not have to ask for help.

❖ LXXVII ❖

The years passed, but not as they had in Troy, when what seemed to be loose, fluffy days were spun into tightly wound yarn, compressing time. No, in Sparta it was the reverse. The threads untwined themselves, spread out, so that one day seemed like ten. So I use weaving and spinning terms to explain my life in Sparta. I spent, it seemed, so much of my time with the weaving and spinning, although I produced nothing of beauty like the lost tapestry I had created at Troy.

Seasons came, seasons went, suspended in that floating timelessness. Father died; after hearing of Clytemnestra's fate, he seemed to shrivel, shudder before what he felt was the fulfillment of the curse brought down on his house. There was only a faint sorrow at bidding him farewell. In truth he had departed long ago.

Now everyone from Sparta was gone. Mother, Father, brothers, sister. Only I, Helen, was left, and my only surviving family was Menelaus and Hermione. Menelaus and I lived in peace with one another, a shuffling, old-person's peace—the peace that descends when all other concerns have either died or fled. Like ancient, stooped warriors, we looked at one another across the battlefield—strewn with perhaps our betters who nonetheless had not survived—as comrades.

Comrades was all it could be. Never again would we be husband and wife in the true sense. Companions, wary friends, battle veterans, fellows, yes, all those things. But not lovers, nor even true husband and wife. Troy and its wounds—physical and of the soul—had seen to that.

There was comfort in that, a finality. I could reach my hand out to Menelaus and resolve to help him through the long years ahead, letting him lean on me if need be, expecting him to let me do the same.

And Hermione? The years likewise softened her toward me. As we worked side by side with spinning, weaving (those woman tasks again! thank the gods for them!), seeing to the needs of the palace, I came to know her, and she came to know me.

She was not like me. One's child never is. But until your child has grown to maturity, you cannot believe it. Your children are part of you forever, from the moment of their birth, therefore you imagine you are part of them as well. But they are entirely apart, seeking their own secrets and bearing their own disappointments. If they choose to reveal them to you, you among mothers are fortunate.

With watchful eyes I saw Hermione as she went about her ways: disciplined, lonely. She was pleasing to look upon, but no man wanted to look upon this daughter of the wayward Helen and widow of the cruel Neoptolemus. Through no fault of her own, she was a pariah, as she had lamented.

She seemed to accept it; she accepted things better than I. Perhaps that was the Menelaus in her, the non-Helen. As I said, she was not like me. Eventually she even became, if not truly affectionate toward me, cordial and pleasant.

And then Orestes came for her. Orestes, so different from the dazed, mad killer I had encountered on the road from Mycenae. This man was reserved, self-assured, polite. He sought out Menelaus to ask for Hermione in marriage, coming as a supplicant.

He and Menelaus withdrew and I was not privy to their words. I knew not what passed between them until they emerged from the chamber and Menelaus muttered, "I am satisfied." But then Menelaus was satisfied with everything now. Later—after Orestes had been treated to the traditional guest-friendship and put in a lofty chamber for the night—Menelaus told me he had at length atoned for the murder. The Furies had pursued him, so that he cut off his thumb to appease them and performed many other demanding deeds until they were finally satisfied. He had been tormented, under two irreconcilable mandates: to avenge the death of his father, and to honor his mother. It had come close to driving him mad. Perhaps he had even become mad for a time.

"It is over, Helen," Menelaus said. "It is finally over."

Yes, everything was over. I looked at him, seeing an old man where once an eager strong suitor had stood. But what did he see when he looked at me? Something equally fallen.

"Is it, then?" I asked, thinking he meant our story.

"Yes," he said. "The curse on the two houses ends now. Hermione is innocent of it, and Orestes has paid its dues, laid it to rest. Think of it—our grandchildren can be ordinary people. No curses, no half gods, no prophecies. How I envy them!"

"They will have a freedom we did not have," I admitted. But the glory would have fled.

We gave Hermione to Orestes, performing all the rites. She was happy, delivered from her house of widowhood and bleakness. She had always fancied him, she confided to me (confided to me! what an unlooked-for gift she bestowed in that intimacy, little knowing what it meant to me), ever since they were children.

"Some things come out right," I told her. "Sometimes we are given our fondest desires."

They had a son, Tisamenus. Hermione asked me to attend her, and I did, joyously, although a midwife was nearby. I held my grandson in my arms even before his mother, gazing on his wrinkled red face and giving thanks for the dull years that had allowed me to be with Hermione and had placed her son in my embrace. A marriage, a birth: things I thought the horror of war had vanquished forever, now quietly resumed.

"He will not be a hero," she said, cradling him. "He will not be called to walk in high places, but merely to do his duty in the ordinary way of mortals." She looked at me. "Mother, can you be content with this?"

I leaned forward and stroked her hair, a gesture she rarely permitted me. But this was a precious moment. "I have had enough of heroes," I assured her. "Tisamenus will have a better life without treading in that realm."

Menelaus stepped into the chamber. "The age of heroes is over," he said. "And I, for one, do not mourn its passing."

Hermione looked up at him, her face full of compassion. "Father, trying to be a hero almost cost you your life, and deprived me of a father."

"All those heroes," he said dreamily. "All gone. We, not quite so heroic, are here to behold the sun." He bent to look at Tisamenus's face. "I can wish no better fortune for you. My grandson, do not be a hero."

The age of heroes had truly passed, and Tisamenus could not be one even if he burned for it. A great bronze wall had been erected around those old heroes, it descended from the sky, and no one could lift it or trespass there. Each age bestowed its own glory, but the age of my grandson could not be the age of Menelaus.

The war at Troy seemed to grow in song, poetry, and story all the while. As it faded from living memory, it grew larger and larger. Men claimed descent from one or the other of the heroes, or, failing that, anyone who had fought in the war, which now assumed the stature of a clash between the gods and the titans.

Were you at Troy? assumed the solemnity of an oath, and *Where were you when the Trojan War was fought?* became a condemnation if the answer was, *Elsewhere.*

Troy, Troy. The world was in love with the Trojan War, now that it was safely over.

LXXVIII

There were fewer and fewer veterans of that war still alive. We saw them seldom. Once or twice Idomeneus came visiting, as did two of Nestor's sons. Old Nestor had returned safely and taken up the reins of kingship smoothly, but others were not so fortunate. Odysseus's son, Telemachus, now a grown man, had stopped in Sparta once to inquire about his still-missing father, who later returned to find Ithaca in a mess. Diomedes, as far as anyone knew, was ruling in Argos. But news did not reach over our mountains easily, and increasing banditry on the roads cut traveling drastically. Our world shrank, cupped in by our mountain ranges, neglected roads, fallen bridges. The more isolated we became, the more people wanted the tales of the Trojan War, when the Greeks had mounted their glorious overseas expedition. It was balm to those who could not travel even within Greece. The Trojan War was supposed to enrich the Greeks, but they were now more impoverished than ever. Who had been served by the shining piles of booty on the beach?

Hermione appeared content with her life, and Orestes doted on her. He had seemingly been cured of all the wildness, the madness that had seized him, and appeared sunnily placid. He trotted about after Menelaus, observing his duties and behavior as king, knowing that he would follow him. The two royal houses had united forever, binding their curses in the past, where they could not spill out to taint the future. Their little son Tisamenus showed flashes of his other grandmother, and in him I felt Clytemnestra and I were clasping hands once again. That this great peace could have grown from the bloody stalk of Mycenae was a miracle.

Just as was the peaceful existence of Menelaus and myself, passing quietly in the palace.

Menelaus still enjoyed hunting and he liked to take his grooms with him, as well as Orestes and little Tisamenus. He said he wanted the boy never to remember a time when he had not known how to hunt. If only my brothers were here, how they would have loved to teach him! I tried to speak of them, to keep their memory alive in the family, but it faded relentlessly. Thus do we pass away, slipping out of mind.

* * *

It was a high summer's day when they all set out, packs of hunting dogs yelping and leaping in eager spirits, spears glistening, grooms carrying buckets of extra arrows. Tisamenus had a little hunting cap with imitation boar's tusks, made of tightly rolled wool, adorning it. His fat little legs would tire soon, and Orestes was prepared to carry him on his shoulders. Menelaus looked stronger and straighter than I had seen him in some time; lately he had taken to stooping and was too eager to sit down, so this was a welcome improvement.

"We'll be gone a few days," he said. "We'll go into the Taygetus foothills, at least, and see what we get."

In other days I would have gone with them, but now I was just as content to stay behind. I could have kept up, but it would have been an effort, and that would have spoiled it.

How old was I now? It was hard to know, because of the odd passage of time while we were in Troy, but I must be over sixty. I did not care; I had long ago stopped caring. Still, sometimes it was a shock to remember it.

They were not gone three days, but at twilight of the second, a mournful procession mounted the hill up to the palace in the twilight. I could see that they were carrying something, very carefully; it was not a stag slung carelessly and proudly from a pole. No, this thing was contained in a blanket, laid straight in a makeshift litter.

I flew like I had in the maidens' race all those years ago, as fleet as that lost girl. I knew it was Menelaus, and when I saw him lying there, staring up, I hated my gift for knowing.

"Poisonous serpent," said Orestes. "He stepped on it." He pulled back the cover and showed the swollen ankle with its angry red fingers streaking upward.

Menelaus's face was rigid, but his eyes moved back and forth with fear. *Helen* . . . he tried to say, but his lips seemed locked.

I took his hand and squeezed it. "Do not talk," I said. "Save your strength. We have antidotes . . ." But did we? Oh, if only Gelanor were here. Gelanor. I still missed him, still mourned his loss. He would know what to do. I sent a slave for our own physician and for medicines. Attendants carried Menelaus to the bedchamber and laid him gently on the bed. I covered him with our finest wool blanket, as if that would save him.

Helen . . . he kept trying to say.

Hermione came running up the stairs. "Father!" she cried. She embraced him, laid her head down on his chest. She did not cry, lest it upset him. But later the physician pulled her aside and shook his head. Little Tisamenus tried to climb up on the bed and Hermione had to pick him up and take him off.

I stood in the corner, biting my fist. I had had no premonition of this. Their hunting trip seemed innocent enough. My special sight did not reveal all things to me, just some things. What good was it, then, if such a big thing slipped in undetected?

I was trembling. I thought I was past all that, past caring, no matter what happened. But I was wrong. Menelaus was dying and I was infinitely sad. I, who years ago had railed at his very existence, now grieved at what one careless step had brought him to.

No one can live forever. We know that, and we also know that some deaths are better than others, but often our deaths come in ways that seem to have no part of us. Menelaus, the warrior, should have died on a battlefield, not in bed of a snakebite in his seventies. So many in our family had died at their own, or their children's, hands. Such a quiet death for Menelaus. But then, he had always been the quiet one.

The antidote and ointment did no good, as I knew they would not. As full night fell, I pulled a stool up to sit by his side, and Hermione sat on the other side. His restless eyes kept flicking from one of us to the other, and he looked both frightened and resigned at the same time. He kept trying to speak but was unable to get the words out. Both Hermione and I tried to assure him it was not necessary. Still, there seemed to be something he very badly wished to say.

I bent my head down to be as close as possible. "I am listening," I soothed him.

"Helen," he whispered, "Forgive me."

I squeezed his hand. "I think we have long since forgiven one another, have we not? Trouble yourself no more."

"No . . . I must tell you . . ."

"I know it all, my dear friend."

"No. I killed your sacred snake. I had him killed, in Troy, because . . . it was the only thing I could do in my hatred. I couldn't kill Paris, so I killed . . . him. Forgive me. It was cruel. And now he has his revenge. I die by snakebite."

The beloved household snake, so horribly killed. I would never forget it. "It was you?"

"One of my spies." He looked plaintively at me. "Say you forgive me. I think"—he sighed—"that is the only deed from the war that I regret. Strange, isn't it, when so many men were killed, that I lament the death of a snake?"

"He was innocent, and not part of the war, so killing him was a crime."

"I knew it would frighten and wound you."

"It did."

"Say you forgive me, Helen. Please. I must hear it before . . . I go. Before he takes me in retribution."

"We did many hurtful things to one another, and yet we are not by nature hurtful people. I forgive you, as I hope you forgive me my wrongs toward you."

"There weren't any. Except . . . the one."

Now I smiled. "That is a monumental *except*." I felt something change in his hand, some heaviness creep across it that was not there before. "Go in peace," I said. "Go with all forgiveness, and care."

He relaxed, and even his lips seemed released into a smile. "Yes," he whispered. He breathed out, but not back in.

Hermione screamed and fell across him. I stepped back and closed his eyes. Might he have peace in his journey.

"My lady, it is time." Someone was touching my shoulder. "You have slept overlong."

Troy . . . I had been in Troy . . . The dream . . .

"I know it is difficult, and sad, but you must rouse yourself. Menelaus can be interred but once. And today is that day. My condolences, my lady. Be strong."

When I wept—but not just for Menelaus—the attendant of the bedchamber put a gentle hand on my shoulder. "I know you sorrow for him. But still, you must—"

Yes. I must. And then, after that, I must again do what I must. And I would be strong. I had no fear of that.

There had been a place Menelaus had loved, in those early days of our marriage. It was on a hill high above the Eurotas, looking down upon Sparta and across to the steep mountains. Tumbled stones hinted that once our family's palace had stood there, and Menelaus had spoken of building another one where we might retreat. It provided magnificent views and, being so high, would be easy to defend. But we had never built it; inertia and familiarity with our old palace had stayed our hands. And after Troy, he had not mentioned it, as if he had put all those old dreams aside. Now he would rest there, in his new palace at last.

I had ordered a tomb structure built of finest cut blocks of stone. It was no easy task, for stone-cutting took time, and carrying them up the steep path was difficult. But I knew Menelaus would wait; he had waited so long for this palace. His ghost would not vex me, for he would understand why his entombment must be delayed.

And now all was ready. The funeral pyre had long since been kindled, the bones gathered and placed in an urn of bronze, the funeral feasts—for there had been several of them on successive days, marking the progress of his shade toward Hades—held. Menelaus was ready for his last journey, and I could rest content that I had fulfilled all his wishes, even those he had not dared to speak. My vision, my knowledge of the thoughts of others, enabled me to do so—a good side of the gift that so often had brought pain.

I was dressed in my finest robes, my most delicate gown, my richest jewelry. We would follow the funeral cart in our chariots, I in front, Orestes and Hermione behind me, little Tisamenus held by his nurse in a third chariot. Creaking, we descended the steep hill, then made slow progress in the meadow path alongside the Eurotas. (Oh, those meadows, where Clytemnestra had taken me, the hill, which Menelaus had labored up, and Paris and I had careened down—good memories? Painful? Bad? Now they all blended together, became one, part of what made Helen, Helen.) There was a place where the Eurotas, swift-flowing as it was, spread out and became shallow and fordable. The funeral cart lumbered across it, the water coming almost to the top of its wheels, but it emerged safely.

More nimble, the chariots crossed easily. I looked upstream. There were no swans there, just the clear water. I had not seen swans since my return. Perhaps they came here no longer, like many things that happen only at a special time.

At last we reached the summit, and I was pleased to see the integrity of the structure I had ordered so hastily built. Its stones never betrayed the quick labor that had gone into them; they were well carved, sharply cut, oblong, as long as a man's arm span. Three tiers made a pyramid, as high as—I suddenly knew—the evil horse of Troy. Perhaps even higher, perhaps as high as four men.

The sky was deep blue above it, with only a few moving fluffy clouds to tell us it was a sky rather than a painting, and behind the Menelaeum—as I meant to call it—the Taygetus Mountains of Sparta rose spiky and jagged. We had not had time to plant trees, but the natural pines hugging the summit had not been disturbed, and the wind sang through them, sending their pungent scent to us, stronger than incense.

There was an opening in the structure to receive the ashes, a little passage-way and a stout door. We would place the remains of Menelaus there after the invocations, the farewells. There was another niche for my own ashes. But they would never reside there, that I knew. So in their place I would leave my silver distaff, a symbol of my duty that I was soon to forsake.

It was I who must convey the urn to its destination. I took the polished bronze in my hands, in wonder that it could contain a man, and all that made him a man. Behind me, Orestes supported Hermione, bent double with grief. The solemnities must be obeyed, and in silence we stepped toward the opening prepared for it. I reached in and felt for the place, setting down the urn. It was so small, such a tiny place. But it would serve, when all else was fled.

The masons, who had been waiting beside the pines, now stepped forward to mortar the stone in place, seal Menelaus behind it. This was the palace where he would reign for eternity.

Stifling a sob, I turned away. I could not bear to think of him there.

But, truth be told, I could not bear to think of any of us contained in the darkness of an urn. Mother, Father, my brothers, all of them were now dust. It must come to this for me as well. Even if it were true I was the daughter of Zeus, mortal offspring must die. Achilles, Sarpedon, Penthesileia, Memnon, all rested in the tomb, despite their godly parentage. Zeus had promised me otherwise, once. But I had ceased to believe his easy promises.

Quietly we descended the steep path, leaving behind the glorious building and its setting. The whistling wind bade us farewell, the pines bowed in token formality.

LXXIX

Menelaus's journey was over; my final one had yet to begin. When we returned from the lofty hill of the Menelaeum, I endured the last, prescribed funeral feast, presiding over it as protocol demanded. I would honor my duty until the end, lest anyone say I shirked or neglected one jot of what was required. And thereafter—I would be free.

Free to rise up and follow what I had been called to do. There was a part of Sparta that still tugged at me, saying, *Do not desert your post.* But I knew Orestes would rule well. Oh, I grieved that I must leave Hermione again, but I would leave her fulfilled and contented, my friend as well as my daughter. And I was growing old—not enfeebled yet, but perhaps soon. I might become a burden, an embarrassing beggar, at the feet of my own daughter, as I aged and became frail. I would spare her that.

I announced my intention to leave Sparta. I hoped not to reveal where I was bound, but that was a foolish hope on my part.

"Troy?" Hermione's hands flew to her throat. "Oh, Mother . . ." She stifled the *How could you?*

"I have had a dream." Dreams dignified all things, gave us permission to pursue them. "I am commanded to go."

Orestes merely nodded. "The gods send us where they will." More practically, he said, "Will you notify us as to when we may expect your return?"

"Yes, if I may," I said. I did not think it likely I should return. But I was obedient to the gods. They might decree it.

In those last days I walked about the palace, as if anointing, consecrating each place I was about to leave. I walked down the steep hill and wandered in the meadows and into the streets of the town of Sparta. The townspeople looked at me, knew me for who I was. But even the most beautiful old woman in the world, the supreme example of autumnal beauty, could not move them, so attuned were they to youth.

I should relish the freedom, the deliverance from the bondage of my beauty. Time had set me free. But I felt a weighty sadness at their failure to see any beauty beyond the most conventional.

Bidding farewell to my daughter and grandson was the most difficult. It is always people who clutch at our hearts, not towns or shrines or duty. I could only console my raging confusion and grief by telling myself that we would meet again. I must believe that. I would.

In Gytheum, the ship was anchored, waiting. Gytheum. Where it had all began. Had I not taken that journey with Gelanor, then . . .

Oh, the old woman's curse! To have lived so long, made so many choices, that everything is a reminder, a tapping on the wrist, saying, *Had I not done that* . . .

I mounted the gangplank. Whatever awaited me, I could endure it, welcome it. My life was not entirely frozen in the past yet. There was an unknown before me—a privilege usually reserved for the young.

"Cast off!" I ordered them. "For Troy!"

The voyage was uneventful, and although I did not fly or float as I had in the dream, it seemed as if we were skimming over the water magically free of hindrance. We put in at various islands, but by my own stern orders we did not drop anchor at Cranae or at Cythera. Those were so holy to me that any revisiting would seem a desecration.

The winds sang in our sail and the oarsmen could rest for long stretches; the winds seemed eager to bring us to the shore of Troy. We made the crossing very quickly.

Standing and shading my eyes, I saw the distant shore of Troy pulling us toward it. At first it was only a long gray line, the place where the beach welcomed the sea, but as we approached I could see all the things I had in the dream, the narrow band of water that is the Hellespont, the heights where Troy had stood.

Rowed ashore, we splashed through ankle-deep water, stepping onto that beach I had once thought never to see again. Gentle little waves were lapping on the shore, which was empty. Nothing remained from the invasion—no huts, no fences, no ship debris. It was as if the Greeks had never come.

Now that I was closer, I could see the blackened stump of what had been Troy in the distance, looking like a dark thumb or a mound. Nothing moved around it. The tumulus marking the tomb of Achilles reared across the plain. It was not as tall as I remembered. Wind and weather must have worn it down.

Nothing was left of the miserable house where I and the other captives had been held, but I knew exactly where it had been. And here, on the beach, I could point to the place where they had piled up the treasures they had ripped from Troy, a tottering heap of bronze and linen and pottery. Seagulls strutted there now, and foamy waves washed over it, their bubbles winking and glistening in the sand, ephemeral jewels, imitation of the stolen Trojan ones.

"Where to, my lady?" My attendants looked around, puzzled. "This way?" They pointed to Troy.

"No. Not yet." I would circle it, visit the plain, sit by the banks of the Scamander, trudge back to the foot of Mount Ida: first see all that had surrounded Troy, edge my way toward it until I had the courage to confront it, behold my dream.

How quickly the fields had recovered. As we walked through them, pushing aside waist-high grasses and wildflowers, I looked in vain for any remnants of the hundreds of bodies of men and horses that had once strewn the fields. I would have thought such a field of death would never vanish. But vanish it had.

This part of the plain flooded in winter, but crowding upon it, at its outer edges, plowed fields and vineyards began. I could see crops growing green under the warm sun, see farmhouses. Here and there oxen were plowing. Carts, half filled with produce, waited in the fields.

On to the foothills of Mount Ida. We passed the springhouse where Troilus had been slain, passed the troughs where once again women were washing, the distinctive slap of their clothes against the stones singing in the summer air. They laughed shrilly as they sprayed one another playfully with water.

The ground rose, and stony outcrops told us we were nearing Mount Ida. Would the hot and cold spring fountains still be there? We rounded a bend and I saw them, the stones crumbling, but the hot water still tumbling out, with its cold twin gushing beside it. Behind it wound the beginning of the path up the mountain. The path I had traveled twice with Andromache.

"A moment," I told my guards. I had to draw away and think of her, wherever she had gone. Oh, Andromache, I pray that you are content. Happiness is impossible, but contentment, yes, that is within reach. I picked a stem of white wildflowers and scattered their blossoms in her honor.

I turned back to my guards and then in the distance I saw the little house from my dream. It was of stone, its tiled roof neatly shining, and surrounded by olive trees. Who was in it? Why had I dreamed of it? Yet I knew my special sight had granted me the vision, and I must honor that.

"There." I pointed at it. "We go there."

It seemed to recede before our eyes. It was much farther away than it looked, sitting surrounded by its fields and masked by the olive trees guarding it. Nothing stirred in the noonday sun; no dogs barked or laborers looked up. But it was too well kept to be deserted. Someone lived there.

We entered the welcome shade of the olive trees, their branches shivering in the slight breeze. The house was in shadow. I told them, "Wait for me." I must go alone—to what, I did not know.

The door was a stout one of painted wood. I knocked on it once, twice. If the door did not open, I would wait. But the dream must not be denied. I was compelled to follow it. I had come all this way to do so.

It did open. A woman stared out at me. I had never seen her before. "What is it?" Her voice was sharp.

"I do not know," I said. I could give no other answer. I should have prepared one. How foolish.

"Who are you?" she demanded.

"I am Helen of Sparta, late of Troy."

Now the door swung open wider. She gaped at me, frowning. "It is even so?" she asked.

"Yes." I pulled my head covering off my hair. But that gesture no longer guaranteed recognition. Helen, the Helen who had called a thousand ships to Troy, would be eternally young. She was in stories and poems, so she must, perforce, be so in life.

She kept looking at me. Then she yelled, "Gelanor! Gelanor!" and rushed from the door.

I was left standing in front of it. Now I knew why I had dreamed of this house.

An elderly man came to the door. At first I did not recognize him, nor he, me. Then we burst into laughter and fell into one another's arms.

"You are alive! You are alive!" I was choked with sobs. I clutched him to me. "I sought you in the streets of Troy, I went to your house, oh, I did everything I—"

"Hush," he said, laying his finger on my lips. In that gesture we were lovers, as we had always truly been in some deep sense—lifelong comrades forged in a bond of utter trust and loyalty. "I know you would."

I pulled back from him, looked into his dear face, the face I had thought lost forever. "How did you know that?"

"Because I knew—know—you."

Stirrings and foot-tappings around us reminded us of the presence of others.

"Yes," said Gelanor, pulling away. "I wish to present my wife, Phaea."

"Wife?" I said. "Truly, you must tell me how all this has come about. I last saw you in Troy, the night before the horse was pulled inside. I know nothing since."

"Come in, take a place at our hearth," Phaea said. "So many years means that it will be a long tale on both our sides."

Their little house was tidy and had unusually large windows, making it bright inside. At first glance I did not see anything that would tell me Gelanor lived there—none of the boys' junk and treasures he used to collect. Perhaps that belonged to the old life that had perished in the Trojan flames. Or marriage had changed him.

Phaea handed me a cup of broth. For an instant I hesitated to drink it, as if by doing so I would shatter a spell, for all this still seemed like a dream. To eat or drink was to embrace where I was as real, bind me there. Defiantly, I sipped it, suddenly aware of my hunger. It was rich with the taste of lamb.

"Now, Persephone, you must remain with us. You have eaten something." Gelanor cocked his eyebrow in that old way. We had been thinking the same thing. It made me smile. They let me finish the broth before telling their story. She spoke a version of the Trojan tongue that was difficult for me to follow. But I was delighted that I could understand as much as I did.

Phaea was the daughter of a herdsman in the area. They had been forced to supply the Greeks with meat; a neighbor who had refused had been killed outright. Secretly they had also provided meat, milk, and hides to the Trojans, but risked their lives to do so. As long as the southern gate was approachable they were able to enter that way, but as the Greek hold on Troy tightened, they were barred from the city.

In the final attack on Troy, they had kept well away, praying they would be spared. Their home was not far from the temple of Apollo—the one beside the springhouse—and they intended to seek sanctuary there if necessary, as that temple was neutral ground between the two sides. Not that the Greeks always honored such things. They hid in their house until they saw the victorious Greeks gathering on the seashore, then they ran for the temple.

Inside the temple Phaea had found Gelanor, dazed and suffering from burns. He was sitting in the underground chamber, his arm draped over the feet of the Apollo statue, staring dully at the opposite wall. At first she had been afraid he was either dead, with his eyes still open, or mad. When he turned his head, his expression was so dreadful she thought this poor man would have done better to die. She brought him food and, when the Greeks had gone, took him from the temple and nursed him back to health in her family's home.

For a long time he did not speak, and her father thought he had lost his wits. He lay in bed, staring, and, even after he was walking again, seemed not to be able to perform even simple tasks. They could not trust him to herd the sheep. They assigned him to gather olives and apples near the house. He could manage that.

"All this while he did not speak. I did not even know what his language was. I did not know if he could understand us."

"It was your Dardanian dialect," Gelanor said. Beneath the teasing I understood the pain of that time. "Such a silly accent!"

She leaned over and playfully pushed him. "It is the most noble of accents. Did not Aeneas and his kin speak as I speak?"

"What happened to Aeneas?" I could not help but interrupt their banter.

"He has never been seen again," she said.

"I saw him alive, fleeing down the street in Troy," I said. My Trojan language was reviving. "I called to him, but he did not answer. I was told by Ilona, when we were miserable prisoners on the beach, that his wife Creusa had died. But beyond that I know nothing." Aphrodite had promised to save him—but had she?

Gelanor sighed. "There is so much we shall never know, endings that we cannot pursue. But mine is simple: Phaea and I were married—after her father was satisfied that I was not half-witted—and we have lived here in peace for many years. I have felt myself to be, in some way, a guardian of Troy. Of what is left of it."

"I am glad for your happiness, dear friend. And Evadne?"

He shook his head. "I think she did not survive that horrible night. So few did." He paused. "And you? I know you were dragged away by Menelaus. But beyond that I have heard nothing. I feared he had kept his promise to his men to kill you in vengeance."

"Menelaus was not a man of vengeance," I said. "In that he was out of place amongst the Greek leaders. He had a tender heart, but they made him ashamed of it. He promised to kill me once we returned to Greece, but we did not return directly there. We spent many years trying to return. Seven of them were in Egypt. Then we returned to Sparta. There I have been, all the remaining years."

He gave a cry, a protest. The old Gelanor spoke. "Oh, how did you endure it?" he said. "To return there, to live with Menelaus—"

"You are not the only one with potions, my friend. In Egypt they taught me how to mix an elixir that protected me from all feelings. And thus I endured those years. But that is over. I left those potions behind. I am longing to feel . . . all that I need to feel."

"Are you sure?" he asked. "I could not allow myself to for a very long time. And it will be worse for you. How could you dare to come back here?"

I looked at him. "How could I not?" I shook my head. "It is my heart, my very self. Am I not Helen of *Troy*?"

They provided a bed for me to rest, and for several days I lived with them, all three of us pretending we were simple people, herdsmen and farmers, with nothing beyond that weighing upon us. We had never known anything but the slow passage of seasons here on the edge of the Plain of Troy, never had any concern beyond when the sheep needed to go to higher pasture or whether the beaters had left too many ripe olives on the branches. Would that not have been lovely? But had it been true, we would not have been ourselves and we would have betrayed the cry of vanished Troy, all those ghosts calling to us.

❖ LXXX ❖

At last I commanded the courage I needed to go to the city of Troy. I must see it all, must revisit it. Gelanor and I set out walking across the plain, leaving behind his household in its sheltered grove. I noted that he moved briskly, for an old man—for that was what he now was. I smiled, remembering Priam and Nestor and how old I had thought them, when they were younger than we were now. But they had *looked* old, I thought, and moved as old men. Surely we did not!

Gelanor directed me toward the shadows of Mount Ida. "First we must go here," he said. "If you would see all, you must see this."

For a long time I did not know where he was taking me, but I was content to follow him. I was still dreading the final sight of ruined Troy, and anything that served to postpone it I welcomed. We passed through groves of olives, their silver leaves all a-tremble, and fields of barley, bowing under the hand of the passing wind.

Finally we rounded a bend in the path and I saw something white gleaming before me. It was large and square. Around it dark cypresses waved, telling me it was a tomb. I felt Gelanor take my elbow to brace me.

"The last casualty of the war," he murmured. "Few come here. She would want you to."

I saw wilting flowers at the base of the tomb, dried enough that I knew he was right; these were old. "Who . . . ?"

"Polyxena," he said. "That poor, useless sacrifice." He stopped and looked at me. In that instant, I saw the old Gelanor, spirited and questioning. "In this lies all the evils of that evil war."

I approached the tomb. There were carvings there, but I did not look at them. Instead I knelt and laid my hands on the cold stone. She lay in there, a morsel to feed Achilles's hunger and vanity. I bent, letting my forehead touch her tomb. "Polyxena," I murmured. "Yours was the greatest sacrifice of all." She had gained nothing from the war, not a single shining moment, and yet she had lain her neck bare like a doomed lamb. There were so few witnesses to her death. Would she be honored? Or would the injustice extend to people coming to Achilles' tomb in ignorance of hers? Paying homage to him and ignoring her?

* * *

We made our way to the tumulus of Achilles, some distance away. Tufts of grass covered it, and there was a discreet altar at its feet. Gelanor circled it, allowing me to take it in in its entirety. It dwarfed poor Polyxena's.

"People come here to sacrifice and pour libations. In the years since his death, his reputation has grown." He shook his head. "Hector does not have a tumulus. But when we go into Troy, or near it, I will show you what has happened with Hector. There is a statue of him, and people sacrifice there as well. In fact, statues are sprouting all around Troy—it's the Egyptian influence, all those statues—and the heroes of the war are being honored. It is a good thing. For Troy must—it must!—live on in the memories of men. There was too much bravery, and too much suffering, for it to vanish without remembrance."

"Paris?" I dared to ask. "Did his tomb survive?"

Gelanor shook his head. "It was too near to Troy. The fire, the destruction . . ."

I gave a cry of despair. Not even a tomb!

He put his arm around me. "Did you not have a private place, a place that you can reclaim?"

Such places were all inside Troy. All consumed. I shook my head. And then, slowly, I remembered. That day we had gone out with the horses. He had taken me to the quiet place by the banks of the Scamander.

"We did not have the chance to spend much time outside Troy," I said. "But there was one place—we were only there once, and I never thought there would not be others, as time went on—I paid little attention—"

"Find it," he said. "Remember it."

I nodded. "I will try." I thought hard, but I could not pinpoint the place. "Perhaps I can find it again in a dream," I said. "But before that, Troy. You must take me into Troy."

He looked at me with that old hard examining look. His eyes might be circled with wrinkles, but his gaze was as strong, as searching as ever. "Are you ready? Are you sure you can endure it?"

"No," I whispered. "But I must try."

Together we approached the ruins of Troy. They loomed larger and larger on the plain as we walked resolutely forward. The first thing I saw was: no walls. The mighty, high walls of Troy had fallen. A bit of their lower courses were still there, only a third of their original height. They guarded only jackals and cawing birds. The towers had vanished. Their stones were scattered like forlorn children at what had been their bases. *And burnt the topless towers of Ilium.* That dreadful phrase that kept playing through my mind, that had come to me unbidden years ago.

"Come." Gelanor was picking his way amongst the stones. Where the mighty south gate had been there was only a gaping hole, and we stepped through it easily. It was nothing like my dream, where everything was intact but deserted. Here all was ruin—blackened, broken, destroyed.

I shielded my eyes. "Take me away," I said. "I can bear no more. Troy is truly dead." And I wept for it, only sorry that my weeping could not be deep enough, could not express the sublimity and the loss of Troy.

He guided me gently through what was left of the streets, the streets that had once been alive and thronged with people. Only when we were outside, sitting beside what was left of the walls and the Scaean Gate, did he say, "You are wrong. Troy lives."

I bent my head over my knees, crying. "No. You have seen it. Troy is gone, swept away."

"And now begins to live," he said. "I tell you, the story of Troy will live long beyond these pitiful, fallen stones."

"So many cities, so many kingdoms, have risen, fallen. Troy is just another."

"I cannot believe that the extraordinary deeds and persons of Achilles, Hector, Paris, and you will disappear. These were different than all those others. Different from Theseus and the Minotaur, different from Jason and his Argonauts, beyond the destruction of Andromache's city of Thebes."

I smiled. At that moment I felt so much wiser than he. "Dear friend," I said, "they all felt thus—felt they, and their valiant deeds, could never vanish."

He had one thing left to show me. He did not tell me what it was until we mounted the steps of a small marble temple modestly hidden behind a grove of sacred plane trees, well out of sight of the ugly mound of dead Troy.

"What is this?" I asked.

"I think it is what you have been seeking," he said. "Are you ready to behold it?"

I looked into his gold-flecked eyes, squinting now with the lowering sun. "You are always full of riddles," I said. "Can you not speak plain for once?"

"Ah, that would spoil it," he said. "Why should we alter what has been our way since the beginning?"

"Because this is the end?"

"Ends should not differ from beginnings," he said. "To do so would impugn the truth of one or the other. We must keep our integrity." He turned me toward the pillars. "Look upon it."

I left him and slowly mounted the steps. It was a small shrine, such as dotted the Greek countryside. But I could feel my heart beating faster. This was no ordinary shrine, or he would not have brought me to it.

There were pedestals with objects displayed upon them, and offerings beneath. They were all from the Trojan War, things I had not thought to see again. There was a knife of Hector's, a sandal of Polites, a comb of Troilus. And then, the largest of all, a shrine dedicated to Paris.

It held his armor! His armor, which I had allowed to be awarded at his funeral games and which I had lamented as lost ever since. It was all there—his helmet, his breast plate, his sword. With a cry, I rushed toward it, touched them.

"I knew you would want to know they were safe," Gelanor said.

Tears spilled down my cheeks. "I berated myself for letting them pass into other hands," I said. "But at the time, my grief blinded me."

"Whoever took them honored them," he said. "That is why I wanted you to see them." He stepped back. "I will leave you alone with them." He touched my arm. "Farewell."

"What do you mean?"

Sadly, he shook his head. "Our brief reunion was all I dared ask. I knew it could not last, if I was honest and showed you what I must."

"I still do not know what you mean," I told him.

"You will," he said. He retreated into the shadows.

I approached the pedestal, boldly took and clutched the tarnished bronze helmet in my arms. If not I, then who?

Dearest helmet, which had protected the head of Paris, I thought as I clasped it. Paris, so long ago. Would he even recognize me now? He had died a young and vibrant man. I was now an aged woman.

Yet I was near him. The nearest I could get to him. *Paris, I have come all this way to honor you*, I told him. *I left Sparta once again and sailed to Troy. It was not a voyage of love and excitement as ours was, but it brought me here.*

And here I am, as near to you as I can come in this mortal life, a life that still binds me. I sat for a long time, recalling with all my might our time together, calling him forth. *If you are not here, I know not where to seek you.* I sat for what seemed an eternity before I set down the helmet. *I thought the helmet was lost to me. I gave it away after your death and bitterly bemoaned my folly. But now I have it. Some things can be recovered. Some things can be restored.*

But, Paris, some lost things we seek forever. I seek you. Come to me. If you are not here, where are you? I sat and waited. I was docile in the hands of the gods, the gods I had so often railed against.

I closed my eyes. I could feel the sun, pouring into the shrine, upon their lids. That was beguiling, luring. It said, *There is nothing but this. Only the sun, shining this day. Why seek anything else? Why look beyond this?*

Paris. Paris. Are you still here, in any semblance? Even as a ghost, a shade, I will welcome you. I want nothing else!

I squeezed my eyes shut. All was silence. And then I felt a gentle touch on my fingers.

"Do not look," a dear voice said. "Do not open your eyes."

They started to flutter open. A sweet touch held my eyelids down. "I told you, do not open them." There was a brush along my neck, my cheek. "Ah, to touch you again."

"Do not torture me," I said. "Let me look full upon you." I opened my eyes.

Then all fell away, and I saw Paris standing before me. Paris in all his glory—young, handsome, and glowing. *Where have you been all these years . . . what has happened since . . . and where are we going?* All surged through my earthly mind. And none could be answered.

"Helen," he said, taking my hand.

"Paris, I come," I answered.

Afterword

One of my treasured possessions is an inscribed copy of Jack Lindsay's *Helen of Troy* in which he confides to his friend, "After the *Cleopatra* was out, Constable suggested another book on a famous ancient heroine, but none of them had the fame of Cleopatra. At last they themselves suggested Helen, apparently unaware that she wasn't a historical character in the same sense as Cleopatra was. But I was delighted at the theme and never raised this point." Like Mr. Lindsay, I, too, had come to Helen of Troy from Cleopatra, and I was under the mistaken impression that she was almost equally historical. Not so. We have no evidential corroboration that there ever existed a Helen of Troy—nor an Agamemnon, nor a Menelaus, nor an Achilles, nor a Paris. Among scholars, there are fierce disputes about Homer, and whether, even if there is an actual site of a historical Troy, there ever took place anything we can truly call the Trojan War.

Like Camelot, Troy is steeped in magic. It may well have its grounding in real people, but the Troy we "know" is mythological. Perhaps there really was an Arthur who was a minor Celtic chieftain in the waning days of Roman Britain, and perhaps there really was a nasty little trade war between a few proto-Greeks and a small fortified city in Asia Minor. But that is not really what the Trojan War is all about in our minds. The grandeur of the Trojan War has come to represent warfare in all its facets—both the glory and the hideous destruction. It acts as a paradigm for all wars.

So, even though Helen is not real in the usual sense of the word, still there were boundaries to be honored. The time period in which she lived and the Trojan War took place is the time of the Mycenaean civilization in the Peloponnese in Greece. We have citadels, palaces, and bridges still standing from that time, and we also have artifacts, so it is possible to locate the characters in a real setting. We have their character descriptions from not only Homer but the wider writings covering the Trojan War. (Homer's *Iliad* only describes seven weeks of the war in its tenth year, while his *Odyssey* briefly summarizes the fall of Troy.) Other writings, known as the Epic Cycle, fill out the entire story, from the Judgment of Paris, when he made the fateful choice that led him to Helen, all the way through the fate of the heroes of the war many years later. The *Aeneid* has vivid details about the fall of Troy, and some Greek lyric poetry also supplies information.

Quintus Smyrnaeus (Quintus of Smyrna), writing in the fourth century A.D., picks up where the *Iliad* ends, with the death of Hector through the departure of the Greeks in his *Posthomerica*, also known as *The Fall of Troy*. Later medieval romance writers added other episodes, and finally Chaucer, Shakespeare, and Marlowe all wrote their own Trojan stories, culminating in the famous line: "Was this the face that launched a thousand ships?" Thus the ultimate description of Helen was written not by an ancient Greek who had seen her face, but by an Elizabethan poet, Marlowe, who only imagined it.

For people who may not ever have existed, the characters in the Trojan War have exceptionally colorful and unforgettable personalities. That is why they "feel" so real, and why we want so badly for them to be real. They speak directly to us and we believe in them. Thus I have chosen to act as though they are all real and truly lived, and we have just lost the official identity papers confirming this. Perhaps one day we will find them. I hope so, as they seem so alive.

I grounded the characters in their proper historical setting and tried to be as accurate as possible. For example, Helen was the daughter of the king and queen of Sparta, and the crown passed through the woman, so it was Helen who bestowed the throne on Menelaus. Sparta at that time was not "Spartan" in our sense of the word, but quite the opposite—literature and music flourished there. Homer only has one instance of writing in the *Iliad*, and although there were palace inventories in very early Greek script, Linear B, no letters from that time have ever been discovered, so unless absolutely necessary—or part of the legend, as in Paris writing his name in wine on a table—my characters do not write letters. The oracle at Delphi may not have been fully developed in Homer's time (although characters in the Trojan saga do visit it), but the Herophile Sibyl, who foretold the Trojan War, was certainly there at the time. Homer does not have horseback riders, but we know acrobats performed on horseback, and Quintus of Smyrna has an episode involving mounted riders, which I kept. That Greek symbol, the Olympic Games, did not exist yet, but local athletic contests were already popular and important.

Besides the historical reality of the characters, two other problems rear their heads in dealing with this story. The first has to do with the mythology, and the second with tone and voice. Both are stumbling blocks for the modern author and reader.

To embrace the mythology or to leave it out? In the original telling of the tale, the gods were major characters as much as the humans were. There were two levels of drama—the humans, who were more or less playthings of the gods, and the gods looking down on them and enacting their own power struggles through their hapless puppets. A squabble between three goddesses over who was the most beautiful led to the love affair of Helen and Paris. Certain gods lined up on either side in the Trojan War, with Athena, Hera, and Poseidon on the Greek side and Apollo, Aphrodite, and Ares on the Trojan side. In addition to that, many of the humans had a god for a parent—Achilles, Aeneas, Helen—so that their parents became involved in their protection. What can one do with this? Eliminating the gods completely makes the motivations collapse, but to us the gods bickering and tricking one another is cartoonish and detracts from the seriousness of the story.

I chose to leave the gods in on an individual level, but not depict what was happening on Mount Olympus. For one thing, since the story is told from Helen's viewpoint, she would not be privy to that. But in the modern world people still have individual encounters with their gods, still pray to them and seek direction from them, and often feel their presence. I also chose to leave intact the idea of having a god for a parent. Thus, Helen is the daughter of Zeus, who came to her mother in the form of a swan, but she did not hatch from an egg. After all, these people believed in such parentage. This was true even as late as the time of Alexander the Great: the oracle at Siwa revealed to him that he was the son of Amun, and he embraced it and believed it.

The tone in telling this story is another question. For such high matters it would seem that a heroic tone is needed, but again, that can seem comical to us now. On the other hand, the modern use of the vernacular, in an attempt to make the characters more accessible, diminishes the story. It somehow doesn't feel right. Being mythological, they should be a bit more lofty. So I have tried to keep the speech and language dignified and a bit "other" without sounding pompous.

I do take the liberty of using terms a modern person can recognize, such as "the Greeks" rather than "the Achaeans" or "the Danaans," to avoid confusion and obscurity. Also, two characters sometimes associated with the story are missing: Cressida and Theseus. Cressida seems to be a later invention of the medieval romantic tradition, not found in the original story, which does include Troilus. Theseus likewise is a later addition, as the Athenians, who did not participate in the Trojan War, that great defining moment in Greek identity, wanted to find some way to link their hero with it, and so invented an episode in which he kidnaps Helen. Neither was authentic—insofar as anything can be authentic in myth—so I omitted them.

Since this is not history as we know it, there are no exact time sequences in the sources. The classically accepted time for the Trojan War is ten years, but the elapsed time to cover all the added incidents, from delayed departure of the Greeks to fight in Troy, to the non-Homeric stories of what happened after the death of Hector, is longer than that. In one instance in the *Iliad* Helen says she has been in Troy for twenty years. The years inside the walls must have passed in an odd fashion, and we do not know what happened to fill them. So I have tried to capture that unusual passage of time and at the same time avoid specific dates whenever I can.

The same problem of history versus mythology applies to Priam and his family. Not all of his children are named; although Hecuba was said in one source to have borne nineteen sons (or children, in other sources), only ten sons are named. Priam's fifty sons has a ring to it, and perhaps it was always symbolic rather than accurate. In any case, I stick only to the named ones.

If you would like to read more about Helen and the Trojan War, of course the place to start is with Homer, the *Iliad* and the *Odyssey*. There are many fine translations, some in poetry, some in prose. The Epic Cycle, which includes the *Cypria, Aethiopis, Little Iliad, Iliu Persis, Nostoi,* and *Telegonia,* now exists only in summary, as the original writings have been lost. The summaries can be found in Apollodorus, *The Library*, Vol. II (Cambridge: Loeb Classical Library, Harvard University Press, 1996) and *Epic Cycle* (Cambridge: Loeb Classical Library, 2000), as well as Jonathan S. Burgess, *The Tradition of the Trojan War in Homer and the Epic Cycle* (Baltimore: Johns Hopkins University Press, 2001). Plays by Aeschylus, Sophocles, and Euripides also cover aspects and characters of the Trojan War and its aftermath.

Continuing the story, there is Quintus of Smyrna, *Posthomerica,* also available in many versions and translations, including *The War at Troy: What Homer Didn't Tell* (University of Oklahoma Press, 1968, reprinted 1996, Barnes & Noble Books).

Biographies exclusively of Helen herself are rare. The most complete, covering every aspect of her story, is Jack Lindsay, *Helen of Troy: Woman and Goddess* (London: Constable and Company Ltd., 1974). In addition, there are John Pollard, *Helen of Troy* (New York: Roy Publishers, 1965), and Ivor Brown, *Dark Ladies* (London: Collins, 1957). Just published is Bettany Hughes, *Helen of Troy: Goddess, Princess, Whore* (New York: Knopf, 2005).

Books on Homer and Troy include: Barry B. Powell, *Homer* (Oxford: Blackwell publishers, 2004); J. V. Luce, *Celebrating Homer's Landscapes* (New Haven: Yale University Press, 1998); J. V. Luce, *Homer and the Heroic Age* (London: Thames and Hudson, 1975); Denys Page, *History and the Homeric Iliad* (Berkeley: University of California Press, 1959); Walter Leaf, *Troy: A Study in Homeric Geography* (London: Macmillan and Company, 1912; reprinted by Elibron Classics); Manfred O. Korfmann, *Troia/Wilusa* (Canakkale-Tubingen: Troia Foundation,

2005); and Michael Wood, *In Search of the Trojan War* (Oxford: British Broadcasting Company, 1985).

Background information about the period is found in *The Mycenaean World* (Athens: National Archaeological Museum, Ministry of Culture, 1988); M. I. Finley, *Early Greece: the Bronze and Archaic Age* (New York: W. W. Norton, 1981); and *The World of Odysseus* (New York: New York Review of Books, 2002); John Chadwick, *The Mycenaean World* (Cambridge: Cambridge University Press, 1976); Nic Fields, illustrated by D. Spedaliere, *Mycenaean Citadels c. 1350–1200 B.C.* (Oxford: Osprey Publishing, 2004); Nic Fields, illustrated by D. Spedaliere and S. Sulemsohn Spedaliere, *Troy, c. 1700–1250 B.C.* (Oxford: Osprey Publishing, 2004); Margaret R. Scherer, *The Legends of Troy in Art and Literature* (London: Phaidon Press, 1964), excellent and inclusive; Susan Woodford, *The Trojan War in Ancient Art* (Ithaca: Cornell University Press, 1993); and Eric Shanower, *Age of Bronze* (Orange, CA: Image Comics, 2001), an award-winning graphic novel in progress that will cover the entire Trojan War and eventually have seven volumes. His bibliography, time lines, and genealogies are exhaustive and accurate.

More specialized information can be found in Henry A. Ormerod, *Piracy in the Ancient World* (Baltimore: Johns Hopkins University Press, 1997); Adrienne Mayor, *Greek Fire, Poison Arrows and Scorpion Bombs: Biological and Chemical Warfare in the Ancient World* (New York: Overlook Press, 2003); Marjorie & C. H. B. Quennell, *Everyday Things in Homeric Greece* (London: B. T. Batsford, 1929); Emile Mireaux, *Daily Life in the Time of Homer* (Toronto: Macmillan, 1959); Hellmut Baumann, *The Greek Plant World in Myth, Art and Literature* (Portland, OR.: Timber Press, 1993); Paul Bentley Kern, *Ancient Siege Warfare* (Bloomington: Indiana University Press, 1999); and Stephen G. Miller, *Ancient Greek Athletics* (New Haven: Yale University Press, 2004).

Greek mythology, being so extensive, requires its own heading. As a child I read Margaret Evans Price's *Enchantment Tales for Children* (New York: Rand McNally, 1926) and *A Child's Book of Myths* (New York: Rand McNally, 1924) at bedtime. Their magnificent artwork made the world of Greek myth very much a part of my childhood imagination. Later sources include Robert Graves, *The Greek Myths, Vol. I and II* (London: Penguin Books, 1990); Michael Grant, *Myths of the Greeks and Romans* (New York: Meridian, 1995); and Barry B. Powell, *Classical Myth* (New Jersey: Prentice-Hall, 2004). In the tangled world of the Greek gods, geneaological charts were both helpful and essential. One is Vanessa James, *The Genealogy of Greek Mythology* (New York: Gotham Books, 2003), and there is also a truly monumental seventy-page compilation, Harold Newman and John O. Newman, *A Genealogical Chart of Greek Mythology* (Chapel Hill: University of North Carolina Press, 2003).

FOR THE BEST IN PAPERBACKS, LOOK FOR THE

In every corner of the world, on every subject under the sun, Penguin represents quality and variety—the very best in publishing today.

For complete information about books available from Penguin—including Penguin Classics and Puffins—and how to order them, write to us at the appropriate address below. Please note that for copyright reasons the selection of books varies from country to country.

In the United States: Please write to *Penguin Group (USA), P.O. Box 12289 Dept. B, Newark, New Jersey 07101-5289* or call 1-800-788-6262.

In the United Kingdom: Please write to *Dept. EP, Penguin Books Ltd, Bath Road, Harmondsworth, West Drayton, Middlesex UB7 0DA.*

In Canada: Please write to *Penguin Books Canada Ltd, 90 Eglinton Avenue East, Suite 700, Toronto, Ontario M4P 2Y3.*

In Australia: Please write to *Penguin Books Australia Ltd, P.O. Box 257, Ringwood, Victoria 3134.*

In New Zealand: Please write to *Penguin Books (NZ) Ltd, Private Bag 102902, North Shore Mail Centre, Auckland 10.*

In India: Please write to *Penguin Books India Pvt Ltd, 11 Panchsheel Shopping Centre, Panchsheel Park, New Delhi 110 017.*

In the Netherlands: Please write to *Penguin Books Netherlands bv, Postbus 3507, NL-1001 AH Amsterdam.*

In Germany: Please write to *Penguin Books Deutschland GmbH, Metzlerstrasse 26, 60594 Frankfurt am Main.*

In Spain: Please write to *Penguin Books S. A., Bravo Murillo 19, 1° B, 28015 Madrid.*

In Italy: Please write to *Penguin Italia s.r.l., Via Benedetto Croce 2, 20094 Corsico, Milano.*

In France: Please write to *Penguin France, Le Carré Wilson, 62 rue Benjamin Baillaud, 31500 Toulouse.*

In Japan: Please write to *Penguin Books Japan Ltd, Kaneko Building, 2-3-25 Koraku, Bunkyo-Ku, Tokyo 112.*

In South Africa: Please write to *Penguin Books South Africa (Pty) Ltd, Private Bag X14, Parkview, 2122 Johannesburg.*